Valor

R.L. STANLEY

Copyright © 2016 R.L. Stanley
All rights reserved.
ISBN: 1505311071
ISBN-13: 978-1505311075

ACKNOWLEDGMENTS

To my friend and editor, April Mullins – thank you for looking at a 480-paged manuscript and saying only "let's do this."
And a big thank you to Tara Komar for giving me the opportunity and encouragement to discover and pursue this idea in the first place. This entire book is your fault. In a good way.

CONTENTS

Acknowledgments	i
Day One, Part One	1
Day One, Part Two	15
Day Two, Part One	30
Day Two, Part Two	46
Day Three	61
Day Four	78
Day Five	93
Day Nine	103
Day Seventy	116
Day Ninety-one	125
Day One Hundred and Twenty-two	138
Day One Hundred and Forty-five	148
Day One Hundred and Forty-six, Part One	160
Day One Hundred and Forty-six, Part Two	182
Day One Hundred and Forty-seven	195
Day One Hundred and Forty-eight	208
Day One Hundred and Fifty-one	231
Day One Hundred and Fifty-eight	250
Day One Hundred and Seventy-two	272
Day Two Hundred and Sixty-four, Part One	288
Day Two Hundred and Sixty-four, Part Two	305
Day Two Hundred and Sixty-five	325
Day Two Hundred and Sixty-six	356
Day Two Hundred and Sixty-seven	358
Day Two Hundred and Seventy-three	377
Day Two Hundred and Seventy-four	379
Day Two Hundred and Seventy-six	381
Day Two Hundred and Seventy-seven	384
Day Two Hundred and Eighty-one	386
Day Two Hundred and Eighty-nine	398
Day Two Hundred and Ninety-three	399
Day Two Hundred and Ninety-four	407

Day Two Hundred and Ninety-six	417
Day Two Hundred and Ninety-seven	428
Day Three Hundred and Five	430
Day Three Hundred and Thirty	435
Day Three Hundred and Forty-five	443
Day Three Hundred and Sixty-five	446
And One More Thing	456

DAY ONE, PART ONE

It's hard to want to be loved by someone, be strong for the universe, and fit in all at the same time. In the beginning, I felt helpless. I felt alone, and, above all, I was scared shitless of everything because I was too small to deal with the universe.

See, everyone likes to think that they're going places, that they're going to mean something in the world and somehow change the fate of the planet in the small blip of time that is their existence. But no one seems to get that in the grand scheme of things, in the massive tangle and bewildering storm that is the eternity stretching out beyond the stars we see at night, we mean absolutely nothing. We're nothing but grains of sand on an infinite beach, only moved to be cycled through the ages by the pounding waves of time. We're nothing. We're *no one*. And we always will be. Nothing we do ever matters or has a difference in this war-struck world we live in.

I couldn't manage this realization. Not until a lot of things changed – some for the better…others, not so much.

It all started with the social hierarchy of the Amaeric War Academy, but then, doesn't every story? Every pathetic little underdog like me always blames his lot in life on the social ladder, but it's true. For the most part, people like big, strong, attractive men – the ones who'll go off to the battlefield and return as heroes with their chests all done up in pins and ribbons and awards for their ability to aim a gun and pull a trigger.

For the record, I'm not *that* bad looking. In fact, a few girls from the town once told me that they like my green eyes, though I think they really just pity me and want to make sure someone says something nice to me at some point in my life. But their pity is the least of my problems. My *biggest* problem is that I'm the runt of my platoon.

In fact, I'm probably the runt of the whole Academy at the moment. Carrying my equipment is a struggle, let alone manning one of the heavy artillery weapons, so when people see me practicing with my fellow cadets, they give me this pitying look.

They know as well as I do why I'm in the army. I'm the human shield, the cannon fodder, the sacrificial lamb. *I* would take the hits and die so the better men behind me could survive.

That's my designation: Cadet Tristan Byrne, weak and therefore expendable. It seemed to be a trend in my family. See, my parents had been war heroes, or so I liked to imagine. My nights were spent spinning wild tales of how they perished at the front lines of the ongoing Great War: my father shot down saving his comrade or my mother braving the flying bullets to reach an injured soldier only to be struck by enemy fire herself as she reached his side.

In reality, their stories were probably mundane.

My father was most likely shot in the trenches, dying as yet another John Doe until someone read his dog tag. My mother probably caught one of the diseases she was trying to heal others of, such as malaria or typhoid – withering away until she died in a delirium of fevers, dementia, and general unpleasantness.

But I'm not here to talk about that or the war ravaging my native Amaeric and all the other nations, leastways not just yet. I'm here to talk about the most stressful and risky time in any cadet's meager social life: the last night of our fourth and final year in the Academy.

This evening of danger was known as Promenade, a formal dance that took place the night before the graduating class was deployed for the front lines. Traditionally, showing up single was the final nail in the coffin of one's social standing – it showed you had no one who cared enough about you to miss you while you were off at war. And I really didn't need anyone reiterating that fact for me.

It would be a really long year on the front lines if they did.

Because it wasn't that I didn't have a date. I *definitely* had a date, but there was the slight problem of our relationship being illegal – explicitly so in some regions, implicitly in others. My partner, just like everyone else's, was smart, strong, loyal, brave, independent, and understood me. That was the most important part: understanding me. Nothing else mattered more to me than being understood by the person I loved.

We cared for each other deeply, had been dating for almost a year, and *no one knew*. As far as I was concerned, no one would *ever* know.

Firstly, it wasn't their business. If there was one thing that I hated more than my lot in life, it was how people seemed to feel entitled to dig around in that lot in life, judge it, and interfere with it accordingly. Secondly, our lives would probably become a living hell if we were found out, leaving both of us to almost definitely face torment for the rest of our very short existences. It was a secret love affair, a relationship worthy of the storybooks, yet undoubtedly different.

I had to admit, though; it was definitely just as star-crossed as some of the literature I'd read.

So it was that I found myself lying in my bunk in my room. That was one aspect that came with being doomed and unwanted that I appreciated. No one liked me enough to share one of the already small, cramped rooms with me. I got to be alone with my thoughts and anxieties, whether they left me screaming into a pillow or just staring vacantly at the rafters. I'd heard in the early days of the war, soldiers had shared giant rooms with each other, rows upon rows of beds filling entire halls. Now, though, the military had resorted to repurposing any site they could get their hands on – like this old missionary that hadn't housed anyone even remotely pious in decades. Our living quarters had adapted accordingly with the space; in fact, our current barracks were once housing for the matrons.

Nothing, it seemed, was untainted by the war.

Outside, everyone was using our half-day off to make plans and get ready for the upcoming dance of cleverly masked tragedy. I, on the other hand, had just finished tying up my unfinished business, contenting myself with the mental outlining of what I wanted my will to be. It wasn't like I had anyone to give my things to anyways, so there really wasn't a point to having one.

But I had to have *something* to do to pass the time.

I decided I would give everything to my S.O., Jax. He was always busy telling me I was going to die, that I didn't stand a chance, but it wasn't like I'd had a choice. The Academy draft was mandatory: four years of military training starting at the age of eighteen. As such, leaving my meager belongings to Jax was definitely the type of ironic, parting prank I'd pull.

No one would be surprised either way. My unit of a little over a hundred young men and women would be leaving with the rest of our class to become heroes tomorrow. I, however, was definitely leaving to die, and this dreaded, stupid dance – my first and last Promenade – wasn't helping my mood at all.

To be honest, I much rather preferred the Hunts that we'd had the three previous years in place of Promenade. They were basically glorified capture the flag games with military personnel. I'd met my significant other at last year's, and with the Hunts I could at least practice strategy – battle planning was one of my few skills. But no such luck this year.

As I stared vacantly at the rafters above me, morbidly thinking about what unsurprised things people would say when they saw my name on the casualty list, I heard my door open. A familiar step graced the wooden floors to come to a creaking stop by my bedside.

"So." I faintly heard boot heels click together. "How do I look?"

I turned my head to glance up at the newcomer, ignoring the self-satisfied smirk on his face. Dressed in our formal olive green uniform with medals and ribbons pinned to his left shoulder from three different assignments to the front lines, Jack Miller was tall with dark hair, dark eyes with arching brows, and a square jawline. He looked like one of those paintings of the long-dead kings that hung in our mess hall: commanding, confident, and compassionate all at once.

The only reason the once-sergeant, now-corporal was back at the Academy three years after he graduated was insubordination. He'd had too good of a reputation and was far too valuable to be shot on the spot for refusing to follow his captain's suicide run order. That and the call had been the right one. But the army couldn't have soldiers questioning orders left and right, so here Jack was – demoted and back with the newbies for what would end up being roughly a year and a half.

"Hideous," I finally told him, teasing as he rolled his eyes at my grumbled response. "Nah, you look great…" The smile pulling at my lips slowly faded as I sighed, anxiety and frustration forcing its way back to the forefront of my mind as our moment passed. "So. Come to see the dead man walking, have you, Jack?"

He sighed, sat on the bed next to me, and lay down so we were side by side. A heavy silence stretched out between us as we gazed at the rafters and the point of the roof high above our heads.

"You're not going to die, Tristan," he finally assured me.

I scoffed, nervously laughing and closing my eyes as if that could quiet the butterflies crowding up my throat from my stomach.

"Do you know that?" I asked, still smiling giddily in panic and grinding the heels of my palms into my eyes. "I'm the human shield, cannon fodder. Everyone knows it. I mean, have you *heard* Jax lately?" I lowered my hands to look at Jack earnestly, and he gave me a small, sympathetic smile. "What, you call that running? How are you supposed to help out your comrades if you can't even carry a daypack and a *snail* moves faster than you?! Come on, Byrne, move those twigs you call legs! Get a move on!"

I stopped my gruff imitation of our drill instructor and supervising officer, laughing unsteadily again as my hands started to shake. It was a nervous tic of mine whenever I got riled up about something like the war, the dance…basically anything that could possibly stress me out. It really didn't do me any favors when it came to combat training, and I could only imagine how horrible it would be on the front lines.

"Hey." Beside me, Jack reached over and gently grabbed my smaller hands in his like he always did, holding them steady until the trembling slowly faded. "You're okay…you hear me?"

I nodded but couldn't help noticing the painful difference between our skins. His was battle-roughened and powerful from years of training and experience. Mine was blistered and soft despite four years of exposure to hard labor, a marker of just how hopeless I would be in war no matter how hard I tried. I tilted my head back a little to look at him and opened my mouth to ask a question, but he cut me off, quickly leaning close and kissing me before getting to his feet and pulling me to a sitting position.

"Uh, where are you going?" I asked, still trying to blink away the brief startlement from his surprise kiss.

It wasn't like it was the first time he'd done that – *far* from it. He just still caught me off-guard sometimes, even after all this time. He looked over his shoulder at me, pulling me up off the bed in his wake.

"*We* are going to the attic."

I rolled my eyes. His ideas for where we could be alone together were getting more and more eccentric by the day. I was still finding hay in my clothing from last week's adventure, and I swore to my boyfriend that the quartermaster's horse had never looked at me the same since. However, Jack honestly didn't seem to care about his sudden bloom of creativity, and he continued leading me down the hall towards the access hatch at the end of the corridor.

"Fine, but can you at least *not* hold my hand?" I protested, pulling away from him and shoving my hands into my pockets. "I don't want people to see us…you know what would happen if they did." Now it was Jack's turn to laugh at me as he reached above our heads and pulled the fold-up ladder down from the ceiling, loud creak of rusty hinges echoing down the stone halls. "What? I don't want to be a victim of the military edition of smear the queer!"

"Come on," Jack responded sarcastically. "Most of the newbies here are bakers, farm boys, stablehands…all the rich, talented kids who'd actually pose any threat already bought their way out of the draft. Unless they're crazy enough to *want* to be here, so I guess, yeah, watch out for those." He started up the steps and looked back at me. "When will you learn that I'm strong enough to protect you from most of the idiots here?"

"I *have* learned that," I said, my trademark sass creeping into my voice. "You're strong enough to protect me from *most* of them. Not *all* of them." We climbed the rickety old steps to our war school's musty catacomb of an attic, and I looked around.

The air up here was musty and heavy like old newspaper, its earthy weight comforting and nostalgic in my chest. Someone – Jack, I assumed – had cleared away all the other cadets' chests and crates to create a massive empty space in the middle of the planked floor. Dust specks drifted through the air, glowing like embers as they passed through the shafts of sunlight piercing the gloom from fissures in the old roof.

And as we stood there, I looked over to where he was holding his hand out to me. I suspiciously narrowed my eyes at him, waiting for some level of explanation or guidance about what exactly we were planning to do here, and my answer came soon enough.

"We're going to have to learn something if we're going to the dance tomorrow," he said, grinning. Panic flooded my veins, and my mind went blank for a few moments, frantically trying to process what he had just said.

"What?"

He smirked, as though he thought I was just playing around.

"Promenade?" he asked, still grinning. "You know, that big social event with food and people and dancing? *We're* going, and we need to learn something."

Is he joking? He has to be joking, right? I mean–

"Tris?"

–he can't actually be thinking we're going to do this –

"You okay?"

Holy crap, what if he's not *joking–*

"Okay, seriously?" Jack sighed in exasperation, reaching forward to snap his fingers in front of my startled deer eyes and making me jump. "Tristan!"

"Sorry, could you repeat that please?"

Okay, maybe it took me more than a few moments.

"I said that we're going to have to learn something because *we* are going to *Promenade*," he repeated slowly and stared at me pointedly until I finally seemed to understand the words.

"Uh, no," I protested, stunned, and my mouth started trying to express all the different ways I thought he and his idea were crazy and could go rot in a hole someplace. "Do you – are you even – we can't just *do* that! You know, Jack," here my voice became patronizing, as though I were talking to a child, "there are these things called *societal norms*, and while I know that you are largely unversed in them, I would think that you would *at least* know this one!"

He rolled his eyes, and I turned away, hands at my head and fists full of straw-colored hair. This was getting out of hand.

"You *really* can't be serious," I continued, turning around and gesturing helplessly at him. "You just…you've *got* to be kidding! Did you just miss our *whole* conversation back there about how I *didn't* want to be found out by people?"

He scoffed, glancing up in irritated silence at the glowing cracks in the ceiling before looking back down at me.

"Do you think I care about what they think anymore, Tris?" His words were brusque, his frustration barely contained, and I blinked, staring at him in surprise. "Because I *really* don't. I never have. We're going off to war in two days, the Promenade's tomorrow, and there's only one person I want to go with!"

I looked down from him to the golden glow of the sun on the floor, shifting my weight from foot to foot and crossing my arms.

"What are they going to do to us?" I looked at Jack as he continued. "Send us to the front lines to die young? We're gonna do that anyways," he said as if he had read my mind and finally delivered the crushing words – the words that I'd known he'd always thought but had just never been able to say to me.

"You were right, okay? You're gonna die after tomorrow, we all will. That's how it works. Front lines do the dying for everyone else. You don't need the added stress of hiding."

"So, you've finally come to terms with the fact that I'm going to die. Congratulations," I managed bitterly, raking a hand through my hair. I swallowed a few times, trying to organize the thoughts in my numb mind. "This dance is my calm before the storm."

Jack shrugged, sitting down on one of the chests and crossing his arms.

"I suppose, if you want to wax poetic. But I'm in the same boat as you." I cast him a weary look that clearly said I wasn't buying a single word he'd just said.

"You've already been to three different stations on the front lines, and you're still standing. You're too experienced to die like me," I scoffed, looking down. There. I'd finally said it. Instead of getting angry, though, Jack just shook his head and got to his feet, putting his hands on my shoulders and looking down at me.

"Tris, you haven't deserted. You're still here even though you know how it's going to end." I met his steady eyes, unable to read what he was really thinking. "You're stronger than all of us." He smiled and kissed my forehead gently before playfully pushing me off balance a little. "Now, then. Shall we get on with our dancing? We've got four hours before our final training evaluation with Jax."

I sighed and shrugged, looking down at the worn floorboards beneath my feet.

"Can't exactly say no, can I? I mean, if you're strong enough to take on most of the people here, there's no way I'm making it down that ladder without picking up something," I said with a wry smile, and his face broke out in his goofy grin as he placed his hands on my shoulders once more.

"See? You're learning, Tristan. You're learning."

Still torn between feeling either freaked out or reluctantly interested, I followed my partner to the center of the open floor as he pulled a battered old record player out of one of the chests.

"Wow...I didn't realize we had one of those up here," I said, surprised and intrigued as he set it up and started looking for a specific record.

"Yeah, well, except for the radios and the war tech, this is now the pinnacle of technology at the Academy. But that's because the world loves two things: bombing the hell out of each other and entertainment." He sighed, moving towards the wall with the cord in his hand, and knelt beside a cracked and yellowed outlet. "Let's see if the wiring's good enough to not short out..."

Please short out, please short out —

"There we go! We're in business," Jack laughed, and I sighed quietly in disappointment to myself. The record slowly started spinning, and he set the needle down on its edge. It looked like I was going to be roped into this no matter what, and the music slowly came to life, sounds of the slower big band piece filling the air. "Now, luckily for you, they play this song every single year. And even more luckily for you, I've been to one of these before so I know the dance."

"You? Dancing?"

"What?" he demanded, indignant as he slowly walked over to me. "Is it really that hard to see me dancing?" I deemed it to unwise to answer that honestly, and, noting my silence, he rolled his eyes and came to stop a little more than a foot away. "So, starting position for the waltz — it's all fairly simple. You'll be the girl, I'll be the guy."

"Really?" I asked, unimpressed, and he shrugged.

"I'm a better leader than you are. Can't have you and your bumbling feet guiding us on the dance floor, we'll look like idiots."

"What, and we're *not* going to anyways?" Before I could continue, Jack grabbed me by the wrist, pulling me close to him and placing my left hand on his shoulder and his left under my arm along my back.

"Hold my hand." I wrapped my fingers around his, and he sighed. "No, not that way. *That* way. There we go." Once he was satisfied with our positioning, he cleared his throat. "Okay, we'll start on three and you just watch my feet and mirror my steps, okay? One, two, three, *now*."

Mirroring, apparently, was easier said than done. Somehow my leg got tangled with his, and with an undignified yelp and loud crash we toppled backwards, Jack landing hard on top of me. I blew my hair out of my eyes, looking up at his unamused expression.

"This is going to be *great*. Isn't it, Tristan?"

There was something unsafe to his question, and I nodded sarcastically, despite my better judgment.

"Oh *yeah*, it's gonna be *great*."

Expression completely unamused, Jack playfully shoved my head to the side and against the floor as he got to his feet to start the song over.

"Okay, let's try this again. I swear to the gods if you can't get your feet to *mirror* mine and not get *tangled* in them, we're still gonna go to the dance, and you're gonna look like a moron in public."

"Oh, I'm so scared…" I muttered, playing disinterested, but Jack knew the truth as much as I did.

I really enjoyed being with him, alone, doing what others could do, without fear of ridicule. We could be the way we deserved to be up here in the lazy heat and drifting dust. The small specks shone like fireflies, illuminated by the spillways of golden light piercing the attic gloom while soft music played in the background.

"On three…one, two, three–"

...———...

"MOVE IT!" I ground my teeth, trying to ignore the shouting giant of a man in my ear. "COME ON BYRNE! YOU CAN DO BETTER THAN THAT, HUSSLE!"

My lungs felt like they were going to burst. My arms and legs felt numb and yet on fire at the same time as I struggled on through the thick mud, crawling with my knees, feet, and elbows while my cramping hands held my heavy rifle above my head. The barbed wire of our recreated No Man's Land littered my way, turning the rather short distance into what seemed like thousands of miles through a hellhole.

I looked up through slightly blurred vision and saw that everyone else had already made it through the obstacle course, and, eyes burning with more than just sweat, I struggled to increase my pace. I groaned as the butt of my rifle started dragging in the mud and the top of my fabric-covered helmet snagged on the rolls of barbed wire crisscrossing above me. I could hear snickering from my fellow cadets, and I fought the urge to just drop the weapon in the mud, pull my pocketknife from my belt, and throw it at one of them. No one would be laughing then.

But just as I was about to follow through with most of my plan, using my blade to cut myself free instead of maiming the asshats standing there and softly cackling at me, the near-silent laughter stopped and the persistent weight of the barbed wire vanished. A big hand grabbed the back of my uniform and hauled me, mud-soaked, to my feet.

"That's enough, cadet." It was Jax. His voice was uncharacteristically low, pitched so only I could hear, and I nodded, dragging a filthy hand across my face to try and obscure my reddened complexion. "Get back in line."

I nodded again and followed his pointing finger, feeling sick to my stomach at the jeering looks people were giving me when Jax's back was turned. But when the drill instructor faced them, they straightened up, expressions square and serious. See, there was a certain way things worked in the military, or at least a certain way things were supposed to work. The drill instructors, S.O.s, and all superiors were entitled in every possible way to make your life as miserable as they wanted. They could make fun of you, embarrass you, physically punish you – which occasionally included breaking "minor" bones – the works.

However, the moment anyone *else* tried to do that, the moment peers turned on each other, our drill instructor started bashing heads in. There was zero tolerance for hounding in the ranks. Unfortunately, there was also zero tolerance in the ranks for snitching, so any lessons people got after hours were never brought to light.

I was a frequent student at these extracurricular classes.

"Alright, ladies, it's time for the ropes. Let's go! Move!"

"Sir, yes, sir!" we chorused and turned as one, jogging off in our perfect lines and rows to the netting stretched out like a trampoline about a foot off the ground. It used to be strung up in a tent-like shape for us to climb up and down, but our instructors decided we needed to practice agility more than climbing to prepare for running in half-destroyed, debris and body-littered trenches and laid it out on the ground instead.

The ropes crossed in two-by-two feet squares, and it was our job to run to the other side by stepping in each of the squares, with all our equipment, and not trip on anything. Year one had been hell; every-one had fallen. Year two, almost everyone made it half way. Year three, almost everyone made it across. By year four, the cadets could have been working in the circuses of the past doing tightrope or something like that. Their balance was amazing, their agility flawless.

And then there was me.

"Byrne!"

I took a deep breath and pulled my helmet down so it shadowed as much of my already reddening face as possible. And then, I started running.

At first, I was pleasantly surprised. I'd gone three feet out of the twelve without tripping and falling flat on my face. Another two feet covered...so far so good. But just as I was about to cross the mid-point, the toe of my boot caught on the taut rope, and I went sprawling, ears burning. I tried to push myself up, but my hands kept slipping on the tarred rope, and my insanely heavy pack kept weighing me down and throwing me off balance. But before I could do anything, a hand that wasn't Jax's grabbed my upper arm, hauling me to my feet and steadying me as he straightened my pack and rebalanced the weight I was carrying.

"Miller, get back in line!"

"Yes, sir," Jack said, clapping a hand on my shoulder and bringing me into line with him. "Just assisting a comrade, sir. We should watch out for our own, not laugh at them."

There was a pointed coldness to his voice that promptly silenced our platoon's quiet laughter, amused expressions going blank too late. Jax narrowed his eyes at the uncomfortable cadets, scowling.

"Is that what we're doing when our comrades fall down?" There was no answer to his bellowed demand, and everyone continued to look straight ahead. "Is that what we're doing?" He paced before the group of cadets and came to a stop before a tall, burly man with a ruddy complexion, sandy hair, and blue eyes. "Jackson!"

"Sir!"

"Are you laughing at Cadet Byrne when he struggles?"

I could see Jackson's jaw working, and I took in a deep breath. Alec Jackson was the son of a blacksmith back in his own region at the center of Amaeric. He was the oldest of six siblings and was therefore a sort of bully. Whenever he could get a foothold in any sort of social hierarchy, he planted himself at the top of the food chain – the leader of what soon became a rabid pack of wolves.

And at this particular moment I was the deer they were supposed to be feasting on.

If Jackson was forced to answer, I would never hear the end of this. As soon as the lights went out tonight, I'd be beaten to death with soap.

"Well, Jackson?"

"Yes, sir," he answered, and I couldn't help but look away from the death glares the other cadets were giving me when Jax's attention was elsewhere.

"Are *all* of you laughing instead of helping Cadet Byrne?" our S.O. shouted, coming to a stop and glaring at the increasingly uncomfortable cadets before him.

"Yes, sir!" they chorused, with the exception of Jack, and Jax seemed to double in size. He pointed in the direction of the trail winding throughout the grounds of the Academy, going up flights of stairs, down hills, and across long stretches of flat ground for approximately eight miles.

"Run the course two times! I don't want to see any of your sorry asses lagging, do you hear me? Byrne, you stay." Silently grumbling, the cadets lined up in their order and prepared to start their punishment. "And I don't care if it cuts into your lunch time, ladies! Start running!" With a rise of dust, the twenty-nine cadets went on their way, matching their paces so that they would last their sixteen-mile run. "Not you, Miller. You stay as well."

Jack stopped jogging, taking in a deep breath and returning to my side. I shuffled a couple of steps away from him, eyes downcast.

No attention. Draw no attention.

Once our instructor was satisfied our platoonmates were far enough away, he turned to face us. I kept my eyes fixed on the ground, shoving my way past Jack to return to the beginning of the ropes.

"What do you think you're doing, Byrne?" Jax called, voice tired, as he pinched the bridge of his nose and looked at the ground. His trademark bellowing was turned almost all the way down, and for once in his life he almost sounded like a normal human being.

"Doing it again, sir," I replied, trying to keep my voice steady, and I blinked back my reflexive tears of frustration as my supervising officer shook his head and looked up at me with a sad expression on his face.

"You're done, Byrne. You've tried. You've tried *really* hard, but you're done. I want you and Miller to go back to the barracks and wash up." He walked towards me, clapping a hand on my shoulder as he passed by. "I'm sorry, son."

With that, he walked off to start cleaning up some of the equipment, and I stood there, staring at the ropes before me in anger and hate. My breathing was ragged and sharp, and I tried to ignore the vague shape of Jack in my peripheral vision, watching me. Maybe he would give me some space.

But after a full thirty seconds went by and he was still standing there, I had had it.

"What the hell did you think you were doing?" I demanded, finally finding my voice as I furiously turned to face him. He looked at me in mild surprise.

"They've been picking on you since day one," he explained, as though it should be obvious. "Someone's got to make them see that you're trying your best, and if your best isn't good enough for them, they should at the very least watch out for you. That's what a platoon does, that's what a unit does. They watch out for each other. We're *supposed* to be a team!"

"*No*, Jack. We're not supposed to be a *team*. We – we're supposed to be farmers! We're supposed to be businessmen! Bakers! Hell, you're supposed to be a gods-damn carpenter! Jackson – Jackson's supposed to be a blacksmith!" I half-shouted, pointing after the rest of our classmates. "We're *not* supposed to be soldiers. We don't even know what we're fighting for anymore anyways. We're just…*fighting*." I yanked off my helmet to reveal my reddened eyes.

"So in the end, all we have is the respect and dignity that we show through our actions and how that respect and dignity is acknowledged by everyone else," I finished, thoroughly annoyed. "Now, I may not have had much of either of those, but at least I had the dignity of always pulling *myself* through everything. I did not need you to come to my – my *rescue!* You just made things worse!" Before he could say anything, I turned away from him, furious and miserable, and stormed off. Then, unable to stop myself, I turned back around and hurled my helmet at him, the throw naturally falling short and coming to a rolling stop at his feet.

"Why can't you just let us be *normal?*"

"Tris. Tristan!"

I ignored his calls and continued on my way, sparing a quick glance back in time to see our S.O. put his hand on Jack's shoulder. He gestured for them to walk a little ways. I had no doubt that they were going to be talking about me.

DAY ONE, PART TWO

By the time I had returned to North Hall, I was hurting all over. Every joint was sore; my whole body ached and throbbed. My skin was going to be black and blue by tomorrow morning, just as it always was. I didn't let anyone know that I was hurting of course. I carried my own weight – I always had. Until today.

I dropped my pack on the floor of my room and removed my shirt, socks, and shoes before exiting my quarters and heading for the bathroom down the hall. I quickly pumped water into the tub, dropping my clothes into the cold water and watching the dirt and mud seep out of the fabric as I lathered up a wire brush with carbolic soap. As I scrubbed at the wool, taking comfort in the routine and familiar motion, I looked down at my abdomen and chest, counting the splotches of purples, blues, and greens until I came to a grand total of eight. Most of them laced my ribs and sternum, but a few were spread across my gut or planted violently along my collarbone. A quick glance at the cracked and stained mirror behind me showed that my back was just as decorated.

I groaned as I got to my feet, pulling my soaking wet – yet clean – clothes out of the tub and hanging them on the clothesline that stretched across the large room. I looked down the spacious hall and sighed, taking in all the impeccably clean tubs that we had all scoured the night before as part of our routine before we went to bed. Normally when I washed up, I was surrounded by people, listening to their conversations and smiling to myself as I heard their jokes and stories, even if they weren't meant for me. Here, I felt like a part of society.

Now, I would be alone, and I couldn't help but feel that this was how things were going to be for the remainder of today and tomorrow – my last days at the Academy. I might as well be in a room all by myself, because no one would be talking around me. They'd all just be silently judging, glaring their hatred at me instead of verbally expressing it.

And I have Jack to thank for that, I thought to myself bitterly as I lowered myself into the water and scrubbed the hardening mud off my skin.

I didn't mind the burning sensation the wire brush left behind as it scraped off layers of my body. It was a cleansing ritual, a ceremony of getting rid of the day's mistakes and slip-ups until I was free, ready to start fresh in the morning. I always went to bed with the delusional hope that maybe tomorrow would be my miracle day. Maybe tomorrow would be the day everything clicked, and I could just keep up with everyone else. Maybe tomorrow would be the day people were proud of me.

It never was.

I eased myself out of the wooden basin, pulling on my spare uniform pants, and headed back to my room with my wet clothes bundled up in my arms. Once I managed to open my door with my full hands, I kicked it shut behind me, setting my still soaked clothes on my mattress and pulling a line of rope from under my bed. I had learned it was best to keep up your own clothesline because the bathroom's line was often pillaged by cadets too lazy to clean their own outfits. Not that my clothes would have fit them; I was a little on the small side.

I backed away from my DIY set up only when I was sure that the cord was firmly tied to the door hinge and the far post of my bed and that it would hold the weight of my wet clothes. Then, I walked over to my trunk and pulled out a canteen full of crushed arnica, chamomile, lavender, and Saint-John's-wort leaves and blossoms. The different herbs were ground up and blended together to form a type of poultice.

Many people would laugh if they saw me using this, call it an old wife's tale and all that, but ever since I could remember I'd been using this stuff. And for me at least it had worked. I took a small amount of the cream and smeared it across the worst of my bruises, the ones that physically kept me from moving properly, and reached back into my locker to pull out some bandages and medical tape. These supplies were not standard issue for cadets, but due to my excessive visits to our medical wing, the Head Nurse, Mrs. Crawford, had given me my own supplies and care instructions.

It really saved both of us a lot of time.

Once I was satisfied that I had treated myself to the best of my ability, I let my locker slam shut and slowly eased myself down onto the mattress until I was lying on my back, practically immobile. It wasn't that it hurt that bad, though it did *really* hurt. I just hoped that if I stayed still long enough I would just melt away, vanish, and I wouldn't have to deal with any of this anymore.

Just as my eyes were drifting shut though, someone tapped on my door, and I painfully sat up, reaching for the nearest shirt I could find and slipping my stiff arms into the sleeves.

"Enter," I called, standing up and fumbling with the buttons down the front. The heavy oak swung open to reveal Jax standing in the doorframe, looking rather out of place and uncomfortable as he stooped to fit in the six foot space. "Sir," I gaped, quickly bringing myself to attention and wincing as he took in the herbs and dressings on the mattress along with the already stained bandages I had taped to my chest.

"At ease, Byrne," he said gently, waving me towards my bed, and I uncomfortably sat down as my S.O. entered my room and took in the small surroundings. A gruff smirk pulled at his lips as he ducked under the clothesline running diagonally across the room. "I remember those days," he commented, looking over his shoulder at me. "Some asshat would always be stealing some part of someone's uniform from the washroom clothesline. You're smart, kid."

"Not really. Everyone does this, sir," I lied, not knowing if anyone actually thought to create their own clothesline in their rooms. My answer came when Jax looked at me skeptically and scoffed.

"Not really. No one does this," he said and sighed, pulling the chair from my desk and sitting across from me. "Why are you here, Byrne?" he asked after a few moments of uncomfortable silence. I frowned, not quite following his question.

"I'm…I'm not sure I understand, sir."

He laughed incredulously and sat back in the chair, gesturing at me as though it were self-explanatory.

"That right there!" There was an air of exasperation in his eyes. "Byrne, are one of the toughest kids I've seen come through this joint. Relatively, you understand. You're nowhere near as strong as the other cadets, but you're one of the most determined kids I've ever had the privilege to meet."

He leaned back in the chair, letting his tall form sag against the wood as he continued. "I just don't understand why you've stayed around. I can't figure out why you haven't bailed on this yet."

"I don't understand why everyone expects me to," I responded quickly and quietly and then, as an afterthought, added, "sir. Service is mandatory, so...here I am. Just like everyone else."

"You really are fearless aren't you?" he mused, staring at me in intense bafflement, but I shook my head.

"No, sir. I'm...frankly, sir, I'm scared out my mind."

He sighed, and when he looked at me I was surprised by the amount of care and inexplicable fear in his eyes.

"Then why in the gods' names are you still here, boy?" His words were earnest, begging. "You know this is a death sentence, and you wouldn't be the first one to desert."

I was quiet for a little bit, staring sullenly at my hands. Then, I scoffed lightly and gave the timeworn answer that every superior I'd ever met seemed to like to hear.

"Because I haven't got any other choice."

"No..." he said quietly, and I looked him in the eye, hoping he couldn't see how tired I was. "No, you're not that bound by honor to blindly go to your death. And being an orphan of the State isn't a death sentence for you, you're resourceful. You could figure out a life outside of here. That's not it."

"Then what is it, sir?" I asked, entertaining his train of thought, wherever it was going. I was too tired to play along and give him another answer.

"You're staying for someone." I looked away from him, hands picking at each other in my lap. "You and the corporal, the two of you are..." He cleared his throat, frowning, and tried again. "How long have you and Miller been...together?"

The question was awkwardly phrased, delivered with even less grace, and I looked up at him with wide, fearful eyes so fast something cricked in my neck.

"Uh – uh, we're – we're not...*together*. At *all*, sir. I mean, we're friends, but we're not...an item, no–"

Jax held up a hand to stay my jumbled words and laughed quietly as he smiled at me. My heart was in my throat, and he waited a few moments to compose himself before speaking.

"Boy, with a secret like that you need to learn how to lie," he warned, expression growing serious, and lounged back in his chair. "You, uh...going steady? That how you say it?"

I cleared my throat and looked down, my face burning.

"Yes, sir. A year now," I mumbled, trying and failing to keep from shaking with fear. He seemed to notice my unease and sighed, shaking his head pityingly.

"I've had my suspicions since last year's Hunt, Byrne. But there's no need to worry about any kind of discipline from me." I slowly looked up at him, eyes wary. "You're not the first couple of cadets to come through here who seem a bit too close one moment and then a bit *too* distant the next – I never got on any of their cases about who they spent their time with." He paused. "And you seem to have forgotten that Miller was here before." I smirked, silently acknowledging that I caught his drift.

"Bottom line, cadet, is this. Life's too short to be imposing regulations on…that type of thing, especially when my job is to send all of you to fight each other to death." He paused, clearing his throat. "And that there is my *personal* advice to you as your S.O." I stared at him in slight confusion, and he got to his feet, huffing and locking his hands behind his back. "Well, cadet." I quickly got to my feet and stood at attention. "There's one other thing I need to address with you. I know that…unorthodox 'training' happens after hours." I swallowed.

"I don't know what you're talking about, sir."

"No. If I was your age, standing where you are now, I 'wouldn't know' either," he sighed, a tired expression on his face. "But the fact remains that it does happen. Your honor code prevents us from knowing about it, though, so I'm going to do something for you." He turned to face the door and gestured for someone to come in, and I clenched my jaw a little when I saw that it was Jack, a mallet looped in his belt. I knew it was a little petty, but I was still pissed. "He's here to put a lock on your door. For tonight and tomorrow, I want you to keep it *shut*. No one gets in unless you want him to."

"I don't need your protection, sir," I muttered, eyes fixed on Jack.

My S.O. sighed in aggravation, stepping up to me and grabbing fistfuls of my shirt.

"Look at yourself, newbie! It's a miracle you've kept up this long if this is how you look after every single day, and I know *this* is an easy pounding for you. If the other cadets get in here, I wouldn't be surprised if we have to scrape you off the walls in the morning!" I didn't answer and just stared at him, expression inscrutable. Whatever he saw made Jax slowly shake his head, and he released my uniform. "Gods, Byrne...you've got too much guts for your own good." With that he turned away, heading for the door. "You take care of that one, Miller. He's gonna get into a lot of trouble." He left the room, adding over his shoulder, "I can tell."

I waited a few moments, just staring at my boyfriend, before I turned to my bed and snatched up the medical supplies, throwing them back into my footlocker. My fingers fumbled with the buttons on my shirt as I hurried around my room, straightening the blankets and sheets on my bed and spacing out my uniform on the clothesline to help it dry faster.

Anything to keep busy.

The door shut.

"Tristan—"

"Why didn't you tell me that Jax knew you were gay?" I interrupted. Jack just shrugged, awkwardly shifting on his feet, and I rolled my eyes. "Look, just put the lock on the door and go."

He clenched his jaw and blew out a huff of air as he pulled a few nails out of his pocket and braced the slide bolt against the door and doorjamb.

"Can you come over and hold this here while I hammer these in?" he asked, voice quiet, and I came over, wincing as I raised my arms above my shoulders to where my boyfriend was holding the lock against the frame. "Watch your fingers."

He quickly and expertly drove the metal slivers into the oak with a single blow from the mallet, and I recalled my angry words at the obstacle course. *Hell, you're supposed to be a gods-damn carpenter!*

"We done here?" I asked as I stepped away, and he tested his handiwork, closing and locking the heavy door. He yanked back on the knob hard to see if it would hold and was apparently satisfied.

"Not quite," he sighed.

He turned to face me, running his hands through his sweaty hair and leaving them there, locked and tangled at the back of his head. He took in a deep breath and braced himself, eyes closed; it was almost as though he were mentally preparing himself for whatever it was that he was planning to say. After a good minute of silence, I rolled my eyes and made the first move – as usual.

"You're not going to make the situation any better standing there and giving your whole speech in your head. You should know that by now." He opened his eyes and let his hands fall back down, arms crossing over his chest. "Just come on. Say it."

"I'm sorry."

I blinked in surprise and stared at him. Straight to the point this time.

"Wow."

"I should have thought before intervening it's just…I'm used to protecting people. It's what I *do* – if I'm not protecting the people that I care about, then I feel like I'm doing something wrong, okay? But I guess that's what happens when you've been to the front lines three times. You learn that it doesn't matter how *good* someone is at being a soldier – you take *care* of them!" He broke off, looking away and lifting one hand to pinch the bridge of his nose as he closed his eyes in aggravation.

"*That* is the mark of a good soldier," he continued, voice hard, and lowered his hand. "Not how well you can shoot a gun, not how much stamina you've got. It's how well you take care of your own. And if I don't start taking care of you here, when I get to the fields I'm never going to forgive myself when I find your dead body in the trenches because *I* wasn't there to protect you!"

"What, you think that helping me when there's no danger around is somehow going to fix your guilt when I die because you suck at keeping me safe?" I demanded, gesturing at him in disbelief. "Because if your idea of helping me out there is the same as your idea of helping me here, then you are going to end up landing me in a heap of trouble. That's why there's a damn lock on my door now!"

That was cheap shot, and we both knew it. Thankfully though he could tell I was just trying to intentionally piss him off, and I watched as he took a deep breath, briefly closing his eyes.

"No," he countered slowly, "my idea of keeping you safe is showing those boneheaded morons currently running sixteen miles around the Academy how to keep each other safe. I teach them that, I won't have to be around to protect you all the time."

"That, and you'll have someone else to blame when you find my dead body," I added in an undertone and immediately regretted it.

"Don't you dare! Don't you *dare* say that!" he nearly shouted, taking a step towards me and pointing at me furiously.

In my mind's eye, I could see Jack, running along the muddy hellhole that was one of the trenches on the front lines, clad in the uniform he was still currently wearing. I could see him finding my body, my dead eyes staring up at him and at the smoke filled skies above us, and I knew what would happen then. It would not end well for anyone: friend, foe, or himself.

Apparently, Jack could tell what I was thinking.

"Don't. Don't think about it, Tris," he sighed, anger dying immediately, but I quickly shook my head, tears pricking at my eyes and hands shaking again as I pressed them over my face, trying to hold myself together. "Aw, man." I took in a shaking, sobbing breath and shook my head again. "Damn it, Tristan...come here."

He stepped over to me, and I took a weak half-step forward, wrapping my arms around him and pressing my face into his shoulder as he stooped ever so slightly to hug me. He was mercifully silent and just let me quietly cry into his uniform and listen to the muffled thudding of his heart in my ear.

"I don't want to die," I finally whispered, voice cracking, and above me Jack scoffed, resting his chin on my sandy hair and rubbing my back to try and soothe me.

"'Course you don't, and I'll make sure you won't."

My reflexive laugh caught in my throat, coming out as a sob, and I tightened my grip on his uniform, pulling him closer to me. He had tried. He had tried to keep that waver out of his voice. But he had failed, and I knew when I pulled away that his eyes would be red-rimmed.

That was the thing about Jack. He never cried, not really. His eyes and nose became red, and he clenched his jaw so tight that sometimes I thought he was going to crack his teeth – but there were never tears. Never.

I don't know where we would've gone from there, but at that moment, someone quickly rapped on the door.

"It's Jones." The words were clipped, filled with simmering anger. I quickly pushed away from Jack, sweeping my bangs over my eyes to hide my tears and ramming my hands into my pockets as I looked at the ground.

"Enter," I called.

The door swung open to reveal a stocky and well-muscled young woman. Her black hair was drawn back from her face in scores of tiny braids, the long tresses wound around each other in a thick bun at the crown of her head. Her hazel eyes were hard and confrontational, and I swallowed as I looked at her hands. They were taped up around the knuckles, the fabric stained with blood from the olive skin beneath. Her tank top was damp with sweat, and when she kicked the door closed behind her, I saw that her right leg was scraped up and bleeding slightly through the drab green fabric.

"Didn't know you were in here, Miller," she said, her smile forced. "Thought you would be out running the course with the rest of the boys."

"You want something, Marcel?" Jack asked, voice leaving no room for small talk. "Or are you just here to be your normal abrasive self?"

"Cool it, hot shot," she snapped, voice dangerous, and I looked at my boyfriend in carefully masked confusion. As far as I knew, neither of us had done anything to piss her off recently. "See, I was on my way back from the punching bags when I saw Jayce running the course with the guys of our platoon."

Oh, fuck.

"I ran with him a little ways," she continued, eyeing me with a bitter expression. "Found out that you two put him out there."

"Your brother had it coming," Jack said gruffly. "They all did."

Marcel scoffed and sauntered up to Jack, jutting her chin out as she glared up at him.

"Oh, aren't you just *saintly* protecting the little weasel. What is he, your little *pet?*" she sneered, and I felt blood creeping up my collar as my hands curled into fists. I could see a muscle working in my partner's jaw as he stared down at her, almost as though she were something unpleasant stuck to the bottom of his shoe.

"Watch the tone you take with me," he whispered, and she laughed, holding up her bloodied right hand and raising her eyebrow as she smirked.

"Bring it, big boy." When Jack made no move to acknowledge her challenge, she stepped up even closer, boots treading on his. "You've seen me at the sandbags, and you know how hard I hit. So *bring it*. That is, if you think you can take me."

A disdainful light glinted in both of their eyes, and when Marcel continued talking, she was addressing me even though her eyes never left Jack's.

"Watch it, shrimp. Our platoon's got a lot of friends…lot of support on campus, and you're not exactly on their good list." Here, her eyes slyly drifted over to meet mine, and a malicious smile pulled at her lips – a bloodcurdling grin that made me want to run the other direction.

"Might get a lot of people visiting tonight…you know, giving *advice*. Who knows? I might even stop by." Here, she looked back up at Jack and smiled sweetly. "You know me. I like the hands on approach."

"I think you should leave now, Marcel," Jack growled, and she feigned innocence, holding her hands up at shoulder height as she began slinking away.

"I'm going." She reached behind herself and wrapped her calloused hand around the doorknob. Her voice became harsh and cruel, her words digging into me and making Jack's eyes blaze. "Not like I want to hang out with a couple of *shags* anyways." My sight went red at the word, and, before I knew what was happening, I was moving.

Much to everyone's surprise, I launched myself forward at my fellow cadet, swinging my arm in a clumsy right hook at her half-opened mouth. My tightly clenched hand collided painfully with the hinge of her jaw in a grating, cracking smash of bone on bone. She stumbled off-balance, swearing viciously, and I quickly regretted my spontaneous strike when she retaliated with her own, punching me square in the nose before grabbing my shoulders and bringing her knee smashing twice into my already bruised stomach and throwing me out into the hall.

"You'll pay for that, you bastard!"

Dazed, the world spinning in nauseating colors, I watched in rather disconnected fear as the livid woman threw herself onto me and grabbed a fistful of my shirt, drawing her arm back to send her iron fist crashing into my face.

"Hey! Hey, knock it off!"

Before Marcel could get any further in pulverizing me, Jack grabbed her around her waist, hoisting her off the ground and throwing her away from me down the hall. Groaning, I pushed myself to my feet, wiping blood away from my face as Marcel and I glared at each other. Jack was poised between us with an arm extended towards each of us. Cadets had gathered in their doorways and were watching us in confusion and open interest, muttering among themselves.

"First off, *language*, Cadet Jones! That was inappropriate and uncalled for, and if Cadet Byrne hadn't been foolish enough to punch you first, *I* would have!" He swung his head around to face me, giving me a look of exasperation meant only for us. "And you! You've caused enough trouble for one day, don't you think? Return to your quarters and *stay* there!"

Unable to speak for fear of spitting blood, I nodded, still glaring darkly at Marcel as she massaged her already swelling cheek.

"Your precious little *pet* busted my jaw!" she snarled, and fear stabbed through my gut as she started towards me again with bloodied teeth bared.

Jack grabbed her by her arms and slammed her back against the wall, glaring down at her.

"Hey!" she spat furiously. "What the hell–"

"Shut up." His words were quick and low, but I could hear them as I limped back towards my room, arms clamped over my stomach. "Listen to me, Jones, and listen well. Cadet Byrne is not my *pet*, nor is he a *shag*." She smirked but then winced as he tightened his grip on her upper arms. "He is *no one's* pet. Your brother is running that course because he can't bring himself to take care of his fellow classmates and instead prefers to laugh at them and pick on them like some schoolyard bully. And you're no better than him." He lowered his head to whisper his final words in her ear, catching her wrists in his hands as she went to hit him.

"If I was as shallow as you, I'd tell you to watch your back. Because if you touch Cadet Byrne or anyone else while I'm here, don't look for me to cover your ass on the battlefield." He backed away slightly, and his eyes were blazing with fury. "Because I won't be there."

He let go of her and moved towards the washroom, back tall and straight, and I quickly closed and locked my door behind me. Despite the heavy barrier, I could still hear Marcel's shouted response.

"Those medals you pin to your shoulder say otherwise, you high-and-mighty, self-important *asshat*–"

The door couldn't block out the sound of the punch my boyfriend landed on her mouth either.

... ‒ ‒ ‒ ...

A few hours later, I groaned in pain as I pulled the tape and bandages off the least painful of my bruises, setting them to the side while I patted around on the mattress to my left for the bloodied rag I had used for my cut mouth and bloody nose. Both had stopped bleeding about twenty minutes after my confrontation with Marcel Jones, and it was only slightly alarming to me that I'd bled that long. Admittedly, I probably should have been more concerned, but for the most part, I was focusing on dealing with my immobile right hand and the purple bruises lacing the knuckles and fingers. Every time I tried to straighten my stiffened joints, burning tears welled up in my eyes, and I was forced to clench my teeth and squeeze my eyes shut against the pain.

It also didn't help my overall state that every time someone's footsteps creaked on the floorboards outside my room I tensed up, waiting for someone to try and open my door only to find that it was bolted shut. But so far no one had dared come near me since Jack clocked Marcel in the face. Sometimes having a guardian did come in handy, it seemed.

Knock. Knock. Knock.

I froze on my bed, staring at the door in fear and anticipation as my stomach churned. If it was Marcel, I was doomed–

"Byrne, it's me."

Sighing in relief, I quickly got to my feet and approached the door, sliding the lock open and letting Jack limp into my room. He had a bucket of cold water in one hand and a wet towel in the other, the bloodied fabric pressed to a rather fresh cut on his forehead.

"What happened to you?"

He smirked bitterly and lowered himself into my chair, slouching tiredly in the hard seat.

"*I* don't have a lock on my door, and Jackson and the Jones siblings have more friends than I originally accounted for." I closed the door behind him and rammed the bolt home, cradling my right hand close to my chest. Behind me, Jack sighed almost smugly with that faux confidence of his. "Nothing I couldn't handle though."

"Soap and towels?" I asked as I headed back to my bed and sat down on the edge of the mattress across from him.

"Nah. Would have been smarter to try that though," he sighed, half-heartedly rolling his eyes and grimacing as his head split with pain. "They tried the old-fashioned boots and fists. Unfortunately for them, I'm a lot better at that than they are. Only one of them got a blow in, and it was a cheap shot." He pulled the cloth away and briefly inspected the blood before reapplying pressure to the wound.

"How so?" I asked, groaning as I tried opening my hand again to no avail. When Jack answered me, his words were painfully reluctant.

"One of them might have smacked me in the head with Hvar's *The Balance and Precision of War*." I snorted, and before I knew it, I couldn't stop laughing. Jack rolled his eyes, giving me a highly unamused look. "Really? It's not that funny."

"It kind of is…I'm sorry, that's almost classic." I snickered and winced, hand going to my sore stomach. I pressed the towel once more against my nose to try to take the edge off the swelling.

"What the *hell* did you punch Marcel Jones for, Tris?" Jack asked in the silence that followed, and I shrugged defensively, avoiding his gaze. "I mean, I know *why* you did it, but what the hell?" I looked up at him and just shook my head. "No. No, no, no, you don't get to slide by on this one with a shrug and a shake of the head. What on earth possessed you to hit *Marcel Jones* of all people?"

We went silent, each waiting for the other to make a move.

"She called us shags," I finally said, not meeting Jack's sympathetic gaze as I picked at the swollen skin of my right hand. "That's not exactly a, uh, an *endearing* term for people like us."

"Tris, the only reason that word has any power is because we let it." I looked at my boyfriend with tired eyes, and he sighed, shaking his head. He got to his feet and sat on the bed next to me, dragging the bucket of water with him as he moved. "Give me your hand."

Grumbling to myself, I reached over and let my hand settle between his own. He turned it over and looked at the bruised knuckles, scoffing as he dipped the cloth he had been holding to his head back into the bucket.

"*Damn*…you hit her hard, Tris." There was a small smirk of pride lurking at the corner of his lips as he brought the wet towel over my hand, trying to cool the hot skin with the cold touch of the water. "Can you pass me those bandages over there?"

I picked up the tangle of dressings and dropped them in his lap, and he sighed, tenderly picking up one end of the fabric and winding it about my palm. Then, he laced it around my fingers until my hand was taped up just like my assailant's own fists. He held it up to me with a slight smile.

"There you go. Next time you hit her, you won't bust up your knuckles as badly." I laughed lightly in response, and his small smile expanded into a grin.

We sat in silence for a little bit, Jack just looking at my hand, until he brought it up to his lips and gently kissed the aching joints – a touch so soft I barely felt the pressure through the fabric. But I did feel the warmth that bloomed in my chest and spread through my body at the gesture. I leaned into his side, and he wrapped his arm around me, letting his left hand hang over my shoulder so it rested against my heart. We sat there in silence for a little until I heard him laugh, and he tightened his embrace.

"Told you that you could handle yourself," he laughed and smiled at me. "You've got guts, Tris."

"Yeah…" I sighed and closed my eyes as the setting sun filtered through the barred window to bathe us both in a soft yellow glow. "Yeah, like Jax said, I've got too much."

"No such thing as too much guts," he answered softly. "Just too much confidence."

"I think those two things come hand in hand, *sir*," I scoffed, rolling my eyes, and he straightened, locking my head under his arm and rubbing his knuckles against my scalp. "Hey – come on, Jack! Ow, get *off!*" He laughed and let go of me, quickly getting to his feet and dropping the rag back in the bucket before heading to the door.

"You going to take your bucket?" I asked, toeing the rough wood. He just waved it away and shook his head.

"Nah, you keep it. I'm sure some of those bruises could use a good soak. I'll see you in the morning, Tris." He smiled at me – a worn, yet ready expression that pulled at the corners of his lips and made his eyes and nose crinkle. "Sleep well."

"Yeah, you, too."

"Like that's going to happen," he scoffed, sliding the bolt free and opening the door. "Between Jayce and the rest of our platoon, especially Marcel and the girls, I don't think that's in the cards for tonight."

"Still…good luck."

Jack just shook his head good-naturedly as he left, and I quickly got to my feet and locked the door behind him. I sighed, leaning back against the thick wood, and closed my eyes in tired resignation. Even though I felt sore and ready to fall apart, there was something relaxed, something heavy that just settled in my bones and left me feeling completely tranquil. That was until someone drum-rolled loudly on my door, and I jumped, suitably spooked. Whoever it was laughed as they walked away, and I headed back over to my bed, lying down and clasping my sore hands over my bruised abdomen.

The setting sun illuminated the sky with a brilliant red through the dirty glass of my bedroom window, and, through half-opened eyes, I watched the blazing orb slowly sink lower and lower in the sky beyond the walls around me. In the hall I could hear people laughing and shouting, their words muffled and tangled up in each other. And as the seconds silently ticked by, I found myself slowly falling asleep, listening to the sounds of a life barred to me.

DAY TWO, PART ONE

It was somewhere between midnight and the early hours of the morning when I heard the first creak of the floorboards in the night. The sound sent me bolt upright in bed with my heart hammering in my chest. Barely daring to breathe, I pulled my covers away from my stiff body and swung my legs off the bed. My body protested viciously against the movement, and I painfully stood, waiting in shivering silence at the foot of my mattress. Someone was in the hall, and if they came through my door, I wasn't going to let them have the pleasure of catching me unaware. Taking in a deep breath, I sat down on my footlocker, back rigid and eyes watching the moonlit doorknob as I waited for the creaking to resume.

"Come on," I whispered to myself, trying to dissipate the anxiety and anticipation building up inside of me. My heart felt as though it was going to burst through my bruised and battered ribcage. "Come on, stop waiting and try the damn door..."

And then, as if whoever was waiting outside had heard me, another shuddering creak broke the still air, followed closely by the softer squeaks of booted feet on ancient wood. I stood up once more, the fear inside me forcing me to get up and move. I felt as though if I didn't do something, didn't keep moving, I was going to pass out. But a few moments later, being the fickle human being I was, I sat down again, dropping my head into my hands and bracing my elbows on my knees.

It's locked, I told myself and looked up at the door once more. *Everything will be fine.*

A thought struck me, and I sat up a little straighter.

Unless of course they got smart and all body-slammed it at once.

That would wake up the overseers. It's fine. They won't do that – it's too loud.

As I sat at the foot of my bed facing the doorway, I turned my anxious thoughts over and over in my mind. My trembling hands tried to find comfort in each other, fingers lacing together until they were inseparable. But still I felt nothing, no sense of safety in the clenched joints pressed against my lips, and I shakily stood up, crossing my arms and clenching my upper arms in my hands. I returned to my bed once more, heart pounding, and fixed my eyes on the shadowed door.

As I watched, the doorknob turned, and the hinges strained against the unrelenting wood.

"What's holding you up?"

I took in a deep breath and released it slowly, calming myself with the knowledge that my fellow cadets weren't getting in unless they wanted to bring our superiors running. That didn't in any way calm the suffocating butterflies that were crowding up my throat, but it was nice to know.

"I don't know. I think he's *locked* it." The hoarse, bickering whispers continued until finally I was able to identify one of the aggravated voices behind the oak slab.

"Open the door, Jayce!" It was Marcel.

I took in another breath and lay back against my pillows, hands folded tensely over my lap and eyes closed. *It would be okay.*

"There a problem here?"

My eyes snapped open, heart stopping.

"Damn you to *hell*, Miller!" Jayce hissed, and I listened to the floorboards creak under shuffling footsteps. "Can't you mind your own business for once?"

"How about you all let the kid rest? He's beat to hell, and he's got a day left to live."

"And we should care *why?* We've all got that death sentence, and I'm gonna spend it sore and uncomfortable thanks to your little show in front of Jax!"

"Told you they were shags," Marcel growled, and I quickly got to my feet, hand hovering above the lock on the door. But just as I was about to open it, something heavy slammed into the wood, making me start, and I backed away, arms locking around my upset stomach.

"I thought you learned your lesson about using that word."

"*He* was the one that knocked you in the mouth?"

"*Down*, Jayce," the young woman warned, and I could almost see her eyes flashing in defiant anger. "You know, I'm starting to think we've got a bigger beef with you than shrimp in there."

There was silence, and my chest was starting to ache from how hard my heart was pounding. I could hear its rapid pulse in my ears, throbbing and roaring like an ocean.

"You really want to go down this road?"

My boyfriend's words were softly spoken, calculating – evaluating whether or not this was really going to be worth his time. After a few seconds of silence, he had his answer. The sounds of blows striking and bodies crashing against the doors and walls practically echoed in the night, and I sighed in exasperation.

"*Dammit*, Jack," I groaned, grinding the heels of my palms into my eyes.

In no time, I heard the overseers' doors bang open down the hall, and their shouted orders to 'cut it out' carried clearly into my room. Feeling sick, I sat down, back against the oak door, and waited. There was no way I was going to be able to sleep now. That and skipping dinner hadn't really done me any favors. I was too wired to let my mind rest, especially knowing that, a mere foot away, Jack was taking a pounding for me.

My eyes burned with tears, and I took in deep breaths to calm myself down. My hands shook in my lap like leaves in one of the winter storms that blew in come December. That damn shaking…

Eventually though, the sounds in the hall died away until all I heard was a shuffling noise just on the other side of my backrest. Something heavy sat down behind me, and I could hear their tired sighs through the closed door. And just when I thought I was going to pass out from holding my breath so long, my sentinel spoke.

"Go to bed, Tristan."

I heaved a sigh of relief and let my head thud back against the oak.

"You want to come in?" I asked, trying not to laugh in relief.

"Nah." Jack shifted behind me, and I could hear the smallest tinge of pain in his voice. "I think I'm good out here."

"You sure?" I pressed, turning my head and speaking to the seam between the frame and the door itself. I heard my boyfriend scoff lightly, and his voice came through a little louder. He must have been talking to the same place I was.

"*Don't* tempt me, Tris." I smiled, and I could almost see his half-grin in my mind's eye. "You go get some sleep. I won't be going anywhere." I got to my feet, pulled a blanket and pillow off my bed, and headed back to the door, dumping my load on the rough floors. "Tristan?"

"I think I'll be sleeping right here tonight," I answered as I lay down with my back to the door, ignoring how the moonlit ground dug into my bruised body. Jack snorted.

"Yeah, we'll see how long *that* lasts."

I rolled my eyes and looked over my shoulder to where he would have been sitting if he were in the room with me.

"I'm not the one who needs the beauty sleep," I teased, and Jack's muffled laugh carried to my ears.

"Alright, Tris. For *real*, go to bed." I smirked as I settled my head back down on my pillow and drew the blanket tighter around me.

"Yes, sir." I didn't know if he heard my sarcastic reply or not, but before I knew it, I was lost in deep, dreamless sleep.

...───...

My eyes opened slowly, and the dusty floor came into focus.

I sleepily shifted my gaze upwards to the frost lining the barred window beside my empty bed. Beyond the glass, the barely risen sun tinted the dark horizon yellow – early morning, then. The air was bordering on frigid, and I could faintly see my breath before my lips. Groaning at how stiff my joints were, I started to push myself up and winced as my muscles and bruises sharply protested. As much as I hated to admit it, Jack had been right.

I *really* shouldn't have slept on the floor, solidarity or no. As I got to my feet, my knees and ankles painfully popped and cracked from the cold, and my back ached from the awkward angle I'd slept in. Overall, I just felt unbelievably lousy.

"Let's see how bad you are," I muttered and unwound the bandage around my right hand. "Ugh…spectacular."

The skin was swollen, a disgusting mix of angry red and purple. A closer examination revealed a little bit of blue around the knuckles. Face twisting into a grimace, I changed out of my sleepwear and into my uniform, which was still a little damp from yesterday. I wasn't exactly in a position to complain. My hands went through the daily routine without much thought, numb to the aches and pains that jolted through my body at every movement in the biting cold.

Yank on the olive green pants that are a little too wide around the waist and pull on some socks. Put on combat boots and tuck the bottoms of the pants into the tops of the shoes. Tie them tight. Put on the belt with the knife and tighten it as much as possible. Pull on the white undershirt. Pull on the button down olive green shirt. Tuck it into the belt.

I was now ready for the day.

The inky velvet of the sky was still all but untouched by the sun, and, yawning, I carefully opened my door, pulling back on the handle and pushing forward on the wood at the same time to quiet the loud groan of unoiled hinges. It was a tactic I'd become very skilled at over the last four years, but as the door swung open to reveal the dark hallway, my stomach plummeted.

"Jackson." The name slipped from my lips before I could think, and I was left staring awkwardly into the face of the tall cadet before me. In the dim lighting, his face looked less red and his hair darker, but his cold blue eyes seemed to have turned to steel, flashing and blazing with anger and a general pent up urge to really beat the crap out of me.

"Morning, Byrne." We stood there in awkward silence while Alec stared me down, and I couldn't help the fear prowling around in my gut as I waited for him to continue. "You ready for deployment day?"

I nodded wordlessly and tried to stare up at him with what I hoped was an innocuous expression as I clenched my trembling hands at my sides. Jackson smirked, crossing his arms and leaning against the doorframe, and forced me to take a step back into my room.

"You know, Byrne, I really hope so." He laughed bitterly and drew the back of his hand across his nose as he stepped closer to me, crossing the threshold into my room. "Because Miller's not going to be there to protect you out there, even if that's what he says. And once he's gone, I swear to the gods we're gonna kick y–"

Without pausing to think, I stepped back and brought the door slamming shut into his face. With a howl of pain, he went stumbling back with thick hands clamped over his bloodied nose. I ran around him, not daring to stick around to see how that had turned out, and tore off down the hall, descending the spiraling staircase two steps at a time while the rest of the floor woke up to the sound of Jackson swearing up a storm.

The air outside was cold, the gloom of early dawn pierced only by the failing flashlights of the cadets on sentry duty and the lampposts scattered across campus. Those were spotty at best with their reliability, seeing as most of the power of the generator below the school was allotted to radio transmitters and other war tech.

So there I was, sprinting across the Academy, the sharp air rushing in and out of my lungs and starting to dry out my lips. Briefly I worried about them getting chapped but pushed the thought out of my head, focusing instead on the way my feet pounded into the ground and how the shock travelled up my legs and rattled in my knees and ankles. I focused on how hard my heart throbbed in my chest, pounding to the point where I thought it was going to burst. I focused on how my muscles ached, and my bruises protested – on how the wind raked through my hair and stung my pale skin until it was red.

These were the sensations that told me I was alive.

"Hey, you!" I came to a stumbling halt, turning around and facing the glaring point of light coming towards me. "Declare yourself!"

"Tristan Byrne, 34927530, Platoon 306, North Hall," I recited and waited as the cadet drew close enough for me to identify him. "Hey, Andrew."

His eyes narrowed as he looked at me carefully, as though determining whether or not I was actually who I said I was. When he was close enough to actually see my face in detail, he smiled, white teeth flashing against his dark skin as he lowered the light from my eyes.

"Byrne, my man," he laughed, coming over and extending his left hand. "How's it been?"

"Good," I lied, awkwardly taking his left hand and giving it a few shakes before releasing and stepping back. "How are things with Chance?" He shrugged, laughing to himself as we started walking down the path once more.

"Same old, same old. She's still going off praying at every hour of the day and night, but you know that's all normal for her."

"That is true," I said, thinking of the deceptively frail-looking cadet draped with amulets of the gods. "Her favorite still Mars?" I followed him closely as he swung his flashlight from side to side, still doing his job as he talked to me.

"Nah, man. It actually hasn't been Mars for a while. She's fawning over Salus now."

"Goddess, right?"

"Yeah, our lady of salvation." He scoffed, rolling his eyes and laughing softly. I frowned as we walked, trying to bring my unsteady breathing under control, and looked at him questioningly.

"You don't believe in them, do you?" My friend initially shrugged, as though he were unsure, but then shook his head.

"Nah, man, and I'm being honest here. I mean, if they did exist they'd have fixed all this already. We're their *charges*, their *kids*. If they're so real, why aren't they helping us out?"

"True."

"What about you?"

"I'd like to…" I began, finally catching my breath, "but they don't like to make it easy do they?" He shook his head, grinning.

I liked Andrew Harris. I really did. He was casual and friendly on the outside, and once you really got to know him, really dug deep beneath the sensitive mask he showed everyone, he was as tough as nails. He also always found time to scratch out beautiful poems and short stories about his home – a mining state down in the south that we'd lost a few years back to the Mezitain. No one had seen it coming, and the takeover had been brutal – enough so to rival our own raids.

Andrew's family hadn't made it out of their home alive, and for weeks afterwards he'd had wild mood swings. He'd call out for his little sister Camille in his sleep, but no one dared to bring it up with him the next day. He'd been falling apart at the seams, and there had been nothing we could do. The instructors just wrote him off as another casualty. All of a sudden though, things just stopped. He was laughing and smiling again; he slept through the night more often. And it didn't take us very long to realize that his recovery had coincided with the arrival of Cadet Idris Chance.

Idris – or Id, as we'd nicknamed her – was an escaped POW from the Mezitain prison camps in the state where Harris used to live, and she was about as shell-shocked as they came. Though Jack said there was also other stuff going on with her, and I had to agree. When she first arrived, she'd start at loud noises, scream at people she almost collided with when walking around corners, and prayed nonstop to the gods. She had amulets and talismans of every single one of them that she alternately wore about her neck. She knew all the prayers, and literally *everything* was an omen.

And from the moment she had set foot on the Academy grounds, Cadet Harris had found a new little sister. They looked nothing alike; he was tall and lanky, yet powerful. She was small and frail, skin so light she looked like a ghost half the time – or something out of a nightmare with her wild mane of black hair framing equally untamed eyes. But whatever she was or wasn't, Andrew had seen something in her worth saving, and now she was much more settled. Now, she only flinched when people startled her, and she definitely spoke her mind more often.

Not everything that came out of her made a lot of sense, but it *was* progress.

Jack was always warning me to stay away from Harris and Chance, though. According to him, Idris was on the verge of breaking. She just hadn't gone off the deep end yet. But whether or not my boyfriend was right – and he probably was – I wasn't going to leave the two of them on their own just because Id was *almost* crazy.

Weren't we all?

"You heading to mess?" he asked, and I nodded. "Okay, I'll walk you there."

"Look, Andrew, you don't have to do that. I'm sure you've got places to be." He held a hand up to quiet me and just smiled, amusedly shaking his head.

"It's my job, Byrne. And you can't be too careful – especially with *you*. You're almost as bad of a troublemaker as Id, except you seem to do it on purpose."

"Thanks," I said, smiling to myself. He cleared his throat and checked his watch. "Something going on?"

"Yeah, Id finishes her morning prayer in ten minutes," he explained ruefully. "I've got to go get her from the Lake."

"What's she doing down there so early?"

He sighed, massaging his forehead. When he spoke, his voice was tired and resigned.

"She's trying to 'commune with the swans' so that she can 'speak with Jupiter.'"

I nodded, digesting what he'd just said.

"So, no luck with the whole making sense thing yet, then?"

"No, not so much."

. . . — — . . .

I briefly waved goodbye to Andrew as I walked up to the stone building before me, watched as his silhouette faded down the dawn-lit paths towards the lake at the far side of the school. No doubt he was on his way to drag Idris possibly from the middle of the water and get her presentable in time for mess hall check-ups. Though, it wasn't like her appearance mattered anymore.

The Academy had become a rather relaxed place as of late, and, according to Jack, it was because our instructors were finally realizing just how attached they'd gotten to us. Idris would be reprimanded for her antics, but our superiors would remember her fondly in the days to come.

I turned back around and looked up at the building before me. It was old, the limestone walls streaked with moss and ivy reaching for the steepled roof. And up at the top of the wall, a symbol of wrought iron was inlaid into the massive bricks, creating a sigil that resembled a two merged with a four. Respectfully, I dipped my head as I passed below the arch, whispering a brief prayer to Jupiter, king of the gods, in my mind as I went.

Jack would've rolled his eyes, but I figured given the odds against me it would be nice to have some divine assistance on my side.

The heavy oak doors were open against the walls, revealing the cavernous hall behind them. Rows upon rows of long benches and tables stretched out before me, and massive, industrial lights hung from the ceiling, bathing everything in a surprisingly soft glow. A furnace burned in the corner, heat from the large woodstove radiating throughout what was once a church thirty years ago — before this war began and the generals repurposed the mission for the War Academy.

At the back of the room I could see Enid bustling around in the open kitchen, shifting the contents of massive basins of rice and beans and questionable meat around with a large wooden paddle. A few other nondescript workers hurried about her as well, laying out the tarnished and scratched steel plates and utensils on the tables.

And, just as they were every time I came into this building, my eyes were drawn to the massive stained window that hung above kitchen area, illuminating the hall floor with patches of colored light as the rising sun struck the glass. Herul — demigod son of Jupiter — knelt before a temple of his father, gripping his sword ceremoniously by the hilt with the tip driven into the ground. He was being blessed for his victory against something; I didn't know nor care what.

I cleared my throat as I made my way into the mess hall, my boots landing with muffled clicks on the flagstone floor. I thought I was being quiet, but Enid must have heard me with those bat-like ears of her. She looked up at me briefly as she checked the rice, gruffly hmphed at my presence, and went back to what she was doing.

"Morning, Enid," I called, unsure as to whether or not she wanted to talk to me today – she never did, but it didn't hurt to try. She made another grunting noise and went to intersect one of the workers carrying plates as I continued to hover nearby.

"Sit down and shut up," she scowled.

Reluctantly, I took my place at the table. For the past four years, I had taken the seat at the very end of the bench, farthest away from everyone else and closest to the kitchen's backdoor. I was a strategist – I *always* had a getaway plan.

"How was your night?" I asked, looking up at the cook as she went by.

"You're gonna get the same answer you've gotten all four years, cadet. So stop asking."

Despite her outward appearance of a grouchy old woman, I could see a gruff smile pulling at the corner of her mouth. Or at least I liked to think I could. As she noisily set the places around me, I sighed, clearing my throat and extending my arms out in front of me to stretch out my stiff shoulders like a cat.

"Mind saying it again? You never know, I might…might find it nice to hear."

She stopped, turning to face me in brief startlement at my softly spoken words. But as soon as the expression appeared, it was gone, replaced with her usual brooding scowl as she bustled along once more. At first, I thought she wasn't going to say anything, but then, something kind sparking deep in her eyes…

"None of your business, you little runt." She slammed a cup down in front of me, just as she always did, and swept back off to her kitchen.

I smirked to myself, taking the empty tin into my hands and twirling it at an angle between my fingers. So it went – every single day when I came down here, I asked her how her night was, and she promptly told me to mind my own self. It was our own little routine, and it was one of many that I was thankful for.

At that moment, I heard a thunder of footsteps on the dirt pathway outside and the flagstone foyer. The workers seemed to simultaneously stop and turn their heads to face the first platoon coming in.

Of course it was mine.

Every floor of the dormitory building was split into three different platoons of thirty-five people – in my case thirty-one of them were men: rough, tough, delusional, save-the-world type men.

The remaining four were the women, and they were some of the most skilled, vicious, and dogged soldiers anyone at the Academy had ever seen. We had actually taken to calling them the Horsemen after the helmsmen of the Apocalypse.

Of course, given that that was their nickname, it was only natural that Marcel Jones was in the front bearing the unspoken moniker of War. Her jaw was set in a tight clench, probably to relieve pain from where I'd hit it last night, and I could clearly see the bruising along the bone from my strike. Her lip, too, was split from Jack's blow. But what puzzled me slightly was the dark splotch around her left eye – a mark that was clearly from a punch to the face. It must have happened last night…

Last night.

I immediately sat up a little straighter, searching through the approaching faces in a mild panic. Where was Jack?

"Looking for your bodyguard, shrimp?" I turned my attention back to Marcel and her girls as she came sauntering over, dropping down onto the bench across from me. She assumed a doubtful expression and shrugged. "I don't know…Jayce gave him a pretty good concussion last night, didn't he, Kat?"

"Yeah." I turned my gaze onto the Mezitain Amaeric who sat down beside me. "In fact, he was throwing up this morning into one of the toilets. Didn't look too pretty." Three of the four girls laughed around me like jackals closing in for the kill.

Katalin "Kat" Soto was a woman of average build who possessed seemingly unending stamina and astonishing strength – though definitely not as much as Marcel Jones. She'd been born in a prisoner of war camp in one of the southern territories after her parents defected from Mezitain. Unsurprisingly, she was raised with a burning hate for her 'home' – that barbed wire-encased shantytown where people starved to death and suffering was the norm.

Predictably, her horseman became Famine.

But before she could continue her mocking comments, Aliyah Moore – a tall, wiry Arikaan with black eyes and dark hair pulled back into a single, long ponytail – leaned forward, forearms braced on the table. She looked skinny, but beneath her dark skin, she was made of steel-cord tendons and titanium bones. Deceptively delicate and wickedly fast, she bore the name Death. She had so far been silent, not speaking, not laughing.

"Marcel," she hissed, her relatively deep voice an even lower whisper. Marcel looked at her and shrugged in question to the woman's pointed stare, and, when War still didn't get what her elder was trying to nonverbally say, Aliyah elaborated with a trademark laconic response. *"Door."*

The other three women looked around at the entrance to the hall, surprised into silence. Jack was standing in the doorway, the bruise on his temple just barely visible under his dark hair. He seemed to survey the room a couple of times before finding us, and I saw his eyes flash dangerously as he put two and two together and started over.

"I *thought* you said he was concussed, Kat," Irina hissed, her ice-blue eyes furious as she glared at her fellow cadet.

Irina Korsakov, the final member of the Horsemen named Pestilence, was a small woman who was barely over five feet tall but had the muscles and build of a weight lifter. With her close-cut, snow-white hair, and surprisingly delicate features, she looked a lot like a warrior fairy.

Katalin shifted uncomfortably under her sharp gaze until Marcel rolled her eyes, gesturing for them to get up and give me space. Around us, the kitchen workers started laying plates of food along the tables, and another three platoons marched in all at once and took their places.

"Come on, girls." She glared at Jack as he came within fifteen feet of us, still smiling that lively, toothless grin that in no way reached his eyes. "Let's give the corporal some space with his pet."

But as the two passed each other, our platoon's eyes watching them, Marcel whispered something out of the corner of her mouth that made Jack's smile falter. A fraction of a second later, he was his normal self again, taking a plate and cup from Enid and sitting down across from me.

"So," he began brightly, reaching for and missing his fork by a good three inches, "how did you sleep?"

I stared at him unimpressed for a few seconds before I spoke.

"You're still seeing double, aren't you?"

"Nah, most things are still in triples." I dropped my fork on the table and rested my head in my hands in defeat. Jack laughed to himself. "I must say...it's *quite* a different way to see the world."

"You do realize that being concussed means you injured your *brain*, right?" I continued, looking up at him, and he shrugged. "No, there's no room for debate here. A concussion *is* a brain injury!" He cleared his throat, and I realized that my voice had gotten quite loud. Sighing, I lowered my volume but made sure that I still sounded just as annoyed. "You should be treating it like you treat any other wound."

"Yeah, around here that means you suck it up and keep going, so…I think I'm doing pretty good, actually." I closed my eyes and pinched the bridge of my nose as my boyfriend accidentally poked himself in the face with his fork. Thankfully, he seemed a little nonplussed by that and paused his efforts momentarily. "Admittedly, the new depth perception may take a bit to get used to."

"You are *impossible*," I hissed in aggravation, but he just smiled and went back to eating at a slower pace while I snatched my fork back up and stabbed it into the gray meat embedded in my rice. "You are going to get yourself killed some day with your stubbornness…"

"Yeah, and you'll get killed by your stupidity, so I think we balance each other out quite nicely." I rolled my eyes and was just about to lift my fork to my mouth when I heard a scuffling sound from my escape door behind the kitchen. I turned my head to follow the noise, Jack doing the same though I could see him squinting in an effort to clear his vision. "What's that?"

"Not sure," I answered and was about to get up and investigate when the sources of the soft commotion made their way into the hall. "Oh, boy."

Apparently, the swans had been *highly* communicative today.

Andrew stepped out of the shadows, soaking wet from about his chest down, with a tired, why-me look in his eyes. His hand was firmly clamped on the shoulder of a wide-eyed, skittish young woman who was equally – if not more so – soaked. Her wiry hair stuck out in every direction, and her doe eyes watched everything at once as she dragged the sleeve of her many-sizes-too-large uniform across her nose.

"What'd she get up to this time?" Jack asked as the South Hall cadet nearly dragged the glowering girl along to sit down next to me. She immediately drew one leg up onto the bench with her, hugging it close to her chest and braced her chin on her knee.

"Why don't you ask her?" Andrew sighed, taking a seat beside my boyfriend. "She's not mute, you know. Or deaf."

I saw Jack's jaw clench slightly as he turned to Idris, a small smile pulling at his lips.

"Hi, Id." She looked at him and tilted her head to the side, making a face. "How are you today?"

She shrugged defensively, making an annoyed noise in the back of her throat and looking away.

"Use your words, Id," Andrew absently chastised, and the unruly mane of dark hair swung around to face him and Jack once more.

"Fine," she said after a little bit, picking at a loose thread on her cuff. "The swans wanted to tell me things…but Andy wouldn't let me listen."

"Id, you were trying to wade out into the middle of the Lake," Harris sighed, and Jack looked between the two of them, eyebrows travelling further up his forehead as the bickering continued. "I couldn't let you go swimming and miss mess. Our S.O. would have killed you."

"Executions are outside of her power," she muttered in annoyance, deliberately missing his hyperbole.

"You *know* what I meant. My point is that you can't go doing things that are going to make you late for the important stuff like mess, Id," he explained patiently, taking another bite of his food. "Talking with swans is one of those things."

"Who are you to disobey the wishes of Jupiter, King of the Gods?" she demanded, eyes blazing, before hunching over herself once more. Andrew, however, didn't react to her outburst and instead continued on with that same calm tone of voice.

"I've told you, Idris – I don't believe in them. That's all."

We unanimously went back to eating until I noticed that the flighty cadet wasn't touching her food. Instead, she was staring at it, and us, in silence.

"You okay, Chance?" Jack asked, swallowing a mouthful of the rice and meat as he spoke. She watched him carefully before quickly shaking her head. "Well, why don't you eat something? It might make you feel better."

Another frantic headshake, and her eyes widened in horror.

"Idris, I know the food doesn't look exactly appetizing," I admitted, taking up Jack's conversation as he shrugged in defeat and went back to his meal. "But it's good food. The beef's a bit stale, but it's still pretty alright." Harris nodded, making a face that said he was reluctantly agreeing but still agreeing, before pushing a bowl over to his ward.

"He *is* right, Id." But instead of trusting us, she wrinkled her nose and drew away. "What's up? Why don't you wanna eat?" She looked around us, as though making sure we wouldn't be overheard, and turned back to stare at us with her intense gaze. "Well?"

"Nothing," she finally whispered evasively, and we returned to our meal.

Once Id made up her mind to not tell us something, we didn't learn anything about it. But I couldn't help noticing that as we continued to eat, she watched us carefully, following the forks to our mouths and back to the plates. Finally, she released her leg from her death grip and lunged forward at Jack, making him jump a little as she pointed at his plate.

"That's rat," she said quickly, before pulling herself back and hunching over her bent knee once more, watching us with those unfathomable eyes.

Jack froze, fork halfway in his mouth, and slowly raised his eyes to look at her to see if maybe she was joking. I cleared my throat and carefully set my utensil down while Andrew frankly looked like he might throw up as he pushed his plate away.

"How do you know this is rat?" Jack asked slowly, fork still hovering before his mouth. She shrugged, rocking back and forth ever so slightly. "*Id*," he warned, and she hunched down even more, slender fingers working the fabric of her sleeves until her skin was pink.

"Kitchens ran out of meat two weeks ago," she explained absently, eyes fixed on the flagstone floors instead of us, and Andrew reached across the table to snap in her ear. She jumped and glared at us.

"How do you *know* this is rat?" her platoonmate pressed.

"Saw them cooking…and the swans told me," she added, perking up slightly as she continued to twist her sleeve.

I coughed, suddenly feeling as though the meat I'd been ingesting all week was reassembling itself and crawling around inside my stomach. Andy and I slowly went back to our food, picking apart the rat from the rice with an utter lack of enthusiasm, but Jack continued to stare at Idris, eyes slightly narrowed in thought and fork still held mid-air.

"You said they ran out of meat *two* weeks ago," he began, and she nodded while Harris and I looked up in dismay. "So what did we eat last week?" She looked once over her shoulder to make sure that there weren't any servers nearby before she leaned forward and whispered her response.

"Cat."

I dropped my fork into my food and pushed my plate away.

"Lovely," I muttered, bitterly sarcastic, and Andrew nodded in agreement, snatching up his tin and downing the water inside in the blink of an eye. Jack on the other hand looked at her in mild amusement.

"Anything else we should know about the food, cadet?" She looked at him in mild fear at his commanding tone of voice and shook her head. "Are you telling me the truth?" She nodded vigorously, and my boyfriend seemed satisfied. "Alright then."

And without another word, he went back to eating his rat and rice breakfast while Andrew and I gaped. Idris giggled.

"Miller, man, that's *rat*," Andy whispered, aghast, and Jack nodded.

"Oh, I know. Can't pass up a good meal though, can you?" He winked at Idris, grinning broadly, and she smiled shyly. "Besides, it kind of tastes like chicken."

"No, it doesn't," I groaned, picking through my food until I'd separated most of the rice from the meat. He shrugged, taking in another mouthful of the rodent-peppered grain.

"It does if you use your imagination."

I couldn't argue with that.

DAY TWO, PART TWO

We had finished eating and clearing away our plates when someone stood up from the staff and officers' table, moving towards the raised dais and podium at the front of the room. Slowly, the soft, pervasive buzz of conversation came to a stop, and all eyes turned to face the austere, straight backed Xiang woman standing before us. She looked around at us, sharply tugging the hem of her navy blue uniform down with white-gloved hands even though the garment was already brutally pristine.

"Oh my gods," Jack breathed, blinking a few times to make sure he was really seeing who he thought he was. "That's G.A. Agathon." I side-eyed my boyfriend, brows furrowing in a subtle question. I never paid attention to the names in modern politics. "General of the Army? She's head of *everything*...her only superior is the Commander-in-Chief."

"Attention!" she shouted, and we all got to our feet, pushing the benches in and staring straight ahead with our hands behind our backs and feet together.

She waited a few moments, looking out over us, her dark, almond shaped eyes meeting every single one of our own. Her intense gaze struck mine and quickly moved on, leaving me feeling sick to my stomach. Her hair was pulled up into a tight bun, and her skin was clear and unbroken save for a thick scar that ran down her left temple and vanished below her high collar. She was dressed in full uniform, and her left shoulder glittered with more awards and medallions than I knew even existed. A ceremonial saber hung by her left side and a standard issue handgun was holstered to her right leg. Her stance was confident, strong, imposing.

Whoever this G.A. was, she meant business.

"Members of the 40th class of the Amaeric War Academy," she began, voice cold and commanding. "I am here today to not only welcome you into the ranks of the Amaeric Army, but also to convey to you the status of our borders – of the fronts our brave men and women are fighting and giving their lives to defend." She paused, weighing her choice of words carefully before proceeding.

"I know that people have been telling you that we are winning, that we are pushing back the enemy on all fronts. And while that may be true for the Mezitain to the south, it is hardly so everywhere else. To the east, west, and north, the Brettain are parrying our every thrust. They are blocking our every strike. And their supplies and resources are unending.

"Simply put, they are better trained, better manned, and better supplied. Reports from intelligence officers abroad have already confirmed what I and many of my advisers already fear. Our navy on the western coasts is losing ground, and the northern fronts are struggling to maintain their positions." She paused again, looking down and setting her hands upon the sides of the podium.

I could see her fingers curl around the wooden edges and took note of how her shoulders rose and fell with a veiled sigh. When she looked back up, her mouth was set in a hard line, and she squared her shoulders, hands clasped once more behind her back.

"Queen Auriane is winning this war. And while I have counseled our Commander-in-Chief on retaliatory measures, he has deemed them unfit. Instead, he proposes that we strike back on all fronts simultaneously, that we continue as we have. As such, I have taken it upon myself to give each platoon their assignments today. Some of you will be lucky. Others will not. But those with less fortune will be graced with the honor of a *good* death for a *good* cause."

In the corner of my eye, I saw Jack's gaze shift downwards though his head did not move.

"Regardless of what your fate may be, I know this. Our country is in need of your loyalty and your sacrifice, and it is my honor to officially indoctrinate you into the service of the Amaeric Army and your nation." The air around us was filled with applause from the staff and officers, and she paused, looking down at the podium as she waited for the sounds of congratulations to fade. "Please be seated."

There was a rasping of wood on stone, and, as one synchronous body, we all sat down, eyes still fixed on her.

"Platoons 280, 281, 282, and 283." The benches scraped backwards, and the men and women stood at attention, eyes fixed forward and expressions vacant. "You have shown great skill and loyalty to your nation through your time here, and it is with great pride that I welcome you to our military. You are to be stationed with Captain Larkspur as Unit 31 at the northern front line. Report to this hall tomorrow morning for roll call and deployment. Dismissed." The four platoons noisily pushed their benches in and left the room, and the G.A. continued once it was silent again.

"Platoons 284, 285, 286, and 287. You have shown great skill and loyalty to your nation through your time here, and it is with great pride that I welcome you to our military. You are to be stationed with Captain Robinson as Unit 32, also at the northern front line. Report tomorrow morning to the obstacle course for roll call and deployment. Dismissed."

I tried to shut out her voice, the monotonous recital of death sentences. My hands were shaking in my lap, and I clenched my fists until I was sure my nails had carved bloody crescents into my palms.

Platoons 288, 289, 290, and 291 went to Captain Capello's Unit 33 of the western front line. Platoons 292, 293, 294, and 295 went to Captain Delacruz's Unit 34 in the same region. And 296, 297, 298, and 299 went to Captain Matthews' Unit 35 in the south.

"Platoons 300, 301, 302, and 303 are assigned to Captain Harper's Unit 36 at the eastern front lines," she continued, and I gave a sad, quick smile to Idris and Andrew as they prepared to leave. "Report to the Lake for roll call and deployment tomorrow morning. Dismissed."

The sounds of movement slowly died away, and I looked around at the final one hundred and forty people left.

Unit 37.

"Platoons 304, 305, 306, and 307." We stood. "You, too, have shown great skill and loyalty to your nation through your time here, and it is with great pride that I welcome you to our military. You are assigned to Captain Howell's Unit 37 at the eastern front lines as well. Report to the Lake for roll call and joint deployment with Unit 36. Good luck, and dismissed."

As we turned to leave, I looked to Jack for a small shred of comfort only to see that he was staring fixedly at G.A. Agathon. His eyes were wide with fear as he remained still in a sea of moving people.

And I realized that something was very, *very* wrong.

Jack seemed to snap out of whatever trance he'd fallen into and set off at a quick pace, shoving through our fellow cadets as though suddenly claustrophobic. And that scared me more than anything else because Jack never showed fear like this. Not in public, not even in private, not unless there was a *really* good reason. As soon as we were out of the mess hall and a safe distance away from the building and our higher-ups, I reached out and caught his shoulder. He turned his head away as I forced him to face me, and I sighed in frustration as he looked to the sky above us to avoid eye contact.

"Jack, what the hell is going on?" I demanded, but he just ran his hands over his face, groaning and muttering to himself. "Jack!"

He looked at me and held his hands out helplessly.

"*Howell*, Tris...Howell, he–" There was a slight tremor to his voice, and he took in a deep breath. As he forcefully released it, he locked his hands behind his head. "Eastern front lines alone is a death sentence, but *Howell*... I've heard the stories. He's ruthless, Tris." He turned away from me and quickly walked back towards North Hall.

"How ruthless?" I asked, but he didn't answer. My heart pounded in my chest and my arms trembled as I clenched my hands and ran after him. "Jack, *how ruthless?*"

My boyfriend stopped and turned to face me just long enough to give his cryptic response before hurrying away again.

"He lets no one out alive."

As I stood there, watching his back retreat from me yet again, I felt a coldness spreading inside me. *He lets no one out alive.* What was the point, then? And suddenly, nothing seemed to matter. Dying was no longer just a possibility that I had to stress out about for the next year. I *literally* wouldn't come out alive, so what was the point?

My hands were still shaking, and I looked down at them, considering the trembling skin and bone before me with wide eyes. Would they be clutching a mutilated or severed limb? Would they be trying in vain to stem a river of blood from my body? Or would they just let go of my weapon and thud limply to the ground with the rest of me as I was shot down?

What would they be doing when I died?

When I died. Not *if* I died. *When.* I closed my eyes and forced myself to continue to breathe in and out in an even, rhythmic pattern.

When.

I opened my eyes and looked down at my hands and released one final breath. Finally, they were still.

"Something the matter, private?"

I immediately dropped my hands and clasped them together behind my back. G.A. Agathon was standing behind me, and I was surprised to find she was only a few inches taller than I was. I shook my head, struggling to maintain eye contact.

"No, ma'am," I all but whispered and dipped my head respectfully. She nodded curtly.

"Good. What's your name, soldier?" I shakily cleared my throat.

"Tristan Byrne, ma'am."

"I believe I saw you with Unit 37, did I not?" I frowned, confusion briefly flashing in my eyes. "Photographic memory, Byrne. I see a face, I never forget it." I nodded mutely, and she stared at me, waiting. "Well?"

"I'm sorry, uh – yes. Yes, I am, general."

She nodded to herself before squaring her shoulders and standing at attention. Uncertain, I reciprocated the action, and she lowered her hand. But before she continued on her way, a faintly sardonic smile played at her lips.

"Remember something, private." She leaned forward until I took a half-step back, gaze transfixed by her predatory eyes. "The hands of the righteous *never* tremble." My gut went terribly cold, and when I managed to speak again, my words were barely audible.

"Yes, ma'am."

Without another word, she walked past me, hands returning behind her back and fingers of one hand wrapping about the wrist of the other.

"Privates!" she called, and I raised my eyebrows in surprise as the Horsemen stood at attention facing her. "I understand you four have a pretty special nickname around here…"

I watched them for a little bit before I started walking in the direction Jack had gone.

For some godsforsaken reason, there was someone I needed to see.

...− − −...

I shifted uncomfortably on my feet as I hovered outside the door of a specific Gaius Jax, staring at the bronze plaque emblazoned with his name. Knocking on a door shouldn't be this hard, and yet there I was – waiting for someone to shove me forward. I swallowed nervously, looking down either side of the hall to make sure that no one was coming and back at the door.

Finally, gritting my teeth and reaching out, I knocked once on the heavy oak, the force of the strike driving painfully up my arm.

"Enter!" I swallowed hard and twisted the antique bronze doorknob, pushing the rustic hinges open. Jax was seated behind his desk, casually cleaning out and reassembling a standard issue rifle. He looked up at me briefly before going back to what he was doing. "Didn't realize you had enough muscle to knock on a door that hard," he muttered to himself, and I looked down. "How did your sleeping arrangements work?" His words were no less gruff in his concern, but they were spoken in a soft, quiet way.

"Fine, sir," I answered, voice equally quiet, and lingered there on the threshold.

Jax looked up at me and made a small, ambiguous noise in the back of his throat. He held up the polished, oiled pieces in his hands.

"Some green cadet broke the thing, and I had to strip it all down. I was just repairing it. Made the replacement part myself."

Awkward silence strung out between us once more, and I watched as his blunt and calloused fingers nimbly put the firearm back together, the pieces sliding together effortlessly and locking in place with soft clicks. The oiled cloth ran over the metal cylinders and catches, wiping away metal dust and grime until it shone like a brand new weapon beneath his hands.

"Was there something you needed, private?" he asked without looking up, and I found something comforting in the uncharacteristically quiet way he was speaking.

It was almost as though I could see into another timeline, another universe, where there was no war. Jax would be sitting in front of a fire, whittling something instead of crafting a weapon of destruction and pain. Grandchildren would be gathered around him or tucked under his arm. He'd be telling stories.

"*Byrne.*"

I blinked and was pulled back into reality. The gun was complete in Jax's hands, and after a beat of silence he cocked and aimed it at me. My eyes widened as he pulled the trigger, and I jumped, eyes closing against the anticipated shot that never came.

My S.O. laughed.

"There's nothing in it, kid, but now I know the firing matrix works again." He scoffed, chuckling at the same time. "You're not dying today, newbie."

I looked down at my hands and finally said what I'd come to say.

"Don't worry, sir. I look forward to the day I do."

Jax looked up at me, surprise on his face, but something akin to pity in his eyes as he took in my defensive stance – my crossed arms and downcast eyes. He sighed, getting to his feet and beckoning me to come into his office. I stepped in, closing the door behind me, and Jax rested his hands on his hips, staring at me. Without saying anything, he turned to look out the barred window behind him and watched the grounds below.

"So, you found out about Howell." A statement, not a question.

"Yes, sir," I answered, voice soft. He nodded and continued.

"Ready to die? No fear?"

"Yes, sir." There was something a little more forceful to my response this time, and he looked over his shoulder at me, eyes almost angry.

"You think you're brave because you've embraced the fact that you're going to die? That you're not in denial or scared?" he asked, expression firm and uncompromising. "True bravery is when you embrace the fact that you're going to *survive*." I looked down at my crossed arms, suddenly feeling guilty, and Jax pressed on, watching me. "Because let me tell you, surviving is sometimes worlds worse than dying." He turned back to face the cadets – no, we were privates now – milling about two stories below, and his voice became wistful, solemn.

"You come back from the war with skeletons in your closet…and don't fool yourself. Everybody's got 'em – even if they don't let you see that they do. And the ones who let those bones see the light of day…" Without turning to me, he beckoned me over, and I slowly approached until I was standing next to him, leaning with him against the wall and looking down into the quad.

Idris was screaming again, hands twisting and pulling at her hair, while Andrew was trying to calm her down. Irina Korsakov was standing off to the side, looking uncomfortable, and I figured that she was the one who'd accidentally set Chance off.

Jax looked down at me, locking his hands behind his back.

"Pity *them*, Byrne. Not the ones who died in battle – they received a mercy far greater than any the living'll receive." With that, my battlemaster sat back down at his desk and set to polishing the rifle once more. "If there's nothing else?" I uncertainly headed towards the door, but before I could leave, he started speaking again.

"Byrne." I turned to look at him, hand on the door. "You stick close to Miller when you get out there, you hear me? And you make sure you don't let Captain Howell know you two are as close as you are." His eyes were serious, pained. "And whatever you do, *don't* pull that lion's tail. His bite is even worse than his roar."

"Yes, sir," I whispered and quickly left the room, the hall, and finally the antiquated administrative building in a blur of tense movement and headed back to North Hall.

The air had a light chill to it, a cold bite that told me the seasons were changing and it would be winter soon. And as I walked down the pathways, looking at couples talking and hanging out, picking out who was from the Academy and who'd come from the town, I was given a sharp reminder that – despite unit assignments – Promenade was still tonight. The knot in my stomach doubled in size, and I increased my pace until I was speed walking down the worn and disintegrating concrete paths back to the North Hall. The ground beneath my feet was now more dirt than cement after so many years of rough treatment, but that was the nature of things in war. Stuff was worn into the ground, used up until there was nothing left.

I looked up as I approached the brick building before me and sighed, stomping my feet a few times on the flagstone steps to dislodge any dirt from the soles of my shoes before heading up the spiraling staircase I had sprinted down this morning. In my mind, I could still hear Alec howling in pain from his smashed nose, and I really hoped that wouldn't come back to bite me in the ass. Breathing unevenly as my injured ribs protested at the quick ascent and steep steps, I gratefully hit the landing and walked out into the hall, hands in my pockets head ducked low.

Best-case scenario: no one paid any attention to me because I looked more downtrodden than usual. Worst-case scenario: people saw that I looked more downtrodden than usual and elected to pick on me.

Miraculously, I made it to my room without any confrontations and gratefully slipped into my room, closing the door and locking it. For some reason, no one had ripped the offending contraption from its place, but I definitely wasn't complaining. Sighing, I turned and was preparing to drop down on my bed when I saw that it was already occupied.

My heart – which had picked up its pace at the sight of an intruder – slowed back to a more reasonable speed when I recognized the lanky form reclined on the mattress.

"Sorry I messed up your bed," he called, not sorry at all, and I smiled softly to myself, pulling off my boots and sinking onto the mattress beside Jack. "I was planning to just sit here and wait for you, but it looked really appealing after my night on the floor. That and the room was a bit fuzzy."

"Your concussion?" I asked, laying next to him and resting my head on his shoulder. I nestled against his side as he wrapped his arm around me.

"Yeah, Jayce got me with another cheap shot a little bit before dawn. I thought everyone had gone to bed, but the next thing I knew he was behind me with some antique knuckledusters. Caught me right behind my ear…"

I sat up and gently pulled him with me.

"Can I see?" He nodded and tilted his head away from me, revealing the barely scabbed over welt beneath his hair. "Did Mrs. Crawford patch you up?"

"I told her I slipped in the bathroom." I snorted, and he pointed at me, tired eyes closing. "That was her reaction, too."

"Maybe you shouldn't be dancing."

He opened his eyes and gave me an unimpressed look that I tried to combat by looking as innocent as possible.

"Nice try, Tristan." He rubbed at his eyes and got to his feet, wobbling for a fraction of a second before centering himself. "We're still learning how to dance." I groaned, sitting up in the bed after him. "What? You were making pretty good headway yesterday up in the attic. We've just got to finish up the base steps and practice your footwork, and we'll look just as perfect as everyone else."

"Tell me again why this is so important?"

He ignored my question and headed for the door. When I showed no signs of following him, he turned to face me, his expression pleading and frankly almost pitiful.

"Come on, Tris. I'm just asking this one thing."

"Yeah, well your one thing has a whole lot of caveats that you're conveniently ignoring," I replied, but when he continued to stare, I sighed and wearily stood up. "Fine. Attic again?"

"Yep. Everyone already got their stuff down from there either last night or this morning, so we should be fairly undisturbed." He stuck his head out the door, checking to make sure no one was there. "Okay, we're good. Come on." His hand wrapped around mine, and I stumbled in his wake, quickly regaining my balance and pulling my hand free. "You'll get there, Tris."

"Yeah. I'll get there when society does."

He didn't respond and focused instead on pulling down the fold-up ladder as quietly as possible. Once the padded ends of the metal silently hit the ground, he flashed a quick, victorious grin and mounted the steps. But before I could follow, I heard a soft thud behind me. Spooked, I turned around and saw a flash of movement in the doorway to my room. My hand dropped to my knife.

"I know you're there," I called, and slowly a hand wrapped around the doorjamb, ring-laden fingers clicking eerily against the wood. A tangled mass of hair peeked from around the corner, wide and skittish eyes fixing on me. I sighed in relief, releasing the hilt of my blade. "Id, what're you doing here? This isn't your hall."

"Well, *he's* not a girl," she hissed back, rocking back and forth on her feet and watching me through her wiry hair. "Someone's gonna get in trouble…"

Her sing-songy words sent chills down my spine, and I quickly walked over.

"Idris—"

"Don't worry," she interrupted, holding up a finger before her lips as she backed away, a laughing smile pulling at her lips and her eyes shining impishly. "I'll not tell a soul…" She giggled and ran off, skipping a few steps before she vanished down the stairwell. "It's our little secret!" she sang, and I could hear her amulets clanking against each other until she was too far away.

Jack looked around at me as I climbed up into the attic, a nonplussed expression on my face, and he straightened from his hunched position over the record player.

"What's up?" I pointed down the open hatch, and he moved over to close it. "Don't worry, I'm on it. Something wrong?"

"Yeah…I mean, not really. But kind of."

The ladder clanged up behind us, and he sat back on his heels, looking up at me with an amused expression on his face.

"Well, which is it?"

"Idris knows," I finally managed, still trying to puzzle out what I'd just witnessed.

"Knows what?"

"She knows that we're gay," I elaborated, and he stood up, eyes wide. "You know, dating, sleeping together, the, uh, whole thing."

"And?" Before I could answer, he started talking again. "Did she go off about the gods, sins – did anyone *hear* her–"

"No, uh…" I frowned, scratching the back of my head. "She was actually pretty calm about it. Minus the giggling and the sing-songy voice and her being…well, you know. Id."

Jack blinked, surprised.

"Well, then." He seemed just as confused as I was.

"That's what I thought, too," I sighed, helplessly shrugging. "I guess the gods don't really care about who people spend their time with."

"Well, I'm not complaining," he sighed, smiling.

I stretched my arms over my head, joints cracking and settling, and my boyfriend returned to the dusty old record player. The air crackled with white noise for a few seconds before the music started playing. I felt Jack gingerly take my right hand in his left, being exceedingly cautious about my bruised skin, and he placed his right hand under my left arm against my shoulder blade.

"Remember, one–two–three count, on me." I looked up at him, at those dark eyes I loved so much, and nodded. "One, two, three–"

. . . — — — . . .

I honestly couldn't recognize the mess hall.

I was used to it being bland and barren, utilitarian and singular in its purpose and design. Now the room was warm and bustling with people, filled to the rafters with lively chatter and colors, and I watched in amazed disbelief from the corner in my olive green slacks and button down coat. My long sleeve shirt of a slightly lighter shade of the same color itched against my skin, and the beige tie pulled annoyingly around my throat. I felt like I was suffocating. That and the peaked cap of that same gods-awful olive color was making my head all sweaty, so I took it off and tucked it under my arm. I'd already been standing there for four hours, and – while I enjoyed people watching – this was getting kind of old.

"Byrne!" I turned around and saw Harris walking over towards me, a smile on his face. "How are you doing?"

"Been better, Andrew," I answered, leaning back against the wall, and he joined me, crossing his arms and watching the mass of people with me.

"Yeah, well, you need to smooth down that hair, man. You look like you just got out of bed," he laughed, and I quickly moved to run my fingers through my disheveled hair. That was, until my body decided to remind me about my bruised knuckles.

"*Ow!*" I immediately jerked my hand down, hissing as I cradled my purpled joints.

"Shit, Byrne," Andy gaped, and I looked up at him, baffled. "What'd you do?"

"You didn't see this at breakfast?" He shook his head. "I got into a fight."

"That's funny, man," he laughed. "Now what'd you really do?"

"…I got into a fight," I repeated after a moment of hesitation, and his smile faded.

"Seriously?" I nodded. "With who?"

"Marcel."

"Ok, *now* you're joking," he returned, laughing again, but I mutely shook my head. "You did not punch War in the face." I shrugged. "If – if you really punched *Marcel Jones* in the face, Byrne, you'd be dead."

"Thanks for the vote of confidence," I grumbled playfully and looked around, searching for something. "You here with Id?"

"Yeah, she's around here somewhere. She looks great. She wouldn't stop humming the dance music to herself all day and spent all her time dancing around. She's *good*."

He was beaming, and I couldn't help but smile with him.

"Well, I'm glad she's enjoying herself," I told him, and he nodded in agreement before frowning.

"How about you?"

I looked at him, all innocence.

"Hm?"

"You don't look like you're exactly having fun," he pointed out, and I shrugged.

"I'm an introvert who's being forced to go to a dance filled with people who hate my guts. Why wouldn't I be having fun?"

"I guess that's true," he laughed, crossing his arms. "Well, I'll leave you to your people-watching." He clapped me on the shoulder and walked off, smiling as Id came sashaying over to him in a floor-lengthed, off-the-shoulder dress as crimson as the blood pumping through our veins.

She smiled shyly and giggled in excitement at the same time, ring-laden hands clasped in front of her. Despite her tangled mane of dark hair, I could still see scars from the Mezitain prison camp crisscrossing her bare shoulders. As I watched them walk off, arms looped between each others, she turned to look at me over her shoulder, shadowed eyes flashing as she lifted a metal-clad finger to cover her lips.

Our secret, she mouthed before she waved at someone behind me and turned around once more.

"So that's what you meant by taking it well."

Surprisingly, I didn't jump at the unexpected voice, though my heart did skip a few beats. Smiling to himself, Jack stepped up next to me, staring at the people as they danced before us.

It was a fast-paced quadrille set to a piece that, based on what I heard, I bet the quartet performing could play in their sleep. Effortlessly, the dancers circled past us in a seamless, beautiful routine of brightly colored dresses, and perfect, pristine uniforms. They looked like little bits of wrapping paper, delicately fluttering away in an absent breeze.

"So, what do you think? Your first big dance: what's the verdict?"

"It's not *dreadful*. But it's definitely not my thing."

"I get that," my boyfriend commented, surveying the crowd. "Still though — you can't say it isn't pretty to look at." We were quite for a few moments before he perked up again. "Guess what song's coming up soon?" I cleared my throat and crossed my arms a bit tighter. "Come on, don't be like that," Jack teased as he elbowed me. "It'll be *fun*, I promise you."

"Mmhmm."

"Really, Tris? We're regressing to sarcastic noises instead of words now?" I rolled my eyes and tossed him a glowering look.

"Shut up."

My boyfriend laughed and put a hand on my shoulder before heading off towards Jayce and Alec, precariously walking backwards into the crowd.

"I need to have a few words with the boys about fighting ethics before we get our thing going," he called, and I tried to ignore the fear bubbling in my gut. I really didn't want to see this, and as Jack tapped Marcel's brother on the shoulder, I turned my attention to the server hovering at my elbow.

"Wine, sir?"

"Why the hell not?" I muttered and took a glass, thankful that my hands were still. This was more stressful than it should be.

Andrew circled past, dancing with Id, and was followed closely by Marcel and some cadet I'd seen around from South Hall. I didn't know his name. At that moment I noticed that the quartet had stopped playing, and I turned to watch as they switched to brass instruments and began playing some kind of swing. Go figure. The slower string pieces were more for tradition's sake – most people liked the fast-paced dances anyways.

Maybe they made us feel alive.

I turned my attention forward again to find Idris shyly standing a few feet in front of me. I could see a question burning on the tip of her tongue, held back by just enough hesitation that she didn't speak. And as I raised my eyebrows in question, she came a few steps closer, fingers twisting the red satin in their tenacious grip.

"I wanted to ask you something..." I gestured for her to continue, and she rocked a little on her feet as she smiled coyly up at me. "Could..." Her voice dropped to a stage whisper. "Would it be okay with you if I asked your boyfriend to dance?"

"*Shh!*" I hissed, holding a finger in front of my lips, and she quickly ducked her head.

"Sorry...but would it?" My heart pounding ruthlessly in my chest, I nodded, smiling in spite of myself, and she grinned, bouncing on her feet again. "Thanks, Tristan!"

Virtually glowing, she turned on her heel and quickly intercepted Jack on his way back to us. I could see her rock on her feet and tilt her head as she spoke, and Jack's eyes widened slightly and met mine over her short stature.

Have fun, I mouthed, teasing him, and he smirked as he offered his arm to Private Chance. I couldn't help but laugh as I watched them do a bewilderingly fast swing together, Id somehow managing the quick, complicated dance in her long dress. The two of them were pretty funny actually, in a cute and adorable way. And I couldn't help but notice as they whirled around each other in an impenetrable yet graceful tangle that Jack hadn't been lying yesterday.

He really was a good dancer.

A few minutes later, the song ended, and Jack came back over, laughing to himself and slightly winded.

"Well, that was fun," he sighed, bracing his hands on his knees briefly before straightening. There was a peculiar expression to his face, a satisfied, happy light in his eyes, and I smiled to myself, looking up at him.

"What is it?"

He shook his head, waving away my question as he regained his breath.

"Nah, it's nothing. I've just never seen Id this happy before." He leaned against the wall, crossing his arms and smiling. "In fact, the lot of you look inappropriately happy."

"Well, we're going to be miserable later," I said simply, and Jack looked at me, eyeing the glass in my hands.

"Are you really so panicked about this that you need something to dull your nerves?" I stared at him dolefully at his playfully disapproving tone.

"I apologize if I'm rightfully scared."

"Yeah, well," he looked over my shoulder at the quartet, "you better drink up."

"Why?" I asked, voice wary. He just shrugged, taking off his hat and resting it on the table beside us as he moved off to the side to grab something to drink himself.

"No reason."

At that moment, the quartet started playing again, the notes of the brass instruments backing the forefront melody of the violin. My heart stopped. I knew this song. I'd been dancing to it in the attic for the last two days. In the distance, I could hear the bells on the administration building tolling the hour.

One...two...three...four...

The voices of the privates slowly started to die down, shouted conversations reduced to whispered questions.

Five...six...seven...eight...

I looked up at Jack, and he sighed, giving me a sad little smile and brushing his fingers against mine.

Nine...ten...eleven...

DAY THREE

...*twelve*.

Everyone seemed to stop and look up at the ceiling as though it was the source of the countdown. And just as they had unanimously looked up, they slowly shifted their gazes down towards each other, smiles fading and sadness settling behind their eyes like a heavy curtain.

Time was up.

The quartet seemed to realize their audience had become distracted so they waited a few seconds before restarting the opening bars to "Sweetheart Waltz" – the song that Jack and I had been waiting for.

Now that it was here, I didn't feel any better.

People slowly found their dates again, hands settling on each other's bodies in preparation for the waltz. The music was gentle, melancholic and yet hopeful at the same time – the violin pulled at my heart while the warm tones of the brass gently whispered that everything was going to be okay. I didn't know what to do or feel.

Watching everyone start dancing again, smiles slowly working their ways back to their faces, made me feel so empty. The ease of their touches brought into sharp relief what I couldn't have. I looked away from the undulating colors before me to my shaking hands, to the red-filled glass between them, and tightened my grip as much as I dared. And as I fought for control over my own body, I saw someone move in my peripheral vision, and a pair of roughened, yet gentle, hands closed around mine. I followed the drab olive green sleeves to the colorful medals pinned to the left shoulder and stopped. I couldn't look any higher.

I knew who it was, had known from the moment he touched me, but I didn't dare look up at him. It didn't matter that we had planned this – I wasn't ready.

Slowly those hands pulled the drink from my own shaking ones and set it down on the white tablecloth, wine standing out like blood on a shroud. His one hand holding both of mine, he began walking towards the dance floor, head held high to meet the gaze of any who looked down at him. I, on the other hand, kept my eyes firmly fixed on the flagstone floors and Jack's shining boot heels. I couldn't look up, and I realized my partner had stopped walking and turned to face me.

Slowly, I reached out and rested my left hand on his shoulder, eyes still locked on his medals. My fingers seized the fabric of his jacket, twisting the material in my grip, and I took in a shaky breath that, when I released it, was even more unsteady than it had been when I inhaled. In response, I felt Jack's sure and steady right hand rest on my waist, snaking around to my lower back, and suddenly people were whispering.

"What's he *doing?*"

"Is that Miller? With *Byrne?*"

"Doing a *waltz?*"

"I think it is…"

I took another deep breath and was about to grab his free left hand when he reached out and, with a touch so soft I barely felt it, tilted my chin up so I was looking right into his brown eyes. Eyes much like the calf's before the blade comes down.

"No more hiding, Tristan. Remember?" he asked, voice low, but I could see the fire behind his words. He wanted to do this, and it wasn't just a whim. It was a need. "I'm right here, okay? We're both right here, and we'll be okay. No more hiding." I took in another breath to try and calm my nerves. It didn't work.

"No. No more hiding," I agreed, wishing my voice were more steady, more confident. I took hold of his hand and briefly closed my eyes, unable to halt the defensively spoken words crowding up my throat. "If this backfires, I'll kill you."

"Stop ruining the moment," he whined, voice low, and I bit back a laugh, smiling down at my feet. "There we go, Tristan. Just relax."

Slowly, led by my boyfriend, our feet found the steps. My mind flashed back to our dances in the shadows of the attic, seeing the dust our feet had stirred from the wooden planks glitter and shine in the shafts of sun piercing the gloom. We were tripping over each other and falling down in my mind while in reality we moved just as perfectly as everyone else.

Vaguely, I noticed that the rest of the privates had stopped dancing, instead opting to stare, aghast, at the two of us. I closed my eyes against them and focused on the man before me, straightening my back, taking a deep breath, and tightening my hold. I wanted to smile, but I didn't dare.

"You're safe," Jack whispered, as though reading my mind. "Smile, it's okay. I'll be right here."

I opened my eyes and looked up at him in mocking disbelief that barely masked my terror, but as he gave me a small, teasing smile, I couldn't hold back my own – though it was more a nervous reflex than a genuine feeling. Thankfully, "Sweetheart Waltz" was a short piece, and the musicians ended the work with stunned silence as we finally came to a stop. I could feel Jack's hand cup the back of my head, and I looked back up at him, eyes filled to the brim with tears.

"I told you you'd be okay," he murmured, smirking, and I grabbed the lapels of his jacket, pulling him down and kissing him.

That set off the audible gasps of shock and disgust, and as I pulled back, I started crying. I was terrified, relieved, feeling too many emotions at once. Jack smiled comfortingly and pulled me into a soothing embrace, locking his arms around me and taking deep breaths that synced with my own. I could hear his heart's frantic tattoo in my ear, and I drew comfort in the fact that he was just as scared as I was. As always though, he didn't let anyone know.

"Told you that you'd come around," he whispered as I pressed my face into his shoulder and gripped the back of his jacket in my hands. It was then I knew everything was going to be okay. I, hopeless Tristan Byrne, was going to be just fine.

At least that's what I thought until Marcel spoke up.

"*Wow.*"

Jack took in a deep breath and turned around, hand gripping mine and holding me steady as we faced her. She had a highly amused, disdainful expression on her face.

"I mean, just *wow*. Corporal Jack Miller, the leader of our platoon…is a *shag*. I called you that jokingly, but I guess I wasn't that far off the mark." She came to a stop a few feet away, crossing her arms over the white gown and formal uniform jacket she was wearing. "That makes you, what? Dirty, inferior? And yet you love to place yourself above us, Miller. How does that work out in your twisted head?"

I could see the other Horsemen shoving their way up through the crowd to stand at her side, and everywhere I looked I seemed to encounter hostile eyes.

"Aw, come on, now, Marcel," Jack began, voice just as patronizing as hers had been. "You're not still sore about the punch in the mouth I gave you, are you?" Her face darkened, and my stomach flipped. "*Oh!* Or is it the fact that my boyfriend here was the one who screwed up your jaw? You did a nice job covering that up with your makeup, by the way."

She snarled, about to start forward, when Andrew stepped between us much the same way Jack had stepped between me and Marcel yesterday.

"Okay, guys, *hold it.*" He looked around at everyone. "These are our last few hours of normal life. Can we just enjoy it, please? You'll have plenty of time to shoot each other in the back starting tomorrow." But his words were lost on our angry platoonmate, and Private Jones surged forward once more, pushing Andrew backwards.

"Get out of my way, you *psychotic—*"

There was a flash of red beside me, and the next thing we knew Idris was whaling on Marcel with a serving spoon she'd snatched from the buffet next to her.

"*Ow!*" Jones yelped, and Idris backed off, glaring at the woman before her, metal utensil clenched so tightly in her shaking hand that her knuckles were white. "What the *hell* is wrong with you?!"

"Andy isn't psychotic!" she shouted back, livid. Her voice was shaky and cracked a little as she increased her volume, but we were all surprised at the rather authoritative and confident way she was speaking.

"*I* am!" She swallowed a few times and cleared her throat. "And let me tell you something. If…if you – or *any of you–*" she brandished the spoon at all gathered, "so much as touch a *hair* on their heads, I will make your lives p-personalized *hell*s. Because *I'm* the psychotic one!"

"Okay, that has to be the most I've ever seen her speak at once in my life," Jack whispered in my ear, and I nodded in agreement, eyes wide.

"No one…*touches them.* A-am I *clear?*" Her words were carefully and clearly enunciated despite her nervous stammer. "Besides, what did they ever do to you? The gods don't care – they *never* have!"

"Great, so does anyone else besides the shell-shocked religious fanatic agree with what she was saying?" Marcel called to the gathered assembly, and Andrew raised his hand, expression stony. "Anyone *other than* shell-shocked religious fanatic and her keeper?"

There was dead silence and then,

"*I* happen to agree with Privates Chance and Harris."

Everyone turned around and parted to reveal the speaker. Jax stood just inside the great double doors of the hall, arms crossed, and clad in full officer's uniform. Despite the fact that his mouth was smiling, his eyes were cold and angry. Marcel immediately stood at attention, as did the rest of us – an odd image given our attire.

"At ease." Everyone reluctantly relaxed and watched as the tall man came toe to toe with Marcel. "So, private. Do you really want to continue this?" Her gaze shifted downwards, and she jerkily shook her head. "Good. Because if you had, I would have told Captain Howell that you are a rabble-rouser. And I know you've heard what his policy is on respect within the ranks." She looked back up at her supervising officer and nodded, voice low and subdued.

"Understood, sir."

"All of you to bed!" he shouted, pushing past her and heading for the back door. "Early mornings from here on out."

There was a general bustle of movement, and Jack put an arm around my shoulders to keep me close as we looked to Idris and Andrew.

"Were you two ever going to clue me in on this?" Harris asked, giving us a tired but playful smile, and I shrugged. "I'm hurt. Honestly."

"Thanks, Id," Jack sighed, and she gave a shy smile, hunching her shoulders and hiding beneath the dark veil of her hair. "I didn't know you had that in you."

"Marcel's bad," she said simply, twirling the spoon between her ring-clad fingers. "You're a nice dancer, by the way."

"Yeah, you, too," Jack grinned. "How do you do a swing in that dress?" She blushed and twirled the spoon once more as she shrugged. "Well, I won't bother you about it if you don't want to—"

"Miller!"

We turned around to see a frustrated Jax gesturing for us to come over, and I sighed, looking at Andrew.

"Well, we'll see you tomorrow morning at the Lake."

Our friends nodded before heading off with the rest of the cadets, arms linked together. I could see them glaring at anyone who so much as looked at us and felt a rush of warmth towards the pair. After a few minutes, the hall was relatively empty, and we walked over to stand before Jax, grabbing our hats off the table as we went.

"I *said* lay low," he growled as soon as we were within earshot. "Is this laying low for you? Good *gods*, Miller! What would you do if I said be as flamboyantly obvious as possible?!"

"You said be subtle around Howell," Jack countered, surprisingly relaxed about the whole affair, and I groaned as I saw Jax rolling his eyes. "You said *nothing* about keeping our relationship on the down low at the Academy."

"Yeah, well, Unit 37 is going to be talking about you bone-headed idiots non-stop, now," our S.O. snapped, clearly frustrated by our stupidity. "No one can prevent that from happening, not even Idris with her colorful threats – though she may be able to stall it a little. The girl's got quite a temper."

"She does," I agreed but quickly shut up at Jax's glare. "Sorry."

"Well, I hope your little coming out escapade was worth it," he muttered before walking out the kitchen door without a backwards glance.

"I have to say that I agree with him."

"Of course you do," Jack sighed.

"I'm just saying that our timing *could* have been better," I pointed out as we left the hall and stepped into the cold night. Our breath fogged before us, and Jack tightened his arm around me, jostling me playfully as he drew me in closer.

"Timing could always be better, okay?" he said softly, and I nodded silently against him. "That's just the nature of life." He took in a deep breath, smiling up at the clear sky, and I looked up with him, head resting against his shoulder. There was something uninhibited and carefree about him I couldn't place.

"What're you smiling at?" I finally asked, and he looked down at me, leaning down to quickly kiss me as we went.

"You."

"Yeah, well, I'm down here, not up there," I pointed out. He tussled my hair, taking my hand in his before looping his arm over my shoulders again so my arm crossed my body.

"Don't I know that," he muttered, mostly to himself, and I elbowed him indignantly in the side. "Ow!" He pushed me to the side, and we laughed quietly at each other. "Come on, Tris. Let's get to bed. Gods know this is going to be the last night of good sleep we'll get for a long time."

We walked in silence for a little longer until I caught him looking up again. That wistful light was back in his eyes, that absent smile pulling at the corners of his lips.

"Come on," I pressed, staring up with him as we walked on, neither of us really paying attention to where we were going. "What're you seeing?" He paused before speaking, still watching the stars above.

"Everything," he said simply and sighed. "I'm looking at the sky, and I'm seeing everything." He paused, looking down at me. "What do you see?"

I hesitated, taking in the sparkling points of light high above us, their cold light peppered across the polluted sky.

"I see the universe," I finally answered, taking in a deep breath and shoving my hands further into my pant pockets. "I see how big it is and how small we are…and then I get stressed out and start panicking. It's all good."

"Really?" I smiled to myself as Jack squinted at the heavens. "That's what you see?" I nodded. "You don't see pretty stars or anything like that?"

"Nah." I shivered in the cold as I continued. "I just see an eternity stretching out forever, and I can't help but think about how small and insignificant we all are in comparison."

"Why do you always have to go and make everything all depressingly philosophical?" Jack complained and then sighed, breath fogging in the cold air. "Sorry. I shouldn't make fun of you for what you think."

"Within reason," I corrected, and he made a gesture of agreement. Our footsteps grew muffled as we left the battered cement road and crossed onto the grass surrounding our hall.

"Of course. Because if you start thinking weird stuff like Id, then I'm gonna be concerned." We stamped our feet on the flagstone steps a few times before entering the hall, the metal stairwell rattling noisily under our heavy boots as we went.

"Don't worry, the feeling's mutual." Jack snickered at that and pressed a kiss to my temple as we reached the landing. "I'm surprised no one's waiting for us."

"You kidding? After Id went off on them, I'd be shocked if anyone so much as breathes in our direction," he laughed. I walked over to my door and pushed it open, looking over my shoulder to him as I did.

"Well? You coming in?" I asked, and he smiled hesitantly, looking down at his hands. "Hey," I began, offering a pointed smile barely visible in the gloom. "We've got a lock now." Lips still curved upwards in that crooked smirk, Jack looked up at me, eyes glinting in the half-light of the full moon outside.

"Why not?"

He closed the door behind him, sliding the lock home, and the next thing I knew we were heading towards the bed, shedding the many layers of clothing between us. Our breath still clouded the air between us, but I knew – as I fell back onto the mattress, Jack on top of me – that the cold wasn't going to bother me tonight.

···———···

When my eyes opened, I found myself face to face with Jack, and I was glad he was still asleep otherwise I would probably have jumped at how close he was. I laid there in silence, staring at his calm and peaceful features, at his sleep-tousled hair. His brow wasn't furrowed in intense thought. His jaw wasn't clenched against words he wanted to say but was in no position to deliver. He was completely relaxed, and for some reason it made me upset.

"It's because we're going to be miserable later," he mumbled quietly, and I propped myself up on an elbow and smiled.

"Hey," I whispered, tucking an errant strand of hair back from his eyes. "I didn't know you were awake."

"Just resting my eyes…but I'd know your thoughtful and melancholic silence anywhere." His eyes opened, and I watched as that peace I'd noticed slowly faded away. "How did you sleep?"

"Great." I rolled onto my back and sighed. "You?"

"Same." The mattress shifted beneath us as he sat up and picked his pants up off the floor, pulling them on and standing. "Come on. We've got to get going."

I didn't want to move. I just wanted to stay in bed, let the world fade away. I wanted everything to just go away. But Jack clearly wasn't feeling what I was, and I watched as he grabbed his uniform jacket and threw it over his shoulder before heading out of the room.

"Bit insensitive much?" I asked to the empty air and sat up, shivering in the cold air. The words had barely left my mouth before the door swung back open again to reveal Jack, dog tags clinking against each other on his chest.

"I'm sorry, that was rude."

I raised my eyebrows, mockingly unimpressed.

"You think?"

"Well, have you looked at the sun?" he pointed out, and I frowned, twisting around and looking over my shoulder. I could just see the top of the golden orb over the mountains and the sky was brushed with yellow along the ridges of the horizon. And that meant—

"Shit!" I shouted, vaulting out of bed and scrambling for my uniform.

"There we go," Jack muttered to himself before vanishing from the doorway and heading for his own room down the hall. The sun was already part way up, and we were supposed to report to our deployment spots by sunrise.

Well, fuck.

Thankfully, we weren't the only ones running late. I could hear the racing tattoo of footsteps as our other platoonmates sprinted for the stairs, and I quickly pulled my t-shirt over my head, followed by the dog tags I'd draped around the bedpost last night.

34927530.

I quickly pulled on my button-down shirt and pants, tucked the bottoms of the slacks into my socks, and yanked on my boots.

Tristan Byrne.

I slung my backpack over my shoulders and was almost out the door when I stopped and looked over my shoulder at my footlocker. Coming to a decision, I jogged back over, opened it up, and pulled out a piece of paper and a pencil. I quickly scrawled a message and closed it in the chest so that it was mostly sticking out but firmly held in place. And, taking a deep breath, I got up and left my room for the last time, snatching up my formal jacket from the floor as I went – just in case.

I didn't really know how cold it was going to get on the eastern front line.

As I hurried down the hall towards Jack's room, I ran the words I'd written over and over in my head, wondering if it was another rash and ill-conceived plan that was going to come back and bite me in the ass later.

I knocked on the doorjamb of Jack's room.

"Hey, you ready?"

"Not really." He shouldered his backpack and gave a wry smile. "But no one never is. Let's go." He clapped his hand on my shoulder, and we ran down the hall while I thought once more about my note. Jack looked down at me, eyes narrowing as we started down the spiraling staircase and slowed down a little so we didn't trip and fall. "What did you do?"

I looked up at him and feigned indignant innocence.

"Nothing!" I shifted my pack on my shoulders and was relieved when he didn't press. I could see my hastily scrawled words behind my eyes, and I still wasn't sure if I hadn't just done something kind of stupid. But as we went on, I saw that Jack was still glancing down at me, brow creased in suspicion. I relented just a little as we hit the second floor landing. "I left a note for Jax with my trunk."

"Ah." He shook his head ever so slightly, expression resigned and unsurprised. "Was it a subtly worded 'go to hell, you giant of a man' note?"

I rolled my eyes.

"You could call it that," I conceded, slightly out of breath from the many flights of stairs. I reviewed the words in my head a final time before finally ignoring them. I could see the dim outline of the open front door below us, and that meant we were going to be running again very soon.

Oh joy.

As soon as our feet hit the last step, we started sprinting, crossing the threshold as quickly as we could. Our breaths fell perfectly in sync as we crossed the grounds towards the Lake. It wasn't far from the barracks; walking, it took ten minutes at the most. When we ran like it was the end of the world, it took closer to five.

Miraculously, we arrived with a few minutes to spare before the sun was fully up, and a quick glance told me that while a vast majority – if not all – of Unit 36 and Unit 37 were present, our respective captains were not. Instead, two hundred and eighty people stood in a nervous, loitering mass on the edge of the dark Lake. I could see a few swans drifting like ghostly ships across the surface of the nearly black water, obscured almost entirely by the early morning mist.

I briefly wondered where Chance and Harris were.

Unfortunately for me and Jack, the fact that our captains weren't here yet meant there was time for the rest of our fellow cadets (privates – we'd officially graduated from the Academy, I had to remember that) to clear the air between us. And, not surprisingly, Marcel was the first one to make a move.

And she started it with clapping.

"Look who decided to show up," she scoffed, mouth curved upwards in a twisted smirk. "Tell me, was last night a *good* night for you guys? Hot and steamy enough?"

"Don't make me punch you in the mouth again," Jack warned, glaring and stepping closer. "Because if I remember right, Jax gave you the warning about roughing us up, not the other way around."

She rolled her shoulders in response, backpack dropping to the grass beside her as she closed the distance between the two of them.

"Bring it on. I've got my Horsemen. Hell, I've got our whole unit. Who've you got on your side?" Jack opened his mouth to say something in response, but someone else beat him to it.

"No fighting." The words were softly spoken, but we all recognized the voice from the night before. "It's really not worth it…"

Heads turned in the direction of the speaker, and I moved through the crowd until I could see her. Idris was sitting down at the edge of the water, fingers trailing in the shallows and drawing minnows to the surface. She looked over her shoulder at me and gave a smile.

"The gods are telling me it's all going to be okay. Especially Neptune… he's very reassuring." She suddenly stopped grinning and looked back at the water, brow furrowing. "But Terra…Mother Terra is very sad. She's sad because we're all going to be returned to her very soon."

We looked at each other, torn between disregarding what Id was saying and actually looking for meaning in her words.

"We're going home to her too soon." Idris pulled her arms away from the water, breathing heavily and looking at her hands with tears in her eyes. "Oh…" The broken word fell softly, sadly, from her lips, and she cradled her wet hands close to her. "I understand…"

"Id? Id, where are you?" She looked around at Andrew's voice and stood up, trying to brush mud off her pants in vain. When he finally made his way through the crowd, he took in her disheveled appearance and sighed. "There you are. Come here, let's try and fix you up."

At that moment, someone called out the words that sent all of us straight to soldier mode.

"The caravan's here!"

Harris put an arm around Idris' shoulders and guided her towards Jack and I, waving to make sure that we got his message to stay still.

"Miller, we're sticking as close to you as we can for as long as we can, you hear?" Jack nodded, taking our friend's outstretched hand and shaking it. "After that...well, I guess we'll see you around."

"Yeah. Of course."

We turned to face the approaching canvas trucks with everyone else, and I was surprised to feel a cold, wet hand creeping into my own. I looked to my right to see Idris staring ahead of herself with wide eyes. But before I could ask what was wrong, she turned me to face her and wrapped her arms tightly around me.

"Whoa, Id—"

"I'll see you on the other side," she whispered, voice barely audible, and I realized that her words were meant only for me. "Take care of Andy for me." She tightened her hold even more for a split second before releasing me and standing closer to Andrew once more, her arm snaking around his to tightly hold his hand. She looked down and furtively wiped at her nearly overflowing eyes.

"What the hell did the gods say to her this time?" Jack asked, voice a low rumble in my ear, and I stared at Idris, gut cold.

"I – I don't know," I lied and hid my sigh of relief when he believed me.

I knew exactly what Idris thought the gods had told her. It was the same realization I'd come to myself, but I didn't have time to dwell on that. About twelve canvas-covered trucks that looked like they could seat probably twenty-five people each were rolling down the dirt roads towards us, dust billowing out from beneath their wheels.

As they pulled up, a tall man dropped from the back of one of them, canvas boots hitting the ground with a dull thud. He was a younger man with an aquiline nose and dark hair clipped close to his skull. His heavy brows arched over light blue eyes, and he took a deep breath as he stared at all of us. He was probably around ten years our senior, broad shouldered and tall. Frankly I was a little surprised. He was supposed to be a captain, so I assumed he'd show up in a fully decorated uniform. Instead, he was clad in a well-worn version of what we ourselves were wearing, and I caught a glimpse of his own Academy dog tags against his shirt.

"I'm Captain Harper," he announced, coming to a stop before us. "Can I get Unit 36 to form a group to my left and Unit 37 to my right?" There was a shuffle of movement, and I shot Harris a wry, apologetic smile as we moved away from each other. He shrugged, and we all looked forward again as our superior started talking.

"Well then, I'm guessing you're the sorry lot I'm supposed to pick up?" He gave a smile that was surprisingly genuine, and we all looked at each other uncertainly. "Don't worry – you're clear to laugh and smile around me. *I'm* not the hard-ass you need to worry about. Thirty-seven, Captain Howell got held up at his post on the eastern front lines – he and his remaining troops are taking pretty heavy fire from the Brettain. Don't worry though. He'll catch up with us in a couple of days."

He beckoned my unit to come forward and started counting us off into groups of twenty-four, taking roll call before pointing each group to a truck.

"He loves new privates," he finished absentmindedly as he wrapped up registering another group, and I couldn't help but shiver at the bitter undercurrent in his voice. As the number of privates standing beside me grew smaller, I started looking at the people left, and my heart sank.

"Oh boy," I muttered, and Jack made a noise of agreement.

"Yep. This'll be fun," he sighed, sarcasm dripping from his words as he crossed his arms.

"And seventeen, eighteen, nineteen, twenty, twenty-one, twenty-two." The Horsemen, Jayce, Jack, and I all glared at each other as subtly as we could. "And we ran out of people. You two over there, you want to join in and make this a twenty-four person truck?"

I nearly sighed in relief as Andrew and Idris came forward to stand beside us. As we started reciting our names, I took in a deep breath as one by one Harper crossed us off the list with a sharp drag of lead on paper.

"Corporal Jack Miller." Jack's voice was softer than the others, almost on par with Idris' nearly whispered response, and I saw Captain Harper's eyebrows lift fractionally at the name.

"You were the sergeant who disobeyed his captain, weren't you?" There was something oddly proud in Harper's eyes. Jack nodded. "Well, don't go doing that with Howell. You'll get a bullet for your troubles."

"I'm well aware, sir. Thank you for the warning."

The captain made a note to himself in the margin of the attendance sheet before resuming roll. After a couple minutes, he set down his pencil.

"Alright, you lot go into that truck over there."

We followed his pointing arm, and I took a steadying breath as I pulled myself up into the long truck bed. The planked ground was gouged in several places, and I watched my feet as I headed for the right hand corner all the way in the back, Jack going with me and Andrew and Idris following close behind. Unsurprisingly, the Horsemen and Jayce sat across from us, staring like vultures. A few minutes passed, and then we all heard Captain Harper's voice carry out over the caravan.

"Full attendance! I'm proud of you guys."

My gut churned, and I took a deep breath, shifting uncomfortably on the hard surface beneath us. The canvas was saturated with the smell of gunpowder, rust, and smoke – a combination that was already making me feel sick. Jack reached over and took my hand, and my heart stopped in my chest before I remembered that everyone knew about us.

"We're going to be driving all day and stopping at Norford around three in the morning," the captain continued. "After that, it'll be another full day of driving, and we'll arrive at the front lines around eight at night. There's a munitions chest in each of the trucks with food. Ration it for the ride." There was a pause. "Gods know you'll need the practice."

There was a slamming of car doors all down the line, and suddenly the vehicle beneath us rumbled to life, making my stomach lurch. I took in a deep breath and looked at the faces surrounding me. They were either masks of stone or just as pained as I felt. But when I looked over at Idris, I couldn't help but feel confused. She was sitting there, cross-legged, with her hands neatly entwined in her lap. Her wild hair obscured most of her face, but I could see that beneath the veil of black her expression was peaceful, her eyes closed against everything that was happening.

Sometimes, I wished I could hear the gods that she claimed spoke to her.

As we drove along, I couldn't help but look out the back of the truck, staring at the buildings as they went by, at the grounds that had become my home over the course of the last four years. And as we went, I could see new cadets lining up on the training grounds. I imagined I could hear Jax screaming at them, even though I knew they were too far away.

Soon, though – all too soon – we left the campus, passing through the one metal gate in the tall cement walls that surrounded the Academy. The early sun shone off the barbed wire that topped the barrier like fire. I closed my eyes and rested my head against the metal side of the truck, skull vibrating with the moving car, and tried to ignore the people around me, tried to ignore everyone but Jack. Jack was my rock in this hurricane, and I tightened my hold on his hand, relief flooding my body as he did the same.

Jax.

> *Thanks for the pep talk, but the thing is I'm a coward. Just thought you should know that when you get all this stuff after my name shows up on the casualty list. Thanks for everything.*
>
> *Tristan*

. . . ‒ ‒ ‒ . . .

I hadn't even realized that I'd fallen asleep until we ran over a pothole in the dirt packed road, and my head slammed down on Jack's shoulder. Blinking in dazed pain, I sat up and looked at my platoonmates, surveying the situation. The sun had set hours ago, and several buzzing and flickering gas lanterns lit up the bed of the truck. Jack was asleep beside me, looking almost as relaxed as Idris had been and – I leaned forward slightly to check on her – still was. Andrew was awake beside her and was currently engaged in a glaring contest with Katalin and Aliyah across from him. They hadn't realized I'd woken up.

"Admit it," Aliyah pressed. "There is something fundamentally wrong about two men together."

I slowly leaned back against the car, watching them out of the corner of my nearly closed eyes.

"I honestly don't think we should care about who Byrne or Miller like to spend their time with. It's not like it hurts you in any way," he countered, crossing his arms and tightening his clenched hands.

"It's just wrong!" Katalin threw back, expression twisted in a grimace. "There's no point to it. Literally, there is no point. It's impossible to have kids, so–"

"It's not natural," Aliyah finished, starting slightly as Irina's head dropped to rest on her shoulder. After checking that her friend was still asleep and reasonably comfortable, she returned her attention to the conversation at hand. "And that is the truth."

Andrew raised his eyebrow.

"Yeah," he began, bitingly sarcastic. "And it's absolutely normal for four girls to spend all their time together. How do we know you're not up to the same shenanigans as Miller and Byrne?"

It was clearly a joke, but I snorted anyways, coughing and choking on the laugh I was trying to keep down. The conversation stopped, and I opened my eyes to look at Moore and Harris, fighting back a grin.

"I'm sorry, that's just a *really* funny image," I finally laughed, and Aliyah's eyes narrowed dangerously. I shrugged, hands raised defensively. "What? It is."

"I am not as lowly and depraved as a *shag*," she growled, crossing her arms and forcefully sitting back against the side of the car.

"Yeah, sure," Harris said, leaning back as well and stretching his arms out in front of him. "Get all defensive about your sexuality. Then we'll definitely believe you when you say you aren't gay." I cackled to myself and closed my eyes, taking in a deep breath and pretending to relax despite the anxiety spiking and prowling inside my gut.

Clearly that was the wrong move.

There was a rush of fabric, and I opened my eyes to see Death lunging for me, hands reaching for my throat. I yelped, scrambling to sit up, but before she could fasten her steel-corded hands on me, Jack's eyes snapped open, and his hand shot forward to grab a fistful of her shirt, elbow locking straight to hold her off.

Heart pounding in my throat, I looked to my right at Jack, taking in the clenched jaw and dangerously flashing eyes. He was completely awake, and I began to wonder just how long he'd been pretending to be asleep beside me. Aliyah's dark eyes were fixed on his, and dead silence filled the rattling truck as people started waking up around us at the commotion.

"Miller, man, cool it," Andrew warned, but he didn't seem to hear.

"Sit your ass back down, Private Moore," Jack ordered, voice low. Her jaw clenched, and I could see her chest heaving with vicious breaths. "I am telling you, as your corporal, to sit...*down*."

He pushed her backwards, releasing her uniform as he did so, and she landed with a thud against the side of the truck, glaring eyes watching us like a raptor. Jack returned her gaze briefly before crossing his arms again and closing his eyes in what I had thought was sleep. I leaned towards him, frowning in question.

"How long have you been awake?" He hummed in response, smiling to himself.

"I wasn't."

I felt a shiver run down my spine.

"What do you mean you weren't awake? How the hell did you know she was coming?" Jack shifted his shoulders against the rumbling car and cleared his throat.

"It's all coming back to me now. The closer we get, I can remember how it all felt." He sighed, clasping his hands together in his lap. "Always need to sleep with one eye open in the trenches. It's like the smell in the air triggers something."

I glanced down at his hands and watched how his fingers ground away at his knuckles until the skin was red and irritated. Within a few minutes, he was asleep once more.

"Yeah, that there is a little thing we like to call *shell-shock*."

I looked at Soto, stomach slowly sinking.

"Hey, will you knock it off?" Harris snapped. She shrugged, smirk playing at her lips, and she locked her hands behind her head, fingers absently playing with her ponytail. "Quit putting things in the kid's head that aren't true. Miller's saner than most of us here."

"I *am* telling the truth. Your 'boyfriend' over there's showing red flags – restlessness, the light sleeping…"

I could feel my hands trembling, and I took a deep breath.

She's lying. She's lying to rile you up – nothing more.

"Just go back to sleep," I muttered darkly, and Katalin chuckled, teeth flashing in the half-light around us.

"I bet I'll sleep better than your *boyfriend* over there." I took in a shaky breath, teeth grinding. "Anyways, I'm not going to sleep. We're almost to Norford, so we're all dismounting and getting some rack time there. I'll save my exhaustion for then."

I swallowed, looking out the open back of the truck in nervous silence. I could faintly see my breath, and I pulled my formal wear jacket out of my pack, pulling it on and leaning against Jack's shoulder. I took his hand in mine, and across the way I could see Katalin laughing to herself.

"As though holding hands could fix *that* mess," she laughed but promptly stopped when Aliyah elbowed her and pointed to the shadowed form beside Andrew. Idris was awake, staring at them with dark eyes as though daring them to make a move. I exhaled slowly and held Jack's hand a little tighter.

South Hall had my back, at least for now.

DAY FOUR

0300 hours

"Alright boys and girls, rise and shine!"

I started at the loud banging in my ear and quickly sat up, blinking away the sleep clinging to my eyes in alarm. Jack on the other hand almost lazily sat up beside me, stretching out the kinks in his back and shoulders as the rest of us scrambled to get up. Captain Harper briefly looked into the back of our truck and did a head count before gesturing for us to get out.

My legs nearly buckled as my feet hit the dirt, and Jack grabbed the back of my jacket to steady me.

"Okay," Harper called from the front of the caravan, and we all started migrating in that general direction, stumbling on our half-asleep legs. "I want you all to go to the inn and tell the keeper that you're new soldiers looking for lodgings for the next four hours. Then we're moving out again."

Jack nodded and herded us in that general direction. The inn was huge. Had the town been a city, it would have probably taken up an entire block. But as we got closer, I started coughing on weird scents.

"What is that?" I asked, and Jack groaned.

"Welcome to The Guild."

I looked at him out of the corner of my eye.

"That sounds like something I'm not gonna like."

"Yeah, it doubles as an inn and a 'source of comfort to weary souls' I think is their latest motto." The disdain in Jack's voice was hardly subtle. "Unfortunately, it's the only place big enough to keep two hundred and eighty troops in reasonable comfort for any period of time."

"So, that smell is—"

"A combination of cigarettes, alcohol, and various recreational drugs that help people forget about the hellhole we call the world today, yes," Jack answered, and I nodded.

"And you're telling me that The Guild is an inn and—"

"A brothel, yes." He rolled his eyes and crossed his arms against the biting air. "Frankly, the whole idea makes me sick, but in today's times of doom and gloom anything that gives you some kind of escape is fair game."

"You're not the only one who finds this sick," Korsakov muttered. "I thought these places were illegal."

"Who really cares what's legal or not at this point?" Jayce asked, and Andrew spoke up from where he was helping Id down from the back of the truck.

"*You* should. Had your sister been born in a different place, she could be one of those girls in there. So respect the people you see when we get in. Okay, Jones?" At that, the brother shut up, and Marcel looked up at him, baffled, as he sidled closer and draped an arm protectively about her.

"What's wrong with you?" she asked, genuinely concerned. He cleared his throat.

"No one's touching my sister."

Jack laughed.

"Don't worry. Given the stigma of gay relationships and the fact that The Guild's got strictly girl workers, I think she'll be fine. That and she can handle herself better than you can," he called over his shoulder, and the siblings glared at him as he opened the door to reveal the smoky interior.

Dead eyes stared at us through the thick air, the men with their arms around scantily clad women. People from all walks of life sprawled across the booths, and cigarettes of gods knew what burned between their fingers. I quickly looked forward, eyes fixing on the bar ahead where the keeper was preparing a few drinks.

"Well, well, well," the man called, coming out from around the counter to intercept Jack. The greeting was strangely forced. "Sergeant Miller! It's been a few years since you came our way, but I still remember your face."

Jack scoffed, ignoring the man's extended arm and clasping his hands behind his back instead.

"Yeah, it's corporal now, Mr. Bentley. And I think you're remembering how I turned down every one of your girls that you sent over to me," my boyfriend responded coldly, and I shifted uncomfortably beside him. "I've got two hundred and eighty soldiers looking for lodgings for the next four hours. We're moving out immediately after."

"All business, as usual," the balding man grumbled and gestured towards an old staircase in the back corner. "You know the routine. The whole west wing is devoted to housin' you guys. Remember, two people per bed – that's the only way all o' you will fit."

As the door opened behind us and more people entered the already crowded room, Jack put a hand on my shoulder and led me forward. The rest of the people who'd been in our truck followed hesitantly behind us, overwhelmed by our surroundings. Idris was just glaring at everyone she saw, muttering something about infidelity, and I tried to hold back my laughter.

"Thanks, Bentley," Jack said as we walked away, and once we were out of earshot, I turned to face Jack.

"Four hours is too long here."

"Don't I know it. Come on. Let's just get in a room, and we'll sleep until it's time for us to go."

We climbed up the rickety stairs and headed down a dingy hallway, Jack pointing to the dormitory like rooms on each side. Each one had about ten beds in it that could easily hold two people, and Jack quickly guided me into a room and towards a bed in the far corner.

"Just put your bag and shoes under the bed. Then get under the covers and try to get some more sleep. You're gonna need it," he told me as he sat on the mattress and unlaced his boots.

"You two had better not start any funny business under the sheets," Korsakov called testily from the door.

I was too tired to engage her beyond an eye roll, and my head reeled with the sights and smells from downstairs. I could still hear shrill laughter below us, accompanied by the low hum of men's voices, and I gratefully dropped down onto the ratty bed, pulling the covers over me. And yet, despite my engaged senses, the moment Jack settled down beside me and draped his arm protectively over me, I was asleep.

I had no nightmares, but as the word started to fade I couldn't help but think about what Katalin had said about shell-shock. And I wondered if Jack's sleep was as peaceful as mine.

...━━━...

When I woke up the next morning, it wasn't to anybody shaking me awake. Instead, it was to the sound of shouting outside the window of our room. Groaning, I rubbed the early dawn light out of my eyes, slipping out from under Jack's arm and sitting up on the mattress. I looked over my shoulder at my boyfriend, taking in his bedhead and peaceful expression, and I couldn't help but notice that there was a furrow in his brow that hadn't been there before. I just wanted to crawl back into bed with him and smooth his skin with gentle kisses. Take us back in time to when things were okay.

But I didn't. I couldn't.

Sighing, I swung my feet off the bed to settle on the cold, rough floors. I stared into space at nothing for a little bit and took in a few deep breaths before standing and making my way to the window. I could still hear the shouting that had woken me up, and I rubbed away the condensation on the glass so I could see into the muddy street below.

Captain Harper was arguing with someone on a horse, and I pressed my face closer to the pane to get a better look. I was too far away to tell anything other than the fact that the newcomer was bigger and meaner than the man who'd brought us this far. And, as I watched, the stranger sent his hand sailing backwards into Harper's face, stunning the younger man and sending him stumbling with the force of the strike.

With that one action, I knew who this was, and I turned to face Jack's sleeping form, heart racing.

"Jack," I whispered, soft voice loud in the cold silence. "Jack!"

His eyes opened, and he looked up at me, disoriented.

"What're you doing up?" he mumbled blearily. I walked over to him, sitting on the mattress and gripping his hand beneath the covers. "What's going on?"

"I think…I think Captain Howell's here."

Automatically any confusion vanished. He looked up at me in resigned defeat and nodded.

"Alright then." Jack slowly began pulling back the covers and sitting up as though his joints and bones were old and rusted. He yawned and ran his hands over his face. "What time is it?"

"Time for us to get moving." We looked around at Andrew, who was sitting up and pulling on his shoes and socks. Id was waking up slowly beside him. "It's about six thirty in the morning. We head out at seven."

Jack groaned, driving his hands back into his hair and leaving them there until the dark locks stuck out in every way possible.

"Well, you heard the man," he finally sighed, standing and grabbing his things while I continued to sit there on the bed. "Let's move out."

... — — ...

Within a few minutes, the twenty-four of us who'd ridden over together were heading downstairs, bags over our shoulders and ready for departure. As soon as I started down the creaking steps, I was assaulted by the dank smell of smoke, and I felt my insides go cold as I took in the people draped over each other, the flat and vacant eyes of the women. They looked like skeletons, ghosts hovering in the shadow of the war only a day's drive away. I looked away to where Harper was sitting at the bar, talking with Mr. Bentley. Even from this distance, through the hazy air, I could see the swelling spot on his cheekbone from Howell's backhand. He briefly looked up at us and dully motioned for Jack to come over. But before he obeyed the unspoken command, my boyfriend turned to face me, urgently grabbing my upper arm.

"Okay, Tristan – I want you to listen to me. Go outside with the others and wait there. Only speak when spoken to, and for the gods' sakes, *don't* say anything snarky." I nodded, and he clapped me on the shoulder. "Go on, I'll be right out." He left my side, and I pushed my way through the cramped booths and tables to the door, fighting to not collapse at my first breath of fresh air all night. Thankfully, I wasn't the only one, and I heard Jayce talking to his sister a few feet behind me.

"Thank the *gods* we're out of there. I swear my lungs were rotting just standing in all that crap."

But before the conversation could continue, someone came over to us, dressed in a fully decorated officer's uniform with a worn holster strapped to his right leg. He was leading five horses behind him, and I could tell that at least a few of them had been to the war fronts. Their legs were scarred, and they seemed to be in a perpetual state of anxiety, teeth grinding away at their bits and eyes rolling back in their heads.

Their handler was an older man with dark hair peppered with grey that framed an angular face. I estimated he was in his late fifties – tall, broad-shouldered, and muscular despite his age. His features were hard, merciless, and his grey eyes flashed with a cold-heartedness that pierced me like ice.

And as I looked at him, I knew that I'd been right.

"Line up," he ordered, and I fought the urge to shudder at his voice as we complied. "Showing up early like fresh meat...well, you'll be standing here in the cold, waiting for the rest of your fellow cadets like the sanctimonious idiots you are." As he finished speaking, he tossed the reigns of one of the horses to Jayce. Startled, my platoonmate caught them and eyed the animal before him with open distrust as we gathered off to the side of the road, waiting in silence.

"Sir?" he asked uncertainly.

"We ride with a sentry set up around the caravan. You're on the first shift." He started walking off when the inn door opened and Units 37 and 36 marched out, standing at disheveled attention with Jack in the lead. Mildly surprised, Howell turned back to face us, hands clasped behind his back. "Well, you soldiers are pretty damn organized, I have to give you that. Even if you're just trying to pander to my better side. You slackers stand over there with the rest of your unit." He smirked as they did as he said.

"You're obedient. I like that in my soldiers."

Beside me, Idris shifted on her feet, dark eyes avoiding his sharp gaze.

A few minutes passed, and I watched as his hawk-like eyes scoured every single one of our faces, the gears visibly turning in his head as he took note of the last few stragglers who ran out and stood at attention. When he was satisfied with his head count, he handed the remaining four reins to Harper and stepped up onto the back of a truck to glare down at us.

"You aren't at the Academy any more, girls." My skin crawled. If he knew what the girls in my platoon were like, he wouldn't be referring to us like that. It was hardly an insult. "This isn't a game, and I will not tolerate anyone who treats it as such." He paused like he was trying to weed out the troublemakers before we got any further.

"There will be no cowardice. You will not flinch in the face of danger, and you will give your lives to protect this country. Anyone who tries to leave, anyone who tries to get out of their duty to our home, and anyone who is disruptive to the efforts of the rest of us I will take aside..." he paused, and his hand rested with careless ease on the gun holstered to his leg. Jack swallowed, and I saw his arms flex in a way that told me he was clenching his hands behind his back.

"And I will pull out my gun..." There was a soft slither of metal on leather as he pulled the weapon free, holding it up for us to see. "And I will shoot you between the eyes."

Before that moment, I thought I knew what fear was. I thought I knew what a monster looked like. But standing there, looking at my captain, I realized I'd had no idea.

"Don't give me a reason to shoot you, and you'll live long enough to die on your own." He holstered his gun, and my heart pounded painfully in my thin chest as he continued.

"I expect full courage from you all. I expect you to be strong in the face of certain death. We are the *last line* between the rest of the country and the Brettain, and therefore it rests on our shoulders to do everything in our power to make sure that our people stay safe. Sometimes that means that we have to do terrible things. We have to commit horrible sins, and we *will* burn in hell." He dropped down to the ground and stepped forward until he was toe to toe with the front line of soldiers. "But you're *martyrs!* Be proud of your place in this war and die with valor!"

He looked down at each of us, a manic glint flashing so quickly behind his eyes that I wondered if I'd actually seen it in the first place.

"We're moving out," he said in a lower voice, walking over to Harper and snatching the reigns from him. "Corporal Miller, Private Jackson, and Private Lee – take a horse and assume sentry positions around the caravan. Let's move! We haven't got all day."

We all rushed to get to our respective positions while Howell stood there, almost basking in our panic. But just as I passed by him, I caught the look he shot my boyfriend as Jack mounted a scarred and battered thoroughbred, tightly gripping the horn to make sure the animal didn't throw him as he settled into the saddle.

"You!" he barked, walking forward, and I hovered by the back of our truck, watching him. Jack saluted unsteadily, other hand smoothing down the neck of the terrified horse beneath him. "You're Miller, aren't you? The one who was sent back to the Academy for disobeying a direct order?" Jack nodded once, brusque and formal, and Howell scoffed, sizing up his subordinate with angry eyes. "If you pull anything like that with me, I'll make sure you pay. And just to make sure you know that I'm serious, I'm going to drive the car with your friends. I hope none of them are skittish."

"They're all model soldiers, sir," Jack replied stiffly, tightening his hold on the reigns and steadying the horse. Howell nodded, eyes narrowing in spite, and I quickly pulled myself up into the vehicle as he turned back to face our truck.

"Oh, I'm sure they are. But you don't mind if I find out for myself, do you?" Unseen behind our captain, Jack's eyes begged me to be silent.

"No, sir," he said.

I quickly sat down near the front of the bed and looked nervously at Andy and Idris beside me.

"What is it, Byrne?" he asked me, noting my wide eyes, but before I could answer, Howell slammed his hand against the side of the car.

"Settle yourselves down, we're leaving!"

I took in a deep breath and ran a hand over my face.

"Howell's our driver?" Marcel asked in a barely audible voice, and I nodded, slowly exhaling. "Shit."

"You can say that again…let's just stay calm, don't say anything, and be as perfect as possible, okay?" I said, looking around at Idris. But my words were lost on her. She was already looking around us with that dazed expression she always had, muttering to herself and running her fingers over an amulet of some god.

"That ship has sailed," Katalin muttered, but her biting humor couldn't hide the fear I saw in her eyes as we watched our shell-shocked comrade beside us. She was a bomb with a broken timer that had ended its countdown long ago. All we could do now was wait for her to go off.

... — — ...

For a long time, there was nothing except farmland – stretches of grain dotted with weeds their owners were too weak or too poor to go out and remove on their own. The ground beneath us was cracked and dry, an effect of the long drought that had plagued the region for the last year. Hollow eyes on gaunt faces gathered to watch us as we went by, and I saw a little girl waving at us as she hid behind her mother's tattered skirts. A few people ran up to the cars and gave packages of food and blankets to us which we accepted with wide, frightened eyes. And as I watched, a young girl ran up to me, holding out a standard issue rifle. Unsettled, I took it from her, taking in her bare feet, sunken eyes, and sallow skin.

"Ma said you'd need it. Good luck, soldier," she panted, still running along with us.

Before she could back away, there was movement at my elbow. Idris had moved up beside me, her formal uniform jacket in her hands, and I moved to the side so she could get closer. Skittishly, Id held it out to the girl, hands shaking, and the child stared up at her in confusion.

"This winter will be colder than most," Chance warned, voice quick and quiet. "It's the start of the gods' vengeance, and you're already sick. Please, take it." The kid ran with us a few more seconds before taking the jacket from Id's hands.

"Thank you, miss," she whispered and finally slowed down, falling away from us until she was out of sight. I realized I didn't even know her name.

Andrew leaned forward and put a hand on Idris' shoulder, getting her attention.

"Id, you'll need that jacket later," he chastised, but she shook her head, sad smile pulling at her lips.

"No. I won't," she told him gently, like she was a mother talking to her child. "But she will. She and the others like her will need protection from the consequences sinners like us bring down on us all."

She slid back over to where she had been sitting and tangled her hands in her hair, pressing her forehead to her knees in silence.

. . . − − − . . .

The landscape changed again almost ten hours later, and just as we were all about to fall asleep due to the monotony of unending fields of dead or dying crop, Irina perked up.

"Hey. It's the Ruins."

I immediately opened my eyes and carefully stood up, walking towards the back of the truck in a precariously balanced crouch. Andy joined me, holding onto my elbow to steady both of us as we went to look at the land around us. We were driving through what was once a city of tall skyscrapers and paved roads filled with cars and people. It was a relic of the old times. Now, there was nothing. It was rubble and scorched metal, a disintegrated model of whatever broken society had existed thirty years ago.

I couldn't help but feel as though the ghosts of the dead were watching us from the piles of trash and wreckage that had once been a living room, an office building…a school. It was as though they were everywhere. Yet *nowhere*. No bodies to be found, but their eyes watched all.

It took us about two hours to pick our way through the vestiges of a civilization that used to be our own, and once we did, we found ourselves in the outlying farmlands that had once surrounded most of our cities. I couldn't help but feel sick to my stomach as the sky rumbled above us, dark clouds brewing low on the horizon.

I swallowed painfully as I watched the gray landscape roll by. I couldn't help but shiver as I took in the charred fingers of farmhouses reaching to the sky, frozen in their last throes to escape the equally scorched and pitted earth below. Weeds and stray crops long dead crunched and disintegrated beneath the wheels of our trucks as we lurched along, and the horses tossed their heads nervously as we slowly moved forward, barrel chests rumbling low warnings as they grated their teeth against their bits. My gut churned nauseatingly, and I tightened my grip on the rifle the kid had given me, fingers tracing over the safety and trigger. Ravens and crows flew in circles high above our heads – some frantically beating their wings to stay aloft, others simply gliding on invisible currents. I cleared my throat anxiously, and Andrew leaned forward to look up at the sky with me, pushing his uniform hat back slightly on his head.

"Ravens," he muttered, normally buoyant personality tensely subdued as he wiped sweat from his dark brow. I looked around at him. "It must look like rain to them." We stared up at the sky, at the black clouds marring the horizon like strikes of charcoal.

"You know what the gods say about the ravens."

We both turned around to look at Idris, and I saw that her hands were tightly wrapped around an ancient looking medallion. Through her shaking skeleton fingers I could make out a metal engraving of a shield with a sword sticking through it at an angle: the symbol of Mars. Her watery eyes were fixed fearfully on the roof of the canvas above us as though somehow she could see through the opaque fabric to the birds circling the air, and her shoulders shuddered with gasping breaths.

"They're heralds."

My heart sank.

"Id, sweetheart, come on. Don't do this right now," Andy whispered, voice wavering as he turned to her. "You've been doing so great, just keep it up."

"They're harbingers!" she insisted, voice growing louder, and I barely managed to keep from shivering.

"Chance, quit it!" Irina barked, standing, and I quickly pulled her down so she was sitting again.

"Calm down, Korsakov. If you freak out, she'll only get worse," I muttered, getting up and stepping back from her as I made my unsteady way to where Id was sitting. She closed her eyes as I approached, muttering garbled prayers under her breath, body swaying along with the truck. "Id." She looked at me, startled, and I swallowed painfully as I saw something unhinged in the back of her eyes. "I know you're scared, okay? We all are. Andrew, Me, Jack, the Horsemen, Jayce – we-we're all scared. But those ravens are just riding the currents. Nothing more." My heart pounded in my chest as she swiftly, frantically, shook her head.

"*No.*" I looked over my shoulder at Andrew who got to his feet and came over to crouch beside me. "No, they mean so much *more*. They're *omens*," she pleaded, and I sighed, backing away and looking at her in worry as Andrew tried to talk some sense into her.

"Idris–"

"They are omens of death and destruction, warnings to those who have committed evil – we're evil!" she shouted, as though she were begging me to understand, and she rose to her knees, gripping her wiry hair in her chapped hands, twisting, pulling, and wailing. Swearing, Andrew knelt before her and tried to quiet her, grabbing her wrists and attempting to untangle her fingers from her scalp.

"Andrew, you're spooking her!" I warned, disconcerted as I hovered just behind his shoulder. "You heard what Howell said about bailing! He hears her talking like that–"

"I know, I *know!* Id – Idris, shhh!" he hissed frantically as we felt the car moving to the side of the road. Howell must have heard her. "Shit. *Shit*, Id, it's going to be okay. *Please*, just be quiet!" When Idris still showed no signs of calming down, Andy lost it, shaking her hard like a rag doll as his voice cracked and rose in panic. "Gods damn it, Id! Shut up!"

Her head snapped up, and, hyperventilating and clenching her jaw, she fixed her red-rimmed eyes on mine. She was baring her teeth at me, a mad light burning in her eyes, and Andrew quickly let go of her. We quickly backed off a bit, my friend holding a hand out to keep the girl at a distance.

"We're evil!" she shrieked, manic. "And the gods strike down those who are evil!" The truck's engine sputtered a few times, and we finally came to a stop.

"What in the hell is going on back here?"

I quickly stood up in the bed of the vehicle, shaking with fear, and turned around to face my commanding officer as he marched over from the driver's seat.

Strategy. Diplomacy.

"N-nothing, sir. Private Chance just got a little excited…sir." My voice wasn't nearly as steady as I'd hoped, and I quickly clasped my hands behind my back to hide how badly they were shaking. His eyes narrowed, and his already hard mouth drew down into a scowl as Idris started wailing behind me, rocking back and forth and scratching at her skin below her uniform.

"We're evil!" she sobbed, and my blood ran cold. I couldn't breathe. I could only stare at my captain in unmasked fear. "I'm tainted. I'm tainted – I can see it on me, I can *see* it! The blood–"

"Id, shut up!" I heard Andy beg, but it was too late. His already dark expression going livid, Howell slammed down the tailgate of the truck and climbed in, shoving Andrew and I aside and grabbing Idris by her upper arm. Her eyes went wide at his touch, and she looked up at him, terrified.

"Monsters…we're all monsters!" Howell dragged her forward, stepping down to the dirt packed road and trying to pull Chance along with him. "I see your face! No!"

"Come on!" he barked, yanking her down from the truck with a jerk that I was surprised didn't dislocate her shoulder. She stumbled and fell to her knees, striking out, hitting him with clenched fists and slashing at his face with her dirt-caked nails.

"Let go!" she shrieked, and he jerked his head away from her as she swung her hand at him, opening three vicious bands of red across his left cheek. When he looked back at her, his expression was stony.

"No!" she sobbed, thrashing, and all along the road, the caravan came to a grinding stop behind us. "No! We're tainted! We're all tainted, evil – we're all going to hell!"

Howell showed no sign that he heard her wailed sermons and started walking, half-dragging and half-carrying Idris with him. I shakily got out of the back of the truck, stepping out with Andrew to see what was going on, and I could distantly hear hoof beats coming towards us.

"We're tainted! Pawns of evil!" she screamed to the watching cars.

I turned to the oncoming tattoo of hoofs on earth to see Jack racing over, scared. *Scared.* What on earth was Howell going to do that would make *Jack* scared? He pulled up beside me in a cloud of dust but didn't dismount.

"Get inside, both of you. Now."

His voice was unsteady, yet firm, and I quickly climbed back inside. I sat down with hands clasped together and pressed against my lips as I tried to control my shaking. Andrew, on the other hand, just stared up at Jack in panic.

"Miller, he's not really gonna—"

"Gods damn it, Harris! Get. Inside. The truck!" my boyfriend shouted. My friend was halfway back in the vehicle when Idris' voice carried down the whole caravan once more.

"The ravens!" she cried, hysterical, still struggling hopelessly against Howell. "We're sinners! Monsters! The tainted of Orcus, and we'll burn in hell for what we've done!"

Her voice was briefly cut off by the sound of a punch landing before she started screaming again. This time, there was something primal to it, something feral mixed in the fear. And just as I grabbed onto Andrew to keep him from pushing by Jack and running out to intervene, her wordless howl was cut off by a loud bang.

I froze, ducking low in the truck, and Jack started in his saddle, eyes wide and the back of his hand covering his mouth in horror. His horse shied away, ears flat against its head and teeth bared as it stamped its feet.

"Jack," I whispered in fear as Andrew began sobbing before me, a horrible, heart-wrenching sound.

My boyfriend just backed his horse away to his guard post, staring at that point beyond my vision in stunned silence as his chest heaved with unsteady breaths. As I watched him shakily retreat, Howell walked past the back of our car, holstering his gun.

"I will have no cowardice!" he shouted viciously in our petrified silence, and I pulled Andrew away from the tailgate by the collar of his shirt and his sleeve before he could do something stupid. He fell back against my legs, both of us shaking violently. I felt lightheaded, concussed.

As my captain made his way back to the driver's seat, he locked eyes with me for a split second, and I swore that the mania that'd been in Idris' eyes blazed in the back of his. A door slammed, and the truck rumbled beneath me. The caravan came back to life, slowly moving forward once more. Every single motion sent my stomach roiling, and I tried taking in large gulps of air, my hands resting numbly on Andy's shaking shoulders.

Nothing seemed to be getting in.

As the car slowly moved along, I forced myself to look to the side of the dirt road where Howell had been standing, and when we finally pulled past it, my heart froze in my chest. Time itself stopped.

Idris Chance, like a marionette with slashed strings, laid in the gutter of the road, sprawled unnaturally on her back with her legs folded beneath her. Her wide eyes stared vacantly at the sky above her, the ravens reflected in her dark orbs. The silvery tears that had fallen shortly before her death left clear tracks on her dirt-smudged face.

But what sent me doubling over the tailgate, throwing up the meager rations I'd managed to choke down earlier, was the bloody hole between her black eyes. It was the blood oozing down her forehead and across her face. It was the spray of red staining her Mars pendant. It was the fact that my captain had just shot an innocent young woman because she'd broken down from a fear that plagued all our minds. As I straightened back up, my eyes found Jack, and I bit my lip against the panicked tears blurring my vision. He was pale, and I could see his hands shaking as they held the reins even from this distance.

"H-he shot her," Andrew sobbed behind me, expression screwed up in a painful combination of agony and uncomprehending shock. "He shot my little sister! He shot – he shot her for being shell-shocked…" I sat down heavily across from him. I was too stunned to be of any use, too devastated to even think about how to make a sound, let alone form words. "He…he killed my Idris. Why would he do that? *Why?*"

I stared vacantly at him, hating how he was begging me in unspoken words to tell him he was wrong, that this was all just a bad dream. I felt my jaw clench, and my eyes slowly looked down at my hands. The first breath hitched in my chest, and Private Harris bowed his head, clasping his hands behind his neck as though hiding from an exploding shell.

"Oh gods, what have I done?"

"You didn't do anything," I heard Marcel tell him robotically, but he shook his head. I still couldn't speak. Couldn't even feel. It was like I was just a passenger in my own body.

"No. No, I should have *helped* her. I should have made her feel safe, all I did was shout at…oh god. The last thing I did was *shout* at her, oh *gods.*"

Suddenly, I couldn't breathe again, and I dropped my head down into my hands, trying to get air. I was shaking violently, and just when I thought I was going to be ripped apart by what I was feeling, that I was going to die and fall apart – suffocating while gulping air – a gentle hand touched the back of my head. I didn't have the strength to look up at who it was, so I just stayed as still as I possibly could as they knelt in front of me. After a few seconds of nothing, of us just sitting there in those frozen positions, I felt them slowly and awkwardly place their other hand on my shoulder. The one that had been resting on the back of my head slid down to grip the back of my neck in comfort.

"I'm so sorry," Aliyah said shakily, moving her thumb back and forth on my shoulder as I finally started sobbing. "Just...just keep breathing, Byrne."

In my peripheral vision, I saw that Marcel was white as a sheet, and Katalin's hands were locked behind her head as she looked up at the canvas ceiling in shaken disbelief. Irina had made her way over to Andrew and was sitting beside him, hand resting on his shaking back. She was speaking to him in gentle undertones. I couldn't hear what she was saying, but whatever it was made him cry even harder.

I could still hear Aliyah's words from somewhere over my head, repeating uselessly like a broken record.

"Breathe...just breathe it out."

I tried to ignore how her voice wavered. I tried not to think about how her words were just as much for herself and everyone else as they were for me. Her head bowed down to rest against the top of mine, shaky breath hot against my scalp, and I tightened my hold on my hair, trying to stifle my cries as my tears burned into my skin and my silent wails tore my throat apart.

And all the while, Idris' ravens continued to scream to the stormy skies overhead.

DAY FIVE

0100 hours

Idris Chance was gone.

I felt dead inside. I couldn't feel the jolting of the car or how my spine protested against sitting in the same position for gods know how long. The dank cold from the pouring rain outside had settled into my joints like a heavy mold. Thunder rumbled overhead and lightning briefly lit up the air at random, jarring intervals. My breathing was abnormally steady, and my eyes stared blankly ahead of myself. Andrew was still sitting beside me, head bowed, and his fingers numbly ran over the fastenings and straps of Id's backpack. He'd long since run out of tears, but his shoulders still shuddered with broken breaths. All twenty-four of us were as silent as the dead, even the Horsemen sitting across from us. They watched Andy and I with sympathy and sadness in their eyes.

Finally, I couldn't bear the quiet any longer.

"She knew she was going, Andrew," I whispered, wiping at my eyes even though they were dry. He finally looked at me, eyes burning with fury.

"That *son of a bitch* Howell dragged her, screaming, to the side of the road and put his gun in her face." His voice wavered but stayed strong. "He put his gun *right* between her eyes and *murdered* her." He took in a shaky breath, wiping at the tears gleaming in his eyes. "Of course she knew she was going!"

"That's not what I meant," I said numbly, expression empty as I tried to block out the image Andrew had put in all of our heads. "Before we left the Academy, she told me something…when she hugged me…" I cleared my throat, trying to find my voice. My words sounded odd to my ears. They sounded like a static voice over the radio, like someone else telling a story. "She told me that she'd see me on the other side." *And that she wanted me to take care of you.*

He laughed, bitter and in pain.

"See — see you on the other side…that's definitely the type of crap she'd spew." He took in a shaky breath, wiping at his face. "Just tell me something, any of you. How does that make what happened to her any better?" I had no answer to that and looked back down at the gun in my hands. "How does knowing that make any of this any better?"

"He didn't even let us grab her dog tag," Irina whispered, and I looked up at her, tired and absent. "It's — you're supposed to keep the tags of the fallen, but he didn't even let us honor her." Aliyah's words broke the silence that followed, and I shuddered.

"We haven't even gotten to the war, and we're already dying."

Suddenly, I became aware of a dull rumbling noise that permeated the air, a sound that reminded me of fireworks going off in quick succession.

"What's that?" I asked, trying to blink away the bell jar that had descended over me, numbing me to the world around us.

"That's the front lines," Marcel answered in the half-light, and I looked at her across the way. Her face was shadowed, barely visible in the gloom. "We're slowing down." Sure enough, the brakes groaned, and the truck came to a creaking stop.

"Everybody out!" Howell bellowed, and we shuffled forward, leaving the vehicle with our packs slung over our shoulders. I gripped the rifle tightly in my hands and looked over to where Jack was dismounting his horse, passing the reigns off to one of the drivers. There was a haunted light to his eyes, and he came over to stand beside me, meeting the eyes of our superior with hard, angry resolution.

"Guess they weren't all model soldiers, were they Miller?" Jack clenched his jaw and didn't answer. Howell smirked, a smug expression that made my skin crawl, and looked at the people slowly gathering before him. He almost seemed to be taking prideful note of how everyone was avoiding his gaze and shaking where they stood as the rain continued to batter down on us. *"Hustle!"*

There was a patter of running feet in mud, and we were soon gathered before him — a trembling, wide-eyed group of soldiers. He rubbed his hands together and turned away from us to face the desolation stretching in front of us. Behind us, I could hear the clatter of horses' hooves as they were loaded up into the backs of the trucks we'd just left.

"Welcome to hell!" Howell shouted above the din, and we looked out over the maze of trenches that stretched for several miles in front of us, at the flashes of artillery and guns in the hazy light. Rain poured down over No Man's Land, and I shakily stepped closer to Jack, fingers brushing against his while our captain's back was turned. A flash of lightning lit up the barbed wire like fire, and when Howell continued, his voice was dark and ominous above the sounds of war and the trucks driving away.

"There's no one left to hear you now."

... − − ...

Units 36 and 37 had split up into their respective groups, and I watched as Howell and Harper coldly shook each other's hands. The younger man's eyes were hard and seething. My captain's were sadistic, taunting even, and I realized why Howell scared me so much. He *liked* the killing. He liked the power of fear. The younger man finally broke away with a disgusted scowl.

"Unit 36 with me!" he shouted, and one hundred and forty people fell in line behind him, following him as he jumped down into the trenches below and headed towards the left. Strangely, though, Andrew didn't follow. Instead, he looked down at the backpack in his hands, torn.

"Hey, Andrew," I called, and he looked up at me. "You're gonna miss your unit."

He sighed, hefting the bag in his hands and tossing it over to me.

"Keep it." I looked up at him astonished. "I don't need anything from there to remember her by. I got it all in my head." He almost dissolved into tears, but he composed himself. "I got every single one of her smiles, her laughs, her wacky stories up here. Clear as day." He nodded to himself, biting his lip. "That's how she's gonna stay, Byrne. You keep that, though. I think you need it more than I do." I nodded my thanks and made a small noise of surprise as Andrew suddenly grabbed me and pulled me into a tight hug.

"Whoa – hello," I managed, and he took in a deep breath, patting my back.

"You're a good kid, Tristan. I'll see you around?"

I backed away, looking down at Id's bag.

"Yeah," I mumbled, not looking at him. "I'm sure you will."

But he got my meaning and nodded, clearing his throat and moving off towards Harper, who was waiting for him down in the trench. As I watched, Andrew dropped down beside him, and his captain put a hand on my friend's shoulder, speaking to him softly before giving him a side embrace. No doubt he was apologizing for what happened to Idris, and I quickly stuffed her nearly empty bag into my own.

It was the last I'd see of either man for a long time.

"Form ranks!"

Startled by Howell's shout, we all turned around and moved to stand in an orderly block of five across and twenty-eight down. I was about to move closer to Jack as we shuffled into place, but a hand grabbed a fistful of the back of my shirt. I stopped, looking over my shoulder at whoever it was.

"Don't get close to Miller. Howell will suspect something's up between you two," Marcel whispered, pulling me back so I was side-by-side with Korsakov, and I caught Jack giving War a quick nod of thanks. As I took in an unsteady breath, Irina stood at attention, muttering to me out of the corner of her mouth as we waited.

"We may not like you two, but we hate Howell's guts." Pestilence paused, making sure that I was actually listening to her before she continued. "So for the moment the Horsemen have your back." I looked at the white-haired girl sharply, startled, and she quickly stomped on my foot in a silent message for me to face forward again.

"Listen up! Front lines are eight miles from where we are, but all the reserve supplies that we'll be using are back here. As you pass between Lieutenants Bates and Wilson over there, they will hand each person a fully loaded standard issue rifle. Sergeant Williams will be issuing two extra clips. Additional munitions will be made available at our station as time goes on."

We started walking, climbing down into the trenches and heading over to the two men our captain had pointed out. Bates was older, a grizzled warrior. Wilson was clearly fresh out of officer's training, and he hesitated as he saw that I already had a gun.

"Donation from along the road," Korsakov explained, and his expression cleared as he handed her a weapon. A few steps later, a young Singh woman, whose uniform told me she was Sergeant Williams, handed me my extra clips, and I was surprised when the three joined our procession after arming the last member of my unit. Apparently, they were our officers, too.

There was no talking as we walked further into the hellscape. In fact, thirty minutes into our trek, it seemed as though the voices of man were being shoved farther underground while the raucous noise of death and destruction grew increasingly louder. I could hear artillery fire booming in the distance, shells whistling as they grew closer to their destinations before exploding upon impact. I could hear the haunting rain of machine guns and rifles, and occasionally I heard a few screams. The air was mostly soot and dust, and as we went, the ground beneath my feet grew muddier and harder to walk through.

People huddled against the embankments, weapons clutched close to their chests. They stared at us with dead, hollow eyes as we walked by, like skeletons with skin stretched over their bleached bones, clad in ratty clothes that were way too big and barely recognizable as uniforms. A few people I saw were missing eyes, fingers. Some were even missing entire limbs, and I shuddered involuntarily, skin crawling as I looked at the wounded lining the walls on either side of us.

"Feast your eyes, kids," one of them called, staggering forward on crutches and laughing as we shied away from him, scared. His hair was thinning, wispy and blonde. A rotten smell seemed to emanate off of him, meaning he had gangrene somewhere. One of his eyes was swollen shut, the angry flesh peaking from beneath soiled bandages. "It's the Hall of Broken Soldiers!" Irina didn't shy away as he hobbled along beside us and reached out to touch her snow-white hair. "You'll be like us one day, too, pretty lady…"

But before he could touch her, she stopped in her tracks, grabbing his wrist and twisting it the wrong way behind his back. As he cried out in pain, she sent her foot crashing into the back of his knee and threw him to the ground. The whole line came to a stop around us at the commotion, and Irina stared down at her victim, a dangerous light in her eyes. Her face was utterly still, expression an unreadable mask.

"This 'pretty lady' would rather die than end up like you," she whispered, blue eyes wide, before stepping back into her place and staring forward again, ready for her next order. Howell smirked to himself, and I could feel the disgust radiating off of my platoonmate at having caused him entertainment.

"Move on!" he shouted, and we started walking again. Fear bubbled in my gut as Howell made his way towards our row. "That'll teach you to keep your hands to yourself, Johnson. What's your name, private?" he called, laughing as he fell into step beside us.

"Korsakov, sir." He nodded to himself.

"One of those Horsemen I heard so much about from G.A. Agathon, then?" She swallowed and continued to stare blankly ahead of herself.

"Yes, sir." Her words were clipped, cold.

"Which one?" The amusement in his voice was making me sick, and I could tell by the way Irina clenched her jaw that it was upsetting her, too.

"I'm the one they call Pestilence, sir."

"Any reason?"

"Luck of the draw, sir," she said with a shake of her head.

My eyebrow rose fractionally at that. She'd just lied. Irina was small and deadly – like a virus. And freakishly pale so she often looked like she was sick. That was why she had the name, but it gave me comfort to know that she was keeping our captain out of our lives in the small, subtle ways that she could. He nodded to himself before slowing down so he could walk behind his command – watching our every move. Knowing I couldn't talk to my companion now, I turned my attention to my surroundings and immediately wished I hadn't.

The first thing I saw was a corpse slumped against a metal crate of ammunition, a raven perched on his shoulder and picking away at the rotten skin of his face. As though it knew I was watching, it stopped its scavenging and turned its beady eyes on me, opening its beak and giving a hissing, hellish caw that sent shivers down my spine. It was the most gods-awful, condemning sound I'd ever heard, like something out of a nightmare. And as we passed by, it vaulted off its grisly post, flapping its wings viciously above our heads like a bat before taking off into the sky.

Feeling sick to my stomach, I kept my unfocused eyes on the backs of the people in front of me for the next forty minutes. My legs burned with each step as we kept up our brutally quick pace.

The cold air was heavy with a pungent smell, a combination of mold and stale dirt and rust that I remembered well from my four years at the Academy. It was the smell of munitions crates and warfare, a stench that burrowed its way into everything, from our skin and clothing to rubber and metal.

And even though I was keeping my eyes fixed ahead, I couldn't help but see glimpses of my new world in my peripheral vision. I couldn't help but hear it, *smell* it in some cases. On a couple occasions, I heard people around me gag quietly at the stench of rotting bodies, fighting the urge to cover their noses and mouths with their hands for fear of what Howell would do if they showed weakness. A couple louder, closer booms made me flinch and the earth tremor, and I closed my eyes for a few seconds, relying on our steady pace to keep me going in the right direction. I wasn't ready for this. *We* weren't ready for this, what kind of joke was a war academy anyways? What good was book learning and theory practice in preparing us for getting shot at?

And the whole while, the further in we marched, the closer and closer we got to the end of the line, I swore I could feel Howell behind me more and more. It was like he kept growing, looming over us like a shadow: a gleeful, twisted, cruel shadow – a demented puppet master warming up to start his show with a grotesque grin on his face. And I found that more and more often my shivering came from thinking about him, from feeling that crushing presence.

The gunfire had become impossibly louder now. I could hear people shouting over each other. Whether they were orders or screams of loss, I couldn't tell. All I knew was that they were yelling loud enough to wake the dead, and I tried to ignore the possibility that that was exactly what some of them were trying to do. At this point, our pace started to get sloppier, slower, as we tried to delay the inevitable and hold out for as long as we could.

Cling to whatever little time we had left as the smell of gunpowder and the taste of metal in our mouths grew ever stronger.

There were no more people huddled against the trench walls here. It was the final segment, the final stretch until we were on the front lines. And gods help me, but I didn't remember any of it. I just remembered staring wide-eyed at the backs of uniforms, trying to control my breathing to no avail and clenching my shaking hands tightly around the farm girl's gun. When I snapped out of whatever fugue I'd settled into ten, twenty, maybe even thirty minutes later, the din of war had become unbearable. I felt like I was going deaf.

"Company halt!"

We stopped in our tracks, and Howell walked up to stand in front of us. "When we turn this next corner, you're gonna be on the front lines. So, weapons at the ready and break ranks." We primed our guns for use and stepped away from each other, staggering our positions. I quickly caught Jack's eye, but he gave me a nearly imperceptible shake of the head.

Stay away.

"I expect complete obedience. I expect bravery, sacrifice – all of it worthy for a king. Because that's what you're doing out here, boys and girls! You're burning for the kings; so let's make your pyres something remarkable, shall we?" With that, he faced forward, squared his shoulders, and rounded the bend with his weapon held at the ready, the rest of us following.

As soon as I saw it all, I balked. People sprinted in every direction, shouting frantic orders and rising over the edge of the trench to fire their guns towards the enemy's trenches not even half a mile away. I tripped over something and glanced down to see a body lying facedown in the mud as though an invisible hand had just dropped him there carelessly. Howell was waving us towards the far end of the trench, near a massive command tent that I assumed belonged to him. As we were walking, someone was shot down beside Jack, and he looked down at the girl's vacant eyes with an expression I'd never seen before.

It was cold. It was as though he didn't care about what he'd just seen, as though it were just an everyday fact of life. And while that was now true for us, it threw me off. Jack wasn't one to not care about life, and this…this was a side of him I'd never seen before.

And it was one that made me feel even more scared than I already was.

"Platoons 306 and 304, I want you down at the south-most end of this line! Platoons 305 and 307, you're manning the artillery weapons on the north-most end! Now, the people you see here are what's left of the command I had before. Another unit of fresh Academy meat like you lot. There were one hundred and forty of them a year ago, too. Now, there's just a dozen of them."

"And you left them here on their own?"

The words slipped out of my mouth before I could stop them, and everyone turned to look at me, eyes filled with fear and plain disbelief. Heart pounding in my throat, I watched as Howell came to a stop before me, gaze hard and angry as he glared down at me.

"Yes, I did. Private…"

"Byrne, sir," I answered, voice wavering, and my captain scoffed, taking in my appearance.

"I trust them to do what's necessary, to *give* what's necessary, for this country to survive. But looking at you…" He laughed. "Well, you're not going to be one of those men, I can see it now. I give you two weeks out here, and trust me. When I make an estimate on how long someone survives, I'm never wrong." He looked around at everyone, eyes glinting. "To your stations!" he bellowed, and we all headed off to our respective places. But not before my captain seized my arm and pulled me close to him, leaning down to speak into my ear.

"I know you were close to that maniac I shot on the truck," he began, voice dripping with menace, and I swallowed down my anger and terror. "I find out you share even the slightest of her convictions or her idiocy, you're next."

With that, he sent me stumbling on my way, and I almost tripped over myself in my hurry to catch up to Jack. But as soon as I was close enough, my boyfriend grabbed me and yanked me out of sight behind Howell's tent.

"What the *hell*, Tristan?" he hissed, angry in his fear for my life. "I give you one job, do not speak unless spoken to, and you–"

"I'm sorry," I floundered, lifting my hands helplessly. "I didn't mean to say it, I swear. It just came out–" Jack sighed and put his hands on my shoulders, looking into my eyes with a worn and serious expression.

"Do not antagonize that man any more, or he will make *sure* that you only live two weeks. You hear me?" I nodded nervously, and he sighed, guiding us both into the stream of people heading for their posts. With every step he took, he seemed to grow older and older, and I snapped my fingers in front of his spaced out eyes to get his attention.

"You okay?" I asked. He nodded but didn't look down at me. "What is it?"

"Back into the saddle I go," he breathed softly before jogging up to the front of our platoon and lifting his hand above his head to get our attention.

"Alright, listen up! Marcel, take half of 305 and go cover the far end of the south side. Use your ammunition sparingly and listen for enemy fire *first* to get a general target." The indicated group of people followed his pointing arm, and he turned to look at the other half of us. "Jackson, take the others and cover the closer end of the south side. Same instructions. The Brettain will most likely try and come over the trenches or bombard us with artillery," he continued, walking down the line and holding his weapon at the ready as we followed close behind, eyes wide with fear on our pale faces. "It's your job to shoot them down before they can hit you. You see something that looks promising, fire. We've got a job to do, people! Let's do it!"

And in that moment, as I found myself actually following the orders shouted at me despite the bullets occasionally whizzing past my ears and the fear pounding in my heart, I was brutally reminded that my boyfriend was a leader of war.

DAY NINE

Four days had gone by.

Four days that had left me utterly convinced that I was in hell, not that that was a surprising conclusion.

In the time that we'd been here, I'd learned that there was no true respite, no such thing as a light at the end of the tunnel. At the Academy, they'd taught us that there'd be lulls between the assaults, but so far there'd been nothing. Everything seemed tiring and dark and hopeless, and we ran on an unending peak of adrenaline that was almost as exhausting as the lack of sleep. It was like being kept at a brutal, stressful high and never allowed to come down.

And yet we were still there, intermittently rising up above the trenches to get a few shots off at the enemy before we were gone again, trying to lock away the instincts that were telling us not to repeat the cycle. As for me, it'd gotten to the point where I was pretending to move with everyone else, but I couldn't put my head over the trench. I couldn't bring myself to deliberately step into the line of fire like a suicidal idiot – or a loyal soldier, depending on whom you asked.

I would just shake as I held my gun close to my chest. I felt like I was separated from everything around me – I could see the terrors of war, but I felt oddly detached, as though a there was a heavy bell jar over me that kept the world out but still let me watch everything as it happened.

Everyone else seemed to be in pretty decent states, or leastways as decent as you could be doing what we were. Mainly, though, I couldn't help but admire and fear the Horsemen. They moved in sync beside each other, setting the cadence and the standard for those around them. They never flinched, and they never backed down. A few times, I saw Jack in the haze around us, shouting orders to Jackson before he moved back to his side of the trench.

That was another thing that bothered me. I'd ended up in Alec's command, not Jack's, and I hadn't been able to talk to him in a non-military way for the last four days. It left me wondering if he couldn't be around me, if he was trying to prepare himself for my death sentence of two weeks.

It made me wonder if he didn't believe in me.

It also made me wonder if I'd sorely underestimated his dedication to the military, and I was just seeing him compartmentalize what he could and couldn't deal with right now. Whatever his reasons, I was feeling alone and isolated. I could sense a shadow looming over me, waiting to descend, and I knew that the moment it touched me, I'd be gone.

Jack would come back down this way and trip over me just as I'd tripped over that kid when I first came in. He'd look down, and he'd see me. And all hell would break loose.

Or at least that's what I used to think. Now, I had no idea how he'd react to finding me dead. Now it seemed more likely that he'd just stare down at me with this impassive expression on his face before running back to whatever he was doing.

He would survive, just as he always did.

"Kid, if you want to survive Howell, you're gonna to need to actually start shooting over the trench before he comes back down here."

I looked over my shoulder at Maggie, a private who was in her late twenties from a platoon a few years back. Apparently, she was the longest surviving member of any unit that had served under Howell, but she wouldn't tell us how she'd done it. Her skin was scabbed over and scarred in more places than I could count, and her uniform was worn and threadbare. Open sores lined her jaw, wrists, and fingers, and her dark eyes were bruised and shadowed beneath bright red hair.

"I am," I lied.

She shook her head, looking up from where she was prepping her weapon for another volley, tired eyes blazing. We were both exhausted, but I could barely see it in her while she fought. She reminded me of one of those mountain cats, ragged yet viciously tireless. I, on the other hand, was falling apart at the seams. In fact, I'd drifted off to sleep a couple times despite the chaos around me, only to be shaken awake by somebody who happened to be passing by.

"Look, kid," she sighed, the words forcing their way through corrupted vocal cords, and she leaned up against the trench beside me. "Howell's a monster disguised as a war hero."

"I know what you mean," I said, thinking about Id, but she shook her head.

"Oh no, you don't," she pressed, smoker's voice cracking with a sardonic bark of laughter. Her hands continued reloading the weapon of their own accord. "I know about what happened to your friend, and I'm real sorry, I truly am. But that was nothing." A cruel, twisted smile crept onto her face as she scoffed and shook her head.

"Howell's a mass murderer, Private Byrne," she finished with solemn finality. "And you'll see that I'm right in the next few days."

She returned to shooting, and I hovered beside her, slightly crouched to stay out of the line of fire. She ducked down behind the trenches in time to dodge a bullet, and she looked at me, eyes sad and angry.

"My unit was only one of *many*, kid. Every single command Howell's received he's driven into the ground." She paused to get off another shot before crouching down beside me again, pushing her hair out of her face so that she could look at me.

"It starts with the small things: longer shifts, less rack time…then it gets worse. Suddenly you're all working twenty-hour shifts, people are dying from exhaustion, and troops start making stupid mistakes that get people killed. And then, when you're all mindless beasts milling around trying to keep your feet under you long enough to get your four hours of sleep, he starts giving the orders." She fired a few more times, and I watched her, noticing how her accented voice had wavered on that last sentence.

"What orders?" I asked, and she gave another dry laugh, eyes trained on our invisible foes.

"Why do you think there's only twelve of us left?" she asked, voice just loud enough to be heard above the din. "Now get up here, kid. Start pulling your weight."

At her scolding, I stepped up beside her and fell into her cycles and routines. The glass cage settled around me once more, and I froze up as I ducked back down below the trenches. She put a hand on my shoulder and roughly turned me to face her.

"Don't think. Point, aim, shoot," she shouted, words still muffled to my ears. "Most importantly, *don't miss*. One shot per person. Don't stop. Don't think. Just pull the trigger, and you'll live."

"Pull the trigger and I'll live?" I asked, incredulous. "You think it's that simple?" She gave a black smile, a cadaver's grin.

"I *know* it is, kid."

A loud whistling filled the air, and we dropped to the ground as an artillery shell from the Brettain crashed into our lines a couple hundred feet down the trench. There were the standard screams, the clatter of damaged equipment, and the explosion of fire and shrapnel that tore apart the air as part of the trench was blown away. Maggie made a gesture for me to stay where I was and continue on while she ran over to regroup the shattered line. But as she backed away, she called out one last bit of advice.

"And with Howell, that's the only way you survive. It's kill or be killed out here, Byrne. So, get used to dirty hands."

I made the mistake of taking in a deep breath and coughed on the polluted air. I clenched my gun in my hands, leaning against the crumbling embankment until I had collected myself. My adrenaline was through the roof. My vision was blurred. My ears were ringing, and I felt light-headed from hunger, fear, and exhaustion. We were already fighting in seemingly absurd thirteen-hour shifts with six hours of sleep in between, and the notion of a twenty-hour day with only four hours of respite terrified me.

It wouldn't take a Brettain bullet to kill me if things went the way that Maggie said they would. My captain would do that himself.

... — — ...

"Thirteen hours!" Howell bellowed, and I heaved a sigh of relief, falling away from the lines as platoons 304 and 305 continued fighting. In six hours, we'd wake up and fight with them until their thirteen hours were up, and they'd get some rack time, leaving us to hold the line until they had their six hours of sleep. And the cycle would continue, each platoon stuck in their pattern of thirteen hours fighting, six hours sleeping.

It was a brutal, unrelenting sequence, and I didn't know how long I'd be able to keep up with it – certainly not a whole year. I was already exhausted. Everything in my body hurt, even my lungs and bones, and I nearly collapsed as I made my way back to the one place I'd found I could be safe and rest without threat of dying by the enemy's hand or Howell's.

It seemed war still respected the sanctuary of the medical tent.

I'd stumbled in there my second day to avoid running into Howell for fear I'd say something else to piss him off, and I'd accidentally bumped into the head doctor as he was setting someone's arm.

It hadn't gone well for the patient.

But the doc took to me instantly.

"I see you're back, Private Byrne," Blackwell called, and I gave a ghost of a smile to the old, salt-and-pepper haired medic. Apparently, my face was pretty amusing because he started laughing in genuine amusement. "Don't hurt yourself, kid. C'mon. I've got a little empty space back there for you to crash in if you like." He gestured to what was probably an operating table, and I frowned.

"Aren't you gonna need that?" I asked, heading in the general direction anyways. The man shrugged and followed a few paces behind me.

"Maybe, maybe not," he yawned, quickly shaking the sleepiness away. "Most of the people I get in here who're that severe aren't going to make it anyways, so I don't try. We're limited on resources out here."

I lay down on the plastic encased vinyl, my eyes flitting closed almost immediately. I listened to nurses bustle around me, and I opened my eyes in time to see the doctor come over and sit next to me. His hands were heavily veined and calloused, yet they were unbelievably steady as he measured out pills and fluids for the swarm of people that were no doubt about to come in. He wasn't fazed by any of the loud booms or rattling gunfire, and I lifted my head a little off the bed.

"How long have you been here?" I asked, and he looked at me over the syringe he was preparing.

"Too long," he muttered, flicking the glass side as he spoke. "You?"

"First tour – hopefully my last, too."

"You're with Howell," he scoffed. "You can be damn sure it's your last." I painfully sat up, curiosity piqued as I propped myself up on my elbows.

"Everyone's been saying that," I said. "Why?" Blackwell looked at me, clearing his throat before going back to his work.

"Howell was part of the border guard thirty years ago – a fresh-faced recruit like yourself." I already felt uneasy. That was around the time the war had started. "They were down by what's now the Mezitain front line when they were ambushed by southern forces. Keep in mind, there'd been no...well, let's just say no *overt* history of ill will between the two of us at that time. Just rising tensions, and he was only a cadet. Wasn't even out of the Academy yet."

"He lost everyone, didn't he?" I asked, glancing between my lap and Blackwell, and the doctor nodded.

"But he survived, and it wasn't because he was a brave soldier, Tristan. He *ran*. He bailed on his patrol and made it back to a base eight miles away. He was the first messenger of the war, the first casualty." He set the syringe and pill bottles to the side before picking up the emergency tracheotomy kit next. "We responded in kind, and, well…things kind of escalated and fell apart form there."

"So, Howell…" I began, confused, and the doctor clasped his hands over the equipment in his lap.

"Howell is trying to atone for his sins the only way he thinks he can. No more running," Blackwell interrupted, looking at me again with his steady, wizened eyes. "He thinks that the more people he leads, the more he stands his ground, sacrifices to the cause that ruined our world, the more his debt to those men and women he left behind will be cleared."

I frowned.

"So, he's crazy?"

Blackwell laughed to himself, closing the kit and setting it aside.

"Aren't we all?" He walked over to grab something from the shelves beside me and patted me on the knee as he walked by. "Rest, Tristan. I'll make sure Howell doesn't come back here." He pulled the curtain closed around me with a small smile.

I was alone and within seconds fell asleep.

My dreams were of the war I was drowning in. They were of Howell fleeing from the massacre of his friends and comrades. They were of his pain and his guilt. They were of Idris drenched in lake water after her communion with the swans, water dripping off of her. Of her dancing and laughing at Promenade, crimson dress pooling and swirling around her. Of her screaming about the ravens and getting shot between the eyes – her head snapping backwards in a bloody arc while the rest of her gracelessly collapsed.

But the nightmare that scared me the most was Jack. I saw him just standing there, shrouded in smoke with skeletons and skulls charred and crushed beneath his feet. His hands were clenched at his sides – fists and forearms drenched and dripping with blood.

When Blackwell woke me up six hours later, I felt as though I hadn't left the war at all. The seconds, minutes, hours, days – they were all starting to blur together.

...———...

When I left Blackwell's tent, I immediately knew something was off. For one thing, the Brettain had slowed their attack. There weren't as many gunshots, and the artillery guns were definitely firing less often. We actually had time to breathe for once.

As I made my way towards the command tent, I saw a crowd gathered before our captain. The tall man was staring at them all like he was daring someone to speak. I noticed that the assembled people consisted solely of the new privates while the twelve soldiers left over from his previous units stood behind him, still and silent. And as I joined the crowd, I could hear Howell talking.

"Total casualty list shows that I've lost five of you useless cogs in nine days, and given that you all need to last me a year, that's unacceptable. We need information on where the Brettain are stationed and firing from so we can thin out their lines before they wipe us all out. So, after consulting my lieutenants, I've come to a decision." He clasped his hands behind his back, and his chin tilted upwards ever so slightly as he surveyed us. "Since the Brettain fire has momentarily abated, the remaining men and women from my previous commands will be sent on a reconnaissance mission over the trenches."

My stomach dropped as I looked at Maggie. She continued to stare at the ground with hands behind her back, head hanging down in submissive stillness. She looked like a statue.

Howell's a mass murderer, Private Byrne, and you'll see that I'm right in the next few days.

"We'll still be firing over the trenches, but we will avoid the area your brave comrades will cover to prevent friendly fire." He turned to face the people behind him and gave a salute, a gesture so utterly empty of respect that it sent my skin crawling. "Good luck."

Without a single word, the twelve people turned around and headed for the ladder, climbing up the rungs without hesitation and stepping out onto the butchering field. But before she vanished from sight, Maggie paused at the top rung, looking over her shoulder at me. One hand fished her dog tag out from under her shirt, and she pulled it over her head, untangling it from her unruly hair and letting it fall to the mud at the base of the ladder. Her eyes were still fixed on mine.

"Told you, kid," she muttered, and as we watched, she pulled herself over the top and started crawling. We all flooded to the edge of the trench, lifting our weapons up and maintaining our normal strategy. But my eyes could only watch the twelve people crawling across No Man's Land.

Almost immediately, the Brettain infantry picked up their pace once more.

My stomach turned as one of the twelve's heads sprayed red, and the poor man fell still. Another two were pelted with broadside fire from some automatic weapon. A fourth got caught in the barbed wire and screamed as she tried to get free, only to give away her position and catch a bullet in the chest. I ducked down to reload and when I stood up again, I could see Maggie in the lead, guiding the remaining five people. At a signal from her, they stood up and brought their weapons to the ready position, shooting down at the trenches. Immediately gunfire erupted from the east, and we quickly directed our own weapons that way and returned fire.

When I looked back to where the last of Unit 26 had been standing, I saw only two people standing, still forging ahead and still firing their rifles. Maggie was one of them, and the ugly truth started to sink into my mind as Howell didn't sound a call for them to return.

He wanted them to die.

As I watched, the two of them ran out of ammunition, and one held up his hands in a gesture of surrender. The Brettain rejected his plea with a torso full of lead, and he collapsed to the ground while Maggie sprinted forward, shouting something. I could see her mouth moving, but I couldn't hear her words. All I knew was that whatever she was saying the Brettain either didn't hear or didn't like, and her legs folded under her like a house of cards.

Just like that, the captain's strategy was over, and we shifted the artillery weapons to face our new position. Checking once to make sure that Howell wasn't watching me, I hurried over to the ladder and picked up the dirty tags, shakily wiping the mud from between the raised lettering.

Margaret Burk 12987265

I pulled the chain over my head, not risking keeping it in my pocket, and headed back to my post. No matter how many times it happened, I couldn't get used to people dying. It was so wrong, unthinkable even, that I would never see Maggie again. Not at the dinner fires telling jokes or at the sleeping giving us advice. Her gruff humor would never again ease our racing nerves; her anecdotes from her parent's farm would no longer help us fall asleep at night.

The more I thought about it, the angrier I got at my captain, and I clenched my hand around the tag hanging about my neck like a noose, taking deep breaths to try and stay calm. I couldn't let Howell see me this shaken. Because then he'd ask what was wrong, and given how pissed off and horrified I was, I would probably tell him exactly what I thought of him.

Howell had just sacrificed people who had risked their lives for a year on the front lines. Maggie...Maggie had been here longer. A year in hell – that was the sentence of our generation. They should have been sent home when we arrived, but instead our captain had kept them there until there was no one left. It was almost as though he *tried* to make sure that no one made it.

He lets no one out alive.

The words Jack had spoken to me in the Academy filled my ears, and I looked around at the rest of my unit. I could tell they were thinking the exact same thing I was. The tears burning my eyes and blurring my vision shifted from grief to anger.

The man we were supposed to entrust our safety to didn't care about us. We were nothing more than a means to an end for him, and with the ever-present threat of execution for any act of insubordination, there was no one left to speak out for us. I tried to find Jack in the throng of people around me, but instead I found Moore and Jones standing side by side, clearly shaken as they talked to each other. I moved close enough to hear what they were saying.

"Maggie told me that he'd do the same to us," Marcel whispered, and Aliyah shot her a pointed look telling her to keep quiet. "I'm not going to stand here while he kills us off group by group, Aliyah!"

"That is out of our control now," the taller woman hissed back, but Marcel shook her head.

"No. No, all it takes is someone who is willing to stand up for what's right. And all it takes is for that someone to have an army behind him."

I looked over my shoulder and saw Jack glaring in barely masked fury at Howell's back as the captain talked with a messenger from Harper's unit.

But just when I thought my boyfriend was going to say something about what we'd just seen, he clenched his teeth and walked away, returning to his post.

There really was no one left to hear us now.

· · · − − − · · ·

Hours had gone by.

Hours of silent obedience and shaking hands and pounding hearts. Hours of wondering if we were going to be next over the trenches, if we were going to face the same fate as Maggie and the others. And hours later, we had our answer.

Not today.

Mercifully, not today.

My skin felt dry and stretched out against my bones. The little moisture that'd been left in my body had been burned out by the small campfire I'd been staring at for the last hour. I pressed my lips together and noted with absent worry the coppery taste working its way into my mouth from the split skin. I ran my tongue over the stinging slits and closed my eyes tiredly – anything to cut through this nothing.

Someone shifted to my left.

Across the fire, someone else cleared her throat.

Nothing more.

"Got food." I looked over my shoulder as Katalin Soto walked over to me and sat down, taking her part of the dried ration before handing it to me. I took the rusting case from her and looked unenthusiastically at the stacked squares of dried meat and centuries old cracker tied together with string.

I wasn't very hungry. I wasn't much of anything right now.

I passed the tin to the next person without taking anything, and looked back at the fire. Sitting here in this quiet, this abnormal silence, was filling enough. But I couldn't help the way my gaze was continuously drawn to the vacant seat to my right. To the note of silence in the constant background noise where a smoker's voice should be. To the muted colors, that missing shock of bright red hair.

Maggie wasn't here anymore. She was never going to be again. Just like Idris. A hollow feeling settled in my chest, and I sighed, forcing myself to look back into the dancing flames. The heat would turn me brittle, and then I'd shatter.

"Remember that story Maggie told us? About her brothers and the rat in their bedroom?" We all looked to the young man who'd spoken. His eyes were red, and he sniffed, dragging the back of his hand across his nose. "She'd had enough of her four older brothers pulling pranks on her, so she caught a rat and set it loose in their room in the middle of the night." A smile touched his face, and he laughed, shifting his weight and looking up at us with renewed life. I felt a smile of my own trying to fight its way to my lips as he got up onto his knees and continued with the story. "And this rat decides that the house is too cold, right? And it finds the edge of the blanket and climbs up into her oldest brother's bed with him."

There was a general tittering of laughter at his impassioned story telling, as though he were channeling Maggie herself.

"And boy did he *scream*," the kid laughed. "Remember how she imitated him? Gods, she was such a trouble maker."

"Remember that other story about how she beat the living crap out of her neighbor when she was like seven 'cause she thought he was a raider?" another girl asked. Another ripple of laughter went around the campfire as we remembered Maggie's description of how six-year-old her had beaten her poor neighbor senseless with a coal shovel when he came to give her mom some fresh bread late at night.

"Hey, how about that time she got stuck up in that tree house she made with her dad?" There was more laughter and smiles, more tension bleeding out of our bodies. I took in a deep breath and closed my eyes, the pain of the gaping hole behind my ribs slowly losing its bite. For a moment, just a moment, it felt like things were as normal as they could be. I could almost see Maggie laughing and smiling beside us, nodding approvingly.

But since when could that last down here?

"What's going on here?" Our bittersweet smiles froze on our faces; our laughter died in our throats. That heaviness settled back in my bones, and I slowly raised my eyes to look up at the newcomer.

Howell stared down at us with suspicious eyes, arms crossed over his chest as he waited expectantly for an answer.

"Nothing, sir," Aliyah said softly in the silence that followed, and we all looked down.

"Nothing?" His voice dripped with sarcasm. "If it's nothing, then why are none of you looking at me?" A tense, long silence dragged out between us, and Death tried again.

"We were talking about Private Margaret Burk, sir. Nothing more."

"Oh? And what *exactly* were you talking about?" he demanded, voice growing sharper, and I risked a glance at him. He seemed agitated, on edge. "We're not questioning my command decisions, are we?"

I felt like ice water had just been dumped down the back of my shirt, and I looked at the others out of the corner of my eye. No one moved, no one spoke. We just sat there in fearful quiet.

"No, sir," Marcel finally answered, and our captain quickly rounded on her, eyes blazing as he grabbed her upper arm and pulled her to her feet. Aliyah straightened a little bit, like she was about to lunge forward but thought better of it.

"No, sir, indeed!" he snarled, and War dug her heels in instinctively, pulling back from Howell enough so that she could stare up at him, anger burning below her skin. "If I hear one more laugh out of any of you, one more comment about your brave comrades who died with valor, I will–"

"Is there a problem here, sir?" a soft voice interrupted, and we all turned around to see Jack hovering at the edge of the firelight. His hands were clasped behind his back, shoulders and feet squared at attention. But there was something daunting deep in his eyes, a low fire that contrasted sharply against the shadows of his face.

"Yes there is. Your people are undermining my authority, questioning my tactical decisions–"

"They're just telling stories, sir," Jack interrupted quietly, voice neutral and controlled. "Or is that against the rules now, too?"

Howell opened and closed his mouth a few times, gaping like he'd been slapped, before shoving Marcel back to the ground and storming off. But he didn't get far before he turned on his heel and jabbed a finger at us in warning.

"Not a word! If I hear even the faintest *whisperings* of doubt, there *will* be consequences!" He turned away and back to us once more. "What did I say I would expect?" We stayed silent, unsure of what he was talking about, and our captain grew even more livid. *"What do I expect?!"*

"Complete obedience, sir," Jack answered smoothly in the frightening silence that followed. "Complete obedience, bravery, and sacrifice – all of it worthy for a king. And you have it, sir."

"I had better. Or by the gods there will be hell to pay," our captain snarled and stormed off to the command tent, tearing open the canvas door and letting the slightly ripped fabric flutter shut behind him. I took in a deep breath, releasing it slowly as I turned to look at Jack. He was still standing in the shadows and slowly looked at us.

"Be more careful, guys," he finally warned, shoulders slowly sagging. "Give her a soldier's farewell, but don't reminisce about her so loudly." He gave a pointed look to Marcel. "I might not be walking by next time."

The Horseman looked down sullenly, rubbing her arm. Katalin scooted next to her, placing a hand on her shoulders as she softly asked a question. War just nodded reassuringly before shrugging off her hand.

I looked back to Jack, unsure of what to say. He let his gaze linger on me a little longer before shifting it to the dirt beneath our feet. And with a gentle scuff of his toe in the earth, he turned on his heel and slowly walked away into the dark.

"Jack?" I called, but my voice was either too quiet or he was too far off. Regardless, he didn't respond, and I looked back to the fire, too tired to get up and chase after him. Sighing, I let myself become ensnared in Howell's silence, and that night I fell asleep to the sounds of burning logs splitting apart and the shaky breathing of the people around me.

DAY SEVENTY

Two months later

Had Maggie's death actually given us something useful, I might have understood Howell just a little bit. I still would've hated him, but I would have been able to understand his choice in the greater context of the war. I would've understood that a leader has to make hard decisions in battle – especially on the front lines. But most importantly, I would've known that my comrades' deaths were in fact worth something.

But the truth was that we'd been pushed back about two miles over the last two months. About ten people had died, so that put our casualty list at twenty-seven, including Howell's suicide run. The living stood strong at one hundred and twenty-five. A few days ago, I heard Wilson and Bates say that those numbers were pretty impressive, but I couldn't believe them. In what world was twenty-seven dead impressive? Ours apparently, but that was beside the point.

I coughed and choked on smoke and dust as a shell exploded somewhere to my right, the heat of the flames flaring against my cold skin and debris scratching and piercing my clothes. I stumbled away from it, tripping and falling down as a few unfortunate souls who'd been closer than me fell to the ground, skin burned and shredded by shrapnel.

Breathing heavy and adrenaline spiking, I turned to face the trench wall before me and fired a couple haphazard shots over the top before ducking back down. My heart pounded mercilessly and painfully against my ribs, and I clutched my rifle to my chest as I crouched at the base of the wall. Artillery shells continued to explode around me, creating sighting points for the Brettain as clods of dirt sprayed in the air and rubble sharply pelted us. A few times they'd shot up flares to try to find where we were stationed, but apparently those had been in low supply because they only used them once or twice.

It didn't matter though. Flares or no flares, our opponents seemed to know exactly how we were set up, and just as I had the thought, one of our artillery guns down the line to my left was hit by enemy fire. The explosion reverberated in my skull, and I fell to the side, bleeding hands dropping my weapon to cover my ringing ears. People sprinted back and forth around me, but I couldn't rise from my cowering position.

"And what do you think you're doing?" I quickly grabbed my gun and stumbled to my feet, shakily reassuming my position as Howell stormed up to me. "*Hiding*, were we?"

"N-no, sir," I stammered, keeping my eyes forward and firing at the few Brettain I saw braving No Man's Land. The opposition seemed to have mercifully eased their assault once more, but they were still coming. Howell crossed his arms and leaned against the wall in a way that kept him shielded from the intermittent enemy fire but still able to watch me.

"If you weren't hiding, then I'm assuming I can stand here and watch you shoot for a little bit, then?"

Panic rose up in the back of my throat like bile, and I reloaded my gun with shaky hands. Taking an equally wobbly breath, I returned to my stance only to drop back down as a bullet tore past my head.

"Oh, come *on*, Private Byrne!" Howell shouted, disdain dripping from his words and sending shivers down my spine. "That's looking pretty damn cowardly to me."

Heart in my throat, I stood up once more, and my raw and chapped hands aimed and pulled the trigger. A few people collapsed, and I ducked back down, breathing heavily and looking up at my captain. His hand was still resting on his handgun, eyes still narrowed, and I felt like screaming. But I couldn't go over again. Instead of moving, I just stared at him, holding his unreadable gaze for what felt like an eternity until he released his weapon and backed away.

"Good enough. But if I catch you slacking off again, I'll make you wish you'd died two weeks in. Like you *should have*," he hissed, and I waited until he'd moved out of sight to sit down, resting my head against the mud bank behind me.

Fear wracked my body, and I closed my eyes, taking deep breaths to try to steady myself. My hands were shaking worse than they'd ever had before, and I tightly crossed my arms over my chest, doubling over to try and calm my racing breaths. But I couldn't stay still, couldn't *not* move, so I shifted my position. I covered the back of my neck, burrowing down into myself to hide from the hellfire and orders screamed around me.

None of the people above me seemed to notice me there, cowering below the shelter of the trench wall. And if they did, they didn't seem to care. They all had the strength to "do what was necessary." Or maybe it was that they were too scared to say no.

I remained there, hunched over and breathing heavily, for the next half hour until Howell sounded the call for sixteen hours. That was another thing: our captain had already increased our shifts, decreasing our rack time by two hours. I could feel the twenty-hour day coming, and I pushed myself up from the ground, joints cracking and protesting as I did so. But while we were taking a break, the Brettain weren't.

"Byrne, get out of the way!" Aliyah grabbed my upper arm and dragged me forward until we were clear of platoons 304 and 305 as they came in to start their shift.

I looked up at her, dazed, and she sighed, guiding me down a ways until we arrived at our small cooking fire. People I didn't recognize were huddled around the flames, eating the smoked meats and dehydrated fruits that we had left from the truck ride over. Someone handed me a small portion, and I gratefully took it as I sat down beside him.

The air was heavy and silent, and the spaces beside some of us seemed to still hold the shapes of the people who once occupied them. But instead of talking, instead of helping ourselves cope with stories or conversation as we had the night Maggie had died, we sat in silence and stared blankly at the dancing fire before us, at the burning embers. Finally, it was War who cleared her throat and leaned forward to look at me.

"I saw Howell coming down on you earlier. You're the fifth person he's done that to today," Marcel commented from across the flames. I looked at her and shrugged.

"I'm still here, so it's fine," I lied, looking down at my scabbed and bleeding hands. My nails were coated with dirt, dry skin of my fingers split at the joints. But for the moment, they were steady. "Can't complain if I'm still alive," I added, the softly spoken words heard only by myself. I took in a deep breath, straightened, and looked around us, trying to find someone in the smoky haze.

"You looking for Miller?" I turned around to see Katalin approaching, a few of her fingers in a splint. I nodded quickly. "Yeah, I figured. Just saw him with Blackwell." Before she could say anything else, I scrambled to my feet, stumbling a little at first as I ran for the infirmary tent. "Wait, Byrne!"

A million different scenarios were pouring into my mind, each one somehow impossibly worse than the last – unpleasant, gory images of Jack bleeding out, dying under the doctor's hands. Missing limbs, shot out eyes, the horrors that I had seen in that tent all inflicted upon my boyfriend at the same time–

"Jack!" I shouted as soon as I pushed entered the tent. Patients groaned around me, some coated in blood, others singed and burned. A few had broken bones, but I ignored their wounds and instead feverishly checked their faces. "Jack?"

"I'm back here. What is it?"

I heaved a sigh of relief as he stepped out from behind a curtained off area, fine except for a rather deep gash across the bridge of his nose.

"Get back here, corporal," I heard Blackwell scold, and my boyfriend rolled his eyes, turning to face the hands reaching for him. "I'm just going to tape this shut, and you can be on your merry way. So *hold still.*" I took a deep breath and scratched the back of my neck as my boyfriend cast a baleful eye at the grizzled medic reaching for his face. The doctor glanced over at me, shaking his head as a knowing smirk pulled at his grim mouth. "Hello there, Tristan."

"Hey, doc." I walked over and sat beside Jack on the operating table, gesturing tiredly to his face. "Shrapnel?" My boyfriend scoffed, rolling his eyes and scowling.

"Yeah. Some green private misfired his weapon, and it ricocheted off a munitions crate. I caught a shard of metal in the face."

"Did you yell at him for it?" I asked, and Jack shook his head, subdued. Blackwell pulled his hands back briefly to shoot his patient a dark glare.

"Sit *still!*"

"Sorry." The irritated doctor grumbled to himself at the apology as Jack continued. "No, Howell got there first."

I took a deep breath and fiddled with my hands. The question I wanted to ask was heavy on my tongue, but I dreaded the answer I'd get.

"Did he shoot the kid?" I finally asked, voice low. To my relief, Jack shook his head.

"Nah, I don't think Howell will shoot people down here. He's got too much at stake to be whittling people off like…" He stopped, the name hanging heavy in the air between us. He cleared his throat a few times before continuing. "Like he did with Id." He winced and hissed in pain as Blackwell pushed the final piece of tape over his injury, and the old man gave a short bark of laughter.

"Come on, it doesn't hurt that bad." Jack tiredly raised his eyebrows.

"I do hope your bedside manner's better than that."

"It's worse," he admitted, voice gruffly teasing, before moving off to his other patients. "But I don't weep and moan about it. I am who I am." With that, we were left alone, and we sat there in almost uncomfortable silence, not looking at each other.

"So, this is first time we've really had to talk to each other isn't it? Since we got here?" Jack asked, finally looking at me, and I nodded.

"Yeah. That is if you're ignoring all of the, uh, business talk." I looked at him, taking in his shadowed eyes and blood marked cheek. He looked normal otherwise. "How are you doing?" He snorted, putting his arm around my shoulders.

"I should be asking you that," he said, his disarming nature breaking through his tired expression. Instead of buying into his mask, though, I just scoffed and stared at him silently. Finally seeing that I wasn't going to let up, he sighed and reluctantly answered. "I'm fine, Tristan. I'm used to this, remember?"

I nodded and rested my head against him, leaning into his side.

"I know. But it never hurts to ask." We were silent for a little bit longer, and I listened to Jack's heartbeat beneath my ear – that calming, unfaltering metronome.

"Well, look at you two lovebirds. It's not often I get romance in here," Blackwell called from the shelves as he prepped a shot for someone. His eyes were mischievous and puckish as he looked at us. "If you like I can put a do not enter sign on the curtains for you two."

Jack rolled his eyes.

"Knock it off, doc," he teased, tightening his arm around my shoulders as I ducked my head and lifted a hand to cover my face. "You're making my boyfriend embarrassed."

Blackwell raised his eyebrows playfully as he went back to work.

"I think you do that on your own, corporal."

We both smiled, and as the man left, Jack's arm slowly moving across my back until we were no longer touching.

"Seriously, though," he continued, softly. "How are you, Tris?" I leaned forward, hands braced on my knees, and sighed.

"Scared out of my mind," I admitted, jaw working. "There's things exploding around me, I'm more scratches and scabs than I am actual skin. I'm pretty sure I'm going steadily deaf in one ear, and I'm constantly at the wrong end of this adrenaline rush that won't go away."

Jack put his arm around me again, steady hand resting on my shoulder and gently tightening around the bone.

"I can barely stay awake sometimes, and then when I'm supposed to sleep I can't get myself to stop thinking, you know?" I explained, struggling to articulate my thoughts. "My – my mind just keeps going…and when I'm supposed to be fighting, I can't bring myself to shoot over the trenches. It's just this brutal, *endless* cycle of fear and adrenaline that keeps repeating over and over and *over* again." My voice started shaking, and I dropped my head into my hands, elbows digging into my thighs. "I just freeze up, and when I *can* shoot I usually miss anyways because I'm so gods-damn *scared!*"

"Tristan, it's okay," Jack murmured gently, thumb moving back and forth on my bony shoulder.

"No. No, it's not. Because now Howell *knows* I'm scared, and he keeps watching me. He just stands beside me and makes me keep shooting with his hand just *waiting* there on his gun." I massaged my temples, bringing my ragged breaths back under control. "It's like he's just waiting for me to screw up."

Jack made a hesitant noise above me.

"I'm not going to lie to you – he probably is." I gave a bitter laugh.

"*Wonderful*. Aren't you the one who's supposed to tell me that it's all going to be shiny and great?" I asked, looking up at him through my hands. "One of those 'oh, don't worry, Tristan. I'll make sure our psychopath of a captain doesn't kill you' type things?" He waited a few seconds after I was finished before responding, his words calm and kind.

"Is that what you want me to say? Because I'll say it."

I took in a deep breath and sat up, tilting my head back to look at the canvas ceiling above us. I thought his words over and shook my head.

"No. No, because I know that would be a promise that you wouldn't be able to keep." I looked around at him and gave a wan smile, moving my hand to catch ahold of his and pull it into my grasp. "And I know you try to keep all of your promises, no matter how ridiculous they are."

"That's true. I'd probably do something stupid," he admitted, staring off into the distance with a playfully pensive expression. "Maybe I'd take a leaf out of Idris' book and put poison oak in his command tent."

Our strange smiles slowly faded at her name, and I looked down at our joined hands, entangling my fingers in his until I was sure our joints were going to snap.

"I miss her," I said softly, and Jack immediately sat up a little straighter. "What's wrong?"

"Oh, nothing. It's nothing. I just completely forgot. I mean, I didn't *forget*. It's just that I haven't seen you in a while." He let go of my hand and reached into his pocket. "After Howell…well, I lingered back. Your truck was close to the front of the caravan so I managed to grab it while the cars were still coming and going." When his hand came free, I saw tiny chains dangling from his hand. And quite suddenly I felt torn between smiling and crying as Jack held them out to me.

"I didn't have very long, but I managed to get her Mars pendant and dog tag off of her." I finally settled on smiling and turned the finely crafted pieces of metal over in my hands.

"Her blood's still on Mars," I whispered, heart breaking. He nodded and rubbed the back of his neck.

"Yeah. I couldn't bring myself to clean it off. All we have left of her… well, it's right there." I nodded.

"I know what you mean…" I looked up at him and asked the question I needed to know the answer to. "How did she look?"

Jack stared down at his hands, sniffing hard and sighing as he tried to find the words.

"Scared," he finally said. I took in a deep breath and stared at the empty air in front of us. "She'd been crying. I could still see the tears on her face when I…" He trailed off, clearing his throat and swallowing a few times. "So, uh, I closed her eyes, straightened her out. You know, made her clothes as neat as I could." I looked back at my boyfriend, taking in his red eyes and nose. "I looked for flowers, but you saw everything." His voice grew slightly defensive. "That ground was completely dead. So I pulled up a few bunches of grain and put them in her hands." He nodded to himself, hands fiddling restlessly in his lap, and I reached out to hold them.

"She was...so *scared* when I first went over to her," he finished, jaw clenched. "I tried to make sure she looked peaceful once I left."

"I'm sorry, Jack." He just shook his head jerkily. "It wasn't–"

"*Sorry* won't bring her back," he snapped, and I stopped talking, slightly stunned. He automatically looked up, utterly apologetic. "I'm sorry. I know it wasn't our fault, it's just…"

I gently squeezed his hand and looked down at our threaded fingers.

"She would've been happy to know you did that for her," I said softly in the silence that followed, and I pulled the pendant and dog tag over my head to join Maggie's. "I'll make sure these stay safe for now and put them in her bag later."

"Where *is* your bag anyways?" he asked with far too much interest, and I reluctantly let him change the subject.

"Blackwell's got it stored somewhere in here. He asked me not to tell anyone though because he doesn't want to become a storage closet." The cold metal settled against my skin, and I sighed. "Id would have liked him."

"Yeah," Jack nodded. "She'd probably skip out on fighting altogether and become a field nurse."

"She would have been good at that, wouldn't she?" We were quiet. "I wonder how Andrew's doing."

"Well, we won't know unless we fall back." I looked at him, confused, and he frowned. "You didn't hear?" I shook my head. "We lost contact with Harper. We think his messenger got killed either on the way back to thirty-six or on the way here. Or they're just gone."

"Aren't they the ones responsible for retreat, though?" I asked uneasily. "If they fell, they were supposed to give the command to fall back for the whole line."

Jack nodded and scoffed as he braced his hands on his knees.

"Yeah, but people get killed. And unless someone notices, no one takes up their job to sound the general retreat."

"So if that's what happened…and if things come to a retreat, we'll just stay here until we all die? We won't fall back?"

Jack got to his feet and turned to face me, placing his hands on my shoulders, and he quickly kissed my forehead.

"*That* I can make sure won't happen."

With a small smile, he let go, turning around and heading for the tent door. I watched his retreating back, taking in his stiff shoulders, and sighed. Blackwell peered back in at me, caught my eye, and smiled in sympathy.

"Special man you've got there."

I laughed, rolling my shoulders and working out the knots in my back as I nodded to myself.

"Yeah," I breathed, agreeing despite my initial reaction. "Yeah, but, you know…you should see him when we're not at war."

He came in and sat across from me, giving me a soft smile.

"Why? Is he even more special then?"

I shook my head, picking at my hands and looking at the doctor before me.

"No." I thought back to Jack smiling and laughing at Promenade. Back to him getting frustrated with his curriculum reading and ranting about the narrow-minded views of our instructors. I thought about how he would bite his lip or chew on the end of his pencil when he tried to focus on his assignments. I thought back to memories of us kissing in the stables at night, nothing but laughter and light-heartedness in our eyes. I lay back on the operating table and closed my eyes as I finished my train of thought, the words wistful and sad.

"He's normal."

DAY NINETY-ONE

Twenty-one days later

Ten more of us had died. That put the number of fallen somewhere around thirty-seven and the number of living at one hundred and three. That was assuming none of the critical cases under Blackwell's care died in the next few hours like he said they would, but I highly doubted that they'd survive. We were up to eighteen-hour shifts now, and people were dropping like flies all around me. They were making clumsy mistakes like that private who almost shot Jack in the face last month.

As for me, more often than not I was getting kicked off the operating table to sleep sitting up on the ground, and I found that I'd become quite used to seeing people get cut open, to watching Blackwell pull bullets out of screaming patients. They rarely survived, but I didn't blame that on him. Most of them, he told me as he sank to the ground beside me, legs unable to hold him up any longer, were dead on arrival. He just had to do something to make the dying think that they had a fighting chance.

I understood. It was the lies that got us through the days now, not the truths.

I flinched as an artillery shell exploded about twenty feet away from me, the shards of metal and rocks scratching my skin through my uniform. Howell had just called another rotation, and I looked around at those who remained from platoons 306 and 307. We hadn't even bothered to move towards the dinner fires down the trench or to the places set aside for sleeping. We'd just fallen back and collapsed against the mud wall, watching with dull eyes as people were blown away right in front of us.

I started counting the bodies as they fell.

One...two...

Another explosion went off, and I covered my face with my hands.

Three.

I was still sitting there, eyes blank and hollow, when I felt someone wrap their arm around my waist and pull my own over their shoulder.

"Come on, Byrne. You can't be sitting here." I looked around at the voice and saw a very blurry Marcel Jones beside me. I blinked a few times, dragged my hand across my eyes, and tried to push away. "Hey. Hey, easy. I'm not trying to pull anything on you. I'm just trying to help."

Something tickled the back of my throat, and I tried clearing it. But that just seemed to make me want to cough more, so I stopped, opting instead to rub at my neck.

"You okay?" I weakly shrugged, and Marcel smirked, finding something funny in my response. "Good answer, shrimp."

She let me drop down beside a couple other hunched troops before joining Pestilence and Famine. The light of the fire before us felt cold and distant despite the fact that its tongues licked the air mere inches away. Our silent vigil was broken only by the thunder the gods on earth hurled at each other. Lightning fell from the sky, scorching and pitting the ground around us, and the earth trembled beneath our feet.

"Can you believe we're the ones doing this?" a young woman asked and looked up at the sky above us. "It feels like we're tearing the sky and earth apart..."

"That's what happens when man decides they're invincible." We looked at Jack as he walked over, easing himself down to join us around the fire. "Can you pass the food tin?" Someone tossed it over, and we were quiet until the girl spoke up again.

"How can you do that?" We all looked at her, confused. There was no malice in the question, just guileless curiosity as she looked at my boyfriend. "I'm sorry, sir. I just mean how can you be so...you know..." Jack smiled to himself, and she pointed at him. "That! How do you do that?"

"Practice," he finally said, and she gave him a tired, disbelieving look.

"Come on, sir. I want to know. I–" A loud whistling interrupted her, and we all ducked, bracing ourselves for the incoming shell and explosion. Once it stopped raining dirt, she locked eyes with Jack once more. "I need to know how you survive it."

We waited quietly as Jack thought out his answer.

"There's always more than meets the eye, private," he began slowly and picked up one of the glowing sticks of wood from the flames, poking at the embers. He opened his mouth to say something but instead just laughed bitterly. The sound was almost anxious, and I frowned slightly as he looked up at us. The firelight cast an eerie glow on his dirt smudged face, and unease churned in my gut. "So, believe me when I tell you that you don't want to know what's going on in my head."

"But I *do*." Jack set down his food and fixed her with a hard stare. She quickly looked down at her hands, voice subdued. "Respectfully, sir." He was quiet for a few moments and nodded to himself until finally something snapped.

"Really?" he laughed, dragging the back of his hand across his nose. "You *really* want to know what's going on in my head?" His voice grew uncharacteristically angry, and another explosion filled the air around us. He was the only one who didn't flinch at the showering debris, and when we looked back at him, I saw something dangerous in his eyes. "Well, then. Let me tell you. I've spent *every* day–"

Suddenly, Korsakov was crouched behind him, fingers digging into his shoulder to get him to stop talking. I couldn't tell what she was saying, but he was clearly listening. And then, as quickly as she'd come, Pestilence was gone, standing and heading back down the trench to find someplace safer to sleep.

Jack stared mutely at the flames before us with eyes that were almost as hollow as ours. That fake smile returned, and he laughed once more. It was a short, harsh sound, and he braced his hands on his knees as he forced himself to stand. He tossed the remainder of his food to me and looked at the young woman watching him.

"Don't mind me. I'm just tired," he sighed, forcing his lips to keep smiling and clapping her on the shoulder as he started to leave. "Trust me, though. You'll be fine." I watched him go for a little bit before looking back to the people around me. They were all staring at me expectantly.

"What?" As soon as I spoke, I realized what they were thinking, and I groaned. "You guys can't be serious. I'm not his keeper *or* his translator." They shifted uncomfortably, and I suddenly didn't feel very hungry. I got to my feet, tossing my food to Famine, and scowled at the faces watching me. "And one other thing – if you're going to look to me to be your mediator with Jack, *stop* talking about us behind our backs when you think we aren't paying attention! You're really not good at hiding your gossip or how often you use the word *shag* when you think we can't hear. So pick a side."

Everyone around the fire awkwardly avoided eye contact, and I turned away from them to head towards Blackwell's tent. I needed to rest, to close my eyes against the world despite the fact that my ears were always ringing, filled with the horrible din. I pushed my way through the tent door, and as I stumbled through the infirmary, half-asleep, I saw Blackwell rushing around tending to people. It would probably be best to stay out of his way, I realized and dazedly opened the curtain to the operating table.

It wasn't empty.

Someone I didn't recognize lay dead on the bed, uniform pulled back to reveal a cut open chest and stained forceps discarded on the vinyl around her. A few crimson-coated bullets gleamed in a steel tray beside her bluing body, and her skin was coated with drying, coagulated blood. Her green eyes stared blankly upwards beneath blonde, mud-stiffened bangs, and I weakly turned around as someone placed their hand on my shoulder.

"Come on, Tris," Jack murmured. "There's nothing to see here." He pulled me back, guiding me back out of the tent and towards a small gully at the base of the back wall of the trench. "Try to get some sleep." I sat down heavily, and my boyfriend joined me and put his arm around my shoulders. I cleared my throat, coughing for a few seconds on the odd tickling noise in my throat.

"You okay?" he asked, voice just loud enough for me to hear him but carry no farther, and he smoothed my hair down before rubbing my back.

"You seemed angry earlier," I managed sleepily, dodging his question with half-closed eyes, and rested my head on his shoulder.

"Yeah, I'm sorry," I heard him say distantly. "I'm just tired. Are you okay?" I felt his hand against my forehead, but before I could answer, I fell asleep, propped up against my boyfriend as the world collapsed around us.

... — — ...

"Tristan, get up." I tiredly opened my eyes to see Jack kneeling before me, hands gripping my shoulders to hold me upright. "Tristan!" I quickly sat up, taking his hand to pull myself to my feet. "It's been four hours. We need to report to Howell."

"I don't want to," I groaned, still half-asleep, and Jack touched his forehead to mine, smiling sadly as he cupped the back of my head.

"I know you don't. But come on. It's been three months, and you're still here. You can do this, okay? I promise I'll be right here beside you."

I nodded, taking in a shaky breath and staggering in the direction of the lines. Jack was still walking tall and steady beside me, and I wondered how he managed it. As we approached, we could hear Howell shouting new instructions to the slumped and tired people gathered before him. As soon as we came into view, he paused for a few moments, eyes locking on us and narrowing suspiciously. After a split second of silence, he continued.

"I'm shifting the positions of the platoons. 306 will be manning artillery. 307 will be guarding them. 305 and 304 will take up position where 306 and 307 were. Get moving!"

Artillery. I took in a deep breath and felt sick to my stomach as the air rattled briefly in my lungs. We all hurried to our places, and Howell stood there, watching us with that hawk-like gaze of his.

And then, Maggie's voice whispered to me, *when you're all mindless beasts milling around trying to keep your feet under you long enough to get your four hours of sleep, he starts giving the orders.*

As I passed by, I looked back at Howell. He was talking to Lieutenant Wilson, expression still and collected in the madness around us. That private last night should have asked *Howell* how he kept that mask up considering what he'd done. I looked forward again and took in the heavy and bulky guns we'd been ordered to operate.

They were massive, the barrels of the battery weapons almost six feet in length. As we approached, an enemy shell exploded nearby, alarmingly close, and I realized that we were the target of the Brettain's own firepower. It made sense, really. Eliminate the opposition's artillery while keeping your own safe, and you're one step closer to winning.

I didn't have time to think any further on it though because the people around me had set to work preparing the guns for use. And when the first one fired, I felt like I'd gone deaf. It sounded and felt like a bomb had gone off right next to me, and I stumbled away from the metal beast, hands over my ears. Almost immediately, I felt someone pushing me back forward, and I looked over my shoulder to see Marcel, eyes flashing a warning as we went back to work.

I soon realized why. Howell was standing a little ways behind us, facing our two platoons. His distrustful eyes were fixed on something a little ways down the trench, and I quickly turned to see what it was. My breath froze in my chest as I recognized the broad-shouldered form he was watching.

"You two idiots came over together," Marcel hissed. "You don't think he's suspicious enough of Miller as it is?"

I glared silently at Jones before picking up one of the large shells and handing it off to someone. She sighed and closed her eyes against the boom of the guns beside us, and within a few seconds, the weapons hit a rhythm, firing in smooth stop and go volleys. With every shot, I felt like my teeth were knocked loose a little more. I felt each reverberating explosion deep in my bones, rattling in my skull, and eventually I couldn't hear anything other than a loud, persistent ringing. The people shouting at me sounded muffled and distant.

I couldn't help but look over my shoulder at my captain, hatred building up in my gut as he returned to his tent. As always, he did the planning, and we did the dying. Another volley went off, and the world went blessedly silent save for that eerie ringing before my senses were assaulted full force once more.

. . . — — . . .

"Pick up the pace!" I ground my teeth at the angry voice bellowing in our ears. "Get their artillery down before I send you over there to do it on foot!" My arms were shaking, muscles tired and spent from hours of carrying the deceptively heavy shells to the gunner's waiting hands. My breath was rattling more and more in my chest, and I coughed and choked on the grainy air around me. Howell muttered darkly to himself before turning around and facing the infantry down the way.

"Stop wasting time! Keep your heads over the trench as long as you've got bullets in your guns!"

Mind blank and body just following muscle memory, I picked up a shell from a damaged munitions box, and my numb fingers slipped over the dented and damaged surface. Warning bells went off in my mind at the cold touch, but before I could put the foreboding sensation into words, my tired hands had already passed the brass shell to the people above me. I watched it travel down the line towards the artillery gun farthest away from me, and my mind struggled through the fog of exhaustion to place what had been wrong.

A few seconds passed, and when the volley started again some part of my slowed mind realized what I'd just done. I turned around and grabbed the nearest person who just happened to be Aliyah.

"*I screwed up!*" I shouted, eyes wide. She put her hands on my shoulders to hold me steady and met my terrified gaze.

"What are you talking about?"

Before I could answer, the barrel of the gun my shell had gone to exploded, and I felt myself knocked off my feet, shoulder crashing brutally into the ground along with everyone else. The ringing in my ears was so loud I could barely hear anything else. Dazed, I sat up. Tears burned in my eyes as I took in the obliterated weapon and the people on the ground, clutching bloodied patches on their uniform. Through the smoke, I could see the lifeless gunner draped over the weapon, blood dripping down his forehead, and I pressed my hands over my mouth, elbows resting on my knees as I stared at what I'd done.

"What the *hell* happened?"

I looked up at Howell with haunted eyes, and immediately someone answered from the wreckage.

"Someone gave us a damaged shell!"

He looked around at the group of people I'd been working with, and I stood up, shaking as I took in the maimed people writhing on the ground around the destroyed weapon. I had done this. When our captain began speaking, his voice was a furious screech.

"Which one of you *idiots*–"

"It – I...it was me." My voice trembled as the confession slipped out, and Howell stepped up to me, grabbing a fistful of my uniform and pulling me close to him.

"You?!" he shouted, and I nodded. "A *first year* at the Academy knows not to do that!"

"I know, sir," I whispered, petrified, and he shook me, absolutely livid.

"You just cost me my best gunner!" I swallowed, watching the hand he had dropped down to the gun at his side. "Are you trying to sabotage our war efforts, private? Because that's all you've done since you've got here!"

"N-no, sir," I spluttered, heart pounding as I looked up at him. "I-it was a mistake, and – and it won't happen again, I swear." He let go of my collar and stared at me, holding my terrified gaze.

"No. It won't," he agreed, and I caught a flash of movement through my blurred vision before the back of his gun smashed into my face. My precariously balanced world flipped, and when things settled back down I was sprawled in the mud, blood oozing down my face. "Get up!"

Shakily, I got back to my feet only to feel my head snap backwards, and I crashed to the ground once more, lip split from a blinding punch. As I slowly, painfully stood, I kept my wary eyes on my captain and saw Jack angrily start towards him, ready to attack Howell from behind. Thankfully, Aliyah intercepted him, slamming a hand against his chest and holding him back with her open palm and a stern look.

"Get your useless ass back to the infantry line," Howell snarled, breathing heavily as he looked down at me. "That way the only person you can hurt is yourself!" Our livid captain stormed past me and motioned for a few of us to take the gunner's body to the collapsed stretch of trench where we'd been keeping the dead. He hadn't gotten very far before he stopped. "And know this!"

I barely managed to stop my forward momentum without falling over and turned to face Howell. I didn't dare wipe away the blood on my face or blink back my tears of pain.

Just stare at him. Take the punishment.

"If you screw up again, I will kill you." With that final threat, he left, and people started moving. Jack pushed past Aliyah, his skin white below the dirt and his eyes wide with fear.

"Tris, let me see."

I pulled away from his reaching hands and caught them with my own.

"No, our shift—"

"I don't care about our shifts right now, Tristan. I'm taking you to see Blackwell," he stated, tone giving no room for argument. He grabbed my elbows, practically holding me upright me as he guided me through my tear-blinded vision to the doctor's tent. The people we passed watched us in tense silence, no doubt wondering if the same thing was going to happen to them. Based on our captain's track record, I could only assume yes.

"Doc, can you take a look at this and make sure it's not broken?" Jack called as soon as we entered the tent. The man looked around at my boyfriend exasperatedly and held up his blood-covered hands.

"I'm a little *busy* at the moment, corporal!" he snapped and went back to treating someone I couldn't see. I could hear their pain though, and it said something that I could handle the sounds of the death and suffering in here better than the ones outside the thin canvas walls.

"Tristan, just sit down, okay?" I could feel Jack's hands leaving me, and I reached out, desperately grabbing onto his sleeve. "Hey." His voice was soft and comforting, and suddenly his arm was solid beneath my hands. "It's okay. I'm just going to go find something to clean this up with."

I shakily nodded and instantly regretted it, crying out as the motion sent pain stabbing through my skull and forced me to release my boyfriend's arm. I felt woozy and numb, like everything I touched wasn't really there.

I looked around for something to sit on, minimizing my movements as much as I could, and finally settled on a box of suture supplies beside the small cupboard the doctor had stored my bag in. As I lowered myself onto the container, I shakily took the bag out and reached inside, pulling out Idris' mass of tangled medallions and amulets. I slowly unwound a couple of them and ran my shaking fingers over the intricate carvings. My blood steadily dripped from my nose and oozed down my face onto my hands, uniform, and shoes. I wondered what would have happened if Id had been here. Would she be dead already? Or would she be sticking it out with the rest of us, hanging on despite all odds?

"Tristan, keep your head up. Come on." Blackwell gently lifted up my chin, and Jack returned to my side, a relatively clean rag in hand. Face feeling puffy and swollen, I took it from him and slowly began blotting away the red. "You look like you got whipped with a pistol, kid."

"Howell," I answered, voice thick. The older man sighed, rocking back on his heels. "What?"

"Did he end this beating with 'if you screw up again, I'll kill you'?" I nodded, and the doctor pinched the bridge of his nose, taking in a deep breath. "He's not kidding around anymore, Byrne. He's marked you."

"What do you mean by 'marked' him?" Jack asked, bristling. Blackwell waved him down.

"When Howell starts leaving physical harm on a soldier, he's stopped considering them to be important," the doctor explained, gently grabbing my chin and turning my head a few different directions before coming to a decision. "You're fine. Just wait here until the bleeding stops." He stood up and looked at Jack. "I assume you can piece together the rest, Miller. Tread carefully, Tristan." He left us, and my boyfriend knelt before me, taking the rag and gently cleaning away the blood on my face.

I closed my eyes and took in several unsteady breaths as I tried to process everything that had happened so far. But all I could think about was the rough cloth moving across my skin, trying in vain to wipe away the mistakes that stained my body.

"Hey." I opened my eyes at the softly spoken word, and Jack wiped away a few of my tears with his thumb. "You're okay." He folded the rag in a different way so that the blood was hidden within the fabric and pressed it back against my face. "Hold this there. I need to go get something."

I did as he said and closed my eyes against my spinning world, wishing more than ever that I could just fade away from it all. Melt away and never wake up. I listened to my boyfriend bustle around, opening and closing drawers and rifling through boxes. A few moments later, I felt his hand on my knee, and I opened my eyes to see him preparing one of the tape strips he'd used for his shrapnel cut last month.

"What's that?" I mumbled and made the mistake of breathing through my nose. A sharp pain shot through the broken skin, and I groaned, pressing the rag a little harder against the angry flesh.

"It's for your lip. Let me see."

I pulled my hand away, immediately missing the cool touch of the rag, and let him examine my bruised face.

"You sure you know what you're doing?"

Jack pulled his hands away and gave me a tired look.

"*Yes*. I took basic field aid. Now, I'm about to put this on your lip, so shut up." I closed my mouth and waited as Jack sealed the split, cold fingers pressing against my red and swollen skin. Once he was done, he rested his hands on my knees as he sat back on his heels and looked up at me. "How's it feel?"

"Terrible," I muttered, returning the cloth to my face, and he smiled wanly.

"I meant the tape." I just nodded, not really wanting to talk, and Jack rocked forward onto his knees, pulling me into a hug as my breath hitched on a sob. "Shh...it's okay, Tris," he whispered, and I pressed my head against his chest, struggling to stay calm. "It'll be okay. I promise I'll keep you safe. I won't let Howell kill you." I scoffed but tightly returned the embrace with one arm before pulling back. Looking down at him now, at his sincere, determined expression, made me want to cry harder for some reason.

"I told you not to go making promises you can't keep," I warned, with a forced playful light to my eyes, and he smiled, resting his hands on mine.

"Think of it as a personal challenge. You don't piss him off, I won't have to keep it." I rolled my eyes, smile pulling at the corners of my mouth despite my best efforts, and looked out at the rest of the infirmary. And my blood went cold.

"Jack," I began, voice strained with fear, and he quickly turned around to look at what I'd seen.

Howell was watching us from the doorway of the tent, and the moment Jack turned to look at him, he started to angrily make his way over to us. I quickly looked to Blackwell and saw that the doctor had seen him too. The medic cast a quick glance over his shoulder to us, mouth set in a tight line, but made no move to intercept our superior officer.

"What's this?" the captain called once he was close enough, and Jack immediately stood up and placed himself between Howell and me. He crossed his arms, shoulders squaring defiantly as our superior stopped mere inches away from him. Nose to nose, forces of nature trying to stare the other down. "Well?"

"Medical attention. Sir," Jack answered, voice hard and underhandedly spiteful. Howell raised his eyebrows, and I tried to swallow the panic rising up in my throat, choking me. I wanted to reach out to Jack, tug on the tail of his shirt to shut him up. But I couldn't. Not in front of Howell.

"Really? Because that was a lot of close touching for simple medical attention. In fact, I've been seeing you two with each other a lot lately." The threat in his words was palpable, the implication so obvious, and my heart raced as Jack shrugged.

"He's a friend."

Behind Howell's back, I saw Blackwell run from the tent, motions filled with nervous purpose. My captain nodded, expression mockingly surprised.

"Oh...oh, I see. A *friend*. And friends pull their friends out of a crucial war effort to baby each other's scratches? Is that what you're telling me?"

"I don't know, sir. Is that what you think I'm telling you?"

I softly groaned at Jack's back talking and hunched my shoulders in an attempt to make myself smaller as Howell made a sound of disbelief.

"Are you getting smart with me, Miller?" he asked, voice dangerously low, and Jack clenched his jaw.

"Might be, sir."

Just shut up, Jack. Shut up, shut up, shut up –

At that moment, the tent door flapped open again, and Aliyah and Korsakov hurried in, Blackwell close behind them and pointing towards us. And as I watched, the two Horsemen quickly walked over to us, practically running as they pushed their way through the crowded infirmary to pass Howell and flank Jack.

"Miller, stand down," Aliyah whispered, pulling my tense, battle-ready boyfriend back a few steps while Irina faced our captain, small frame bold and strong.

"Sir, I'm Private Korsakov. We met before. I understand that these two may be thorns in your side, but I really wouldn't do anything you would regret later," she said placatingly, and his eyes narrowed.

"Meaning?"

She paused, and I could see her mind racing to come up with something. Unfortunately, what came out of her mouth wasn't improvisation, and I swallowed hard.

"Because Corporal Miller is a respected and well-liked person with Unit 37. If you kill him, we won't be happy with you. And you know, sir, what happens when a captain has no hold over his people."

"Are you threatening me, private?"

She swallowed, jaw clenched in mute fear, and Aliyah stepped forward.

"No, sir. She is merely being honest and tactical with you. Miller has considerable influence on most of our unit. If you do anything that would put you on his wrong side, you are going to be on the wrong side of a lot of people."

He looked between the four of us, anger glowing in his eyes.

"This is sounding *a lot* like blackmail," he growled, and Aliyah lowered her crossed arms to her sides.

"Take it as you will, then, sir. But it is the truth."

He swung his head side to side as he looked at us, like a dog being poked and prodded by too many people from too many sides. But as he sized up the three young adults standing up to him, he clenched his jaw, vein ticking in his neck. Moore stood at attention, expression cold and unfathomable, just as tall as my towering boyfriend – almost like she was his shadow. Jack's arms were crossed over his chest, expression hard and angry. And Pestilence…her eyes blazed with cold warning as she shifted closer to my side, her hand creeping onto my shoulder and clamping down until I was certain her fingers would leave bruises.

This was a battle he wasn't going to win. With a snarl of anger, Howell turned on his heel and walked off, storming past people easing down onto gurneys and nurses carrying medication.

The tent door flapped shut behind him, and I released my tensely held breath. I dropped my head into my hands. This...this wasn't good. Jack turned to face the Horsemen.

"Okay, you just blackmailed *Howell*," he hissed furiously, and Aliyah glared at him.

"If you two kept your hands to yourselves or at least had some sense of situational awareness, we would not have had to," she returned, voice even but reprimanding at the same time. Beside her, Korsakov closed the curtain around the operating table with a firm nod, crossing her arms as she faced my boyfriend.

"The fact is, Miller," she began, voice grim as she met his gaze, "we didn't lie to him. At all. We haven't seen a single Brettain soldier since all this began. And yet, here we are – being told that they're the enemy by the one man who has so far been the most dangerous to us. People don't know what we're fighting for anymore, sir, but they do know that they can gather behind you." *Sir.* Irina just called Jack *sir.* They were *dead serious* about this. "Because you don't fight for the war, you fight for survival. That's always been your goal." She stopped talking, and Aliyah brought her friend's point slamming home.

"Miller, whether you like it or not, you have an army behind you," she finished, cutting my boyfriend off as he opened his mouth to protest. "An army that Howell does not have."

Jack looked at us all in disbelief, like he didn't recognize us. As though we were suddenly strangers.

"You're talking about *mutiny*," he finally said, the word heavy in the air between us.

Pestilence nodded as she leaned against one of the tent poles, eyes flashing dangerously, and I wearily braced my forearms against my knees.

"Yes," she said gravely. "Yes, we are."

DAY ONE HUNDRED AND TWENTY-TWO

Thirty days, four miles, twenty more people dead.

That was what we'd lost, and there wasn't much we could say that we'd gained except for the confirmation that threatening to blackmail Howell hadn't been one of the Horsemen's brightest moments. In fact, it was alarming how quickly the man established that we'd crossed a line.

It started with the twenty-hour shift. If we'd been exhausted before, we were now dead on our feet, and it didn't help that the Brettain were now raining constant fire down upon us. It was almost as though they gained more supplies as time went on instead of running out. And more and more often, the Brettain soldiers dared to cross No Man's Land. A few of them had gotten all the way to our trenches before we feverishly managed to shoot them down to save our own lives.

The first time that happened had been the first time I'd ever seen the enemy in my life. I'd seen pictures in the Academy, of course, but this was the first time I'd seen a flesh and bone person from the other side. Two soldiers, a man and a woman, had fallen down into our trenches, shot down once they'd gotten close enough, and they'd tumbled to the ground beside me with pained screams. Their eyes were open, staring blankly at the sky; their skin was dirty and bruised, cut with shrapnel. They could have been people from our own side.

The one thing we didn't have in common with them though was the fact that their bodies weren't starved. They weren't skeletons. Beneath the grime they looked like whole people, but I didn't have long to think about that. Bullets pelted the ground around me, sending mud and dirt flying up at my face, and I looked around at the eighty-nine people left standing. There were no such things as shifts now. Everyone was fighting constantly, and some were forced to stay up twenty-four hours before alternating out so there was someone holding the line while the others slept.

The only thing powering us now was adrenaline and fear since the next thing Howell had done was to restrict the food rations. No one wanted to say it, but the truth was that we were running low on supplies, and since we'd lost contact with Harper and the resource station there was no way to replenish them. Someone had suggested sending a runner down to check on Unit 36, which was only a little over a mile away at this point given our rate of retreat, but Howell refused. He'd said that best-case scenario they were in the same state that we were and couldn't afford to send us anything. Worst-case, they were all dead and knowing that would destroy our morale.

I'd laughed to myself when he said that. As if we had any morale left.

We'd already given up. Even fighters like the Horsemen had abandoned trying to find a way out and had just decided that they were going to go down in a blaze of glory and pull as many of the enemy down with them as they could. And I had to admit – it was a tempting mindset.

But for me, I just wanted out. Whether that meant I died bravely or like a coward or somehow made it out alive I didn't care. I just wanted it over.

And yet, here I was, still dodging bullets when I could have let them hit me and had everything over with. Survival instinct was sometimes a shitty thing. Life just seemed to enjoy struggling on in the face of total adversity, even if the quality of that life was frankly not worth the trouble.

The girl who'd asked Jack how he survived was currently in Blackwell's tent with pretty advanced scurvy. Her hair was falling out in some places, and her joints were swollen. Patches of her skin were dried and browned, and her gums bled sometimes to the point where her teeth were stained red. Unfortunately, the doctor had nothing left to give her, and there had been no fresh food since we started. It was bitter irony to me that Jack had told her she was going to be fine.

As for Jack, Howell had been making sure my boyfriend had minimal contact with the rest of us. I'd rarely seen him outside of the command tent, and when he was fighting alongside us it was always too intense for him and I to get a moment to talk.

Today, however, it seemed I might get lucky. As I passed by Howell's tent, I could hear Jack's frustrated voice carry through the fabric.

"Sir, we don't have the supplies for that—"

"What else do you have in mind, Miller?" Howell demanded. I stopped outside the tent, listening carefully. "Is it retreat? *Again?* Because you listen to me and listen well, I refuse to retreat any further!"

"I'm just saying that your plan physically isn't going to work, sir. We don't have the ammunition or man power available to pull this off."

"Watch the tone you take with me, *boy!*"

"Sir, you keep claiming that the Brettain will slow down – that they'll ease up. That *still* hasn't happened!"

"They *will!*"

There was a sudden rustle of movement, and I quickly ducked behind the corner of the captain's tent as Howell left, heading somewhere down the trench without a backwards glance. Wilson, Song, Williams, and Bates all filed out, looking uncomfortable, and Jack came out last, looking irritated enough to punch something.

"Twenty hours!" the captain shouted, and I took my chance.

"Jack!" I whispered, and my boyfriend turned around, expression clearing and a relieved, loving light flashing in the back of his dull eyes.

"Oh thank the gods. You're still here."

I gave a darkly humorous smile at that.

"Don't know about that. I feel like I died last week and just didn't get the memorandum."

He came over, rubbing at the bruised circles beneath his eyes.

"How are you? I know your cough's been…" He trailed off and made a vague gesture with his hand.

"It's fine," I said, and he nodded, too distracted to even notice the lie. "How did it go with Howell?" Jack tiredly sighed in response.

"He can't find a way out, and he's too stubborn to fall back again. But that's nothing new." I hummed in agreement, thinking the conversation was over, but he started talking again. "And he doesn't take into account the views of others. I mean, there're only two ranks to him, and it's captain and private. He completely ignores Lieutenants Wilson and Bates, and he barely even *looks* at Sergeant Williams and Song because they're ranked lower than the other two." He groaned in frustration, raking his hands through his hair and sighing heavily.

"And let me guess. The only reason he takes what you say into account is because of what Moore and Soto told him."

Jack nodded, massaging his temples.

"I'm almost glad they blackmailed him just because of that," he muttered before trudging towards our usual refuge. The moment we pushed open the tent door, though, Blackwell turned to face us, haggard from the constant stream of patients.

"Boys, you can't be in here today. It's too crowded," he shouted, and we nodded, backing out and sitting on the ground just outside the door.

This had happened the last few times we'd tried to hole up in the med tent, and we didn't even stop to think that people were dying in there anymore. We didn't try to help or intervene. We just nodded and went back outside, listening to those behind us and watching those before us battle to stay alive and fail.

This time, though, we hadn't been sitting beside the tent for more than a few seconds before I started coughing. And once I started I couldn't stop. I noticed Jack moving beside me, shifting so that he was kneeling in front of me, eyes wide and scared, but I couldn't pay him much attention. I was too distracted by the painful, hacking sensation that stabbed my lungs every time I tried to breathe. Too distracted by the incessant coughing that was preventing me from catching my breath.

"Tris? Tris, you okay?" I managed to get one gasping breath in before it started all over again, and the tent flapped open behind us. Jack's hands grabbed my shoulders, panicked and rough. "Tristan!"

"Miller, get that kid in here!" Blackwell ordered, appalled that we hadn't brought up my cough before. My boyfriend helped me stand, picking me up by my elbows and walking me towards an overturned crate in the corner of the infirmary. "How long has this been going on, son?"

"A month," I managed and took in a deep breath as the doctor instructed. He made a small sound of annoyance as I started coughing again, the air tickling the back of my throat and my lungs seizing up on me when I tried to inhale too much.

"You should have come to me sooner. If you had, I might have actually had medicine for you," he chastised, his gruff nature failing to mask the genuine concern in his eyes. "As it is, I can't tell what this is at the moment. Breathe in." He rested his hand against my back as I followed his directions, and I glanced up at Jack. "Breathe out." He was watching me with a tense expression, pacing back and forth with his eyes fixed on me. "Well, it could be many things. TB, simple aggravation from all the particulates we're breathing in…" He sighed, pulling his hand away from my rattling back. "Again, had you come in sooner, I'd have had something for you. But not now – my supplies have all but run out."

"Yeah, everything's running out," Jack sighed, taking a deep breath and resting his hands on his hips. "Food, ammunition, meds…we're scraping the bottom of the barrel now." Blackwell made a sound of agreement before returning to his other patients, checking stitches and pulling a few pills from his pockets.

"Nothing you can do about that now, gentlemen. Ride out Howell's anger. All that's left is the crash and burn." He looked over his shoulder at us, eyes backlit with something akin to a challenge. "That is, of course, unless somebody decides to do something first."

Heart sinking, I looked back up at my boyfriend and watched as he rocked back on his heels, teeth grinding against each other.

"What did you hear?" he finally asked, taking in a sharp, deep breath and crossing his arms. The doctor shrugged and went back to changing the bandages on a young private's leg.

"There are a lot of rumors going around. Courtesy of the Horsemen, of course," he said, almost as though he weren't even paying attention to us. "One of them has been spreading word down the proverbial grapevine about deciding whose side we're on. It seems that they're fairly keen on the idea of rebellion."

"I'm gonna kill them," Jack growled, turning to go, but I reached up and grabbed ahold of his sleeve.

"Don't fuel them," I warned, relieved when he looked down at me. "If you want this all to stop, go to Marcel." I broke off coughing and nearly doubled over, waving my hand at him to indicate that I had more to say. "She was the one who put the idea in Moore's head a couple months back," I finally gasped, breathing heavily as I sat back up. "Aliyah must have filled Soto in on the situation after their run-in with Howell."

Jack growled in frustration, grinding the heel of his palm into his eyes.

"I swear to the gods…" he sighed and looked over at Blackwell. "You know that if Howell finds out about this, he's going to kill Tristan."

That startled me out of my half-awake state.

"What? Why me? I'm not the one planning a mutiny!" Jack rolled his eyes at my indignant tone and looked down at me.

"He can't touch me, okay? But he can sure as hell touch you."

"I get it," I told him and got to my feet, shaking my head free of the shadow of sleep looming over me. "I'll talk to her. Okay?"

"You?" he asked incredulously. "No offense, but why would she listen to you? She doesn't really listen to anybody."

"She probably won't," I admitted, groaning as I straightened my back. "But it's better that I get caught talking to Marcel than you." He clenched his jaw and tensely ran his hand through his hair.

"True," he admitted, though he looked like he still wanted to argue. I took in a deep breath and squeezed his hand briefly before letting go and heading for the tent door. "Tristan!"

I stopped and looked back at him, taking in the burning fire in his eyes.

"What's wrong?" I asked. *What's not wrong?* my mind bitterly returned, but I quickly turned my attention back to the man before me. He shifted anxiously on his feet and picked at his nails, suddenly less confident.

"I want you to know something." Slowly, I walked back over, holding his gaze, and Jack took in a deep breath as he looked around at Blackwell. "Could you give us a moment, please, doc?" The old man nodded, yanking the curtains closed around us as he walked off to check someone's blood-soaked rags.

"What is it?" I asked, unease prowling in my gut as Jack shifted on his feet and reached out to put his hands on my shoulders. "Jack, you're scaring me." He gave a forced smile and shook his head.

"No, it's not...I just want you to know that if Howell – if he tries to kill you, he's got another thing coming."

I laughed, the utterly mirthless sound a reflex to cover my rising anxiety as tears burned my eyes.

"Jack, don't do something stupid –" I began, looking up at him in pain, but he just shook his head again, expression set.

"Because if he takes you from me, I've got nothing left to lose."

I closed my mouth, shaken and unsure how to respond.

"Jack, I–"

He clapped his hands on my shoulders once before nodding to himself and backing away, still cautious of physical displays of affection. His forced, strained smile finally faded as a curtain dropped behind his eyes. He ruefully shook his head.

"I...I just wanted you to know that," he whispered, looking at his worn boots as he shoved his hands into his pockets. "I *needed* you to know that."

Before I could even begin to think of something to say to him, Jack turned and walked out of the tent, the canvas flapping shut behind him. In the silence that followed, the weight that my boyfriend's words had created crushed down on me, replaying in my head until I was certain I was going to lose my mind unless I started moving. Claustrophobic panic crowded up my chest and into my throat, and I stumbled out of the tent, tripping over legs and arms as I struggled through the maze of bodies and pushed open the flap.

The chalky air clung to my lungs, and I coughed until I thought the ash lined organs were going to come out of my mouth. When I was finally able to breathe again, I found myself kneeling in the mud, staring down the littered and scorched trenches. Jack's words continued to whisper in my ears. There was no doubt now as to what he would do if he found me dead. And I knew now more than ever I had to shut down the talk of mutiny. I pushed myself back to my feet and headed past the dinner fires towards the gully Jack and I had slept in. I could only hope the Horsemen hadn't found a new place to hang out.

The people I passed were exhausted, dead men walking with skin that was paper thin and translucent. Their eyes were sunken holes in their faces, and their clothes hung loosely about their arms and shoulders. I could already see a few people exhibiting signs of scurvy – scabbed over skin, missing hair, bleeding mouths. And as I continued on, several people sank to the ground, letting their bodies fall apart in their exhaustion like puppets propped up on a dark and forgotten shelf. Our lack of sleep and overall malnourishment was crushing us, leaving enough desolation in its wake to compete with the war we were somehow supposed to be fighting at the same time.

As I went, I couldn't help but start to agree with what the Horsemen and Blackwell were saying. We needed someone to help us out because we were too afraid to help ourselves. And as I realized that, I got angry. Angry at myself, at them, at Howell, maybe even a little at Jack. I was angry with them for suggesting that my boyfriend should pull a stupid stunt that would get us all killed. Yet…at the same time, I was angry with Jack for not doing that on his own in the first place.

I had to remember whose side I was on. And as I saw the Horsemen gathered by the wall of the trench, glow of the fire illuminating their faces like the hounds they were, I knew.

"Jones!" I shouted, hoarse voice cracking over the name, and she looked up at me. I caught a glimmer of taunting laughter in her eyes as she got to her feet and came over to me, wiping her muddied hands on her uniform as she went.

"How's it going, Byrne? Miller still up?" Once she was close enough, I grabbed fistfuls of her uniform and slammed her into the trench, seething. "Hey!" she shouted, grabbing onto my own shirt and trying to shove me back. "The hell is wrong with you?!"

"Oh, I don't know," I began sarcastically, choking on a cough. "Maybe it's the fact that you're spreading rumors of a gods-damn *mutiny!* Do you have any idea what Howell will do to me, will do to *Jack*, if you keep talking about this?"

Understanding flashed in her eyes, and she roughly let go of my shirt, holding her hands up defensively at her shoulders.

"Gods, Byrne! Calm down, I'm not talking about that!" I frowned but released her uniform and backed away. She scoffed at me, straightening her clothes and throwing me an insulted glare. "What do you take me for, an idiot?"

"Then who's talking?" I snapped, crossing my arms with a shiver.

"Did it ever occur to you that people may be arriving to this conclusion by themselves?" Katalin asked from where she was sitting on the ground beside us. She was poking at the flames before her, not meeting our eyes. "We need some hope around here. I mean, you've seen us. We're falling apart at the seams, and Miller just so happens to fit the bill."

"True, but Miller has a track record," Irina countered.

"He is on thin ice," Aliyah said solemnly. "The captain doesn't trust Miller at all. It makes him perfect for a threat to keep Howell on his toes, but a poor candidate for actually leading a mutiny."

"*Thank you*. The more you fuel this thing, Kat, the more you're putting him and everyone else at risk," I scolded. "Challenging Howell's hold on us is just going to make him even more insecure and even more jumpy than he already is. He'll make more brutal decisions to reassert his control, and when he does, Soto, you're going to regret ever trying to promote mutiny." She had the decency to look down at that, and I continued, frustration building as I spoke. "Luckily for you, he's keeping Jack close by, and now he's got some say over what goes on in the command tent. But you push Howell anymore, Jack's not even going to have that!"

Her eyes met mine for a brief second, but at my furious expression, she bit her lip and looked down again. As I stared at Famine's hunched form in frustrated silence, Marcel snapped her fingers before my nose, making me jump.

"There are other ways to get my attention," I growled, turning to her, but she didn't engage my anger.

"You've made your point. What do you want us to do?" she asked, for once business-like with me as she crossed her arms. Her dark eyes danced in the light of the fire before us, and I took in a deep breath, looking away from her and into the flames as I came to a decision.

"Tell those of us left that Jack in no way wants to be a part of a mutiny. Okay?" I demanded, looking at each of them, and I was relieved when Korsakov nodded. "You make sure that they know – and that *Howell* knows – that Jack poses no threat. He's just a soldier. That's all he wants to be, okay? He just wants to keep his head down and make it out again." I broke off and turned around, shoulders shaking with barely suppressed coughs. Once I'd forced the tight sensation back down my throat, I turned back to them and continued speaking. "We have to start relying on ourselves. Now if you don't mind, I'm going to get what sleep I can before we're back on our feet for another twenty hours."

With that I left the Horsemen huddled around their fire and found a small corner of the trenches that I could sit down in, shielded on almost every side from the chaos of war. And as my body hit the ground, my mind went blank while the world fell dark behind my closed eyes. As I sat there, fading away into the mud walls, I wondered if this was what death felt like. One day, you just couldn't fight anymore so you sat down, laid down your arms, and let everything go.

And the maelstrom of life washed away to leave you alone once and for all. If that was what death was, I couldn't wait. It was a blessed alternative to where I was now. And in fact, the more I thought about it, the more convinced I became that I'd actually gone and died in my dazed stupor, and I finally fell asleep.

But when Aliyah and Marcel shook me awake four hours later on their way to our stations, I realized I hadn't in fact died. It had been nothing more than a brief taste of the peace that waited at the end for us all, and as each breath rattled in my chest, I realized couldn't wait until my next four hour block of sleep.

Not because then I could rest, but because it seemed it was the closest I could get to dying.

DAY ONE HUNDRED AND FORTY-FIVE

Twenty-three days had passed, and the Brettain hadn't let up in the slightest like Howell had claimed they would. They were still firing at full force, as though they had no such things as supply shortages, and we'd been pushed back yet another mile as the trenches collapsed and became rubble behind us – extensions of No Man's Land. It was almost as though the Brettain were getting more men, more medicine, more supplies. More food. Hell, even more rest. Anything we didn't have, they had to have had in abundance, because there was no other way that these people could fight as long and as hard as they were without some kind of advantage. We even had the home ground, and still we were failing to hold them at bay.

The worst part though was that our increasingly frequent mistakes and failures were starting to show in Howell.

Over the past few weeks, he had taken to locking himself away in his tent for longer and longer periods of time, pouring over outdated casualty reports, information on the Brettain that I had no doubt was at this point useless. And he kept calling his lieutenants and sergeants – even corporals – into his tent to scream at them for things they couldn't possibly help.

After one of those meetings, Jack burst into Blackwell's infirmary and sat down beside me on the operating table in angry silence, hands braced against his knees and eyes furious.

"Not a good day, huh?" I croaked, my words tickling something in the back of my throat and making me cough long and hard.

"It never is," he sighed, a glimmer of his normal self in his grim words, and rested a hand on my rattling back. "Gods…Tris, how are you feeling?"

"Like I'm going to throw up my own lung pretty soon," I rasped, looking up at him. "How about you?" He scoffed slightly at my nonchalance and wrapped his arm around my shoulders, pulling me close to him so that my head rested against his chest. "Doc says it's not TB."

"He's sure?"

I nodded and cleared my throat as Jack kissed the top of my head.

"Yeah. I've got none of the other symptoms, so he's thinking maybe it's some kind of asthma." Jack frowned, hand subconsciously tightening on me and pulling me closer.

"But you're not asthmatic."

I laughed, the sound bitter and harsh.

"Tell me something I don't know." I ran my hands over my face and lay back on the table, gently pulling away from my boyfriend. Thunder clapped overhead, drawing cries of fear from some of the more disoriented patients beyond the veil. A cold rain started pouring down on the waterproofed canvas above us. "So, what did Howell have to say to you guys this time?"

Jack rolled his eyes and cleared his throat in preparation for another tired rant.

"The usual. That he's seen kids fight better than this, that we're the only chance this country has, that we're a critical tactical outpost, and so on and so forth." He ran his hands through his hair, eyes tired and distant. "The thing is I wouldn't mind this as much if he was actually out there fighting with us. Instead–" he laughed, the sound disdainful and cruel, and he rested his hand on my bent knee, thumb tracing out the bone, "instead, he's cooped up in his tent looking over papers he won't let us see while we do all the dying."

"There's a reason for everything, Jack," I warned, putting my hand over his and holding tight, and he looked down at me as though I were suddenly an alien. Somewhere down the line a long, loud whistle carried through the air, ending in a loud, earth-shattering boom.

"You can't *possibly* be with Howell on this one."

I coughed, nearly choking on my sharp breath, and propped myself up on my elbows.

"Of course, not! The man's a gods-damn monster," I finally managed. "I'm just saying that all leaders have reasons they keep secrets. Sometimes we're better off not knowing them."

Another whistling sound filled the air, and three booms went off in rapid succession. The ground trembled beneath our feet, and Blackwell pushed the curtain open, disheveled.

"Get out there," he barked, shooing us away, and I reluctantly swung my legs off the bed. "That was three artillery shells within the span of five seconds – the Brettain are picking up their pace." We were halfway out of the tent when Jack turned around to face the doctor, eyes pleading.

"Look, doc...I know we're low on meds, but is there anything at all you can give him for the cough?" Blackwell sighed, and Jack hurried to explain, voice strained. "I know he's not a priority, it's just...it's gotten a lot worse."

"I don't know what he's got, Miller. But even if I did, there are others who need that medicine more."

Jack reluctantly nodded his understanding, and we left our refuge.

The air was filled with smoke and dust, and I could see people dragging corpses in the general direction of our burial dumpsite while others forced their weary bodies to retaliate. My heart pounded painfully in my chest as I took in the damage that had been done in that last artillery volley. Suddenly, Jack's hand fastened around my forearm, dragging me back to a covered position as he placed himself in front of me and quickly surveyed what remained of our force.

The Brettain shells had collapsed parts of the trenches, the ridges blown apart so that the approaching infantry had a direct line of sight into our lines. The opposite side's soldiers were coming en masse while our own troops struggled to find covered positions to retaliate from. It was looking like we were going to retreat again or else run the risk of getting trapped in a kill box.

So, of course, that was when our elusive captain decided to emerge from his tent.

"Howell," I whispered, pulling my arm from Jack's hand and gently nudging him towards our superior. He gave me a quick, pained glance over his shoulder, and I nodded, offering a small smile. "It's okay, I'll be fine." I pushed him away by the small of his back, the pressure kind but firm. "Go do your job."

He gave me a quick nod before looking back at Howell. The man was still occupied with someone else, and when Jack turned to me, there was something desperate in his expression. He quickly stepped forward, hand going to the back of my neck, and kissed me. It was rough and quick, and I could feel in his lips the fear he kept hidden in his eyes as I rested my hand on his waist.

"Stay safe," he whispered, breaking the kiss and looking down at me through the rain. The water beaded on his skin and dripped from his hair, and I nodded, my heart in my throat.

"You, too."

He turned away and ran over to where our captain was finishing up his conversation with Sergeant Williams.

"Sir, do we fall back?" he called once he was in earshot, and Howell spared him a single, vacant glance before walking away. Jack hurried to fall into step with him, and I felt something heavy and cold settle into my gut as I caught a glimpse of our leader's face. The captain's eyes were glassed over and absent as they took in the destruction around us, surveying how the line was collapsing around our ears.

"Sir?"

Finally, he seemed to make a choice.

"No," he answered, voice shaky and stubborn. "No, we don't fall back. No more surrendering!" The last words were shouted, and those closest to him stopped what they were doing to look at him. "We are *not* falling back anymore!"

Jack exhaled sharply and nodded, playing along.

"Then what's the strategy, sir?" he asked as people rushed to shore up the damage to the trench. The man clenched his jaw, taking stock of who and what we had. When he came to a decision, his words were sickeningly familiar.

"I want you to send part of your platoon over the trenches to charge the enemy," Howell ordered, nervously licking his lips as he moved down the trench, hand fastening around Jack's upper arm to keep them alongside each other. Heart pounding, I followed, making sure to keep my distance. "They'll draw the Brettain fire, give you and me down here an opportunity to see where their shots are coming from. We can *finally* retaliate."

I could see my boyfriend's face contort into an expression of confusion, and he looked at his superior in disbelief, stopping in his tracks as the rain pounded the earth around us.

"Captain, that's suicide," Jack replied, unable to hold back. "We've used that tactic before, and it ended with a massacre that we learned nothing from! *Respectfully*, sir, there's only eighty of us left—"

Howell looked back at the sudden deadweight behind him, expression darkening and frenzied eyes blazing dangerously.

"Do as you're told, *corporal*," he growled, tone cold and warning.

All around the two officers, people stopped rising over the trenches, opting instead to turn and stare. Marcel was one of them, and she slowly made her way to my side, eyes fixed on the situation unfolding. Jack's eyes flickered to mine over our captain's shoulder, and his lips pressed together in a tight line.

"Oh, gods," I whispered, and my chest suddenly tightened as my lungs stopped working. War glanced at me in worry, and I quickly wiped the rain from my eyes as though clearing my vision would change what was about to happen. "Don't do it, Jack."

"Byrne, what is it?" she asked, but I couldn't answer her. A few yards away, Jack took in a deep breath and squared his shoulders, jaw clenching in preparation for that one word I knew he was going to say.

"No."

Beside me, Marcel took a sharp breath, running a hand over her mouth in apprehension as the rest of us felt our hearts stop.

"What did you say to me?" Howell's words shook with disbelief, and Jack shook his head again, eyes flashing.

"I said *no*." His voice was firm, but I could hear a slight tremble in the back of his throat. The older man's eyes widened in shock. "You're asking me to order men and women under my command to certain death. There is *no* tactical advantage in that, sir. In fact, it's nothing short of *insanity*."

The captain shook his head, stepping over the dead bodies strewn around us until he was toe to toe with his subordinate.

Stay safe.

"They warned me about you," he hissed, fuming. "They warned me about you, and I should have listened. Jack Miller: the *sergeant* who thought he was a *captain*. Well, allow me give you your final warning here, you insubordinate *coward*." I could see Jack's jaw clench in anger, and his hands tightened into fists at his sides. "I call the shots here. If you try and override me, your road ends right here with one of *my* bullets in *your* brain." Howell's hand drifted down to his waist to rest on the cold metal of the revolver strapped there. "Now order your men to move out."

Jack took in a shaky breath, gaze shifting to stare at the weapon ready to be drawn and fired at his head. When he spoke, his voice was impossibly colder and more commanding than the captain's, and his eyes never left the glinting steel of the weapon.

Stay. Safe.

"No." He looked back up at the dark eyes boring into his skull, eyes filled with malice and hatred, and I felt my stomach drop as my heart leaped into my throat at the defiance in Jack's gaze and the resignedly set angle of his jaw.

In one swift motion, Captain Howell pulled his gun free from his side and leveled it at my boyfriend's head, the barrel pressed nearly against Jack's forehead. My blood suddenly turned to ice, and I was about to run forward and tackle my superior to the ground when someone ran up and grabbed me from behind, steel arm trapping my arms against my sides and hand clapping over my mouth to keep me silent. As I reflexively struggled against my captor, she tightened her hold and whispered lowly in my ear, her voice strained and harshly sympathetic.

"I'm sorry, Byrne. But you are not going anywhere."

I slammed my head back against Aliyah's bony chest, but she didn't relinquish her grip. I could only watch in muffled horror. Howell's finger tightened on the trigger, and Jack's eyes shifted ever so slightly to meet my own that screamed at him above Death's silencing hand.

You, too.

Instead of giving me some shred of comfort, Jack looked back at his executioner, a daring light burning ferociously in his eyes, and then, the picture of defiance, he said something. I couldn't tell what it was, the world was drowned out in the sound of the rain and my pounding heart, but whatever he'd said pushed our captain over the edge. With a snarl of rage, Howell reversed his grip on his weapon and brought the back of the gun swinging around into Jack's temple, knocking my boyfriend flat on the ground.

I kicked and shouted muffled curses in Aliyah's arms as our captain followed Jack to the mud, swinging his weapon into his subordinate's face a few more times to disorient him. I could see the blood glistening on the metal, and tears pricked at my eyes as I imagined the brutal gashes marring my boyfriend's face. Then, finally tired of pummeling the unarmed man before him, Howell seized a fistful of Jack's shirt and pulled him close. My heart shattered at the way my boyfriend's head fell forward, eyes struggling to stay open beneath the bloody rain, and I screamed behind Aliyah's hand.

"Let's see how much you like disobeying my orders, *corporal,* when it hurts someone you care about!" he snarled and got to his feet, sending a few more well-aimed kicks to Jack's gut that made him convulse on the ground, dazed and overcome with vertigo.

Finally, Aliyah released me, and I pushed away from her, breathing heavy and erratic, to face the horrible scene before us. Howell was facing us, hawk-like eyes roving the fearful faces watching him and searching for one in particular.

When our eyes locked, I knew he'd found it.

"You were right, Miller!" he shouted as he pushed through the troops towards me. He didn't even need to touch anyone. They shrank away from him like he was parting an ocean, and I looked at Jack in stricken terror as he continued to lie unmoving on the ground.

He looked so still, so small, lying there with his head tilted at an almost odd angle against the earth. Unmoving save for the wind pulling frantically at his clothing.

"Sending half the platoon over makes no sense." I looked back at Howell and saw he was almost upon me, viciously shoving one private out of his way. "It's a waste of men. As you said, we only have eighty left." He lunged forward to grab me by the arm and dragged me along with him as he started back the way he'd come. And as my eyes followed our current path, my heart stopped. We were heading towards the ladder leading to the level ground, the killing field above the trenches.

"I'll just send Private Byrne."

"No," I whimpered, trying to drive my feet into the ground, but there was no point. Howell continued forward like an angry bull, and I realized there was no slowing him down now.

"He's useless anyways, wouldn't you agree? Couldn't hit the broad side of a barn if he tried."

People tripped over each other and their own feet in their desperation to get away from us, turning away from me as I tried to catch glimpses of their faces. Only Aliyah met my eyes, and I was shocked to catch sight of tears before she too looked to the ground. Her jaw was set, arms crossed defensively.

They're all scared, I realized, and my throat went dry.

Howell pulled me close to whisper in my ear, his breath hot and vicious against my skin.

"And you know what? I never liked you shags anyway." I stumbled as the captain swung me around towards the rickety steps, and I crashed into the wall, losing my balance and falling into a sitting position in the mud. "Alright then." He nodded at the ladder, glaring down at me. "Go."

I stared past my superior's legs, catching a glimpse of my boyfriend's still unresponsive body on the ground. *No* – it was a powerful word.

And Jack had given us the courage to use it.

"No," I whispered, looking up at him and shaking my head as my throat closed in terror.

Out of the corner of my eye, I could see Jack finally turn his head, dazedly blinking on the ground and clearly struggling to separate up from down. His face was streaked with blood, and I could see his skin already swelling around his nose and eyes. As I watched, he tried to get up, lifting himself a few inches above the ground before crumpling again.

"*No?*" The word was nearly shrieked, and Howell closed the distance between us, shoving me to the ground as I started to get up. "Move!" he bellowed, livid, but I couldn't comply. I couldn't push myself back into a standing position, couldn't pick up the gun that lay discarded beside me. I could only stare up at him in shaking, petrified silence, back pressed against the bloodstained trenches and arms drawn up against my chest as I silently cried. "I said *move!*"

I cried out as he brought his steel-toed boot swinging forward into my rib cage. I fell to the side, elbow holding me out of the mud as I curled in on myself, unable to breathe past the pain. His iron fingers grabbed hold of my shirt, nails scratching against my skin, and pulled me up so that we were nose to nose. His eyes blazed with an insane fire, and I took in a shuddering, sobbing breath as I fought in vain to keep down the hysteria pounding mercilessly in my chest.

"Now you listen to me, you spineless, *pathetic* excuse for a soldier," he continued, pulling his handgun from its holster and pressing the barrel against my left temple; I sobbed and tried to shy away. "You are nothing more than a body to me. *Nothing!*" His words were shouted, venomous and shaking. "And if I tell you to march out there and get yourself shot, you *march out there* and you *get yourself shot.*"

He let go of my shirt, and my legs folded uselessly under me, leaving me to stare up at him in utter terror as, expression foully dark, he lowered his gun until the barrel pointed at my head.

In my mind, I could see Idris sprawled on the roadside, and I closed my eyes, turning my head away and biting back a scream as I held my hands up before my face in vain.

"I'm counting to *three*." I took in another shuddering breath, struggling to ignore the man before me. "One." People started moving away, their boots shuffling in the dredge. "*Two*."

They were all torn between watching and turning their backs on the scene unfolding before them. I couldn't help my quick glance up at Howell and fought down a scream of painful anticipation for him to just pull the trigger already. Through the heavy sheets of rain, I could make out Jack struggling to his feet, panic-stricken, and I closed my eyes against my tears and sobs, caving in on myself below the sight of the gun above me.

"*Three*."

I screamed as the gun went off and went silent, shivering in the wet cold. Waiting for the piercing pain and then darkness.

But instead there was…nothing. I slowly opened my eyes and looked up, flinching, my shaking hands holding my knees against my heaving chest. Howell was just standing there, looking at me with a perplexed expression on his face. And that was when I saw the red staining his coat, spreading and dribbling down his chest.

The gun slowly slipped from his hand and thudded, harmless, into the mud below.

A second shot rang out – a shot that sent a bullet tearing through his throat from behind – and Howell dropped to his knees, eyes glassing over as near-black blood spilled from his mouth and throat. And as he finally slumped forward, splashing into the sludge beside me, I looked up at whoever it was that had just saved my life.

And I saw a sight that made my blood run cold.

Jack stood there in a drunken sort of way, legs braced against his spinning world and arm extended, smoking gun in his hand. His bloodied head was bowed under what was no doubt a splitting migraine. His brow was furrowed with pain, concentration, and tortured relief.

He was facing me. Was facing where Howell had been standing.

And as we all watched in stunned silence, he re-holstered his weapon and slowly sank to his knees, hands locked behind his head in a gesture of surrender. He blinked rapidly, taking deep, steadying breaths as he knelt there in the rain and mud, hollow gaze fixed on the corpse lying beside me.

He couldn't believe what he had done — I could see the haunted shock in his eyes. To be honest, I couldn't believe it either.

"I've shot and murdered my capt...my superior officer," he began, monotoned voice tripping over the formal wording as he tried to shake his head clear. "I place myself at your disposal for disciplinary measures."

He looked down, jaw clenched, but his eyes remained open, stormy gaze finding and holding me steady through the rain and blood dripping down his face. Nobody moved for what seemed like an age, and overhead thunder rumbled low across the sky while artillery fire continued to shake the ground beneath our feet.

Finally, Aliyah stepped forward, but she didn't go towards him. Instead, she went towards me and knelt beside Captain Howell's body, rolling him over and undoing the belt and buttons of his jacket. Slowly, Jack lowered his arms, watching her in confusion, but she gave no indication of what she was doing. Not even when she pulled the bloodied garment off the dead man and draped it over her arm.

But as she turned to face my boyfriend, her expression grew solemn, bordering on ceremonious. Jack shook his head.

"Moore, *no*," he warned, voice shaking, but she came forward anyways, stopping before his kneeling form. Silently, she presented the coat to him, the sleeve's blue captain's insignia facing him.

"Captain Miller," she shouted, moving to stand at attention. Jack was forced to take the jacket into his hands and looked at all the determined, dirty, and grimly bloodstained faces around him. "We await your orders, sir!"

He looked up at her, disgusted and shaken.

"I can't wear this. I just *killed* him—"

"From what we saw, sir, Captain Howell was killed by enemy fire," she interrupted, still at attention. "Wasn't he?"

I couldn't bring myself to join in with the chorused response. All I could do was look at my boyfriend's tortured expression through my tear-blurred vision as my ragged breath echoed in my ears.

"Yes, sir!"

She looked down at him, expression giving no indication of the lie we were all taking part of — the enormity of it.

"We await your orders, sir," she repeated, voice lower this time, and she fixed her dark eyes on his. Jack's expression was downtrodden, devastated, but nonetheless he swung the coat over his squared shoulders and got to his feet. He moved slowly, as though the jacket bore the weight of the worlds, and he looked at the people watching him, sickened.

"We hold this line," he finally announced, voice shaking as he walked among his new command. "No one comes over that ridge do you hear me? *We hold this line!*"

"Yes, sir!"

He closed his eyes at the chorused response, and I could hear his heart breaking. And I knew why. I knew the look in his eyes as he took in and memorized each face that he passed. It was the same way he had looked at me on many occasions since this began, though he didn't know that I'd noticed.

We were all just kids — kids he had the honor of killing.

After giving a few more quick orders, he jogged unsteadily over to me and dropped to his knees. Ignoring the dead man beside us, he pulled me close to him, kissing my forehead, my temple, and hugging me as tightly as he possibly could.

"Oh gods, Tristan. I'm sorry. I'm *so* sorry," he whispered.

I shook my head, burying my face into his shoulder and pulling him close by the front of his shirt as I finally cried, sobs making me cough and choke. I wrapped my arms tight around him, and I didn't know if the tears were for him or me.

"Come on. Let's get up." Wearily I stood, grabbing my weapon as I did, and looked up at him with reddened eyes. He gently cupped my face in my hands and blinked the crimson rainwater from his dark eyes. "I told you, Tristan. I told you I wouldn't let him hurt you."

He kissed my forehead once more before turning and facing the people waiting for his next order. And as he went, I could see his shoulders start to sag under the new weight.

"Byrne, you all good?" I turned to see Marcel walking over to fall in step beside me, and I tried to wipe the tears from my eyes. I nodded mutely, waiting for the other shoe to drop. "Great. 'Cause my *own* pride hurt to see you so undignified. *Gods*, have some respect for yourself, shrimp."

And there it went.

She slapped me on the back with a sincere expression before jogging off to join up with the rest of the Horsemen, and I found it odd that a comment that once would have humiliated me actually made me feel a little bit better. But up ahead, I could see Jack shakily smirking at me. Clearly he'd heard Marcel's taunt, and I realized it really wasn't that strange at all. I was okay.

For now.

The rest of the night passed in an endless blur of gunfire, artillery, screams, death, and smoke – as most nights did now. More people got killed. More people got hurt. And I saw Jack die a little each time someone went. I saw him struggle to breathe each time someone choked on their own blood and chapped lips turned a frothy pink as shrapnel-pierced lungs drowned. I saw him stumble and pale with every maimed kid that screamed and writhed in the sludge that was quickly becoming more viscera and dead than mud.

That night, I watched my boyfriend waste away from caring too much, and I realized that – in a twisted, cruel way – Howell had been just as sane as any of us. A front line captain in this war had to see his men and women as bodies. To see them as anything more would kill him, very slowly, from the inside out.

DAY ONE HUNDRED AND FORTY-SIX, PART ONE

Hours later – hours that seemed like decades – Jack gave the order that made me heave a sigh of relief, and I stumbled back a few steps to collapse just inside the door of the med tent.

"Platoons 304 and 305, take a break! 306 and 307, stay at your posts. We'll swap again in four hours!" He knelt by me, taking my hand in his and tightening his grip in comfort. "How are you holding together?"

I didn't answer. I just stared at him with my hollowed eyes and coughed on my shallow breaths. His left eye was almost swollen shut, the skin already discolored beneath the many wounds and streaks of drying blood marking his face and temple.

"How are *you?*" I croaked and nearly choked on my rattling lungs.

His jaw tightened, and he looked down at our hands, his thumb grazing over my bloodied knuckles in thought. But just as he opened his mouth to answer, two field nurses rushed in, carrying a screaming man on a stretcher. Jack pulled me to my feet and moved me out of the way.

"What happened?" he asked, captain once more. I watched in shaken silence as Blackwell came over, took one glance at the bloodied young man before him, and shook his head, shooing away the gathering nurses. "Doc?" The old man pulled Jack to the side, speaking in undertones that I could barely make out.

"There's nothing we can do for him, Miller. One of our shells exploded in his face." Jack looked over at the young man despairingly. "This isn't the first time I've seen faulty equipment kill one of our men, and I doubt it will be the last. I'm sorry." Blackwell quickly returned to his work, treating and patching up the many other patients he had groaning and bleeding out around him.

I wearily sat back down on an empty crate, leaning my head against the trench wall. And as I listened to the drumming tattoo of rain on the tent above us, I watched Jack hesitantly walk over and sit beside the choking private. Gingerly, he rested his hand on the bloodied shoulder before him. Blue eyes fixed on his dark ones, and the private's mouth opened in a small, gurgling gasp of pain.

"Hey, Jackson," our captain said softly.

My tired eyes widened slightly. How had he recognized him? Looking at the shuddering, bloody, burned mass of flesh and clothing before me, I could see nothing of the loudmouthed bully that had hunted the halls at the Academy.

"Miller…" he whispered, voice a soft creak of sound passing through his scorched throat. He fell silent, breath rattling in his chest as his eyes closed against the glaring light of the medical tent.

"Told you I'd have your back out here." The man choked, some part of his shredded body catching in his throat, and Jack eased him back down as he tried to rise off the table. "Just lie still. You're gonna be okay, kid. You hear me?"

Alec weakly opened his eyes. The blue stood out strangely against his blackened, yet shiny and red-slicked skin, and a scoff pulled at his bloody lips.

"Liar," he coughed, shaking hands splayed and held above himself in an effort to keep his raw skin from coming into contact with anything.

"Nah, I'm not lying, son," Jack assured him, voice kind and soothing in the chaos around us. "Doc's just gone to get you something for the pain. Then, he's gonna come back and bandage you up. Make you look like one of those old mummies for a bit, sure, but you're gonna be fine."

Something childlike shone in the private's eyes, and Alec took in a breath that shook with something more than just pain.

"Don't want to die, sir," he croaked, fastening his hand on Jack's and refusing to let go despite the pain that was undoubtedly searing his skin at the contact. "Don't let me die."

I could see my boyfriend floundering for words, stricken. His bruised eyes were red and glistening, and he opened his mouth a few times without speaking before he managed to find his voice again.

"You're not…you're not going to die. I promise. Just…go to sleep." Jackson shook his head, the motion sloppy and desperate, and Jack tried again. "You need your rest, Alec."

"No. No, if – if I sleep, I'm not gonna wake up." Instead of conceding the fact, our captain brought their clenched hands into the younger man's line of sight.

"I'm right here. See? And I promise you that I'll make sure you wake up when it's time to move." But Alec just laughed in bitter fear, coughing as his lungs slowly failed and filled with fluids from his burned flesh.

"You *shags*…always lying," he muttered in a coarse taunt as his head lolled to the side, leaving a bloody stain on the bedding below him, and Jack smirked.

"Well, that's why we're so good at it, private," he joked, but he looked up at me with pained eyes as he spoke, careful to make sure Alec wasn't watching.

"I'm sorry," the soldier whispered urgently. Jack looked back down at him and gave a small, reassuring smile, shifting his sticky hold on the man's hand.

"It's okay. It's all okay." But Alec was beyond hearing. He just stared at Jack's face with open fear, begging with bloody words.

"Please, I'm sorry…just don't – don't let me die. I don't want to die." My boyfriend swallowed, gathering himself as he listened to the dying man's pleas.

"Then go to sleep," he finally whispered, leaning forward and resting his elbow on the mattress beside Jackson. "I promise you won't die if you just go to sleep."

"Promise?" the delirious man whispered, and Jack nodded stiffly.

"Yeah. Yeah, I promise. I'll be right here to wake you up when it's all over." Jackson nodded, eyes blearily blinking against his undoubtedly fading vision. "It's going to be okay."

And as I watched, our captain bent over him, easing a hand under the dying man's neck and locking their eyes together. There was still something there, something begging Jack for mercy, and the elder sighed. For a split second, he looked so much older – greyed and wise beyond his years.

"Just sleep, son."

And, slowly, fighting the inevitable the whole time, our companion's eyes drifted shut. Thirty seconds that felt like hours passed with the two of them in that position until finally Jack let him go, hunching his back and bracing his hands against the operating table.

"Alec?"

There was no response, and Jack bowed his head, glassed-over eyes fixed on the oddly peaceful corpse before him. A few moments passed in silence, and, still looking gutted, he stared up through a tear in the ceiling of the tent to the smoke filled sky above us, searching for something I did not know. In the din, I could hear him speaking softly to himself.

"Diana, bless this soldier for he has fought in your name to his final breath." He paused, clearing his throat and taking a deep, steadying breath. "Grant him peace in the afterlife and guide him to Proserpine, wherein she may take mercy on his immortal soul. I ask this in the name of Alec Jackson, slain this day – valiant goddess, may you vouchsafe to me what I ask of you in prayer. So may it be."

Slowly, painfully, I got to my feet and practically dragged myself over to him, bracing myself on every possible thing I could as I went.

"Come on, Jack," I whispered, resting my hand on his shoulder as he stared listlessly at our dead platoon member. I closed my eyes against my spinning vision and swallowed back another painful cough. "Jack, he's not the only one who's died…you have to come on."

When he still showed no signs of moving, I linked my arm through his and pulled him into a standing position, guiding him down the trenches to Howell's personal tent.

"What are you doing, Tristan?" he finally asked, slowing what had been up to this point a rather steady and willing pace.

"You need to sleep," I responded and groaned as Jack pulled away.

"I can't do that. Not now."

"You're captain. *Not* invincible," I countered, trying to keep my voice steady. He hesitated, biting his lip as he looked around us at the frayed line we were barely managing to keep together. "Look, if we want to do this and succeed, we're going to need our captain. And we won't have our captain if you're asleep on your feet." He looked down at me and opened his mouth to protest, but I quickly cut him off.

"*No.* You're no good to us half-dead." I pointed to the tent. "Go get some rest. I'll wake you up if there's anything we need from you." He still looked on the fence about listening to me though, and I continued, jumping to the next thing he'd be worried about. "I'll get Marcel to take over."

"No." I turned back to face him and took careful note of how choppy his sentences were in his exhaustion. "No, uh…get Soto. She's…she's more reliable. Marcel just gets angry. Katalin can compartmentalize. Send her in to me once you find her." I nodded and set off at a limping jog, my stomach cramping on me from hunger, and I groaned, pressing a clenched fist against the tight knot.

Kat…where *was* she?

I finally caught sight of the powerful young woman directing a few people to take up position a little farther down the trench, waving her arm in a sweeping motion to indicate where the gunfire was coming from. Without even questioning her, the four men and women ran off, hands gripping their weapons tightly.

"Katalin!" I shouted when I was ten feet away, and she glanced over her shoulder to me, giving a couple last orders before coming over.

"What do you want?"

I blinked at how sharp her tone was and stammered a little.

"Uh – um, Jack wants you. He's over in Howell's tent." She nodded and started heading in that general direction when a thought struck her, and she turned back to face me. "Yes, I do know how stupid I looked when Howell was about to blow my brains out, and I apologize for making you feel embarrassed to know me," I interrupted, staring at her with tired eyes. "Marcel beat you to that one." She frowned.

"I'd *never* make fun of you about that. Never. That's cold." Her words were hurt, affronted. "I was just gonna say that I think you should stay with him."

"Care to elaborate?" She grasped what I meant and waved for me to follow her as she started walking away.

"I know that you've seen it. How attached he is to his troops."

"What, and you want me to get him to be unattached? Distance him?" I asked in disbelief and fell into step beside her. "He just sat with Jackson while he died." She looked at me, startled.

"Alec's dead?" I nodded, voice matter-of-fact as we went on.

"Faulty equipment. Artillery shell exploded right in his face."

"Gods…" She shook her head, at a loss for words. "Awful way to go."

"Yeah." *I killed someone that way.* "And Jack sat with him the whole time. So, don't tell me to detach him from everyone because it's too late for that. He's in too deep."

She nodded, bronzed face torn between speaking and processing the information I'd just given her. We were silent until she reached the captain's tent, and as she reached out to grab the thick canvas, she stopped. She hesitated before speaking.

"Then at least be there for him," she said, looking back at me. "Make sure he has someone to lean on, because with a heart like that it's gonna be hard to keep going."

With that, she vanished into the tent, and I trudged over to where Jayce and Marcel were sitting against the wall. They looked up briefly as I came over, but gave no other inclination that they'd seen me. Not that I minded. It was nice to just sit there in silence for once, ignoring everything that was going down around us. But just as I thought that to myself, Jayce looked up at me again.

"How's he holding up?"

"Hm?" I returned, not following, and he rolled his eyes.

"*Miller*. Corporal to captain's a big jump. Unrealistic, really."

I shrugged.

"He's always been a good leader. Probably would have made it there anyways…he just fast-forwarded a bit." *A lot*. But Jayce was shaking his head, and Marcel continued her brother's point.

"That's not what he meant. Miller's always been very protective of his troops. I mean, that's why he shot Howell," she explained, snapping a piece of wood she'd been twirling between her fingers clean in half. "It wasn't because you two are in love or whatever. Howell was a threat to all of us – one that, in Miller's eyes, had to be eliminated. Frankly, I agreed with his call."

Her brother picked up her train of thought.

"But he's not designed to make those types of calls day after day. He–"

"He cares too much," I finished, and Jayce nodded, surprisingly not angry at the interruption. "I get what you're saying, and…and I know that it's true. But that's how he's always been. I mean, if he's lasted this long, he should be fine. Right?"

Marcel took in a deep breath and shook her head, leaning forward to brace her forearms on her knees.

"Byrne, one of these days, Miller's going to have to make a call. He's gonna have to make a call that's going to cost a lot of lives in the short run but give us a tactical advantage in the long run. You know that's how war works. For all of your many shortcomings, you *are* a strategist." Reluctantly, I nodded, and Marcel continued. "That call will be a turning point, a watershed in this war: whether we hold the line or the Brettain break it. Under Miller's command, Queen Auriane's armies are going to press forward, and we are going to fall back. And you *know* it." But I shook my head.

"No."

She raised an eyebrow, unimpressed.

"All the evidence says *yes*."

"No." I shook my head more emphatically. "Jack will be able to make that call, I promise you. When it really matters, he'll pull through. I know him." The siblings shrugged in defeat, and I looked over at the tent in time to see Katalin ducking out from under the canvas flap. Her eyes met mine, and, after a subtle tilt of the head, I got her message. "I need to go."

Groaning slightly as my joints cracked and popped, I got to my feet and made my way back over to Jack's tent, ducking inside and blinking a few times to adjust to the light of a few gas lanterns. And I was met with an odd, disconcerting sight.

The tactical table was uselessly cluttered with pencils and bits of wood that I guessed Howell had been using as figurines to represent the Brettain forces. Papers, reports, maps, and telegrams were all strewn across the floor and the sparse furniture as though a small hurricane had just blown through. Most, if not all, bore some type of seal. Some I recognized as G.A. Agathon's.

"Is everything okay in here?" I asked tentatively from the door. Jack looked at me from where he was examining a report and absentmindedly nodded.

"Yeah, yeah...just looking at casualty reports that Howell had radioed in from the rest of the front line outposts." I nodded, coming closer to him. Jack seemed distant, distracted, and I wasn't sure if he even realized I was moving. "I mean, they aren't brand new reports, but still..."

"How are things?" There was silence, and I stepped a little closer until I was standing so close to him I could feel his body heat through his clothes. "Jack?"

He pinched the bridge of his nose and let the paper fall to the ground. He took in a deep breath and looked up at the canvas ceiling above us.

"It's not good. The Brettain are decimating us." He turned around and picked up another few reports, quickly flipping through them. "Command strategists don't think we can hold out for longer than a week, and Howell got this five days ago via wire. What's more, according to this report–" he slapped the paper in his hands in frustration "–they've predicted that the Brettain are going to spearhead their attack right through *our* outpost."

My stomach dropped, and I shifted on my feet, trying to come up with something to say.

"We can hold them off." I hid my shaking hands behind my back while Jack laughed bitterly and looked back at me in disbelief.

"Have you *looked* at us recently?" he scoffed, making a sweeping gesture to the world around us. "We're running on empty. When the Brettain come through, they'll be able to walk right over us and not even break a sweat."

I searched for something else to tell him to drive that caged expression from his face.

"Well, um, that could be alright, couldn't it?" I offered, my words weak and comfortless. "I mean, maybe they'll take prisoners. Maybe we'll all be fine." Jack laughed again, a short bark of noise, and crossed his arms over his chest.

"Since when have the Brettain taken prisoners of war?" he asked, and I avoided his gaze. "Look, I appreciate what you're trying to do, Tris, but don't." Another frightened laugh. "Just don't. Not you. Don't try and make this better." He sat down heavily on the cot and dropped his head into hands.

"Gods," he whispered. "That's why Howell was trying to find out where they were stationed. That's why he wanted that charge – it wasn't suicide, it was a last ditch effort to prevent *this*." He pointed angrily at the fallen report and looked up at me, hopelessness shining in his eyes. "In the next two days, the Brettain are going to come swarming over No Man's Land, and we're gonna be overrun."

He let his hand fall back to his lap and stared up at me with powerless eyes. He looked so fragile, hunched over himself with his fore-arms braced against his knees. When he spoke, his voice was strained and quiet.

"I can't stop this."

After a few seconds of stunned silence, I nodded, watching my boyfriend carefully. He didn't need a shoulder to cry on. He didn't need reassurances or platitudes. He needed defiance.

"So," I began, stepping closer to him and crossing my arms, "how do we go down?"

"What?"

"How do we go down?" I repeated, stance resolute. "If we're not going to survive, we had better find a good way to go out. Make the Brettain pay when they come down into *our* trenches." He stared at me for a little bit, as though trying to figure out who he was looking at. "What?"

"That's something one of the Horsemen would say," he said slowly, standing and waiting for the whistle of an incoming shell to end in an earth-shaking explosion before continuing. "Not you."

"Well, I've decided I'd like to live," I said with an off-handed shrug. "And they've got a pretty nice mindset for that." He shook his head, wryly smiling to himself. "But none of that matters right now. Come on." I grabbed his hand and pulled him back towards the cot. "We can deal with this in a few hours. You need to rest."

He sighed once before sitting down and reluctantly letting me push him back into a sleeping position. But his eyes wouldn't close. He just looked up at the roof of the canvas tent above us, hands tightly clenched on his stomach. I took a deep breath and turned down all the gas lamps before gently nudging him. He moved over a little bit, and I joined him on the narrow bed, joints aching.

"Talk to me," I said softly. I reached over and took his hand in mine, moving it over to rest on my own chest. As we lay there, I could feel his fingers tracing out my ribs.

"Why?" he asked, voice low and defeated. I rolled onto my side and protectively draped my arm over him, resting my head on his shoulder.

"Because I'm your boyfriend," I said with a gentle smile. "It's my job to deal with all the crap you've got bottled up inside that head of yours." Jack sighed, smiling sadly, and I frowned as I felt him flinch beneath me at the sound of another artillery shell striking home nearby. I mean, I flinched too, but Jack...he never did. That just wasn't something he did.

He was used to the noise, the nightmare. He wasn't supposed to be like the rest of us. He seemed to know what I was thinking and shakily rested his hand on my head, letting his fingers nestle in my sweaty and mud-streaked hair.

"You really want to know what I'm thinking?" he asked, voice rumbling in my ear. I nodded, and he gave a soft laugh, a saddened scoff. "I'm *scared*. I look at you, at the rest of them, and I get so gods-damned *scared*. I want this over as much as you do." He paused. "Maybe even more so."

I didn't say anything in response to that. There was nothing I could say. He'd caught me off-guard, just as he'd known he would, and we were left to lay in silence until finally we drifted off to sleep.

... — — ...

I woke up to someone gently tapping my arm, and, blinking rapidly, I turned my head to look at the person standing next to our cot. Despite my fatigue-blurred vision, I managed to recognize the half-dead private swaying before me.

"Kat," I stammered, sitting up and disentangling myself from Jack at the same time. "Oh my gods, what happened to– " She held up her hand to stem my questions.

"Look, I've been awake for practically forty-six hours." She shook her head to clear it, coming back to what she was going to say. "Shift's over. We're swapping out the platoons again."

I swung my legs off the edge of the cot and massaged my temples. I tried and failed to ignore how my head throbbed with the booms of heavy artillery and my heart beat in sync with the rapid tattoo of the machine guns and rifles. She backed up a little, waiting for me to wake up completely, before continuing.

"I'm going to get some rack time. Wake up the captain."

She turned unsteadily and left, and I looked over my shoulder at my restlessly sleeping boyfriend. His bruises had settled on a nasty combination of blue and purple, and the cuts had stopped oozing. Surprisingly, his eye wasn't swollen shut. He was worse for wear, but he wasn't broken.

Not yet.

"Jack?" I whispered, putting my hand on his shoulder and shaking him. "Jack?" He started awake, chaotically vaulting out of the cot and wiping at his eyes.

"What? What's going on?"

I stared at him for a few moments before speaking, waiting for him to settle back down and get his bearings.

"It's been four hours – time for us to rotate." He sighed, running his hands through his hair before looking at me and clenching his jaw. With a slight pang, I realized I had just scared him awake, and I knew his heart was racing. "Sorry. I guess I shouldn't have woken you up like that." He shook his head, straightening his clothes and looking everywhere it seemed but at me.

"No. No, it's okay."

I didn't press the matter and watched as he snatched Howell's blood-stained coat from across the top of a chest, pulling it on and leaving the tent. Exhausted and achy, I got to my feet and followed him out. People hurried past us, and I gagged slightly on the strong stench and taste of gunpowder. I could see Jack and Soto talking through the haze, the Mezitain woman shakily giving her report of the last four hours. As I watched, I saw her sway dangerously on her feet, and Jack barely managed to catch her as she collapsed to the ground.

"Can I get some help?" he shouted, and Irina seemed to appear out of thin air, her nearly white hair dyed gray with the soot and powder from the artillery.

"She needs to rest. Take her to Howell's tent and let her sleep in there." She nodded and pulled Katalin's arm over her shoulder, half-dragging and half-carrying her towards the tent.

"How long was she up?" Jack asked, still watching the two women go on their way, and I looked around, expecting to find someone else standing there with us. But we were alone, and I realized he was talking to me.

"Forty-six hours with only seven hours of sleep in all that," I answered, watching the two women go. "Between Howell's 'shifts' and those last four she picked up for you...she's done in."

"We all need rest," Jack said, looking around us.

I tried laughing at the statement, but instead I immediately started coughing – a deep, rattling sound that had me doubled over, hands braced against my knees. Vaguely, I felt Jack's hand on my back, and I quickly forced myself to stand up straight.

"I'm okay," I lied, the words automatic now, but he firmly shook his head.

"Tris, that's sounding even worse than before." I shrugged, trying to ignore the now ever-present scratchy sensation at the back of my throat. But I was deliberately stalling, and he knew it. "Tristan, it's *bad*."

"It's *been* bad for over a month now," I said and turned away before he could say anything else. "Come on. We need to go."

"You should see the doc," Jack pressed, walking after me. I snorted.

"What? Afraid I've got TB?" I joked, rolling my eyes, but Jack's answer made me stop in my tracks.

"Yeah. I am."

"There's people bleeding out from missing limbs and gunshot wounds, their guts held in by bandages..." I began, watching him carefully, "and yet you want me to take up Blackwell's precious time and resources yet again over what might be a simple case of TB?"

"I've seen it kill people before, Tristan," he warned, catching up with me as I started walking again. "It's not as 'simple' as you put it."

"Jack, I'm not going to take up space other people need because I've got a *cough*. It'll go away on its own soon." My voice grew gentle again, and I looked up at him. "I promise. I mean, you haven't seen anyone else here with it, have you?" I pointed out and quickly continued as he looked away. "Jack, I'm breathing in gods know what out here. I'm bound to get a cough now and then. Just relax."

"I know," he finally muttered, and I heaved an internal sigh of relief. "It's just–"

"Incoming!" someone bellowed, and a loud whistling tore through the air, hurtling towards us. But before I could turn around to look for the shell and hide, Jack slammed into me from behind, knocking me to the ground and landing on top of me.

A fraction of a second later, the air throbbed with the shockwave of the explosion, shrapnel flying through the air and embedding itself in everything it could reach. I gritted my teeth against the loud boom and clapped my hands, bleeding anew, over my ears. As soon as the dust and sound dissipated, Jack pushed himself up off the ground, pulling me with him, and ran over to the edge of the trenches, hauling soldiers back to their feet as he went and shrugging his weapon off his shoulder and into his hands.

"Pull yourself together, let's go!" he shouted, voice cracking as he ran along the mud wall, pointing and gesturing towards the direction the noise had come from. "Fire that way! Moore!" The tall woman looked around at him from where she was checking a body, eyes flashing. "Run down to the artillery battery and tell them to concentrate their fire in the direction of that shot! We can't have them sending any more of those down here!"

Aliyah nodded briefly and ran off in the direction Jack had pointed, shouting her orders as she went. I followed the rest of the troops as we ran to take our positions at the trenches and forced my body to show itself over the top of the trench with the others, firing a few times before dropping back down behind the surface. The half-eroded embankment didn't offer much protection any more, and for some it was enough. But as the people around me turned back and fired again, I froze. I sat there, hyperventilating with my back pressed to the wall. I gripped my rifle tightly in my hands and clenched my teeth against the chaos around me.

Not again.

I couldn't stick my head over into the line of fire and stare down death. That wasn't in the cards for me, not today. It never had been.

You think you're brave because you've embraced the fact that you're going to die? That you're not in denial or scared?

I took in deep breath after deep breath, trying to steady myself and build up the courage to take part in the next volley. I wasn't about to die, not after being out in this god-forsaken hell for nearly five months. That wasn't how these things were supposed to work. I'd almost made it halfway – wasn't that when we were supposed to know we might make it? Wasn't that when we were supposed to know that we got to evade our fates for a little longer?

"Come on, Byrne!" Irina shouted above the tattoo of fire, and I turned around to face her. Her eyes blazed with defiance as she reloaded her gun, and she grabbed my shoulder, turning me to face the wall with her. "We go on three. Let's go." But when I made no move to accompany her, she forcefully turned me to face her, hands brutally tight on my shoulders. "I'm right here. *Trust me.*"

I swallowed and looked forward once more. She started the cadence.

"Let's go on three. One, two, *three!*"

The fifty of us remaining from 304 and 305 unanimously rose up and fired across the barren stretch of land between our lines and the enemy's. The clamor of sporadic gunfire tore through the air for a few minutes until we dropped back down to move down the line and restart the process.

True to her word, Private Korsakov was right beside me, hanging on tenaciously despite it all. As we went, though, I noticed a stain of inky red across her right shoulder and chest, and I was reaching to point it out to her when she swatted my hand away. Her eyes flashed briefly with anger at the fact that I had noticed her injury, but when she looked away I could see her jaw working nervously.

"Irina–"

"*Don't* call me that," she snapped, and I tried again.

"Korsakov, did you get shot?" She shrugged defensively, a lopsided motion given her wound. "When did that happen?"

"Yesterday. Shortly after Miller took command." My head was spinning and I struggled to find something to say.

"Did you go to Blackwell?"

She snorted.

"What's that son of a bitch gonna do? Stitch me up? Stick me with his needles? There's no point now anyways, the bleeding's stopped. It's not like I'm dying."

"That's going to get infected, Korsakov," I pressed. "You *need* to go see him."

She rolled her eyes as she took up a new position and waited for me to catch up with her

"The world's ending, and you want me to go get a bullet wound looked at because it *might* get infected?" she asked, disdainfully. I nodded. "So what if it gets all crappy?"

"You could die," I said like it was obvious, and when she didn't show a reaction to that, I realized what was going on. She just didn't care anymore. She was here to fight, and she was going to fight until she ran herself into the ground.

She'd embraced death.

"Guess I'll finally be Pestilence, then," she muttered to herself before looking forward again. Her jaw clenched. Her eyes blazed with a feverish light. "On three!"

And so the cycle continued.

... — — — ...

It was ten hours later, and our platoon was two hours into our second four hour rotation when, suddenly, everything went quiet. There was nothing, not even the slightest sound of a flag rippling in the air. The Brettain had just stopped firing, and Jack silently gestured for us to hold our fire. Even the other two platoons that were supposed to be resting came out of their various hideaways, and a few nurses left the med tent, asking in soft undertones what was going on. A few voices proposed that the Brettain were withdrawing. Others said that they'd run out of supplies.

But as I looked over my shoulder at Jack, I knew what was really going on. And I could tell that he did too.

"I want all sergeants and lieutenants in the tent now," Jack ordered, heading in the direction of Howell's canvas citadel. "And anyone who graduated from the Academy with commendations in strategy feel free to accompany." I tried to ignore the strain in his voice and fell in line with the people following our captain. But before we got very far, Jack stopped and turned around, pointing at the gathered people warningly. "And I want no one firing at the Brettain! Buckle down. Organize what ammunition we've got left and set up watches."

Somewhere, a voice I didn't know called out in protest.

"But sir, they're exposed. We should take them on right now!"

"No. *They're* not exposed," Jack countered, voice hard. "*We* are. Storm's coming, private. Best get ready for when it hits."

Somewhere in the desolate world around us, a raven's rasping cry carried out over the smoky hellscape, and I shuddered, continuing on with the others to the command tent. Jack walked in first, followed by most of the other lieutenants and sergeants until I was left face to face with Wilson.

"Where do you think you're going?" he demanded harshly, and before I could answer, Jack's voice carried out to us.

"Private Byrne received a commendation in strategy from Battlemaster Jax at the end of his third year. He's cleared to be here."

Without saying a word, I pushed past the peeved lieutenant and took up a position behind Jack, standing off to the side like his sentry. We were silent for a little bit as Jack gathered up the papers scattered across the tent, and finally he looked up at us all.

"I'm not going to spare any niceties here. I hope you know that." Some nodded, others just continued to meet his gaze in acknowledgement as Jack set the papers on the map of the trenches.

"Upon taking over his position, I discovered that Captain Howell had received reports that the Brettain were going to punch through the front lines and overrun us. Most likely," he explained, drawing the line with his finger, "they're going to spearhead their attack through our outpost. Recent intelligence reports told him that this was slated to happen either today or tomorrow." He paused, looking down at the red casualty numbers in his hands. "And it looks like it's going to be today."

"So when Howell told you to send your platoon over..."

I took a deep breath and looked at Wilson as the man trailed off. He looked almost younger than Jack, and I realized that the lieutenants and the sergeants surrounding us were either rather old or surprisingly young. And the more I looked, the more I saw that the young were still wet behind the ears, and the old were too battle-worn to care.

"Yeah," Jack answered, waiting a few seconds to let the challenge hang in the air. "It had a point. It was a last-ditch, poorly thought-out point, but a point none the less." Grizzled Bates spoke up in the silence that followed, voice hesitant.

"Are you…are you gonna go through with his plan?"

Jack seemed to grow in size at the mere suggestion, and when he spoke his voice was a furious growl.

"I would *never* do that. No potential strategic advantage is worth sacrificing our men and women. I'm not going to ask you to send your troops over the trenches to die." He looked down at the table before him, hands braced on the war map. His voice grew quiet. "I'm not going to do that. So. Tell me what our options are."

There was silence.

"Well, if they're going to break through, they're most probably going to rain us with artillery fire. That's assuming none of our artillery crews managed to knock their weapons out of play," Williams began, clearing her throat and pointing to a circled portion of the Brettain trenches. "While that's going on, they'll start sending people over the trenches. Once their artillery stops shooting, their infantry will be upon us. We'll have no time to regroup, and…" She looked up. "It'll be a bloodbath."

"That's assuming the Brettain are still at full force and in the same positions as before," Jack pointed out, but another lieutenant just scoffed and shook his head ruefully.

"They always are. I don't know how the sons of bitches do it, but they seem to have unending men. It's a miracle we've held off this long."

Jack was quiet for a few moments, eyes intensely roving the layout, numbers, assets, and weaknesses before him.

"Well, what if we split our artillery?" he asked, pointing to a point on the map that was farther down the trench on the opposite side of where our artillery was currently lined up beside our infantry. "And we created a false location—"

Williams cut him off, her expression grim.

"That won't work, sir. We've been firing full force since this began. The Brettain know exactly how many guns we've got, and if we don't use all of them, they'll suspect that something's off right away."

Jack blew air out of his nose in aggravation, raking a hand through his hair. His jaw worked tensely as he stared down at the table, and I couldn't help the fear building up in me. Jack didn't know what to do. None of them did. My throat went dry, and I stepped forward until I could see the canvas map before me.

"How about you, *master strategist?*"

"Knock it off, Wilson," Jack growled, fixing the man with a dark glare, and the lieutenant piped down. "You got anything, private?" I narrowed my eyes, scrutinizing the information before me.

Out of the box. Think out of the box. Bend the rules.

"I might," I began slowly, stepping forward and rearranging the artillery and infantry on our side until the board was unrecognizable. Satisfied with my work, I stepped back and waited for a response. The one I got wasn't exactly comforting.

"What the *hell* is this supposed to be?" the older sergeant demanded, and I looked up at the people standing around me. Behind the confusion I could see the start of comprehension, and their eyebrows rose fractionally as the plan took shape before their eyes.

"I can't tell if this is madness or brilliance," Williams finally said, and Jack caught my gaze, offering me a small smile of pride as we stared at each other.

"Both. It's Tristan's primary state of existence." He cleared his throat and stepped forward, breaking our eye contact to address the plan I'd laid out. "So, take us through how this would work."

"Alright," I began. "First, we would have to set up the troops a good distance down from the artillery weapons. Line them against the sides of the trenches; create barricades with whatever supplies we've got left. That'll be our cover when we're waiting for the Brettain to arrive."

"What do you mean *waiting* for them?"

I looked at the woman who'd spoken and sighed in annoyance.

"Every strategy we've used when the Brettain charge is to line up facing them and try and narrow down the playing field while we get decimated by artillery fire," I explained, pointing at the map. "We *always* give the enemy something to shoot at. This way, we'd let the heavy artillery do the job for us. Infantry *has* to hold their fire in order for this to work." I cleared my throat, uncomfortable at how everyone was *actually* paying attention.

"You said the Brettain never change their positions. So we stagger our artillery guns a little bit in two different divisions at opposite ends of the trenches — sort of like bookends with the infantry between them. We aim both wings of artillery at the same point and volley in alternating sequences – make sure it's a constant stream of fire right down on the opposing side's own artillery. Or at least wherever we think they are. Absolutely *ignore* the people. Infantry will deal with them once they get close enough. The battery weapons' only focus should be on taking out the Brettain's artillery."

"That's simple enough, but your plan won't do shit when they drop down on us." I held up a hand to silence the older officer once again.

"We halt our artillery fire once the Brettain get within twenty feet of our trenches. Best-case scenario, we'll have incapacitated their guns by this point and only have to worry about the people. That's when we move *our* artillery."

"*Move* the artillery? Those guns weigh a fair amount, Private."

"I know, Sergeant…" I squinted at the elder's uniform, "Song. We've got rope though. Tie it to the guns, and at Jack – at Captain Miller's order we move everything into place. The infantry falls back behind the artillery. Turn the guns to face No Man's Land where the Brettain are coming from, drop the angle of the weapons, and set up a crossfire. Thin out the crowd. Make them less eager to come after the artillery.

"Infantry will have two jobs. One half will start firing with the artillery to slow enemy troops who will start heading over to us to take down our artillery weapons. The other half will take down the people coming into the trenches."

"This actually may work…"

Jack was clearly fighting the urge to roll his eyes.

"Thank you for the input, Wilson," he sighed. "To maximize casualties, our infantry should wait as long as possible. Have them hold their fire until as many Brettain as we can afford are in the trenches before we break cover and start firing. The troops will *have* to stay hidden behind the barricades until the last possible second."

"We'll have to make those barriers as inconspicuous as possible, then," Bates mused, and I nodded in agreement. Then, the older man heaved a tense sigh. "Well, if this doesn't work, we'll go out in a blaze of glory."

We were quiet for a little, staring at the map, and I made the mistake of glancing over at Jack. He was staring at his lieutenant with a baffled light in his eyes, a confused expression on his face.

"What makes you think I'm going to let us stay here and get slaughtered?" he finally asked, and everyone looked at him uncomfortably.

"Well, sir, we are the last tactical outpost. If we back down, the whole front line's going to fall behind us."

Jack went quiet, staring hard at the map before us, at the unwinnable scenario we all faced. He sighed in aggravation and rested his hands against the table, chewing his lip as he tried to find a way out. I knew he wasn't going to. I knew he was going to be forced to make the hard call. But I'd be right there for him when he did, just as I always was. This would be how it ended. But when he straightened and looked at each of us in turn, his eyes were icy and stubborn.

I felt something heavy and ominous settle in my bones.

"Then it all falls," he stated, voice leaving no room for argument. "The lines, the outpost, *hell*, this whole war front! It *all* goes. It all falls down. We leave nothing behind." My stomach went cold as Jack shoved his hands into Howell's pockets and headed for the tent door. "No cause is worth this."

In the silence that followed his exit, the officers and I looked at each other in helpless silence until Bates cleared his throat.

"Look, I know Miller's been under a lot of stress lately. Maybe we should prepare to counter his orders in the event that we can't hold the line."

My heart leapt into my throat, but before I could speak up in defense of our captain, Sergeant Williams started talking.

"I agree. Miller's a good soldier, don't get me wrong," she began, obviously uncomfortable with what she was saying. "He's a good leader. In fact, I believe he'd be one of the greats if this were a war with honor. But it's not. This war is as far from honorable as you can get. And as it is, Miller cannot make the type of calls a captain needs to make on these lines. We can. We've done it before."

Finally, I managed to speak up.

"No." They looked at me, unimpressed by my betrayed outburst. "No, you chose to follow him! You all *chose* to follow him as your captain. If you'd had issues when Moore made that call, you should have spoken up then. So you damn well had better listen to him now!"

Blood pounding in my temples, I pushed through the officers before me and left the tent. The stillness of the air above us sent shivers down my spine. This was wrong. This was all so wrong. For months, the air above us had been exploding, filled with cacophonous, man-made thunder.

And now...now there was nothing.

This was the calm before the storm, and the anticipation was making me sick to my stomach. I scanned the faces I passed for Jack. He couldn't have gotten far.

"Jack?" I called, and people parted before me as I quickly walked along. Sullen eyes met mine and then slid away, and I coughed on the smoky air. "Jack?" I found myself weaving my way to the field hospital, and Blackwell straightened from his hunched position by a private's ravaged leg. It looked like another artillery shell injury.

"Get that bandaged and put some anti-septic on the wound. Sparingly, mind you...it seems we're running low on that now, too." He looked at me as his nurse ran off and gave a sad smile as he wiped blood from his hands onto a sullied towel. "He's back there." I followed the tilt of his head to a missing panel of the tent and felt my heart sink.

This wasn't good.

I nodded my thanks to Blackwell and headed towards the abandoned length of trenching that ran behind the infirmary. A terrible, over-powering stench reached my nose, and the muddied ground slipped beneath my feet as I stumbled along. I had never been back here, had *made sure* I never came back here. I heaved a pained sigh as I rounded the corner to see barbed wire fencing, the razor sharp wall the only barrier between the living and the dead.

"Jack?" I called softly. The man standing a few feet away looked over his shoulder at me, turning something over and over in his hands. "Look, I know you don't want us to stay here when the Brettain come over, but–"

"Stop talking, Tristan," Jack said softly, looking back ahead of himself at the body dump of a graveyard before us. "Just...stop. I know you want to run. We *all* want to run, save for those idiots back there who want to die martyrs. They think death in war is some sacred gift." He scoffed and looked back at his hands once more, taking in a slow, shaking breath as he did so.

"But look at 'em all," he whispered, voice breaking. "*Look* at them, Tris." I took a hesitant step towards him, heart pounding in my chest as my boyfriend continued speaking, staring at the bodies before us. "There are sixty people lying there. *Sixty people* who died thinking it was some great release, some reward after everything they'd been through." He shook his head and looked down, pinching the bridge of his nose. "They don't get it. None of you *get it*."

"Jack," I began gently and reached out to rest my hand on his shoulder, but he spun around to face me before I could get close enough.

"Howell sent every single one of his commands to their deaths. Every single one of them died, to the last man, *except* for him!" His eyes were red with unshed tears, and I backed away as my boyfriend continued in pained anger, stepping forward and trying to articulate what he was saying with his hands. "He was so...so *enamored* with this idea that death is glory that he brainwashed his people, people who *trusted* him, into jumping the trenches to certain death, into sticking it out to the bitter end. No matter what that end tuned out to be!"

"Jack–"

"And the Brettain *shot them down* as they came!" His furiously shouted words reverberated off the walls of the trenches. And as he stood there, struggling to breathe, he shakily extended his hand towards me, showing me the objects he'd been holding.

Dog tags, I realized, feeling sick. At least sixty of them.

"This is what they've become! This...*this* is the end they come to!" he shouted, voice cracking and shoulders heaving with unsteady breaths.

"Jack, I'm not saying that Howell was right–" I tried, voice shaking as I eyed the tags, but he didn't seem to hear me.

"I *won't* be him! I will not make this–" he pointed to the scores of dead, voice rising in anger, "–*okay!* It's *not!*"

"I'm not saying it is," I pleaded, trying to placate him. "We just don't have a ch–"

"*We shouldn't be looking forward to this!*"

His shout echoed in the abandoned trench, and he backed away from me, tears in his eyes as he gestured helplessly to the air around us. When he continued, his voice was treacherously on the verge of breaking down.

"They – you shouldn't be *okay* with dying. Those officers back there, they shouldn't be trying to make martyrs of us all as though that somehow makes everything we've been through *okay!* You're all *kids*." His eyes were as helpless and pained as his voice as he struggled to continue. "You're *kids!* Dying shouldn't be the endgame for you guys, it should be going *home* – wherever the *hell* that is!"

"Jack..." I tried again, but he just shook his head, stopping my words as he placed his hands on the back of his head, tags still clenched in one hand while the fingers of the other twisted and gripped his hair until his knuckles were white. "Jack, please–" He just continued to shake his head, backing up hard into the trench wall and falling into a sitting position. His forearms slowly moved to brace against his knees as he bowed his head. I felt shaken, numb, standing there like a stranger.

Jack never sounded like this. He never *did* this. He wasn't the one who broke down. That was the rest of us.

And then, in the silence that followed, came the first sob.

DAY ONE HUNDRED AND FORTY-SIX, PART TWO

My breath froze in my chest at the ragged, broken sound. It was worse than any terror I'd seen on the battlefields, an image more distressing than the countless soldiers I'd seen die screaming. Jack Miller – my anchor, my strength – was sobbing into his arms, shoulders heaving shakily. His tears slowly cleared away strips of blood and grime that had hidden his face since this hell started, and I could see that his cheeks were flushed, his eyes swollen beneath the purpling bruises blotched across his skin. His brow furrowed against the pain burning in his chest, and his jaw clenched down on his sobs, teeth grinding together as his body tried to keep the sounds from escaping. He curled in on himself impossibly tighter, drawing his knees up closer to his body and locking his hands down on the back of his neck.

"Jack?" I whispered, slowly approaching and kneeling before him.

My own vision was blurred to the point of blindness, and I reached out to him, gently moving his hands from his neck and lifting his head so that we were looking at each other. His eyes were redder than I'd ever seen them, the strength of his dark irises lost in the spilling tears. As I looked at him, his brow furrowed painfully, mouth opening in a gasping sob, and the dam finally broke. The movement reopened some of the gashes on his face, and I gingerly wiped away the fresh blood, avoiding his bruises.

"Hey. It's okay," I whispered unsteadily and pulled him forward so that his head rested against my chest. I wrapped my arms tightly around his shoulders. "It's okay…you're okay."

A keening sob forced its way out of his throat despite his best efforts, and he locked his arms around me, seizing the back of my uniform in his hands and twisting the fabric in his fists until there was no way I could have pulled away. Not that I ever would have. I knew this pain too well.

"I know all their names," he sobbed into my shoulder. I took a deep breath, stroking his hair and tightening my grip. "I know *all* their names…"

"I know. I know you do," I whispered, blinking away my tears.

I looked at the rotting dead beside us, at their bloated, split, and discolored skin. I could hear the dog tags clenched in Jack's trembling hand shake against each other like dead leaves as he sobbed harder, and I flinched as he suddenly screamed in wordless pain and anger, slamming his fist repeatedly against my back in his anguish.

"It's okay," I whispered again, ignoring the sharp points of pain along my spine that I knew would turn into bruises. "It's okay, Jack. I'm here. It'll be okay. Just let it out…let it all out." My heart broke at the shuddering gasps in my ear and the soft cries of pain that accompanied each breath. I rubbed my hand in calming circles on his back and pressed my head against his shoulder.

"I'm right here, Jack. It's gonna be okay." A few minutes passed, and I was relieved when his breath's erratic pattern evened out slightly, though it was still peppered with brutal sobs. "You know, you're still a kid," I said softly. "At the Academy, four years seniority may have meant some-thing, but out here…you're just a kid, too."

"No," he whispered, voice a tortured gasp as his tears picked up again, and he weakly shook his head against me. "No one is…not after their first tour, not anymore."

I pulled away enough to look into my boyfriend's haggard face, at the haunted glaze in his eyes and the quivering of his chapped and split lips.

"You never told me about–" He shook his head, releasing a shivering sigh and looking down.

"I can't." I opened my mouth to say something, but he looked away from me to the graveyard. "Tris, I *see* their faces…every single one of them. And I don't mean just them." I looked to the dead beside us, body swaying with every unsteady breath Jack struggled through. "I mean from my *first* assignment…my second…*third*." He shook his head and pulled away from me, dropping back heavily against the mud embankment and staring up at the sky above us. "I see them every minute of every day." He forcefully wiped tears from his eyes and looked down at me. His voice broke down into a pained whisper over his next few words. "And...and I can't help but see you in them, too. Because I know..." He took in a deep breath and centered himself, driving the heels of his palms into his eyes. "I know that before this is over more of you are going to die, and *you* might be one of them." He looked disgusted with himself, filled with self-hatred as more tears fell. "And I'll most likely make it out *again*."

Exhausted, he let his head drop down to rest on his knees. His fingers ran over the lettering of the dog tags, committing to memory every number, every name.

"I just want to go home," he finally whispered, voice gummed up by sobs, and another wave of tears forced their way to his eyes once more. "I want us all to go home." He ran his free hand through his hair, trying to shake away the heavy blanket of desperation still clinging to him. "And that's...*that's* why I'm not waiting for the Brettain to kill us all. That's why we're all falling back when I tell us to." He looked back up from the tags, staring out over the putrid bodies we'd grown accustomed to smelling. He looked beaten, defeated, as he continued to cry. "I want...I want those of us still left to make it home. Just this once, I want us to go *home*."

We fell silent. And as I carefully watched my loved one wipe away tears he hadn't realized he was still crying, I couldn't help but hear Jax's voice from so long ago. His words from that morning in his office so long ago just kept repeating in my head, so I kneeled in Jack's zoned out line of sight and placed my hands on his knees.

"Jax told me something the day of Promenade. Well, actually, he was telling me off for accepting the fact that I was most probably going to die out here. Wasn't like I listened, of course."

My boyfriend looked at me silently, his eyes flat and dull. Listless. Once that comment would have made him smirk. I continued gently.

"He said that true bravery is when you embrace the fact that you're going to survive. Because surviving is sometimes worlds worse than dying." I gave a sad smile, and Jack took in a deep, quieting breath. "At the time, I thought he was just talking about Id. But then he told me that when people come back from the war, they've got skeletons in their closets. And...well, Id's weren't exactly hidden, were they?"

Jack looked down, fingers running over the bloody and rusted chains. I continued, tightening my grip in comfort.

"He told me not to fool myself...that everyone had them, even if they didn't let me see that they did. And I didn't realize it then, but I think he was talking about you that time." I paused, waiting as Jack tried to scrub the tears from his lashes and hide his flushed skin and puffy eyes. "Hey." I reached out and stilled his hands, leaning forward to gently kiss him. His lips were rough and tasted like salt – from the tears or blood, or both, I wasn't sure. I pulled back enough to continue talking.

"I love you. You hear me?" He nodded, and I could feel his unsteady breath on my lips. "*I love you*. And I'm sorry I never saw that you had all of this inside."

Jack laughed lightly, a tired, exhausted sound, and slowly got to his feet. I rose with him, hand resting on the small of his back, and he gave me a quick, habitual kiss on the forehead as he started backing away. It left me feeling empty and gutted instead of comforted.

"Don't be," he mumbled, straightening his shoulders and rubbing at his eyes. "I made sure you didn't see it."

I watched him drop the tags back into his pocket and start back to the rest of our unit. I knew that he needed space after what had just happened, but there was one question I had to ask.

"Do you get the nightmares?" I called after him, my voice surprisingly steady. My boyfriend stopped, shoulders sagging, and looked back at me as though debating whether or not to tell the truth. Then, heaving a sigh and running his hands over his face, he gave his answer, his grim confession.

"Some days are worse than others."

And with that he was gone, leaving me to watch the ravens settle upon the corpses and restart their morbid work.

· · · — — — · · ·

"Sir, we've gotten 'most everything into position!" Bates shouted, and I watched as Jack went about his responsibilities, pointing people in different directions and giving orders.

"Captain!" Jack joined the younger lieutenant Williams and gestured for him to continue. "We've got the barricades up." I followed my boyfriend and looked at the stacked boxes, crates, and tarps. "The containers used to hold medical supplies, food, ammunition. Jayce and the Horsemen emptied them, filled them with debris and mud instead."

"Where did we put supplies?" he asked, looking sharply at his officer, and the man made a face.

"Well, sir, there isn't much left," he admitted but pointed down a ways to the obscured infirmary. "We used part of what was left over to give the doctor as much protective shielding as we could. He's got the rest of the supplies back there with some spillover into the body dump. We tried our best to keep the munitions out of the way of direct gunfire so they don't, well, you know."

Jack nodded and took a deep breath, rubbing his hands together to try to banish the cold.

"Alright, good work Williams. Assemble the people we have left."

As the man ran off, Jack walked through the gathered knot of soldiers and climbed up a few rungs of the ladder to the surface so he could look over us. I headed over to him, leaning up against the trench wall below him.

"Time for a rousing speech?" I asked, looking up at him, and he took in a deep breath, nodding.

"Seems like it's about time for one of those, doesn't it?" he admitted, voice too even, and I scoffed, forcing myself to seem calm, and crossed my arms.

People slowly filed out to stand before us, staring up at our leader with sunken eyes. I could see people from platoons 304, 307, and our own 306. But as I looked closer, I realized that no one remained from 305.

"One hundred and forty people," Jack began after a few moments, and I looked at the people gathered before us. "There were one hundred and forty people when we first left the Academy, and even then...we were already losing friends before we even set foot in these trenches." People looked down, battered bodies shifting on blistered and weary feet. "And now – now, there are eighty of you here, eighty of you who've either made it this far or just gotten real damn lucky.

"Whichever it is, you've survived, and if you survive just a little longer, we'll be home by month's end." People looked at each other, eyes glimmering with something akin to hope. "I know our orders were to hold this line for a year until the next group comes to take our place. But that's not going to happen – not this time. Like the G.A. told us, the Brettain are winning this war, and their queen is making sure no one pulls any punches.

"At the moment, our opponents have stopped firing. This is not a sign of weakness or reprieve. They're gonna come running over No Man's Land while their artillery makes it hell down here for us. We are going to die in a massive bloodbath if we sit here, so that's not what we're going to do."

I could see Marcel and Jayce muttering to each other, and my temper flared.

"You have something you want to say, Jones?" I called, voice cracking, and Jack looked down at me in surprise. "Either one of you?"

Marcel looked at me, eyes speaking volumes more than her mouth as she mutely shook her head.

"Nothing you don't already know," she answered, arms crossed. Jayce nodded in agreement.

"Then shut up and listen," I snapped. Jack dropped down into the mud beside me and put a hand on my shoulder.

"Easy, Tris," he whispered before addressing his command once more. "I know you think that this is a tactical disadvantage. And I'll be honest with you – it is. But we stand a larger chance of surviving and making it out of here if we fall back and regroup with Captain Harper at the last possible moment." He paused, as though contemplating what he was going to say next. When he continued, I looked down, the first genuine smile I'd had in months pulling gently at my lips. But it felt wrong – ghoulish, even – on my face, like the grin on a skull, so I stopped. It really wasn't anything to be smiling about anyways.

"But that's not what you were all programmed to think, is it?" Jack was saying, and I looked back up at him. "We've been taught to think that our lives mean less than a tactical advantage. That's why there are only eighty of us left – eighty stubborn, battered soldiers.

"You have to be some of the bravest people I've ever had the pleasure of serving with. But I was told something about bravery that you need to know." His eyes flickered briefly to my hunched form. "You've always been told that death is the end goal, that it's all we have to look forward to. Don't listen to them. Don't embrace death. Embrace living. Embrace the idea that you're going to survive, because surviving…" He paused. "Surviving is sometimes so much worse than ending up like those sixty people who aren't standing beside you anymore. Surviving means that you'll see their ghosts every day for the rest of your lives.

"But someone has to live. Someone has to survive long enough to have something other than war. Let it be us. Fight now not for death but for life. Fight for survival. Fight for a future with your loved ones and your families – whether they are waiting for you at home or don't exist yet." He stopped and saw that everyone was staring at him a bit oddly.

"Don't fight until you die. Fight until you're *about* to die. And then run for your lives. That's my final order." He walked forward, his expression unreadable as the remains of our unit parted before him. I quickly set off after him.

I didn't get very far.

"We need to talk." I looked down to where Marcel's hand was latched onto my upper arm and glanced up at her mildly. "You told me he could make that call," she hissed, livid.

"I guess I was wrong," I responded coldly and pulled my arm free from her grip, continuing on and rubbing my bruised skin and bone as I went. For some reason I didn't really care that Jack hadn't been able to make the call. Part of me was relieved.

In fact, as I looked around at everyone, I couldn't help but notice that there was a light of hope in their eyes. There was something defiant in the desperation that we all faced. Five months of hell, and finally, *finally*, there was a light at the end of the tunnel. I made my way towards the med tent and pushed open the flap to see Blackwell bent over a nearly empty drawer, collecting everything he had and putting it into a battered leather satchel. It looked like it had seen nearly as much as the old man.

"What're you doing?" I asked, weaving my way towards him through the bustling nurses and troops.

"Mobility, Tristan," he said over his shoulder, grizzled face tired as he continued to pack. "When the Brettain come over the trenches, we'll need to bail fast. And I'm not going to have time to take down this tent *yet again*, so I'm grabbing what I can now. You want to help?"

"I'd love to, but I'm needed out there. I made a plan."

He raised an eyebrow and walked over to me to grab some equipment behind my legs.

"Oh, is that right?" he muttered as he bent over, and I nodded, crossing my arms.

"Yeah. It's a pretty good plan, too. A bit out of the box, but it's solid."

He sadly shook his head, setting the supplies he'd gathered on one of the gurneys and putting a hand on my shoulder.

"Don't hold too fast to hope, Byrne," he warned, expression grim. "I've been in this situation more times than I can count with Howell, and the only reason we weren't all butchered was that he held his ground. He made it too costly for the Brettain to continue."

My stomach churned.

"If you're trying to say that Jack made the wrong call trying to save our lives, you had better shut up right now," I warned, and he backed off a few paces, holding his hands up at shoulder height. But I could tell he didn't mean it, wasn't convinced, and when I continued, I was almost shouting. "He has done nothing but give and give to this war! And now when he finally has a chance to make the war give *us* something, everyone's hating him for it!"

"Calm down, Tristan," Blackwell ordered, gesturing to the wounded around us. "I have patients in here, and you're being disruptive." He put a hand on my shoulder and guided me towards the back of his infirmary, voice low as he spoke. With every word, my anger mounted. "I understand what you're feeling right now. But you must also understand that whatever you two have planned countermands the very nature of this war."

"Maybe that's how people need to start thinking in order to end it," I snapped and pulled away from him, blindly leaving the tent and looking around at everyone. People were moving with purpose, hefting crates and any bit of debris they could to create shielding for themselves. This was it.

"You've got that look."

I turned my head to see Irina leaning against an artillery gun, injured arm held close to her body.

"What look?" She shrugged.

"The one of a person not sure they're going to survive."

I glanced at the angry skin visible beneath her torn shirt, the red flesh swollen around her collarbone.

"You speaking from experience?" I asked, my words almost indifferent, and she followed my gaze.

"It's nothing," she lied, pulling the torn strips of her uniform back over her wound, and I shook my head.

"Look, I've spent enough time with Blackwell here and the nurses at the Academy to know that's infected. And if you don't get that looked at, it's gonna get really bad."

She rolled her eyes.

"I've already got a fever, Byrne," she snapped, voice dripping with false bravado. "I've got the tremors and the cold sweats. It *is* really bad."

Her eyes flashed defiantly, daring me to say something, challenging me to tell her what to do. But I said nothing. The silence between us dragged out, leaving us standing there and looking at each other while everyone else continued to hurry by. When she continued, her voice was dogged and soft.

"So, you can either drag me to Blackwell when we both know that he doesn't have the medication for me, or you can let me die with a gun in my hands, doing some good for the rest of us." I looked down, shifting on my feet. "It's your choice."

Something heavy settled in my gut at those words. Something cold and detached started to freeze over my heart. And finally, I shook my head and looked up at her with solemn eyes. I couldn't bring myself to fight her anymore.

"No. It's yours. And I'm going to respect that."

She nodded once in thanks before we both moved off to help tie rope to the artillery and pull them into place. We had work to do.

··· ─ ─ ─ ···

In a matter of a few hours, we had completely reconfigured the landscape of our trenches. Debris from collapsed sections had been carried over on gurneys to create earth barriers for infantry while we used whatever we could to shield the combat-facing side of the infirmary. The artillery guns were primed and loaded, facing the Brettain lines, and the infantry were lined up in their corresponding places. Jack and I stood side by side next to Aliyah's artillery gun, and Jayce stepped up to man a second one, Marcel taking the position of his guard.

The battlefield was hushed, silent, held captive in a frozen moment in time. Smoke and fog slowly invaded the air around us, the ghostly masses waiting with bated breath as it covered everything in a thick, unearthly dusk. And in the silence crushing down on all of us, suffocating us with its heavy, cold air, I looked up at the sky above us. The clouds seemed unending, just as they had been since we'd arrived. But closer examination revealed something glittering just beyond the leaden veil.

"Jack," I whispered, pointing upwards, and he followed my gaze. "Are those stars?"

He squinted at the smudge of light high above, and I looked at him, taking in the bruises, dirt, and blood streaked across his face. His skin was broken with fresh cuts and scabs from shrapnel and Howell's abuse. Yet, below the trauma, there was something pure.

"You know what?" he breathed, a smile ghosting over his features. "I think it might be."

"Will you two shags quit star-gazing?" Unamused, the two of us looked down from the sky and over our shoulder at Katalin. She was tensely shifting from foot to foot, hands wrapped tightly around her rifle as she stared out over No Man's Land. It didn't matter. The enemy lines were invisible in the eddying, ever-changing gray. "You should be more focused on what's down here." Her eyes flickered to us briefly, and she cleared her throat as Jack continued to look at her in amusement. "Respectfully. Sir."

Suddenly, a loud whistling pierced the air.

"Incoming!" Aliyah called.

Before the shell even touched down, we were returning fire of our own, the guns executing their staggered volleys flawlessly as hands loaded round after round of shells. A loud explosion went off a couple hundred feet to the right of where our artillery was, and I felt relief flicker in the back of my mind. Our opponents were still using our gunners' old locations, as they should be.

We had some time before they regrouped.

"They're coming! Thirty feet!"

Jack looked around at the shout and ran forward to the edge of the trenches with me close behind. He set his gun up against the top and waited as the last of Unit 37 fell into place beside him. The shadowy figures of the Brettain infantry were approaching through the haze, and my breath caught in my throat as I realized just how many people were coming towards us.

There had to be almost forty of them.

"That's twenty feet," I whispered, and Jack nodded.

"Ready!" We pulled back the hammers in unison, our captain's hushed voice guiding us. "Aim...fire!"

We pulled the trigger, and most of the Brettain collapsed, falling back like targets we'd shot at in the Academy. But just as I was starting to get excited, the shadows' guns went off in a crack of lead rain, and our own people snapped back like the target boards I'd seen the Brettain as. It was a cycle – a vicious, cruel cycle. And as we settled into a routine, I couldn't help but wonder how long we would last.

Because no matter how many times we shot or how well we aimed, the Brettain just kept coming.

... — — ...

"Get down!" Jack ducked as the closest rank of enemy soldiers fired at an almost point-blank range into our trenches. Unfortunately, some weren't fast enough, and my boyfriend swore under his breath as Bates and Song collapsed beside us. Two hours later, our gunners had still failed to take out the enemy's artillery all the way, and we were still hanging on by our fingernails.

Twenty-three of us had paid the price for it.

"Another volley!" Jack shouted, and we fired over the trenches. "Fire at will!" Another section of the wall collapsed under the bombardment of the Brettain artillery, and my boyfriend shouted wordlessly in frustration, spinning on his heel to face the guns beside us. "Moore, get those guns *down!*"

"Shift us to the left!" she yelled back, and Jack signaled for a few of our infantry to run over and pull the guns to a different angle. "Restarting!" I covered my ears as the booming began again but nearly jumped for joy at the sound of an explosion from the opposite side. The Brettain artillery stopped firing.

"Finally! Keep it going!" Jack shouted, and I quickly glanced over the top of trench, eyes wide and heart pounding. "Tristan, how are we doing?"

I quickly, vehemently, shook my head.

"Jack, they're right on top of us, and there're a lot of them. I'd say around fifteen feet and–" I risked another quick look before ducking back down "–at least seventy people. I'm pretty sure there's more though. And no one's coming to take out the artillery."

Jack paused, expression vacant as his mind raced, and I spoke the hated words that had started growing in the back of my mind over an hour ago. "We need a new plan. I'm sorry. I'm sorry, Jack, mine's not gonna work." Finally he came to a decision and turned to shout his new instructions.

"Moore, drop the plan! Keep alternate volleys with the artillery while we narrow down those on foot further down the trench. Let's go!"

But before we could move, the Brettain infantry returned fire, and four people went crashing down into the mud. My heart sank as I saw that two of them were Lieutenants Wilson and Williams. We'd just lost all of our trained officers. Immediately, we returned to their positions, shooting down the approaching Brettain, and Jack quickly grabbed my shoulder, pulling me back hard against the trench beside him.

"Tris, I need you to go tell Blackwell to start clearing people out. This isn't going to last much longer. Go!"

I nodded and set off running, tripping and falling over the debris of collapsed barricades in my blind rush. The shock of the ground beneath my hands spiked violently up my arms, and my cheek slammed painfully against the boot of some dead private. My vision tilted, and I faintly heard something crack in my shoulder before I was pushing myself back up, brushing the dirt and blood off my scraped hands as I ran.

"Doc!" I shouted as soon as I was in earshot, and the man stuck his head outside the tent, frenzied and wide-eyed. "You need to start clearing out! Jack says we're not going to last." He nodded, and, with seemingly inhuman speed, nurses started helping patients out into the open, guiding them down the trench and towards Harper's unit.

That was if Unit 36 was even still alive, I realized and quickly ran back over to the site of all the fighting. Fifteen more people laid dead on the ground, and Jack was motioning for the troops to fall back down the line. I hurried over to his side, the farm girl's rifle at the ready, as he shouted his orders.

"Keep the volleys coming just a little longer!" Someone else screamed as a bullet hit home, and Jack looked around to where Aliyah and Jayce were still firing the artillery. "Moore, Jones, let's go!" The two of them waved their team away and dropped down to the mud, lifting their weapons to the ready position and joining us.

My hands were shaking as I trained my sight on a dark figure atop the ridge and pulled the trigger. It toppled forward, and I looked into the face of the enemy for the first time in months. The soldier laid there in the mud, dead eyes staring at nothing.

He still looked just like us.

But I still didn't have the time to dwell on that. I still only had time to point, aim, and shoot – just as Maggie said so long ago. And *don't miss*. But as fate would have it, it seemed none of us had a lot of time. Two more people collapsed along our thinning line, and our captain had enough. Jack's hand clamped down on my shoulder, pulling me away with him.

"Fall back!" he shouted, voice cracking.

And we did. We turned tail and ran, firing over our shoulders when we were certain we weren't about to hit our friends. But mostly though, we just took Jack's order to heart. I dug my split and dirty nails into my boyfriend's hand as we sprinted through the killing field and wove through the debris, scrambling over our collapsed walls to retreat farther and farther back into our own trenches.

Fight until you're about to die. And then run for your lives.

So we ran.

And with every step I could hear Jack's breath come punching out of his lungs. His abandoned rifle thudded sharply against his running legs, and I followed the bloodied strap up from the metal to his body. To the hand gripping tightly to mine. To the arm crossing his own torso. To the other hand pressed tightly against his skin. To the long fingers struggling to find purchase along the curve of his ribs.

And finally to the dark veins of blood seeping between them.

DAY ONE HUNDRED AND FORTY-SEVEN

0100 hours

"Okay," Jack gasped, finally allowing our company's jog to slow to a staggering walk. "Okay, I think we're far enough." He sighed in relief, the breath coming to a painful halt as he jerkily stopped mid-step, groaning and brow furrowing in pain. His hand was completely red against his side, and I quickly pressed my hand on top of his, grabbing his shoulder to hold us both steady.

"I'm getting Blackwell," I whispered tensely to him, but Jack doggedly shook his head.

"It's just another graze. I'm okay," he mumbled above me, and I gently pulled his hand away from the singed and soaked fabric of his shirt to look at the bloody score across his ribs.

"Yeah, and it only *just* stopped bleeding," I countered, eyes flicking once up to him before returning to the burned skin before me. "Don't think I didn't notice. I would have said something but–"

"We were a bit busy running for our lives," he finished. He placed his hand on mine and gently pulled it away from his side to hold it tightly in his. "It's just a graze. Hurts like hell, but it's a *graze*."

"You've lost blood–" I tried repeating.

"And I can stand to lose just a little more," he pressed, voice tired and pained but kind. "Look, we keep walking until we get to Harper. Then we can stop to patch up our injuries." I looked down at my red-stained hand, slowly watching my fingers curl around his. "Okay?" I nodded reluctantly and looked back up at him.

"Okay. But I'm—"

"If I start to feel dizzy, I'll let you know."

I rolled my eyes, and he grunted in pain as I wrapped my arm around his waist, pulling the hand I'd been holding over my shoulder.

"I'm not waiting for you to feel dizzy, you idiot. 'Cause if I do, you're not gonna say anything," I muttered, and we headed after the rest of our unit, Jack steadily leaning on me more as the adrenaline and shock wore off and the pain fully set in.

I didn't know how long we had been running. All I knew was that we'd outpaced the Brettain behind us and were in the clear for the time being. But as I looked at the people around me, I couldn't help but wonder if we would ever be in the clear. Five months ago, we had started out as one hundred and forty. Then we were eighty. And now...

Now, we were thirty-five.

As I watched my boyfriend's tightly drawn face beside me, Jack looked down at the pocket of his jacket and slipped his bloodied hand inside.

"What is it?" I asked, but he just wearily shook his head and pulled a tangled mass of dog tags just far enough out of their hiding place that I could recognize them for what they were. "Jack..." I whispered sadly, and he cleared his throat, withdrawing his hand and staring at the trench ahead of us with empty eyes.

"So close," he breathed, voice heavy and exhausted. Those two words, coupled with those eyes, the tags, and the blood – *his* blood – drying on my hands...they made me feel sick.

"Tristan!"

I looked over my shoulder to see Blackwell hurrying over, breathing heavily.

"You okay?" I asked, and he waved my concern aside.

"Just an old man. You forgot something in the med tent, and I thought I'd..." His eyes lit upon my stained hand and quickly shifted to Jack, catching glimpse of his shirt beneath Howell's jacket. *"Miller!"*

My boyfriend gave the man a wan smile as the medic reached out for his bloodied side.

"Hey, doc."

"Gods damn it, kid! Why didn't you say something?" he snapped, glaring at Jack and shooing me aside with disapprovingly narrowed eyes.

"We were a bit busy," he offered half-heartedly, and Blackwell scowled.

"That is not a good reason to not say something about being shot," he hissed, yanking his bag open and pulling out a suture needle and thread.

"No, doc. *No*," Jack groaned, pushing forward again. "I'm not going to have everyone stop moving so you can stitch me up." But his retreat was quickly stopped when the older man reached out and grabbed the back of Jack's collar.

"You are going to sit down right now, and you're going to let me stitch you up. Or I will call Marcel and Korsakov over to hold you down," the man growled, and Jack slowly sat down, shooting the doctor a dark look. "Thank you. *Sir*."

"Why're we stopping?"

Jack and I looked over our shoulders to see Marcel heading towards us just as Blackwell roughly pulled off Howell's coat. I winced as my boyfriend stiffened and hissed in pain.

"Will you *watch* it?" he groaned, but the doctor didn't answer him. He just set the coat to the side and opened his bag.

"Miller!"

I waved Marcel back, and her quickening pace slowed a little. Katalin and Korsakov hovered a few feet behind War, as though trying to decide whether or not to follow, and I gave a small sigh of relief when the two women pressed their lips together and turned away, calling for a company halt. Marcel kept walking.

We didn't need any more prying eyes at the moment.

"Why're we stopping?" the shorter woman repeated, and I looked to Jack in response, to the blood seeping through the side of his shirt.

"Jack got shot." The words sounded hollow in my ears, unreal, and their weight suddenly hit me. *Jack got shot*. Marcel's eyes widened in fear, and she quickly shouldered past me to kneel before our captain. "Almost," I amended, and my pounding heart slowed just a little.

Jack almost *got shot*.

Marcel heaved a sigh of relief, her tense shoulders slumping as she let her head drop down against her knee.

"Well, *open* with the 'almost' next time, shrimp!" she laughed, the sound tight and reflexive as she looked over her shoulder at me. "You damn near gave me a heart attack!" She turned her dirtied face back to look at Jack. "You okay?" There was a hard concern to her voice that made my stomach turn, and my boyfriend gave her a wan smile.

"Picture of health," he offered half-heartedly but then nodded almost imperceptibly when Marcel continued to glare. Blackwell pulled out a suture kit and expertly threaded the needle, moving the sharp point to the ravaged skin in the same, practiced motion. "I'm *fine*. It practically missed me."

"Practically being the important word there," I countered.

Jack raised an eyebrow in tired acknowledgement only to grunt in pain and brace a fist against his knee. Blackwell looked up at him with a withering expression, bloodied fingers holding the hooked needle still where it was embedded in my boyfriend's side. I suddenly felt queasy.

"Holding still would be much appreciated," he said dryly. Jack took in as deep of a breath as he could before tensely nodding and looking forward again. His eyes glassed over as he forced himself to relax and spaced out. "Brace yourself, kid." Blackwell's lips pressed together grimly as he bent his head closer to his work, pulling the torn skin back together and preparing to plunge the needle in.

And Jack immediately tensed again, eyes squeezing shut. His breathing was painfully controlled.

"Hey," I whispered, slowly sinking to my knees in front of Jack. Marcel quickly got up to give us some space as he opened his eyes to look at me. I couldn't read them. "It'll be fine." I blindly reached out and grabbed his hand, smiling despite the way our skin stuck together, the coagulating blood tacky between our fingers. "Just focus on me. Doc'll be done before you know it."

Another terse nod, and I nearly swore as he tightened his hand around mine, his fingers grinding my joints together as we both clenched our jaws for different reasons.

"Try to stop getting shot, and we can all avoid this more often, Miller," Blackwell chastised, his gently scolding words spoken for no other reason than to break the silence as he continued to stitch up Jack's side. "What is this, the second time?"

Jack didn't answer. Instead, he just closed his eyes and shifted his grip on my hand so that he was no longer trying to snap my bones. I glanced at to his wound and saw that the doctor had been moving at a ruthless pace, and he was already finishing up, tying off the heavy black thread holding Jack together. Honestly, I was surprised that Jack hadn't passed out.

"You keep this up, next time you're not gonna be so lucky, kid," the doctor continued, sighing as he rocked back on his heels and put his tools back in his bag. "Third time's the charm." He handed Howell's coat back to Jack, his expression serious. "And the way I see it, the Brettain have missed twice already."

I swallowed painfully at those words and quickly stood, pulling Jack's arm over my shoulder to help him stand.

"Thanks, Tristan. I'm okay," he whispered, words soft and reassuring, before looking back to our medic. "Then, I'll make sure they don't get a third chance, doc." He gave that same cavalier, crooked smirk before pressing a quick kiss to my temple and stepping away to address the rest of our group. "Okay, guys. Let's get moving again."

I sighed and crossed my arms, watching him as he all but sauntered off and waved people's concern away. As though he hadn't just literally dodged a bullet.

"I can't tell if he's brave or foolish," Blackwell grumbled, rising from his crouched position and dusting off his knees. "Ah, well. I'll just keep patching him up for you." I scoffed in tired thanks, and his eyes lit up as if he'd suddenly remembered something. "Oh, here. I grabbed this for you on my way out."

My eyes widened as he pulled two objects from his bag.

"Oh my gods." I reached out and took them into my hands.

"I couldn't grab the whole bag given how much else I had to carry, but I did manage to get these two for you."

It was Idris' dog tag and Mars pendant – the one still stained with her blood even after all this time.

"Given the state of this one, and the fact that the other's a tag…well, I figured they were the important ones."

He was right. They were the only two that mattered.

"Thanks, doc," I whispered and stared at the necklaces with saddened eyes before pulling them on over my head, tucking them in with Maggie's and my tags. "Won't lose them this way."

"Tristan!"

I looked up at Jack and waved to let him know I heard him.

"The captain calls," I said apologetically, but the old man just smiled and shooed me away. Thanking him once more, I headed over to my boyfriend, limping slightly as my weary legs protested at the fast movement. Apparently I'd landed harder on my knee than I'd originally thought when I'd fallen in my mad dash to the med tent. "What is it?"

"Oh, nothing." He draped his arm back around my shoulders and immediately shifted his gait so he could lean on me a little bit, alleviating the strain on his side. "I just wanted to see you before everything goes to hell again."

"What do you mean *again?* We're out."

"No," he sighed, shaking his head and staring off with distant eyes. "I won't be able to convince Harper to fall back." A bitter, wry smirk forced its way to his mouth. "But I'll try my best." I thought about that for a little before a rather dark thought came up.

"What if Unit 36 was overrun, and he's dead?"

He thought about it for a little bit.

"Well, in that case, screw this. We're going home."

... — — — ...

We weren't so lucky.

When we arrived at Harper's command, we were greeted with a setting very much like the one we'd just left. A few stalwart privates had managed to stay alive, and they were running around trying to patch up the holes in their sinking front line and effectively ignoring us as we stumbled into their encampment. Not that we could blame them. We knew what was coming as well as they did because the Brettain were silent and still, biding their time across the way.

It was the same strategy that had taken us down and left us here.

"Look, I don't care how low our supplies are!" a highly frustrated voice shouted, and Jack motioned for us to wait where we were as he approached the sentry outside the captain's tent. "We need to hold off the Brettain or else we're all going to die. You understand me?"

"Private," Jack began, coming to a stop before the man and nodding a greeting. "I'm Corporal Miller from Unit 37. It's urgent that I speak with your captain."

The soldier stared at our leader with narrowed eyes for a few seconds before turning and opening the flap of the tent, relaying the information at a volume too low for us to hear. The captain's response, though, was clear as day.

"*Miller?*" The tent opened up to reveal a disheveled and bearded Harper staring at Jack like he was a miracle. "My gods, it *is* you!" Giving a disbelieving laugh, the man seized my boyfriend's hand and shook it. "It's so good to see you right now, corporal. You've got no idea."

"The feeling's mutual, sir," Jack replied, lying through his teeth, and his superior shook his head, smiling despite himself.

"We thought you were all dead. Where's Howell?" he asked.

Jack swallowed, averting his gaze, and I fought the urge to step closer to him.

"He didn't make it."

Harper's expression faltered strangely, and I saw his gaze flicker down to the nametag on Jack's coat, to the old blood staining the bullet hole to the chest and the fresher red along his side.

"Well, how about Wilson? Bates? Williams? Song?" But Jack just shook his head, and the man let out a sigh of incredulity. "Who's left?" Silently, my boyfriend pointed over to where we were standing, expressions grim, and Harper massaged his forehead. "Gods. So few. So few of you made it."

"The Brettain broke the line behind us," Jack explained, drawing the captain's attention once more. "We held them off as long as we could before we got out of there." The man before us suddenly looked guilty, and Jack sighed and looked down with a bitter grimace. "Let me guess. You're not falling back." Harper had the grace to at least look ashamed.

"I know you want to get out of here. Given what you've been through, I can't blame you," he began, and I watched as Jack nodded in reluctant acknowledgement of what he was saying. "But...look, you have to understand. I *need* more men to hold the Brettain off." At that moment, Jack's expression grew stony and harsh. "I know you all want to bail, but I can't afford to just let replacement troops go–"

Bone crushed against bone, and Harper stumbled away from the nearly six-foot mass of rage before him, nose bloodied and probably broken.

"You *son of a bitch*," Jack spat, infuriated. "You're no better than that bastard Howell!"

Harper stared at his opponent, measuring him up as he slowly stood up straight. Neither of us missed the way Jack swayed slightly on his feet as he raised his voice. His hand subconsciously touched his wounded side, and I could hear him softly groan.

"You're the one wearing his coat," the captain pointed out, words quiet and challenging, but my boyfriend shook his head.

"I am *not* like him! *I* know how to be a decent human being!"

He turned back to us, pointing Blackwell and his six remaining patients towards the medical tent and waving the rest of us over.

"Alright, this is your call," he began once we were gathered. "We can either walk out or we can stay here."

"You're not walking out," Harper called, wiping blood from his face. We looked over to him, disdain glowing in our eyes. The memory of *liking* this man felt so distant.

"Why is that?" Marcel demanded, crossing her arms angrily.

"Because you know how to help us. The Brettain used this strategy on you. You know what's coming." Howell seemed desperate, his eyes slightly wild. "Help us prepare. Help us fight!"

But Jack just shook his head, and his bloodied knuckles tightened into fists once more.

"We've seen enough fighting for a lifetime."

"You're an honorable man, Miller," Harper pressed, earnestly, and I rolled my eyes, disgusted at the lowness of his plea. "Don't throw that away because you're homesick."

"I am not *homesick*," Jack snarled, anger mounting exponentially as he turned around all the way to face the ragged captain. His eyes were blazing, his words malicious and livid. "I am *sick* of warmongering bastards like you treating us like we're disposable!"

Around us, I could see Harper's unit turn their fearful eyes to watch us. As I looked at them, I couldn't help but see our own scared faces, couldn't help but hear the first incoming shell when the Brettain relaunched their attack. And, feeling sick to my stomach, I knew the only course of action available to us. I reached out and put a hand on Jack's shoulder, voice soft as I got his attention.

"Jack." He looked to me, his temper abating ever so slightly. "Harper's right." His brow furrowed in confusion, and my heart broke at the light of betrayal in his eyes. "Look, I want to go home more than anything, but we are talking about abandoning people who need help. We'd be leaving them to their deaths."

"We deserve to go home," he protested. I just stared at him, waiting for him to calm down.

"So do they," I whispered, and he stopped his arguing. "Look at us and then look at them. They deserve to go home, too." His focus shifted over my shoulder, and I half-turned to look at the last of us with him.

Miraculously, the Horsemen were still standing. Jayce hovered over his sister's shoulder, and Korsakov looked like she was about pass out. Twenty-nine other privates I didn't know by name stood at attention as well, and a closer examination proved what I had already suspected. The Horsemen, Jayce, me, Jack...the seven of us were the only ones left from Platoon 306. Everyone else was gone.

"Fine," Jack muttered, looking around at Harper. "We'll help. But I swear to the gods, if I lose any more men I am taking it out on you." He faced us once more as he backed away towards the command tent. "Get some rack time, thirty-seven. You've earned it."

"Brave of you, Byrne," Marcel commented as we headed for the field hospital. "You know, almost suicidal."

"I'm not trying to get us killed," I retorted as we went, staying close to each other. "I'm just trying to give the others a fighting chance, too." I pushed open the flap to the med tent and immediately was overwhelmed by the metallic smell of blood and the moans of the wounded.

"How noble," Kat deadpanned, but I didn't engage either her or Marcel further. Instead, I searched the dying and the injured for a single face. Maybe, *just* maybe he was still here...

"Byrne?"

I turned around at the tired voice and found myself face to face with the man I'd been looking for. A bandage wrapped around his head, passing over his left eye. His right hand was also heavily taped and bandaged, and from the way it was wrapped, I could tell he was missing several fingers. His skin was burned in a few places, though not horribly, and I knew what had happened.

"Faulty artillery shell?" I asked as I sat on the bed beside him. Andrew nodded wearily.

"How'd you know?"

"Same thing killed Alec Jackson." I looked down at my friend, taking in the same drawn features that had come over us all. "You look like hell."

He laughed.

"Not so hot yourself."

I snorted, a non-verbal ghost of a smile, before reaching inside my shirt and pulling Idris' dog tag and Mars pendant over my head. Immediately, he gasped and gratefully took the objects from my extended hand.

"Oh my gods."

"Jack managed to hang back and grab those from her on the road. He closed her eyes, too. Put her in a peaceful position with some grain in her hands since, uh, since there were no flowers. But he did his best to give her the respect she deserved. He didn't have a chance to get them to you before we split ways."

He looked up at me from the two necklaces, suddenly fearful.

"Did your boy make it, too?" I nodded, smiling ever so slightly. "Gods, Miller's one tough son of a bitch."

"He's our captain now. Though I guess now that we're back here he's a corporal again." His eye widened in surprise, and I lowered my voice as I leaned towards him. "Don't tell anyone, but he killed Howell. The running story is the bastard was killed by enemy fire if anyone asks. I just figured that you deserved the truth."

Instead of looking disturbed or startled, Andrew just smiled to himself, closing his eye and leaning back in his bed with a content expression on his face.

"I knew it. I *knew* that gods-damn monster had it coming," he sighed, finally at peace, and I rested a hand on his shoulder. "How's it looking out there? It's been quiet for a couple of hours now..."

"The Brettain'll be coming over the trenches soon," I sighed, squeezing his shoulder a little. "That's what they did to us." Harris nodded and then, to my surprise, sat up, swinging his legs out of the bed. "Um, where do you think you're going?"

"Oh, I'm not in here for treatment," he explained, noting my scolding eyes. "They haven't got any more medicine for us, so I'm here for the rack time." He gave a lopsided grin. "I'll be right there alongside you punks when this all goes down."

Suddenly, the tent door opened up, and I looked over my shoulder to see Jack standing there, panicked and breathing heavily with a hand pressed over his injured side. I rose from the mattress, heart in my throat.

"What is it?"

"The Brettain are half-way across No Man's Land," he panted, gesturing to the line. "They must be going for a gods-damn ambush, must have figured we'd warn thirty-six about their tactics. Get everyone ready at the trenches to start firing." He was about to go sprinting back to wherever else he was needed when he stopped and turned back around. "Good to see you, Harris."

"You, too, *sir*," he joked and clapped me on the shoulder, grabbing my arm and using me to stand up. "Time to go kick some ass. Right, Byrne?"

Despite myself, I smirked and nodded, quickly walking alongside him to reload our guns at the weapons station and load up on what additional ammunition we had left. There was something realer about everything this time. Something that truly felt like camaraderie, and Harris smirked at me as we silently ran into position, taking up our posts along the embankment. Jack and Harper came up behind us, talking in quick undertones, before turning forward again. Harper's whispered orders carried to all our ears.

"Ready...aim..." I took in a deep breath and looked at Andrew, a little nauseous, and he grinned. "Fire!"

The Brettain were caught completely off guard, and within ten seconds we had gotten off another volley before they could retaliate.

So it started again.

... — — — ...

It was surprising what an additional forty-five people could do. Instead of being almost entirely decimated within a few hours and retreating, we were standing fairly strong at ninety people left after seven hours. But as I pulled the trigger on an empty clip and frantically dropped down to reload, I knew this wasn't going to last.

The little ammunition we'd had left was all but gone. A few people had given up trying to find bullets and were reduced to throwing rocks and large pieces of shrapnel. Some people had even taken to lighting fires and hurling the burning pieces of wood into the ravaged No Man's Land in the hopes that we'd slow the opposition down with the additional barrier.

Andrew was still shooting beside me, aim surprisingly good despite his missing eye. Bodies had piled up across No Man's Land, and I briefly felt sorry for the Brettain who were no doubt struggling over the corpses of their friends to get at us.

When I couldn't find another clip, I sat down against the embankment and watched as the people around me managed to find more and more to keep throwing or shooting at the people coming at us. They were relentless in their desire to stay alive just a little longer, and I couldn't help but feel sick to my stomach. Because all of this, it was in vain. There was no way we were going to last the night – this alone had been a miracle. Now, we were truly running on empty.

"Keep going!" Harper shouted as he saw people falling into sitting positions, ducking down to avoid the bullets flying overhead. "We can hold them off, just keep it up!"

He was frantic, eyes scouring the people on the ground as he tried to figure out who was dead and who was just hiding. His pained eyes met mine briefly, and he motioned for me to get up, silently pleading with me. But I couldn't move.

"Captain!" Jack shouted and ran over, grabbing Harper's shoulder and violently twisting him around so they were face to face. "We need to go!"

"We can hold them!" he shouted back, as though bellowing the words would make them true, and Jack shook his head.

"No, we *can't!* Trust me, they had almost the exact same strategy with us. You won't be able to hold them off. They'll start coming en masse any second now, and they won't stop." My heart stopped as gunfire spattered the ground around them, and my boyfriend quickly fired one shot, killing the man who'd almost killed him. He looked back to Howell, eyes flashing. "You need to fall back *now.*"

Another shell exploded some distance down the line, and I threw my arms over my head to protect myself from the shrapnel, coughing so hard my chest was in agony. And as I pulled my grimy hands back from my lips, I saw that they were sprayed with blood. *My* blood. Heart racing, I looked up at the person beside me and saw that it was Irina. Her skin glistened with a feverish sweat, and her dull eyes darkened as she saw the blood on my hands.

"Get to Blackwell," she ordered, and I laughed, wiping away the blood on my pants.

"What, like you did?" My voice was scratchy, hollow.

"If that's TB, you could get all of us sick. I've got an infected gunshot wound while the doc's got no antibiotics left. Do the math."

"I'm *fine.* He said it's not TB—"

"Sicknesses evolve," she pointed out before firing again and handing me her spare clip. "Take that and get back up here. It's time to go out." But I couldn't lift the weapon any more. My ears were ringing, and I felt numb, dizzy even, as I sat there and looked around me.

Rocks and clods of dirt sprayed off the ledges barely managing to keep us alive. Our safety was literally disintegrating around us, finally done in after so many months of constant battery. Someone fell to the ground beside me, his face a bloodied, unrecognizable mess, and I nearly threw up, breath catching in my throat. A quick death absolutely bereft of mercy.

Was *that* what I was asking for?

I looked over to where Jack and Harper were still arguing and took in their wild gestures and stubborn expressions. My breath rattled loudly in my chest, and my eyes just wanted to close against it all, to finally block out the horrible sights around me. Instead, I kept my eyes opened and forced myself to breathe in the heavy air, to feel the soot and smoke grating against my throat and filling my lungs. I forced myself to face everything around me, to let myself go deaf to the world around me save for the unrelenting shells and bullets. And as I sat there, forcing myself to feel what life was left in me, I couldn't take my hands completely off my gun, nor could I look away from Jack.

"Look at them!" my boyfriend shouted and turned the captain to face us. Our eyes met again, and I took in a deep, resolute breath, tightening my fingers around my weapon. "They are finished! They are *dying*, and you can let that all end!" He stepped back into Harper's line of sight. "Let us fall back. This line is *falling*, the G.A. told us herself – just sound the retreat!"

And as I stared at them, the words we'd been praying to hear slipped from the captain's lips.

"Fine. Fine…fall back!"

Jack nodded in relief and turned to face the enemy lines. But the brief respite in his eyes faded away to horror as his eyes lit on me and he started running. Slowly, I became aware of a whistling sound growing louder and louder right behind me.

Artillery.

"Incoming!" Jack shouted and pulled me up from the ground, throwing his arm around me. But before we could run for cover, the shell hit the ground behind us and exploded. The air suddenly erupted into fire, dirt, and shrapnel. Jack's hand was torn from my shoulder as the trench collapsed around us.

My vision went dark.

DAY ONE HUNDRED AND FORTY-EIGHT

0000 hours
   Nothing.
   There was absolutely nothing, save that eerie, fateful ringing.
   Our screams were silent, distant – the gunfire hushed. The only sound I could hear was my heart pounding its steady funeral beat in my temples, my breath rasping loudly in my ears as it dragged evenly across my throat. Dazed and weightless, I forced my heavy lids to open, to take in the tilted world around me. The air was filled with dust and smoke, the people above me nothing more than vague silhouettes running for their lives. I watched their shadows convulse and arch in pain as Brettain rounds hit them in the back, and they collapsed to the darkened ground, vanishing – disintegrating – into the cloud of dust and smoke.
   Heartbeat growing louder and breath coming harder, I lifted my aching head from the dirt below and stared at the faces above me.
   Jack.
   As I managed to twist my left arm under me, a brutal scream pierced the stunned fog of my mind; a spray of rounds blew someone away. I felt out of sync with everything, as though the world was moving around me, and I was just a few seconds behind.
   Jack, I thought to myself again, dazed. *Where's Jack?* He had been right beside me, I'd felt him…just before the world had been lit on fire, and the air exploded in our faces.
   My vision tilted and swam, fading in and out as my heart synchronized with the pain throbbing in my veins. My breath dragged across my throat

like knives, lungs unable to sift through the dirt in the air and find the stale oxygen I so desperately needed. As my senses slowly came back to me, the numbness in my legs and right arm that I'd sensed before slowly transformed into pain. More specifically, a dull, pressing ache. Still numb, I tried turning onto my back only to find that I could barely move, and I forced myself up at an odd angle with my left arm to look over my shoulder.

The Brettain shell had taken out the trench work, plowing into the top of the ridge and leaving me pinned beneath what felt like a ton of dirt and rock that had collapsed in on us. My legs were trapped beneath a mountain of rubble. My right arm was bent back at an odd and increasingly painful angle – pinned just above my elbow beneath a massive rock that had been hidden in the banks that shielded us for so long.

People continued to run past me, shouting garbled orders to each other that either they couldn't say properly or my ears couldn't seem to decipher. A few people tripped and fell over the bodies and debris on the ground, struggling to get back to their feet as soon as they hit the dirt. I tried to duck down farther than I already was as bullets pelted and spattered the now exposed trench, downing my comrades as they tried to escape the direct line of fire and get to safety.

But even in the mayhem that surrounded me, I could still only look for one person, one face. Part of me could still feel his hand on my shoulder, pulling me close as his call of incoming rang through the air. But no matter how many faces I looked at, those of the living above and the dead around me, I couldn't find him.

I felt like I was trying to cough up my lungs as I struggled to blink the ash and dirt out of my eyes, to clear my throat enough to call out, to make some sort of noise. I quickly dragged the back of my hand across my mouth and felt light-headed as it came back stained red. This wasn't good. At that moment, I heard a bugle sound out over the battlefield, a frantic, cold resonance that was quickly cut off and silenced, ending in a discordant and shattering note. And with that I knew it was over, and I watched as the few remaining people left fled past me, sprinting down the trenches to fall back.

Harper had gotten the word to the bugler. The line, the line we'd been supposed to hold – no matter the cost – was breached, and we were falling back once and for all.

And as I realized that, it occurred to me that I was pinned on the butchering field, a waiting target with my back exposed and inviting to bayonets and bullets. Fear burned in my stomach, howling and tearing like a caged animal at my gut until I couldn't keep it in any longer. I screamed in fear and frustration, tears burning in my eyes as I dug my one free arm into the mud beneath me – clawing at the earth, straining to pull myself from my trap. Howell's words from so long ago resurfaced, voice shouting at me as though he were right beside me, leaning over me and bellowing directly into my ear.

I trust them to do what's necessary – to give what's necessary – for this country to survive! But looking at you…well, you're not going to be one of those men. I can see it now. I give you two weeks out here!

"I proved you wrong!" I sobbed, choking on my own words as I fought to pry myself free. "I made it through for months!"

My fear, my terror, my panic, it was all falling away. It was pushed out of my head and my body until I felt only one sensation, only one emotion blazing in me, giving me strength and driving me. It was anger.

"I'm not going to die out here!" I shouted, almost seeing my murdered captain hovering above me in my delirious and fevered state. "I'm not going to die now! Not now and not fucking here!"

But no matter how hard I forced myself, no matter how I twisted and pulled at the weight on my body, I couldn't seem to budge. I couldn't get myself free. I looked up at the crumbling ridge of the trench above me in time to see a Brettain soldier come into view, gun held at the ready position as he fired down into the dugout. Men and women crashed down to the ground around me, blood soaking the mud and staining uniforms like red ink.

Dying. We're all dying.

I groaned as I struggled to pull myself forward just enough to grab the rifle lying outside my reach. My fingers brushed the cold metal, slipping uselessly over the muddy surface, and I made a choked sound of desperate frustration, coughing on the smoke from the small fires that blazed along the trenches.

"Come on. Come *on*," I panted to myself, lurching forward so that I swore something cracked in my pinned right arm, and my hand closed on the stock of the rifle, fingers tightening around the weapon. *"Come on!"* I shouted and, with the most coordination I'd ever had in my life, propped myself up with my elbow, swung the gun around while keeping the joint planted firmly in the ground, and braced the weapon across my chest and right shoulder with my forearm. My gaze found my target's as his found mine. I could see his eyes, could see the sweat and blood mottling his skin, and knew that he was just as scared as I was.

Don't think.

Point.

Aim.

Shoot.

I squeezed the trigger just as he swung his rifle around, and he toppled out of sight, the recoil of the weapon slamming the gun painfully back into my jaw and making me see stars. I had seen his eyes widen in shock as my bullet struck home, and I choked back bile as I realized a few seconds later that he'd looked terrified of the dark he knew was coming.

We were all scared in war. Didn't matter which side we were on.

Just then though, more people started coming into view, and I took in a shaky breath, repositioning the gun so the recoil wouldn't hit me in the face and pulling the trigger as soon as I had a target.

Don't miss. One shot per person. Don't stop, don't think, just pull the trigger, and you'll live.

Just pull the trigger, and you'll live.

But no matter how many rounds had been left in the gun when I had managed to grab it, there was no way there was enough to keep the whole opposition at bay. And finally the time came when I pulled the trigger and nothing came out. Mercifully, someone else farther down the trench fired his own weapon, and my would-be-executioner fell out of sight.

My mouth and throat were dry, and I looked at the bodies above me – bodies I had put there. I pushed the gun to the side, gagging and throwing up nothing but acid. *Pull the trigger, and you'll live.*

Why did we need to be here to pull the trigger in the first place? We weren't fighting for our countries. We were fighting to survive. All of us. And I was ready to go home, ready for it all to just be over.

Who the hell knew what those people up there had been like? They could have had families, could have been parents. They could have owned shops or worked in factories. They could have had farms, or just lived quiet lives with their families. I knew for a fact they *hadn't* been monsters.

Or, at least, no more of a monster than ourselves.

My breath was coming hard and fast, the shallow, rattling gasps filled with dust and the dank smell of mud as fearful hysteria crowded my mind.

What have we become?

I wearily looked up to see a group of Brettain march into view about thirty feet down the trench, stepping around the bodies before them. Their eyes roved the littered ground, weapons held at the ready.

This was it.

I was going to die, just like they'd all said.

But just as I thought they were going to find me, that I was going to be killed where I lay, a gunshot went off right behind me, and the lead Brettain collapsed. Startled, the rest of the soldiers looked around and started firing at whoever had just saved my life, and a few more crumpled to the ground before the rest hid behind our own barricades. As I threw my free arm over my head, keeping low as bullets ricocheted and missed around me, I looked at who my savior was. And my heart stopped.

Jack.

He looked terrible, bleeding from several nicks and cuts on the sides of his face and neck as he ducked behind the trashed barriers. His uniform was stained with what looked like more than just mud, torn in some places by the shrapnel from the explosion that had left me pinned here. His free hand pressed against his wounded side, and I could see his breath hitch on each inhale.

He spared a quick glance towards me, eyes hard and scared, and jerked his head at the opposing men. A bullet shattered the crate beside him, and he flinched, the splinters dusting his sleeve. Grasping what he was thinking, I nodded and took note of where the Brettain were standing before looking up at him.

"They're reloading *now*."

Just as the Brettain paused in their assault, Jack stepped out from his cover, firing his rifle four times. We were alone once more.

I groaned and dropped my head down onto my arm, exhausted from the fear and adrenaline.

"Tristan, you okay?" I nodded, not looking up at him. "Tristan!"

I glanced up at Jack and nodded once more, unsteady and trembling. I knew my eyes were red, that my dirty face was pale with terror beneath the grime. But given the circumstances, I frankly couldn't bring myself to care.

"I'm fine," I croaked, running my hand over my face. "Thanks for that. That was – that was some nice shooting."

He rolled his eyes at my tired compliment before heading over to me.

"You're an idiot," he returned, forcing a smile of strained relief. He let the gun swing down to his side, held in place by the weapon's strap over his shoulder, though his hand still lay ready on the trigger as per training. "I'll be right there. I'm just checking…"

He trailed off as he quickly looked down either side of the trench, as though hoping that someone from our side would be coming, that one of the dead bodies would magically rise up and help us out. But when he saw that there was no one coming, friend or foe, he turned back to me. He briefly stooped down to kiss my forehead, breath ghosting across my skin, and headed for the mass of rocks and dirt pinning me to the ground.

His finger left the trigger.

"Okay, Tristan. Just hang tight, I'm gonna–"

Red exploded across his abdomen, and my breath stopped in my chest.

Paralyzed.

The world went silent, like someone had flipped a switch–

Horrorstruck.

The booming fire of the artillery weaponry, the carrying shouts of men, the haunting tattoo of gunfire in the distance, all of it, it was just *gone*.

Gutted.

I couldn't register anything.

I couldn't even hear my own scream of agony as it tore out of my throat, dragging claws along my insides and ripping away the skin of my throat.

"JACK!"

It seemed slow motion to me, the way that he caved in on himself. His hand let go of the gun as his arms reached out for the empty space before him, trying to find something to hold on to.

Trying to find me.

The weapon hit the mud before he did, and his legs quickly collapsed under him. His whole body crashed down on its back like a marionette whose strings had been slashed without warning, casting him to the ground mid-movement. His eyes were wide with shock, mouth slightly open in a painful, futile effort to draw in the gritty air around us. The thick red spread across his abdomen, soaking his clothes, and his shaking hands pressed numbly against the slicked fabric, quickly turning crimson themselves. I looked over my shoulder, expression a mask of pain and helplessness, to find the top of the trench empty.

Whoever had been there, whoever had pulled the trigger, was gone – leaving me helpless, and Jack, oh *gods*–

"Jack!" I shouted again, straining and digging my fingers into the mud as I tried to drag myself forward, to pull myself free of the mound of dirt and rock. "No!" He was gasping for breath, chest shuddering in brutal spasms as he fought to breathe. "Jack! Jack, you look at me! *Look at me!*" I screamed, and his head lolled to the side to face me, skin somehow even paler than it had been before as his hands slipped uselessly over his blood-slick stomach.

"T-Tris," he whispered, eyes pained and terrified. The tortured word, my *name*, was barely audible. And as I watched helplessly, he groaned, coughing on the blood that rose up to his lips.

"No! No, no, no," I babbled, voice breaking as tears filled my eyes. Jack's breathing was shallow and rapid, each hitched, useless gasp pulling at the hole in his gut.

"I – I can't–" His words were whimpered, his expression terrified and confused at the same time.

"No! No, you stop it! Stop it!" I shouted frantically and tried to wrench myself free again. "It's gonna be okay, Jack! I *promise*, I promise it'll be okay!" I knew this was where we would be okay. W-we had to be. *I* was the strategist. *I* figured out how to make things work. I looked back to him.

"We're a team, okay? We're a team. Tell me what type of gun it was!" But Jack was beyond hearing, let alone speaking, and he coughed and choked as his attempt to answer me pulled on his injured stomach. "No, you *focus!*" I was hysterical, frantic. "You focus, and you tell me what type of gun it was!"

His shoulders rose off the ground as he convulsed with the pain, red-frothed teeth grinding against each other as he weakly pressed down on his blood-soaked gut. I felt like screaming, like sobbing. I wanted to tear my hair out as I watched him.

Focus.

"R-rifle...standard..."

Jax's voice rattled off in my head, lessons of field first aid quickly coming back to me. *Respond. Don't think about the person, just the scenario.*

"Okay. Okay, stan-standard rifle. There was no exit wound, so apply pressure to the entry wound until I get out of here." Oh gods, I sounded so cold, so heartless. Clinical. "Try...try not to move. What was the range?"

He didn't answer, and I desperately grabbed a fistful of dirt and threw at him in an attempt to keep his attention.

"Hey!" He slowly, jerkily looked at me. "Just – just stay with me, okay? You're going to be okay, please!" I begged, voice breaking, and Jack gave a small whimper of pain, shuddering as his hands slowly started slipping away from where they had been weakly clutching the torn fabric of his shirt.

"No. No, not you! Not you! Don't you dare!" I shouted and reached out to pull a bayonet from one of our side's corpses, using it to pry away the boulders trapping my legs.

To my great relief, one of the heavy rocks tumbled free, and I looked over my shoulder at Jack, taking note of his erratic breathing and his pale and waxy skin – especially around his eyes and lips. I tried to ignore the crimson staining his teeth and trickling down the corners of his mouth. And how horribly his bruises and cuts stood out against his gaunt skin.

"Jack? Jack!" He blinked, weakly looking over at me. He was scared, but what frightened me more was the helplessness in his expression, the tears of pain in his eyes. "Jack, stop it! You stop it right now!" I shouted, wrenching another rock away and managing to free my left leg.

My breath grew just as chaotic as his as I used my legs and left arm to work on shoving away the rest of the debris weighing me down. My right arm. That was all that was left now, just my right arm.

"You are Jack *fucking* Miller!" I turned back to face him, panting and blinking away a burning sensation in my eyes. I couldn't tell if it was from tears or if it was fever-induced sweat dripping down my forehead and my brows. "You are *my* Jack!" I bellowed, slamming my fist into the ground. "You are *my* Jack, and you are not going to give up! Do you hear me?"

Something distant and yet at the same time vaguely dogged glimmered behind the growing emptiness in my boyfriend's eyes.

"*I* made it this far!" I continued, desperate and angry in my terror. "*I* made it this far, alive, and if I can make it, so can you! You are not going to give up. *You* don't give up!" My cracking voice seemed to echo down the trenches in the silence between us, and I waited for him to speak, waited for him to respond. "You – you *can't* give up!"

As I watched, his breath hitched again, and a few tears slipped from his eyes, running parallel to the blood from his mouth. I choked back a sob of my own and ground the heel of my palm into my tear-filled eyes.

"Don't..." I begged, voice breaking. "Don't, *please*..."

"'M sorry," he whimpered. His slurred words were barely audible over the Brettain's distant chaos, and I screamed in anger, bucking against my final restraint and trying to wrench my arm free.

"*Stop*," I sobbed, grabbing my upper arm and jerking back, trying in vain to twist my elbow and wrist. But it held fast, unable to move even the slightest bit. I sobbed, sending my bloodied fist crashing into the stone, screaming at it with fury. "Stop it! It's not supposed to be like this!"

I shifted my position, trying to get to my knees and pull away. I only stopped when it felt like my arm was going to snap and my shoulder was going to dislocate, and I had never felt more helpless in my life. I howled in wordless anger, looking up at the clouded sky above me before turning back to face Jack.

His eyes still watched me, tired and distant, like he wasn't really there any more. Blood stained the inside of his white lips red as more trickled down the corner of his mouth, and his crimson-stained hands barely held onto his drenched shirt. I rested my forehead against the ground, pulling in vain against my imprisonment, and stared at Jack in defeat out of the corner of my eye.

Abdominal wounds are the worst. They look nasty, and they are nasty. In some cases, the stomach has been punctured, and there's acid corroding their insides. They'll go into septic shock. In that case, you've got to get them to a field hospital as soon as possible before they die. Tops, you'll have fifteen minutes. If the descending artery has been severed, the best you can do is give them their last rites. However, there are some that look nasty, but there's still hope. The stomach hasn't been punctured. Maybe, if anything, it was the diaphragm or the liver, maybe a lung. It's still very serious, there will be a lot of bleeding, but you can't let that spook you. Get to your partner, stop the bleeding, and seal the wound if you can. Get them somewhere safe. If you have medication to clot blood, give it to them. You don't want to move them any more than necessary, so use one of the stretchers to either carry or drag them to help. Don't panic.

The most important thing is you get your comrade to safety. That is paramount.

I swallowed painfully as I reversed my grip on the bayonet I'd been using before and began wedging it between my right arm and the rock pinning it down. The flat edge, streaked with mud and a dark substance I didn't want to identify, pressed dangerously against my sleeve. It was angled just enough that the blade wasn't slicing down into my skin, and I took in a deep breath, applying pressure and slowly letting the air hiss out between my teeth. The weight on my trapped hand and wrist slowly began to lessen.

Behind me, I heard a strangled groan, and I looked over my shoulder to see Jack staring at me with fear in his fading eyes.

"Jax said that getting you help is more important than anything else. Is paramount to anything."

I took in a shaky breath and refocused, increasing the pressure of the flat of the blade on my arm and using it as a lever to lift the rock weighing down on me. My hand shook under the strain, wrist fighting to stay locked and straight. But just when I thought I was going to be able to wrench my arm out from underneath, bayonet holding the stone at bay as I moved the metal along with me, my left arm shook with a fatigued tremor, and my wrist slipped to the side.

My breath caught in my throat, and my heart stopped beating as I immediately forced my hand back to its original position. But I could feel hot blood oozing down my right forearm, and I swore to myself as I realized I'd cut my trapped arm with the bayonet. My adrenaline was racing too much for me to feel the pain, but from the sudden warmth spreading down my skin and the slippery, tickling sensation buzzing in my arm, I guessed it was fairly deep.

"Okay. Okay, one more time," I whispered to myself, voice tight and unsteady. I looked over at Jack and saw that he was still watching me, half-closed eyes filled with that same fear. "It'll be okay," I told him, trying and failing to be reassuring as I looked back at what I was doing. "It'll be okay." I repositioned the bayonet and began lifting upwards once more. *Almost there, almost there, just a little higher.* "It'll all...be...oka—"

Crack.

My chest seemed to freeze, and my stomach dropped out. My breath came in unsteady gasps, and I shakily released the end of the bayonet, staring in stunned silence as the length of soiled metal remained at its odd angle. My trapped arm felt odd, swollen almost, and I slowly pulled back. I felt like I was in a trance, like nothing was real, and I gasped in agony, unable to scream from the sharpness of the pain, as my arm dragged along the blood-slicked underside of the boulder. As soon as my elbow came free, I knew I was in trouble.

My sleeve was soaked in red, and I could see the place in my arm where the bloody bayonet impaled my skin. Breath growing hysterical and heart pounding in an erratic, fatal beat, I pulled the rest of my arm out of its imprisonment, movement eased by the blood spilling from my forearm.

The blade had slipped in my left hand. The dirtied metal had plunged diagonally through my right arm so it entered my body close to the inside of my elbow and exited once more in my wrist near the back of my hand. And despite the buzzing haze of shock blinding my senses, I could feel the pain stabbing through my bones.

"Oh gods," I whimpered, voice small and scared as I slowly wrapped my trembling left hand around the base of the weapon.

Immediately, at that slightest of taps, my nerves shrieked in protest, and I stopped, gritting my teeth and closing my eyes as I almost blacked out. It seemed that as soon as I so much as touched the metal, the shock vanished, and I could feel everything. But I had to take it out. Every part of my mind screamed to remove it.

Take it out, take it out, take it out —

I howled in agony as I jerked back on the bayonet, the damaged blade catching on tendons and bone and flesh as it tore unevenly out of my arm. I could *feel* the razor sharp metal dragging along the inside of my body, slicing into my already ravaged muscle as I removed it. As I screamed through my clenched teeth, I fell away onto my side, left hand clapped over the searing pain jolting through my right arm. Dark blood seeped through my fingers, drenching my hands as the dark fluid coursed in rivulets between my shaking fingers and spattered onto my shirt.

As I lay there on the ground, groaning and hyperventilating, I forced myself to a sitting position, pressing my wounded arm close to my chest.

The pain was incredible, paralyzing. I couldn't breathe. I couldn't see. Everything was white static, everything hurt, and my nerves screeched in anger and pain. My mouth was lined with blood from where I'd bitten the inside of my cheek, and I pushed myself away from the red-stained rock. I clenched my hand over the ragged hole in my arm, gritting my teeth as I felt the fragments of bone shift painfully beneath my skin. Hot blood continued to pulse through my fingers, and I dazedly heard Jax's voice.

Artery damaged. Potentially severed. Tourniquet.

I stumbled to my feet, staggering forward towards the destroyed med tent ten feet away. The small distance felt like miles, and I nearly fell flat on my face, overcome with nausea and dizziness as I pushed through the tattered canvas.

"Tourniquet. Tourniquet," I groaned, desperate, and pushed through the trashed mess to a scorched cabinet in the back, yanking open the door and grabbing the combat medic's kit for the dressing. My forearm throbbed painfully, but I didn't have time to stop and think about the implications of my injury. I quickly tied the strip of cloth around my upper arm, twisting the wooden bar into the fabric until it effectively cut off all circulation to the lower half of my arm. I clumsily tied the wood down, fingers shaking almost uselessly.

Okay, now you need to tend to Miller. What's his condition?

I unsteadily turned on my heel, nearly falling over like a drunk, and ran out to Jack, kneeling beside him and quickly placing my fingers against his neck. I could barely feel the thready and faint pulse and estimated a rate before reaching down and pulling away the lapels of his open jacket. His eyes dimly watched me, and my lips pressed together into a grim line. The bullet hole was large, too large for a standard rifle, and I felt the first inkling of doubt worm its way into my mind.

FOCUS! How much bleeding? Location of the injury? Exit wound? Come on, *kid, think!*

I took in a deep, shaking breath and looked at how low the wound was on his body, ignoring the fogged eyes begging me for reassurance, for help.

I couldn't give it to him. I angrily blinked tears out of my eyes.

The shot couldn't have missed his organs, and that meant there could be acid and gods knew what else leaking into his body, slowly poisoning him. And with my arm...

I couldn't do anything. The realization hit me like a battering ram, and I stared down at Jack with a stunned, sickened expression. I couldn't do anything. I couldn't do anything but *watch* as...

I sank back on my heels beside him and slowly leaned forward, resting my forehead against his and burying my fingers in his hair. My words were whimpered, begging him for forgiveness.

"I'm...oh gods, I'm...I'm so *sorry*."

His eyes fluttered momentarily at my touch and the sound of my voice, and his lips parted slightly, a faint, whispering breath escaping his dying lungs. I sat back up, and his eyes slowly fixed on mine, his fingers moving weakly on his stomach, as though trying to grab me. I moved my bloody hand from his head and grabbed his stained hands in mine, sobbing.

"Don't – I don't–" he choked, words stuttering and broken as he fought to speak. His brows were furrowed, expression contorted in pain as his eyes frantically pleaded with me. Eyes like Jackson's, I realized in horror.

He tried to speak again, and I shakily shushed him, afraid of what he was going to say. I lifted our bloody hands to my lips, silently begging him to be still. To be *silent*. "Don't – don't let me go–" I sobbed in response, clinging to his hand and bowing my head over him. "Tris, I don't – I don't want t-to go–"

"I'm sorry," I gasped, words barely audible and wrenched out of me as though I were being gutted. It was all I could say, all I could manage, and my voice cracked. The useless apologies continued to be drawn out of my throat like the cries of a frightened child. "I love you, Jack. *I love you...*"

His chest barely moved with his shallow breaths, and as I watched, his hands finally slid away from himself and dropped into the mud. I shakily grabbed them and pressed both back over the still oozing wound, as though that small gesture could reverse what was happening.

He's still alive, boy. I blinked against my dizzy eyesight and my tears and looked around myself, deliriously trying to find the source of Jax's voice. *You can do this, newbie. You can't help him here, but you can still help him elsewhere. There's still time.*

"No. No, I-I can't – I've got nothing, I–"

Stop the bleeding. Compression, pack it down.

I pushed away from Jack and half-ran, half-tripped over to the medical tent. I headed to the cabinet and opened it, staring at the limited materials before me. My mind went blank.

Strategy, kid, Jax scolded. *That's what you can do. What's the* strategy?

"Stop the bleeding," I whispered, reaching forward and fumbling for sterile gauze, bandages, scissors, and a canteen. "Stop the bleeding." It was a mantra that kept me calm and kept me moving. My hands were shaking like dead leaves, and I almost scattered my supplies as I ran off to where Jack was laying, still and white, and dropped to my knees.

My right arm was basically useless, the bloody and crippled fingers able to get little traction or grip as I set the canteen to the side. I braced the package of sterile gauze between my knees and ripped the top open with my left hand, pulling the fabric out and folding it into a thick square big enough to cover Jack's wound. Then, as quickly as I could with my numb and bloodstained fingers, I clumsily tucked the loose end between the layers of the padding so it wouldn't come unraveled.

I set the makeshift press on the cleanest spot of Jack's uniform I could find, quickly twisted open the canteen with my teeth, and poured some of the precious water onto the gauze to get it a little damp. Not soaking wet, just a little damp, I had to remember that. Next, I picked up the scissors and quickly cut open Jack's shirt a little more around the bullet wound so I could see what I was working with.

It was welled up with blood, skin ragged and twisted around the entry point. I couldn't see very well, and I knew what I had to do next. I clenched my jaw as I picked up the canteen and poured some water over the gaping wound. Jack made a small, startled noise of pain, and I quickly hushed him, squeezing his shoulder and holding him down as he reflexively pushed up against me.

"It's okay, Jack. You're doing great," I whispered, tightening my hold before I picked up the gauze pad I'd made. "Okay...Jack? This is really gonna hurt, but I promise it'll be okay." And, taking a deep breath, I slowly pushed it down over the wound, packing it into the hole a little.

"*Agh!*" Jack's eyes squeezed shut in his delirious state, and his bloodied teeth ground against each other as he pushed weakly at my hands, trying to make the pain stop.

"Shh, Jack, leave it alone. It's okay," I whispered, voice shaking until my words were almost unrecognizable. I finished patting the gauze into place and began folding the long lengths of bandages into an even thicker and bigger pad, tears burning in my eyes at his pained, wheezing breaths.

"Y-you're doing great, Jack. Just stay with me...stay with me," I panted, the pain in my arm reaching the blinding point. The blood loss was making my vision swim despite the tourniquet.

I laid the thick layer of cloth over the blocked wound to hold the gauze and his insides in place and fumbled with pulling his belt off, yanking it free from his waist. Groaning, I propped him up a little with my knee and shoved my uninjured arm under him, threading the leather to the other side of his body. I reached across him with my maimed right arm, shakily and clumsily grabbing the buckle so I could use my good hand to cinch it down over his wound. I awkwardly fastened the belt once I was satisfied that the bandage wouldn't move and that there was sufficient pressure to slow the bleeding and protect his organs.

Okay, private. You've stopped the bleeding for now. What's next?

"Help...I've got to go get help." I started to get to my feet when Jax's voice shouted in my head again, like some kind of invisible, angry angel.

No! You can't leave him here. You can't go get help. What are you going to do?

I sank back down to my knees and looked at Jack, at my nearly six-foot boyfriend bleeding out on the ground before me. I looked at his ashy skin, at its strange wax-like complexion. I looked at his eyes, his half open eyes that were so dull and flat and *pained* that I almost couldn't remember how they looked when he was happy, when he laughed…or even when he cried.

STRETCHER, Byrne! For the gods' sakes, pull yourself together, you're useless like this!

"Stretcher, stretcher," I muttered to myself, as though repeating the word would somehow keep my mind focused on the task and myself sane. I quickly pushed myself back to my feet and ran into the med tent again, eyes roving the wreckage. "Come on…come on…"

But no matter how many sheets or blood stained beds I overturned, I couldn't find a stretcher. I couldn't find anything I could salvage, let alone turn into something I could carry Jack on by myself with a lame arm. With a scream of anger, desperation, and exhausted pain, I brought my foot crashing into an empty crate, sending the object skittering across the ground to come to a stop beside my boyfriend.

"I-I can't…I can't do it," I sobbed, sinking to my knees a few feet away from him. "I can't…I'm sorry, I can't–"

I broke off in a cry of pain as my arm burned with agonizing fire, and I doubled over, gasping and choking on my hurried, panting breaths as they caught in my throat. Jack made no move to look at me, eyes blinking slowly as he stared emptily at the smoke filled sky above us. The pauses between his breaths slowly grew longer.

And as I sat there, tears blinding me and throat closing up, a spark lit up in the back of my mind. A stupid, dangerous spark.

"I don't need a stretcher." I said to the empty air, voice shaking. I bent over Jack, breathing shakily, and kissed his furrowed brow, smoothing his mud and blood stiffened hair from his face. "I love you, Jack." And as I looked down at him, at that sunken, deathly pale mask, I leaned down and kissed him again – properly this time. My unsteady breaths ghosted across his still lips and against his skin. "I love you. I won't let you go."

This had to work.

Gritting my teeth, I rolled Jack onto his right side and knelt facing away from his chest, leaning back so that my shoulders nestled against the inside of his left shoulder and hip. This had to be done perfectly. It had to, or else this wouldn't end well for either of us, especially Jack.

Taking in a deep breath and praying to the gods, I hooked my left arm behind his left leg, making sure that the inside of my elbow nestled against the inside of his knee. Then, I reached up with my left hand to grab Jack's upper left arm in a harsh grip while my throbbing right hand weakly held his wrist, locking his body across my chest. He groaned softly behind me, and I fought to steady my breath and block out the now constant pain in my right arm.

"It's okay. It's okay."

The words were pitifully weak and unconfident. I shook my head to clear it, and something in me burned. Desperate resolve flooded my system, and my heart rate increased until it was pounding painfully in my ears, the vessels in my temples feeling ready to burst.

"Come on. Come on!" I grunted and shifted my knees in the mud below us, struggling to find purchase and balance. *"Come on!"* Groaning with the effort, I rocked forwards, straining upwards until my vision almost blacked out, and I finally settled on my knees. Jack was poised precariously on my shoulders, his head limp against my bleeding arm. "Come on. Come on…" Shouting through gritted teeth, I brought one knee up and planted my worn boot in the mud. "Just one more time. Just. One. More. *Time.*"

Muscles shaking, I lurched upwards, finally standing and bracing my legs apart until I was unsteadily balanced. Chest heaving and heart beating so hard I was sure it was going to shatter my ribs, I raised my head and looked at the smoke filled trench ahead of me. It seemed impossibly long, an eternity. How was I supposed to carry him that far?

I staggered forward, Jack's body pressing down on my back in the fireman's lift until I was about to fall over.

"Jack?" I whispered, coughing as I stumbled down the body littered trench, adrenaline pounding through my system with every throb of my heart. "Jack!" I heard him moan weakly behind me, or at least I thought I did. I couldn't be sure. "Jack, it's going to be okay," I continued, mindlessly talking. "I'm going to make this okay. It's…I'm going to make this okay. I promise." My vision tilted and swam, but I squeezed my eyes shut, pressing stolidly forward and planting my blistered and weary feet one step ahead of each other only to repeat the cycle.

Keep talking. Keep him engaged.

"You remember how we first met?" I began, raw voice just as grating as the sounds of the battlefield. His right hand thudded limply against the back of my leg with each jolting stride I took. "I-it was the third year at the Academy. You...you came into my quarters before the annual Hunt. Told me you needed a strategist. Someone to make your game plan." I laughed deliriously at the memory, chin quivering as I plowed on, stepping over bodies of people I had grown to know over the course of the last four and a half years.

Don't think about them. Think about him. Think about him.

"I told you what I thought you should do. I laid it all out on the map. You all thought I was crazy..." I sobbed and coughed, pain in my arm radiating into my shoulder and chest as I continued shakily on. "B-but you got them all to listen. You got them all to listen to you...to listen to me. An-and we got the flag. We won."

A shaking, tearful smile forced its way to my lips as I remembered the moment Jack had sprinted across our team's border with the underclassmen's flag in his hands. Relived the moment back in North Hall after the festivities had finished in the mess when someone knocked on my door, and I opened it to find him standing there, smiling shyly at me with the damn thing in his hands.

"Y-you ruffled my hair that night..." I continued, voice a broken rasp. "When you came to congratulate me."

"...then...y' kissed me..."

I gave a breathy laugh and turned my head to the right, looking at Jack as his eyes opened a mere fraction of an inch to look at me.

"R' you..." His gaze drifted down to look at my feet stumbling along under his weight, and his brow furrowed in incomprehension behind the pain as his sight fixed on my right forearm, at the sullied skin and blood. "Your arm..."

"I've got you, Jack. I told you we'd get through this. I promised you," I rambled, tired vision swimming and blacking out for a second. "And I don't break promises. I mean, you should know that. We've only been dating f-for what now? Almost a year and a half?" His eyes slowly drifted shut again, and he didn't answer, his head resting limply against my side. "W-what are we going to do for our two year anniversary, Jack?" Tears burned my eyes, and I looked back forward, not wanting to trip and fall. Or maybe it was so I wouldn't have to look at the still face beside me.

"We...we should do something special," I rambled. "It's kind of a big one. Maybe we should go dancing..."

At that moment, I heard the all too familiar tattoo of machine gun fire farther down the trenches behind us, and my heart stopped.

"Oh gods," I whispered, stopping my forward movement and turning around slightly to see if I could see any of the enemy approaching in the haze. "Not now."

I couldn't see anyone yet, but I knew that sound. It was the dull march of approaching footsteps. Another wave had started. I turned back around and increased my pace until I was sure I was going to fall over, my battered body protesting against the strain. Jack groaned behind me as my jerky steps no doubt sent pain shooting through him.

"I'm sorry, Jack. I'm sorry." There was no response, and I tightened my grip on his wrist, fingers finding the pulse there. My heart lurched as I felt the faint beat against my thumb. He was alive, but it wasn't good.

"Hang on, Jack. You have to hang on," I whispered, my vision blacking out on me and fading back in repeatedly as my legs nearly buckled. "Hang on, hang on..." More machine gun fire came from behind us, and something broke inside of me. A cold fire flooded my gut, a burning sensation that sent my body numb and my heart pounding.

All of a sudden, I couldn't feel my legs. I couldn't feel my right arm. I couldn't feel the pain building in my back. All I could feel was my feet numbly dragging quickly along the ground, catching on debris as I stepped around the bodies and scattered equipment before me. But whatever short burst of energy my sudden adrenaline rush gave me, it didn't last nearly as long as I needed it to.

My lungs started burning like they were on fire, making me choke on my ragged coughs. My knees and ankles cried out with each step I took. My maimed right arm was a mass of pain that my mind had just accepted it couldn't combat, but my body was too dehydrated for me to cry any more. My breath burned dryly in my throat instead of bringing me air. My eyes stung, and every time I blinked it felt like my lids were lined with sand. Vaguely, I noted that we had moved a good distance from the front lines, that my blind following of the maze had led us farther inland. And for a brief moment a flicker of hope burned in my mind.

Field hospitals were off-limit war targets. If I just made it to the central field hospital we'd passed when we'd entered the lines, whoever was behind us couldn't touch us. We would be safe. Jack would get help. Jack would be okay.

Jack would live.

And with that, my mind went blank. There was only one thought in my head, one thought driving my empty body forward. *Jack will live.* With each word I struggled to plant my feet in front of each other.

My head dropped down against the locked cross of Jack's leg and his arm, and my half-open eyes fixated on the ground in front of me, oblivious to anything or anyone else. I just watched the mutilated dead, the broken bayonets, the discarded guns, the fallen tents and scattered gear as I stepped over them.

But eventually, my hard, quick pace died down into nothing more than a tired, lop-sided stagger, and the toes of my boots dragged through the mud as I went. My back was wet with Jack's blood, and I faintly realized I hadn't bound his wound tightly enough. I had no idea how long I'd been walking, though I was sure it wasn't as long as it felt to me. It couldn't be. If it was, the words I'd been using to keep myself going meant nothing.

That was when I heard the first voice. Wearily, I raised my head and looked up, breath wheezing out of my chapped and pale lips – lips like Jack's. I could dimly see shadows of people moving around, calling orders that I either couldn't hear or couldn't understand. All I could hear was my heartbeat pounding in my ears, my breath rattling in my chest. But as I continued on, I saw it: a massive white tent surrounded by a sprawling, chaotic maze of smaller ones, all emblazoned with the purple cross of Vediovis, god of healing.

"Jack," I whispered, voice raw and croaking. "Jack, we're okay. You're okay. Y-you're okay…"

There was no answer.

As I drew closer, I thought I could hear people whispering, pointing at us as we went along from where they were sprawled against the walls of the trenches, nursing their injuries.

"Looks like Byrne–"

"Oh my gods, what happened to his arm?"

"Is that Miller? I think that's *Miller*–"

Someone broke away from their path towards the main large tent and came running over, shouting for someone to bring over two stretchers.

"*Byrne!*" There was something shocked and scared in the way she said my name and looked at us. "Byrne, it's okay. Shrimp, it's *okay*. You can let go." I looked up into the face of the newcomer and saw that it was Marcel.

Let go?

We weren't with a doctor yet. I couldn't *let go*.

"No," I mumbled, trying to push past her. "No, I-I have to get him – have to get him safe. I have to get him safe!"

She didn't move. Behind her I could see the stretchers, the stretchers Jack so desperately needed, and I blearily made eye-contact with her. There was something there, something – something *terrified*.

"It's okay, Tristan. It's okay. You did *great*," she said gently, reaching out to try and take Jack from me, but I shook my head.

"No. No, he needs help. He needs *help*."

"That's what we're here for. Okay?" Her hands were at her shoulders, showing me she wasn't going to take him from me. "You both need help, Tristan. You did great, now let us do the rest."

"I–" I groaned, and my knees finally buckled, my hands losing their hold on Jack as I crashed to the ground. Thankfully, War's reflexes were faster, and she caught my boyfriend before he hit the ground, letting his heavy body rest against her as she quickly applied pressure to his wound.

"*Shit*," she whispered, and I looked at her listlessly as I swayed on my knees. Her fingers rested against his throat, urgently checking for a pulse.

His calm, peaceful face was tilted towards the sky, sunken eyes closed and blood-lined mouth slightly open. There was so much blood covering his stomach beneath Marcel's shaking hand. Yet…he looked so calm. I was dazed, unable to think clearly.

So calm.

My vision blacked out, and I was about to fall forward when someone grabbed my shoulders and pulled me backwards onto one of the stretchers. I opened my eyes to watch as the medics set Jack's deathly pale body on the length of fabric beside me and lifted him up. Dazedly, I tried to sit up, but Marcel quickly pushed me back down onto my gurney with gentle hands.

"They're both in a bad way. Let's get going," I heard one of the nurses say.

I blinked dazedly as Marcel ran next to me, holding my blood-soaked hand in hers as the medics carried me to what I would later find out was the critical care side of the tent, just behind Jack. But as they set him down, they started to carry me farther away, and I made a small noise of protest in the back of my throat. Thankfully, Marcel still hadn't taken her eyes off of me for some reason and followed my hollow, pained gaze.

"Hey!" she barked, and the medics turned to face her. "Over there. Keep him with captain – *Corporal* Miller." They nodded their understanding, but she wasn't finished. "You *keep* them side by side, and you don't even *think* about separating them! You hear me?"

"Yes, ma'am."

I looked up at her in bleary confusion, but she just stared down at me with an ashen complexion before running off to some part of the tent I couldn't see. The world around me was spinning with colors and in speeds I couldn't understand, and I groaned as the four medics set me down on a bed. They quickly lifted me off the stretcher onto the mattress, cutting my uniform away and dragging a rolling tray over with surgical equipment.

"Ok, it looks like the arm is the only big injury. Samantha, clean it out. We can't seal anything in there when we do this."

My breath started growing ragged and panicked, and I looked away from the bottle of rubbing alcohol "Samantha" was bringing over. Instead, I focused on Jack. He wasn't moving. His eyes were closed. I couldn't even tell if he was breathing, and his lips looked slightly blue.

"Jack?" I whimpered, eyes burning and throat tightening. I tried to sit up, the attempt nothing more than a twitch of my shoulders. "Jack?"

One of the nurses who was working on pulling away my handiwork of the now blood-saturated belt, bandages, and gauze looked over at me, her eyes grim, and lips tight.

And as we stared at each other, I understood.

"No," I whispered, shaking my head in denial and horror, and suddenly screamed as the disinfectant made contact with my arm. Samantha pressed her lips together at the sound but just tightened her hold on my arm as I started to thrash, cleaning it at a quick, brusque pace.

"Someone hold him down!" a voice barked, and suddenly there were multiple people on me, keeping me from trying to throw them off. "Look, kid! You need calm down!"

"Jack!" I shouted, tossing my head as I tried to see my boyfriend lying on the bed only a few feet from me and yet too far away. I reached out, struggling to grab his hand where it hung stiffly off the bed. My fingers just groped at empty air. *"Jack!"* Deft hands pulled my dog tag from beneath my shirt and pulled it over my head.

"Jemma, his name is Private Tristan Byrne, number 34927530," the hands' owner said, passing the pieces of metal off to another nurse. "Private

Jones said he served in Howell's Unit 37, deployed with the latest batch from the Academy. Find his blood type in the register, get some, and start him on a transfusion."

There was a new type of burning in my arm, and I looked over to see the ragged cut bleeding anew as Samantha pulled away, the tourniquet in her hands. The cloth she'd used to clean me was covered in mud, bits of flesh, grime, and sullied blood.

"How did this get cut, private?" a younger man asked as he hurried over, prepping a shot of something he swiftly injected into my arm.

"It was an accident," I babbled, looking at him with wide, tearful eyes. "I-I had to get out – to save Jack – is Jack going to be okay?" I couldn't focus on the questions he was asking, couldn't think straight.

"We're doing our best for him, Tristan," the doctor said firmly, drawing my scattered attention to the current situation once more. "Now, I need you to tell me what you cut your arm with."

"Bayonet. I-It was sharpened against protocol, but it – it was all I had. I was tr-trying to lift a rock, I had to help Jack, he–" One of the nurses ran over with a rudimentary IV of blood to the still body beside me and quickly slipped the needle into the inside of his forearm, starting the flow and pulling over a bright white light and surgical kit. "Jack...Jack?"

There was still no response, and I felt like screaming again.

"Tristan, the bayonet you cut yourself with was very dirty. And it looks like you cut the bone when you got injured." The doctor kept talking to me, telling me something that looked important, but I couldn't hear him. I couldn't understand. "Tristan!" I focused on him again, eyes wide. "Do you understand what we're saying?"

"I don't care. I don't care what you do to me, I just need Jack safe!" I snapped, trying to jerk my arm away from them, and the nurse looked at the blood stained cloth in her hands, biting her lip. The doctor nodded.

"Okay, Tristan. We gave you a drug that will knock you out and numb your body. That'll let us operate, and when you wake up, you'll be on the mend. It's all going to be okay, son," he said gently, his still-pure voice echoing in my ears as whatever they gave me kicked in.

"Jack?" I whispered, turning my head to face my boyfriend as my vision darkened, and my heart stopped as I saw the nurses start running, flocking around his bed to start CPR.

Then, I saw nothing.

We need to cut it, someone said.

Prep his arm.

DAY ONE HUNDRED AND FIFTY-ONE

Three days later

I woke up a few times over the course of the operation on my arm, but never long enough to ask about Jack or see what was happening with him. I did catch a few blurry images: nurses bringing doctors scalpels and forceps, gauze and sutures. At one point, it looked like they were pricking his legs and feet with small needles. A few times I thought some nurses were doing CPR again, but I could never be sure of what I saw. I felt like I was seeing everything through a frosted pane of glass, catching fuzzy glimpses of what was going on before the world went dark again.

Finally though, I woke up.

My eyes opened slowly, gradually taking in the light and colors around me. I felt exhausted, battered, and utterly drained. There wasn't one part of me that didn't hurt, and the longer I was awake, the more I wanted to close my eyes and go back to sleep. My breath still rattled painfully in my chest. My head still burned with the heat of a fever. My bones still ached, and my body pulsed and throbbed with pain.

I was tired, and it wasn't because I needed more sleep than was physically possible, but because I was just tired of this life we all had. I was tired of the pressure. I was tired of the stress and trauma. But I was only awake for about ten seconds before I remembered. Before everything came crashing back on me.

My heart leaped into my throat, and I roughly pushed myself into a sitting position only to gasp in sharp pain as I inevitably shoved my right arm against the sheets and pillows. I felt lopsided, off somehow. I was still disoriented, breathing raggedly, and I quickly looked down at my right arm, the phantom pain of the bayonet slicing through me again. And I froze.

It was...*gone*.

I blinked a few times, unable to comprehend what I was seeing. It was just *gone*. That doctor, whoever he was, had *cut off my fucking arm*. I dizzily lifted my hand to the bloodstained bandage and almost cried out as what was left of my right limb erupted in pain at the slightest touch. It had been amputated about an inch above my elbow, and I took in a trembling breath, even more frightened and unsettled than before.

Shaken and nauseated, I looked at my surroundings and saw that I was in a separate wing. Everything here was cleaner, the bedding and bandages whiter. The people around me weren't screaming or crying in pain like the patients had been in the main tent I'd come into with Jack. In fact, most of them seemed to be comatose – some bandaged so much I thought they were wrapped in burial shrouds.

Jack.

Panic rising in my chest and nearly suffocating me, I turned to look at the bed next to me and heaved a sigh of relief, tears welling in my eyes. Jack was safe and sound beside me, propped up on a couple pillows so he wasn't lying flat on his back. He was either asleep or unconscious; I wasn't sure which. But all that mattered to me was that he was alive. Jack Miller, *my* Jack Miller, was alive and breathing. I took in a sharp breath, and before I could stop myself I was sobbing, crying in relief with my one hand shakily pressed over my mouth. I was terrified that if I took my eyes off of him for a second, if I so much as blinked, he'd be gone again.

"Jack?" I whispered, moving to get out of my bed and go over to him but stopping when I realized I was attached to an IV. "Jack?" There was no answer. He just continued to lie there, complexion pale and washed out, the skin around his eyes bruised purple-black and sunken. His face was scabbed over in some places, angry and infected in others. "Jack? Can you hear me?"

"Oh, good. You're awake, private."

I jumped, suitably startled, and looked in the direction of the voice, scrubbing quickly at my eyes. There was a woman heading over to me from the other side of the tent, and I quickly recognized her as the nurse who'd tended to Jack. She'd looked at me with that grim expression.

"My name is Tama Weiss," she greeted, brusque and indifferent. "I've been assigned to take care of you and Corporal Miller."

"Is he going to be okay?"

She smiled, a forced expression on her austere face, and sat beside my legs on the bed.

"Why don't you tell me what happened to you two?"

I took in a deep breath and reluctantly looked over at my unconscious boyfriend. There was some more blood in his face than before. Not a lot, but certainly more, and the waxy texture was all but gone even if the bruises and cuts weren't. I could stand to wait a little longer before demanding to know about him…and whatever had happened to my arm.

"You were with thirty-seven, but you were found with Harper, private," the nurse pressed. "They were stationed a little over a mile away. Did…did you carry the corporal all that time?"

I shook my head, voice answering automatically.

"Thirty-seven and thirty-six got pushed back." I could smell the smoke and hear the explosions, and the ringing returned to my ears as though something had just blown up next right next to me all over again. Oddly, I didn't even flinch at the sensory assault. It felt natural after everything. "We joined up with Captain Harper after Captain Howell was…"

My breath hitched, and the shot fired. Jack stared down the barrel of his gun at our dead captain, and I could see him kneeling in the rain, could see Aliyah stepping over to him, Howell's coat in her arms. I struggled to breathe evenly and looked down at my hand, heart stuttering at the sight of just the one.

"After he was killed by enemy fire," I finished, and she nodded.

"That's still a quarter mile through some very rough trenching, Byrne," she said gently, and I looked at her.

"Yeah, I carried him from there to here," I stated, answering her silent question with more than a hint of anger. "What else was I supposed to do?"

She nodded easily and held up her hands in a placating gesture.

"I'm sorry. I was just impressed at how much you managed to do with your injuries, unassisted," her voice said somewhere above me as I stared at the sheets over my legs. "The shock alone would keep most people from forming even a rational thought."

Tears started pricking my eyes again, and my chest constricted with fury and helplessness.

"If you want to gawk at me or – or try to figure out how an adrenaline rush could let someone like me to do everything I did, save it for when I'm sleeping," I finally snapped, glaring at her, and she floundered as she tried to explain herself.

"That wasn't what I...I'm sorry. If it's too soon, I can leave you alone. I only asked because Doctor Nagai wants to know what happened, and–"

"Then tell *him* to ask me," I interrupted, words hissed through clenched teeth. I knew I was being unfair, but I couldn't help it. "I just...all I need to know is if Jack's okay."

"You care a lot for the young man," she said, evading my question.

"Yeah, well, I should." The retort slipped out of my lips before I could stop it, and I quickly clamped my mouth shut, staring at Jack's unconscious body in silence.

"I'll leave you two alone. Doctor Nagai will be in shortly to talk to you about your arm and the corporal." She turned to leave, but before she left, I called after her.

"The line – is it really broken?"

She looked back at me and nodded.

"Yes. The Brettain halted their movement three days ago, around the same time when you and the corporal were brought in. As far as we can tell, they haven't started advancing again. But...it's strange."

I frowned.

"How so?"

She shook her head in bafflement as she answered.

"The scouts they're sending out? They're brandishing white flags."

"That's surrender," I said, mostly to myself, and she nodded.

"Exactly. But the thing is...they aren't surrendering." She looked down at her hands. "Reports say that any wounded that they come across they're taking in and treating as their own. The relatively whole people they come across are made prisoners of war, but from what we've heard, they're treated like equals." She looked back up at me. "It makes no sense."

"It makes perfect sense," I answered, voice quiet as I pieced together what was going beyond the canvas walls boxing us in. She looked at me in curiosity. "The Brettain are done fighting. They know we've lost, so what's the point of continuing to fight?"

"They're still shooting our soldiers," she protested, growing indignant, and I scoffed, letting my head thud back against the pillows.

"Did our people shoot first?" I asked softly after a few moments, and, she finally left, a thoughtful, reflective look on her face. However, it didn't last long. No sooner had Weiss left than the tent door re-opened to reveal the young Xiang doctor who'd cut off my arm.

"Hello, Tristan," he sighed, pulling a chair with him and sitting between my bed and Jack's, his back to my boyfriend. "I'm Doctor Nagai. I did your surgery there." I glanced down at *it*, unable to comprehend that what I was staring at was actually part of my body.

"Yeah, well...nice work."

He gave a sad smile in response to my bitter words.

"It was never our intention to amputate, Byrne. But whatever you cut yourself with, I believe you said it was a bayonet, it didn't make a clean cut. It splintered and scored your bones, depositing bacteria and necrotic flesh inside the tissue. It was a very grisly wound, and, given how low we are on supplies, you almost definitely would have gotten gangrene. We wouldn't have been able to treat it, and it would have killed you in the long run."

I scoffed at his explanation. It felt woefully inadequate.

"So you decided to just...cut it off," I muttered, unfairly cold. Instead of engaging me, he cleared his throat and carried on with his own train of thought.

"I heard you chase Nurse Weiss out of here." I didn't answer, looking past him at Jack. "Corporal Miller is going to be *fine*, private. And he's got you to thank for that." Still staring at the sleeping man beside me, I gave a small, absent smile – nothing more than a barely visible quirk at the corner of my lips. But most of what I felt was in my eyes. I sniffed once, drawing the back of my hand across my nose. "You okay, son?"

"Yeah." My voice was thick and unsteady. "Yeah. Yeah, I'm great. *Peachy*, even." He nodded at my sarcasm, once again refusing to participate in an argument, and for some reason it was just making me more and more pissed off.

"I got in touch with your S.O. Gaius Jax," he continued, and I looked at him in apprehension behind the frustrated anger. *Please tell me he didn't say anything. Please, please–* "He's coming out with the next caravan of troops to talk with you and the corporal if he's awake."

"What do you mean *if* he's awake?" I asked, the familiar and nauseating sensation of fear starting to build inside me again.

The doctor sighed, leaning forward to rest his forearms on the edge of my bed with tired eyes. His expression was sympathetic and kind, but for some reason I felt anything but comforted.

"That's why I need you to tell me what happened to the two of you." His voice was gentle, even kind. "If I know what happened, I can explain everything. But right now, there's some confusion, and I can't confidently explain what happened to your friend." I nodded, breathing as deeply as I could as I sat in silence. My left hand shakily clenched and unclenched in my lap, and a sharp pain stabbed through the stump of my right arm, making me wince. "You can take your time. I'm sure this was all very stressful for you."

"Yeah," I laughed, voice shaking. "Yeah, you have no idea." I pinched the bridge of my nose and tried to take deep breaths in the hope that that would be enough to clear my mind and let me focus.

Fine. Fine...fall back.

"There was an incoming shell from an artillery aimed for the trenches where Jack and I were stationed..." I began, eyes deliberately unfocused and expression vacant. "It missed and buried itself in the mud just above us. About eight feet out into No Man's Land. When it exploded..." I trailed off, remembering how the very air around us erupted in flames. "Part of the trench collapsed, and I got pinned under the rubble. I managed to hold out for a little, but I...I was about to get gunned down when Jack showed up."

I could feel the fear rising up in my throat, suffocating me. The scream was building in my gut once more as I remembered being unable to move, trapped, certain I was going to die.

"He was coming to help me when..." I stopped, biting my tongue until I tasted blood to keep myself from crying.

"I get what happened next, Byrne. You don't have to say that part, if you don't like."

I sighed in relief and quickly nodded as I closed my eyes and cleared my throat.

"I, uh...I tried to get out, but I couldn't pull my arm free. I was almost out of the rubble, but–" I laughed in bitter, helpless anger and opened my eyes once more. "I just...I just couldn't get my right arm out. So I, uh...I tried to use leverage with a bayonet I pulled out of one of the – one of the peo...the bodies on the ground."

"It slipped, and you got hurt," Nagai finished. I nodded. "Gods, son." He shook his head, pitying expression making me feel sick. It felt wrong somehow, that level of sympathy, that word *son* coming from a man who was only a few years my senior.

"Next, I, uh, pulled the bayonet out and put a tourniquet on my arm." My words felt robotic, detached. "Tried to stop Jack's bleeding. Then, I picked him up with a fireman's lift—"

"You did that with your arm in the shape it was in when you got here?"

"You'd be surprised by what you can do when it's a matter of life or death," I said quietly. *And when it's someone you love more than life.* "When a person's survival depends on you not screwing up for once and doing the impossible, you usually find a way to make it happen." I paused to refocus myself, words grim and barely audible. "You know the rest."

Nagai sat there, mulling over what he'd heard, and nodded.

"Well, that certainly explains what happened to your friend," he sighed, pulling a small notebook from his pocket and scribbling a few lines down.

Something heavy and cold settled in my stomach.

"What do you mean?" I whispered, looking up at him slowly.

"It probably happened when you lifted him up onto your shoulders and stood up. Or when even you set him down and passed him off to Private Jones," he explained, standing and walking over to check on my still-unconscious Jack. "You saved his life, of course. If you hadn't been there, Corporal Miller would have bled out and died alone."

"What did I do?" I asked, coldness spreading, and watched him with wide eyes. My breathing was growing ragged again, and I choked down a cough. "What did I do to Jack?"

"I'm assuming that the battlefield was a bit hazy, yes?" I nodded, heart in my throat. "Was it Miller who told you what the gun was?"

"Yeah," I answered with a nod. "It was a standard issue rifle."

Here, Nagai shook his head, and the ice spreading throughout my body reached my blood.

"I'm afraid the bullet we pulled out of Miller was a much larger round than the ones used in standard issues. My forensics nurse says your corporal was hit by a sharp shooter."

My heart stopped as I remembered the size of the entry wound.

Large, too large for a standard rifle —

"Oh my gods," I breathed, hand shakily covering my mouth. "Oh my gods, I moved him." I looked at the doctor in horror. "A bullet that big in that sensitive of an area – and I moved him…"

"Byrne, you were following the protocol for a standard issue rifle," the doctor interrupted gently. "You couldn't have known."

"That's why I didn't see anyone on the ridge after he…but why would Jack lie to me?" I asked, confused and betrayed. "Why didn't he tell me he hadn't seen the shooter?" My voice was getting louder, and Nagai raised his hands placatingly.

"Private, I need you to calm down. Please."

I rested my forehead against my left knee, struggling to keep calm while my life lay in the bed beside me, fading away. Somewhere in front of me that damned doctor was still talking.

"Now, Corporal Miller probably didn't say anything to you about not having seen the shooter because he didn't want you to feel even more helpless than you already did. If he'd told you he hadn't seen the gunman, you wouldn't have known the caliber, and you'd have been in the dark. You wouldn't have known how to help him, and Miller would have died. By telling you it was standard issue, he gave you something to do – something to focus on. Tell me." I looked up at him, tears burning in my eyes. "Would you have been able to do what you did for that young man if you hadn't known the gun? The supposed extent of his injury?" Mutely, I shook my head. "That's right. You both would be dead right now."

"But I moved him," I protested, voice shaking. "Doctor, I moved him while he had a sharp shooter's slug in his stomach."

The man sighed.

"Seeing as the enemy only uses sharp shooters for designated targets, I'm guessing that the bullet was fired by some greenstick Brettain private." He spat the last words out, obviously disgusted, but I couldn't share in his displeasure. I could only wait for him to get to the point. "Clearly, he didn't know who he was supposed to be shooting at in the first place, otherwise he never would've wasted a bullet on Miller. In fact, given that it was still in Miller when we got to him, I'm guessing the sniper had to fire through something else first–"

"Doc. *Stop* procrastinating and just tell me," I interrupted, voice harsh and panicked. "What did I do to him when I picked him up?"

"My guess is that when you decided to move him in a fireman's lift, you shifted his spine, which was already damaged from the bullet. You moved it, jostled it around, and it…" He paused, as though assessing whether or not I was really ready to hear Jack's prognosis. "The movement coupled with the severe damage to his body irreparably damaged part of either his spinal cord or nerves. We're not sure which. If…when he wakes up, he's going to be paralyzed from his hips down. If he's lucky and listens to our treatment plans, the damage won't go any higher than that."

I couldn't breathe. Everything had just stopped. Time was non-existent, and all I could do was stare at my paralyzed Jack, at my brave, foolish, *stupid* Jack and hate him for what he'd done.

"How could...how could he have done that?" I whispered, pressing my hand over my face as the tears in my eyes reached the tipping point. "How could *I* have–"

"This isn't your fault, Byrne, and it isn't Miller's. You both did every part of this exactly right."

I didn't believe him. Couldn't believe him. How was this – paralysis and amputations – supposed to be doing things right?

Nagai got to his feet, gathering his clipboard from where he'd dropped it on the foot of my bed and transcribing the notes from his notebook.

"Nurse Weiss will be back in a little while to check on you and change your bandages." He was about to walk away when he saw that I still hadn't looked up from my knees – that I was still silently crying to myself. Sighing, he reached out, gently putting his hand on my shoulder. I looked at the tent wall across from me with vacant eyes. "What is it, Byrne?"

"Nothing. Nothing, it's just..." I sighed, blinking slowly as I looked up at him. I felt empty. The man's words had hollowed me out like the scalpel he'd used to cut into me and...oh *gods*. "Jack...Jack just loved to dance."

... — — ...

Nagai gave me something for my cough that also knocked me out, and I was asleep almost instantly. But this unconsciousness was deep and dark, something almost worse than the dreams that had been plaguing me for the last several months. I was staring down the endless abyss of my own mind, and the blackness I saw scared me. Occasionally, the sound of gunfire woke me up in a cold sweat, but the shots were always distant and never repeated. I often wondered if my mind was playing tricks on me.

But every time I woke, I immediately looked to my left. And every time Jack was still lying there, unconscious and unstable. Sometimes a little paler than before, other times with a bit more color...but he was still there.

It was near sunset when I woke up for the third time that day. Despite my several naps, I still felt heavy and exhausted. I just wanted to fall back asleep and pray that when I woke up everything would be okay again.

It never was, but it didn't hurt to hope.

The air was cooler, and the light from outside was dim, barely strong enough to pass through the canvas walls of the tent. I slowly sat up, taking care to keep my body clear of the IV line and my throbbing right arm away from the rough fabric. And, just as I always did, I looked to my left.

Jack was still there, still sleeping. But he wasn't alone. I blinked in confusion as I stared at the raven perched on the foot of his bed, its long talons clicking against the wood as the bird shifted slightly. It stared at me intently for a bit, beady eyes wide and unblinking, before giving a low chuckling croak and looking to Jack.

"Get out of here!" I hissed, flapping my hand at it. It sidled away from me down the length of the footboard railing. "Go!"

Instead of flying out the open tent door, the raven hopped down onto Jack's bed with a disgruntled croak, landing awkwardly on one of his legs and flapping its wings to regain its balance.

"Stop it, get out of here!" I snapped, jerking the sheets back to get out of bed before remembering I was still connected to the IV. The bird didn't listen. It just continued to walk forward, pausing and flapping its wings whenever its nails got caught in the threads of the blanket.

"Fucking bird, get *out*," I scolded, looking around for something to throw at the corvid as our unwanted guest hopped off Jack's thigh and onto his hand before continuing its walk up his arm. All the while, it continued its innocuous croaks and gurgles, picking at some parts of the blanket and dragging it up a little higher.

"I swear to god, bird," I began, getting out of bed and slowly dragging my IV around the bed with me. It stopped and looked at me, now perched on Jack's shoulder. "If you don't get out of here right fucking now, I will–"

"It's okay."

My heart stopped. That voice. I hadn't heard that voice in months. I shouldn't have heard that voice again, *couldn't* hear it again. That soft, gentle voice with a lilt of melody to it, innocent–

"It's okay," the voice repeated behind me with a familiar giggle, and I could almost hear that smile in the light laughter: that blinding smile that had been so rare. The bird bobbed its head up and down a little bit in preparation for flight, looking towards the speaker. "He's just a herald."

I couldn't breathe. Couldn't speak. I couldn't move until the bird took off, and I quickly turned, following its flight over my shoulder to someone standing at the end of the tent, and all I could feel was fear at what I'd see–

"Private!"

My eyes snapped open, and I awkwardly sat up, slipping to the side and crying out in pain as my amputated arm dug into the mattress.

"Easy, son. Easy, that's it."

Warm hands gently lifted me back up into a sitting position, easing me back against the pillows. The room was still dim, but definitely not as dark as it had been a moment ago.

"Wh-what?" I stammered, disoriented, and looked up into Nagai's face as he loomed over me. He gave a comforting, understanding smile and sat back on the mattress.

"You were having a dream, Tristan."

Dream. Of course it was a dream. Dead people don't come back.

I took in several deep, calming breaths and closed my eyes.

"Nightmares are to be expected given what you've been through. Have you experienced any dreams like this before?"

I didn't answer him, couldn't. Instead, I started dragging the inside of my arm against my side, struggling to drag the IV needle from the inside of my elbow out without my other hand.

"Tristan. Tristan, I need you to leave that alone."

"Get it off of me," I hissed and looked up at the doctor with a strained expression. "Get it off, I don't need your medicine! I don't need to sleep anymore, just get it out!"

I don't want your dreams.

My voice had picked up in volume and franticness, and Nagai reached out to still my arm.

"Okay. Okay, Tristan, we'll take you off the meds. It's fine. I can't force medicine on you, so I'll take this out now. Alright?" I nodded and stopped pulling against him, letting him ease the needle out of my skin. "See? Good as new."

I yanked back the covers and moved my legs towards the edge of the mattress. My right knee twinged painfully at the movement, and I paused. I was still wearing my uniform pants, but my shoes and socks were gone, replaced instead with some kind of canvas hospital slipper. I was wearing a worn old tank top that was a few sizes too large instead of my long sleeve shirt, and I looked up at the doctor.

"Where are the rest of my clothes?" I asked softly, and the man reached over to the chair beside my bed.

"Here, but..." He trailed off and handed me the shirt. He left the boots on the ground, and for that I was thankful. I wasn't quite sure how I was going to tie my shoes without my right hand just yet.

"But what?" I mumbled, taking the shirt from him, and immediately I knew what he was talking about.

"There was quite a lot of blood," he explained, crossing his arms. "And from what I can tell, most of it was the corporal's." I felt nauseous, and the blood-hardened fabric scratched against my fingertips. *Jack's blood.*

"Oh," I managed, voice quiet.

"I'm already searching through the, uh...let's call them *recycled* clothes for something in your sizes. Your friend Private Jones took the corporal's jacket before his surgery, as well." My heart started pounding, and I looked up at the doctor. "I think she burned it, but it was stained pretty badly. No one could have reused it – too much blood. I told her to take yours as well, but she said that was your choice, not hers. She did figure out a way to knot the right sleeve so that you can't see the blood as much, but the back was pretty soiled as well..." he was saying, but I wasn't really listening.

"It's fine," I mumbled, turning the sleeve over in my hand.

A dark brown stain covered the knotted end of the right arm, most of the discoloration confined to the tightened loops of fabric. But as I turned the entire garment over, I remembered the hot, sticky press of blood against my shoulders. The entire back was mottled with brown and maroon stains, the fabric scraping against my skin and leaving trails of rust along my hands.

It wasn't fine. I wasn't going to be able to salvage this.

"Actually, um," I whispered, voice unexpectedly hoarse, and I looked away from the fabric to Jack's body. "Can you, uh..."

"I'll throw it out for you, private," Nagai said gently, reaching out and taking my uniform from me. He started towards the door, the shirt folded over his arm. "If you would like, you can walk outside now. The sedatives will make you a bit dizzy and disoriented, but they shouldn't hinder you too much."

"Thank you," I said. The words were pitched so low that I doubt he heard them, and he stepped out of the tent without another word.

The world was silent, suspended in a pensive, easy quiet that for once didn't have my skin crawling. I slowly finished easing my legs over the edge of the bed, and I immediately clenched my teeth, groaning. My right knee, the one I'd hurt repeatedly during the chaos of the last five days, erupted in a new wave of pain, and I gingerly pulled my pant leg up to get a look at the aching joint. The kneecap was purple and blue-ish black, the skin swollen and hot to the touch, and I flashed back to when I'd run to tell Blackwell the line was falling. I remembered the way my cheek had slammed into somebody's boot, palms grating against the ground and shoulders cracking at the impact. I must have slammed my knee into a rock or something, too.

I took in a deep breath and slowly eased myself to the ground, inhaling sharply through gritted teeth as I put my full weight down on the unsteady joint. This was the first time I'd felt the ground beneath my feet in days. My right arm throbbed with pain as I stood up straight, the blood pounding heavily in the new base of my arm. I took one wobbly step forward before I almost lost my balance and braced myself on the edge of the mattress. My breath shuddered in my lungs, and angry, helpless tears blinded my vision at how broken I felt. I couldn't even *walk* properly.

"Jack?" I whispered and slowly hobbled around my bed, using it as a crutch to cross the space between us. I finally came to a swaying stop on his left side and balanced myself with his IV stand. "Hey…Jack?"

His eyes remained closed. His features were still slack. And as I looked at the cuts and bruises marring his vulnerable face, I felt my gaze dragged downwards.

"Oh, gods," I whispered to myself and slowly reached out, grabbing the edge of the blanket dragged halfway up his bare chest.

The scars and freshly scabbed over nicks seemed to point the way, and I gingerly pulled the sheet away from his battered body until I caught sight of the edges of the bandages tightly bound around his abdomen. I closed my eyes and took in a slow, steadying breath before quickly glancing over my shoulder. No one else was awake, and there were no orderlies, doctors, or nurses around to scold me.

"Okay," I whispered and looked back at my boyfriend. "Okay."

It couldn't be as bad as Nagai had said it was. This was Jack Miller. *Jack Miller*. He survived three tours to the front lines. He always found a way to beat the system. He always managed to come out on top even when he was beaten down to the bottom. But as I slowly pulled the blanket back the rest of the way, I saw the rest of his bandages.

It was as bad as the doctor had said.

"What the hell are they doing?" I whispered, shaken and disgusted, and glanced briefly at Jack's unconscious face. "*I* can do better than these guys,

Jack. Can you believe this?" I scoffed, forcing myself to be lighthearted, and looked back at his stomach.

His skin was bruised and swollen around the edges of the gauze. The fabric itself was bloodied, the color growing progressively darker the closer to the center of his wound it was until it was nearly black. I reached out and gently brushed my fingers along the surface, and when I pulled them back they were stained red. Fresh blood, then. Nagai was either an idiot going for open wound healing, or they had just finished stitching him up.

"What are you doing?"

I looked over my shoulder to see Nurse Weiss storming over from the tent door, expression reprimanding. I didn't care, though. I was just pissed enough to deal with her.

"This is supposed to be dry!" I snapped and furiously pointed to Jack's wound. She looked suitably startled at that and brushed past me, following my shaking finger. "You need to keep GSWs dry and clean. This isn't dry and clean!"

"We were planning on changing his bandage in a few minutes with the others, Private Byrne," she countered stiffly and looked over my shoulder at something. She jerked her head towards Jack's bed, and I turned to look. A few other nurses had entered the room behind her, and they pulled me back out of the way. "Now, if you would please stop harassing our patients and let us do our jobs—"

"I want Blackwell," I interrupted. The nurses looked at each other in confusion as they started changing Jack's dressings. "Doctor Blackwell? He was with Unit 37 under Howell. I want him to treat Corporal Miller."

"We'll find him once we're done here," another girl said gently from beside Jack's head, and I looked at her. She looked very familiar, and I stared at her for a few seconds until I placed her. She was Samantha, the girl who'd helped treat me with Nagai. "If you could just step outside for a few minutes, we'll be done here shortly." She gave me a calm, reassuring smile. "I promise we'll take care of him." I reluctantly nodded, backing away, and slowly left on my shaking legs.

As I exited the tent, I gingerly moved my left hand to the remnants of my right arm and slowly allowed the fingers to curl around the ravaged flesh. There was something grounding in the sharp pain that drove through me, something that twistedly reassured me. The cloud cover that had been hanging over us for so long now had almost entirely dispersed, and the sky was darkly vibrant as the sun sank towards the horizon. The dusky blue was fading into indigo, the orange turning red, and I looked around at my dimming surroundings.

There weren't many people walking around outside. The few that I saw looked busy or preoccupied, and some I didn't even dare to go up to. And finally, as I stood there, turning in circles, trying to find even the slightest inkling of where to go or even a familiar face, I realized something.

I was alone. I slowly released my hold on my arm. All of the faces I saw around me were unfamiliar. I had no idea where anyone I knew was. I knew that Marcel had made it, and if Marcel had made it and wasn't walking around out here, that meant…

"Korsakov," I whispered in sickened realization and picked a person to approach. "Excuse me," I called, limping over to a private sitting against the trench. His leg was poorly bandaged at the thigh, and a crutch rested across his lap. He looked up at me, an uninterested light in his eyes until he saw my arm. "Have you seen a group of four girls walking around anywhere?"

He didn't answer me. He just stared fixedly at my right shoulder, and I self-consciously crossed my left arm over my chest, grabbing the point of my shoulder and obscuring my amputated limb from view.

"Sorry, man," he mumbled, hesitantly looking me in the face.

"No, it's…it's fine," I said, not meeting his gaze. "But the girls – have you seen them?" I finally looked at him, and thankfully he was still paying attention. "Two of them are Mezitain, average height. Third one's Rusikan, pretty short, and the fourth one's a really tall Arikaan." A faint glimmer of recognition flickered in the back of his eyes, and I quickly continued. "Um, the short one's got blue eyes and white hair – looks kind of sick." He sat up a little straighter and pointed at me, cutting me off.

"Yeah. Yeah, I saw them." He gestured towards the medical tent across from the one I had just come from, and my heart dropped. "In there. Blue eyes and white hair's definitely sick."

"Thank you," I said, nodding my thanks before turning on my heel and half-jogging, half-stumbling back inside, scanning the beds for my friends as soon as I crossed the threshold.

"Byrne. Is something wrong?"

I looked around at Nagai, the man's expression kind and sympathetic – concerned in that same manner that rubbed me the wrong way. The words felt heavy on my tongue as I spoke them.

"I'm looking for Irina Korsakov."

He pointed towards a curtained off bed at the far corner of the room before turning back to his patient. I slowly walked over, stomach uneasy, to stand just outside the half-closed curtains. Marcel and Katalin were sitting in chairs to either side of the bed, and Aliyah was perched at the foot of the mattress, hand resting on her friend's leg.

"How are you feeling?" she asked, and Irina scoffed.

"How do you think, Aliyah? It's like my blood's on fire," she groaned and wearily closed her eyes. "I asked for it, though, not getting checked out by Blackwell."

"Should've listened to me," I said, and the others turned around, eyes widening in surprise.

"Well, well, well. Look who's back from the dead," Marcel teased, and I scoffed, meeting her gaze. "You look good, shrimp. You know, despite the fact three quarters of your right arm's gone."

"How's Miller?" Kat asked softly.

"Not good," I said. "He hasn't woken up yet, and I had to chew out his nurses for not keeping his wound dry." I double-checked my headcount. *Four.* My heart skipped a beat. "Did Jayce..." I began and trailed off, unable to finish my question. Marcel nodded quickly.

"He's fine. Busted up his arm a bit, but he's alive. He's fine."

I sighed in relief, a little tension leaving my shoulders as I nodded. We went silent, awkwardly hovering around each other until I walked over and sat on the opposite side of the bed from Moore. Its occupant smiled slightly at me, and I forced myself to return the expression.

"Are they keeping you comfortable?"

"It's enough," Irina responded, eyes closing sleepily. "They keep giving me something that knocks me out, but they've got nothing else. They ran out of gangrene meds weeks ago."

"Yeah, they were giving me some of that stuff, too. Doesn't do shit," I sympathized, and she wearily shook her head in agreement.

"If the Brettain catch up with us, maybe they'll have medicine," Marcel said softly, and Irina laughed deliriously.

"Marcel, there is no way I'm taking meds from the Brettain. Not after everything they've put us through." We didn't press the issue and instead sat there, watching our hands. Only Moore seemed able to stare our dying friend in the face. "What is it?"

"Nothing. I'm just making sure that someone is watching over you," the woman said gently, patting the girl's leg. "Rest, Irina. We will be here when you wake up."

At those words, I got to my feet and started to head towards the door.

"Where are you going?" Katalin called, challenging me out of force of habit, and I looked over my shoulder at her.

"I'm gonna go sit with Jack until he wakes up. They should be done changing his bandages by now." I took a couple more lopsided steps before turning back to them again. "Take care of her." The three women nodded, and I sighed, dragging my weary body back to my own hospital wing.

When I got there, Nagai was hunched over Jack's body, lifting his eyelids, raising and dropping his hands, and taking notes. As though Jack was a mannequin for study, a cadaver the surgeons practiced their technique on.

"What's going on?" I demanded. Nagai looked up at me and straightened, completely unfazed by my tone.

"I'm making sure your friend hasn't slipped further into his coma."

"Is that...do you think he will?" I asked, suddenly feeling clammy. He simply sighed and shrugged.

"He might. He might not. The damage to his small intestine was very extensive, and the septic shock almost killed him. It's actually miraculous he pulled through. He still has a fever, but his chances of beating the infection are good." He trailed off, lost in his own thoughts as he stared at Jack, and I noisily clearly my throat. He looked back at me, apologetic. "I'm sorry. As I was saying, having no response after intensive surgery is to be expected, but it *has* been three days since we operated. We were hoping for some kind of reaction by this point."

My throat constricted, and I crossed my arm over my chest to grip my amputated limb as tightly as I could. I focused on the sharp pain burning through my arm and shoulder.

Ground yourself.

"Is..." I cleared my throat and tried again. "Is he dying?"

This time the doctor readily shook his head and was about to continue when another voice interrupted.

"*Always* with the questions." We both looked over our shoulders to see Blackwell approaching, medical bag in hand. Relief flooded my body, and a weight that I hadn't even realized had been on my shoulders lifted. "Hello, Steven. I'm here to take over care for my patient."

"*Your* patient?"

The old man nodded, wincing as the motion pulled at some stitches on his neck.

"I've quite the bond with these two idiots, and I understand how they work," he explained and gestured to my boyfriend and me like we weren't even in the room. "So, I'd like to take them off your hands."

Nagai leafed through the papers on his clipboard before shrugging and handing off the chart.

"Feel free. But if Corporal Miller over there wakes up, I want to be the first to know," he warned and quickly left the tent. Blackwell looked at me and rolled his eyes.

"As if," he snorted. "*You*, Tristan, will be the first one to know."

There was a twinkle in his eyes as he smirked at me, and I walked over to him, locking my arms around him in a hug. I just barely managed to keep down my cry of pain as I accidentally pressed the ragged, bandaged end of my right arm against his side.

"Well, someone's happy to see me," he laughed, and I nodded vehemently, not trusting my voice just yet.

"You made it out," I finally said, tightly closing my eyes and taking in a deep breath. Everyone was alive, if that was even possible. *Everyone had lived.* He pulled back and clapped a hand on my uninjured shoulder.

"I told you, kid. I've been on the front lines for too long. I know when and how to retreat." With that, he pulled the makeshift clothesline curtains shut around both my bed and Jack's to give us a bubble of privacy. "Feel free to hop into bed with him now, son. I know that's what you've wanted to do since you woke up."

I gave a wry smile, and as he left, I pulled myself onto Jack's bed and settled down next to him. My head nestled against his shoulder, and I moved to rest my right hand on him only to remember it wasn't there anymore. Hissing slightly in pain, I moved to Jack's other side and lay down on my right side. Struggling to ignore the pain of my amputated limb against the mattress, I carefully rested my left hand over the clean, dry bandages wrapped about his torso and let my fingertips trace over the rough material holding him together. I could feel his pulse through the fabric, could count the slow beats.

After several moments of feeling his heart fight to stay alive, I reached out and pulled the covers up over us, closing my eyes against my tears as I returned my one hand to his wound. I wished that my touch could make it all go away – like in the fairy tales and myths. But instead of feeling renewed flesh under my fingers, all I felt was the same funereal tick of his heart.

"Jack?" I whispered, pleadingly. When there was no response, I gently kissed his cheek and rested my head back down on his chest. I listened to his heart beat in my ear as my breath rattled in my lungs. "Jack, if you can hear me, please…wake up."

Seconds turned to minutes.

Minutes to hours.

And still he slept on, leaving me to hold onto his empty body and softly cry into his shoulder until I fell asleep.

DAY ONE HUNDRED AND FIFTY-EIGHT

Seven days later

"Should have known." My eyes opened at the angry statement, and my sleep-blurred vision slowly focused on Doctor Nagai glaring down at me. "And here I've been calling you two *friends*."

"Shit," I groaned.

I sat up and coughed, grinding the heel of my palm into my eyes and trying to drive away the situation at hand. But when I looked up again, he was still there. For a whole week, thanks in part to the efforts of Blackwell, I'd managed to sleep next to Jack at night and not get caught by what I'd discovered was a rather homophobic staff with the exception of Samantha. But it seemed that was over.

"Out of all the social taboos for me to get, I have to get the shags," he growled to himself as he angrily scribbled something on his clipboard, and I eased myself to the ground, slowly straightening my back.

"And out of all the doctors," I countered, voice tired, "I have to get the asshole." His expression darkened, and I smiled coldly. "By the way, if I still had my right hand I'd punch you right about now, because I *really* don't like the word shag." Before we could continue passive aggressively threatening each other, a welcome voice interrupted us.

"I thought I told you these were my patients now, Nagai," Blackwell called and came to a stop between us. He looked at each of us in turn with scolding eyes. "Am I interrupting something?"

"Apparently, not everyone in the world of medicine is as enlightened as you," I said pointedly before making my way back to my own bed and lying down. Another cough forced its way out of my throat as I shuddered with chills, and my friend shot Nagai a dirty look before moving to tend to me.

"Sit back up, Tristan," he said gently, placing his hand on my back, and I obeyed. "Breathe in…and out." I could feel my breath rattling against his palm, and he sighed, placing the inside of his wrist against my forehead and looking at the other medic. "Now, if you had stop gawking at his boyfriend and taken a look at Private Byrne instead, you'd have realize that you had a patient in need of help, Steven."

"I'm sure you can handle it. After all, he is *your* patient," he said stiffly before leaving the tent in an indignant huff.

"Shame on him," Blackwell scoffed beside me. "Nothing wrong with people like you, and you're patients just like everyone else which means he gets to treat you regardless of personal issues. If he's got a problem, he can talk to Harper about a transfer," he grumbled as he continued to examine me, and I snorted, amused. "Well, Tristan, you will be happy to know that I just diagnosed that cough of yours. Bad news is that we don't have the antiviral meds for you. Those ran out a long time ago."

I blinked as he got up and started to check Jack over.

"You gonna be that cryptic, or are you going to tell me what it is?"

"Pneumonia. Don't worry, it's probably viral – I've had a few patients with it recently. Wait it out, take it easy, and it'll be gone in a week or so." I nodded and looked to Jack's pale face in the bed next to me as I sat back against my pillows. Blackwell noticed. "Sorry, kid. There's still no change."

"He's been asleep for more than a week, doc," I protested. He nodded, sitting on my bed and resting a hand on my knee. "And you're telling me not to worry about that? He's in a *coma*—"

"I know. But the fact is that Jack underwent some serious trauma. That he hasn't woken up isn't good news, I'll admit. But he's not dying either." I nodded, picking at my fingernails and coughing. "He's just taking his own time to mend, Tristan. He'll wake up soon enough, though you feel free to tell him to hurry it up. We're getting old waiting," he teased, and I snorted, the sound nothing more than a light exhale through my nose. After a few beats of quiet, he reached for my bandaged arm. "Can I check?"

I nodded and involuntarily shivered as his calloused hands touched my scabbed skin, unwinding the gauze and examining the sutures.

"Well, that's a relief. Your arm is healing quite nicely. It seems Nagai at least knows what he's doing when it comes to amputations."

He replaced the bandages and got up, moving to leave.

"How's Irina?"

He looked down at his hands wrapped around his clipboard.

"She's still hanging on," he sighed and shook his head in grim wonder. "I don't know how, but she's making death work to get her."

"How much longer do you think she has?"

"I'd be surprised if she lasted past tonight," he admitted, eyes shining with remorse. "Are you gonna be okay, kid?" I nodded, pinching the bridge of my nose. I felt like I'd just been punched in the gut. "Are you sure?"

"Yeah. It's just…" I let my hand drop back to my lap, and I shook my head, staring at the tent wall with listless eyes. "I told her to go to you to get her wound checked out." I looked at him helplessly. "I *told* her."

"We all make foolish choices on the battlefield, Tristan. Don't hold that over her head."

I shifted my gaze over to Jack's sleeping form, drained and exhausted despite the fact I'd just gotten a full night's rest.

"Don't worry," I told the doctor as he left, eyes trained on the bandage around my boyfriend's abdomen. "I won't."

. . . — — . . .

Nurse Weiss kicked me out of the tent to sit outside, claiming that the fresh air would do me some good. I didn't see how, considering that the air was still pretty bad from the non-stop fighting it had been subject to, but I wasn't about to argue with someone who looked at me like I was something stuck to the bottom of her shoe.

Apparently she didn't like gay people either. And to be fair, I probably hadn't endeared myself to her with my backseat nursing. But mostly, it was the homophobia. In fact, none of the field staff seemed to be very progressive in that regard. Blackwell was the only one who would bring me meds now, and I had learned to ignore the obscenities people whispered about me as I passed them. I didn't have a right hand to punch them with, and my mind was still too exhausted to come up with witty, biting comebacks in a timely manner.

On the flip side, the outside world did have one thing the inside didn't, and that was the warm sun. I walked down the trench until I was pretty far from the med tent and found a singed and half-destroyed munitions box to turn over and sit on. I settled back against the wall and closed my eyes.

I hadn't been there for more than two minutes when I heard him.

"Byrne!" I opened my eyes and sat up to see Andrew Harris running towards me, a ridiculously relieved grin on his face. "I can't believe it, you son of a bitch!" I stood up to meet him, and he wrapped me in a tight hug, carefully avoiding my arm. He broke away to look down at me after a few seconds, happiness in his eyes. "You're alive!"

"So are you," I said, clearing my throat a few times and offering a small smile I didn't feel comfortable giving. "It's good to see you." He nodded, clapping my shoulder, and we both sat down.

"You too, Byrne. You, too."

In the time that followed, Andrew and I talked off and on about little things like the warming weather and impending summer months. He asked about my arm, and I explained what happened. Then, he asked about Jack, and I told him about that, too. But after a few more half-hearted attempts to continue our small talk, the conversation quickly went south. It was filled with massive, dragging silences and awkward, half-started sentences neither of us moved to finish.

And I couldn't help but realize that in the span of a single day we'd finally become too different. He seemed to notice it too and got up, going to shake my right hand with his three-fingered one before realizing I didn't have that arm any more. He cleared his throat, looking ashamed, and awkwardly shook my left hand, nodding once to me as he walked away. And as I watched him leave, I wondered what it was that made people change so much. It wasn't like we'd undergone anything different. We'd started off as similar people, came here, and survived the same hell.

If anything, Harris was more adjusted than anyone else I'd seen. Except maybe Aliyah.

Whatever it was, I couldn't help but hope that Jack and I ended the same way that we'd began — side by side. That was, if he ever woke up. At that moment, the phantom pains started in my arm again, and I groaned, rubbing at the skin a few times to try and drive it away. It had been getting worse over the last couple of days. I finally gave up on my arm, accepting the fact that it would be hurting with flashes of stabbing pain for the next couple hours, as per usual. I took in a deep breath, holding it in as I closed my eyes and tried to focus on the warmth of the sun instead.

The world was strangely quiet after the din of war, though I could still hear people arguing in the distance and others crying out in pain in the med tents. A few flags and canvas walls rippled in the wind. The absence of gunfire, the stillness of the earth after the shattering booms of artillery guns…it was all so foreign, so strange. It was like I'd never experienced peace before in my life. The adrenaline high was gone, and I was finally able to let myself relax, to be still, to close my eyes without straining my other senses to compensate for the lack of vision.

I soon found myself on the verge of dozing off, breathing a little less labored than it had been lately and my tired heartbeat relatively steady. But just as I finally finished relaxing, tense nerves finally calming and my brutal anxiety dying away almost completely, I heard it. Footsteps. Someone was approaching from the open trenches to my right, beyond the field hospital.

Brettain territory.

I kept my eyes closed and fought to keep my breaths light and shallow. Maybe I could play dead, and whoever it was would pass–

At that moment a raven cawed practically in my ear, and I scrambled to my feet, heart pounding. The bird flapped noisily into the air from where it had been perched above my head at the ridge of the trench. As I watched it go, I took a deep breath to calm myself back down.

"Hellish little buggers, aren't they?"

My stomach dropped into my feet at the accented voice, and I slowly turned around to find myself face to face with seven people dressed in unfamiliar formal blue uniforms. They looked healthy enough, though I could see the tired marks of war on their faces. The woman who had spoken was probably in her early fifties with short blonde hair that framed an austere and angular face. But despite her stern features and intimidating height and posture, her hazel eyes sparkled with amusement.

"I must say though, they are useful for some things. For instance, I was under the impression you were dead there, private."

I couldn't say anything for a few seconds. I was stunned, terrified. And what finally came out of my dazed mouth made me want to smack myself.

"You're Brettain."

"Observant boy, isn't he?" she said, smirking at her fellow officers, and they laughed. She turned back to address me. "Yes, we are Brettain, and I'm General Mayworth. My people and I are here to negotiate a proper ceasefire with your front lines. Is there a captain or perhaps someone higher ranking that I can speak to?"

I floundered, staring up at her mutely before pointing towards the tents behind me.

"It's a field hospital," I stammered, mind racing as I thought of all the rumors I'd heard of the new, unpredictable face of the Brettain army. "It's a safe zone, you can't kill anyone. I can make sure no one shoots at you, just don't...*don't* kill anyone."

She looked at me solemnly, a pitying smile teasing her lips.

"You have nothing to worry about, soldier. We've no longer a need for violence to back our words." I stared at her, uncomprehending, and she shook her head. "Of course. Your post hasn't heard the news, yet."

"What news?" I asked, voice all but a whisper.

"The front lines have collapsed all along your borders," she said simply. "Arikaan, Mezitain, Xiangon, Brettain – we're winning. It's only a matter of time before your ally Rusika falls as well." I took in their defiant, successful expressions, and couldn't help the words I spoke.

"That doesn't make you the good guys in this," I coughed and groaned softly as I saw the blood mixed in with the mucus on my palm. She nodded in agreement.

"True. But you and your people are hardly free of fault yourselves." She caught sight of my stained hands before she could continue and turned to face one of the men behind her. "Leftenant Richards, call our medics in. Tell them to bring supplies." She looked back at me with her hawk-like gaze and straightened her shoulders. "We're not here to hurt you. We only want to talk to your captain."

She's lying. She's lying, pretending to be kind.

She seemed to know what I was thinking and took in a deep breath, the kind light in the back of her eyes quickly replaced with hard steel.

"Allow me to outline a few facts here, private. As noble as your hesitation is, you're clearly ill. You're unarmed and missing most of what appears to be your dominant arm." I subconsciously tightened my hold on the stub of my right arm and fought the urge to back away from her. "My men and I are healthy, whole, *and* well-armed, so you make the call. You can either take us to your superior, or we can walk right through you."

Let them walk through you. Say no, a voice whispered in my mind.

I swallowed painfully and looked over my shoulder to the tent I knew Jack was in, still unconscious and trapped in his coma. There wasn't even a choice to make. I turned back to Mayworth and nodded, unease prowling in my gut. The woman smiled to herself.

"That's what I thought."

Feeling scared and oddly numb, I turned around and began walking as fast as I could down the trench, leading the head of the Brettain army into the heart of what was left of our front lines. I felt vulnerable leaving my back to them. My whole body tensed up as I walked, my motions jerky and stiff. As we walked further into the camp, people pointed and whispered to each other, sending runners to go warn Harper that the enemy had arrived. Battered and bruised Amaeric troops lined up outside the tents. Some were wounded, others sick, but they were all survivors. My scattered attention was quickly pulled forward again when I saw someone coming towards us, and I realized it was Jayce. The brother of War's expression was livid, and his heavily bandaged hand fell to the gun at his side.

"Byrne, move!" he barked, and I held up my hand to him as I heard the Brettain draw their own weapons behind me.

"Jayce, hold it. They're here to negotiate."

"As if," he growled, drawing his weapon and holding it at the ready.

"Your comrade is telling the truth," the general said behind me. "But while we come in peace, we will not hesitate to shoot if you fire at us first." Jayce tightened his grip on his weapon, and she pressed her point, using the same waterproof logic she'd used with me. "Look at us and then yourself. Who do you think will win that engagement?"

Reluctantly, Jayce backed off. Behind him, I could see Harper coming over, his face stitched up in several pieces from shrapnel wounds. His arm was held tightly against his body in a sling, and I was relieved to see that he was unarmed.

"General Mayworth," he called, voice cold, and she forced a smile.

"Captain Harper. I take it you were the head of that last outpost?" He nodded, crossing his arms and coming to a stop a few feet away. "Well, that explains how stubborn they were. You cost us a lot of good men."

"As did you," he returned. "In fact, a lot of them are dying as we speak because we don't have medicine. I assume you can fix that?"

She inclined her head.

"Certainly. On one condition."

"There's *always* a condition with you," he said through gritted teeth and bitterly shook his head.

"War's a business, Harper," she replied in that same simple manner of hers. "You should know that better than most. How many times have we traded resources in the winter months?"

"That was *different*," he spat, eyes disbelieving, betrayed. "We were both stranded, cut off from our suppliers. We needed each other's equipment to survive! We called ceasefires to help each other bury our dead for crying out loud!"

"But now we've no need for your services or supplies. You just need medication from us, and I'm happy to oblige," the woman said, voice cool and collected. "As a matter of fact, the young private who walked us in here needs medicine himself. But we *need* to have a trade off. That's how my superiors like things to work."

"Fine," Harper conceded, taking a deep breath. His gaze slid away from hers. "What do you want?"

"I want you to surrender." Harper looked up at that, motion sharp and eyes blazing. "We would then turn your field hospital into a fully furnished prisoner of war camp, and you would send notice of the line's surrender to your superiors." Our captain opened his mouth to protest in anger, but she cut him off, procuring a document from a pocket in her jacket. "Read it," she ordered, voice giving no room for negotiation. "Then, you'll know this is the only choice you have left."

He snatched it away from her, seething. But as he started reading, his eyes widened.

"These are our casualty numbers?" he asked in disbelief, looking up at her, and she nodded, eyes sympathetic. "They didn't tell us this." He flipped through a few more pages, expression growing more and more shocked and betrayed as he went. "They didn't tell us *any* of this."

"You've been used, Michael," she said gently, and he shook his head in denial. "We do have surveillance photos if you'd like confirmation of what you're reading there."

He held out his hand for them immediately, as though to call her bluff, and Lieutenant Richards stepped forward, handing a manila folder to him. Our captain quickly opened it, and whatever he saw made his shoulders sag in defeat. He sighed and handed them back, looking sick to his stomach.

"I have your word we'll be treated as well as the rumors say?" he finally whispered, voice stunned and quiet. She nodded, and he reluctantly held out his uninjured hand, jaw clenched and tears in his eyes. As we watched, Mayworth gripped his outstretched forearm as he grabbed hers, and they shook hands once. "I guess...I guess you can send word back to your own higher-ups that you've secured the eastern front line."

"Thank you, captain. I understand this is hard for you." They released each other's arms, and she gestured for her officers to start calling in more troops. Harper scoffed bitterly.

"It could have been harder."

She made a noise of agreement.

"Very true. Calvin Howell could have been here, and there would have been a blood bath." My heart froze in my chest as Harper's eyes narrowed, and Jayce came over to stand beside me.

"Yes. How did you know he was dead?"

"You mean aside from the fact we were able to have that conversation just then?" She gave that same cold smirk before beckoning one of her formally dressed troops over. "Meet Sergeant Jacob Clarke. He's one of our greener recruits, but he's a fairly decent shot over long distances, if you follow my meaning." The young man inclined his head respectfully towards Harper. The gesture wasn't returned. "It's no secret what Howell does to those under his command. He's a war criminal. I myself have given several reports on the man. You Amaerics, of course, dress him up as a hero while he butchers the innocent people who entrust their lives to him as some kind of patriotic propaganda. We knew he'd never face justice in your courts, so we took the matter into our own hands."

"Meaning?" Harper asked.

Brettain soldiers started dropping down into the trenches around us, directing each other towards their tasks as our own troops shrank away into the shadows of the tents. We were uncomfortable and far out of our depth, and I wanted nothing more than to retreat into the medical tents with them, return to Jack's side and ignore what was happening. But I couldn't. I could only watch as the Brettain invaded the last of our line, and while I knew that meant this was all over, that our role in this war was finished, I couldn't help but feel a little upset.

"Clarke here is a sniper," Mayworth was saying. "As you know we only use them for targeted killings. The sergeant was entrusted with the assassination of Captain Howell and was successful just as your line fell."

Her words jarred in my half-focused mind, and I turned to look at our captain and her.

"Howell wasn't killed by a sniper," Jayce protested, stepping forward, and my stomach plummeted as my heart jumped up into my throat. "He was killed by *Mi–*"

"Machine gun fire," I quickly interrupted, mind racing, and Jayce's jaw snapped shut as he realized his mistake. "We all saw it. We let one of your men get too close to the trench line, and he killed Howell. He died. Right in front of me." That last part wasn't a lie at least. Mayworth looked around at the confused sergeant beside her. "I-it was machine gun fire. Clear as day."

"You *said* you got Howell," she began, voice low, and he hurried to explain himself.

"I did, ma'am," he said, truly confused. "Or...at least I thought I did."

"What made you so sure?" she pressed. I could see the sergeant trying not to panic at how angry she seemed.

"He – he was wearing his uniform, ma'am. I could *read* his name on the uniform, it said *Howell*. There was a captain's insignia on the arm." My heart stopped. I couldn't breathe. "Tall, broad-shouldered...he definitely fit the description you gave me, ma'am. I honestly don't know what's happening."

"It's okay, Tristan. Just hang tight. I'm going to –"

"JACK!"

"Byrne, you okay?" I was gasping for breath, eyes filled with angry tears as I stared at Sergeant Clarke in furious disbelief. Jayce put his hand on my shoulder, peering into my face. "Byrne?"

"The bullet we pulled out of Miller was a much larger round...my forensics nurse says your corporal was hit by a sharp shooter."

Aliyah stood before Jack's kneeling form, presenting him with Howell's coat, the sleeve's insignia of captain facing him.

"You son of a bitch," I hissed. Mayworth, Clarke, and Harper looked at me as I shakily pointed at the sniper. "You! You were the one who shot him!" I started forward at him, but Jayce caught me, locking his arm across my chest and holding me back. "You shot Jack!"

"Who?" the Brettain asked, nonplussed, and Harper's mouth opened in silent dismay.

"Oh no..." he groaned, and Mayworth looked at him.

"What is going on?"

"Corporal Jack Miller...he took over Howell's position after he died. This was his fourth tour–"

"He was just wearing his jacket!" I shouted, my voice cracking as tears blurred my vision. "Jack's half Howell's age! *How* did you not see that?"

"Byrne, settle down!" Jayce grunted as I bucked back against him, livid and desperate.

"You *shot* him!" I screamed as my comrade backed away, dragging me with him, and part of me savored the shaken looks on the Brettains' faces. "If he dies, I'll kill you!"

"Wait. *If?*" I looked at the general, taking in shaky breaths and calming slightly in Jayce's grip. "Let him go." Reluctantly, Jones backed away, and I stumbled forward, breathing heavily and glaring at them all. "You said *if*. So, he's not dead yet?"

I laughed, the sound hysterical and taunting. My words were bitter and sarcastic.

"No. No, you just paralyzed him and put him in a coma. But at least he's not dead, right?" Before she could say anything, I turned on my heel and fled, wiping at the tears burning in my eyes.

. . . — — . . .

"What the hell are you doing?" I demanded as soon as I stepped into the tent. Nagai was standing over my boyfriend, checking his vitals with gloved hands. "I thought Blackwell made it pretty clear he was only one who treated us." He looked up at me, disdain gleaming in his eyes as his explanation rose readily to his lips.

"He's busy with Korsakov. The girl's on her way out." I stood by Jack's side, taking his lifeless hand gently in mine and running my thumb over his scabbed knuckles. "Was that you I heard theatrically shouting outside?"

"If you don't shut up, I will stab you with your pencil," I muttered, glaring dangerously at him, and he moved away to another patient. "By the way, we just surrendered the front line to the Brettain. They're sending doctors, nurses, medicine, and supplies to turn this place into a POW camp. So, you should probably go talk to Harper."

I listened to him run out of the tent as I dragged a chair over to Jack's bed. The legs scraped hollowly across the wood platform floor, and I sat down heavily. I felt tired, worn thin, and my ears rang with silence. Right here, it was just Jack and I curtained off from the world. I closed my eyes and took his hand in mine, squeezing the cool skin as tightly as I dared. The world was changing outside. In here, I could pretend that everything was normal, center myself on my breaths and the hand tightly clasped in mine.

Howell.

The name was a furious curse in my mind, a cruel bane to my existence. If the Brettain decided they were going to recover Howell's body, they'd see that we'd lied. They'd put two and two together.

And Jack. The trouble that Jack would be in, that trouble that we'd all be in–

"Trist'n…"

I opened my eyes at my barely audible name and looked to the man before me. He looked just as bad as he had the last few days. His skin was still drained of color, eyes still bruised and sunken into his skull. His lips were still pale and chapped. I must have imagined his voice, but…

"Jack?" I whispered, leaning forward and watching my boyfriend with bated breath.

His relaxed brow furrowed in pain or confusion – maybe both – and he slowly turned his head to face me, eyes still screwed shut.

"Tristan…"

My heart soared, and I nearly laughed in giddy disbelief.

"Jack? Jack, I'm right here." I stood up and sat on the bed beside him, and relief surged through my body as he almost imperceptibly tightened his hand around mine. "Hey…Jack? Can you hear me?"

He groaned, grimacing in pain, and I gently kissed his hand. He slowly opened his eyes, staring up at me in a dazed and half-asleep way.

"Tristan?"

I smiled down at him, tears blurring my vision.

"Good afternoon, sleepy head," I teased, tightening my grip on him until I was sure I was going to break the bones in his hand. But he didn't smile back. Instead, his gaze weakly shifted around us, brow still furrowed. His breathed words slurred together as he continued.

"Where 'm I?"

"We're at the central field hospital," I whispered, forcing myself to stay calm and patient. "You got shot, remember? By a sniper?" He looked up at me, still confused, and I saw he was looking at my arm. "You were coming to help me, and you got shot. You told me it was a standard rifle, and I had to fix you up." He continued to stare up at me, lost, and my heart started to sink, fear rising in my throat. "Jack, we're on the front lines. We fell back. Do you remember?" He looked away from me, and his already unsteady, hitched breathing became erratic. "Jack. Jack, look at me." His eyes shifted towards me once more, and I swallowed painfully. I had to ask the question I'd been dreading. "Jack, what's your last name?"

"Miller," he whispered after a few seconds, closing his eyes. "59…27… 8530…Corporal. Jack Miller…"

"No, Jack." I hurried to cut him off, heart breaking as he continued to mumble through my reassurances. "I'm not interrogating you. It's me. It's Tristan."

He looked up at me again, eyes hollow, and I brushed his hair from his eyes, gently kissing his forehead.

"I can't..." He blinked slowly at me, expression pained and confused. His words were slurred. "Why...why can't I move?"

My stomach churned. I wasn't ready to have this conversation, not yet. It was cowardly and selfish of me, but I couldn't do it.

"You're safe," I whispered soothingly instead, continuing to stroke his hair back from his forehead. "You're safe, okay?"

His gaze fixed on something over my shoulder, and his brow furrowed even more, eyes guarded. I felt his hand tighten feebly around mine.

"No...we're not," he whispered, voice strained with pain and fear, and I turned around to see Clarke and General Mayworth standing behind me. The sergeant came forward, and I protectively tightened my grip on Jack's hand. He noticed and stopped moving, addressing me.

"I'm...I'm sorry, sir."

I looked away from him and back at my boyfriend.

"I'm not the one you should apologize to," I said coldly, and he looked down at his feet.

Jack didn't react anymore to their presence. His tired eyes just watched me blankly, and Mayworth stepped forward, beckoning her soldier away.

"Private Byrne, your partner's not completely aware of his surroundings right now, and he probably doesn't know half of what he's saying or hearing. The best things you can do right now are to get him his doctor and give him some space."

"How would you know what's best for him?" I snarled, and she sighed. "You put him here!"

"I've seen people in this state before. What he needs right now are rest and a doctor." She paused, looking over my shoulder at him, and I quickly followed her gaze. "See? He's already gone back to sleep."

Feeling somehow worse than I had before Jack woke up, I released his limp hand and got to my feet. When I looked at the two officers behind me, I felt nothing but rage.

"I'll be right back," I warned, glaring. "If you so much as touch him, I swear to the gods..."

She nodded her understanding and walked out with me, Clarke in tow. I had to find Blackwell.

...———...

When I did, I wished I hadn't. He was standing a few feet away from Korsakov's bed, watching the girl with crossed arms and too wide eyes. As soon as he saw me approaching, he met me halfway across the room.

"Now's not the best time, Tristan."

"Jack just woke up," I whispered, sighing helplessly. "He didn't know what was going on or where he was. He couldn't remember anything that had happened."

"Okay." Blackwell looked over his shoulder at the Horseman's bed and took in a deep breath, releasing it slowly. "I'll go check on him." He looked back at me, expression grim and sympathetic. "I'm sorry, Tristan, but Irina won't last much longer. I give her half an hour, tops…if she's lucky. But she'll probably be ready to go in the next few minutes." He shook his head, eyes distant. "I'm truly sorry. I tried my best, but…she's too far gone. The Brettain got here too late."

I nodded silently and hovered just within earshot of her bed as he left, putting a gentle hand on my shoulder as he did.

"Do you want me to fix your pillow?"

I bit my lip and forced myself forward until I could see past the curtain into the bed.

"Aliyah, that's the fourth time you've asked me that in two minutes," Irina croaked, pale skin flushed from the unrelenting heat of her fever. She shivered with chills a few times, and Marcel pulled the blanket higher up over her body. "Thanks…"

"Are those Brettain meds doing you any good?" Soto asked from the foot of her dying friend's bed, and Korsakov gave a lopsided shrug.

"I'm just feeling sleepy. I'm…I'm ready to go home." She closed her eyes and fell silent. "Winova…Winova's pretty this time of year. All those spring flowers…and the birds…" She was quiet for a few seconds that felt like hours. "Don't…don't let those foreigners bury me."

"Of course we won't. We'll do it ourselves," Aliyah told her gently and reached out to hold her hand while Marcel swapped out the wet cloth lying over Pestilence's forehead.

"You don't have to keep changing it," the girl whispered weakly.

Jones smiled down at her, the expression heartbreakingly sincere.

"Don't worry, Irina. I like doing it."

"I just...I just want to go to sleep," she whispered, voice hoarse and barely audible. Moore and Marcel held her hands and smiled comfortingly at her. Katalin on the other hand looked down, tears in her eyes. "Oh, don't cry, Kat..." But Soto just shook her head.

"It's not fair," she sobbed, wiping at her eyes in frustrated denial as she looked at her pale friend. "*This* isn't fair! You made it out! It's *not* supposed to end like this! *We* were the ones who were supposed to walk away!"

Irina looked away from the people around her and saw me.

"Well, it's not our choice how things end up, is it?" she asked, watching me. I gave a sad smile, saluting her, and she laughed quietly to herself. The other Horsemen looked over their shoulders at the sound in sync, and if the circumstances were different, I'd have laughed. "Hey, Byrne."

"Hey, Korsakov." I walked to the foot of her bed and sighed. "You feeling any better?"

"Been better. But I'm feeling okay," she sighed, groaning as she shifted herself in her bed. Her eyes were tired and red. "Jayce came in here earlier. Told us about that Sergeant Clarke."

"Yeah. Yeah, they were going after Howell," I scoffed, looking down at my white knuckled grip on her footboard. "Apparently, he's a war criminal to the Brettain, so they're going to want his body to confirm cause of death. When that happens, Jack's screwed."

Irina nodded, expression peaceful as she met our eyes around her.

"We know. But don't worry," she began, coughing harshly for a couple moments before continuing. "We've got it all figured out."

She made a vague gesture towards Aliyah, and the woman held a piece of folded paper towards me. It was a sheet from a doctor's chart, but when I took it from her, I could immediately tell it wasn't a patient's profile.

"What the hell is this?" I demanded, voice low and a little angry. Irina sighed contently and closed her eyes as she spoke.

"*That* is a fully signed confession stating that I, Private Irina Korsakov, shot and murdered Captain Calvin Howell." She cleared her throat, forcing her eyes open again. "We got those of us left from thirty-seven to sign on as witnesses verifying that that's what happened." She broke off into a fit of coughing, and I shook my head.

"I can't let you do this," I said, handing the paper back to her. "I won't. You can't do this to yourself."

"It's my choice, Byrne," she snapped, the words losing most if not all of their bite in her weakened state. "Respect it like you respected this one." I followed her shaking finger to her infected shoulder, and, hating myself for doing so, I reluctantly nodded.

"Fine." I took a pencil from the clipboard at the foot of her bed and with my left hand awkwardly wrote my near-illegible initials in the witness section before handing it back to Aliyah. "*Fine*. I'll…I'll let you give that to Mayworth."

"We owe Miller this much," Marcel whispered, not looking at me, and I watched as she fiddled with the wet cloth on Irina's forehead.

Korsakov just smiled, closing her eyes and releasing a long, slow breath. She seemed to sink into the pillows and blankets, becoming even smaller than she already was. She looked like a child. A child dying with a bullet hole in her shoulder. When her eyes opened, they seemed fogged over, and she reached out for Aliyah, grabbing her friend's hand with her frail one.

"It's over, now. Right?" she breathed. The tall woman nodded. "Oh… I'm just glad you're all here…"

"So are we," Aliyah said gently, reaching forward to check her friend's wound. I caught a glimpse of blackened, rotting skin beneath the collar of the shirt and felt viciously sick to my stomach. Katalin apparently shared my discomfort, and she stared fixedly at the sheets before her.

"I'm ready to go home," Irina whispered, voice even quieter and more childlike than before. Moore nodded, letting her friend know someone was still listening with a gentle squeeze of her hand. "I just want to go home…"

Pestilence's fevered eyes were distant now, and Aliyah leaned over her with a gentle smile, hugging her tightly. Irina's pale arms slowly encircled her back and her bony fingers gripped her friend's uniform.

A few seconds later, the skeleton hands released the back of Aliyah's jacket, slowly slipping away to thud dully on the mattress. Marcel released a shaking breath, leaning forward and bracing her elbows on her knees as she steepled her hands over her face. Katalin raised her fist to her mouth, biting down on her knuckles as she drew her feet up onto the chair with her; tears slipped down her face as she fought to keep in her sobs. But before Death could pull back, I turned around and walked away with my stiff gait, teeth clenched and eyes burning.

I knew how it had ended. I didn't need to see it.

. . . − − − . . .

Within a few hours, the Brettain had revamped everything. They'd set up living quarters above the trenches on one side, and the hospital had been expanded and replenished with additional medication, equipment, and staff. People with the slightest of colds and infections were getting the medicine they needed, and when Blackwell pushed open the curtains around Jack and I around midnight, he was holding a bottle of pills in his hand.

"I managed to find some antiviral meds for you, Byrne."

I nodded and took the tablets he offered me, feeling empty and listless. I could still see Soto crying, could still hear the hollow thud of Irina's arms on the mattress as she faded away in Aliyah's arms. Could still see Marcel hunched over herself in heartbroken defeat. And, just to make things worse, my boyfriend hadn't opened his eyes since he'd briefly woken up earlier.

As I took the medicine and continued to stare blankly ahead of myself, Blackwell joined me on the edge of my bed. He put a hand on my shoulder and spoke so softly into my ear I had to strain to hear him.

"Tristan, there's something you should know. Now, don't say anything. Just listen." I nodded uneasily at his grave demeanor. "Jack has been awake for the last three hours." I pulled away from him, startled and hurt, but he pulled me close again. "He's relatively lucid, and I explained what happened to both of you."

"What?" I stammered. I felt gutted and hollow, like someone had just slapped me across the face. "If he's awake, then…then why hasn't he talked to me?"

"Tristan…you have to understand something about Jack. You lost an arm. He can no longer walk. In one moment, he's lost his independence, his self-reliance. And to someone like him? That's going to be devastating. He will never be able to do certain things on his own ever again." I looked over at my boyfriend, seeing how his hands were folded tensely over his stomach and cursing myself as I realized how blind I'd been. I'd grown so used to having him unconscious beside me that I hadn't even noticed he'd woken up. "This silence is his coping mechanism."

"Look, I know him–" I whispered, but the doctor continued on in the same hushed voice.

"That's the point, Tristan," he interrupted. "You don't anymore. Look, kiddo. You need to understand that the Jack Miller you knew before all of this is not the same man next to you now. Just as the Tristan Byrne next to him isn't the same man he knew." He paused pointedly, and I looked down.

"You understand me, kid?" I nodded mutely, refusing to look at him. He just sighed and got to his feet, speaking in his normal voice once more. "Do you want me to turn down the lamp? You're the last one up."

My response was unenthusiastic, empty as I mulled over what he'd just told me.

"Sure."

He turned down the gas lamps until their light was a faint flicker, and I pulled up the blankets, waiting until I was sure he'd left. I turned onto my side to face my boyfriend in the dark. Even if he wasn't going to talk to me, there was one thing he needed to know.

"Irina Korsakov died a few hours ago," I whispered to the dark.

All I got in return was silence, and I sighed, rolling over onto my back. I was about to drift off to sleep when I heard Jack take in a deeper breath than normal. I knew the question he wanted to ask, could sense it, and part of me wanted to make him say it. But the other part of me, the better part, remembered what Blackwell had just told me.

"It was gangrene," I continued, and I could feel his relief as I answered his question. I smiled to myself in the dark. "See? I still know what you're thinking. And I know why you don't want to talk. I understand. And...and I respect it." Silence. "Just remember that I'm always here for you, Jack. No matter what."

Just as I fell sleep, I could have sworn I heard a voice whisper to me – a rusty, quiet voice that I still recognized despite the undercurrent of tortured pain.

"Thank you."

. . . — — — . . .

When I woke up an hour later, I was freezing. My breath hung above my lips in an icy cloud, and my body trembled with violent shivers in the half-light of the infirmary. At first, I thought it was just the cold that had woken me, but as I sat up, I became aware of a shuffling noise behind me outside. I turned around in my bed to see an odd, flickering shadow moving past the tent.

"Where are you lot going?" I heard a Brettain call, and I felt a heavy sense of foreboding in my stomach when there was no response. "Hey!" I cast a quick look over my shoulder to where Jack was sleeping, expression fitful. I considered waking him but quickly decided against it. Whatever this was, I could handle it myself. Would *have* to handle it myself.

I shivered as my feet touched the cold ground, and I pulled my new jacket over my bare shoulders, screwing my eyes shut at the strong stench of gunpowder and mud that stung my nose. Well, new was a strong word. The jacket was a "recycled garment" as Nagai called it. It'd belonged to someone who…wasn't around anymore. I took in a deep breath and yanked on my battered boots, not bothering to tie the laces since I hadn't mastered that yet with one hand. I stumbled towards the door of the tent, looking down the trench in the general direction of the voice I'd heard.

A group of people stood in the light of the sentry's blazing torch. Their body language was confrontational and angry, and I groaned to myself as I recognized the three silhouettes before me as well as the shrouded figure lying on the stretcher between them.

"Damn it," I whispered and quickly picked up my pace.

"Step aside," Aliyah warned, voice cold, and the Brettain sentry leveled his weapon at her.

"You can't be wandering around at this hour. It's past curfew," he said, and Marcel scowled from the back of Korsakov's gurney.

"Hey, asshole! We just want to bury our friend!"

I sighed to myself and headed over to stop the impending disaster. This wasn't good.

"Then leave the body with the doctor. He'll organize her burial with the others tomorrow," the soldier stated, giving no room for argument, and Katalin bristled, storming up to him.

"We're not letting your people touch her," she said, expression coldly furious as she pointed to the covered body beside them. "You did this to her!"

"Guys!" I called once I was in earshot. Moore looked over her shoulder at me, dark eyes blazing as I came up beside them. "Just hold it for a second, alright? Don't do anything stupid."

"Irina's last wish was for us to bury her. *Us*. Not *them*. You heard her, Byrne," Death growled, dark skin shimmering in the firelight. "I will honor her request." She turned her bottomless gaze back on the unsettled soldier before her, and her hands tightened on the handles of the stretcher behind her. "Even if it means I have to walk over your body to do it."

"Moore!" I barked, but none of the Horsemen shared my appall at her behavior. "Will you calm down?" I shifted my gaze to the Brettain, who was staring with wide eyes down the sight of his raised weapon. "You, too!"

"Is there a problem here?"

My blood froze in my veins, and we all turned around to see Mayworth approaching, her step quick and purposeful. Her angular features seemed skeletal in the flickering torchlight, and I quickly placed myself between her and my friends.

"They just want to bury her, ma'am," I explained, voice shaking as she came to a stop and surveyed the situation. "That's all they want. Please."

The general's eyes narrowed slightly, taking in War's tense shoulders and her furious grip on the handles of the makeshift pallet. They shifted to Famine's gritted jaw next, her averted gaze and clenched fists. And finally, she looked at Death's predatorial, fearless eyes – the stubborn light that told the Brettain officer she would not be swayed.

And instead of speaking, Mayworth simply stood at attention, her hazel eyes resting on the covered face of the body War and Death bore.

"Was this a friend of yours?" she asked, words quiet and respectful, and Katalin nodded, still refusing to meet the officer's eyes. "How did she die?"

"By your hand," Aliyah answered, voice cold. "Though it was slow to kill her." The general nodded her understanding.

"May I know her name?"

"No," Marcel bit, the word short, vicious. "No, you bastard–"

"Korsakov."

Aliyah, Jones, and I looked at Katalin in surprise.

"Her name–" She stopped and cleared her throat. "Her *name* was Irina Korsakov."

"Any relation?"

"Our sister," Famine continued, swallowing as she answered and avoiding her companions' accusing eyes. "One of our own."

"And she wanted us to be the ones who buried her. Not you and your men," Marcel muttered, words losing none of their hatred in their softness. Mayworth nodded and gave a respectful, ceremonial salute to Pestilence's shrouded form. And then, she started speaking.

"Ath...*Diana*. Bless this soldier for she has served in your name to her final breath. Grant her remembrance on earth and peace in Elysia. Guide her to Pers...Proserpine, wherein She may take mercy on her immortal soul." My chest ached at the familiar words spoken to unfamiliar faith. "I ask this in the name of Irina Korsakov, slain this day. Valiant goddess, may you vouchsafe to me what I ask of you in prayer. So may it be."

The three women looked away as Mayworth ended the prayer, torn between giving their grudging thanks and pretending it hadn't happened.

"Bury your dead," the general finished. "Sergeant Harding will oversee your work – for security measures. You understand."

"Thank you, ma'am," Moore finally said, and I heaved a sigh of relief as they continued on their way, Harding shadowing them with his light.

"Wait," Soto sighed, and the procession stopped. She shook her head bitterly, reaching forward and pulling a folded piece of paper from Aliyah's jacket pocket. I shivered as she trudged back to where we were standing and handed the confession over to the Brettain leader. "Ma'am."

"What's this?" she asked.

Katalin didn't answer. Instead, she and the other Horsemen continued solemnly on their way. Mayworth watched them go in perplexed silence, but the expression soon cleared as she looked down at me.

"As for you, private." I met her eyes and hoped I seemed calm. "You should return to bed. She will be there for you to visit in the morning."

I looked away from her and watched the trio walk into the rudimentary cemetery the Brettain had set up. I could almost sense Mayworth following my gaze, and my heart pounded in my ears as I heard the sound of the paper unfolding in her hands. Above us, the Horsemen gently set the body of their fallen friend on the earth and started digging in the firelight.

"So." I closed my eyes and released a slow breath as the general began speaking, voice cold and assuming. "It wasn't machine gun fire."

"No, ma'am," I whispered, mouth dry. "It wasn't."

She laughed, folding the paper back up and putting it into her pocket.

"I suppose it's for the best that she died," she began pointedly, standing beside me and watching the shovels move dirt back and forth. "We would have considered her a hero, of course. But protocol would have mandated we try and convict her of murder."

She looked at me, and I could see her smirk in my peripheral vision. She hadn't bought the confession. We both knew it. But she seemed to be going along with it anyways.

"Goodnight, ma'am," I whispered, quickly turning around and heading back to the tent.

"The Brettain have a saying, Private Byrne," she called. I turned back to face her silhouette. She was looking out over the trenches, and her knowing words carried on a cold fog into the night air.

"Living or dead, the blood of the covenant is thicker than the water of the womb."

DAY ONE HUNDRED AND SEVENTY-TWO

Two weeks later

"How are we today?" I continued to seethe at the wall opposite where Marcel and I were sitting beside Jack's bed and made a noncommittal noise at the approaching doctor. Jones just continued to glare at our mutual item of concern while Jack stared at the ceiling in frustrated silence. "That bad, huh?" Blackwell sat down on the foot of Jack's bed and put a hand on the man's leg, drawing a glare from his half-paralyzed patient.

"We were just trying to explain to Jack that it's *still* too early for him to sit up on his own," I said pointedly.

Jack sighed and lifted his hands defensively.

"Gods! All I want is a change of scenery, Tristan! Is that such a crime?" he snapped, voice hoarse. The doctor nodded easily.

"No, Jack, that's quite understandable. In fact, if you'd like to sit up on your own, go ahead and give it your best shot. Just know that I won't stitch your stomach back up *again*," he warned, and Jack just stared at him, coldly unamused. "See? Even you know that's not a good idea."

The doctor stood and moved to his side, pulling away Jack's shirt and lifting the taped bandage to examine the wound. It was still red and angry, scabbed in most places and freshly scarred over near the edges. But it was healing – slowly, from the inside out.

"Does it hurt?"

Jack mutely shook his head, and Marcel scowled, reaching across me to punch his arm and making his upper body sway to the side ever so slightly. Those few millimeters of movement made his body lock up in pain, and I winced at the small groan of discomfort that escaped his clenched jaw. Marcel on the other hand just sat back in her chair, crossed her arms, and smiled tightly at Blackwell with flashing eyes.

"He's hurting," she answered, voice overly sweet.

The doctor sighed, shooting her a warning look before scribbling down a note on his clipboard.

"I'll see about getting some pain meds from the Brettain."

Jack didn't acknowledge him. He just glared at Marcel beside us.

"I swear to the gods, once I get out of this bed I'm gonna kill you."

She smirked in amusement and raised her eyebrows in silent challenge.

"What are you gonna do? Run me over with your wheelchair?"

Jack's face became an emotionless mask, fury burning behind his eyes.

"Private Jones!" Blackwell scolded, and I gaped at her. Thankfully, she at least had the decency to look ashamed at what she'd just said.

But just when I thought we were going to be able to avoid a scene, Jack just *had* to pipe back in.

"You know, sometimes I wish Korsakov was still dying. That way you could go poke fun at her for rotting alive instead of me!" he half-shouted, and Blackwell threw his hands up in defeat.

"Corporal Miller, some decorum! Please!" he began, exasperated, but Marcel was already on her feet, infuriated.

"That is *it!*" she shouted, fuming. "Don't think I won't punch a cripple, because I will—"

"Both of you, *knock it off!*" I shouted and was so glad that Jack had been moved to one of the single person isolation tents. I couldn't imagine what this situation would have been like in front of a whole hospital wing.

Reluctantly, Private Jones sat back down, doggedly avoiding the three of us. Jack ground the heels of his palms into his eyes, trying to block out the world around him.

"I'm sorry about the wheelchair comment," she finally said in the tense silence that followed, and Jack scoffed. "And the punching a cripple thing. That...wasn't very professional of me. Sir."

"Just...leave me alone." His voice was sullen and muffled by his hands.

Blackwell looked at me and gestured for me to get up with him. I knew this routine pretty well by now. As I got to my feet, I gently placed my hand on Jack's shoulder and gave it a gentle squeeze.

"I'll check back in on you in a little bit," I whispered.

He just stared impassively at the canvas roof above him. It didn't really bother me. This was his standard response for most things now. The truth was that Jack had become increasingly moody over the last two weeks, and when I'd brought it up with Blackwell, he'd said it was to be expected.

That didn't make it any easier to deal with.

"I don't get it," Marcel said, exasperatedly, and turned to face Blackwell and I in irritated confusion as soon as we left the tent. "We've been busting our asses taking care of this guy, and that's how he treats us?"

"To be fair you did hurt him. Both physically and verbally," I pointed out, and she gave me a thoroughly unimpressed look.

"That's not what I meant. He's so wrapped up in his own issues that he can't see how much we're struggling to help him! Doesn't that bother you? I mean, you're his boyfriend. You *literally* gave your arm to save his life, and he's acting as though that doesn't even mean anything!"

I turned away from her, refusing to respond to the uncomfortable truth she'd just brought up.

"Private Jones, what you have to understand that Miller is undergoing a psychological trauma as much as a physical trauma," Blackwell explained. I nodded in agreement, crossing my arms and growling to myself when I was lopsidedly reminded yet again that I only had the one. "He's trying to adjust to his new life, and we can only help him once he wants us to."

"You just need to be patient," I finished, looking up at her. "And trust me, as his boyfriend, I really want to hit him over the head once in a while. In fact, it's more on a daily basis at this point, but I understand that what he needs right now is patience. So, I'm not going to go in there and dump all my baggage on him when I know he's got more than enough for himself."

"But you can't let him walk over us like this though without letting him know that it's not okay, Byrne," she protested, hands on her hips. "You let him keep on like this, he's never going to heal. You need to snap him out of it and make him realize that it could be much worse – and that if he doesn't start listening to us it's going to *get* worse."

I looked to Blackwell for his input, but he just shrugged.

"She has a point, but I'm not getting mixed up in this. If you choose to take her advice, that's on you." He sighed. "Now, if you'll excuse me, I have to go get our problematic patient some pain medication."

After he'd left, I turned to Marcel, double-checking that Jack was out of earshot before speaking. This time, my tone was a lot kinder, even grateful.

"Look, I just want you to know that we really appreciate all your help." She nodded, taking in a deep breath, and rocked back on her heels. "But I need you to take it down a notch with Jack."

"I know. I know, I'm sorry," she sighed, pulling her long braid over her shoulder. "I just needed a distraction after we buried Irina. Kat and Aliyah volunteered to be on the work crew to take down the trenches – you know, to start rebuilding on top. By the time they told me, all the spots were full. I figured I'd make myself useful to you two idiots – gods know you need someone to watch out for you…but I keep trying to interact with you like I did with them." She shrugged. "Old habits die hard, I suppose."

"Jack's got a different sense of humor, I'm afraid," I commented wryly, but she shook her head.

"That's the thing, though. Before all this…he didn't." She rammed her hands into her pockets and smiled sadly at the ground. "But I guess that's what this type of crap does to you, right?"

"Yeah," I sighed. "I'm just glad you and the Horsemen are still working out together." She nodded.

"Me, too. And Jayce and I are even closer than before, so that's great."

"Silver linings." I laughed bitterly and rubbed the inside of my shoulder as another phantom pain shot up the ravaged arm. "I wish I had a couple of those."

"But you *do* have them," Marcel said, comforting and yet baffled at the same time. I frowned, and she continued. "You both survived, didn't you?"

My expression cleared, but I closed my eyes at the dull ache I felt in my chest at her words.

"Yeah." I looked over my shoulder and through the tent door to where Jack was laying perfectly still, hands steepled over his nose and mouth as he took in deep, unsteady breaths. "Yeah, we did."

… — — — …

Everybody had a job in the camp. Some helped prepare the meals with the Brettain cooks. Others helped record inventory. Most were tasked with building barracks and basic facilities like bathrooms and showers, which were really just curtained off tubs we filled with water and scrubbed off in.

Of course there was some animosity between us and Brettain, but that was only natural. We'd been at war for thirty years, that wasn't something that just went away overnight. So, understandably, there were always several fights a week when one of us snapped at something smug the other side said and vice versa, but there were always about six people lunging for the altercations to break them up. That was the hopeful part. There were always people from both sides rushing to settle things back down.

In fact, I'd found that a lot of the Brettain soldiers were just as battle weary as we were, and I'd come to be on a first name basis with a lot of them. Strangely though, there was only one I really seemed to connect with, and I wasn't quite sure how I felt about it.

A few hours had passed since I'd left Jack to his own thoughts, and that familiar fear and concern was forcing its way back up my throat. I should have checked in on him by now to make sure he was okay, but I was busy with my own job: hauling baskets of firewood to the main buildings and tents that needed it. And that was pretty much everyone, so it often took me about three hours to get enough wood to all the people who wanted it. And it really didn't help that I was short an appendage – in fact, I was pretty sure the rope was starting to chafe my left shoulder from the weight. I was almost done with my route of sorts when I heard a familiar voice speak softly behind me.

"Hello, private."

I stopped and turned around. My Brettain friend handed a report off to a subordinate and closed the distance between us, a veiled smile of greeting in her eyes.

"General Mayworth." She fell into step beside me as I went to my last post, letting the heavy bag of wood slip off my shoulder and to the ground. "How're you?"

"Fine," she said with her usual laconic style. "How's your boyfriend?" I made a sound, and she raised an eyebrow. "Well, that's hardly helpful."

"His wound's healing," I told her and waved at the cooks to make sure they knew their firewood had arrived. When I turned around, she nodded to herself.

"But his mind is a different story. Isn't it?"

I nodded, and we walked down the trench. I could barely recognize it. The debris was all but cleared away, and the scores of dead had been buried systematically over the last two weeks in individually marked graves. It was nice to not have to throw them together in mass burials…to have the time to treat them with the respect they deserved.

"Byrne."

I jumped and looked back at her.

"I'm sorry. I just got distracted." I paused, debating whether or not to tell her and coming to a decision. "Yeah. He's just…I don't recognize him."

"You have to give him time, Byrne. He'll come around. As will you."

"How do you know?"

"I told you that I'd seen people in his state before," she began with a sad smile. "I know how they recover…and I know how they don't." We walked in silence for a bit, not really heading anywhere specific, before she continued. "He'll have a break soon. Everything will come crashing down over him, and he may say some things that you'll wish you'd never heard. But at that point he will recognize that he needs help, and that's when you can step in and provide him with the support he needs."

She finally came to a stop before a bench crudely made of repurposed metal from munitions crates and empty shell casings and sat down. I joined her, and we watched the people come and go around us.

"Why do you let me spend time with you?" I asked, looking at her, and she stared down at me, confused. "I'm a private from the Amaeric army. You're a general. Isn't this some level of fraternizing with the enemy?"

"I find you fascinating, Byrne," she answered, clasping her hands over her crossed knee. "By all rights you don't have the personality or skill level to have survived this war, and yet here you are." She looked at me, a wondering gleam in her eyes. "At the end of all things, you were left standing. Clearly there is something in you we've all missed that's crucial to survival."

"So, I'm an amusing oddity," I summarized.

"If that's what you'd like to call it, yes," she said, looking forward. "But you are a personable oddity, and quite frankly I like you for that. You've got spirit in you." We sat quietly in the sun for a little longer, and I let out a soft snort of laughter. "What?"

"I was just thinking about your accent. It's *weird*."

"I beg your pardon?"

"I just mean that I've only ever heard Amaeric accents my whole life. Then, I hear the Brettain accent, and it throws me off." She continued to look at me in unconvinced amusement. "I mean, you guys say 'left-tenant.' What's the direction have to do with anything? Why not the right? Do these people rent apartments on your left? Where's the logic?"

She raised her eyebrows, unamused, and crossed her arms.

"Well, you Amaerics say 'loo-tenant,'" she pointed out. "'Loo' for us is the *toilet*."

"Point taken."

"Also, we don't say apartment, we say flat," she added, and I looked at her, mockingly offended. "And we don't say rent, we say let."

"Your language is bizarre," I sighed, playfully giving up, and she rolled her eyes.

"It's the same language as yours!"

"I don't know *what* you're speaking," I said, askance, "but it's definitely *not* what I'm speaking."

She laughed and got to her feet, straightening her uniform and dusting off her pants.

"It was good talking with you, Byrne. As always, your sense of humor is quite a relief. Just…don't forget to smile," she sighed. I looked up at her, expression serious once more.

"Then give me something to smile about, ma'am."

"Fair enough," she conceded. "And remember, private: just give your corporal some time. He'll come around, I promise."

I nodded my thanks and watched as she returned to her tent, no doubt to face the mountain of responsibilities waiting for her. I could hear the sounds of rebuilding in the distance, of hammers falling on foundations and nails pinning down the floors.

Things were starting to come together.

・・・ — — ・・・

I was still sitting there a couple hours later, dozing in the half-light and listening to my breath rattle in my chest, when I heard the low rumbling in the distance. My eyes opened, and my heart stopped in my chest as I sat there with bated breath. I knew that sound. Brettain soldiers started running along the tops of the trenches, shouting hurried orders down to their fellow troops. Confused and uneasy, I got to my feet and climbed up the ladder to what had once been No Man's Land, approaching the barbed wire fence.

That was the thing. No matter how well we were treated down in what had once been hell, we were always reminded that we were still prisoners by the sharp, rusty wire roping us in.

A single armored vehicle approached down the dirt-packed road to our camp, and as it drew closer I saw the battered Amaeric flag emblazoned on its rusted hood. All around me, the Brettain lined up, weapons held at the ready in silent warning, and I turned to see Mayworth walking towards us, with Harper at her heels.

"I thought you sent message telling your people that this was over," she growled, and the captain shrugged, at a loss.

"I did. I swear to the gods, I sent a signed and sealed message with your liaison to the Academy," he protested.

She shook her head, brushing past me and stopping at attention before the fence. The car came to a halt a dozen feet opposite us, and the engine shut off, the shadowed driver throwing back his seatbelt and opening the door. Immediately, my throat closed up, and my eyes smarted with tears as I took in the tall, burly man before me. His strawberry-blonde hair was streaked with more gray than I remembered, and his face was creased with more worry lines, too. But I recognized him.

"I'm unarmed!" he shouted, voice booming across the land. He raised his hands to his shoulders as he stepped away from the car.

"Oh, really?" Mayworth called back dryly. "If you're so unarmed, why did you come in that?"

Jax met the general's eyes with an equally cold gaze.

"We've been at war for three decades, General," he began and slowly approached the fence line. "I've learned it never hurts to be too careful."

At a subtle gesture from Mayworth, the soldiers trained their weapons' sights on the man before us. My S.O. got the message and stopped.

"Declare yourself and your intention," she ordered, and he lowered his hands.

"I'm the battlemaster at the Amaeric War Academy. I was sent by G.A. Agathon to broker an agreement for this section of the front line."

"She couldn't come herself?" she asked, and I stepped forward a little bit, trying to catch my superior's eye.

"She has bigger fish to fry than you, General." He paused. "Besides. I was the supervising officer for the kids in thirty-seven and the battlemaster for everyone you've got in this camp. Also, I received a radio message from a Doctor Blackwell that one of them was in serious condition, and the punk was enough of a smart-ass to leave a note naming me his beneficiary when he left the Academy."

Mayworth smirked, a barely noticeable movement of her lips.

"I think I know the private." She glanced over her shoulder, making sure I was still standing a few feet behind her before waving Jax towards the gate. Unanimously, all the Brettain soldiers relaxed and lowered their guns. "We can discuss your proposals, Mr. Jax, over a meal. Dinner is in an hour, and I'm sure *he* can point you in the direction of my tent." The barbed gate clanked shut behind my S.O., and he looked at Mayworth in confusion as she walked away.

"Who?" he called, but she didn't answer him. Instead, she just gave me a baffled look as she walked back towards the ladder.

"You named him your beneficiary?" she asked, and I shrugged.

"It was a shortsighted move, ma'am," I admitted, straight-faced.

She shook her head and climbed back down into the trenches below us. The soldiers and few Amaeric prisoners of war who'd come to see what was happening started returning to their posts, and the once-crowded space slowly cleared. And in the bustle of movement, Jax found himself face to face with me.

I don't think he recognized me at first. He just stared down at me with this frown on his face – this look in his eyes as he tried to put two and two together. And I had to remind myself that the last time he had seen me had been almost six months ago. I knew I looked different.

In fact, the first time I'd glanced at a mirror in the showers the Brettain set up for us, I'd just stood there, unable to recognize the person staring at me. He'd been a stranger. My already angular features looked sunken in. The circles under my eyes were so dark they looked bruised, and my collarbones jutted out of my skin while my clearly visible ribs shook with each breath I took. And, of course, where my right arm had been, there was nothing more than a sutured and bandaged stub. My hair had grown out despite the downtime we'd had to keep ourselves relatively cleaned up in the trenches, and the tips of my hair now brushed against my ears and the nape of my neck. A few times I'd had to swipe my bangs aside in order to see. My mouth hadn't smiled in what seemed like an eternity.

But mostly the change was in my eyes. They weren't optimistic, weren't the eyes of kid. Not anymore. They were cold and glimmered with sarcastic, dark humor.

It was like Jack said. After the first tour, no one was innocent.

"Byrne?" My name was a whispered question, a sound of denial, and I took in as deep of a breath as I could, meeting Jax's eyes.

"Sir," I answered.

He reached out to me, fingers catching the chain of my dog tag and pulling the cool metal free from my shirt, and I looked away as he read the name. I understood. His mind needed confirmation for what his eyes were seeing. When the tags thumped against my chest, I glanced back at him. His hand had drifted down to examine what was left of my right arm, and his eyes locked onto mine as I reflexively jerked away.

"I'm sorry," he apologized, voice brusque, and he took a few uncertain steps back. I shook my head, shifting on my feet and staring at my boots.

"It's not a problem, sir." My voice cracked, and Jax slowly knelt before me, hands on my shoulders. His eyes were kind, yet sad, and he gave me a shaky, relieved smile.

"Don't you 'sir' me ever again, newbie." I looked down again, uncomfortable with the eye contact, and the man quickly pulled me into a tight embrace. Bearlike arms locked across my frail back, and he took in a deep breath as he felt my one arm reciprocating the action. "I have more respect for you than you could ever have for me."

"Um. Thank you, sir." I cringed as soon as the word left my mouth, but he just laughed, pulling away and standing.

"That'll take you a bit to get over, so I'll cut you some slack now. But in a few years, I want you to be calling me anything *but* sir. You hear me?"

I nodded, unable to fake a smile in response to the genuine one he was giving me, and started heading towards the ladder.

"Byrne."

I paused on the top rung, looking at him. He sighed, avoiding my gaze as he gathered the courage to ask the question I could tell he wasn't sure he wanted the answer to.

"How's Miller?"

There was a hopeful pitch to his voice, and I felt some kind of twisted amusement at the fact that he couldn't bring himself to ask if Jack was alive. But instead of commenting on it, I just sighed.

"That's something you should see for yourself."

. . . – – – . . .

"So, you're telling me he's being a general pain in the ass."

"No – I mean, kind of, but no. It's a psychological thing."

"Doesn't excuse it," Jax argued, and I rolled my eyes.

"You're sounding like Marcel."

"The Horsemen are still alive?" he asked as we headed towards Jack's tent, and I shook my head.

"Three of them are. Irina died two weeks ago of gangrene." He shook his head bitterly before looking at me again, urgent.

"What about Harris? Harris and Chance?"

"Harris is fine. Well, mostly fine. He lost an eye and a couple fingers on his right hand from a faulty shell." I was quiet for a few steps. "Howell shot Chance before we even got to the front lines. She had a full-on episode, and that was a good enough excuse for him." I looked up at Jax, surprisingly collected as I continued. "He got what was coming to him."

"That's not the cadet I knew at the Academy," he said softly, stumbling on the uneven ground and narrowly avoiding walking into people. I didn't break pace, weaving with ease through the crowded, chaotic space. "Being thankful for someone's death."

I looked over my shoulder as we neared Jack's canvas-walled room, catching and holding his gaze.

"No," I agreed. "It's the private."

I pushed open the flap of the tent and stepped to the side, watching Jax as he came in. He had to stoop slightly so he could fit through the doorway. A plate of untouched food lay on the side table, and Jack was staring at the wall opposite us, watching as a light breeze made the fabric billow in and out like breathing lungs.

"Jack?" I called. He turned to look at me, surprise flickering in his eyes. "I've got someone here to see you."

"Sir." He went to sit up, and I sharply cleared my throat, earning myself a quick glare. "What are you doing here?"

Jax pulled up a chair beside my boyfriend as I settled on the foot of the mattress.

"I'm here to try and broker a deal with Mayworth to bring you home. Though by the looks of it, this is a better place for you to be than anywhere under Amaeric control."

"That bad?" Jack asked, clearing his throat, and our S.O. nodded.

"We've been losing ground on all fronts. Turns out our allies brokered their own treaties and flipped sides without telling us. We've got the whole world coming down on us, now. Won't be long before we're stamped out."

"The G.A. wasn't kidding, then," I mumbled, and Jax shook his head.

"No, the she wasn't. But enough about the rest of the world. How are you doing?"

Jack scoffed once before lifting up the hem of his shirt and pulling back the bandaging to reveal his injury. Our battlemaster sighed, shaking his head with sadness in his eyes, and Jack covered up again.

"How long has it been?"

"Three weeks." Jack dug his palms into the mattress, pulling himself upwards a little into a more angled posture and ignoring my scolding eyes.

"Type of gun?"

I jumped to answer this question.

"Sniper rifle. Some greenstick idiot thought he was Howell," I told him, pinning Jack with yet another warning glare when he tried to sit up again. Jax caught the look and frowned, glancing between us.

"Something the matter with you two?"

Jack crossed his arms.

"No. We're just fine," he said, and I nodded in agreement. "Of course, Tristan won't let me move the slightest bit without yelling at me to either stay put or get a nurse to help."

I bristled, anger and frustration coiling in my chest and making it hard to breathe.

"Well, I'm *sorry* if I'm worried about you hurting yourself!" I snapped, voice rising. "It's only been three weeks, Jack. You're still healing."

"That doesn't mean I can't move around in my own bed."

"Do you remember what happened the last time you tried to move on your own?" I demanded, irritation building. "You reopened your stitches, and Blackwell had to redo them all because Nagai's a homophobic ass who won't touch either one of us."

"That was only a few days after I woke up. I was more fragile then," he countered, and I narrowed my eyes. He rolled his eyes and held his hands up. "Look, I *realize* that was a mistake, but I swear I can move myself into a sitting position on my own, now. Okay?" I stayed quiet, refusing to feed into our now-old argument. "Look, I'll prove it." He started bracing himself to sit up, pressing his palms against the mattress, and I reached over and grabbed his hand.

"Jack, *stop it*. I don't want you to hurt yourself more than you already have. If you want to move, get help."

Jack jerked his hand away from mine and ran both through his hair, groaning in frustration.

"You don't *get* it, Tristan! No more nurses, no more doctors!" his voice was frustrated, strained. "I'm *done* with them! I just want – I *need* to be able to move myself in my own bed. Why can't you get that?"

Finally, Jax had had enough.

"Okay, *clearly* I've missed some things, and I just opened a whole can of worms I really didn't need to know about," he said loudly over our mixed voices, hands raised, and we both looked at him. "But the fact of the matter is this, Miller. Your legs are paralyzed. That means there is some kind of damage to the spine from the bullet, and if you are trying to move yourself before that heals all the way, you risk making your injury so much worse. You think being unable to move your legs is bad? Imagine being unable to move your torso."

Jack looked away, obviously ignoring what the man had just said, and our S.O. nodded grimly to himself, getting to his feet and looming over us.

"I'll tell you what," he began, and my boyfriend slowly looked up at those words. I felt nauseating unease settle in my stomach. That talking-to-a-child tone was never good with the battlemaster. That tone meant he was about to start bashing heads in. "You can start moving yourself around on your own when *this* doesn't hurt anymore."

With that, he reached over to Jack's stomach and pressed down with considerable force on the bandaged wound.

"What the *hell?!*" I shouted and reached across the bed to grab Jack's shoulder as he cried out in pain.

He twisted his upper body away from the man beside us as much as he could, violently tearing his shoulder from my grasp with his arms clamped over his stomach. I felt sick as I sat there, helplessly watching and listening as my groaning Jack forced himself through the pain. His breathing was ragged and broken, hissing between his teeth as he tried to fight back what was probably close to agony burning through him. Heart pounding in my temples, I cast a dark look at my S.O. who uncomfortably met my gaze. He leaned over Jack, putting a hand on his shoulder and forcibly turning the injured man to face him.

"Rest, Miller. I know what I'm talking about." Jack didn't answer, just took in deep, shaking breaths and stared at him in hurt betrayal. "And one other thing." Jax's voice became hard and reprimanding. "That young man over there is your *boyfriend*. He *cares* about you. Gods, he lost his arm making sure that you survived!" I looked away from his hissed words, but I couldn't block out his voice as he continued. "So you straighten out this issue you've got, and you let him help you. Stop acting like a child!"

"Now." He turned to face me, and I could feel myself shaking in fury. "Where's that Brettain general?"

I shook my head, rage barely contained, and got to my feet, storming out of the room with my superior close behind me. As soon as we were far enough away from the tent, I turned around to face him, livid.

"How was that helping?!" I practically shouted, but Jax just walked past me. "I told you he's struggling to adapt to the whole paralyzed thing, and you just—"

"And I told you that's not an excuse," he countered without looking at me, and I hurried to catch up to him. "Look, Byrne. I know this is hard on you, and it's definitely hard on him. But the sooner he comes to terms with the facts of what's happened to him, the sooner he can start healing. He's in denial right now, and you need to help him accept what happened to him."

"What do you think I've been trying to do?" I asked, infuriated, but he shook his head.

"You've been arguing with him. You've been trying to tell him what to do and what to feel and what to think. Make him start to realize things on his own." He paused and put a hand on my shoulder. "Now that I've given him the shock he needed, he might start to respond by himself. And when he does, listen. That's the most important part, Byrne. *Listen.*"

He headed off to General Mayworth's tent but stopped, turning back to face me.

"It'll probably be past curfew by the time I'm ready to leave, Byrne. So I guess this is goodbye for a long while." I nodded stiffly and took his outstretched hand. "Stay in touch. I still have your stuff to give back to you at the Academy."

Despite my anger, I managed a tight laugh.

"I'll send you a forwarding address when we get out of here."

He nodded curtly before leaving me, and I watched him go. It was odd. I had no idea when I would see that man again, and it was disconcerting to me that my last memory could be his back walking away and the feeling of anger in my chest.

· · · − − − · · ·

A few hours later, after a meal of beans and stale bread that was worlds better than the jerky and dried fruit leather we'd been eating the last five months, I headed back into Jack's room. I had been rehearsing an apology in my head, rewording it over and over again all throughout dinner while I unenthusiastically poked at my meal. And I felt like I'd finally come up with one that would cover all my bases – from how uncalled for Marcel and Jax's actions and words had been to my own insensitivity. I could make this right again, smooth over the rough patches like I always did. But all confidence I'd gained walking to his tent vanished as soon as I cleared the threshold. My stomach dropped while my heart raced, blood pounding mercilessly in my temples.

His bed was empty.

"Jack?" I called nervously to the half-lit room and slowly made my way into the space. My nightmare from the day I'd woken up resurfaced in my mind, and I walked faster, breathing shaky and panicked. His blankets were tossed about, tangled in each other, and I could see bits of food from his overturned dinner tray scattered across the ground. "Jack?"

As I stepped a few feet closer to his bed, I saw the hand on the ground.

"Nurse!" I shouted, running around the bed and dropping to my knees beside my half-conscious boyfriend. He lay in a heap on the floor, one hand over his blood soaked abdomen, and I took in a sharp breath as I saw the red stain seeping between the floorboards. "Oh, shit...Jack, look at me." I gently pulled him into my lap and turned his head so that he was looking up at me. At my touch he seemed to wake up a little, brow furrowing as he tried to focus. "Jack, talk to me, okay? What happened?"

"I didn't...I wasn't trying to–" he protested, pain-filled voice dazed and pleading. "I promise, Tristan. I wasn't trying to get up."

I nodded and tried to keep myself calm as a few nurses came sprinting into the room. They started giving each other orders and sent someone off to find Blackwell. I gave him a shaky smile.

"I know, Jack. I know you weren't," I said gently, brushing his sweaty hair away from his skin. I realized too late that my hand was coated in his blood and hesitated for a few seconds before resuming the calming motion. "Just talk to me. Tell me what happened."

He took in a shuddering breath as the nurses pulled the bed away from us and turned the lights up. As they tended to his reopened wound, not daring to move him more than he'd already moved himself, he answered my question.

"I-it was just a nightmare," he whimpered, confused. "We...we were in the trenches, and I had to get away." I nodded, biting my lip as I ran my fingers through his hair. His eyes nearly fluttered shut. His breathing was painfully erratic, and I wondered how awake he truly was. "But I swear, Tris, it was j-just a nightmare. I wasn't trying anything."

"Don't worry," I whispered, kissing his forehead and reaching down to hold his bloody hand as he gritted his teeth against the pain. "It's okay. It's okay, Jack. The nightmare's over now, it's done....I'm here. It's okay."

But as I sat there, cradling him and fighting away the nausea of holding his bloodied hand for a second time, I couldn't help but think the truth. It wasn't okay. It wasn't okay at all.

"Private Byrne? Doctor Blackwell is probably going to want to redress his wound here – he's lost quite a lot of blood, and moving him might make him bleed more. Can you keep the corporal still?"

I looked up at Samantha, heart pounding. But instead of looking at me with that reluctant contempt that most of the other staff did, her gaze was kind and reassuring. I nodded, eyes wide with fear, and she reached out to put a hand on my shoulder.

"He's going to be okay," she said gently. "Just stay with him."

As soon as she finished talking, Blackwell came running into the tent, batting the canvas door out of his way as he hurried over and knelt across from me. He gave the two of us a cursory glance before making a calming gesture with his hands that I realized a few seconds later was meant for me. He turned his focus to Jack and sighed.

"I told you not to move yourself, Jack," he scolded, voice gentle despite the words he was saying. "Why didn't you listen?" My partner looked at the doctor with tears of pain and betrayal in his eyes, and his disoriented words slurred as he tried to protest.

"I wasn't – Tris, *tell* him, I wasn't–"

"Shh, Jack...it's okay," I whispered soothingly and looked at Blackwell, trying to keep my tears back as he tended to my boyfriend and pulled back his bloodied shirt. "He had a nightmare. He wasn't trying to move himself. It...it was a just a nightmare."

"Okay," the doctor said kindly, gravelly voice calm as he patted Jack's shoulder. "It's okay, Miller. You're not in any trouble. I understand."

As I sat there, my tears finally spilled over. I bent over Jack's delirious form, whispering shaky reassurances into his ear and smoothing his hair back. He continued to stare dazedly at the ceiling.

I don't think he heard me.

DAY TWO HUNDRED AND SIXTY-FOUR, PART ONE

Three months later

 I took in a deep breath and stretched my left arm over my head, the bones cracking and noisily realigning themselves after last night's awkward positioning. Jack was still asleep beside me, his head pillowed on my right shoulder and arm thrown protectively cross across my chest. It was a comforting sensation, and one I hadn't felt in a long time. But it wasn't perfect. I could still feel the sore spots on my ribs from where Jack's nightmares had gotten physical.

 But I didn't really care about the bruises. I cared more about what was causing them. After three months Jack had regained considerable mobility. He could move himself around in a wheelchair now with some help from us when he got tired, and he could sit up in bed on his own. He still needed help getting in and out of bed and probably always would, but he was healing.

 His nightmares, on the other hand, were a different story.

 Every night he had at least one, and recently it had become more than that. They ranged anywhere from remnants of his first three tours to more traumatic memories from his fourth. Sometimes, he was running away from something, and then his legs collapsed under him, leaving him stranded for whatever was chasing him. Other times he was getting shot all over again. All I knew was that he'd fallen off the bed a few times and after the third time I'd abandoned my bed and started sleeping with him.

I hadn't gotten a decent hour of sleep in a while, but I didn't care. Jack was a little safer than he had been, and that was all that mattered to me.

"Good morning, Byrne." I half-heartedly grunted at Blackwell, and he cocked an eyebrow at me, shoulders heaving with a resigned sigh. "I take it last night was just as restful as the others?"

"Hilarious, doc," I countered, voice dry as I slowly sat up. Jack was still sound asleep beside me, brow slightly damp with sweat. His eyes weren't screwed shut, though, and his mouth was relaxed, so he wasn't having a nightmare. I saw Blackwell start moving again in my peripheral vision, and I looked back at him. "How's the med tent looking?"

"Wonderful," he beamed, quickly engaging our new conversation and picking up my empty bottle of pneumonia antivirals. "Most of the patients have been dismissed, and those that are left are mostly just for monitoring reasons like Jack." He sifted through the pages of his clipboard and crossed something out. "But we've already packed up the equipment and supplies we don't need and stowed them in the trucks waiting to take you guys back to the Academy."

I sighed and carefully extracted myself from underneath Jack.

"I can't believe that's today," I finally said, and Blackwell smiled at me.

"It's a day that's been long in coming, kid. You should probably get to the showers before they start disassembling them."

"I thought the Brettain were keeping this as an outpost or something," I yawned as I got out of bed and pulled on my socks and shoes to go get cleaned up before eating.

"Oh, they are. They just want to fill in the trenches and rebuild everything on top. You know, bury the past and move on...that sort of thing."

"I don't know. It feels like a cheap move to me," I said after a little bit. "It's like they're just wiping away everything that just happened here. That happened to us." The older man just shook his head, methodically folding my bed's sheets as he spoke.

"They can't ever wipe it out, Tristan. Not when you, Miller, Harris, and so many others look the way you do. Those are scars they can't hide."

I smiled wryly to myself as I headed towards the door. The Brettain had finally gotten around to making actual buildings for the field hospitals about two months ago. The nights were *much* warmer now.

"Hey, uh, if you're in here when Jack wakes up, can you tell him where I went?" I asked, over my shoulder.

He nodded, absently waving me away, and I quickly left, walking along the wooden pathways we had set up down the trenches. We'd been getting intermittent rain in the early fall, and the ground was spongy and sticky with the combination of humid air and warm showers. But I'd become used to the trails and could walk them without even thinking about where I was stepping.

A few minutes later I arrived at the showers and opened the door to get a face full of steam. Apparently others had had the same idea as me but had had enough foresight to heat up their water over a fire beforehand. I could see a shadowy silhouette in the fog turn their head to look at me.

"Get in or get out."

"Sorry, Moore." I stepped in and closed the door, heading for an empty stall and pulling off my clothes as I opened the tap and cold water poured into the basin. We were silent for a few minutes while we continued our separate routines, and then I heard Kat from the other end of the hall.

"How's Miller doing?"

"Fine," I called back.

"I saw him moving around in his wheelchair a few days ago," she said after a few beats of silence. "By himself. How's that going for him?"

"Alright."

Suddenly, Marcel's voice spoke from right outside the curtain around me, and I jumped.

"Okay, shrimp? We're looking for something more than single word answers."

"He's *fine*, okay?" I said and continued to wash off in the cold water. "He's can move around on his own fairly well, but the nightmares are still there. And they're not pretty," I snapped, stepping out of the water, drying myself off, and pulling on my pants. "Is that enough information for you?"

I pulled back the roughly made curtains, shirt bundled in my hand, and saw Jones standing there, waiting for me. Her wet hair was free from her usual style of meticulously tight braids and instead hung loosely down her back, soaking her tank top. I could make out Katalin standing behind her, moving her heavy curls back and forth to put it back into its normal style.

"Yeah, that's good enough." She winced as Soto pulled on her hair, and I caught a mumbled apology from Famine. "It's fine, Kat. I'm used to it." She turned her attention back to me. "So, where are you two planning on going after today?"

I shrugged and pulled on my shirt and jacket.

"I assumed back to the Academy to grab our belongings that we left there, but after that…" I picked up my socks and shoes. "Who knows?"

"You're not going to Miller's family in the mid-west?" Aliyah asked as she pulled on her shoes a few feet away.

"How the hell did *you* know about them?"

She shrugged, lacing up her boots.

"I have my ways."

I looked at the other two Horsemen, mutely demanding an answer, and Katalin rocked up on her toes to look over Marcel's shoulder.

"We may have asked Jack where you two were planning on heading a few weeks ago. He wasn't sure either, but he mentioned that he has some family left back home."

"Yeah, highly religious, conservative family members who have no idea he's gay–" I broke off, brow furrowing as I struggled to pull on my socks and shoes with the one hand "–and could quite possibly be dead. He hadn't heard from them for over a year at the Academy. Besides, I got the feeling he doesn't really like them all that much given that it's like pulling teeth to get him to even mention them." I straightened, finally satisfied with my shoes, and headed for the door. "Bottom line is I wouldn't rely on them too much."

"Good luck, Byrne," Kat called, and I waved at her as I left, the door slamming shut behind me.

"Hey, Byrne!" I looked over my shoulder to see Andrew running over to me, eye alight with excitement and a grin on his face. Humoring him, I stopped and raised my hand at him, a smirk pulling at my lips.

"Hey, Harris. Nice eye patch."

He laughed, reflexively reaching up to run his fingers across the fabric as he fell into step on my left.

"Thanks. It was a gift from that Doctor Nagai." My stomach churned at his name, and my companion seemed to notice my discomfort. "Don't worry, I wasn't too nice to him. I heard what he said about you and Miller and gave him a piece of my mind."

"Well, the world can't be filled with nice people, can it?" I asked, voice sarcastically understanding. He laughed again, and I took a closer look at him. There was a lightness to his gait, something almost buoyant. I squinted at him suspiciously. "How are you, Andrew?"

"Great, man. I mean really great," he grinned, looking down at me and crossing his arms importantly. "I just got out of Mayworth's tent, and she asked me to come with her to some big peace talk. Apparently the Brettain are assembling a whole bunch of soldiers form all over the world, and they want us to share our experiences with the International Summit. Deal out some reparations, you know? Set the record straight."

I gave a crooked smile, clapping my friend on the shoulder as he let his arms relax from their tight cross over his body.

"That's great. You'll finally get to tell the top brass about the hell their orders cause." Andrew nodded, but his smirk faded as he looked down at his hands. "What is it?"

"I, uh…look, Byrne, I need you to just listen to me, okay? Hold off on any judgment until I explain myself." I nodded, nonplussed, and he took in a deep breath, squaring his shoulders as we walked along. "I…I also asked her if I could join the Brettain forces." What little remained of my smile slid off face as I looked at him in stricken confusion. "She said yes."

"Y-you what?" I stammered, stopping with a betrayed expression, and he turned to face me. "You *what?!*"

"See, I *knew* you'd take it like this," he sighed and immediately assumed a debater's stance. "Look, what has Amaeric ever given us except war and pain?"

"That's…the Brettain aren't any better than us, Andrew," I protested, still reeling and baffled by what was happening. "Sure, they gave us this, but the fact is that we're in this situation because the whole world couldn't stop throwing a selfish tantrum for thirty years!"

"Yeah, but the rest of the world is changing now, Tristan," he pressed, earnest. "They're drawing up treaties and – and *surrendering*. But look at us! Amaeric is still clinging to this…this depraved ideal of honor and righteousness, and it's killing *everyone* within its borders. The Brettain aren't doing that anymore!"

I opened my mouth to protest but slowly closed it again. I tried to see the situation through his eyes. Mostly though, all I saw was a young woman with wild hair trying to commune with the swans.

"I get what you're saying, Andy," I said after a few beats of silence but despite my supporting start, shook my head. "But that doesn't mean I agree with it."

Andrew scoffed, dragging the toe of his boot through the dirt.

"Wouldn't expect you to. I mean, look at you and Miller – you're the very picture of valor." I defensively crossed my arm over my chest and grabbed my right arm, quickly looking at the ground. "But as long as you understand me, I'm happy." I nodded and, sighing, extended my hand to him. He smiled wanly and took it, locking eyes with me. "Thanks, Tristan."

"No problem," I said softly. I could barely maintain our tenuous eye contact. "Good luck out there, Andrew."

He nodded his thanks and started walking to the Brettain barracks, pulling an orders envelope from his pocket. Even from this distance I could see Queen Auriane's seal on the outside. But before he reached the sentries, he turned back to me.

"I'll make sure the world knows about Idris," he called to me, walking backwards, and I informally saluted him. "Who knows? Maybe she'll be the one that ends the war."

As I stood there, watching him walk away, I suddenly spoke, the words falling from my lips without me even pausing to think.

"Hey, Harris!" He turned back to face me, eyebrows raised in a silent question. Mouth dry and words pityingly hopeful, I continued. "I'll see you around?"

A sad light filled his eye at the familiar words, and he looked down at his feet, the rest of his body impossibly still. His shoulders heaved with a sigh, and I swallowed painfully, watching – waiting for his answer. Finally, he looked back up at me, expression solemn.

"Yeah," he began, voice heavy. "I'm sure you will."

There was no point in either of us trying to hide our lies.

With that he turned on his heel and walked to the sentries, extending his envelope to them. They quickly took it and looked it over, and suddenly I couldn't watch anymore.

I walked a ways down the trenches, my direction aimless. There was no purpose to my wandering except a need to move after the conversation I'd just had. I felt a little nauseous, and pain suddenly shot up my right arm. I came to a stop with a wince and quiet groan and carefully wrapped my hand around the stump to tentatively massage the healing skin.

That was when I heard a low, gurgling croak behind me.

Used to the sound, I turned to see a raven perched on the handle of a shovel that had been driven into the ground not a foot away from me. Her intelligent eyes fixed on mine, and she bobbed her head up and down as she continued to make innocuous little noises at me. Her feathers were ruffled against the warmth of the sun, and I heard the voice in my head again. That gentle, forever-lost voice.

It's okay.

I took in a deep breath and, for a reason I wasn't quite sure of, slowly reached out to her.

It's okay. He's just a herald.

Idris had been terrified of these birds, had seen them as omens of evil, had died screaming about them. But then, in my dream, her voice had been calm. She'd *giggled*.

"You're not all good or bad are you?" I asked. The bird tilted her head at me and croaked once. "You're just a herald."

Feeling breathless and oddly calm, I managed to lightly stroke her silk feathers a few times before, with a disgruntled squawk, she snapped her beak shut on the air beside my fingers and flapped off.

"Geez!" I yelped, snatching my hand away, and I heard someone snort in amusement a ways off to my right. "Shut up."

"I see you're making friends in your usual way," the voice continued, and I turned to see Jack coming over, his bandage-wrapped hands resting lightly on top of the moving wheels of his chair to slow down. "What'd you think was going to happen?"

I shrugged, thumb rubbing at my index finger.

"Just to make things even better," he began with a mischievous lilt, and I cast him a baleful eye, "have you ever stopped to think about where a raven's beak has been in the trenches?" I glared down at my inappropriately amused companion. "They dig through all the trash, eat rotting food, not to mention corpses–"

"It didn't actually bite me, Jack, so you can stop now," I interrupted and headed towards the field hospital while my boyfriend followed me, still invisibly smiling to himself.

"Dammit. Seriously, though, what'd you think was gonna happen?"

"I don't know," I called back to him and slowed down so that he could keep up without straining himself. "Maybe I was going for a little fairy tale action back there."

Jack smirked at my sarcasm, but the expression seemed to sit wrong on his face in the same way I felt uncomfortable smiling.

"Don't blame you. Looked like you actually got kind of close."

"I did," I agreed, and he playfully raised his eyebrows. "Raven feathers are nice and soft. But enough about the bird. How'd you sleep?"

"It was okay," he said after hesitating for a few seconds. "I had another nightmare, but I don't remember what it was about. So, I suppose that's an improvement?"

"Yeah," I reassured him, putting my hand on his shoulder as we went. "That's good." It wasn't, but I couldn't exactly tell him that to his face. "So, ready to leave?"

"Definitely," he said, nodding vigorously. "Where to is the question, though." He looked at me expectantly, and I shrugged.

"I don't know." My footsteps and his wheels creaked and groaned over the wood beneath us. "Do you really want to try your family?"

"Hell, no," my boyfriend bitterly laughed. "I just told the Horsemen that because they wanted an answer."

"Well, wherever you go I'm going to be right there beside you," I said firmly, and Jack looked up at me, visibly touched. "What? Jack, I'm your *boyfriend*. That's kind of my job description."

He looked forward again, distant, and I felt uneasy all of a sudden. My worry was barely allayed when he resumed talking.

"Well, we'll stop at the Academy to get all of our stuff, but other than that, I've got no preferences about where we go next."

We pulled off the path to stop at the bench Mayworth and I had sat at so many months ago. I stepped in front of Jack and hooked what was left of my arms under his, waiting for him grip the back of my jacket.

"One," Jack began, "two...three."

I stood up and swung Jack around so that he landed on the seat of the bench with a rather loud thud, and I winced as I pulled back from him.

"Sorry?" I offered as he painfully pressed a hand to his back.

"We need to work on that a little bit," he groaned.

I sat next to him and waited as he arranged his legs into the position he wanted. People were moving around us, packing things up that belonged to the Amaerics and reorganizing what belonged to the Brettain. All in all, it was very busy, and I watched Jack as he settled back, his shoulder pressing against mine.

"What if..." I trailed off, thinking over the words in my mind before I spoke. "What if we picked a direction and just drove? Just keep going until the gas runs out and where we end up is where we stay."

"That's a *bit* risky," Jack said with a grimace, and I shrugged.

"Well then, what do we want for the rest of our lives? Because once we settle down, I don't want to move again."

Jack sat in thought for a little bit, and I noticed his hand subconsciously massaging his knee.

"I'd like to see the ocean," he finally said, voice quiet.

"You've *never* seen the ocean?" I asked, shocked.

"Tris, I lived in the mid-west, and then I went to war," he explained, a burned-out light in his eyes. "I never got stationed near the water so I never saw it. You're from a coastal city – you were luckier than me. Than most of us." I nodded, lacing my fingers in his.

"Okay. Okay, we'll do that." I paused in thought. "We'll want to stay away from the southern and the eastern borders. What about the west?"

"That could work. I mean, the navy pushed most of the fighting away from the shoreline fairly quickly over there. It'll be a little better off than most other places," he mused, and I nodded in agreement, running through the geography of the region in my head.

"So, what…central coast of Calin?" Jack nodded absently at first and then grew more confident as he thought about it more. "If you drive non-stop, that's just under two days away from the Academy."

"Yeah, that'll work. We'll figure out where exactly when we get back to the Academy," he said softly, half to himself and half to me. He took a deep breath and clenched his hands on his knees. "It'll work out."

"Hey." He looked at me, wide-eyed, and I gripped his hand tightly. "It *will* work out. I'll make sure it does. I promise." I felt us both go still as we remembered the last time I'd made the promise that everything would work out, and I quickly tried to cover it up. "You know me," I continued, vaguely lighthearted. "I don't break promises."

Jack gave a quiet, wobbling laugh, and quickly draped his arm across my shoulders, pulling me close to him. This feeling…I'd missed it. I tightened my hold on the hand in his lap and rested my head on his shoulder, just breathing and thinking about the fact that he was still breathing, too.

"So central Calin," I said, breaking the silence. "That's home, then."

Jack shook his head, resting his chin on top of my head.

"No. Home's us. Wherever we are, that's where home is." I smiled and closed my eyes against the warm sun as he spoke. "It's not a place, Tristan, not for us." He looked down at me and smiled. "It's us."

"Alright then, Mr. Waxing Poetic," I snorted, untangling myself from him and leaning forward to rest my forearm across my knees. I looked back at him over my shoulder and gave him a very small smile. "If I'm home enough for you, I guess you're home enough for me."

"Now you're the one waxing poetic," he countered, playfully pushing me sideways.

I didn't engage him any further. I just smiled, staring ahead of myself with tears burning in my eyes. For a split second there, we'd had our old banter back. And in the silence that followed, Jack took in a deep breath, expression conflicted, and I turned my full attention on him.

"Jack, what is it?"

He blinked, like he was startled I'd noticed he was upset, and an iron curtain dropped behind his eyes. A heavy mask settled over his features until I couldn't read him at all. He swallowed and looked down at his hands, fingers running over his scabbed knuckles and tracing the fading scars.

"I need to see them," he finally said, voice low. "Before we go, I need to see them." When he looked up at me, there was a fire blazing in his eyes like coals, and I took in a deep breath, nodding to him in understanding. "I need to see *him*."

I squared my shoulders and got up, pulling his wheelchair closer to us and lining it up for him. In a fluid series of motions, he wrapped his arms around my neck, and I lifted him up and moved him into his chair, settling him down and backing away.

"Come on. I'll follow you," I said.

He nodded, leading the way to the ramp the Brettain had built into the side of the trenches. And as he went up, I walked behind him, watching as his hands slid a little on the wheels of his chair with each forceful thrust forward. It took us a little bit to get to the upper level, and my heart jumped into my throat whenever one of his hands slipped completely off the wheels, making him swear under his breath. When he had to stop close to the top of the ramp, his breathing was heavy and uneven.

"You okay?" I asked, coming up behind him.

"Yeah." He roughly cleared his throat, pushing himself forward. "Yeah, I'm fine."

I ignored his lie. I'd said the exact same words enough times over the course of the last few months, and I wasn't about to start calling him out on it. I was many things, but I wasn't a hypocrite.

We moved in silence down the dirt-packed trail that ran alongside the crude cemetery, and while Jack kept his eyes focused forward, I watched the markers go by. The square crosses of Orcus weren't more than a foot tall, constructed of scraps of wood that had been roughly lashed together with half-disintegrated twine. The charcoal names were barely legible on the cross-sections, shakily scrawled out on the rough wood. The Brettain said they would work with the Amaeric government and military to eventually replace them with real markers – complete depictions of Orcus' symbol instead of just the cross – but I wondered if by then it would be too late. If the names would be long gone.

And I couldn't help but notice that they were alarmingly close together. How did each person have their own grave? They were nearly buried on top of each other, and as I looked out over the field of stakes, I saw only a field of dead plants scorched in a crop fire long ago. The earth was freshly turned but still stained a dark, bitter color that for some reason I knew wouldn't fade until years into the future.

"She's here."

I looked down at Jack and saw that he had come to a stop in front of one of the headstones – if they could even be called that. I took in a deep breath and knelt beside him, resting my hand on of his and staring at the marker. There was no name, and for a moment I wondered how Jack had identified this as her grave until he pointed to the silver chain tying the two pieces of wood together.

"They used her tags," he whispered, leaning forward so that he could run his fingers over the metal, and turned the rectangle towards me so that I could read the name.

Irina Korsakov.

"It won't fade," I offered, looking at Jack, but he was too focused on our friend's grave.

"Why hasn't Mayworth come to me about killing Howell?" he finally asked, wide eyes unblinking and fixed on the dog tags between his fingers. I shifted on my knees, trying to maintain my calm, collected demeanor.

"Someone else took the fall for you," I told him, my voice surprisingly steady, and watched as my boyfriend's suspicions were confirmed. He went still, hunched over in his chair like a statue for the longest time. And then, he just nodded, clenching the tags in his fist and taking in a deep breath as he bowed his head. "No one pushed her into it, Jack. She volunteered."

Jack laughed once, a bitter sound that shook dangerously.

"Stupid punk," he muttered, voice angry and resigned as he looked back up at her marker, his eyes red with tears. "That stupid, *stupid* punk…"

I took in a deep breath and put my hand on his back, rubbing smooth circles into his taut skin with my thumb. I could feel his spine shudder and hitch with his unsteady breaths, and I looked down at the ground.

"It was her choice," I whispered, and he slowly let go of her necklace to brace his forearms on his knees. "It was her choice, Jack. So, please. Let her have the dignity of that choice."

"I wasn't worth it," he mumbled after a few moments. His voice was barely audible as he steepled his hands over his mouth. "I wasn't worth it."

"Hey," I snapped, the word gentle despite the force with which it was said. "You *are* worth it. You hear me? She thought you were worth it, so don't you dare say that you weren't. Don't you dare cheapen her decision like that." I grabbed his shoulder and leaned forward to look him in the face, eyes blazing and voice hardening.

"You are worth dying for, you hear me? You are worth a reputation. You are worth a court martial." I sighed and paused as Jack finally met my eyes. There was something guarded and carefully vacant about his expression, and I softened my tone, giving a comforting smile. "None of us are ever going to let you get put away for killing Howell. You saved our lives."

Jack stiffly sat back in his chair, mulling over what I'd said. But just when I thought he was going to say something, he grabbed the wheels of his chair and forcefully turned himself around, heading back towards the ramp.

"Where are you going?" I called, standing up but not turning after him. When he called back, his voice was hard and cold.

"I've got someone else to visit." The words were spat, heartless and angry, and his back was stiff and tense as he moved. I quickly headed after him, jogging a little bit to catch up with his quick descent back down into the trenches.

... — — ...

It soon became clear where he was heading. At first, I was confused. He gave no indication of where he was going, just kept heading south down the trench and pushing himself against the flow of people without a single glance to me over his shoulder. But then, the crowds of people started to thin out, and I was finally able to see we were going.

"Jack," I called, voice changing from confused to utterly serious. "Jack, you're gonna have to stop pretty soon." He ignored me and kept going, and I rolled my eyes and increased my pace until I was nearly running after him. "Jack, the planking runs out in, like, three feet!"

He stopped and bowed his head, hands tightly gripping his chair until his knuckles turned white. I sighed to myself, slowing down to an awkward, shuffling gait as I rammed my hand into my pocket.

"You want to get to fence, don't you?" I finally asked once I was a few feet away, and Jack looked over his shoulder, eyes following me as I came up beside him.

"I need to see him," he whispered, voice strained yet determined. He looked forward again to the abandoned length of trench before us that turned a corner not ten feet away. We both knew what lurked just out of sight, and he took in a deep breath beside me, the air shuddering in his lungs. "I *need* to see him."

I nodded, taking my hand out of my pocket to rest it on his shoulder.

"Okay," I assured him, squeezing, and he looked back up at me. "Okay, you'll see him." I swallowed and searched the trench around us. "Let's see what we have to work with here." Immediately, my eyes lit upon the long boards the Brettain had wedged up into the mud walls in an effort to shore up the abused earth a little longer. "Uh-huh."

"Tris, those – those are actually important," Jack began as I stepped away from him and grabbed the closest plank of wood.

"What is this? A three by six? Eight…nine feet long?" I asked looking back at him, and he reluctantly nodded, watching me with wary eyes. "That should work."

Without further ado, I braced myself under the piece of lumber and slammed myself upwards. In a showering of dirt and pebbles, the heavy piece of wood came free of the trench wall, and I held it still over my shoulder. Most of it was still dragging in the earth behind me, but I adjusted my grip on the two feet or so that was sticking out in front of me, pressing down on it and lifting the back end off the ground.

"So, you'll need what, four of these?" I asked my wide-eyed boyfriend, but Jack just pointed me back the way I'd come.

"Tristan, put those down. You're gonna hurt yourself–"

"Jack, I carried you though here with an impaled arm and a concussion. A plank of wood isn't gonna kill me," I said dryly, giving him a look.

I walked past him and let the end of the three by six hit the ground in front of the right wheel of his chair. And as I cautiously walked down its length, easing it to the ground with my one hand, I risked a glance up at Jack. He was staring at me with this odd expression on his face, almost as though I'd slapped him, and I quickly ran through what I'd said.

"Did...did I say something?" I asked, and Jack quietly shook his head. I straightened my back and walked over to another plank of wood, doing the same thing and wincing as a rather sharp rock scraped across my cheek. "I know I said something," I pressed as I walked past him again. I hissed in pain as I let the wood down a little too quickly and my elbow locked up.

"It's nothing," Jack muttered, and I gritted my teeth a little.

You never tell me what you want. Or what you're thinking, I growled to myself, rolling my shoulder as I walked a little further back to grab a third plank. Already I could feel my shoulder smarting beneath my shirt from where I'd been slamming it up into the beams.

That's gonna bruise.

I let the wood slam down a little too quickly and swore viciously as a large splinter stabbed through the space between my thumb and forefinger.

"You okay?"

I glanced at Jack and nodded, gripping the offending shard with my teeth and yanking it out of my skin.

"Yeah, yeah, fine. Just a splinter," I mumbled. "Cut myself a little, but it's not bad." I wiped my bleeding hand against my pant leg and grabbed the last plank of wood, ramming my shoulder up into it. Once it was free, I carried it over and lined it up with the end of the length of timber stretching out before Jack's right wheel.

"You're expecting me to keep myself balanced on those?" Jack asked, unamused, and I shrugged, wincing as it pulled at my left shoulder.

"Well, you've got six inches, don't you?" I asked, breathing slightly heavy, and he continued to bitterly stare at me. "I'm sorry. C'mon, just try it. I'll walk on your right to make sure you don't fall."

Jack laughed once but slowly moved himself forward anyways, leaning to the left so he could keep himself centered.

"You know..." he began, voice tense. "Used to be you couldn't even run with a backpack without almost passing out."

His words had an odd timbre to them, and I shrugged, watching as he continued, perfectly centered, on the narrow pathway.

"Well, adrenaline," I supplied, and a nervous laugh bubbled up in my throat, not quite making it out of my mouth as he cautiously rolled himself onto the next set of boards. "Okay, this'll take you up to the bend, but we're not gonna get a track going around the corner. So, I'll carry you from there."

"Carry me?" Jack asked in disbelief. "It's gonna be more like dragging, isn't it?" I shrugged, kicking a clod of dirt along our path.

"I've...I've done it before. I *can* carry you," I said quietly in the silence that followed, and Jack scoffed, a quiet huff of air that escaped his dry lips.

"Yeah." His words were sullen and gloomy. "Yeah, you can." He came to a stop at the end of the second set of boards and looked up at me. "So. How does this work?"

There was something decidedly confrontational and bitter to the slump of his shoulders and the tightness of his hold on the wheels of his chair. He was grinding his teeth, and I carefully knelt before him, resting my hand on his. I wrapped my fingers around his clenched joints.

"Jack," I whispered, staring intently at my boyfriend, but he continued to stare down at his lap, breathing too even and controlled. "Jack, look at me. Please?" Slowly, he looked at me, eyes lined red, and I gave him a weak smile. "If you don't want me to carry you, that's okay. I can get one of the Horsemen or Jayce to help us out, or–"

"No," he interrupted, eyes flashing, and I pulled back from him a little. "No, I...if we're doing this, it's just us. No one else." His voice grew softer, and he stared at the ground again. "I don't want anyone else to..."

Touch me.

The end of his sentence hung unspoken between us, and I nodded in understanding.

"Okay," I said and briefly squeezed his hand before sitting back on my heels. "Okay, I understand. Just talk me through how you want this done." Jack nodded, swallowing and taking a deep breath.

"Um, well, you'll need to somehow lift up my legs. Or just get a good hold on my waist, otherwise my upper body's just gonna stretch."

"Okay. We'll, uh..." I looked at my left arm and nodded wryly. "We'll figure this out. I promise." I stood up and took in a deep breath, rotating my shoulders to loosen up the muscles. "Alright, if you reach up and lock your arms around my shoulders I think we can do this." I leaned over him, and Jack wrapped his arms around my shoulders, forearms crossing just behind my neck and hands gripping his arms. "Alright, I'm just gonna reach behind you and grab onto your belt. Okay?"

Jack nodded tensely against my shoulder. I took a deep breath and wedged my arm between his back and chair, wrapping my fingers around his belt.

"Alright, you count," I told him gently, and I could feel his breath hot against my neck.

"One, two, *three*." I stood up and turned around, stumbling slightly as Jack tightened his hold on me and threw me off balance. "You okay?" he asked, slightly panicked, and I quickly nodded.

"Yeah. Yeah, I'm fine. We're fine," I assured him, my words quick and slightly strained. "Let's just move quickly, shall we?"

I started off at a quick stumble, the leather of Jack's belt digging into my fingers, and my boyfriend's arms painfully dragged my shoulders down. Only twelve feet to the corner, to the front lines. I could do this.

Move. Quickly, quickly, quickly, quickly. My breathing grew ragged, and I tightened my hold on Jack's body, heart hammering painfully. *Move.* I could feel his feet dragging along the ground beside me, heavy and still, just as they had been before – locked across my chest and stained with blood.

Don't stop moving.

"Tristan, stop," I heard Jack say, but for some reason I didn't register his words. They were just sounds strung together in a meaningless series, and I quickly staggered around the corner, half-running, half-falling the last ten feet to the barbed wire fence. The hellscape stretched out before me, that damned, blackened stretch of land that was still strewn with debris, the earth still stained with old blood.

Get him to the fence. Get him there safe, whole, don't drop him.

"Tristan, stop. You're gonna fall or hurt yourself—"

And suddenly I felt like I was walking in the opposite direction, that the world before me had flipped, grown darker, louder, thicker. I was supposed to be getting Jack *out* of the trenches, why was I going back in?

Blood's soaking my back, Brettain are coming down the trench, Jack's stopped talking, my arm is on fire, I need to carry Jack—

"Gods damn it. Tristan!" Jack shouted and violently twisted his upper body down to the ground. My world was suddenly thrown off kilter, jerking me out of my memories as the earth slammed painfully into my cheek.

"Tristan, *snap out of it!*"

I quickly sat up, slipping to the side as I tried to use my right arm in my disorientated state. Jack looked at me with weary eyes from where he was sprawled on his back.

"Jack," I began, shaken, and my boyfriend pushed himself up, dragging himself sideways until he was sitting up against the opposite wall of the trench. "Jack, I'm…I'm so sorry." I grabbed what was left of my right arm in my hand and drew one of my knees up to my chest. "I don't…I didn't mean – I'm *sorry*."

Jack closed his eyes, leaning his head back against the dirt and taking a deep breath.

"It's okay," he sighed, voice tired as he wiped his face with his scraped hands. "Wasn't your fault."

I laughed, the sound sudden and manic.

"Wasn't – wasn't my fault?" I scoffed, disbelieving, and tried to slow my racing heart. "I just lost my *mind* back there. If you hadn't pulled me down, I probably would have gone plowing into the gods-damn fence!"

Jack just shook his head, subconsciously rubbing at his bruised elbow.

"PTSD's never your fault, Tristan."

DAY TWO HUNDRED AND SIXTY-FOUR, PART TWO

His words hit me like a battering ram. Like the bullet he'd taken. I took in a shaky breath and let my leg slam back down to the ground as I looked everywhere except at the remains of the war front beside us.

Post-traumatic stress disorder.

No. No, that wasn't going to be me. That couldn't be me. How the hell was I supposed to move on now? How the hell was I supposed to *forget* all of this when–

"–it won't leave me alone? This can't be me!" I quickly shut my mouth with a loud click as I realized I'd been shouting the words I thought I'd been saying in my head. Jack had dragged himself forward a few feet, and one hand was fastened on my leg while the other held himself up.

"Tristan. Tris, please, just – just stop. Listen to me, okay?" I took in deep, shaking breaths and met his eyes. "You're fine. We'll figure this out, alright?"

"But I can't do that to you." I stopped, heart frozen in my chest. *Oh gods. I didn't just say that.* But Jack's stricken and hurt expression told me I had, and I noticed he'd pulled his hand away. "I just meant that...well, what with your nightmares an-and everything, that I can't do this. I need–" I forced myself to shut up, to carefully plan what I was trying to say. I closed my eyes, blocking out my boyfriend's betrayed face, and cursed to myself. *You're in deep enough as it is, just say it.*

"After everything, I want to take care of you. To be there for you," I said slowly, breathing slowly. "And I can't do that if I'm constantly jumping at gods-damn shadows." I reluctantly opened my eyes, expecting to be met with a furious, insulted glare.

Instead, Jack just looked worn down and defeated.

"So that's what I am to you now?" he asked, voice low and monotoned. "A charity case? An *obligation?*" The last word was laced with anger, and I quickly shook my head.

"No. No, you are *not* an obligation! I'm not staying with you out of pity or something," I countered, growing defensive. "Gods, how could you even think that of me? What kind of person do you think I am?"

"Well, isn't that what you just said?" he challenged. "That I'm a broken man that needs someone to take care of him?"

"No! *Gods damn it*, Jack, I can't let you down again!" I shouted at him, tears burning in my eyes. "I can't be fucking weak anymore! If I hadn't been so…*pathetic*, I could have gotten out of the rubble sooner. I wouldn't have needed you to rescue me, and I wouldn't have gotten you shot!"

That shut him up, but I couldn't stop. I had to get it all out, purge my system. I had to tell him all the things that had been weighing me down and keeping me awake at night. I gestured shakily at him.

"If I hadn't been so weak, I could have carried you to help properly. I wouldn't have fucking *dropped* you. I wouldn't have snapped your spine or whatever it was, and you would be walking! I–"

"W-what?" Jack interrupted, face pale. He looked like he was about to be sick, and I stopped talking, tears blurring the world until it was unrecognizable.

"You…they told you, didn't they?" I asked, voice shaking. "Blackwell, he…he said he told you."

Jack stiffly shook his head, dazed.

"He just said it was the bullet," he stammered, utterly lost and guileless. I looked down, a panicked, hysterical laugh bubbling up in my throat.

"Well, uh, *no*. No, it was me. Both of us, I guess," I giggled, feeling sick as I looked at him. I couldn't see his expression through my tears, and my chest tightened as my reflexive laughter died on my lips.

"It…it was an *accident*," I finally whispered and gestured helplessly at him as the first sob hiccupped in my throat. "I didn't know your spine was damaged 'cause I thought it was a standard rifle. But–" I gave that brittle, defensive laugh again before dissolving into tears. I pressed the heel of my palm into my eyes, trying to grind everything away. "Gods, I'm *sorry*…"

"When you carried me...you..." Jack said somewhere in front of me, and I hunched my shoulders, slowly pulling my knees back up to my chest.

"I didn't mean to," I whispered, voice choked and small. "I just wanted to keep you safe. And Jax said that—"

"Jax?" My boyfriend now looked thoroughly confused and concerned. I made a sound of frustration and gestured to my head.

"I could hear him. In my head, I could hear his voice telling me what to do, to keep going. S-so I did, and I'm *sorry*," I finished, looking up at him through my tears. "This is all my fault. *My* fault. Because I wasn't strong. I wasn't brave. I just sat around while everyone else died protecting me, I—"

"Hey." I stopped talking, chest shuddering with wheezing gasps, and stared at Jack's white-knuckled hold on my leg. "Look at me." He dragged himself forward so he was sitting just two feet away from me and tightened his grip even more. "Tristan, *look at me*."

I slowly followed the path of his arm up to his shoulder and stopped, expression slack. How long had it been since that ragged shoulder had been clad in a clean, fresh-pressed uniform – decorated with ribbons and pins? And how long ago had his body danced?

Oh gods, what had I done to him?

"Tristan." He pulled himself closer, a foot away now, and grabbed my shoulder. His thumb pressed firmly against my collarbone. "Look at me." Slowly, I shifted my gaze up to meet his, and I took in a deep breath, dragging my hand across my eyes. "You're strong. Okay? You're brave."

"No," I said, shaking my head and glancing up at him like I doubted his sanity. "No, I'm not—"

"Hey!" His fingers dug comfortingly into my shoulder. "You feel that?" I didn't answer, and he shook me slightly. "Tris, d'you feel that?" I nodded, hesitantly looking into his eyes again.

"Yeah."

"If you hadn't been strong, if you hadn't been brave, you wouldn't have been able to." He paused, waiting to see if I was listening, and I held our eye contact. "We wouldn't be here without you. *I* wouldn't be here if you hadn't patched me up and carried me out of *there*."

He jerked his head to the left on that last word, and I followed the motion to stare at the fenced off trench beside us. Just looking at it made me feel drained and exhausted. Suddenly, Jack's hand shifted from my shoulder to the side of my face, and I silently looked back at him.

His skin was rough and warm against mine, the small strips of bandaging he used to protect his hands from blisters from his chair surprisingly soft. I took in a deep breath, holding it in as long as I could before I slowly released it, leaning into his touch. He leaned forward, resting his forehead against mine and letting his hand slide back to cup the back of my head.

"I don't blame you for what happened to me, Tris. Okay, hon?" I took in a shaky breath and nodded against him almost frantically. "I never will. And I would do all of it again. *All* of it. Getting shot, the coma, paraplegia, whole thing."

"But why?" I asked, genuinely confused as I reached out to him, fingers brushing against his stomach.

I felt his muscles tense at my touch, shying away as though burned, and I stopped, pulling my hand away. He sighed, pressing his head a little harder against mine. Hot breath ghosted across my lips in an apology, and I pulled away to look up into his eyes, trying to blink away the swollen feeling in my face.

"Why would you want all of this?"

Jack drew himself a little closer, legs dragging across the earth. I folded my legs to let him come closer, staring intently at him, and when he looked back up, his face was flushed from exertion and something else, something that burned deep in his eyes. And without answering my question, he closed the distance between us, fingers tightening in my hair and drawing me close as he kissed me.

There was something desperate in the way we pressed against each other, and I reached for his side to hold us steady as I leaned into him. My nose briefly bumped into his as I titled my head, and he opened his mouth into the kiss, his tongue tracing over mine and breath burning my skin as he gently bit down on my lower lip.

The sensation, so long absent, sent shivers through my body, and I rose up on my knees, briefly breaking the kiss but staying close enough that our breath warmed each other's lips. Once I was straddling his immobile legs and sure his back wasn't uncomfortably twisted anymore, I moved my hand from his side to his neck and bowed my head to kiss him once more, sliding my arm around his shoulders. His mouth was warm and familiar, and for the first time in months I truly smiled. His hands moved from my waist to my sides, pressing against my skin as they moved up my back and held me as close as he could without either one of us losing balance.

My hand moved to cup the back of his head as his own hands slowly moved down my body and returned to my waist, holding himself upright with only my body. I burrowed my fingers into his dark hair just as his fingers dug into my hips, and I slowly sat back on his thighs, closing my eyes and just kissing him, memorizing his taste and the way he felt against me. The way he made me feel alive, and the way he made me do the same things to him that he was doing to me.

Relearning things about him I had known for over a year, but had forgotten in the span of a few months.

I opened my eyes and looked into Jack's face. His eyes were still closed, his expression relaxed and at peace for the first time since the trucks first rumbled into the Academy. The worry lines were gone from his forehead, the tired shadows wiped from beneath his eyes. His scars seemed to fade back into his skin. He looked like he used to, for just a brief moment, and my heartbeat slowly evened out, my breathing growing calm as I sat there, kissing him and just being with the man I loved more than life itself.

Then, his eyes opened, and I could see the difference.

I could see the darkness lurking behind the love and kindness in his eyes, and I slowly, reluctantly, pulled away. My arm moved back to my side, and my hand rested on his forearm, fingertips smoothing circles into his sleeve. I was relieved when he sat back as well, hands running down my arms – his right hand trailing all the way down to hold my left while his other hand traced out what remained of my right arm.

"It's, uh, it's been a while," I finally managed, clearing my throat a few times, and Jack gave a light huff of laughter and a small smile.

"Yeah," he breathed as he looked at me. "Yeah, it has."

He lifted his right hand to gently cup my face, and as his thumb rubbed soft, gentle patterns on my skin, he lightly caressed my amputated limb with his left hand, sending pain spidering up my skin that I couldn't bring myself to tell Jack about. He looked at our joined hands and squeezed gently.

"*This* is why," he said, smiling as he fiddled with our hands and tangled our fingers. "*This* is why I'd do it all again, Tristan." He looked back up at me. "Because I'd rather have you, stump arm and all." He paused, smiling as I gave a shaky laugh.

But when he continued, his expression grew serious and earnest.

"I'd rather have us, with your anxiety attacks and my paralyzed legs and nightmares, than not have us at all. Than not have this." He let his hand slide down my neck to grab my shoulder again, and he took a deep breath, thumb sweeping back and forth against my throat and collarbone. "I'll hold you together during the day, and you'll hold me together at night. Okay?"

"Okay," I whispered, and Jack leaned forward to kiss me once more, the touch registering as nothing more than a ghost of a sensation across my lips before he pulled away.

"Now...ready to say goodbye?"

The warmth that had blossomed in my chest and flooded my body with reassurance and a sense of safety, started to freeze. My expression stiffened. I looked to my left, staring at the barbed wire fence two yards away and at the unmarked burial mound a few feet beyond it.

"Yeah," I whispered, voice hollow. "Yeah, I am." I slowly got off Jack's lap and knelt beside him, asking an unspoken question.

"You sure?" he asked, and I nodded.

"Yeah, Jack. I'm sure," I told him, and he clasped his arms around my neck and shoulders. I grabbed ahold of his belt. "You count."

"One...two...three." I stood up, staggering to the side and bumping into the side of the trench before quickly regaining my balance. "You sure you're okay?"

"Yep," I managed. "Yeah. I'm okay."

I started walking, pace slower this time and much more deliberate. For some reason his weight settled more easily on my shoulders this time, and my hand found a more comfortable grip. And as we closed the final six feet to the barbed fence, Jack's arms tightened around my shoulders, and I could feel his chest shake with a heavy breath.

Finally, we stopped, just standing there in the silence – my boyfriend using me to hold himself up and my arm barely managing to keep him close. Not three feet away, Howell's grave stared back at us, the disturbed mound scattered with debris and vulgar messages carved on sticks of wood. I could read a few of them, and I smirked to myself, amused and satisfied at the amount of hate poured into those rugged words.

See you in hell.

I hope you're burning, you monster.

Fuck you. Sincerely, Unit 37.

That one was probably Marcel. But then I saw one that made my eyes burn with tears, and the dry amusement I'd been feeling faded away.

For Platoon 305.

"I'd forgotten about them," I whispered, and Jack tightened his hold in comfort. "How did I forget about 305?"

My boyfriend was quiet for a little, weighing his answer carefully, and I shifted on my feet, bracing my legs to compensate for his weight.

"It's easier to forget those that didn't make it than to remember them," he finally said and spat through the razor wire. There was something dark and angry burning in his eyes, blazing through the cracks in his armor like light on a shattered mirror. "Fuck you, Howell," he gritted out between clenched teeth, and I winced as his fingers dug painfully into my shoulders. But then, as quickly as it'd come, his anger slowly started to fade – the fire ground down to embers that eventually burned out into black smoke, and Jack's shoulders started shaking.

"Fuck you," he repeated, voice a strained whisper, and his head rested gently against my aching shoulder. A hot wind wound its way through the trenches, and I tightened my hold around his waist, taking in a deep breath as he silently sobbed. "Damn you to *hell*."

My left arm shook with a fatigued tremor, and I gritted my teeth, gripping Jack's belt a little tighter and trying to ignore how the leather bit into my hand.

"It's okay, Jack," I heard myself say, and I shifted precariously on my feet, almost losing my balance. "He's already burning. It's okay."

Jack nodded against me and took in several deep breaths in an attempt to collect himself. Finally, he was quiet, head still propped up against my shoulder as he watched the desecrated grave.

"You okay?" I asked after a few moments of silence, and he nodded again. It was a silent, subdued motion. "You ready?" All I got was another nod, but it was good enough for me. I shifted, and my aching knees cracked painfully in protest. "Alright. Let's go home."

I slowly turned around and started heading back towards the camp. But something burned on my tongue, and I stopped. I bowed my head and took a deep breath.

"Tristan?"

I took a half step back and looked over my shoulder to Howell's grave. And as I stood there, catching my breath, a raven swooped down from over the trench to land on his grave, picking away at the dirt in search for food.

"You hear that, captain?" I asked. My voice was shaky yet confident in a way that it hadn't been for a long time. "We're going home."

I inhaled slowly, briefly clenching my jaw. Time to go. I slowly walked away, my gait lopsided but resolved. We didn't look back, and as we left, Jack gave a wry laugh. I looked down at him, confused, and the sound built until he was almost dragging me down, trying not to double over with pure, unrestrained laughter.

"What? What is it?" I asked, fighting back a reflexive smile of my own. He looked up at me, a tearful grin spread across his face.

"We just made out in front of our homophobic captain's grave."

I rolled my eyes and kept staggering forward as my boyfriend dissolved into another giggling fit.

"You can be really immature sometimes, you know?" I said, forcing a light-hearted tone into my voice. He made a noise of agreement somewhere in the vicinity of my ribs, and I looked back up ahead of us.

Somehow, I still didn't feel like smiling or laughing just yet.

... — — ...

Jack and I had been sitting in relative silence for a couple of hours. Just resting side-by-side against the wall of the trench, watching people go about their business and listening in on the snippets of conversation we could catch. We occasionally said something to each other, but we felt off. After the intimacy with Irina and Howell's graves, everything else felt superficial in a way. Maybe we kept trying to connect and just kept missing our marks.

"Well. What do we have here?"

Jack and I both looked up to see Blackwell standing over us, eyebrow raised in amused silence.

"Hey, doc," I said, assuming my best questioning expression.

"Very cute, Byrne," he drawled. "Do you want a chair so you can at least be a *comfortable* sack of lazy bones? I've got medical supplies that need organizing back in the infirmary if you want to make yourself useful."

"I think we're good here, doc," Jack replied, voice pleasant, and the older man rolled his eyes.

"Yeah, I bet you are. Sitting there on your ass while the rest of us bust our chops getting work done around here."

"Tell you what," my boyfriend began, spark of dark humor in his eyes, and Blackwell looked down at him amusedly. "If you can somehow figure out how to get me *off* my ass, I will gladly become your personal medical assistant."

I dropped my head into my hand and ruefully shook my head.

"I see," the doctor mused. I looked at him with a wincing expression. "It seems you have passed your wonderfully dark and sarcastic sense of humor on to your boyfriend, Tristan. Strong work." There was an entertained light in his eyes though, and he started to work his way back into the stream of people passing by. "You boys take care."

"We will, sir," Jack smiled, and Blackwell gave a sloppy, informal salute.

"Sorry, doc," I called after him. He waved me away, smirking, before vanishing into the crowd.

Speaking of vanishing into the crowd...

"Hey, have you seen the Horsemen since we got back from the fence?" I asked, looking up at Jack, and he shook his head, not really concerned. "I wonder where they are. I mean, there aren't many places for them to go, so you'd think we'd have seen them after sitting here for a couple of hours."

"Why don't you ask Jones?" my boyfriend mumbled, closing his eyes and leaning his head back against the trench. I looked at him in confusion, and he cracked an eye open to point at the man quickly walking past us.

"Hey, Jayce!" I called, waving at him to get his attention

Marcel's brother stopped and turned around at the sound of his name. The moment he saw us, he smirked and shook his head.

"Byrne. Miller. Didn't see you down there," he greeted, cutting through the traffic of people to stand before us.

"Kind of the point," I sighed, rolling my shoulders. "We're avoiding getting drafted to do work."

"That and socializing," Jack added.

"It is kind of the same thing," I said. Jack hummed in agreement.

"Mind if I join in?" Jayce asked. "Because I've been running errands for these Bretts all day."

Jack made a vague gesture that our friend took to mean *by all means*, and the man grabbed a crate from the side of one of the tents and dropped it in front of us. He sat down with a content, tired sigh and braced his forearms against his knees.

"Have you seen your sister anywhere?" I asked, and he shook his head, looking down.

"No, uh...she and the others have been a bit on edge since the rumors started going around about us leaving, you know?" he began, rubbing at his knuckles. "My best guess is that they're sitting with Korsakov. Saying their goodbyes."

"Yeah. It's hard to leave someone behind like that," Jack said softly and looked down at his hands. I gave him a quizzical look. "It's nothing, Tris," he sighed, waving me off. "Just some old friends from a long time ago."

I didn't believe him, but I changed the subject anyways.

"Are they planning on bringing her tags back for her family?" I asked, turning my attention back to Jayce. He shrugged.

"I've got no idea. They don't want her to end up in an unmarked grave, that's why they used her tags for the marker instead of charcoal." He sighed and shook his head, fingers continuing to grind away at his knuckles. "This would be so much easier if we had two sets of tags, you know?" He looked up at us slightly. "One for the body, one for the family."

"I didn't know Korsakov had a family," Jack said, stricken.

"Don't beat yourself up over it, Miller," Jayce said with a wan smile. "She didn't tell any one other than the Horsemen, and I only learned about them from Marcel."

"And Aliyah told me after Irina died," I added. "She had family back in Winova. Both of her parents are still alive, and she had a younger brother and sister. Paternal twins apparently."

"They'll probably be coming to the Academy, then," Jack said heavily, and I frowned.

"What do you mean?"

He cleared his throat and sat a little straighter in his chair, hands tapping out a slightly nervous beat on his legs.

"When troops come home, you have a day where families come to pick up their kids. Get them out of there as quick as they can before their sons and daughters get dragged out there again." His fingers traced out patterns on his thighs, his eyes distant. "It's always tough, you know? Because some families go home with their kids. Others take home flags or dog tags. Some even get caskets." He paused and sighed, looking up from his lap to the dirt wall opposite us. "And then there are some families that don't come at all. Their kids survive the war, but…they don't survive the home front." His lips quirked in a sad, hollow smile, and he looked back at us. "It's a luck of the draw how it turns out."

I was about to say something when Mayworth's voice cut through the air.

"Amaerics!"

Jayce sighed, rolling his eyes.

"Guess that's our cue, huh?" He held a hand out to me, and I took it, pulling myself to my feet while Jack slowly wheeled himself after us.

People were moving towards the center of the camp, so we fell in line with them, hoping that we were heading in the right direction. Turns out we were. Soon enough, the mob made its way past the tents and buildings to the open space we'd made at the center of camp. General Mayworth was standing on a crate, surveying everybody, as if just by looking she could tell if we were all present and accounted for.

It reminded me eerily of G.A. Agathon.

She waited a few more minutes while everyone else crowded in, and, looking around at us, I found it painfully obvious that we looked healthier than we ever did under Howell. We were clean and composed. A little more battered and bruised, some of us maimed or scarred for life, but we were still standing. At that moment, Aliyah, Katalin, and Marcel dropped down from the top of the trench across the crowd, and I nudged Jayce.

"Found your sister," I said, pointing.

He nodded his thanks, putting a hand on my shoulder before he set off to force his way through the crowd. I watched his back for a couple yards before looking back at Mayworth. Even from this distance, I could see her chest slowly rise and fall, and I knew she was about to start talking.

She cleared her throat once, and the buzz of conversation died down as all eyes fixed on her.

"We've received a final report from Battlemaster Jax. They're ready to receive you at the Academy." Everyone started talking at once, and she held up her hands, waiting for us to settle back down. I reached forward and gently squeezed Jack's shoulder. He didn't react.

"We'll be able to spare a few of our own vehicles for transport to your War Academy, but no further. You'll convene there and will then be sent to your respective destinations as Amaeric resources are made available," she continued, raising her voice as people inevitably began talking again. "The trucks have been packed with any spare equipment you had left over, and if you take your personal belongings up there within the hour, you'll all be on schedule to arrive home in two days. May the gods bless your journeys." She paused, watching us, and I could see the smile veiled in her eyes as she gave her final command.

"Dismissed."

Dismissed.

As soon as the word left her mouth, as soon as she stepped down from the crate, chaos erupted. Around me and Jack, people were shouting and screaming, hugging each other and laughing. Some were even crying. And it wasn't just Amaerics. Brettain soldiers with familiar faces started to mingle with the crowd, clapping people on the back and drawing others into hugs.

Joy. There was...*joy* in the trenches. Between nations.

As I stood there, hovering behind Jack's wheelchair, I watched people from enemy countries embrace and start their goodbyes, and my eyes found Clarke. He started towards us, expression asking permission to approach, and I quickly shook my head. He stopped and nodded once, offering us an apologetic smile. Then, he squared his shoulders and gave a formal salute – left arm straight at his side, fist clenched, and open right hand lifted to his brow, palm facing outwards. I lifted two fingers to my brow in an informal response, and he nodded once before turning away to talk to the Brettain woman beside him.

"Who's he?" Jack asked, looking up at me, and I feigned innocence.

"Who?"

"The kid who just saluted you." I shrugged. *"Tristan."*

Just bite the bullet and get it over with.

"That's Sergeant Jacob Clarke," I began and sighed, shaking my head. This was going to be interesting. "He's, uh...he's the sniper who shot you." My boyfriend went quiet, and I tightened my grip on his shoulder, feeling the tense muscles beneath his shirt. "That's why I didn't tell you. He's a good kid, but–"

Before I could explain myself further, Jack pushed himself away from me, moving through the crowd and muttering apologies to people when he bumped into them or ran over their feet.

"Where's he goin' now?"

I looked over my shoulder to see Marcel, Jayce in tow. I sighed resignedly and looked forward, listening as the siblings drew up alongside me.

"He's got someone he needs to talk to," I said, mostly to myself, and the three of us watched Jack stop in front of Sergeant Clarke.

The Brettain sniper quickly stood at attention once more, and I could see my boyfriend shaking his head as he looked down. Apparently Jack said something, because Clarke looked down at him with a baffled expression and asked him something with a perplexed tilt of his head. Jack looked back up at him and shook his head in turn in a silent answer. Slowly, the sniper's hand fell from his brow back to his side, and his nose and brow wrinkled against something. And as he quickly dragged the back of his hand across his eyes, I realized they were tears.

This time I could easily read the man's lips as he looked down at my boyfriend, speaking in earnest.

I'm sorry, *sir*.

"Miller's gonna kill that poor boy with guilt," Marcel commented to my right, crossing her arms.

I shook my head absently just as Jack reached out to shake the man's hand and pointed to a spot on the man's stomach a little higher than where the sniper had shot him. And Clarke, despite himself, laughed a little, and an ashamed smile crept onto his face.

"No," I said softly. "No, he's good at this sort of thing."

"Did your boyfriend just show Clarke where to shoot him next time?" Jayce asked in disbelief, pointing at them.

I snorted to myself, shoving my hand in my pocket and looking back at them as Jack turned his chair around and headed back towards us.

"Yeah. Yeah, he did. Where are Soto and Moore?"

Jayce shrugged and looked to his sister.

"Aliyah's probably with Irina again," Marcel admitted, letting her arms relax and slipping her hands into her pockets. "We're not sure about Kat."

"Soto's over talking to some Brettain guard." The three of us turned to look at Jack, and he sighed, fingers tapping an anxious beat on the wheel of his chair. "We gonna get out of here? It's a bit crowded."

"Yeah, c'mon."

I stepped in front of Jack to part the crowd before him while Jayce and Marcel flanked him on either side, making sure that he had room to move without bumping into people. As we went, people spared us passing glances but not much else. They ignored us almost as quickly as they noticed our presence.

They'd gotten used to us: the private with one arm and the corporal in the wheelchair with their posse of generally argumentative and intimidating soldiers who shadowed their every step. It didn't bother me at all, and I could tell Jack was quite content blending in with the crowd. But I knew once we reentered the world, we wouldn't be treated as such a commonplace sight. And I realized as I spared another glance over my shoulder to my boyfriend that not all of us would handle the prying eyes with grace.

"Hey." I jumped as Marcel dropped a hand on my shoulder and glared at her as she smirked. "Sorry, shrimp. Look, we hate to leave you, but we have to go grab our belongings out of the barracks."

"Go." We all looked at Jack, and he made a shooing gesture towards the sleeping quarters. "I'm sure Tristan and I will figure out something to do to pass the time." She playfully saluted our corporal before throwing her arm around her brother's shoulders and sauntering away. "You okay, Tris?"

"Sure," I said with a shrug. "Why do you ask?"

"I caught you staring at me a few times," he said after a little hesitation. "You had that look."

"What look?" I scoffed, walking forward once more. His response was quiet and cautious.

"The one you give me when you think I'm not watching you." I sighed and stopped, turning to face him. "You know, the one that's focused more on my legs than my face."

"It's not you. Trust me, it's—"

"Let me guess," my boyfriend cut in, voice dripping with sarcasm. "It's you."

"No," I countered, rolling my eyes and gesturing to the people around us. "It's them. Or I guess, more accurately, it's the people at the Academy. Out in the...the real world, as it were." I scratched the back of my neck and rocked on my feet a little as I shifted my gaze to the wood planking beneath us. "And yeah...it is a little about your legs."

"Told you. You've got a look," Jack teased, nudging me as he rolled past. I scoffed, rolling my eyes. "Don't worry. I'll try not to bite anyone's head off once we're back in 'proper society' as doc likes to call it."

"We'll see how long that lasts," I muttered only half-jokingly, the softly spoken words hanging in the air – meant for no one.

"Oh, boy. Tris," Jack began, tugging lightly on my sleeve. I looked back at him. "We've got incoming."

I followed his pointing finger towards the center of the crowd and saw Mayworth easing her way through the smiling and laughing people towards us.

"Miller. Byrne," she greeted, nodding to each of us in turn. I let go of Jack's shoulder as we saluted her, and she gestured towards the ramp to the surface with a single sweep of her arm. "I'll walk you to the trucks."

"Thank you, ma'am," Jack began, "but it won't be necessary."

"As you wish," she said, respectfully inclining her head, "but at least let me walk you two to the ramp."

We slowly walked with her in companionable silence to the incline Jack and I had gone up earlier in the day. People were packed tightly together, nearly stopped in a bottleneck effect as they tried to move too quickly up the narrow path. We came to a stop at the base of the ramp, and she looked down at us, sighing heavily. Her expression was carefully neutral, and she stood at attention, saluting us.

"Private. Corporal. I hope we're never in a situation where we must see each other again," she admitted.

"The feeling's mutual, ma'am," I answered, returning the gesture, and my lips quirked in something close to a smile.

She lowered her arm, turned on her heel, and quickly departed. Her back was straight and stiff, and as I watched, she ducked through a tent door and was gone. I knew that while we were heading home, while we got to leave, her role in this war was far from over. I thought of Howell and how I'd once believed that a front line captain had to see his men as bodies in order to stay sane. But then...

Then, I saw Mayworth. And Harper. Two commanding officers who'd called cease fires just to help bury each other's dead and exchange medicine and food. A foreign general who'd fraternized with enemy troops. Pawns in a war who bent the rules where they could and acted honorably where they couldn't.

What did we rationalize to justify our actions?

"Come on," I said gently, putting my hand on Jack's back and shivering as my skin brushed against the sweaty canvas of the chair. "We should get going."

My boyfriend gave a curt nod and pushed himself forward, struggling slightly to make it up the incline a second time. The workers had tried to make the angle as gradual as possible, but I could see Jack's hands shaking as he went. Going up it once had been hard enough, but twice in one day, even though he'd had time to rest...

"Jack, you want some help?" I asked and tentatively placed my hand on the right handle of his chair. He cleared his throat, hesitating.

"Yeah," he finally muttered, bowing his head and straining to hold the wheels still so he didn't slide backwards. "Yeah, some help would be nice."

"Okay. I'll take the right, you take the left."

He changed his grip on the left wheel and I leaned into the right hand side, quickly matching my pace with his so we would go straight. Slowly, we cleared the ramp, and once we hit the flat ground, Jack quickly took over, roughly shoving the wheels forward. We were nearing one of the trucks when I heard someone shout my name.

"Tristan!"

I turned around and Jack shifted his chair so that he could see over his shoulder. Blackwell waved at us from the crowded pathway, and Jack sighed theatrically beside me.

"Damn. I should have known we wouldn't get away clean," he joked, and we waited as the older man pushed his way through the crowd with his medical bag slung over his shoulders and a relieved look in his eyes. "Hey, doc."

"Miller. How're you holding up?"

"Well enough," my boyfriend replied, offering the physician a small smile. Blackwell nodded, clearing his throat, and gruffly turned to face me with searching eyes.

"Byrne?"

"I'm fine, doc," I told him, playfully exasperated with a smile pulling at my lips. He nodded to himself, sighing and wrapping his battered uniform coat tighter around his shoulders.

"Good, good..." He trailed off awkwardly. "Well, then. I guess this is goodbye, huh?" I pulled the man into a hug and clapped him on the back. "I hope I'll see you two again." We broke apart, and he reached down to shake Jack's hand.

"Us, too," my boyfriend said and tightened his grip on the man's hand. "Thanks for everything, doc. I really mean that."

The jaded physician scoffed.

"Don't call me that anymore, kid. No more titles. It's just Blackwell," he scolded, but the normal bite to his words wasn't there. There was only a distant sadness to his eyes. "But, um...that aside...if you boys ever need a physician, and I mean *ever*, you track me down. Alright?" We nodded, and he shoved his hands into his pockets. "I'll always be your doctor."

He cleared his throat again and gave a quick smile before turning away and trudging off towards the truck designated specifically for officers and specialists. But as he placed a hand on the rough bed, he paused and looked back at us. He seemed torn, unsure, and Jack quickly gave him a hand.

"Get outta here, doc!" my boyfriend shouted, smirking, and the man bowed his head with a grin. As he looked back up at us, he waved goodbye with tears in his eyes. Harper held a hand out to him, and he took it, climbing up into the back of the truck. "And just like that…"

"We'll probably see him at the Academy," I offered, pulling myself up into the bed of our own truck, but Jack shook his head.

"No, he'll leave as quick as he can," he said, mostly to himself, and I sat down on the edge of the bed with my feet dangling off the end.

"Why do you say that?" I asked, and he shrugged.

"Ah, it's nothing. He's just been here too long, you know?" He tilted his head back to look up at me. "He'll want a change of scenery."

"Hey, Miller!" We both looked around in perfect sync to see Jayce and Marcel heading over, Moore and Soto not far behind. "Need some help?" the man asked.

Jack smiled, overly-sweet, and turned his chair to face them.

"Only if it'll make you feel better."

"Yeah, yeah…" Soto grumbled, rolling her eyes. "Talk us through this, you jerk."

I watched as the Jones siblings each took one side of my boyfriend – pulling one arm over their shoulders and supporting his back as they slid their free arms under his legs. In a coordinated lift, they sat him down on the edge of the truck bed, and Katalin pulled his chair out of the way.

"Jack, I'm going to grab you from behind and drag you over to the side of the truck, okay? You can take it from there," I said softly, putting my hand on his shoulder to let him know where I was.

He nodded tensely, and I knelt behind him, wrapping my arm under his arms and across his chest and pulling up and back. I quickly backed against the wall, and he pulled himself into a more comfortable position.

"Thanks, Jayce" he grunted, repositioning his legs. The Jones brother lifted the wheelchair into the truck and folded it up beside us.

"No problem, sir."

Jack looked at our four companions as they joined us, climbing up into the back of the truck and sitting around us.

"No more sirs."

"No problem, *Jack*," Marcel said, smirking, as she sat down a few feet in front of us with Katalin and Jayce taking the spots on either side of her. My boyfriend grimaced, and Aliyah settled down across from me.

"Hmm...not that close yet," he teased.

"No problem, shag." Kat looked up at Jack, eyes wide and innocent, and he rolled his eyes as we all smiled – private expressions only meant for ourselves. And for some reason, coming from her, the word didn't hurt. I thought back to what Jack had said so long ago.

Tris, the only reason that word has any power is because we let it.

"I give up," Jack sighed, and I absently scratched the back of my neck, still mulling over Soto's words.

We were quiet for the next fifteen minutes as the rest of us loaded up into the available trucks, but it wasn't an awkward silence. If anything, it was one of the most comfortable silences I'd ever experienced. There was no tension, no metallic taste of fear tainting our mouths. We were relaxed, some of us even buzzing with excitement. And as I looked around at the Horsemen, at Jayce, and at Jack – took in their peaceful expressions that so achingly reminded me of an unruly-haired girl – I realized I wasn't alone.

"Attention!"

We looked out the back of the truck to see Mayworth standing before the barbed wire fence, backed by her soldiers. Their weapons were slung over their backs or holstered. Their backs were ramrod straight, arms stiff at their sides, feet shoulder width apart, and gazes fixed forward. Something settled heavy and aching in my chest, and my eyes pricked with inexplicable tears. A fraction of a second behind their general, the Brettain company snapped their feet together and brought their right hands to their brows while their left arms bent at the elbow behind their backs.

"Safe travels, Captain Harper," she called, and there was no response. I could only hope Harper was giving her some kind of nonverbal acknowledgement.

Behind Mayworth's shoulder, I could see Clarke staring at me, and I awkwardly returned the salute. He flashed me a quick, small smile before reassuming his stoic expression. The something coiled tightly in my chest loosened slightly, and I leaned against Jack's shoulder, linking my arm in his and breathing deeply as I held his hand. His skin was warm and dry, and his tendons shifted beneath my touch as his fingers interlaced with mine.

Without warning, the engines roared to life, and we started moving, jostling and bouncing along the uneven road. As we bumped into each other, I shifted and craned my neck to watch the trenches and scarred earth move away from us. The others around me did the same.

It was a terrible picture. The blackened ground and barbed wire permanently marred the landscape. No Man's Land was the worst. We could still see it all – the scorch marks, the stained ground, the barricades that were too entrenched into the earth to be removed just yet. The trenches where we'd spent the last eight months were nothing more than deep furrows in the earth, their contents mercifully hidden from our vantage point. The only remnant of the war we could see beyond the tortured landscape was the blue swarm of the Brettain's uniforms, still respectfully standing at attention as we departed.

Jack tightened his grip on my hand even more. I glanced at him to find him staring at the destruction before us with wide and vacant eyes. I didn't know where he was, but I *did* know one thing – he wasn't sitting next to me. I leaned against him a little harder and hoped that wherever he was he could feel me beside him.

The hardest part was passing the cemetery. Everyone seemed to crowd towards the back of the truck to watch as their friends and family went by – to see them one last time, no matter how fleeting the moment. The crude markers adorned with equally sloppy names of people we'd cared for went by too quickly to read. As the trucks picked up speed, I heard a few people start crying. I didn't look to see who they were.

This was a private moment.

But as we passed a certain point, I forced myself to look over at the Horsemen, heart heavy. They were teary-eyed and silent, huddled together as they watched the headstones go by. Jayce hovered anxiously beside them, unsure of what to do. I noticed that his hand was on his sister's shoulder, his thumb smoothing back and forth across the bone. She reached back and held his hand with a white-knuckled grip.

Suddenly, I felt Jack shifting beside me, and I sat up a little as he extricated his arm from mine and reached out to put his hand Moore's boot, getting her attention. Once she looked at him, he sat up as straight as he could against the side of the truck and saluted the graves. I quickly grasped his meaning and slowly stood up, clumsily lifting my left hand to my brow.

"For Irina," my boyfriend said quietly, but Death shook her head as she stood up, the rest of the Horsemen a mere fraction of a second behind her as more people followed their example.

"No," she said, her low voice quiet as her unblinking eyes watched the rows of crosses go by. "For all of them."

Eventually, the truck started going up a hill. I took a shaking breath and watched in tears as, in the dying light of day, No Man's Land, the trenches, the graves…they started to fade away in a red tinted haze. Once we crested the hill, people slowly started to sit down, and I felt warm fingers creep into my hand, trying to pull me down.

"Tristan…"

"Not yet," I whispered, closing my hand around Jack's and watching as the earth rose up. Soon it would block the horizon and the trenches from view. "Not yet."

The truck dropped sharply as it hit a dip in the road, almost making me fall, and, just like that, it was gone. I let out a shaky sigh and reluctantly sat down, quickly dragging the back of my hand across my eyes. Jack pulled me close and wrapped his arms around my waist.

"Wait." We looked at Marcel, and I felt uneasy as I saw her scanning the faces of the people around us. Her voice was tense, panicked. "Harris. Where's Harris?"

I looked back out of the truck and watched the dusty road grow longer and longer behind us.

"Tristan?" I heard Jack murmur in my ear. I could feel everyone's eyes on me, and I swallowed painfully as my tears burned my eyes.

Byrne, my man! How's it been?

"He's, uh…" I paused, clearing my throat and looking down at my lap. Jack gently squeezed my hand, and I took in another deep breath.

Yeah…I'm sure you will.

"He's not coming," I finally muttered, refusing to look at the betrayed expressions I knew were on everybody's faces. I just continued to stare at my hand – our hands – and held on tighter.

The sun set in a bloody display of red, charcoal clouds slashed violently across the horizon. None of us really noticed.

. . . − − − . . .

That night – the sky near-black, the world almost impenetrably dark – we drove past Idris Chance.

She wasn't there.

DAY TWO HUNDRED AND SIXTY-FIVE

We pulled into Norford around ten the next morning, but none of us really felt like dismounting. Even that shantytown seemed different after the our time away. The rundown buildings were now in shambles. Hollow eyes watched us from every window, peering out from behind tattered curtains. The air was stale and cold. A sharp wind keened through the streets. Overall, it was a very unwelcome setting. But we needed some rest, and we were definitely not going to get any in the back of the cramped trucks. Well, that was a lie. We could all sleep almost anywhere now. In fact, the truck was a nice alternative to some of the nights we'd had in the trenches.

But there were beds not twenty feet away, and the officers were set on us getting some decent sleep before we returned to the Academy the next day. So, we reluctantly filed out, dropping to the ground and looking to our superiors for instructions as they dismounted as well. Unsurprisingly, they gestured for us to head to The Guild, and I yawned while Jayce unfolded Jack's wheelchair and passed it down to Aliyah.

"You okay?" I asked, and Jack nodded. "Just tell them how to help you." I slowly eased myself down from the bed, stepping back without so much as a stumble.

"Okay, Miller," Marcel began, rubbing her hands together as she knelt beside my boyfriend. "Kat will take your left side, I'll take your right. Aliyah will help you down into the chair. That okay with you?"

"On three?" Jack asked in response, with a wan smile. War smirked and pulled his right arm over her shoulder, working her other arm under his legs while Famine did the same on his left.

"You count," Jones said softly, and Jack took a deep breath.

"One…two…three."

The two women stood up and shuffled forward to the end of the truck bed before slowly easing Jack down so that he was sitting on the edge.

"See? Easy enough," Moore said gently, offering him a calming smile before pushing the chair up under his feet and shoving her foot under one of the wheels so it wouldn't roll. "Put your arms around my neck, I'll ease you down." Jack hesitated for a few moments before reaching out and wrapping his arms around her neck. "You count again."

"One, two, three." She straightened her back and pulled Jack forward in the same motion, one arm tightening around him to keep him from slipping out of her grasp while the other held under his legs. "You okay?"

"I'm okay, Miller," she said easily, but I saw Jack nervously tighten his grip on the back of her shirt, struggling to hold onto her.

"You sure?"

"You're no lightweight, Miller," she admitted with a gentle smile that I was relieved to see was genuine. "But I'm not either." She settled Jack in his chair and backed away, squaring her shoulders as she looked down at him. "See? We're both fine."

"Yeah, yeah," Jack grumbled as he pushed himself forward towards me. "Thanks, guys. Now, let's go get some rest."

His chair moved surprisingly well over the hard-packed dirt, and I nodded my thanks to Aliyah as I walked after him. But we didn't get very far before we realized a problem.

"Shit," Jack muttered.

He came to a stop and smiled in grim, twisted amusement at his lap. As soon as he spoke, I came to the same realization and paused mid-step, closing my eyes and mentally kicking myself over what had just happened.

"What is it?" Soto asked, stepping up to us.

Jack gave a short bark of laughter before bitterly turning himself away from The Guild and heading back towards the truck. Around us, people continued to disembark and head up the steps and into the building.

"You need to go up a staircase to get to the beds," he sighed, looking up at Famine with that same forced smile. "And, uh, as is *painfully* obvious, I'm not climbing any stairs any time soon. Let alone the three steps just to get into the building in the first place."

"Jack, I'm sorry," I sighed, and he waved me off.

"No, it's fine. The stable's probably cleaner than this place, anyways," he joked, and I inwardly cringed.

"Can't argue with you there," Jayce sighed, expression a little disgusted. When he continued, he gently nudged his sister. "Come to think of it, I'd probably prefer to stay in the stable, too. Wouldn't you, sis?"

"*No*," Jack said, quickly and firmly shaking his head. "You lot are going to go get some sleep in actual beds tonight in an actual inn. Alright?"

"C'mon, Miller. We've never slept in a stable before," Marcel whined, playfully kicking at the wheel of his chair. "It'll be an experience."

"Look, when I was a kid, my best friend lived on a farm. I've done this before," Jack said, but the Horsemen and I continued to look at him with dubious expressions. "Look, it's fine! I've had the luxury of one of doc's beds for months now. Don't go losing sleep over me sharing a room with horses for the night."

"Us," I corrected. The five of them looked at me – Jack in confusion and the others in amusement. "Don't go losing sleep over *us* sharing a room with horses for the night." Jack rolled his eyes and sighed, crossing his arms over his chest. "You aren't kicking us out of a gods-damn stable, Jack," I scolded, rolling my eyes. "I don't think that's even be physically possible, there're way too many entrances to cover."

"Yeah, forget it, Miller," Katalin added, stepping up next to Marcel and putting her hands on her hips as she eyed our corporal. "We're sticking with you and Byrne." A crooked smile pulled at her lips, and Jayce nodded.

"You're not getting rid of us that easily," he finished, and Jack seemed torn. "Come on, Miller. One last hurrah. The seven of us hanging in the stables while the rest of the crew shacks up in Bentley's flea palace."

"One last night together," Moore pressed gently, calm and collected as always, and I looked up at her. "Who knows the next time we'll all be in one place like this?"

"You mean tired, hungry, freshly released prisoners of war?" my boyfriend asked, voice dripping with sarcasm.

She shook her head, gestures fluid and graceful as she moved her hands behind her back and tilted her head ever so slightly to the side. Her hair for once wasn't pulled back and instead framed her face in shadowed black. She looked surprisingly…kind. Gentler than I'd come to expect of her.

"Alone," she said, eyes sympathetic. "With the company of only those who know. And who understand."

We were quiet for a moment, and I looked at the four people standing opposite Jack and me.

I looked at the Jones siblings' battered olive skin, at the stray scars that marked their arms from shrapnel. I looked Marcel's playful – if aged – eyes as she shifted her weight onto one foot and crossed her arms. Her brother stood beside her, his aggression gone, replaced instead by a need to care and protect.

Katalin, I noticed, seemed more quiet than normal. I realized that she reminded me more of Irina now than anyone else. Her stoic silence was interrupted only by brutal sarcasm instead of acting as the sharp watchdog attached to Marcel's hip.

And Aliyah. She just stood there, watching us as if she already knew how everything was going to go. Like she knew what we were going to say and how we were going to move long before we ourselves did. I didn't miss the way she looked down and smiled knowingly to herself as Jack sighed and threw his hands up in the air.

"Okay, fine. If you guys don't want to shack up in the flea palace, as Jayce so eloquently put it, feel free to join me in the stable." But despite the aggravated defeat he was projecting, there was a pleased light in his eyes as he looked up at me. I smiled slightly down at him.

"Great," Marcel sighed, rubbing her hands together to generate some heat and heading towards the back of the Guild. "Let's get going then. Find ourselves a nice stall, it's freezing out here." Jack laughed once to himself before following her.

"So tell me, Miller," Marcel continued. "Is hay really as scratchy and itchy as people say it is, or can you actually make it comfortable?" I shook my head at the playful, teasing burr in her voice and followed a few feet behind them, Kat and Aliyah beside me.

"It's…pretty scratchy," he began, sounding a little less than confident in his response. "I mean, last time I did this I wasn't really concerned with how itchy it was, though I was pulling hay out of my clothes for a few days afterwards."

"Well, that and you were a kid. I mean, kids don't care if something's itchy," Jayce added, looking down at him, but Jack shook his head, voice casual as he continued.

"No, actually it was the last month at the Academy." Panic flared up in my mind, and I quickly jogged over.

"Uh, Jack?" I started, trying to get his attention, but it seemed I was too slow.

"What the hell were you doing spending the night in the stables at the Academy?" Marcel asked, completely confused.

I cleared my throat, stepping a little in front of Jack's wheelchair so I could make eye contact.

"Yeah, Jack," I asked, staring at him pointedly. "What were you doing in the stables?"

The question's intended meaning of "shut up" was completely ignored as Jack looked at me with a far too innocent expression that I knew usually preceded a smart-ass comment. And, too late, I realized my mistake.

Oh, don't do it –

"You."

"Dammit, *Jack–*" I groaned, turning red and dragging my hand across my face while Marcel made a choking noise next to me.

"*Miller!*" she practically shrieked, taking several, nearly-running steps away from us in horrified disgust. Her brother stopped dead in his tracks and doubled over with laughter. "*I don't need to know that!*" she shouted, gesturing to herself with a flustered and disturbed expression on her face. "*None of us* needs to know that – oh my gods, what is *wrong* with you?!"

"Well, that explains why you weren't concerned with how itchy it was," Kat said from behind us, expression carefully composed.

Marcel made another horrified and disgusted noise and violently shuddered. Behind her Jayce finally had to sit down he was laughing so hard. Aliyah at least had the decency to cover her face and turn around while she laughed at us.

"I am *actually* going to kill you," I groaned between my fingers, but Jack just laughed, grinning up at me.

"You know you love me, Tristan," he sighed, still smiling proudly like an idiot, and started on his way again.

After delivering a frustrated, yet playful, kick to Jayce as I walked past him, I headed after Jack. And that was when I realized that my boyfriend's smile, his laugh as he'd completely embarrassed me…they'd been genuine. Jack was actually happy and actually laughing. That didn't mean I wasn't still frustrated with him, but at least now there was a silver lining to my utter humiliation.

"Are you all going somewhere?"

I turned around at the shouted question, struggling to become serious once more as I cleared my throat a few times. Out of the corner of my eye, I saw Jayce trying to do the same, wiping tears from his eyes and getting to his knees. Captain Harper was standing expectantly in front of The Guild, arms crossed and eyebrow raised. And, belatedly, I realized that none of us had thought to tell our superiors where we were going. I suddenly wished my face wasn't as flushed as it was.

"Sorry, sir," I began, seeing the reprimanding look on his face, and was about to continue when Jack eased his wheelchair to a halt beside me.

"We realized I'm not getting up those stairs you're standing on, sir," he explained apologetically. "Or the ones inside that lead up to the bedrooms, so we were thinking we'd just crash at the inn's stable. If that's alright with you, of course, captain."

Jayce slowly got to his feet and put his arm around his still-disgruntled sister's shoulder, smiling amusedly. The two made their way towards us, Kat and Aliyah following.

"Well, we'd prefer it if all of you were somewhere we can keep an eye on you," Harper began, shifting awkwardly on his feet as people continued to walk past him and into the building. I stepped closer to my boyfriend and dropped my hand to his shoulder. "I'd hate for something to happen so close to home, so close to everything being over. Especially for you, Miller. These people are more jumpy than usual."

"We appreciate your concern, but he won't be alone, sir." Jack and I looked over at Moore as she closed the distance between us, once again perfectly composed with Katalin lagging a few paces behind her. "We're planning on staying with him, sir. The six of us."

Harper hummed in response, expression unchanged.

"That's why I'm worried. Whenever the lot of you start hanging around each other, I know to brace myself for some trouble," he said, surveying our rag tag group and taking in how we were clustered around Jack. How the Horsemen and Jayce protectively flanked us – whether it was intentional or subconscious, I didn't know. But regardless I loved them for it. Finally, Harper sighed. "As you were. Gods help me, as you were."

"Thanks, captain," Jack called and gave him an informal salute. "You won't regret it."

"Don't say that, corporal," he warned, pointing at Jack as he headed to the door. "I'm already worrying." He twisted the doorknob, and we caught a brief cacophony of sounds from the inside of the rickety building before the door closed behind him. In the silence that followed, we all looked to Jack.

"What?" There was a distinct twang of defensiveness to his voice, and I shrugged.

"You still ready to turn in? Or do you want to look around first?"

He cast me an unamused, withering gaze.

"You guys can do that," he offered, eyes darkly humorous. I smirked as he turned his chair around and started heading down the road, chair jolting slightly as it passed over the uneven surface. "I won't be there to bail you out when these people chase you out of their town."

But there was something tense to his words that started to raise the red flags in my mind. I wanted to ask him if he was okay, but instead, I looked at the others questioningly.

"Well, I'm following him to make sure he doesn't roll himself into a ditch," I said. "Anyone else wanna come?"

"Sure," Kat said, hooking her thumbs into her pockets as she walked after Jack. Her worn boots kicked pebbles along the dirt road as she went. Jayce and Marcel followed her, the older sibling still with his arm slung around his sister's shoulders.

"There's something wrong," Aliyah said once they were out of earshot. I looked at her as she approached, folding her jacket over her arm. I tried and failed to ignore how her dark eyes bore into me. She continued, "you heard it in his voice."

"Why do you think I'm going with him?" I said softly, and the two of us turned to walk down the road together. "I know he needs space – time to be alone. But that's not what this is."

"He's looking for something," she said after a few moments of silence and moved her hands from behind her back to clasp in front of her. I didn't say anything, just watched the clouds of dust our feet created as we walked along the abandoned stretch of road. "I don't know what it is, but…he is looking."

"You always seem to know more than you let on," I said, looking up at her and holding her gaze. "How?"

She gave a small smile and looked ahead of us again.

"By doing exactly this," she answered softly, and I followed her eyes to see she was watching Jack like a hawk. "We give everything away with our body language, Byrne. *Everything*. Our futures are written in the way we hold our head around our superiors, the way we confront obstacles. Even in the way we hold our pencils or tie our laces." She took in a deep breath. "Even in the way we joke and tease each other. But what's most important is *when* we do these things – *when* we react the way we do, and in what order.

"Our habits become our tells," she finished and looked at me. "I've just learned to anticipate them before you give them away. Predict what you're going to say before you speak, what way you're going to move before you do. For all our irrationalities, we are very methodical creatures."

"So what's he gonna do now?" I asked softly, watching my boyfriend's back. "Can you tell me that? Because I'd kill to know what's going on inside his head right now. Or at all. He just hides everything behind jokes and stories…"

"And you hide them behind an emotionless mask," she replied without looking, and I found something of immense interest in the clear skies above us. "Don't think I haven't noticed that you don't smile any more. Not truly. You'll smirk sarcastically. You'll let your lips pull a certain way at things that once would have had you grinning, but you never smile. And I can't remember the last time I've heard you *genuinely* laugh." I cleared my throat and kicked a rock out of my way, watching as it skittered across the road. "You're just as much an enigma to him as he is to you."

"So that's your grand advice?" I asked and looked forward again as we walked along. "Talk about my feelings?"

"He *is* your boyfriend, isn't he?" she asked, and I felt something twist ashamedly in my gut as I looked at my shuffling feet. "I thought the whole premise of having a significant other was that you had someone to confide in." I shrugged defensively and crossed my arm over my chest to grab my stump. "I suppose that is the question you need to answer for yourself before you approach Miller, then."

I didn't answer. I just pointedly avoided the ugly truth she'd revealed, and we were silent for a little bit before she sighed, looking at the buildings as we passed them.

"But what do I know?" she said and crossed her arms with a slightly frustrated air. "I'm just a soldier."

"Why do you care so much?"

"You're not half-bad together," she began, taking in a slow, deep breath and looking at Jack in front of us. I rolled my eyes. "I am being serious. I may feel unsettled by the notion of two men or two women together, but you two...let's just say I wish you a happy ending."

"It's progress, I suppose," I admitted, gently mocking her, but she just smiled before increasing her pace to catch up to the others.

The sharp air filled with dust from our shuffling feet, and I glanced to the windows of the shops and homes we passed. Curtains swayed as invisible people pulled away, and I could have sworn I caught glimpses of faces peering out at us. The sensation of being watched by people I couldn't see sent shivers down my spine, and I forced myself to a jog, the battered soles of my boots absorbing little to none of the shock as my feet slammed into the ground.

"Nice of you to join us up here, shrimp."

"Shut up, Jones," I grumbled, slowing down to a walk and falling into step beside Jack. "How you feeling?"

"Fine," he replied, a little surprised. "You?"

"I'm okay," I said but then remembered Aliyah's words. "I guess."

At that moment, we heard a gentle clatter of metal to our left, and Jack gripped the top of his wheels, easing himself to a stop as we all froze. The sound had come from one of the alleyways, and I felt anxiety start to gnaw at my stomach as we stared at the cluttered space. The trashcans smelled like they hadn't been emptied in weeks, and flies hovered in a thick cloud above the tops in search of a rotten meal.

"It was probably just a cat or some kind of animal looking for food," Katalin said, slowly starting forward again though her eyes were still fixed on the alley. My heart pounded painfully in my chest, and I realized that all of us were a little tense.

"It was just an animal," Marcel agreed, voice a little rigid. She cleared her throat and pulled her brother along with her. "Come on."

Jayce followed her, still watching the shadows, and I looked at Jack. He was still sitting there, staring into the dark with a pained expression on his face, and I started to feel uneasy. Aliyah noticed him, too.

"Is he here?" she asked softly, and I shrugged.

"Jack?" I whispered and tentatively reached out to put my hand on his shoulder. He didn't jump at my touch, so that was good. I risked kneeling beside him. "Jack, you okay?"

"It's alright," he called, still not looking at me. I frowned and looked back into the empty alley. "We're not gonna hurt you."

The heavy feeling in my gut was suddenly gone, replaced with an aching pain in my chest as a little girl slowly peeked out from behind one of the garbage cans, grimy fingers curving around the tarnished metal.

"Are you here to kill us?" she whispered, voice small and shaky, and Jack shook his head, smiling kindly.

"No, sweetheart," he answered gently. "We're just going home."

She slowly stepped out from behind the can, and I could see her a little better in the half-light. She looked skittish, bare feet shifting nervously in the dirt as she watched us.

"My name's Jack. And this is Tristan," he explained, pointing at me. I gave her a tiny smile, and he looked over his shoulder to where Aliyah was standing. Her expression was nonplussed and little confrontational. "And that's Aliyah. She looks kinda scary, but she's alright."

The little girl pulled her arms behind her and tilted her head to the side, dragging her toe back and forth against the ground as she watched us. Her hair was wild and mousy, her eyes openly distrustful as Jayce pulled Marcel and Kat back into view.

"Who're they?" she demanded, voice surprisingly firm. My eyebrow rose fractionally in response, but Jack just smiled.

"Well, the shorter girl with the cool braids is Marcel. The man next to her is her brother Jayce," he began, pointing to each of them in turn. "And she's Kat."

A hesitant smile started pulling at the child's lips, and she looked down at the ground.

"I like cats," she said shyly, glancing back up at us, and I looked at Soto in mild concern that turned out to be well-founded. The woman looked uncomfortable, and I realized, looking around at us, that Jack seemed to be the only one at ease with the situation.

"I'm more of a dog person, myself," Jack continued. She cautiously stepped forward until she was standing on the edge of the road. "So, what's your name?"

"Hope," she whispered.

I followed her blue gaze to Marcel and was surprised to see a reassuring smile slowly appear on War's face.

"Do you like my braids, Hope?" she asked, slowly kneeling, and the girl nodded. "Do you want to come see them?" The child suddenly looked less enthusiastic, fingers toying with the sullied fabric of her dress. Jayce slowly backed away from his sister, pulling Kat and Aliyah with him. "I promise they don't bite," Marcel assured her and pulled a handful of the small braids over her shoulder to hold them out to the girl. "See?"

The little girl approached slowly, cautiously, walking with that shy, sashaying gait that all children seemed to know as she reached out to the Horseman's hair. As we watched, she slowly ran her fingers along the tight braids, eyes widening at the touch.

"They're so pretty," she whispered, awed.

"Where's your mom, Hope?" he asked, watching her with saddened eyes, and she looked at him, brow furrowing as she took in his wheelchair.

"What happened to your legs?" she asked, avoiding the question as she shifted her attention from Marcel's hair to the metal and canvas curved around my boyfriend's body.

"I got hurt real bad a few months ago," he said simply, and she looked up at him with wide eyes as she stepped closer to him. "But I'm okay now."

"My daddy got hurt real bad, too," she said softly, tilting her head and reaching out to touch the smooth spokes of the chair's wheels. She looked back at Jack, expression painfully guarded for her age. "You won't kill us?"

"Why do you think we're here to hurt you, Hope?" I asked. She looked up at me and shrank away a little as she saw my arm. "It's okay. I just got hurt, too." She nodded solemnly, eyes wide, and I asked her again. "Why do you think we're going to hurt you?"

"'Cause they came and killed my daddy," she answered, voice small as her fingers curled around the spokes of Jack's chair. "And Danny's daddy, too. And they took my cousin, Sarah."

I looked sharply to Jack, but his attention was fixed on the little girl.

"Hope?" Jack asked softly, and she looked up at him with serious eyes that were far too old for her face. "Who came?"

She shrugged, running her fingers back and forth across the metal and creating a low thrumming sound.

"I dunno, I never saw 'em before. Momma said they were bad men. Wanted food 'n stuff. She called 'em raiders." The last word was carefully enunciated, obviously new vocabulary, and Jack looked over his shoulder to Katalin. She shook her head, expression sour.

"It's probably people from neighboring towns or farms," she explained, crossing her arms. "People are starving and scared. They lash out, do stupid things to survive. I saw it happen enough in the camps growing up."

"But *taking* people?" he asked, clearly disgusted.

She shrugged again, looking down at her feet. Hope was still engrossed in Jack's wheelchair and thankfully wasn't paying us any attention.

"Some people want different things," Kat answered, voice low as she slowly ground the sole of her boot into the ground. "Not everyone's starving for food, Miller." Her nails tore softly at the fabric of her sleeve. "And some people are sick in the head."

"Or they may be collecting bodies," Marcel offered in an equally grim alternative, standing back up.

"Bodies?" I echoed.

"For fighting," she elaborated in an undertone, sighing in distaste. "If word got out that Amaeric was planning to surrender, some of the more stupid warmongers in the south and midland may have decided to take things into their own hands." She crossed her arms and sighed before she continued. "It happened a lot in Rusika about ten years back when that armistice rumor was going around. People would raid their neighboring towns, kill those who fought back, and capture the young men and women. Draft them into makeshift militias, you know?"

"Will they come back?"

We all looked to the little girl staring up at us with wide eyes, and Jack sighed, smiling at her.

"You look like a kid who can handle the truth," he began, eying her carefully. "Am I right?" She nodded diligently, and Jack leaned forward in his chair, forearms resting lightly on his knees as he looked her in the eyes. "Do you want me to tell you the truth?" She nodded again, this time more carefully, and Jack's eyes grew sad. "Well, then, Hope…they'll probably come back. But I don't know for sure." She looked down at her feet, and Jack reached out to put his hand on her shoulder, the small bones vanishing completely beneath his touch. "Now, where's your mom?"

The girl looked over her shoulder and pointed back the way we'd come.

"She's workin'," she said simply, and I followed the line of her skinny arm to the building on the corner. My heart sank. "Momma says it's the best job in the whole town 'cause she gets paid more'n anyone else."

There was a note of pride in her voice, and she beamed at us, not understanding our pitying and almost horrified expressions.

"Your mom works at The Guild?" Marcel finally asked, voice shaken, and the girl nodded.

"She told me people wouldn't get it," she said defensively, crossing her arms and looking up at us as though daring someone to say something else. "But she says it's a good job and there's nothin' wrong with it 'cause she gets to take care of me."

I glanced at the alley we'd found her in and saw it was no more than a stone's throw from the back entrance of the inn.

"Is that why you were hiding back there?" I asked, looking back at her. "You were waiting for your mom?"

She nodded, smiling shyly.

"Yeah, she gets off work soon." Her demeanor suddenly shifted, and her smile faltered. "You won't hurt us?" she asked again, and we all shook our heads, expressions as sympathetic as possible. She defiantly crossed her arms and squinted at us suspiciously. "Well, momma will be able to tell if you're lyin'. She *always* can."

"Well, we'll be glad to meet her, then," Jack said kindly, and the shy, cautious smile slowly crept back onto her face. She glanced quickly over her shoulder again to nothing but an empty alleyway before giving her attention completely to the Horseman.

"You don' talk very much," she stated matter-of-factly, looking up at Aliyah, and the woman shrugged. "And you don' seem very nice."

"Appearances can be deceiving," she said simply, and Hope frowned.

"Momma used to say that."

Looking around us, I understood why she didn't anymore. The world looked like it had gone to hell in a hand basket, the people seemed starved and violent — and, well, both observations it seemed were right. As I took in the battered town around us, I looked over Hope's head to see the back door of The Guild slowly creak open. The air groaned with the sound of rusty hinges grinding against each other, and a woman with tangled blonde hair stumbled out onto the landing, softly closing the door behind her.

Her eyes were dark with smudged make-up, and I could barely see the edge of her skirt beneath the oversized military jacket she was wearing. Her legs were thin and bruised, and she leaned against the heavy door, pulling battered, too-large boots onto her bare feet. She dragged a shaking hand through her hair, and the quick action segued into a fluid, practiced motion of her reaching down into her pocket and habitually pulling out a cigarette and disintegrating matchbook. Her blue eyes were ancient in her youthful face, and she looked over her shoulder to us, fogged gaze disinterested.

That was, until she caught sight of the girl.

"Hope!" she shouted, voice cracked and panic-stricken as she vaulted over the railing, stumbling as she landed hard on her left leg. "Get away from her!"

I raised my hand up to my shoulder and backed away from the child before me, the others doing the same.

"Momma!" Hope grinned, running over to the frantic young woman and tackling her around her waist. The woman quickly threw the smoke over her shoulder, wiping frantically at her mouth as she knelt down and wrapped her arms around her child.

"Hope, what have I told you about talkin' to strangers?" she hissed, pulling back from her daughter and tucking the little girl's messy hair out of her eyes. "What have I told you, Hope?!" The girl's eager expression slowly fell, and she stared sadly at her feet.

"To not to," she mumbled, and the mother nodded vehemently before standing, pulling her child close to her side. "But they're nice, momma. I *promise*," she pressed, looking up at the woman as she wrapped her arms around her leg. All the mother did was pull her child even closer, practically clutching at her.

"Alright, what the hell do you want?" she demanded hoarsely.

"Nothing," Jack told her, his expression open and frank. "We were just talking to Hope. She was telling us about the raiders you got a while ago."

"Last month," she spat, shifting on her feet as though preparing to run. "So you'll understand if I don't believe you aren't up to anythin'."

"Think about it," Marcel said forcefully from Jack's left, drawing and holding the woman's fierce gaze. "If we were raiders, we wouldn't bring along an amputee and a paraplegic."

"Ma'am, we're just some troops coming back from the eastern lines," I said, slowly lowering my arm, and her sharp gaze immediately shifted to me. "The rest of us are staying up in The Guild. You, um…you might've seen them come in."

The woman's brow furrowed briefly, as she tried to remember through the haze of the indoors. As she nervously licked her lips, I caught sight of a painful sore at the corner of her hard mouth.

"We understand that raiders killed your husband, miss," Aliyah said kindly, breaking the tense silence. "And you don't trust strangers, rightfully so. But we are not here to cause any more harm."

The mother's expression seemed to soften almost imperceptibly around her eyes for a second as she looked down at her daughter. She slowly let her grip loosen.

"They didn't hurt you, Hope?" The girl dutifully shook her head, and her mother took in a deep, unsteady breath, looking back up at us. "Are you really from the eastern lines?"

"Yes, ma'am," Jack answered, pointing back down the road. She leaned forward slightly to check our story. "Those are our trucks right there."

"Yeah, well, don't get comfortable. We don't take kindly to strangers 'round here. Not anymore," she snapped and quickly picked up her child, holding her close as she brushed past us and down the street. Just before the woman ducked down an alley, her pace picked up into a nervous run, and she threw us one last panicked glance over her shoulder.

"It's only been what? Eight months?" Jayce asked, still staring at the space the mother and child had vanished into. "Almost nine?" He looked at the rest of us, an uncomprehending look on his face. "How'd this happen? I mean, yeah, the town wasn't that great when we drove through the first time, but this…" He scoffed, gesturing around us. "Norford's hung on for thirty years. Why'd it fall apart now?"

"It's just the bottom of the barrel, Jayce," Marcel said gently, hooking her arm through her brothers and pulling him down the road with her. "The war's closer, it's been thirty years…it's just the bottom of the barrel. Come on. Let's just get to the barn."

He looked down at her, expression pained and troubled.

"We did this," he said, the words a stricken realization. "Didn't we? We did this to that little girl."

Marcel tightened her hold, pulling her brother closer to her and looked down at their feet as they walked. Katalin set off after them, eyes fixed on the ground in sullen silence. Aliyah waited a few seconds to catch my eye before heading after them.

"Yeah, Jayce. We did," War sighed. I looked at Jack. His hands rested in his lap, and his eyes stared sadly at nothing. "It wasn't just us, but yeah. We're just as guilty."

"Jack?" I called.

My boyfriend cleared his throat and quickly blinked to bring himself out of whatever reverie he'd fallen into. He quickly moved his chair forward and looked over his shoulder at me. I fell into step beside him.

"Yeah?" His expression was too questioning, too blank.

"What's wrong?" I asked, and he looked at the four people walking in front of us.

"They're finally getting it," he sighed. Marcel wrapped her arm around Katalin's waist and pulled her to her side, Famine's arm resting across War's shoulders. Aliyah continued to shadow them, hands gently clasped behind her back as she watched their tells and waited.

"Getting what?" I asked.

Jack started moving forward, and I walked beside him, making sure I was easily in his field of vision and holding eye contact. He gave me a tired, closed-lip smile before shifting the worn expression towards our friends.

"War's messy. It gets everywhere. It stains everything and everyone…it doesn't come out." He scoffed, eyes unfocusing as he continued to shove his wheels forward in rough, rhythmic thrusts. "We get it on ourselves, and everything we touch is tainted."

"I think we already figured that out," I said, but Jack shook his head.

"No. You figured out that the front lines are messy. That the battlefield is a horrible nightmare." He looked up at me, expression sad and knowing. "Now you guys'll figure out that none of it stays out there. We track it back in with us when we come home." He looked forward again, taking in a deep breath and slowly releasing it – the weight of four tours heavy in his lungs. "And then everyone else is part of it, too."

We walked in silence after that conversation. My hand rested gently on Jack's shoulder as we went down the road, following the Horsemen as they turned a corner into an alley wider than the others and cleared a path for Jack as they went. The sides of the buildings stretching up on either side of us were stained with mud and other substances I didn't care to look too closely at, and the ground beneath our feet shifted and gave under our weight. I didn't dare look down to see what we were walking in, and Jayce quickly walked back towards us to start pushing Jack's wheelchair.

"Thanks," Jack reluctantly said, and Jones just shook his head.

"You're not touching your wheels while we go through here," he told him, and I slowly let go of my boyfriend's shoulder so we could move more easily. "Gods know what's on the ground."

The air was putrid and rank around us, sheltered from the cold wind whistling down the main road. I wondered if the locals could even smell it anymore or if they'd grown accustomed to the stench. We definitely could.

The reeking odor was overpowering, and I lifted my hand to my nose and mouth, gripping the cuff of my sleeve between my palm and fingers so I could press the smoky fabric against my nose.

The lingering, pungent combination of gunpowder and disinfectant was preferable to the nauseating stench of sewage and rot that seemed to cling to my throat and lungs every time I breathed. Out of the corner of my eye, I could see Jack doing the same thing, and the Horsemen picked up their pace until we had escaped the alley, clearing our throats and taking deep breaths of the fresher air.

"Could I – well, I'm gonna continue to push you once we're clear. If that's alright, of course?" Jayce began awkwardly, and Jack twisted around in his chair to look up at him, brow furrowed. I could see his discomfort in the way his lips pressed against each other in a thin line, and Jayce tried to explain. "It's just that you got a lot of crap on your wheels going through here. If I can keep pushing you, it'll eventually get cleaned off, and you can take it from there."

Neither of us missed the way Jack's jaw clenched, and his eyes quickly shifted downwards.

"Yeah," he answered, nodding and stiffly turning back to face forward, crossing his arms over his stomach. "Yeah, that's fine. Thanks, Jones."

Jayce just nodded and leaned a little more into the handles of my boyfriend's chair as he pushed him along, the three of us exiting onto the back lot of The Guild. The air was sharp and cold once more, the smell of rain heavy in the draft. As I walked beside them, I couldn't help but reach across my body to grab onto my amputated limb, cracked nails digging painfully through my shirt and into my skin. I should have been the one helping Jack, and I had no one but myself to blame for not being able to. Jayce caught my stare, and I quickly looked forward again.

"You were a carpenter, weren't you, Miller?" he asked suddenly, and both my boyfriend and I looked at him, confused and a little suspicious. War's brother just looked at us with guileless eyes, and Jack slowly replied.

"I mean, my dad was. He taught me until I was eighteen, but I wouldn't call myself a carpenter per se–"

Jayce cut him off with a shrug.

"Maybe you could look into making some kind of brace for the right handle on your chair. I don't know, something that can detach and reattach when needed."

I looked away and uncomfortably cleared my throat, quickly letting go of my arm and shoving my hand in my pocket.

"I'm not an artisan, Jones," Jack sighed, crossing his arms a little tighter and watching the ground pass underneath him. "I can build a crappy table, but…" He trailed off and looked over at me. I barely caught the movement out of the corner of my eye. When he continued his words were softer and apologetic. "I can't make prosthetics."

I felt something twist in my stomach, and I looked at my feet, kicking another rock down the road and watching it vanish into a pile of trash. Anything to avoid Jack's eyes and the unnecessary apology in his dark irises. Jayce cleared his throat, hands tightening around the handles of the chair as he focused on what was in front of us.

"Well, there's your stable."

Jack and I looked at the large, decrepit building. It was abandoned, or at least I assumed so. Given the trashed feed and hay scattered outside the structure, there couldn't have been more than one or two animals in there, and since the raiders had come through, any livestock left were probably either sick or very old.

The stable was about twenty-five feet long and thirty feet wide, which meant three stalls and a tack room most probably. There were several sun-bleached boards missing on each wall, and the holes and gaps created an eerie whistling sound as the wind blew through them. The large door was knocked off its hinges – again, probably from the raid – and as we stepped in, the already cool temperature dropped even lower. The straw beneath our feet was dry and brittle, its warm, heavy smell all but gone, and as we slowly spread out and took in our surroundings, I realized I was right. Three stalls, one tack room – all empty.

"This place hasn't been used in a while," Marcel commented, looking up at the cobweb-strewn rafters and at the rays of sunlight slicing through the gloom from holes in the roof.

"It'd be too dangerous," Katalin said, looking over her shoulder as she approached the tack room. "This place wouldn't survive a storm, and all of this?" She kicked at the dead hay beneath our feet. "It's kindling. If a spark landed in here, the whole stable would go up like a match." She caught our stares and shrugged, opening the tack room door and stepping inside. Her voice carried out to us from the shadows. "It happened a lot in the camps. Except with people inside instead of animals."

"Well, that's a pleasant image," Jayce muttered and stepped away from Jack, rubbing his arms to either generate heat or drive away the chills from what Kat had just told us.

"You tell us this as we're planning to sleep in here?" I asked Katalin in disbelief, and she re-emerged from the darkened room carrying a battered saddle, the leather split and unusable from sun exposure and improper care.

"It's too cold for a fire, and the sky is clear," Aliyah said reassuringly. "We'll be fine for a few hours of rest."

The Horsemen and Jayce following Kat back into the tack room to pick out ratty horse blankets and discarded saddles to use for pillows given the sparseness of the hay. Jack looked at me and shrugged.

"They are right, you know."

"Doesn't make it any more comforting," I replied.

"Byrne." I looked over to Soto, and she handed me a battered Eastern saddle, draping it over my arm. "Not much back there."

"It's fine," I assured her before turning back to Jack. "I've got us a pillow." I lifted up the object, and he rolled his eyes. I could hear the others shuffling around in the tack room behind us.

"How luxurious," he drawled with a tired, amused smile and headed over to a stall with an already open door. "This one'll work." I joined him and looked into the space.

"Guys, we've got one," I called.

Our four companions came over, arms laden with ratty, dirty blankets and abused equipment. Marcel surveyed the room and hmphed. It was probably twelve by twelve feet – not too small, but big enough for six of us to fit without much of a problem.

"Good enough."

She and her brother went in first, sitting down farthest from the door. Aliyah and Katalin settled beside them in that order, leaving a little space between themselves and the siblings as they set up their makeshift sleeping areas. This stall seemed to have more hay in it than the others at least, and I dropped the English saddle to the ground and looked to Jack.

"You ready?" I asked, and Jack nodded silently. I reached behind him to grab his belt while he wrapped his arms around me. "You count."

"One, two, three."

The count was faster this time, spoken as though it were a nuisance, and I pulled up and stepped back as he tightened his arms around me. And as I turned and slowly bent at my waist until Jack was sitting gently on the ground, I saw Jayce over my boyfriend's shoulder. There was a warm, kind glow in his eyes as he watched us, an invisible smile that vanished as soon as he realized that I was making eye contact with him. He looked away.

Jack pulled his arms away, and I sat down heavily beside him, our backs against the stall's battered wood paneling.

"You can use the saddle," I offered and nudged the black leather with my toe as I relaxed against the wall. Jack frowned.

"You aren't gonna use it?"

"I sleep better sitting up," I lied, and Jack nodded absently, looking at his palm pressed flat against the ground holding him up. "Hey." He looked back at me, and I reached for his shoulder. "Come on. Lie back."

I caught a brief glimpse of the relieved quirk of his lips as he grabbed my outstretched hand and used me to pull himself a little closer to my left side. A loud rasping sound filled the silence as his legs dragged along the hay-strewn ground. In a series of practiced movements, I brought my knees up closer to my chest and Jack let himself fall back against the angle formed by my body, adjusting himself as I slowly let my legs lay flat with Jack's head and shoulders pillowed against them.

"How many times have you two done that?" Marcel asked. We looked at her and shrugged.

"A couple," I answered vaguely and looked back down at Jack. "Back or side?"

He paused before answering, brow furrowing in thought.

"Side," he finally responded. I nodded easily. "Can you help with…"

In response, I reached out and grabbed his pant leg just above his knee while he twisted his upper body as far as he could to face me. With a few quick, hard jerks that pulled painfully at my nails, I managed to get Jack's lower body to turn with the rest of him. The Horsemen and Jayce had the decency to not awkwardly watch us at this point, for which I was thankful. Once he was settled, Jack slid his left hand under my leg, the way he used to with his pillows, and rested his right arm over his side so that his hand lay across his stomach. I reached down and gently ran my fingers through his hair, the movement natural and subconscious. Usually, the motion calmed him down and allowed Jack to finally start drifting off to sleep. But today, for a myriad of reasons, he remained tense and wound up, breaths deep and controlled.

"How long do you think before we leave?"

I looked up at Marcel and shrugged while Jack propped himself up on one arm to look at her as much as he could over his shoulder.

"We'll probably head out around six. So, a little under eight hours at this point."

She nodded to herself and lay back, turning onto her side and crossing her arms over her stomach. The air seemed impossibly colder now that we weren't moving, and Jayce dragged his equestrian pillow a little closer to his sister so he could wrap his arm around her slightly smaller frame and keep her warm.

"Jayce, what the hell? Get off," she grumbled and elbowed him hard in the chest. He just rolled his eyes, laying his head down and closing his eyes.

"It's freezing cold in here, and I don't have a blanket," he whined, and War growled in frustration, crossing her arms tighter against her body and scowling at the hay-strewn floor.

"I am *not* your personal heater," she returned bitterly, but I could see the very faint spark of amusement in the back of her eyes.

Very faint.

Aliyah was already asleep somehow. She was lying on her back, head resting comfortably against a gaudy, weather-beaten western saddle with her eyes closed. Her hands were folded neatly over her stomach, and I marveled at how easily she seemed to be handling everything.

Katalin also seemed to be on the verge of drifting off as well, though her sleep was like a glimpse into the past. She was curled up beside Aliyah, arms tucked close against her chest behind her drawn up knees. Her head was bowed down, chin resting against her half-curled fingers, and I thought back to the comments she'd been making since we'd returned to Norford. Looking at Katalin now was like seeing a ghost of the ten year old who'd grown up in the squalor of a prisoner of war camp. Except we weren't behind barbed wire in the south. We weren't on the front lines under the control of a foreign army. We were in Amaeric, our own home, and all I could see – all the towns and cities – all I could see were death camps.

I was still running my fingers through Jack's hair, and I looked down to see that he, too, had drifted off to sleep. The tight fist he'd made against his gut was now relaxed, and his fingers rested, half-curled, against his skin. But his breathing was light and shallow, and I knew he would probably wake up at the slightest movement.

At least there'd be no nightmares. Belatedly, I realized that was probably why he'd been so against the idea of all of us sleeping in the same place as him. I was the only one who knew the explicit nature of his dreams. The others only knew *about* them. I'd only been able to make up excuses for my bruises for so long before the Horsemen had confronted me, demanding to know if some Brettain troops were roughing me up and asking if they had to go kick someone's ass for me.

Oh, the irony.

So I told them, and now they knew about the dreams. But they hadn't seen them firsthand, and as far as I was concerned, they never would. I brushed a strand of hair out of Jack's eyes, tucking it back behind his ears. His nightmares were private.

"I wish I could fall asleep that fast," Katalin said softly, and I looked up at her. "I envy him sometimes."

She was sitting with her back against her saddle, arms around her knees and holding them close to her chest. While I'd been staring down at Jack, it seemed everyone else had slowly sat back up, propping themselves up on an elbow or a saddle to look at me. All except Aliyah – she'd simply tucked an arm behind her head, dark eyes half-open.

My hand stilled protectively on my boyfriend's head.

"Count your blessings, Kat," Marcel muttered, picking half-heartedly at the laces on her boots. "He doesn't just fall asleep quickly." I nodded and slowly let my thumb sweep back and forth across Jack's scalp, careful not to get tangled in his hair. She looked up at us, expression tired. "That girl, her mom…" Her head dropped against her knees, and she sighed. "I thought going home meant it was over."

"It's a stain," I said quietly, thinking back to what Jack had told me. Jayce looked up at me, an attentive light in his eyes. "War, it's – it's like mud or something. It sticks onto whatever it touches. And we just track it all over our homes when we come back."

"Miller?" he asked.

I nodded, smiling wryly to myself as I looked back down at Jack's head in my lap, gently continuing to run my fingers through his hair. His face was quiet and still. His bone structure and unbroken skin looked like porcelain in the shadowed half-light around us, and his chest moved lightly with each sleeping breath. Peaceful. Completely unaware that in the waking world we were talking about him.

"He has a knack for phrasing these things in a way we can make sense of," I admitted, and the Jones brother nodded.

"Benefit of four tours, I guess," he said softly.

I rested my head against the stall and looked up, my fingers continuing to absently trace out Jack's skull as I prayed to the gods that for once his dreams were free of demons.

"Or the curse," I muttered.

The shafts of golden sunlight pierced the gloom above us, and dust and hay and fragments of cobwebs drifted lazily through the bright spillways. Somewhere far away, I could hear "Sweetheart Waltz" crackle out of an old record player, and I closed my eyes, hand still so that my fingers were nestled in Jack's hair, arm gently cradling his head. The air was heavy and sweet in my lungs, and my mind drifted as I remembered the last time I'd breathed air like this – in the solitary dark of the night, standing with my back against the wall of any empty stall and my arms wrapped around Jack's neck, holding his taller body against me.

My head slipped to the side, and I quickly woke up to the teasing smiles of the Horsemen and Jayce who just rolled his eyes and turned over as his sister crooned,

"Aw, aren't they adorable?"

I snorted, blinking tiredly and looking down at my boyfriend's body, at how it seemed smaller now – one arm tucked under my legs while the other curved over his stomach. At how his legs were bent slightly beside us from where I'd pulled at him to help turn him on his side. He looked almost child-like. I moved my imaginary right arm to rest against his side, the non-existent fingers holding his hand, and my eyes slowly slid shut again.

How things changed.

... — — — ...

I felt him jerk once at probably close to four. I woke up long enough to run my hand through his hair a few times, whispering gentle reassurances to him under my breath. He settled back down, brow creased fitfully, and I ran my thumb along the furrowed skin as if that small gesture could chase away the monsters and memories. My head tilted back against the wall again, and within a few moments I was asleep once more.

I was so tired. Abnormally tired, really. In fact, it was pretty odd when I thought about it, all I seemed to do now was sleep...

... — — — ...

"Byrne," a voice whispered, and I slowly opened my eyes, looking up at Marcel and wincing as my neck twinged in pain. "Harper just stopped by. It's time for us to pack up."

The rays of light were gone from the air above us, and I shifted my spine, the bones cracking almost painfully as I worked out the kinks. As I moved, Jack's eyes opened, and he quickly looked around, eyes a little dazed.

"We moving?" he asked blearily, still half-asleep, and I nodded, patting his shoulder in case he couldn't see me in the dim lighting.

"Yeah. Come on," I yawned, gesturing to Jayce's shadowy form as he walked towards the door. "We'll help you up."

Jayce reached down, and Jack took his hands and pulled himself into a sitting position. I got to my feet and arched my back, wincing as the last of my misaligned and aching joints fell back into place. The girls gathered the saddles and took them back to the tack room.

"Alright, Jayce? Can you bring his chair?" I asked sleepily and stepped in front of Jack, straddling his legs. I vaguely registered Jones moving off as Jack wrapped his arms around my neck, and I grabbed his belt. "On three?"

"Just go."

I rocked backwards, pivoted on my left foot, and, grogginess making me a little overenthusiastic, turned Jack a little too forcefully into his chair. I winced at his small grunt of pain.

"Sorry."

"Too asleep to care," he mumbled dismissively, grinding the heels of his palms into his eyes a few times before grabbing his legs and lifting his feet onto their rests. He yawned loudly, resting his hands on the handles of his wheels. "Let's go."

I led the way towards the broken threshold, shivering and wrapping my arm around my stomach. A cold, piercing wind rushed through the stable without any kind of warning, filling the air with that same sharp whistling sound from earlier, and I wondered vaguely how the horses had survived in here. The Horsemen joined the three of us just as we left the building, and I looked up at the sky.

The sun had finished setting. The last light was slowly fading from the ridge of the horizon. Given the season and the region, I guessed that it was probably somewhere between six and seven.

Right on schedule with what Jack had said.

As we left back the way we'd come, Jayce taking over for Jack when we passed through the putrid alleyway again, I couldn't help but look to that back entrance for The Guild. Couldn't help wondering if Hope's mother was working an evening shift or if she was home with her daughter.

My answer came soon enough.

As we neared the trucks at the front of the institution, people walking half-asleep to their respective vehicles, I caught sight of the small-framed woman draped in a military coat standing at the edge of the building. Her blonde hair was still just as tangled, and a dying cigarette rested between her fingers.

"Go on." I looked at Jack questioningly, and he jerked his head towards her. "We won't leave without you, I promise."

"Ha ha. Very funny," I returned dryly but put a hand on his shoulder in thanks.

I broke off from the group, waving slightly to get her attention as I approached. She scoffed as she saw me, taking another deep breath of her smoke that burned it out, and she dropped it to the ground, crushing it beneath her heel.

"What do you all want now?" she asked, defensively crossing her arms, and I shrugged.

"I just wanted to let you know that we're leaving," I told her, standing beside her and shoving my hand into my pocket. "No harm done. At least, none that I know of."

She watched me carefully out of the corner of her eye.

"You get shot?" she finally asked, eyeing the knotted end of my right sleeve.

"Stabbed." She nodded to herself, watching what was left of the eastern front line start the disorganized process of cramming everyone back inside the trucks. "My name's Byrne."

Her arms remained firmly crossed over her chest, eyes turned away from me.

"Mel." The single syllable name was bit out, and I nodded, the two of us falling silent once more. I watched as the Horsemen and Jayce helped Jack towards one of the trucks. It would be a while given the large crowd of people before them so I had a little time to try and figure out how to talk with this woman.

"My husband was on the eastern lines," she said abruptly.

I looked over at her and waited for her to continue. I was surprised that she'd decided to keep talking to me. Her eyes were wide and distant, staring at something no one but her could see.

"He came home with his leg all shot up. It was a gods-given miracle we kept off the gangrene as long as we did." She looked down at her jacket and half-heartedly picked at the hem of the massive sleeves.

"I thought Hope said the raiders killed her dad," I said, and she looked up at me, face half-hidden in the dying light. Her expression was dark and solemn.

"They did," she whispered, clearing her throat and rubbing at her eyes with the coat sleeve. "You ever…I'm sorry, what was your name again?"

"Byrne."

"You ever see someone die of gangrene, Byrne?" she asked me. Her face was so tired and worn I felt like I was staring into a mirror. "You ever see someone's body start to decompose while they're still livin' in it?"

My gut twisted nauseatingly as I thought of Irina, of the black, rotting skin beneath her shirt.

"Yeah, I have. It's…not pleasant."

She scoffed at the understatement, shaking her head and lifting empty fingers to her lips.

"No. No it's not." She took in a deep breath, closing her eyes as she exhaled. "He was sick, laid up in bed. I told him to stay put, to not go out there, but Sarah was screamin'…" She trailed off, slipping back in time.

"Sarah – your niece?" I prompted, and she nodded, looking back at me with a startled expression.

"How did you–"

"Hope mentioned her," I said. She nodded and looked at the crowded trucks.

"He went out there, draggin' that rotten leg behind him." She laughed shakily, looking down at the battered olive green fabric encasing her body and her boots. I knew both once belonged to her late husband. "He didn't even get off the porch before they shot him down."

"I'm so sorry," I whispered, and she shook her head, hands resting on her hips as she turned to face me. A hot anger burned in her eyes, turning them cold and furious.

"We don't need your pity," she snapped, voice shaking. "We need this war over! We need food! We need someone to realize that the war isn't just on the borders anymore!" A heavy silence hung between us, and I stared at her impassively as she sighed and shook her head, smiling in a reflexive way to herself that was painfully familiar. "Sorry. Guess you know a little more about that than most."

"We got firsthand experience with the whole killing and trying not to get killed thing, yeah," I agreed.

"How can you talk about it like that?" she asked accusingly, a disturbed expression on her face. "You said it yourself, you *killed* people."

"And how exactly do you deal with what you do?" I demanded, voice sharp and angry, and I turned to face her completely. "You let people abuse your body and infect you with gods know what just to make ends meet. So tell me, what exactly do you tell your daughter when she asks about your sores, your bruises?"

She was silent, staring at me like I'd slapped her, and beneath the anger part of me felt ashamed.

"Do you tell jokes?" I continued, voice softening, and broke our eye contact. "Do you make up stories about how you were just clumsy or block her questions with some black humor she won't get until she's older?" I swallowed painfully and looked back at her. "Do you hide behind masks and lies, hoping she can't tell that even though you're smiling, all you want to do is scream?"

She closed her mouth and paused, expression softening and turning sad and defeated.

"Sometimes," she admitted, voice quiet and small. "Sometimes, yeah. I do. But I try to hide it from her. Makeup when I can spare it, you know?"

"I do," I said softly, and she looked at me in puzzlement. "My, uh, best friend, he has brutal nightmares about the things he's seen," I explained and rocked back on my heels. "Some nights – well, most nights – I get bruised pretty bad, but I make sure he doesn't see them." I tilted my head a little and shrugged. "So, I get it. A little."

"No, you don't," she sighed and reached into her pocket to procure another cigarette. Her words weren't judgmental or condemning. They were just sad and pained. "And I hope you never do, because…"

"Lying to your daughter is much different than lying to your friend," I finished, and she nodded, meeting my eyes as she finally managed to light a match and touched it to her smoke. I looked over her shoulder to see Jayce, Aliyah, and Marcel helping Jack up into the back of the truck while Katalin packed up his wheelchair. "I have to say it. I have no idea how you manage to keep going."

"Why do you think I named her Hope?" she said softly, voice thick as she crossed her arms tighter over her stomach. Our soldiers continued to pass us by, climbing into their respective trucks. In the bustle of movement, I shrugged, trying to keep track of how things were moving along.

"I named her 'hope' because I needed somethin' to come home to," she said, voice hard and genuine, and I looked at her. "Somethin' that's stronger than all of this – the war, the death, the starvation, the sickness. I need hope, and my daughter is all that I have. I need her to remind me that everythin' can be okay, that maybe if I put myself through hell now she won't have to sell her body to desperate men to make ends meet, too." Her eyes were filled with tears, and she shakily raised the cigarette to her lips, inhaling deeply and closing her eyes. "So tell me, soldier…" She exhaled her lungful of smoke and opened her eyes to look at me, gaze intense. "Is she gonna have to do what I do?"

I looked back at the battered and tired men and women climbing up into the backs of the trucks. They were almost done loading, and I sighed as I caught a brief glimpse of Blackwell moving further back into his car. Harper was waiting outside the truck bed, counting heads as they loaded up. I noticed he held his arm a little stiffly against his body, a painful remnant of the once broken joint.

And as I watched the Horsemen help Jack sit against the side of the vehicle, backing off so he could make himself comfortable and leaving a space beside him for me, I knew my answer.

"No," I finally said, looking back to Mel and giving her a gentle smile. "Your daughter won't have to do what you do."

She looked at me with her daughter's serious eyes, taking another drag of her cigarette.

"Are you sure?"

"Let me tell you a secret," I said, checking over my shoulder to make sure that no one else was within earshot. It didn't look like it. Most of us were already in the trucks, and those who weren't were hovering outside the battered automobiles, waiting for their turn to climb in.

"The war's gonna be over soon." Her eyes widened in disbelief. "It's not a rumor. We were just released by the Brettain yesterday, so trust me. Next couple of months, this is all gonna be over. Your daughter won't have a war to fight." My next words stirred something inside me, a combination of emotions I couldn't even begin to explain. "We made sure of that."

An irrepressible smile of relief broke out over the young woman's face, cracking the dried skin around the sore at the corner of her mouth. Blood welled up in the spidering cuts, but she didn't seem to care. The cigarette fell from her fingers, and she gave a breathless laugh, pulling her much too large sleeves over her hands as she lifted them to her mouth.

"It's over?" she asked.

"Soon," I corrected her, but she just shook her head, eyes shining. "So, just do me a favor and keep it quiet for the moment."

"Soon, now – there's no difference. After thirty years, they mean the same thing." She tilted her head back to look at the ashy sky above us, the cold air turning her sallow cheeks red in the porch light of the Guild. There was nothing but relief in her eyes, and she heaved a great sigh, looking back down at the ground and grinding out the cigarette with the toe of her boot, crushing the embers back into the earth.

"I need to go tell Hope," she breathed and laughed to herself, shaking her head. She looked up at me, smiling crookedly, but then she grew serious once more. "Are you lot drivin' through the night?" I nodded. "Watch out for raiders."

"Will do."

She nodded and took in a deep breath, lifting the sleeves to her lips and smiling into the fabric as she turned around and headed down the road. There was something lively and ridiculously close to some sort of half-skip in her step. I laughed once to myself and shook my head. I was probably going to regret this, but at the moment I couldn't bring myself to care.

"You told her, didn't you?"

I jumped, turning around to find myself face to face with Katalin. Even though she'd been the one to speak first, she wasn't looking at me or even Mel. She was just staring off into the distance, looking through and beyond the crooked rows of houses.

"I mean, look at her," I said. Hope's mother shifted the oversized coat on her narrow shoulders and stepped down the same alley she'd gone down earlier with her daughter. "She deserved some good news, don't you think?"

"You better hope this war ends, then, Byrne," she muttered.

I looked up as a raven flew off its shadowed perch on the edge of The Guild roof, silently catching the wind twisting through the empty streets of the town and gliding effortlessly over our heads. The night air was so quiet I could hear the wind run through its feathers like the sounds of rippling military banners and white flags.

"It will," I said softly, and the bird vanished into the darkened sky.

"Come on. They're waiting on us." I looked at back at Kat, suddenly tired. She started walking, catching hold of my arm and pulling me with her. "Let's go home. Come on."

"I'm coming, Kat," I grumbled, pulling my wrist from her grasp. "You don't need to pull me like I'm on some kind of leash."

She rolled her eyes as we climbed up into the truck and sat down across from me and Jack. As I sat on Jack's right, my hand immediately and readily holding his, I looked at the order we were sitting in. Jack's wheelchair sat between Aliyah and Marcel instead of an empty space, but I could still see who would have been sitting there. Could still see her white-blonde head falling against Aliyah's shoulder, making the tall woman jump. And as I looked to my right I could see Andrew and Id where now there were two strangers. I felt a heavy pang in my chest, and I rested my head against Jack's shoulder.

"Does it get easier?" I asked quietly, and Jack rested his cheek against the top of my head, sighing. I could feel his breath against my skin, and he tightened his hold on my hand.

"Afraid not," he sighed, thumb sweeping back and forth. "You just get better at living with it."

Seeing nothing but ghosts around me, I closed my eyes and pressed my head a little harder against his shoulder. I felt Jack shift beside me, and his arm wrapped around me, pulling me close. I briefly opened my eyes to look at the Horsemen, and I found that they were glaring in judging silence.

But not at us.

Their eyes were fixed on the strangers around us, and I saw that Jack had already closed his eyes against the rest of the world, limiting what he experienced to touch and sound and smell. And as I closed my eyes as well, I realized that this really wasn't that bad of a world to be in. I couldn't see the sidelong glances unknown people were giving us or the protective glares the Jayce and Horsemen were shooting back at them. I could just feel Jack beside me, just hear his breath rush in and out of his chest and his heartbeat in my ear. It was a tiny world that belonged only to us. No war, no pain, just each other. As I fell asleep, I wished that it could stay that way.

But even with my eyes closed, I could feel the accusing and repulsed stares of the people around us, and another phantom pain shot up my arm.

DAY TWO HUNDRED AND SIXTY-SIX

We drove past the old farmlands today.

They were completely gone now. The scorching suns of the summer had started wildfires, turning everything to black char. Then the northern winds had blown in, and any husks of ash that had managed to retain the shape of the crops they'd once been were scattered. The remnants of the homes of the people who'd once lived there, the burned skeletons reaching for some kind of respite in the heavens above, were nothing more than now.

The Ruins loomed ominously on the horizon, and the ravens and crows riding the currents above us shadowed our battered caravan as soon as we passed under them.

...— —...

The destroyed city was no longer empty. Throngs of people had started living in the wreckage, trying to find asylum and safety in a world that no longer existed.

...— —...

The farmhouses we'd driven past, the ones whose inhabitants had given us food and supplies, were now in shambles. Doors stood crooked in their frames, barricaded with tables and chairs. Rocks and termite-riddled wood shored up the windows. Starved people armed with pitchforks, hoes, and scythes watched us from the meager safety of their homes.

I saw a girl standing barefoot in one of the doorways, rusted axe in her grimy hands. She was wearing an Academy coat and a heartless steel in her eyes.

·· · − − − ·· ·

    Some of the people riding with us started getting "motion sickness". At least, that's what the driver had told us it was when we yelled at him to pull over. I don't think that's why they were throwing up though.

    We'd driven by a house hit by raiders. But judging by how decomposed the bodies on the porch were, it had been a while since the attack.

    We should be fine, Katalin had said.

    Jack had laughed at that. Someone threw up over the side of the truck.

    I was reminded of black eyes, silver tears, and a pale face streaked with blood, and suddenly my own stomach wasn't quite as settled as it had been.

·· · − − − ·· ·

    The sun set. It wasn't anything spectacular, but at least now it was dark. This way, we couldn't see the horrors we passed, and I stared blankly into the rumbling night. Best to not focus on anything in particular.

DAY TWO HUNDRED AND SIXTY-SEVEN

0230 hours

 Fittingly, it was a pothole in the road that woke me up. And despite the pain in my temple from where my head had slammed, yet again, into Jack's shoulder, it wasn't nearly as bad as the cracking sound my boyfriend's jaw made on the top of my head.
 "Ow!"
 "*Gods*," Jack groaned, massaging the sore bone while I rubbed furiously at my skull. "The roads got worse."
 "Are you really surprised?" I mumbled, stretching my arm out in front of me and quickly blinking. "How close are we?"
 In answer to my question, the brakes came to a squealing halt, the worn down pads screeching like nails on a chalkboard.
 "Declare yourself," a tired voice shouted, sounding more annoyed than commanding.
 "Matthew Gratner," our driver answered. "45038621. I'm heading the convoy bringing troops home from General Mayworth's camp. We should be right on schedule."
 The heavy sound of unoiled hinges grinding open carried out to us, and I looked at the silhouette of Jack's profile. I couldn't bring myself to speak. Everything felt wrong all of a sudden, like there should be something else, something more. It shouldn't be this simple.
 I jumped as someone shone a flashlight into the back of the truck and our eyes, checking our faces and taking note of our lack of guns. Security measures, I supposed. Couldn't be letting just anybody through the gate.

"Alright, let's see your tags. Come on!" the man behind the blinding point of light ordered, still sounding annoyed.

We all fished around beneath our collars, pulling the rectangles from inside our shirts. The chains and pendants rattled against each other in a gentle tinkling of metal. Whoever the guard was, he seemed satisfied that the bare minimum of his job requirement had been filled, and he turned the light away from our faces to trudge back to the gate of the Academy.

"Alright. First car goes through, but I'm under orders to inspect all the others before allowing entry."

"Doesn't matter to me," I heard our driver respond gruffly.

We started moving again, suspension protesting as the truck dropped about a foot into some kind of ditch at the gate's threshold, and we all slid and crashed into each other. The girl next to me yanked her arm away and held it close to her chest as though she'd been burned. She fixed me with a disgruntled gaze like I'd somehow tainted her, and I awkwardly looked away and took in a deep breath, hunching my shoulders.

This was going to be fun.

The back of the truck slowly filled with more and more excited chatter, the people growing antsy and shifting on their folded legs as they eagerly looked out the back of the truck into the darkened landscape. We could see the light at the guard's house and a little bit of the tall, barbed wire gates of the Academy, but little else. As the trucks rumbled down the road, I noticed there were far fewer sentries on patrol than usual, and the few I saw were carrying gas lanterns instead of the bulkier flashlights.

It seemed that even the Academy was running low on supplies, and the institute had direct lines to the factories up north. I suddenly thought back to what Mayworth had told me the first time we'd met.

The front lines have collapsed all along your borders.

It was likely, if not probable, that the factories had been lost or at least cripplingly damaged. And if the military was running low on supplies, I could only imagine how little the people had. I let myself sway slightly as the truck moved along the gently curving road leading back up to the main cluster of the Academy's buildings. That tight, anxious feeling was back in my chest, and I couldn't understand why. I couldn't understand why I felt this terrible, nauseating feeling in my gut. It slowly crept up my throat, suffocating me.

Home.

I clenched my left hand into a fist against my bent knee, taking as deep of a breath as I could with the strange pressure on my chest. My right arm started to ache, and I involuntarily flinched, groaning as a sharper pain shot through the bone.

"Tristan?" I heard Jack whisper next to me, concerned. His hand gently gripped my shoulder while his other reached out to brush my hair from my eyes. I shook my head stiffly.

"It's nothing." I saw Aliyah watching me, a stern light in her eyes, and I amended my lie. "It's just my arm. It's nothing." Now, it was a half-lie, a half-truth. Whichever one preferred.

The nausea became nearly overwhelming, and I closed my eyes, sweat beading on my brow as I tightly pressed my lips together and breathed shakily through my nose. I was going to throw up.

"Hey, shrimp, you're not looking so good there."

I shook my head at Marcel's concern, sitting up a little straighter and then resting my forehead against my drawn up knees. I took in several deep, gulping breaths, and Jack smoothed gentle circles against my back.

"Tris, just keep breathing," he whispered, and I sensed rather than saw the people around us shift away. "I'm right here. It's almost over."

"It can't be this easy," I breathed, air wheezing in and out of my lungs. "It can't be this easy."

It's not fair to those who didn't make it if it is.

"It's not," Jack assured me and gently wrapped an arm around me.

The truck came to a rumbling, jerking stop, the rusty brakes screeching beneath us. I listened as the driver's door opened and slammed shut, and suddenly the blinding flashlight was back in our faces. I could faintly see the bouncing points of light behind us as the other trucks approached, and the car bed shook beneath us as Gratner slammed the tail down and beckoned for us to get out.

"Alright, come on. Trip's over." Everyone around us got up at once, and the shorter man held up his hands to halt our movement. "Whoa, easy there." Despite his overall gruffness the whole trip, he seemed kinder now. "Let's do this in an orderly fashion, alright? Front row first, then second, then third, and so on. Come on, let's go."

The first line shakily dismounted from the back of the truck, stumbling as they acclimated to the sensation of standing on still ground once more. The second row followed them. And then the third.

And then it was our turn.

The people behind us grumbled impatiently as I half-dragged and half-carried Jack over to the edge of the bed. The Horsemen quickly dropped to the ground on either side of us, Jayce handing them Jack's chair like a well-oiled machine. Tentatively, eyes watching Jack for any kind of discomfort or protest, Katalin reached forward and grabbed his ankles, gently moving his legs over the seat of his chair and backing away once I'd helped him sit down. Marcel and Aliyah stepped up and took Kat's place, dragging one of Jack's arms over each of their shoulders and sliding their other hands under his legs. I gently squeezed my boyfriend's shoulder.

"On three?"

He didn't count this time. He just nodded at Marcel to show he was ready, and the two women gently lifted him and moved him into his chair, backing away so he could arrange himself. Once he was done, Jack slowly moved away, looking up at me where I hovered uncertainly on the edge of the tailgate. That feeling of anxiety and distress was still tight in my chest.

It can't be this simple. It can't be this easy.

It's just a single step.

"Tris, come on," my boyfriend urged, voice still gentle but with a slight edge. "People are waiting."

I glanced over my shoulder at the crowd of people impatiently waiting to get out of the cramped truck, and Jack moved himself a little closer to me, one hand holding tightly to one of his wheels. The other reached up to me, and I took in a deep breath, leaning forward to grab his hand and let myself drop. My knees knocked against each other, and I stumbled to the side, Jack's hand immediately going to my waist to steady me.

"Hey," he whispered, smiling softly up at me as I looked down at him in the dark. "You okay?"

I grabbed his arm, waiting for the world to balance out again. We were standing in front of the mess hall, and the battered temple of Jupiter glared down at us in the gloom. Its rusted symbol was barely visible beneath the creeping veil of moss and ivy, and I shivered and stepped away from Jack, crossing my arm over my chest to hold onto my stump. People continued to get out of the truck, and I took in an unsteady breath.

There was a dull, fiery light coming from inside the double doors of the mess hall, probably from the candles and gas lanterns they were no doubt using to light its massive interior. The air was frozen around us, and I felt light-headed. I turned around and looked at the Academy grounds, at the absurd normalcy of everything. It was all the same, still standing strong. The only thing that had changed was the landscaping, and even then it was only for the better. The ivy and mosses were flourishing, the undergrowth creeping up the trunks of the trees and tangling in with the bare branches to try and choke them out with their tendrils.

"Tristan," Jack repeated, voice a little louder. "You okay?"

"I think so," I said numbly, turning to look at the mess hall in time to see a familiar, brawny figure step over the threshold, lower half of his face covered in an unfamiliar beard. "Is that Jax?" I heard myself ask before my vision blacked out, and I was falling.

··· ─ ─ ─ ···

I usually woke up slowly. My mind crawled out of that inky black sleep on its own while the rest of me reluctantly followed – hearing, smell, touch. I became aware of my surroundings slowly, and sight was always last.

That wasn't how it worked this time. This time, my eyes opened first, and I blinked rapidly, eyes screwing shut against the blinding brightness of the wall lamps. My head throbbed, and I dragged the back of my hand across my eyes, groaning softly as the rest of me slowly woke up. The glaring lights slowly dimmed to their normal levels, and I turned over to find myself nose to nose with a leather couch cushion.

I recognized this couch. Maybe.

"He's up," a gruff voice announced somewhere to my right.

I twisted onto my side and reached out, grabbing onto the back of the couch and using it to sit up. I felt dizzy, and when I looked up, someone promptly shoved a tin of water in my face. A quick shift of focus showed my boyfriend's anxious eyes behind it.

"What happened?" I asked, awkwardly taking it from him and lifting the cold metal to my lips.

"You fainted," Jack answered, his voice strained. I hummed and looked around for something to set the glass down on. "Here. Let me take that." He reached out and took it from me, and I blinked tiredly.

"Why'd I pass out?" I asked, clearing my throat, and that gruff voice from earlier answered me.

"You were dehydrated, newbie."

Ah. That was why I recognized the couch. I looked around at the dark wood panels and sparse décor. I also recognized the office.

"Sir," I began slowly, looking at Jax. He was sitting behind his oak desk, pouring over papers and flipping through reports. He looked up at me from beneath thick brows and grunted in response. "Why am I in your office?"

"The administration is still working on assigning rooms and registering everyone, and your boyfriend over there is convinced you're a shrinking violet and insisted we get you somewhere quiet," he said, looking back to his papers. "Not sure I agree with the assessment that you're a dainty little thing, but I *did* agree some quiet would be good."

"Thanks, I guess," I yawned. He just waved me off, and I took the cup back from Jack, taking another sip.

"You two can stay in here for the night," he offered, utterly serious. "If I've figured out how to sleep on that couch before, you two will manage."

"Why don't we just go get a room assignment?" I asked, baffled, and looked to Jack for support. But my boyfriend just looked down at his lap, expression carefully neutral.

"The world's gotten a bit angrier since you two left, Byrne," Jax sighed, scribbling his signature on something before moving it to a steadily growing pile at the corner of his desk. "It's going to take a little more planning than a random room assignment to keep you and Miller in one piece."

"I'm not sure I–"

"Homophobes, Tristan," Jack interrupted softly, looking up at me with eyes that said he knew this routine well. "When a war starts going south, the people start to lash out. They find new groups of society to start hating and attacking, people that are a little more within reach than foreign armies."

"Oh," I said softly and absently nodded. "Makes sense…"

"I'm not happy about it either, Byrne," Jax sighed, glancing up at me. "But the admin has started breathing down my neck about watching out for people like you because even though there's no explicit national law against homosexuals, there isn't one protecting you from the states either." He paused as someone knocked and set his pencil down, sighing and looking to the heavy oak door. "Enter." It swung open, and Aliyah walked in, nodding once to Jack and me before presenting our supervising officer with a heavy folder. "Moore. That it?"

"The last of the eastern line prisoners of war have been registered and casualties have been recorded, sir."

He nodded resignedly, taking it from her and flipping open to the first page. She continued to stand at attention, staring down at him impassively as he read. His shoulders sagged in defeat, and he took in a deep breath, pinching the bridge of his nose and letting his elbow slam onto the desk.

"You're dismissed, private."

She nodded curtly and turned on her heel, leaving just as quickly and gracefully as she'd entered. I felt the hair rise on the back of my neck as she caught my gaze, eyes unfathomably dark as she shut the door behind her.

"Sir?" I asked uncertainly, and Jack balanced the tin on his lap, turning his chair so that he could look at Jax without craning his neck. Our supervising officer shook his head and looked up at us, expression worn.

"How many?" Jack asked softly.

I thought back to the nine hundred and eighty of us who had left the Academy two hundred and sixty-seven days ago. Nine hundred and eighty people. Nine hundred and eighty beating hearts and vibrant souls.

"We'd already received final reports back from all the northern and western lines," Jax began, getting to his feet and sitting on the edge of his desk, the folder heavy in his hands. "Your caravan was the last of your class assigned to the eastern lines to come home, but we haven't gotten the rest of you back from the south. The Mezitain are holding on a bit tighter to them – bad blood, you know."

"That's not an answer," my boyfriend pressed, firm but not unkind, and Jax stared levelly at him.

"According to our analysts' reports, our final count will be around one hundred and ninety six."

"Lost?" I whispered pleadingly, voice hoarse and unsteady as my throat went dry and closed up on me. "That's...that's a casualty number, right?"

Jack moved the tin of water off his lap, reaching out to set it shakily on the side table beside the couch I was still seated on. He was as white as a sheet, his eyes wide and seeing things miles away, and the anxiety and denial prowling in my stomach started clawing its way into my throat. Jax looked ragged, ancient as he stared at me with downtrodden eyes.

"One hundred and ninety-six alive."

Jack's hand missed the edge of the table, and the cup toppled noisily to the ground, water spilling across the old floors.

"Shit," he mumbled, responses numb and slow as he backed his wheelchair away.

I stared down at the slowly expanding pool of liquid as it coated the ground in a transparent lacquer, seeping into the cracks between the ancient floorboards. My heart throbbed in my temples. My breath echoed in my ears. I felt like the world around me was closing in, the old walls crushing the breath out of me.

"That's eighty percent," I heard myself say, and Jax's enormous hands were suddenly blocking my view of the floor, using his own jacket to mop up the mess.

"It's fine, Miller," Jax was saying. Neither he nor my boyfriend paid any attention to what I'd just said. "It was just a slip, don't worry about it."

"That's *eighty percent*," I repeated, voice sharper this time as I continued to stare at the floor.

Jax stopped, rocking back onto his heels and holding the soaked fabric in his hands as he looked up at me.

"Yeah. It is," he finally said, standing up and bracing his hands on his knees as he did so, like the joints were causing him pain. Jack's hands tightened until his knuckles were white around his wheels, and our S.O. sighed, draping the wet uniform over his arm. "Welcome to the twenty percent, Byrne." The door opened. "I'll see you two in the morning."

With a hollow, agonizing thump, it closed behind him, leaving Jack and I to sit there in stunned silence. As the quiet dragged on, I suddenly found it harder to breathe.

"Jack," I whispered, panicked, looking up at him with tears in my eyes. "Jack, I–"

"Come here," he said softly, reaching out to me.

I stood up and walked over to him, sitting on his lap and swinging my legs over the arm of his chair. As I rested my head against his shoulder and hid my face in the crook of his neck, he wrapped his arms around me.

"That's...Jack, that's seven hundred and eighty-four dead," I gasped, unable to breathe properly. "Seven hundred and–"

"Don't. Don't think about the numbers, Tris," Jack said softly, cutting me off. I turned into him, unpinning my arm from between us and looping it around his neck. "That's it...just let it all go," he whispered.

I pulled myself tight against him, closing my eyes and gently kissing his exposed skin. I felt Jack's arms tighten protectively around me like that one small gesture could change everything.

Welcome to the twenty percent.

"I don't want to be part of the twenty percent," I whispered shakily, and Jack looked down at me with a sympathetic, pained expression.

"Would you rather be part of the eighty?" he murmured, and my heart skipped a beat as my response didn't come as readily as I thought it would.

"No," I finally answered, voice hushed, and shook my head. "*No*. No, I don't want to be a part of *any* percentage."

I rested my head against his shoulder and let my eyes slide closed as I thought about all the cadets who'd been crammed into the Hall almost nine months ago. Nine hundred and eighty people. *Seven hundred and eighty-four* of whom I'd never see again. I thought about my platoon, my exercises. Was there anyone left besides me and Jack? Besides Aliyah, Katalin, Marcel, and Jayce? Despite Jack's warning, my mind started running the numbers, doing the math. Thirty-five people in my platoon. Eighty percent of thirty-five…

Seven.

Only seven of us hypothetically left. Jack, the others, and I made six, and I briefly wondered who the seventh was before I remembered. Irina. Irina had been our seventh survivor until the gangrene took her.

"Let's lie down," Jack's voice rumbled beneath my ear. I reluctantly got to my feet, waiting for Jack to get close to the couch before I helped him move. We went through our routine in silence.

"Back, side, or stomach?" I asked once his back was braced against the arm of the couch, but he waved me away.

"I'll just lie down on my back, it's fine," he sighed, rubbing at his tired eyes. "C'mon." He lifted his legs onto the cushions and winced as his shoes streaked the leather.

"Here." I sat down beside him and slowly picked at the laces, working them loose and awkwardly pinning his legs beneath mine so I could pull the boot off. "You okay with me getting the other one, too? I just figured your balance would be off."

"Yeah, of course." There was no discomfort in his voice, no defensiveness like there usually was.

I smiled half-heartedly at him as I set to work on his left foot. Soon, the second boot had joined its twin on the ground beside us, and I started to work on my own shoes. My boyfriend tapped the back of the couch to get my attention.

"Hey." He motioned for me to kick my legs up to him. "You helped me, now I help you." I followed his instructions, and he easily removed my boots, dropping them to the ground with surprisingly loud thuds. "Alright, help me lay down without hitting my head on this damn couch."

I offered him my hand and leaned back as he grabbed onto my wrist, pulling him down the couch so his head would clear the arm of the chair. Once we reached that point, I leaned forward slowly, letting gravity take its course and easing him down onto his back.

He sighed and closed his eyes as soon as his head rested against the stiff upholstery. I smiled softly at the brief moment of peace that flickered over his face, my expression invisible to him, before getting up and turning down the gas lamps bolted to the walls. Soon, the room was bathed in dull warmth instead of blinding light. I walked back over to where my boyfriend was lying down and slowly straddled his legs, frowning as I tried to think through how I was going to lie down without just falling on top of him. I hadn't gotten anywhere before Jack cracked an eye open and reached out to my right shoulder, gently grabbing the joint.

"Come on. I would actually like to sleep at some point."

His words were teasing, yet tender, and I braced my left arm against the cushion just beside his head and slowly let myself sink down on top of him. Jack's own arm acted like my absent limb until I was resting against him, my head heavy on his chest. I counted the metronomic beats of his heart, the five pulses per breath beneath my ear, and threaded my arm under his back, palm up so my fingers could curve along his bones. I sighed contently, and his arms came up around me, hands lazily crossing over each other near the small of my back.

"I love you, Jack," I whispered and shivered as I recalled the harrowing circumstances of the last time I'd said those words. His hands moved a little higher on my back and stilled just under the hollows of my shoulder blades.

"I love you, too."

I inched forward and angled my head so I could lightly kiss his cheek before lying down again and falling still. As we lay there in the half-light of Jax's office, feeling the other breathe each time our bodies pressed against each other as our lungs expanded, I realized I wasn't tired. I'd slept for long enough, and I tightened my half-embrace a little more. I could tell from Jack's breathing pattern that he wasn't feeling drowsy either, and I knew if I looked up at him he'd be wide awake. The anxieties that had been plaguing my mind on the drive here suddenly started to manifest once more, taking truly terrifying forms.

"Where do we go from here?" I suddenly asked, propping myself up a little lopsidedly to look down at Jack. He frowned up at me.

"What do you mean?"

"You and me," I elaborated. "Where do we go?"

"Well, we decided on Calin, didn't we?" he asked, clearly a little lost as to what was going on. "And we're staying together…aren't we?" There was a sudden burr of fear in his voice, and I quickly nodded.

"Yeah, 'course. But what then?" I asked, voice a little unsteady. "What do we do after that? Jack, *look at us*. What the hell do I do after this? Where can we go where we won't have to hide, where we won't have to constantly look over our shoulders?"

I felt his heart start to race beneath me, and he reached up to me, hands gently cupping my face.

"Tristan, where's this coming from?"

"I don't know," I finally admitted with a nervous, breathy laugh, and shifted anxiously above him. He gently pulled me back down to lie against him again, one hand behind my neck and his other arm around my waist. And I realized something in the silence that followed. "You didn't answer me."

He took in a deep breath, and the hand on the back of my neck reached up to gently hold the back of my head.

"I wish I could," he sighed. I closed my eyes, taking deep, controlled breaths. "I don't know what we do next, Tris. All of this…it's all I've ever done for the last…gods, how long has it been? Almost eight years?" I felt something flip sickeningly in my stomach as his fingers started tapping out the years against my back. "Four years at the Academy the first time, three years fighting, one year back at school…gods, it'll be nine years in a few months." We were quiet, digesting the news in shocked silence. "*Nine years*. Gods," he repeated and then looked at me, eyes wide. "You turned twenty-two in the trenches."

I blinked, suitably startled, and tried to think of something to say.

"H-huh," I finally stammered, clearing my throat and pulling my arm out from under him. "I guess I did…" I pushed myself up so I was sitting back on Jack's legs and clumsily got to my feet, walking over to Jax's desk and searching through the chaotic mess for a calendar.

"What are you looking for?" I heard Jack ask, and I finally found one, yanking it out from beneath an improvised bookend made out of a warped artillery shell. I quickly looked at the month, scanning the crossed out days until I came to today's date. I slowly set it down. "Tristan?"

"I guess we both forgot things," I mumbled, and Jack lifted his head up off the couch, forcing his elbows beneath himself so he could sit up a little. "Your twenty-sixth birthday was two weeks ago."

"Really?"

I felt angry all of a sudden, disappointed in myself.

"Yep. Happy belated birthday, I guess," I offered weakly, walking back over to him and sitting down in his chair.

"We had other things going on, Tris," he said gently, but I scoffed and shook my head.

"You had an excuse. For my birthday, we were in the trenches trying not to get our heads blown off. Two weeks ago..." I stopped and shrugged half-heartedly. "I don't know. I just hoped that I'd remember something like that. Regardless of what was going on."

Jack gave me a pitying yet loving look before settling back down on the couch.

"Come on." He patted the sofa. "Consider it a belated birthday present. I want to be able to fall asleep with my boyfriend without people disturbing us."

"I wouldn't count too heavily on that happening," I said wryly, but Jack just shrugged, the movement awkward given his reclined position.

"It's *Jax's* office. Anyone with even half a brain wouldn't come in here without his express permission."

"Fair point," I said softly and smiled before standing and climbing onto the couch with him, lying down until we were back in our original positions. We were silent again, waiting as the world continued around us, and I felt Jack take in a deeper breath than normal, clearing his throat.

"Tristan," he began, and I looked up at him, taking in his furrowed brow and tightly pressed lips.

"What's wrong?"

He looked at me, eyes softening at my concern, and gently rested his hand on my head. There was something reverentially tender to the gesture, and he looked up at the ceiling above us with tearful eyes. His answer was whispered, quiet and raw.

"Thank you for saving my life."

I felt my whole body go still at those words, that shaking confession. I tightened my one-armed embrace around my boyfriend ever so slightly and turned my head into his neck a little more.

"You're welcome."

We didn't say anything else that night.

The twenty percent, like the eighty, were silent.

...———...

I woke into that bleary, confusing in-between of sleep and consciousness at some early hour of the morning, unaware that I'd ever fallen asleep in the first place. The wall lamp had been turned off long ago, but the black sky beyond the barred windows overlooking the Academy was tinted with a barely perceptible mist of color.

So, I was at a bit of a loss as to what had woken me up until I saw a tall, broad-shouldered silhouette moving towards me and Jack in the dark. Panic surged through my chest, and I struggled to get up, mind running on automatic. But the shadow quickly shushed me.

"Easy, newbie. It's just me." The fear sluggishly faded, and I lay down against Jack once more, drowsiness quickly returning as the man draped a rough woolen blanket over us. Jack hadn't stirred. I felt the heavy warmth of my S.O.'s hand on my shoulder. "Rest easy, boys."

He straightened and moved back to his desk. He sat down and lit the gas lamp, but the light was so low I could barely see the flame. With a heavy sigh, he went back to work, typing condolence letter after condolence letter on his typewriter and signing his name off on the bottom as he added up the dead. Despite the noise, I slowly drifted back to sleep.

I'd learned to fall asleep listening to much worse.

...———...

"I do, in fact, need to get some work done in here." I cracked open an eye to be greeted with a sunlight-filled room and a drill sergeant smirking at me in amusement even though he looked like he hadn't slept in a hundred years. "Important meetings with important people, you know how it goes."

"What time is it?" I asked groggily, sitting up, and Jack quickly opened his eyes as I moved on top of him.

"About a quarter to ten."

I awkwardly crawled off of Jack, my boyfriend grunting as I accidentally kneed him in the stomach.

"Sorry," I yawned, but Jack just waved me off, slowly propping himself up on his elbows.

"We'll get out of here. Is the mess hall still the mess hall?" he asked, and Jax hesitated.

"Most of it is. The twenty feet in front of that stained glass window has been turned back into a church, though. They've got an altar, incense, and everything." I made an interested noise in the back of my throat as I helped Jack into his chair. "But the rest of it is still set up the way it was when you two were here."

"Thanks for letting us sleep here," Jack said, but he waved us off.

"It was nothing. By the way, I got your housing figured out while you were sleeping. North Hall, room nine. The Jones siblings will have room seven next door. Moore and Soto will have eight across the hall from you. I already put your footlockers in your quarters."

"Thank you." The sir died in my throat when I remembered his request in the trenches, and Jack and I put our shoes on, my boyfriend helping me with my laces.

"You two have a whole system down, don't you," Jax said dryly from his desk. Jack nodded as we headed towards the door, responding to the man over his shoulder.

"We've had some practice."

... — — ...

The mess hall was…different.

In my head, I could still hear the faint music of Promenade, could see the faces of people no longer here, and the room briefly came to life again with familiar colors and smells. Then, I was brought back down to reality, to the barrenness of the walls and the musty smell that hung in the air.

The benches and tables were closer together, cramped into the part of the building closest to the door. Despite the proximity, they were crammed with people, and as I looked around, I realized that they weren't just cadets. There were older people, children, and a handful of men and women who were probably in their mid thirties and forties. They reminded me of the farmers we'd passed on our way to the front line, and I thought back to the people we'd seen moving into the Ruins.

"Refugees," Jack said softly, confirming my suspicions as we joined the long line for food. "They can't live off their land anymore, and the raiders are getting more and more violent. They come here or go to cities, though most of those were on the borders, so now…"

"They're long gone," I finished, and he nodded. It took us about ten minutes to get to the front of the line, and I looked in surprise at the lady about to serve me my food. "Enid."

She looked up at my voice, just as surprised as I was. We stared at each other blankly for a few moments, trying to figure out what to say, and I saw my boyfriend laughing at us out of the corner of my eye, a hand covertly covering his mouth. Just when the silence was starting to get uncomfortably long, I knew exactly what to say.

"So, how was your night?" I asked, voice perfectly innocent.

Enid *laughed*, shaking her head and rolling her eyes as she whacked her serving spoon on the edge of the bowl and handed the oatmeal to me.

"None of your business, you little runt." This time, I wasn't imagining the grin on her face. "Now, get out of here."

I gave her a small smile before I left the line and walked over to one of the tables, moving to the end so Jack could sit his chair at the head. A few people stared at us as we went, but not many. As we sat down I looked a little closer at the prayer area.

There were probably fifteen people kneeling on the stone floors, heads bowed while an elderly matron guided them in a prayer. I couldn't hear her over the noise of the people eating, but apparently the service-goers could. Most of them were refugees, but I saw a few troops among them. I noted with interest that there were no cadets. Behind the matron was the altar Jax had been talking about. It used to be the podium, but now it was draped in a red blanket – decorated with candles of different sizes and colors, flowers, and garlands of grasses decorated with weed blossoms. A whole array of photographs and personal memorabilia covered the ground around it, and I realized it was a memorial. I suddenly felt like I was intruding and looked around at the other people in the room.

Very quickly I started feeling uneasy. Most of them were cadets, and their expressions were sullen, fingers drumming out intense, wired beats on the tables. Their shoulders were stiff and hunched, legs bouncing anxiously. Their eyes were shifty, nearly glaring at every private who passed them, and I saw a few mutter darkly to each other as Marcel and Katalin walked by.

"What is their problem?" I asked lowly, and Jack followed my gaze to the three cadets scowling at our friends.

"They blame us," he said around a mouthful of food. "To them, we lost the war. Not to mention the fact that Kat's full Mezitain and Marcel's half."

"Us?" I asked in disbelief. "They're blaming *us* for that?"

Jack nodded with a sigh, and I scowled at my food.

"They've spent at least the last year training for war, Tristan. Some of them the last four," Jack explained softly. "They've been raised in a world with nothing but war, and now that their time's come to actually contribute, to do something, it's over. We were the last class of the Academy." He took another bite of food, chewing slowly before swallowing. "In their eyes, we let them down. Now, they've got all that anger, frustration, and hate, and nowhere for it to go except inwards. Anyone who's not 'normal,' who's not born and bred Amaeric is gonna have to watch their backs."

I felt an icy shudder run down my spine, and I turned around to see a boy and girl probably nineteen years old glaring viciously at us. As I looked at them, they leaned a little closer and started whispering to each other.

"This place is gonna implode," Jack finished, spoon scraping along the bottom of his bowl, and I looked at my mostly untouched meal. "And it's gonna get ugly."

As soon as he finished speaking, there was a loud clatter near the door accompanied almost immediately by expletive-laden shouting. We turned to see two cadets at each other's throats – one had his fists clenched in her hair while the other raked her nails down his face, leaving bloody tracks down his cheek. My heart jumped into my throat as Marcel stepped in and shoved the two apart with brutal force.

"Hey! Knock it off!" she bellowed, and the girl started forward again. "I said stop it!" War body slammed her hard, and the girl practically flew back, tripping over a bench and crashing to the ground. "I didn't just come back from nine months of fighting to have to deal with this shit, knock it off!"

The younger girl glowered at her new opponent, ignoring her original target as she wiped blood from her mouth.

"I'll get you for that, bitch," she snarled before scrambling to her feet and storming out the door.

Jack scoffed lightly and pushed his empty bowl away as Marcel looked around in annoyed disbelief, hands on her hips.

"Told you."

. . . ─ ─ ─ . . .

Jack's words were still playing over in my head as I walked along the Academy grounds. I wasn't sure where I was going, didn't have a direction or a purpose. I just needed to walk around somewhere that wasn't a trench or enclosed by barbed wire and cemeteries, and I found myself moving further out towards the stables. The horses weren't used anymore so the only people who came out this far were usually caretakers in the mornings and evenings. Since it was about four in the afternoon, I was alone.

The sun was warm on my back despite the chill in the air, and I took in a deep breath, blinking a little drowsily as I neared the stable. I considered going inside but decided against it. Instead, I just sat down on top of the feed barrel beside the open door, head resting against the paneled wall as I listened to the animals inside shuffle around.

I wasn't alone for long.

I saw three Academy cadets heading towards me down the road, and I recognized two of them as the boy and girl who'd been glaring at me in the mess hall. The third was older, probably a fourth-year, and I nodded to them once they were about ten feet away. They just stared at me, and I took in a deep breath.

This felt wrong. I watched the strangers out of the corner of my eye as they wandered a little inside the stable and listened to the low rumble of their voices. All the warning bells were going off in my head, and I cleared my throat, sitting up a little straighter as the fourth-year walked out towards me.

"Hey." I gave him a mute, closed mouth smile. "You just get back?"

"Yeah," I answered hesitantly and eyed him cautiously.

"Eastern front line, right?"

"You know, I should get going," I said apologetically, chest tightening with fear. I quickly got up and tried to move past him, but he just laughed, a dangerously cold sound, and stopped me with a hand to the chest.

"Come on, what're you afraid of?"

"Nothing, I just realized I'm late meeting someone," I lied, mouth dry, and the two second-years sauntered out of the stable. The boy had a hoof pick in his hand.

"Aw, is it your boyfriend?" the fourth-year asked, voice drawling, and I stepped back from them, heart pounding in my chest. "Maybe we'll pay him a visit when we're done with you."

"Touch him, and I'll fucking kill y–"

He punched me in the mouth, cutting off my threat, and I crashed into the feed barrel, knocking it over.

"Did you just *threaten* me?" he demanded in angry disbelief. I looked up at him through watering eyes as the other two started closing in. "Are you fucking kid – a *shag* threatening *me?*"

I scrambled backwards, stumbling to my feet and looking around for something to defend myself with. There was nothing, just a pile of hay bales that the three people were slowly backing me towards, and before I knew it, my back slammed into the scratchy grass. I was trapped in the angle of the hay and the wall, and my breath turned shaky as I eyed the metal hook in the second-year's hand. My mouth tasted like blood and fear, and I was torn between cowering and fighting as he passed it off to the fourth-year.

"Maybe I'll carve his name into you once we're do—"

There was a loud, sickening clang, and the man pitched forward, dead unconscious. The makeshift weapon clattered harmlessly across the ground. I looked up on the verge of a complete breakdown to see Marcel, legs braced and shovel clenched in her hands like a baseball bat. I saw dark hair stuck in bloody clumps to the riveted shoulder, and I looked back down at the prone cadet. The back of his head had been gashed open.

"Get away from him," she snarled, voice a menacing growl.

"What did you *do*—" the girl began.

"I said get away!" Marcel's expression was feral, eyes blazing, and the two second-years slowly backed away with hands at their shoulders, shaking with fury. "Byrne, you okay?" she asked, gaze flickering to me briefly before returning to the cadets, and I nodded. "Get over here." I quickly stumbled behind her, carefully avoiding the shovel, and she turned her attention fully to the others.

"You stay away!" she warned, shifting her grip on the tool and holding it in front of us like a boar spear. "Because next time, I spill your brains!"

Slowly, she started backing away, the cadets quickly kneeling by their friend and glaring murderously up at us. Subconsciously, I grabbed Marcel's arm with trembling hands, using her to hold my shaking body steady as we quickly retreated. Once we were near the main road, the shovel clattered to the dirt, and we ran.

· · · − − · · ·

"What were you thinking?" she panted as we ran into North Hall and finally slowed our pace to a staggering walk. She stopped, roughly turning me to face her. "They could have killed you, what were you *thinking?!*"

I couldn't answer. I couldn't really think about anything – I was still too shaken and scared, struggling to process what had almost happened. Finally, she seemed to notice, and Marcel sighed, gently grabbing my shoulders and looking at me sternly.

"You can't go wandering off alone, shrimp," she said, voice hard in its fear but still kind. "Okay?" I nodded mutely, still shaking, and she roughly put an arm around my shoulders, keeping me close as she walked me to my room. "Come on. You've got some stuff to tell Miller."

...———...

I was sitting numbly on our bed when Jack came in, opening the door and talking almost immediately.

"Hey, I saw Blackwell as he was leaving, and guess what? He's got us set up with some physical therapist named Dr. Simmons..." He trailed off as he saw Marcel standing in the corner of the room, expression grim and arms tightly crossed. "What happened?"

I looked up, mouth still slightly bloody and lips a little cut and swollen, and Jack went white.

I softly started to explain what happened, and the door shut with a soft click.

...———...

That night, Jack and I lay in bed with our arms wrapped tightly around each other. All I could do was stare at the familiar lock on our unfamiliar door. My heart was still racing five hours after the attack, and I pressed my head against Jack's chest.

"We go nowhere alone. Okay?" he said softly, and I nodded, tightening my hold on him even more.

Right here, we were safe.

DAY TWO HUNDRED AND SEVENTY-THREE

Six days later

After the incident with the cadets, Jack and I had taken to waiting for each other outside our PT sessions. If possible, either one of the Horsemen or Jayce walked with us, but sometimes they were busy or we couldn't find them. On those days, Jack and I just kept our heads down and returned to our room as non-conspicuously as possible.

Today was one of those days.

I sighed as I left Dr. Simmons' office, opening and closing my left hand to try and relieve the painful cramping. I was greeted by Jack and an otherwise empty hallway.

"How'd it go?" he asked, and I shrugged.

"I can sort of form letters now. It looks like a kid's handwriting, but it's something," I answered sullenly. "How about you?"

"Alright. Mostly it was just making sure that my core muscles stay in good shape. Or as good as they can be." He looked once down each end of the hallway. "Come on, we should get going."

We quickly crossed the small section of the Academy grounds in about five minutes, and I helped Jack get over the rugged threshold of North Hall and into our hallway. So far, no one had stopped to bother us, but as we neared the corner to our room, I heard a strange, coarse noise. It sounded like something rough being quickly dragged back and forth across wood.

"Do you hear that?" I asked. Jack nodded, brow furrowed in confusion. "What is that?"

"No idea," he said slowly, half-paying attention.

We rounded the corner to see the Horsemen and Jayce huddled around our door, and Jack and I frowned quizzically at each other. I loudly cleared my throat.

Our four friends looked around at us, simultaneously guilty, apologetic, and even a little fearful. As we drew closer, I saw the red-stained brushes in their hands and the soapy bucket at their feet. I was about to ask what was going on when my boyfriend and I saw the door. Jack sighed heavily, easing himself to a stop, and Jayce and the Horsemen looked down at their feet, red hands picking at the stained wood and coarse bristles of their brushes.

The word *shags* had been written across our bedroom door in red paint, the slopes of the letters ragged and vicious, and despite our friends' attempt to wash it off before we got back, it was still legible beneath the watery haze of color. As Jack and I stood there quietly, unsure of what to do or say but unsurprised at what had happened, Katalin sniffed once, expression fragile, and dunked her brush into the bucket before scrubbing at the wood once more.

"We'll clean it up," I heard her say softly. I noticed that her knuckles were a little scraped. "You can stay in our room while we're working."

"Thanks, Kat," I said softly, and Jack reached out to gently pat her on the arm, nodding his appreciation to the other three as we retreated to the relative safety of Katalin and Aliyah's room.

It took them three hours, but they finally got it out.

DAY TWO HUNDRED AND SEVENTY-FOUR

It wasn't even ten in the morning yet, and a new story was already spreading through the Academy like wildfire. Apparently, one of the field nurses from the eastern front line had been attacked, beaten to a bloody pulp, and left unconscious behind the mess hall. Some private had found her and taken her to the infirmary, and it wasn't clear yet if she was dead or alive. No one had seen the attack, or so they said, but I couldn't shake the feeling that the assholes who'd cornered me were behind it. The Academy had become a toxic place, filled with angry, warmongering people who wanted nothing more than to hurt to someone – anything to vent their hate and frustration.

I knew my feeling was right when I heard a man in the quad proclaim loudly that apparently the nurse was "another one of those fucking shags." I looked at Aliyah, terrified, and she quickly got up, arm protectively circling my shoulders as we walked back to my room. Jack was already there with Jayce and Marcel, and as I walked through the door, my boyfriend looked at me with sad eyes.

"I was the one who found her," Jayce whispered, staring at his bloody hands with haunted eyes as Katalin came in behind me and closed the door. "She – gods, she looked horrible…I thought she was dead."

I sat on the bed next to Jack and took his hand in mine, watching Jayce as Marcel rubbed her brother's tense shoulders.

"Is she alive?" I asked quietly, and Jayce nodded.

"It's not good though," he mumbled, running his hands over his face. "The doctor said she's in a coma. He doesn't know if she'll wake up."

"You did the best you could, Jayce," Jack said softly. The man nodded, slumping down in his chair with tears in his eyes. "Jayce, look at me." He slowly looked up at my boyfriend. "You *did*. Okay?"

"I know." His voice was a hoarse whisper. "I know."

I went to go see her that night, Kat accompanying me to stand guard. And as I sat at her bedside, looking into her battered face and holding her splinted hand, my suspicions were confirmed.

It was Samantha.

DAY TWO HUNDRED AND SEVENTY-SIX

Two days later

Jack was in the middle of his session with Dr. Simmons when the main door of the building burst open with a resounding bang, knob chipping the wall. Jayce stumbled inside a split second behind it, eyes wide and breathing heavy, and I immediately stood up from where I'd been seated against the wall. As soon as he saw me, he ran over, and I realized I'd never seen this kind of fear on his face before.

"Jayce, what's—"

"Kat," he gasped, coming to a staggering halt. "Katalin, she – she got jumped." He gestured urgently behind him towards the door and struggled to catch his breath. "Infirmary."

I cut Jack's session short.

... — — ...

Katalin could have looked a lot worse.

She had a black eye, split lip, and broken nose as well as a few cracked ribs, but she was conscious with all her appendages and fingers intact. We'd have to stay with her overnight to monitor her concussion, but other than that she was gonna be fine.

"Did you see their faces?" Marcel asked, sitting by her friend's side on the mattress.

"Yeah, I did." Her voice was sharp and wobbly. "But I can't remember them very well. I was kind of busy." Bruises mottled her skin beneath the collar of her uniform shirt, and her breathing shook as much as her words.

"How many were—"

"Four, okay? There were four of them!" Katalin snapped and looked down, taking a shaky breath. She lifted her scratched hands to her face and ground her palms into her eyes. "What does it matter?!"

"I'm sorry," Marcel whispered. "I didn't...I'm sorry."

"They jumped me by the stables," Kat continued after a little bit, voice shaky and subdued. She kept her focus on the sheets under her, picking at the loose threads. "Kept calling me a dirty Mezitain and a fucking spy and a camp rat. One of them tried to pull me down by my hair, but I've been able to get out of that one since I was nine." Her eyes glistened with tears about to fall, and she clenched her teeth. "I shattered one guy's hand. Broke the other's nose. Dislocated the third guy's shoulder."

"Well, that should be enough to find them, they'll have to get treated—"

"I don't *want* to find them, Marcel! I just want to forget about it!" Kat shouted, and Aliyah quickly stepped forward and put a calming hand on her roommate's shoulder. "I could have been *her!*"

My heart broke as we all followed her shaking hand to Samantha's still unresponsive body. Her bruises had turned dark, nasty blues and purples, and her skin was swollen and scabbed between the many bandages, casts, and splints. The IV in her arm was the only thing sustaining her.

"I could have been her," Katalin repeated brokenly, and Jack moved his chair close enough to her bedside that he could reach over and gently hold her hand as she started crying.

"Come on, Kat," he said softly, and she looked up at him, complexion flushed. He smiled gently. "Let's get you back to your room. Tristan knows how to patch you up."

"Yep," I confirmed, forcing my voice to be light. "I've got the stuff in my room. It's old-school poultice shit, but it gets the job done."

She nodded jerkily, and I stepped forward with Jayce to help her out of bed. As soon as her feet were under her, we both backed off to let Marcel and Aliyah take over. I knew how stiff bodies could get after a solid beating.

... — — ...

Fifteen minutes later, we were back in Jack's and my room, Katalin seated on the bed as I pulled all the supplies out of my trunk and laid them all out on the mattress. As I worked, Kat cleared her throat.

"Could you guys step outside?" she asked softly.

"Oh, I was just gonna talk Aliyah through how to do this and have her put it all on," I began, but she cut me off.

"No, I…it's fine." She looked up at everyone. "Could you…"

"Of course," Aliyah said kindly. Jack led everyone out into the hallway, Moore exiting last and closing the door behind her.

The room was awkwardly quiet for a few seconds before, with a pained breath, Famine gingerly reached up and started unbuttoning her shirt. I immediately grimaced. The bruise I'd glimpsed in the infirmary branched across the inside of her left shoulder, massive and purple. I got up and knelt behind her on the bed, helping her ease off the shirt. Her back was covered in large splotchy bruises like the one on her chest, and there was some dried blood on her back from where the hook of her bra had torn into her skin. I moved back in front of her and saw that her sides and stomach bore the same splotchy bruises.

"They kicked you, didn't they?" I asked, and she nodded. "Okay. Let's get you taken care of." I handed her the canteen, and she looked at me in a little confusion. "I need you to put some of the cream on my hand for me."

She gave a soft "oh" of realization, and the rest of the time passed in silence, save for the occasional hiss of pain as I touched the worst of her bruises. She helped me with the bandages as well, holding the end in place while I wrapped it around her body.

"Your mom…she was a nurse, right?" she asked quietly. I looked up in surprise. I never spoke about my parents, let alone thought about them.

"Yeah."

"Must run in the family," she said with a small, bruised smile.

"Yeah," I repeated softly as I looked back to my work. "It must."

By the time we were done, her shoulder and abdomen were completely wrapped in bandages.

"Okay, you're set," I said lightly, handing her back her shirt.

"I'm sorry," she blurted suddenly, twisting the fabric in her hands, and I blinked at her in confusion.

"For what? This wasn't your fault—"

"We used to do this to you. To Miller," she whispered, tears filling her eyes again, and she took in a shuddering breath. "I'm sorry. I'm so sorry."

Before I could think of anything to say, she started crying. I hesitantly let my hand rest on her back, her abused skin hot to the touch. And as we sat there, I realized there was nothing to say.

All I could do was let her cry.

DAY TWO HUNDRED AND SEVENTY-SEVEN

It was around eleven at night when Jack and I were startled awake by a loud bang. It was quickly followed by voices screaming and the sounds of furniture and bodies crashing around, and it took us a few seconds to place where the racket was coming from. When I did, my heart stopped.

Next door. Marcel and Jayce's room.

"No!" I heard a voice shout, followed by a scream that made my blood run cold.

Jayce.

I vaulted out of bed and, ignoring Jack's calls for me to wait, threw open our bedroom door just in time to see Aliyah sprint from her room to the one next to ours. I caught a glimpse of something long in her hand and after a few seconds heard three loud, sickening cracks followed by pained screams. I heard more doors opening and looked over my shoulder as four overseers sprinted from their rooms at the end of the hall and tore past me.

"What the hell is going on in here?" I heard one of them shout. Jayce's voice was hoarse as he yelled back.

"Those fuckers broke in here and attacked me and my sister!"

"You broke my leg, you bitch!" a voice howled, and I walked over to the open doorway, looking inside.

The room was completely trashed. The two chairs were thrown across the room. The dresser had been pulled out of its corner and turned on its side. Two strangers lay in pain on the ground at the foot of the bed, one of them holding his bloodied kneecaps and groaning while the other grabbed at his thigh, the limb bent at an odd angle like something was trying to tear through the skin. Aliyah stood barefooted between them and the Joneses, bloodied crowbar held at the ready and expression murderous. The white bed sheets were torn half off the bed, and I followed them down to where Marcel was pressing the corner against her brother's leg. In the moonlight, I caught sight of a discarded, bloody knife on the floorboards, and I felt sick as I looked at Marcel's face, at the fear as she held onto her brother and tried to slow the bleeding from his thigh.

"Alright, come on. We're taking you two to Jax," one of our overseers scowled.

"Fucking Mezitain half-breed!" Broken Femur spat, voice high with pain as two overseers grabbed him and hauled him to his feet. The other two grabbed Broken Kneecaps. "Shag-loving spies!"

As they were being taken from the room, Kneecaps caught sight of me and snarled. I took a step back, heart pounding.

"We're coming for you next, you fucking shag!"

"Shut up, Lucas," one man carrying him barked while the other rolled his eyes. "You're in enough trouble as it is!"

As soon as they were gone, Aliyah dropped the crowbar.

"Jayce, you okay?" Marcel whispered frantically, smoothing his wavy hair back from his forehead. "Jayce?"

He nodded, teeth gritting painfully and groaning as Aliyah quickly tore off part of the bedding and tied it off around his leg.

"Yeah. Yeah. I'm fine…"

I looked over my shoulder and saw Katalin standing in the doorway to her room, a little on the pale side beneath her bruises with a knife clenched in her hand.

"I'm fine."

DAY TWO HUNDRED AND EIGHTY-ONE

Four days later

Today was...complicated.

Almost two weeks ago, Jax had sent out letters and telegrams to the families of the people in my graduating class. One hundred and ninety-six of them got good news. One hundred and ninety-six of them received today's date to pick up their kids.

Seven hundred and eighty-four got condolence letters. Seven hundred and eighty-four families were told that their sons and daughters, their nieces and nephews, their granddaughters and grandsons weren't coming home. They never would be. Jack had brought his dog tag collection to Jax and helped him sort through the ones they had to pair them with a condolence letter and recruitment photograph that the Academy had on file from each soldier's first year.

Some of the names had no families on record. Others had family in areas that had since fallen to foreign control or had been wiped out to the best of our knowledge. Some lucky, or unlucky, families were among the refugees who'd been brought in, and Jax gave them the news personally. There were a couple times I'd hear wailing coming from his office, and my heart broke as I thought about what was happening behind that heavy door.

At the end of the day, Jack had seven tags that remained unclaimed. Two of them were because there was no family on record. Five of them were because their towns had since fallen to foreign armies. He told me that those five families might show up anyways within the next few weeks or so. At our time of graduation, the Academy had sent letters to our families with a tentative date for pick-up. The letters that Jax had just sent last week gave them the new date.

Irina Korsakov had a valid address on record.

When I said that was a silver lining, Jack hesitated. He told me that some families showed up anyways, especially if their child's dog tags weren't enclosed, because they were convinced that someone made a mistake. Their child wasn't dead, they were just missed in registration. Someone in records screwed up and accidentally marked their child as deceased instead of alive. Their kid's name got put in the wrong list for whoever was writing the letters, but really they were actually alive. It was just a mistake.

He said those were always the hardest. Those and the ones where the kids made it back, but their families didn't.

I asked him if he'd ever seen a family told their kid was alive when they were actually dead. Mercifully, he said no.

... — ...

Jack and I were in the mess hall, picking slowly at the bland oatmeal that had been served for breakfast for the last week. As usual, the room was packed to the rafters, and I thought back to when I'd thought mess during school was crowded. These days, we had staff, students, returning soldiers, refugees, military officials and workers from other regions of Amaeric all crammed in here. It seemed like everyone who could possibly be in the area was represented in this room in some way shape or form.

"Do you think your family will come?" I asked, and Jack sighed, wearily closing his eyes and dropping his spoon into his bowl.

"Gods, I hope not," he groaned, massaging his temples as if the very idea gave him a migraine. "I really don't need to see them right now, I've got enough on my plate as it is."

I quickly shook my head.

"Not do you *want* them to come. Do you *think* they'll come?"

Jack paused, mulling it over, but after a few moments of silence, something darkened in his eyes, and he quickly snatched up his spoon.

"No." There was a click as the metal utensil stabbed through the grain and struck the bottom of the tin bowl. "They won't."

I could tell that whatever he'd remembered had upset him, weighing down on him like a heavy cloud, and I quickly tried to lighten the mood.

"Well, if my parents came, I'd definitely have a bigger migraine than you would if yours came."

Jack's spoon stopped halfway to his mouth, and he slowly looked up at me, a long-suffering expression on his face.

"Tristan. Your parents are *dead*. They've been dead since you were, like, five."

"Exactly." Jack groaned and let his spoon drop down again. "If they showed up it would be a whole undead situation and—"

"Please stop," he moaned from behind his hands, but I could hear the unwilling smile in his voice. "This shit was funny when Harris was here, but now it's just sad."

Success.

"I'm wounded," I teased back, expression still neutral, and Jack looked up at me, a strange sort of sad half-smile on his face. I slowly grew serious. "What?"

"Windows to the past, huh?" he said softly, still smiling wistfully, and went back to his breakfast. Unseen by anybody, I smiled slightly to myself, letting my gaze slide to the left to where Andy and Id would have been sitting before I went back to eating.

"Do you know if the others will see their families today?" I asked with a mouthful of food. "Or at least whether or not they had letters sent out?"

Jack nodded and finished swallowing before answering.

"Yeah. Jayce and Marcel had a letter sent out, so did Aliyah. But Kat's family was probably just released from the camps at some point in the last couple months, so we have no idea where they are."

"Damn," I sighed, stirring my food around. "She could really use some family right now."

"We all could." I gently nudged his wheelchair with my foot.

"Well, you've got me. And I've got you."

Jack smiled and nodded, pushing his plate to the side.

"That I do." He yawned, stretching his hands over his head. "Alright. Let's head out. We're supposed to meet the girls and Jayce in the quad for pick-up."

I stacked our dishes and carried them over to Enid, nodding to her as she quickly took them from me and scraped the uneaten food back into the pot with everything else. Waste not. It was still disgusting, but it was better than eating cat or rat.

I jogged over to Jack's side, falling into step with him as we headed out the doors and down the wooden ramp. The walk to the other side of the

Academy was quiet, save for the bustle of people getting ready to go home, and for once I didn't feel as anxious crossing the grounds. Pretty soon we crossed into the quad, and Jack immediately scoped out Jayce. The man was perched on top of one of the tables, Marcel sitting next to him on one of the benches instead. Katalin was next to her, and Aliyah was on the bench opposite them behind War's brother. His hand rested on his injured leg, gently massaging the skin around the wound.

"Survived feeding time?" Marcel joked, and Jack snorted.

"It has gotten crowded," he admitted as we joined them. "But at least the Brettain are sending staple foods." He rubbed his hands together in the cool air, trying to generate some heat. "So. You guys ready?"

"I'm just here for moral support. Family's still MIA," Kat said, looking around at her friends. Her movement was a little easier now and the cut on her lip was slowly starting to heal. Her nose and eye were still really bruised though, the colors shifting towards green instead of blue and purple.

"How about you three?" he asked.

"We're ready," Marcel said, leaning to the side to bump her brother's hip with her shoulder. Jayce nodded, and I could tell they meant it.

"It's been nearly five years since I've seen my parents," Aliyah said quietly, a small smile pulling at her lips. "It will be very good to see them again."

"When do people usually get here?" Jayce asked, a little antsy, and we all smirked at him. "What?"

"People started arriving this morning," Jack answered and turned his chair to face the road that lead to the gate of the Academy. "So, now we wait."

I walked over to his side and slowly sat down, resting my head against the side of his chair. The tension bled out of my body as his hand dropped down against me, heavy on my chest, and held me close. Sighing, I leaned my head against his arm and reached up to hold his hand.

"Now we wait," I echoed.

... — — ...

We'd been sitting there for about four hours, watching families reunite with their kids with tears and screams of joy or sometimes nothing more than overwhelmed silence. It was touching in an amusing way to watch our fellow classmates stand up on their toes and crane their necks to squint at the people walking down the road from the gate, trying o identify them as quickly as possible. Some sagged back down in disappointment when the faces turned out to be strangers'. But others got lucky, and those were the ones that made the waiting a little easier.

It was about two-thirty in the afternoon when Marcel sat up a little straighter and elbowed Jayce in the thigh. He started awake, having lightly dozed off in the sunlight, and slowly stood up on the bench. His hand pressed against his leg, and he squinted slightly at the three women making their way down the road. They were on the shorter side with dark, tanned skin, and greying black hair drawn back in single braids. Two of them were on the stouter side, wearing long skirts and shawls while the third was a little thinner and wore pants instead.

"Is that..." I trailed off, looking up at Marcel to see a wide smile slowly spread onto her face.

"Jayce, that's mom," she laughed giddily, getting to her feet and pulling her brother after her. "That's mom and her sisters, come on!"

She quickly helped Jayce down from the table and tightly grabbed his hand, walking towards the approaching women. You could see the moment the two saw each other. The women stopped in their tracks while the kids started walking a little faster, Jayce's gait on the stiffer side. I squeezed Jack's hand a little tighter, and he laughed.

"Marcel?" the woman in the green skirt called. Her accented voice bordered on hopeful hysteria, and she shaded her eyes. "Jayce?"

Marcel started running, dragging Jayce along with her. He was clearly struggling to ignore the pain in his leg, and their mother started running, too, tackling her children in a giant bear hug. She pulled them down to her height and kissed them repeatedly on every inch of skin she could reach. She was crying, smiling widely and saying things in a language I assumed was Mezitain as she directed her attention first to one child and then the other and then started the cycle over again. Their aunts hurried over, too, adding themselves to the tangle of limbs and Mezitain endearments. Somehow everyone ended up sitting down, arms wrapped tightly around each other, rocking back and forth ever so slightly. I could see Marcel's mom reaching for her daughter's hair, picking up the small braids and holding them up in an admiring question. Marcel laughed, wiping at her eyes, and pointed over her shoulder to us, more specifically at Aliyah.

"Come, come. You have to introduce me to your friends," the woman said eagerly. Marcel groaned as her mom dragged her and Jayce to their feet.

"Mama," she whined, still smiling, and her mom clicked her tongue.

"No," she scolded, loving pride in her eyes. "You *must* introduce me to your Horsemen." As they started walking over, Jayce subtly pointed to the side, and Jack tapped my shoulder.

"Scoot over." I looked up at him, clearly confused, and he continued pointedly. "Remember how Marcel and Jayce were at the beginning of the year? These are the people that raised them."

I quickly stood up and moved to the bench where Marcel had been sitting.

"So, guys, this is our mom," Marcel introduced, still grinning tearfully. "And these are our aunts Maria and Adela. Mom, these are our friends Jack, Tristan, Aliyah, and Katalin."

The women shook our hands and hugged each of us in turn until they saw Katalin.

"*Dioses*, what happened?" Marcel's mom gasped, bee-lining for her. "It was one of those no good supremacists, wasn't it? Adela beat one with a shovel last week—"

"I'm fine, Mrs. Jones," Katalin reassured her and smiled as the woman checked the tape on her nose and the stitching on her lip. The older woman hissed in sympathy as she took in the bruised eye. "Aliyah broke their legs for me."

The woman turned a sharp eye towards Aliyah and reached across the table to tightly hold her hands.

"Good girl."

Well, I definitely knew where Marcel got her personality from.

Aliyah smirked and nodded her thanks.

"Are your families coming?" Adela asked, and I shook my head.

"No, Jack and I've got no family. We're just here for moral support."

"Why don't you come spend the day with us?" Maria pressed, resting a hand on my shoulder, and I looked at her. "You shouldn't be alone today. Join the family!"

"Thank you for the offer, but we really couldn't," Jack smiled, gesturing to Jayce and Marcel. "This is your day with them. Though, you could take Katalin along. She doesn't have family coming either."

"No family?" their mother asked, looking at Kat in near outraged. She wrapped her arm around the girl's shoulder and guided her off the bench. "Come, mija. You'll spend the day with us."

"O-okay," the girl stammered, and Marcel mouthed 'thank you' to Jack, arm around her Aunt Adela's waist. We watched as they headed towards the Lake, and Jack laughed once.

"Well, that's a colorful family."

"Indeed," Aliyah agreed and was about to continue when a deep voice cut her off.

"Aliyah."

We all jumped and turned around to see a tall Arikaan man and woman standing about ten feet behind us. The woman wore a simple red dress, her hair braided the way Marcel's was and woven into a bun. The man was dressed in slacks and a worn button-down that was some kind of maroon color. As I looked at his straight, slightly poufy hair, I glanced at Aliyah and took in the long straight hair that hung down her back. Both strangers looked remarkably young, but I could see some gray in the man's shadow of a beard and some very light wrinkles at the corners of the woman's eyes.

As Aliyah slowly got up, their eyes filled with tears. Her mother smiled, hands pressing together before her lips. Her father reached up and adjusted his glasses, wiping at his eyes beneath the lenses.

"Baba?" Aliyah asked softly.

He gave a broad smile, opening his arms as she ran forward, jumping up and locking her arms around his neck. He leaned back, lifting her feet off the ground and beaming.

"Oh, Aliyah," he laughed, looking up at the sky and sniffing back his tears. "It's been so long, Ali. So long." Aliyah just nodded, and when he set her down, she let her forehead rest against her dad's, just smiling with her eyes closed and her hands gripping his collar.

"Five years," her mother sighed, and Aliyah let go of her dad to latch onto her. She was too overwhelmed to even speak. "Five years, and you're finally here." Aliyah nodded again, pressing her face into her mother's neck and breathing deeply. "Oh, we've missed you, baby."

"Everything is just as you left it back in Olean," her father said, running his hand up and down his daughter's back. "We kept the restaurant through the Mezitain occupation, so home is the same. Everything is ready for you."

Aliyah finally pulled back, breathing deeply, and wiped at her eyes.

"It's a little more complicated than that," she said gently and gave her parents an apologetic smile. Their joyful expressions slowly faded, and she looked over her shoulder at us. "I need a moment to talk to my parents."

"Of course," I said and got up. Jack followed me over to the other end of the quad; it was far enough away to give the Moores privacy but still in shouting distance in case anyone tried to harass us. They only talked for a few minutes before Aliyah beckoned us back over, her parents' expressions crestfallen but supportive.

"Mama, baba, these men are Corporal Jack Miller and Private Tristan Byrne." They shook our hands, flawlessly shifting from their right to left hands with me. "Corporal Miller saved our lives in the trenches."

Her father tightened his hold on Jack's hand looking from his daughter to my boyfriend.

"Thank you. I don't know what we'd do without our girl."

"She's exaggerating," Jack said with a wry smile, but Mr. Moore shook his head, letting go of his hand.

"My Aliyah does not exaggerate. She only tells the truth."

"That she does," her mother agreed and wrapped her arm around her daughter's waist, holding her close. Aliyah looked down self-consciously. "She is a person of honor. And even though you're not coming home, I am very proud of you."

"You're not going home?" I asked, and she shook her head.

"No. Marcel, Jayce, and I are going with Katalin to Alama to help find her family." She looked at her mother and smiled gently. "Olean is only one state away. I promise to visit often."

"You had better," the woman scolded and took a deep breath. "So. If you're not leaving with us, what do we do now?"

"I can take you to meet my other friends," Aliyah offered. "They're by the Lake with their family."

"That sounds perfect," her father smiled, taking his daughter's arm and letting her lead the way.

"They're not what I expected," I finally said. "They're very…warm."

"And Aliyah's not?" he asked, and I shrugged.

"I suppose she is in her own way," I said and frowned as Jack turned his chair back to face the road. "Who are you waiting for? No one else we know is coming."

He took in a deep breath, hands wrapping tightly around the push rings of his chair. When he answered, his voice was quiet.

"Hopefully."

... — — — ...

Hours went by. Hours of people and excited voices climbing over each other, of lucky privates loading up their belongings into their families' cars. A few people left on horseback. One or two of our classmates had nothing but a backpack with them and started the long walk home with their loved ones. And still we sat there, watching the sun sink lower and lower in the sky. Whoever Jack was hoping wouldn't come hadn't shown up yet, and I watched him grow more and more relaxed as the daylight faded. Around five, the sun finally setting, Aliyah and the Joneses came back with their families, apparently getting ready to say goodbye and go their separate ways. Katalin trailed a little behind them, engrossed in conversation with Adela.

That was when she came.

"Excuse me!" we heard a frantic voice call. We looked to see a young woman with familiar blue eyes and a pixie face coming over.

She was dressed in a simple cotton dress, and the dark blue contrasted prettily with her reddish blonde hair that was tucked under a green bandana. Two children hovered behind her. They were clearly twins, except one was a boy and the other a girl. Their skin was very pale, just like their cropped hair. The little girl was in corduroy overalls and a short-sleeved shirt, the boy in patched-up suspender pants of the same material and a button-down shirt with rolled up sleeves. A battered cabbie cap a little too large for the boy's head hung over his blue eyes.

"Oh gods, no," Jack breathed, and I closed my eyes as he hunched his shoulders and sighed.

"Is that..." Marcel stopped, unable to say her name.

"Yeah," I whispered, opening my pained eyes. "Yeah, it is."

"Excuse me, please!" she ran over to us, her children trailing after her a with a little less enthusiasm. "I'm looking for my daughter." She pulled a photo from a pocket sewn into the side of her dress and handed it to me. "Please, I've been asking everyone I can find, but no one's seen her."

I bit my lip and looked down, keeping the photo turned away from me. I could hear Jayce gently telling their families to come with him, to give us some space.

"Please. *Please*, just look at it, I need to know if she's alive," she begged, and I glanced at the little girl peaking at me from behind her mother's dress.

"Are you Mrs. Korsakov?" I asked softly, and she paled even more.

"Yes. Yes, that's me." Her voice was nothing more than a breathless whisper, and I swallowed painfully, handing her back the photo.

"I..." My throat closed up, and I looked down again.

"We need to talk about Irina," Aliyah said softly. The mother's breath painfully hitched in her chest. "My name is Aliyah Moore, and this is Marcel Jones and Katalin Soto. I don't know if your daughter ever talked about us to you, but we were her–"

"Her friends," the woman finished, voice shaking, and I looked at her sadly. "You all...you were her best friends."

"Yeah," Marcel said kindly, stepping forward and gently putting a hand on her shoulder.

"She talked about you in all her letters," the woman whispered dazedly. "What happened to her?"

"Let's sit down, Mrs.–"

"Catharine."

"Catharine," Marcel repeated, still smiling kindly though her eyes shone with tears as she led the woman to the bench. "Let's sit down here."

"Mama, where's Rina?" the little boy asked, eyes wide, and his mother gently shushed him, hand smoothing through his hair.

"Shhh, Oliver." She looked up at us. "Is she...is Irina..." We all looked at each other, at a loss as to how to answer kindly, when Jack spoke up.

"Yes. She's dead." My head whipped around, and I gaped at him, horrified at the blunt way he'd answered. "I'm very sorry for your loss, but Irina is dead."

Catharine nodded, biting her lip and slowly breaking down into tears as she held her children tightly to herself.

"What happened?" she whispered, voice strained.

"She got shot, and the wound got infected," Katalin explained gently, sitting down across from the mother along with Marcel. "We'd run out of meds, and by the time we got some from the Brettain, it was too late."

"We were all there with her," Marcel added. "She wasn't alone."

"Was she in pain?" Catharine asked smally.

"No," I lied, and Aliyah nodded once to me in thanks. "She was talking about how pretty Winova was during the spring."

Her mother smiled shakily and nodded with a faint laugh.

"That's my mountain girl," she breathed, taking in a deep breath and kissing the tops of her kids' heads.

"Mama, is Rina coming home?" the little girl asked, tilting her head back to look at her mother.

"No, Isabel," she whispered gently, smoothing her hair back. "Irina's not coming home. I'm sorry, baby."

The little girl looked down, sniffling quietly, and Catharine held her tightly. We were unsure of what to say or do next, and Aliyah reached out and put her hand on the woman's back, standing behind her like some sort of silent guardian. The mother nodded quickly at the contact, clearly getting something from the gesture, and Aliyah let her thumb sweep back and forth across the nubs of her spine. Catharine took in deep, shuddering breaths as she tried to keep herself together for the sake of her two remaining children huddled in her lap.

"She wasn't alone," Aliyah repeated, echoing Marcel. "I held her as she went, and I promise it was very peaceful. She just fell asleep."

The woman started to sob, slowly losing the little control she had left, and both her children wrapped their arms around her, trying to hide their faces in the angles of her body as she cried. Aliyah slowly knelt beside her, one hand smoothing up and down her spine in comfort while the other gently rested on Oliver's back as the little boy started crying – confused and scared. I looked to where Jayce was standing with his and Aliyah's families, and saw that they were on the verge of tears as well.

Mr. and Mrs. Moore's arms were wrapped around each other in silent comfort while the Mrs. Jones, Adela, and Maria held each others' hands like they were the only things keeping them grounded. I looked up to the dusky sky and sighed, heart breaking as I listened to the Korsakovs' crying sobs. When I finally looked back to the family, I noticed Jack moving away from the table. I followed him until we were standing side by side at the edge of the quad, looking down the dusky road to the gate. The sun was about to vanish below the distant mountains, and I put my hand on his shoulder.

"Your family didn't show up." Jack nodded silently, still staring at the gate. "That's good news, isn't it?"

"I suppose," he said dully, and I knelt beside him, putting my hand on his. "I know they hate me. The gods know I hate them. Give a matron a gay son, and there's bound to be friction, right?"

"I thought you said they didn't know you were gay." Jack gave a bitter laugh at my confused comment, eyes tired as he stared at the fading road.

"No. They just think they cured me of it." My heart stopped, and he looked over his shoulder to where Marcel and Katalin had moved to sit on the edge of the table on either side of Catharine, talking gently to her while

Aliyah continued to rub her back. "It just would have been nice to know that they still cared about whether or not I was alive." He shook his head, and together we started back towards North Hall.

"I guess that's just too much to ask of a man of the gods."

"I'm sorry," I said in the silence that followed, and he sighed.

"So am I, Tristan."

DAY TWO HUNDRED AND EIGHTY-NINE

Eight days later

Jax finally managed to convince the Academy administration that they needed to separate the cadets from the privates.

Apparently, the incidences of bigotry-driven attacks had increased quite a bit since we came back from the eastern front lines, and the incidents with Samantha and then me, Katalin, Jayce, and Marcel had finally tipped the scales in the admin's eyes. Now, the cadets were housed in the eastern and southern ends of campus along with the refugees, who had also started to show intolerant behavior towards people. No doubt, they were encouraged by the cadets' actions. Privates, other returned troops, and active officials were moved to the northern and western sides of campus. Thankfully, since Jayce, Jack, the Horsemen, and I were already at North Hall, we didn't have to move.

It was quieter in our building now, and I looked out our window at the sound of trucks approaching. Another convoy was passing through the gates, and I idly wondered what it was bringing this time. Refugees, troops, equipment, prisoners of war, soldiers from the front lines that hadn't fallen yet…the possibilities seemed endless. But mostly I wondered if they were finally going to stay long enough for us to get our chance to leave yet.

I wasn't sure if I could stand being here much longer. Even though a new system had been put in place to keep the peace, it was no longer home.

DAY TWO HUNDRED AND NINETY-THREE

Four days later

It was probably seven in the morning when someone started knocking on our door. I groaned, pulling a pillow over my head, and Jack swatted at me in protest as I pulled the blankets away from him.

"Tris, get the door," he yawned, and I made a noise in the back of my throat.

"You get it."

"Tristan, seriously?"

"Fine," I grumbled, tossing the covers aside and stumbling towards the door. My vision was still a little blurry, and my hair felt like it was sticking up in every possible direction. Honestly, whoever this was had better have a good reason for making me get up. I wrenched open the door and stared blearily up at Jayce.

"What?" I croaked, and he smiled widely. "What is *wrong* with you?"

"Samantha's awake."

And now I was too.

... — — ...

Fifteen minutes later, Jack, Jayce, and I were in the infirmary, hanging back a little bit as Jax spoke to the still mostly immobile girl. She was sitting up in bed now, propped up against her pillows, and even though she still looked awful, there was a dogged strength in her eyes.

"Alright, well, I'm going to make sure that we've got someone standing guard at the door for you, okay? I don't want anyone coming in here to hurt you again."

She smiled lightly up at the officer.

"Thanks, sir." Her voice was brutally hoarse, and she let her gaze shift over to us. Her eyes lit up. "Hey, you two." Jack and I headed over, taking the side of her bed opposite Jax. "How are you?"

"Seriously?" Jack asked, smirking. "You're asking us that?"

She gave a breathy laugh and closed her eyes.

"I'm alive. Can't complain," she sighed and looked at Jax. "He said he's got the guys who did it, too."

"The two guys who attacked Jayce and Marcel were part of the group," the man explained. "In exchange for a slightly lighter sentence, they gave up the other names."

"Good," Jayce said gruffly, and she looked at him curiously.

"Who're you?"

"Oh. I'm...I'm the guy who found you."

"Come here," she said, and Jones slowly came over, gingerly taking her weakly beckoning hand. "Thank you."

"Hey, I'm just sorry I didn't get there earlier." He looked at Jack and I. "I should leave you guys to it."

"Alright, see you around Jayce," Jack said, patting his arm as he passed.

"I'll check in on you later," he called to Samantha, and she smiled as he left.

"He's a good man," she said softly before looking to Jax. "Didn't you have something you wanted to tell them?"

We both looked to our S.O. questioningly.

"Well, someone's excited," he said gruffly to the patient, but Samantha just smiled. "The northern, western, and eastern line troops are all getting shipped home tomorrow. Or at least to the destinations closest to wherever they want to go."

"Wait, seriously?"

"No, Byrne, I'm lying," Jax said dryly. "*Yes*, seriously."

I looked to Jack, and he grinned at me, reaching an arm up and around my waist.

"Ready to get out of here?" he asked, and I nodded vehemently.

"Oh, hell yes. Please."

"You two should go to Calin," Jax said seriously, interrupting us. "It's the most liberal of the states, the farthest west...I really don't see you two fitting in anywhere else."

"That's what we were planning, don't worry," Jack assured him. "We were thinking somewhere on the central coast—"

"Estercliff."

We all looked to Samantha blankly.

"It's a really small seaside town," she elaborated. "Good people, really liberal. My sister Casey lives there with her boy Colin. I was going to go live with her, but…well, I'm a little too fragile for travel right now." She nodded slightly to the pencil and notepad on her bedside table. "I can tell you the name of the place if you'd like to write it down. It's an apartment complex."

"Yeah, yeah. Definitely," Jack said eagerly, taking both objects into his lap and getting ready to write. "Estercliff?"

"Yeah. The complex is called the Seaside. If you ask anyone about it, they'll be able to point you in the right direction. And my sister's name is Casey Roman. She's also a nurse…works for the local VA hospital." Her voice had become really scratchy and tired, and Nurse Crawford came over, fixing us all with a scolding glare.

"You're tiring her out," she said sternly, pointing us towards the door. "It's time for her to sleep and you to go."

"Thank you, Samantha," Jack said kindly, reaching out and taking her hand. "We'll see you out there when you're well enough to travel."

"No problem." We were about to leave when she called after us. "Take care of yourselves out there." She swallowed painfully. "It's not as safe for us as it used to be."

Jack nodded solemnly.

"Thanks. You, too."

...———...

The sun was setting as Jack and I got dressed, helping each other out when necessary. The room was a little on the cold side, and I shivered despite the spare coat I had on over my casual uniform. When I'd left the Academy, I'd also left my clothes in my trunk – including an extra pair of socks that I was currently wearing over the ones I already had on. Jack was wearing his coat as well, and I'd draped a blanket over his legs, careful to fold it so it wouldn't get caught in his wheels.

Someone knocked on our door, the sound piercing in the unsettling quiet of North Hall.

"It's probably the others," Jack said, buttoning the top of his coat as I opened the door.

"Yep." I stepped back from the door to reveal Aliyah and Katalin. Both were dressed similarly to me, and I glanced into the hall. "Where're Marcel and Jayce?"

As soon as I spoke, the two siblings left their room, similarly bundled up, and walked somberly over to us.

"You got the stuff?" I asked, and Aliyah held up the bag in her hand.

"I picked it up at mess today," she said, walking into our room and setting the canvas bag down on our bed. She pulled out a small pillar candle first, then some tinder and a small, husk-like boat. "Put the candle in the boat first, then nestle the tinder in around it. Make sure the tinder is up high enough that it can catch fire from the candle when it burns down."

She demonstrated with the supplies she'd pulled out and passed the finished product to me.

"Thanks," I said. She nodded, passing out materials to everyone else and watching as they each made their own boat.

"Alright," Jack said softly, placing his boat on his lap. "We should get going. We don't want to be late."

We filed out after him, expressions solemn and pace deliberate.

No. We certainly didn't.

··· — — — ···

When we finally got where we were going, we were surprised to find that we were one of the first people there. There were probably only forty people huddled around the edge of the lake, wrapped in ratty jackets and layers of clothing, the small ships clutched tightly in their cold-bitten hands. I knew there would be more. Hopefully lots more. I had no idea why they did this after people had already gone home with their parents, but it was better than not doing it at all. Though, it did give the families of the dead a chance to make it to the Academy on time, and I supposed it was kinder to not make them see the reunions that could never be theirs.

"Could one of you take over for me?" Jack asked as we approached the muddy banks of the Lake. "I want us to be as close to the water as we can possibly be."

Katalin quickly nodded and pushed his wheelchair along.

We kept walking, threading our way through the gathered people until we were right on the edge, the dark water washing gently against the coarse shore only a few inches from our feet. The sunlight was all but gone now, the last of it fading away behind the mountains, and I watched as throngs of people headed towards the water from the mess hall. I realized that they must have held some kind of service beforehand.

At the head of the procession was Jax, holding a large lantern in one hand. In the other, held close to his chest, was a small leather book with a burned symbol of Pluto on the cover. His expression was solemn, just like everyone else's, and as he drew nearer, I saw others approaching from different parts of campus. We'd be starting soon, then. I took in a deep breath and looked at the Lake, at the smooth, mirror-like surface that stretched out before us, fading into the tree line at the far bank. Its trademark fog hadn't rolled in yet, and in the distance I could see the swans drifting across the water, still ghostlike in their gliding stillness.

The gods are telling me that it's all going to be okay. Especially Neptune. He's very reassuring. But Terra…Mother Terra is very sad. She's sad because we're all going to be returned to her very soon.

I looked around at the people crowding around us, all armed with the small candle-laden crafts. A couple people were already sniffling, wrapping their arms around their friends and loved ones. I became aware of a warm light piercing the gloom as I watched them, and I turned to see Jax and a young cadet coming towards me. He looked at me with sad eyes as they passed, stepping into the water and wading forward until they were up to their knees. He passed the lantern off to her, and she held it up as a raven started to caw and croak in the tree above us.

We're going home to her too soon.

"Diana." His voice carried over the water, bold and clear. "Bless these young men and women for they have fought in your name to their final breaths. Grant them peace in the afterlife and guide them to Proserpine, wherein she may take mercy on their immortal souls. I ask this in the name of these children, honored this day." He paused, and I felt Jack slowly take my small boat from me, setting it in his lap so he could hold my hand in his. I looked down at him, but he wasn't looking at me. His eyes were closed, body still.

Jax's breath fogged before him in the light of the lantern as he opened the small book, flipped to a page towards the end, and started reading. He paused for about four seconds between each name.

"Joseph Abbott. Kathleen E. Amato. Jeffrey Atkins. Jessica Avery. Mia Banting."

I closed my eyes and felt Jack tighten his grip.

Distantly, I could hear Jax continue to recite names, but I wasn't paying attention. All I could think about was Private Banting. I hadn't realized that she'd died…my last memory of her was of Blackwell trying to treat her for scurvy. Jack tugged gently on my arm, and I opened my eyes as he passed me back my boat. People had started lighting their candles, bringing the lit boats to the water's edge and gently shoving them off into the dark. Beside me, Aliyah lit a match and gestured for me to pass her mine.

"Patrick Breen. Simon Caldera. Andrew Cera."

She handed it back to me, and the small flame warmed my hands just as Jax said the next name.

"Idris Chance."

I took in a deep, shaky breath and knelt in the mud, delicately placing the vessel in the water. The raven started making noises again, gurgling and croaking. Once I was sure it was steady, I gently pushed the boat off and watched as its bow cut through the black water to join the dozens of other pyres drifting further and further out on the Lake. The swans still hovered at the far shore as though they were a part of the proceedings themselves.

"Asmara Dalak. Rebecca Delaney."

Idris.

I put my hand over my face, struggling not to cry as I knelt practically in the water. Jack gently rubbed my back and whispered soothingly to me. I wasn't sure what he was saying, but the sound of his voice helped a little.

"Jonathan Evans. Eliot Ford." More names, more boats, more people crying. But we weren't alone. "Ari Fukumoto. Amelia Grayson. Mark Gru." We were all here, all of us mourning the loss we all felt. "Robert Harold. Nicole Harris. Palma Hart."

Seven hundred and eighty-four names from our class alone. I watched Jax as he continued to list the fallen, and I wondered how many times he'd done this. It wasn't too long before another name we knew personally came up, and this time Jack prepared his candle.

"Alec Jackson. Erin Jacobs. Felicia Jasso."

I stood up as Jack bent over in his chair, reaching down and setting his small pyre in the water. He gently shoved it off, and the names continued. As we neared the K's I saw the Horsemen and Jayce light their tributes.

"James Kafka. Jennifer Kendall. Richard Kearns." They all knelt down, waiting.

"Irina Korsakov."

As one, the four people set their boats in the water and gave them the lightest of pushes before standing up. Aliyah put her arms around Katalin and Marcel, dark eyes dancing with the pinprick flames of the water before her as her friends quietly hugged her back. Jayce tagged on at the end, arm around his sister and head resting on her shoulder.

"James Novak."

The names just kept going. Natsumi Okuyama. Megan Peraza. Kibra V. Robel. John Robinson. Anthony Solorio. Dorian Spencer. Finally, it seemed like we were nearing the end of the alphabet, and the Lake was filled with the small boats, flickering with the lights of at least seven hundred burning pyres.

"Hiro Uchida. Ling Wei. Steven Wolfe."

The endless litany of names stopped, and the air suddenly went quiet. It felt eerie. I took in a deep breath, feeling oddly weightless and heavy at the same time as I stared at the burning water. The candles would burn on their own for another half-hour. Then, the tinder would catch fire. The flames would spread to the boats themselves, and then every trace of this memorial would be gone. It would drift down to the bottom of the Lake with the rest of the ashes, thirty years worth of names and people. The silence continued for about a minute, and then Jax continued.

"Valiant goddess, may you vouchsafe to me what I ask of you in prayer. So may it be." The people around us chorused their response.

"So may it be."

I noticed none of us had spoken.

There was a soft click as Jax closed the book and took the lantern back from the cadet.

"Let us observe a moment of silence for our friends, our brothers, our sisters, and our cousins that we have lost. May they never be forgotten, and may the living never be left behind."

The moment of silence lasted for ten minutes, and once it was over, Jax turned to face us, slowly trudging back to dry land.

"There will be an all night vigil. For those of you who want to stay for its entirety, you are welcome to. I'll be staying to make sure no one disturbs you and to pay my respects as well. If you do not wish to stay beyond this point, that's also okay. Do not think you're disrespecting anyone by leaving. We all mourn and remember in our own ways. Thank you."

As people moved around us, I looked at Jack and the others.

"Do you want to leave or stay?" I asked. Marcel took in a deep breath, wiping at her eyes.

"Stay. Just a little longer...until the boats start burning," she whispered, and we nodded.

"Okay," I said gently. "We'll stay as long as you like."

And so we stood there in silence for another twenty minutes, huddled close to each other. As the time passed, the seconds ticking by in agonizing slowness, the Horsemen slowly stepped back from the water and instead moved over to stand behind me and Jack. Katalin tentatively put a hand on my shoulder, her other arm still wrapped around Aliyah. Jayce clapped a hand on Jack's shoulder, and my boyfriend rested his free hand over his. He looked up at Marcel and Aliyah behind his chair and smiled before looking back at the water. And so we stood there, watching and waiting for that first boat to catch fire.

Without warning, it did. As the small flame suddenly flared brighter, the boat next to started burning as well. As we watched, the light spread in a gentle ripple across the Lake until the water looked like molten silver.

"Okay," Marcel sighed, slowly untangling herself from her friends. "I'm ready to go now."

Jayce moved his hand from Jack's shoulder to the handles of his chair and began pushing him back towards campus. I walked alongside them, still gently holding my boyfriend's hand. We were nearing the walkway back to North Hall when I cast one last look over my shoulder.

"Wait."

I let go of Jack's hand and ran back over to the water, pulling a set of dog tags from beneath my shirt and weighing them in my hand. I noticed Jax watching me from the boulder he was sitting on, and I glanced back to where my friends were waiting expectantly. Resolve hardening, I pulled my arm back and threw them, watching as the metal soared through the air and caught the light of the flames. And finally it splashed next to one of the boats, vanishing with barely a ripple below the surface.

I took in a deep breath and whispered the name softly to myself.

"Margaret Burke."

I ran back to the others, taking Jack's hand in mine as we slowly walked back to North Hall.

DAY TWO HUNDRED AND NINETY-FOUR

You couldn't even tell there'd been a memorial service here last night, I reflected as I skipped yet another rock across the Lake. Or, rather, tried to skip. My left-handed throw just plowed into the water.

"You're throwing it at an angle, Byrne."

I looked at Katalin, unimpressed.

"I'm sorry, how about you cut off your dominant hand and then try to skip rocks?" I snapped, and she shrugged, whittling away at the reed whistle in her hands.

"I'm ambidextrous."

I rolled my eyes, my next words spoken more to myself than her.

"Of course you are."

Plunk.

"Shouldn't you be with Miller at his PT?"

I shook my head and threw another stone.

"No, Aliyah's waiting for him. I needed some space."

Plunk.

"How's your PT going?"

"Okay. I'm writing pretty well now."

Katalin hesitated before asking her next question.

"You ever consider other forms of therapy?"

I hurled another stone as far as I could, no longer trying to stay above the water.

"I'm sound in the head if that's what you're asking."

SPLASH

"Really?" I side-eyed her before throwing something else. "So, if I run up behind you on the way to mess tomorrow morning and drop my hands on your shoulders, you won't have an anxiety attack?"

I stopped my arm mid-drawback and looked at Famine, jaw set.

"Marcel told you about that?"

"Uh-huh," she answered, eyebrows arching. "Don't worry, though. She told Aliyah and Jayce, too." I sighed, picking up another stone and chucking it. "Byrne, that's the fifty-eighth rock that you've pitched into the Lake. I'm actually surprised you keep finding stuff to throw."

I stopped, turning to look at her.

"What?" I demanded, hand on my hip. "What do you want?"

"I want you to think about getting yourself a therapist," she said after a second of hesitation, and I laughed, picking up a surprisingly heavy rock.

"I'm sure you'd love that." I hurled it, finding satisfaction in the loud splash. "Tristan Byrne, the broken toy soldier."

"Is that what you think of Miller?"

I threw another stone and stopped in surprise as it skipped once before crashing.

"No." I glanced at my feet and kicked at the muddy earth beneath me. "He's allowed to have some problems."

I started looking around for more to throw when Soto walked up to me and shoved the inside of my right shoulder so I was forced to look at her.

"And you're not?" she challenged, stepping closer to me, and I backed away, crossing my arm.

"Look, it's just this place, okay? I'm just always jumping at shadows here. Once we leave I'll be fine," I protested and headed closer to the water to find some pebbles. "You know how it is. I saw you in Norford."

Kat retreated back to her boulder and climbed to the top. As she sat down, she crossed her legs and finished the final touches to her whistle.

"Yeah," she said. "I do."

I threw a bunch of smaller rocks at once so they shattered the peaceful water like buckshot.

"I can't believe I miss how it used to be," I sighed.

She nodded to herself, testing out a few notes on the reed. They were cold and clear, perfectly in pitch. I shivered.

"I get that."

. . . ‒ ‒ ‒ . . .

We walked up the path towards North Hall about an hour later, and I felt a little odd as I reached the tall building. This was the last time I'd see this place, the last time I'd consider it a home. Well, home was a bit of a strong word. It was at best a living space. As we were walking, I heard a familiar rumbling noise behind us, and Kat and I habitually stepped off the road and watched as battered and dirty trucks rolled past. Tired, gaunt faces looked at us out the open back, and I wondered where they'd been brought back from. I also wondered if this was the convoy the admin would spare to take us away from here today.

"I can't wait to leave," Katalin sighed, and I nodded, eyes following the trucks as they went by. There had to be at least thirty of them.

"Yeah, tell me about it." We started down the road again and ignored the people passing by. "The sooner I'm out of here, the better."

By the time we reached North Hall, people were already disembarking from the trucks and following the new streamlined process the Academy had come up with to give people room assignments: take a room number from the person standing at the door and go on up. As we walked to the door, the newcomers ducked their heads and avoided eye contact as though we were scrutinizing them. Really though, we were just passing by.

This was nothing new to us.

As we passed Marcel and Jayce's room on the way to our own, I heard the brother call me over. I stopped and stuck my head in the open doorway.

"Those our rides?" he asked, jerking his thumb over his shoulder to the window, and I shrugged.

"Your guess is as good as mine. Is Aliyah back with Jack yet?"

"No, we haven't seen them," Marcel said. "They should be here soon, though."

"Okay, thanks."

I walked into my room and dropped down on the bed, taking in a deep breath and closing my eyes. The world was so quiet. The noise of the trucks outside was minimal, more background static than anything else, and the sounds of newcomers walking down the hall or up the stairs were nothing compared to the things I'd heard. I wondered if anything would be loud to me again. Because of the silence, I was able to hear the sound of something rolling across floorboards and immediately sat up. A few moments later, Jack came into the room, talking over his shoulder.

"Thanks, Aliyah. Yeah, tell the guys. I'll tell Tristan."

"Tell me what?" He looked forward.

"Jax has a meeting in thirty minutes for western and eastern front line privates about the move out procedure." He reached behind him and pulled the door shut. "Dr. Simmons told me to tell you goodbye."

"Oh, that's nice of her. How'd your last session go?"

"Good," he yawned, stretching his arms over his head. "She gave me some new half-finger gloves for my chair and said as long as I keep up my exercises, I should be able stay this mobile."

"I'll make sure you do," I smiled, the expression a small, wry quirk of the lips. Jack rolled his eyes as I got up to help him onto the bed.

"No more drill sergeants, please. I've had enough of those for one lifetime."

"No more drill sergeants," I agreed and helped shift him to the bed and sit him against the headboard. "I'll pack our stuff into my footlocker, okay? You should take a nap, you look tired."

He nodded gratefully, and I patted his leg once before getting up and opening Jack's chest. He didn't have much in there: just a spare button-down shirt, an extra t-shirt, his formal jacket, and a few other pieces of clothing. I pulled all the clothing out and set it on the floor. Tucked at the bottom was a small tin case I'd never seen before, and I reached in, picking it up and setting it with the rest of his stuff. This would be easy enough to consolidate. I opened my footlocker and pulled out my jacket before piling in all of Jack's clothes, also setting his coat aside with mine. After making sure my medical supplies and Jack's strange case were nestled safely in the center of all the clothing, I laid both our formal jackets across the top. I breathed out slowly, rocking back on my heels before shutting the lid with a sharp click.

"Done already?" Jack asked sleepily, and I nodded.

"We don't have much," I admitted as I climbed into bed and lay down next to him. "We'll have to buy new clothes and shit when we get to…what was it called? Estercliff?" He nodded wordlessly, not meeting my gaze and instead finding something of great interest in his hands. I frowned, turning onto my side and looping my arm with his. "What's wrong?"

"Aliyah told me you had an anxiety attack this morning," he finally said, voice soft, and looked up at me.

"Oh, Jack, it was nothing," I assured him. He sighed. "She just startled me." He looked at me earnestly.

"You'd tell me if it was anything else?"

"Of course." He smiled, leaning forward to kiss me gently.

"I'm here for you, okay? I get this stuff. You don't need to hide things from me," he pressed, and I nodded, nestling my head into the crook of his neck and feeling his heartbeat under my hand.

"I'll tell you the moment I start," I joked, and he snorted, hand resting on my head.

"I love you, Tristan Byrne. You're an idiot, but I love you."

"Love you, too," I said softly and we lapsed into silence.

We'd been doing this a lot – just lying together and taking comfort in the peace and quiet of our room. It definitely helped now that we had Jayce and the Horsemen standing guard in a way. Unfortunately, we couldn't stay that way for long. Soon, Jayce was knocking on and opening our door.

"Hey – oh, sorry." He quickly lowered his voice. "We need to go to the meeting." I turned to Jack only to see that he was asleep. I smiled softly to myself and kissed his forehead before getting out of bed and heading to the door. "He's not coming?"

"No, he should sleep," I said and gently closed our door. "The meeting shouldn't take too long anyways."

Marcel, Aliyah, and Kat joined us in the hallway, and we headed down to the mess hall.

"So, where are you and Miller off to?" Marcel asked.

"Estercliff, Calin?" I answered, and all I got were blank stares. "It's this tiny seaside town on the central coast. Apparently it's really liberal and gay-friendly."

"Jackpot," Jayce mused, and I nodded. Marcel looked less thrilled.

"That's all the way across the country," she whined, and I laughed. "I see how it is, shrimp."

"You can always send us a letter if you miss us too badly," I teased, and she raised an eyebrow.

"You joke, but I will do it, Byrne," she warned.

"Oh, I know," I laughed. "Jack said to mail the letters to the Academy, and they'll forward it through once we give them our new address."

We stopped talking as we neared the mess hall and joined the masses of people trying to make their way inside. Jax was speaking with someone at the podium, and I looked around as we sat down. I recognized a few faces, but not many. Most of these people were from the western front line.

"Okay, listen up!" Jax called once we were all seated. "One of the convoys came back today, and we've got forty-five trucks all lined up at the Lake. Fifteen of them will go west, fifteen will go south, and fifteen will go north. We won't send anyone east because the land isn't ready for people to live on just yet, and it's still mostly under Brettain control." Those of us from the eastern lines muttered in agreement. "So, the first fifteen will go all the way out to Calin's coast. The next fifteen will go all the way down to Alama's coast, and the last fifteen will go all the way up to Winova's foreign border. Get your belongings, say your goodbyes, and report to your desired area in an hour. Dismissed."

I looked at Jayce as Jax quickly gathered up his papers and left.

"Told you it was gonna be short. Jax looks like he's got places to be," I noted as the burly man quickly left out the back door.

"Yeah," Jayce said and looked back at me, lightly hitting my arm as we stood. "Hey, at least our truck sections are right next to each other. We'll have a bit longer to say our goodbyes."

"Let's use Jax's exit," Katalin interrupted. "We'll get back to North Hall before everyone else that way – have a little more quiet time to ourselves."

The five of us quickly ducked out the cook's entrance and headed back to our building at a fast pace. Thankfully, our plan worked, and we stayed ahead of the noisy crowd behind us. As the others stepped into their rooms to finish packing up, I slowly opened my door to see if my boyfriend was still asleep, grimacing as the hinges creaked noisily. Jack looked up from his pillow, hair sleep-tousled but eyes awake, and I smiled at him, leaving the door open behind me.

"Get a good nap?" I joked.

"It was only like...five minutes," he mumbled, sitting up and yawning again. "We get a departure time?"

"Yep. One hour." I gestured to the door. "The others are packing up, but we're ready to go."

"Thanks," he smiled. I pointed in a silent question to his chair. "Nah, I'm good on the bed right now."

"Okay." I sat back next to him, head on his shoulder.

We lapsed back into one of those silences for another five minutes until Katalin came and gently knocked on our doorframe.

"What's up?" Jack asked, and she slowly walked in.

"Can I sit down?" she asked quietly, pointing at the foot of the bed.

"By all means," I said, Jack nodding beside me, and Famine slowly sat cross-legged on the mattress at Jack's feet. There was something troubled on her face. "What's bothering you?"

"I...don't want us to leave," she slowly answered, frowning slightly as she tried to figure out what she meant. "Or I don't want you two to leave. One of the two, I'm not sure." She looked down at her hands. "I guess I just got used to having you two around."

"Aw, we'll miss you, too," I teased, and she looked up at me sharply.

"I mean it, Byrne." She paused. "You're good guys."

"The world's not ending, Katalin," Jack said gently. "We'll see each other again. Promise."

There was another knock at our door, and we looked up to see Marcel. She wore similar expression to Kat's when she'd come in, and Jack sighed, patting the mattress. She came in and wordlessly sat down in the center of the bed against the footboard. She tucked her legs under her and didn't say anything, just sat there silently and picked at the hem of her pants.

There was another soft knock, and Jack and I looked up at Jayce. He seemed a little embarrassed, but I just smirked and motioned with my head to the empty side of the bed. He sat down next to me, head thumping back against the headboard as he stared at the ceiling. War gave her brother a sympathetic half-smile.

It was another thirty seconds before the final knock came, and we all turned to Aliyah. She was the only one who looked utterly calm and at ease, and Jack waved her in.

"Join the party, Moore."

She gave a barely perceptible smile and came into the room, shutting the door quietly behind her. She climbed on the bed and sat down between Marcel and Jayce, cross-legged like Katalin. There wasn't a single space left on the mattress now, and I waited for someone to say something. But there was nothing. This was the last time we'd all be in a room together for gods knew how long, and we were just sitting in silence. Finally Marcel spoke. It was nothing more than a whisper.

"This is our goodbye...isn't it?"

She looked up slightly to where Jack and I were sitting together, staring at them all. Jayce continued to glare at the ceiling with a clenched jaw, and Katalin stared at her lap with her arms crossed over her stomach. Aliyah sat with perfect posture, looking at everyone openly. No one spoke for a bit.

"Yeah." Jayce didn't look down from the ceiling, just cleared his throat and repeated himself. "Yeah. It is."

We went quiet again, and Jack and I looked around at our friends sadly. Aliyah was the only one looking up, and Death gave that same, secret smile to us. A farewell all in itself.

Goodbye.

· · · — — — · · ·

Fifty minutes later, we'd finally had to start moving, and we did that in silence, too. We each went to our own rooms, grabbed our own trunks, and left the building. No one really waited for anyone or said anything beyond what was necessary. Jack and I were the last ones out, and I picked up one end of the footlocker by its rope handle.

"Ready to go?" I asked, hovering by the door. Jack nodded, taking one last look around.

"Yeah. Yeah, let's get out of here."

We left the room silently, Jack leading the way down the hall. I listened to the sounds of his wheels and the scraping of our trunk against the worn floors. Both were in time with our gaits, echoing off the barren walls, and I felt something odd in my chest as we finally stepped outside.

"Take one last look, Tristan," Jack said, and we stared at the building looming above us. "Good riddance."

"Couldn't agree more."

And just like that, we left North Hall for the last time, heading across the grounds to the waiting trucks. Our moods seemed to grow lighter with each step – the air fresher, the world brighter.

"Is this what the world normally looks like to you?" Jack asked, and I looked down at him, confused.

"What do you mean?"

"Everything's so *short*."

I aimed a kick at the wheel of his chair and almost fell over.

"I can't believe it took you this long to make that joke," I said, and he smirked to himself. "I'm a little disappointed."

"You don't mind."

That was true, I reflected and fell into step with him as we approached one of the westbound cars.

"Hey, Miller! Byrne!" I turned to see Katalin and Marcel running over, a smile on the latter's face. "We had to say something before you left."

Jayce wasn't far behind them and quickly took my footlocker from me, sliding it into the back for me. Jack smiled ruefully.

"Sorry," he said, shrugging. "I kind of liked the morose silence."

"Shut up, Miller," Marcel returned.

"Good luck finding your parents," I told Soto, and she smiled sadly.

"Thanks, Byrne." She stepped forward and gave me a quick hug before bending down to hug Jack. "You take care of your one-armed boyfriend. He's a troublemaker."

"Don't worry," Jack laughed as Aliyah approached. "I plan to."

Kat backed off, crossing her arms and staring at her boots while Marcel stepped forward to tackle me in a bear hug.

"Gods," she whispered and tightened her grip even more. "I'm gonna miss you, shrimp. You and your bodyguard."

"I'm gonna miss you, too," I managed before tapping her back to tell her I couldn't breathe.

"Sorry." She quickly let go and stepped over to Jack, wrapping him in an equally tight embrace. My boyfriend smiled into her shoulder, and while they hugged, I shook hands with Aliyah and Jayce.

"You keep in touch, okay?" Marcel ordered, voice roughly kind and muffled as she spoke into my boyfriend's shoulder. "And you take care of each other." Jack nodded as she pulled away.

"You, too."

Aliyah and Jayce shook Jack's hand as well before Soto and Marcel offered to help him into the car. As I watched, I couldn't help but tear up. Once I helped my boyfriend get himself and his wheelchair situated against the side of the truck, I noticed that only a few strangers were joining us. Apparently the south and north were the popular choices. And for the next five minutes we sat there silently, our friends awkwardly standing a few feet away. It was the bedroom all over again.

None of us knew what to say. What was there *to* say? Thankfully, our awkward standstill was cut short by the driver's shouting.

"Westbound trucks are rolling out! If you're planning on heading west, get on now, otherwise you're getting left behind."

The Horsemen slowly backed away, Jayce practically dragging his sister, and the engines roared to life.

"Tell Jax we wanted to skip out on goodbyes," I called, voice cracking, and Famine nodded, face still marred with fading bruises.

"We will."

"We'll see you around," Jack shouted over the noise of the engine, his smile strained. Death just shook her head in regret, earning a scathing glare from War at her parting words.

"No. You won't."

As we pulled away from them and turned along the curve of the road, Jayce waved. I raised my own hand in farewell, choked up.

Twenty minutes later, Aliyah's voice still echoed in my ears as I sat in Jack's arms, and we watched as our friends and the one place we'd ever been able to call home – no matter how twisted it had become in the end – finally vanished into the distance.

DAY TWO HUNDRED AND NINETY-SIX

It had taken us a little over a day and a half to get to Calin due a couple detours along the way. It seemed the roads were more damaged than we'd initially anticipated. In fact, there were some particularly rough patches where I actually missed the rugged roads we'd bounced across nine months ago. But when we finally crossed the mountainous borders into Calin and drove through the forests, I felt, inexplicably, as though I'd come home.

The air was crisper, fresher than the sky we'd become used to at the Academy. The trees and bushes were greener, healthier, fuller. As I watched the landscape rush by, I caught glimpses of birds and small animals flitting through the trees.

"You last two are Estercliff, right?"

I started at the sudden static voice and got to my feet, walking over to the radio transceiver bolted to the wall.

"Yeah," I confirmed and waited for the driver's response.

"Alright, that'll take us about another seven hours."

I hung up the radio and sat back down beside Jack, our cheeks and hands red from the cold air and the wind that whipped around the inside of the truck. He sighed and leaned his head against mine.

"This...this feels like home," I sighed after a few moments of silence.

I crossed my arm over my chest and rested my head against the rattling side of the vehicle. The truck weaved gently through the woods along the dirt-packed road, and we stared almost absently out the back of the car and watched the redwoods go by. Squirrels scampered along the branches in search of food, leaping from tree to tree.

"I don't know why…but it just does," I continued, and Jack nodded in agreement beside me, wrapping his arms tighter about himself and clearing his throat.

"Kinda weird seeing as you were a city kid, and I was country," he said, but I shrugged.

"Maybe that's why it feels like home." I made a vague motion with my hand. "It's a new start. Of sorts."

He nodded sagely, thinking something over.

"A change of scenery," he concluded, forcefully optimistic as he looked at me.

I slowly got to my feet, groaning as my joints protested, and headed over to our footlocker. The object sat innocently in the corner, and the closer I got, the harder my heart seemed to beat. I took in its scratched and battered surfaces, the chipped paint and crookedly printed letters spelling my name. I kneeled before it and released a breath of hot air that hovered in a cloud before my lips as I lifted the lid and pulled our jackets out.

"Here, you'll probably want to wear this." I tossed it over to Jack, and he caught it, leaning forward and pulling it on.

"First thing we're doing once we find a place is getting civilian clothes," he grumbled.

I nodded in agreement as I put on my mold and gunpowder-saturated jacket. No matter how many times I washed it, I couldn't get that smell out. The pungent stench assaulted my senses, and I clenched my hand around the edge of the trunk, arm shaking as my knuckles turned white. It wasn't long before Jack noticed.

"Tristan." He reached out to me with one hand and held himself steady with the other. "Tristan, breathe. It's okay." I stared down at the contents of the trunk, at the meager relics of our lives and took in another deep, shuddering breath. "Tris…c'm here."

I closed the trunk and moved over to sit in his lap. My boyfriend's arms wrapped around me and held me close. His breath felt like fire on my neck compared to the cold air around us, and I closed my eyes, holding onto his crossed forearms. I felt his heart pounding against my back, and I took in a deep breath that strained against the tightness of our hold on each other.

"If I open my eyes," I said unsteadily, "will we be leaving the Academy for the eastern lines?" Jack drew me in closer and rested his chin on my shoulder.

"No." His voice rumbled safely against my back, and I took in a deep breath, focusing on the pressure of his arms across my chest.

"You promise?"

"Always."

When I opened my eyes, we were swaying in the back of a truck, backs pressed against the side of the vehicle. We weren't looking at starving fields or ruins of long ago. Instead, we faced a simple forest road that was eerily peaceful in its winter stillness.

We were alone.

As I released the shaky breath I'd been holding, Jack kissed my temple.

"I promise you're safe with me."

I turned so that I could lean into his chest, and I closed my eyes again, painfully aware that my stump was pressing against his stomach.

"I know I am."

...---...

"Tristan?" I felt a hand rest on my head, and I quickly sat up, blinking dazedly.

"What's going on?" I asked, quickly shaking myself awake to assess the situation. But Jack just put a hand on my shoulder and pointed out the back of the truck.

"Look." There was a breathless, child-like wonder in his voice.

I watched as the road started to bend behind us, and as we rounded the corner, Jack gasped beside me.

The ocean stretched out beyond the horizon, blending with the sky and glittering in the late afternoon sun. The water was a deep blue ridged with the white crests of waves, and I could hear the calls of gulls as we drove along the curve of the harbor. I leaned out the back of the truck slightly, Jack holding onto the back of my jacket, and looked down the side of the road. The sloping, forested hills gently leveled out into a small town. Most of the buildings had a cottage or Brettain style to them, and I smiled as I saw how little traffic there was. There were only a handful of cars, one or two trucks, and what looked like lots of bicycles. There wouldn't be a lot of noise here at all.

"Jack, it's perfect," I whispered and glanced over my shoulder to my boyfriend. He wasn't paying attention. He was just staring wide-eyed at the ocean, a dazed sort of smile on his face. I looked back to the water and saw it through his eyes. "It's beautiful, isn't it?"

"Yeah," he breathed, and I sat back with him, looping my arm with his and resting my head on his shoulder. I felt him absently kiss my temple, and I smiled. "It's so big. I knew it would be big, but it's just...*huge*." I laughed and looked up at him.

"That's kind of what an ocean is, Jack," I teased, and he kissed me.

"Stop trying to ruin my moment," he murmured, and I leaned my head against him again.

"Not trying to," I whispered. We looked at the water together. "We'll be just fine here."

"Yeah." I watched Jack, and my heart ached with joy at the wonder on his face, the pureness of his expression. "Yeah, we will."

... — — — ...

The truck came to a stop near the edge of town, and the driver helped Jack and I disembark. Our footlocker dragged behind me as I grabbed the rope handles at one end and took a look around. The street was calm and leisurely, just like it'd seemed from the road. The few people who were out walking around looked healthy and happy, free of the anger and suspicion that had filled the Academy. There was no tension in the air, nothing to put me on edge.

Estercliff, Calin. It really was perfect.

"Alright, take care you two," the driver called, and we waved to him as he got back in and slowly drove away.

"Well," I began as Jack pulled up alongside me, "where do we start?"

We slowly headed down the chipped sidewalk, ignoring the people who glanced at us from the shop windows. It started drizzling, and I closed my eyes blissfully at the gentle touch.

"Let's head to a coffeehouse or something. Get out of the weather and then we can ask where 'the Seaside' is."

"Sounds like a plan," I said.

We picked one of the small businesses to our right at random called the Sandpiper Coffeehouse. As I opened the door, a small bell jingled above my head, and I started, heart pounding. As Jack wheeled himself in, the people inside turned to look at us for a couple seconds, open curiosity in their eyes, before turning away.

"There's a table in the corner if you like," I said quietly, pointing, and he went one way while I approached the counter. I dropped my hand to my pocket and pulled out a little bit of the reparation money we'd gotten from the Academy. It wasn't a fortune, but it was enough for us to get by on our own for a few months while we got situated.

"Um, two…" I trailed off, struggling to think of something to order. "Coffees. Black, please," I finally stammered.

The young woman gave me a small smile as she took the few bills I'd handed her and prepared our drinks.

"You just come home?"

I looked at her, hand fiddling with the knotted sleeve of my right arm.

"Yeah. Me and my b…my friend over there."

She nodded, awkwardly clearing her throat.

"Where were you stationed?"

"Um, eastern front lines," I answered, thrown by the continued small talk.

"That's a long ways away," she continued, preparing the first coffee.

"Well, uh, that's how we like it," I returned clumsily. She smiled kindly at me, filling up the second mug.

"Well, that makes sense," she said evenly, squaring her shoulders as she walked back to the counter. "It's gotta feel good to be out."

I nodded anxiously, more than ready for this stressful conversation to be over. She slid the mugs across to me, and I took one and reached for the other only for both of us to be reminded that I only had the one hand. She reddened in embarrassment and hurried around the counter, picking up Jack's mug.

"I'm so, so sorry. That was so thoughtless of me," she blurted, moving quickly.

"No, it's okay. I, uh, I forget that I'm missing an arm sometimes, too." My joking words fell on deaf ears, and I sighed, following the woman over to Jack.

"Here's your drink, sir." She set the ceramic down and stepped to the side so I could sit down. "Are you gentlemen new to the area or have you been here before?"

"We're new," Jack admitted. "By any chance, could you point us in the direction of 'the Seaside'? A friend recommended it."

"Oh, of course! Here, let me write it down for you." She pulled a note pad from her apron along with a pencil, writing as she spoke. "You just go to the end of this street you're on here, take a left at Dover Avenue, and go all the way down to the water." She straightened and handed us the paper with a smile. "There you go. I know the man who talks to the applicants – just tell him Kate sent you."

"Thanks," Jack said, taking it from her and tucking it into his pocket.

"My pleasure." She was about to go back to the counter when another thought struck her, and she quickly wrote something else down, long black braids swinging around her as she turned around and handed me a second piece of paper. "I don't know if you're interested, but these are a few places that are looking for employees."

"Thank you," I told her sincerely, and she dipped her head.

"Most of us here lost family members to the navy, so we go out of our way to help veterans." We gave our thanks again before turning to face each other as she returned to her post.

"Wow," I whispered, and Jack nodded as he took a sip of his drink.

"Yeah. We're veterans, now." He gestured to the paper. "What're the jobs?"

"Postal service, the Veteran Affairs Hospital, the local soup kitchen – which apparently pays pretty well. Or at least that's what she's written here. And...huh." I looked up at Jack. "Lady Minerva's Orphanage. Apparently the matrons are looking for people to help with extended care teaching." We were quiet for a few moments, and I gently continued. "I know you and religion have a complicated–"

"I'll apply."

I blinked, surprised.

"Really?" I asked, and he nodded.

"Don't know if they'll take a paraplegic given it's working with kids, but it's worth a shot."

"Well, I think you'd be good at it." I looked at the list again. "I could look into postal service," I said with a shrug. "My left arm has gotten pretty good, and I could always just sort the mail." Jack snickered. "What?"

"You'd be wearing another uniform," he laughed.

"Way to ruin a good job, Jack," I said dolefully.

"Oh, we don't do uniforms here." We looked up at Kate as she walked by with another order. "Sorry, I wasn't trying to eavesdrop, I was just–"

"No worries," I told her and looked back at Jack. "*Ha*, no uniform."

He rolled his eyes, and we finished our drinks, awkwardly avoiding the terribly hidden glances of the other patrons.

. . . – – – . . .

"I think this is the place," I said as we approached a wooden, six-story building. Its simple style was clearly influenced by old Brettain architecture.

"Yep."

A sign hung above the lobby's bay windows that read "The Seaside", and thankfully, there were no steps at the front door. I held open the door for Jack, and as I followed him inside, I took in the clean, hard lines of the building's interior. It was very austere but homey at the same time.

"Can I help you?" An old man exited an office, and I walked over while Jack looked at some photos on the wall.

"Good evening, sir," I greeted, unsure of how to proceed. "Uh, we're new in town, and we're looking for a place to rent. Oh, Kate recommended you."

"Fresh out of the military?" he asked, eyeing the footlocker in my hand and shifting his hold on his cane.

"Yes, sir," Jack said easily, coming to a stop beside me. "We've already got a few potential jobs in mind, and we have enough to pay rent for two months."

"Assuming you charge the standard rate," I amended, and the old man smiled.

"Well, you two seem to have everything in hand," he began, shuffling a few papers and signing his name a few times. "And anyone Kate sends me I'm obligated to take in otherwise my girl will kick me out of the house."

"Family?" Jack asked.

The old man laughed as he checked a few drawers.

"Daughter. Doesn't look like it does she? Fortunately, she took after her mother that way." He took in a deep breath, scratching his head as he tried to remember where he'd placed whatever it was he was looking for. "Well, I have a lower price for vets, and by the looks of you two, you'll be wanting ground floor. Ah!" His eyes lit up, and he fished around in the top drawer, pulling out a key. "Let's go look at thirty-seven. It's a good little corner unit. Previous owners bought a house, moved out a few weeks ago."

My stomach flipped a little nauseatingly, but I followed the man to the door at the end of the hall anyways. He pushed open the salt-coated hinges to reveal a two-room apartment.

"This used to be an inn, so everything's fully furnished: dishes, utensils, bedding, furniture. There's a fireplace right here, and the kitchen is in the corner to the right of the door," he grumbled, cane thumping against the ground as he shuffled through the space. I leaned the footlocker against the wall just inside the door. "There's one bedroom over there in the back. I hope you boys don't mind sharing a bed."

"Not a problem sir," I assured him, and next he pointed out the small bathroom opposite the bedroom.

"There's a bathtub with the shower. Should make life a little easier for you, son."

Jack nodded his thanks to the landlord as he moved through the space. There was a couch with a radio on the side table and a four-person dining table next to the window Jack was at. I walked over to him and noticed his look of wonder. I followed his gaze.

"Wow," I whispered.

"Yeah, you can see the water from here. It used to be prettier – not that it isn't nice now, of course. A lot of debris from the war washes up though. Kids come home dragging guns behind 'em. Course, they don't work 'cause they're all waterlogged, but still."

I put my hand on Jack's shoulder, squeezing.

"You okay here?" I asked. He nodded absently, eyes fixed on the dark blue ocean stretching past the horizon. I turned to the old man. "I think we'll take it."

"Alright, I'll get the paperwork, and we can settle on a payment plan tomorrow."

I wasn't listening. I was too busy kneeling beside Jack and holding his hand in mine as he continued to stare at the ocean. We stayed there in that position for several minutes.

"Alright, you two." We turned at the sound of the old man's voice and joined him at the table. "Just sign at these three places, and we're good to go." As Jack and I read through the papers, the man continued talking. "We do communal meals here by the way. They're not mandatory, but they're there if it makes things easier. Dining room's at the opposite end of the hall, and we do meals at seven, noon, and six. A staff cooks everything – it's all pretty straightforward."

"Thank you, sir. We'll definitely take you up on that," Jack said with a smile and slid the papers back over to our new landlord.

"It's always good to meet new people," he smiled and shook our hands before hobbling out the door. "Have a nice evening."

The door clicked shut, and Jack gave me a tired smile.

"Well that could have been a lot worse."

"Don't tempt fate," I warned and fetched our footlocker, dragging it towards the bedroom. "I call the shower first."

Jack laughed, sitting back in his chair and looking out the window.

"Fine by me."

... — — ...

I had no idea how long it had been since I'd taken a shower in an actual bathroom with actual water pressure, but it was too long. After scrubbing my body as clean as possible, I just stood there, letting the water pour over me like rain, and closed my eyes. This was a new place. A new life. New everything. I took in deep breaths and ran my hand through my hair, letting all the tension bleed out of my body. Fresh start. I looked down and slowly opened my eyes, examining the scarred end of my arm and letting my fingers run over the shiny patches of skin, tracing out the permanent marks. A phantom pain dug into the tissue, and I tilted my head back up.

Fresh start.

I took in a deep breath and shut off the water, drying off quickly and pulling on my pants. Then, I ran the water in the tub until it was filled up a good amount and opened the door. Jack was still by the window, watching as the last of the sunlight faded from the sky and water.

"Hey. Ready to take a bath?"

Jack nodded quietly to himself and joined me in the bathroom without a word. I helped him out of his chair and sat him down on the floor to help him take off his clothes. From there, we somehow got into the tub, and I helped him wash the parts of his back he couldn't reach. We were mostly quiet through everything though, and when it came time to help Jack out of the shower, I had to practically drag him. I winced as I most likely bruised his hip on the lip of the ceramic basin, and as we sat there on the cracked tile floor, working together to dry him off and get him dressed, he cleared his throat.

"Thank you."

"For what?" I asked, frowning as I lopsidedly stood.

"Helping me." He looked up at me with solemn eyes as he pulled on a t-shirt. "I know it's hard. And…well, let's be honest, probably not how you planned to spend your life."

"Jack," I said softly. I shook my head, sat next to him, and lightly kissed his cheek. "You are the way I want to spend my life. All of this right here, this is what I want. Sure, it's got a few twists I wasn't expecting, but it's still what I want. I promise." I held his hand tightly. "But you're welcome."

We sat there for a little longer until I noticed he was shivering, and I helped him back into his chair and took him to our bedroom. As we settled in for the night, Jack pulled the covers up over us both as I threw my arm across his stomach, and his arm curved around my shoulders. I realized that what I'd said was true. Sure, I'd love to have my arm back. I'd love for Jack to be able to walk again. But this was where we were now, who we were.

And I was okay with it.

...———...

It was eleven forty-five when Jack started tossing and turning. I had just started to doze off, courtesy of all the sleeping I'd already done, and I sat up slightly, blinking in the moonlight from the window.

"Jack?" I mumbled, rubbing my eyes.

He made a small noise of fear in the back of his throat, and I quickly fumbled to turn on the lamp on the nightstand. I groaned, squinting in the sudden brightness, and looked at Jack. My boyfriend was breathing heavily next to me, drenched in cold sweat and muttering to himself under his breath with his eyes screwed shut.

"Jack," I mumbled, still half-asleep, and reached for his shoulder. "Jack, wake up."

My hand settled on his skin, and things took a very sharp turn south.

"No! Get off me!" he shouted, lashing out and clipping my cheek with a glancing blow. I stumbled back and nearly fell out of bed as he started thrashing even more, struggling to move his legs and continuing to shout in a harsh, terrified voice.

"Jack." I got to my knees and caught hold of one of his wrists, ignoring the smarting pain in my face. "Jack, wake up!" I shouted. At the loud noise, Jack's free hand latched around my throat, eyes staring at me in wild, blind fear that I now shared.

"Jack," I choked, letting go of his wrist and pulling at the iron fingers slowly crushing my neck. He propped himself up on his elbow, eyes empty of recognition, and tightened his grip. Black dots swarmed my vision, and my pulse throbbed painfully in my temples. I gagged, struggling to breathe. "Jack, it's me...Tris-tan!"

A few tense seconds later, seconds that felt like eternities, he still hadn't let go, and I clawed at his arm, slamming my knee forward into his side and throwing him a little off balance. Just as my vision blacked out, Jack's eyes widened in realization, expression horrified.

He let go, and I crashed down to the mattress, body heavy and limp. I took in a shuddering breath, coughing and choking on air.

"Oh my gods. Oh my gods, what did I – what've I done?" I heard Jack whisper in terror, and he grabbed me, shaking me and struggling to turn me over. "Tris? Tris! Tristan, *please!*"

"'M okay," I groaned. My voice was a hoarse rasp, and I slowly opened my eyes, still coughing and gasping. "It's okay. 'M fine, it's okay." I reached for Jack, grabbing his shirt and pulling myself towards him as I sat up.

"I'm sorry. I'm so sorry, Tristan, I'm *sorry.*"

He looked terrible. His skin was waxy and pale. His eyes were haunted, his hair sticking up in every direction. I could tell he still wasn't fully present yet, and as I tightly wrapped my arms around him and pulled him up against me, I could feel us both shaking.

"Y-you...you shouldn't sleep with me," Jack whispered, voice as hoarse as mine, and I shook my head, gently kissing his sweaty hair.

"It's okay, Jack." I cleared my throat again, trying to ignore my pounding headache. "That was my fault."

"I almost...I nearly killed you," my boyfriend protested, his voice weak and breathing ragged.

I tightened my embrace, exhaustion and adrenaline competing viciously inside me.

"We'll figure it out, Jack. We'll figure it out, I promise."

DAY TWO HUNDRED AND NINETY-SEVEN

0330 hours

Jack finally fell back asleep, his arms wrapped tightly around my waist. But I couldn't. No matter how hard I tried, I couldn't fall asleep. I slowly lifted Jack's arm off of me, got up, and walked into the bathroom. Wincing, I tilted my head back slightly and checked my throat. The skin was already starting to bruise, and I swallowed painfully, staring at myself in the mirror.

I knew what had happened was my fault. I grabbed him before he was awake, shouted at him. This was my fault.

But as I walked back into our room and slowly climbed back into bed, I realized that for once in my life, I was afraid of Jack.

I was afraid of my boyfriend.

··· — — — ···

That day, we kept busy. We should've talked about what happened, but we didn't. *Couldn't.* Instead, we left our apartment as early as we could and went to the communal breakfast at seven to grab some bread and a couple apples. We didn't really look at anyone, just grabbed what we needed and then left.

From there we got directions to the nearest charity shop to get new clothes. Most of the garments were made of repurposed canvas sails, the fabric dyed and softened so it'd be more appealing and comfortable. There were a few old uniforms tucked into the racks that both of us deliberately passed over. I saw a few Academy jackets as well. They'd been stripped of their insignias and ranks. The weather was colder here, so most if not all the clothing we grabbed were pants, long-sleeves, and sweaters.

After a quick stop at the apartment, Jack and I went our separate ways. He went down the road one way towards Lady Minerva's, and I went the other way to the post office. I didn't know how Jack's meeting went, but I was greeted with a smile and eager, kind words.

... — — — ...

When we met at our apartment later that day, we both had jobs, though Jack said he'd have to get a character reference sent from Jax as a formality. And later that night, as we figured out a payment plan with our landlord Ben, the old man pointedly said he also offered a couple's discount, and I realized that we couldn't have gotten more lucky.

After everything we'd been through, things were finally going our way. I felt like I could finally stop waiting for the other shoe to drop.

DAY THREE HUNDRED AND FIVE

8 days later

It was a shift on the mattress, nothing more – a single, barely noticeable tremor that made my eyes open. Heart beating quickly in my chest, I slowly sat up, minimizing my movements, and looked at my partner beside me. He seemed peaceful, hands resting lightly on his stomach, but I knew better. I cautiously pulled my covers back and got up onto my knees. I could see Jack's muscles tense beneath his shirt, and I took in a deep breath, leaning away from him as I reached out my arm.

"Jack?" I whispered, hand progressively coming closer to his shoulder. When he didn't respond to my whisper and instead took in a sharper breath than normal, his brow furrowing and jaw clenching, I finally let my hand rest on his arm.

Since that first night, I'd learned to lean away from him.

Eyes fogged and fearful, Jack pushed himself up with one arm while he lashed out with the other, fist just missing my face as I jerked backwards. He was disoriented, breathing heavily as he looked around himself, and I carefully put my hand on his, placing myself in his line of sight.

"Jack, it's just me. It's just Tristan."

His breath came in ragged gasps, and he let himself fall back down, staring up at the ceiling above us. We'd been in the apartment nine days now, and his dreams had swung back and forth between pleasant and night terrors. Tonight, it seemed he got a night terror. The nice thing was that I'd learned to wake up at the slightest sign of distress instead of waiting until he was shouting to realize something was wrong.

"You're safe," I said softly, returning to his side and pulling him against me. His back was clammy with sweat, and I could feel him shaking. "Do you want to talk about it?" He ran his hands over his face and shook his head. But a few seconds later, he nodded. "Okay…come on, let's sit up."

Once we had gotten situated, I waited for him to speak, careful not to rush him.

"It was you," he finally said, voice a hoarse croak, and I tightened my arm around him. "Instead of shooting me, Clarke shot you. I couldn't get the rocks off you, and you were just looking at me, screaming and begging me to help you, and I couldn't, I–" He broke off into shuddering breaths, and I held him close.

"That's not what happened, Jack," I said gently. "I'm here. I'm fine. I didn't die, okay?"

He nodded, and I reached out to turn on the light. I'd done this enough times to know that we wouldn't go back to sleep, and I was relieved to see that it was already six in the morning. I had to go to work at the post office at eight and Jack had to go to Lady Minerva's, so we weren't losing that much sleep.

"I didn't hit you, did I?" he asked, looking up at me. I shook my head.

"No. Not this time."

"Good," he sighed in relief and pinched the bridge of his nose as he bowed his head. "That's good."

. . . ‒ ‒ . . .

We were eating breakfast when the woman across from us pulled out a newspaper and flipped open to a story inside. I glanced up at the movement and was about to return to my food when I looked back at the headline and the photograph half-covered by her hand.

"Excuse me." She looked at me, startled. "Could I see the front page?"

"Oh, of course." She untangled it from the rest of the pages and leaned over the table. "Here."

"Thanks." I quickly laid it out and slowly smiled. "Jack. Take a look at this."

"International Summit tensions rise with eye-witness accounts," he read and was about to shrug when he looked down at the picture I was pointing to. He quickly took the paper from me. "No way."

"Yeah. That's Andy," I said. We looked at the photo of a man in a suit and eye-patch, maimed hand resting visibly on the side of a podium as he spoke to the Summit members. "He's looking really good. A lot better than the last time I saw him."

"You know him?"

I looked at the woman I'd taken the paper from and saw that everyone was now paying attention to us.

"Yeah, uh, he's Andrew Harris," I replied hesitantly. "We served with him, graduated from the same Academy class." Everyone's expressions had grown increasingly intrigued. "He's a good man. A good friend."

"So, everything he said in that speech is true?" a balding man at the far end of the table asked cautiously, and I hesitated again.

"Well, what did he say?"

"There is no enemy in this war." I looked at Jack as he read from the paper. "There are no heroes, no villains. There are just good people, people who are angry and suffering, and those who take advantage of them. There is just a broken system that has long forgotten what it stood for and instead of fighting for a purpose now fights for the sake of fighting and the whims of powerful people. I have seen friends, people I considered family, killed by bloodlust-driven men. I have seen good men and women maimed and killed as they tried to make the best of situations bad leaders put them in." Jack paused, eyes growing sad.

"One man, Captain Howell, murdered a girl I loved as my own sister for being shell-shocked. Her name was Idris Chance. She was twenty-one years old when he dragged her to the side of the road and shot her between the eyes. He was cruel and sadistic, and he murdered without abandon. And he was not an unusual find on the front lines, which was even worse. I use the word murder because that is what it is. I do not use execute, I do not use kill. Call what he did, what we have done, what it is. We murder each other in droves for petty, empty reasons. Ask anyone at the Academy why we started fighting, and we'll say because the Mezitain attacked us thirty years ago. Ask them why we continue to fight, and they'll give the same answer. The world has become toxic. Generations of people have been all but wiped out, and for what? Nothing more than a vendetta of pride. We are not expendable. We are not pawns in your games. And we will not march silently to your commands anymore."

Jack stopped reading, and I looked around the table. Everyone was still, heads bowed as if listening to a prayer. Their expressions were solemn, but as I looked at Jack we couldn't help the smiles that crept onto our faces.

"Yeah," I answered. The girl looked up. "Everything's true."

"Even that Captain Howell?" the bald man pressed, and I leveled a cold stare at him.

"Howell was *our* captain," I said coolly, gesturing to Jack and I. "So yes. The parts about him are especially true."

The rest of the meal passed in silence, and as we left the room, leaving the newspaper folded on the table, the woman ran out after us.

"Excuse me!" We stopped, letting her catch up. "Are you two Tristan and Jack?" She nervously fiddled the skirt of her white nurse's uniform, and we looked at each other.

"Yeah," Jack began. "How do you—"

"I'm Casey Roman." She quickly shook our hands and pointed down the hall. "I just got Samantha's letter a few days ago, and as the gods would have it I believe I'm your neighbor." She cleared her throat and smiled. "So, I suppose if you need anything, just ask. My son, Colin, is usually home if I'm at work."

"We will. Thank you." She returned to the dining hall, and I looked at Jack as we left the building. "So, what did you think about what Harris had to say?" I asked, and we started down the sidewalk, the rising sun warming the sea-chilled air. Jack smiled.

"I wish he'd been born thirty years ago."

I nodded, shoving my hand in my pocket.

"Me, too."

. . . ‒ ‒ ‒ . . .

That night, Jack and I sat together on the couch, listening to the radio in the dark. One of the stations was broadcasting parts of the Summit talks, and I shivered as I listened to Andrew speak. His voice crackled over the airwaves, strong and commanding despite the static interference, and Jack held me a little tighter in his lap. I rested my head in the crook of his neck and pulled the blanket up higher around us.

"We do not want reparations. How would you assign blame in a war that's been going on for thirty years? How would you decide who was guilty of inflicting the most harm or who suffered the most losses? No, burdening a couple countries with reparations to pay the rest of the world is nothing more than a surefire way to guarantee another war in the near future. All it will do is feed the resentment and hurt in those nations, and those sentiments have torn us apart for long enough. There is enough anger as it is in the world. There are enough attacks on minorities within our own borders driven by hatred and racism, by xenophobia and homophobia, by starvation and desperation. Our world is sick. We do not need to add to its problems, and simply ending this war will not fix them. We need to stand together. Send each other resources. Rebuild our infrastructures, feed our starving people, and treat our wounded and ill.

"In the trenches, there are stories of enemy armies calling ceasefires to help bury each other's dead, trading supplies so that they could all make it through the winter months. And if they can realize the value of binding together to survive greater threats, then entire nations should, too. We need to take a step back from our emotions and realize that without each other this planet will never be able to fully heal again. What I'm describing will be a long, slow recovery, but it will be a recovery. Maybe our children will not reap the benefits, but our children's children will. All we need to do is be strong enough to say no more, to counter hate with care. Call it an idealist's fantasy, a naïve boy's pipedream. I know this won't be easy. But I have faith that it can work. I have faith in the world that our desire to live and rebuild will overcome our old ways. Thank you for listening."

As the air was filled with the static of polite applause from somewhere far away, I gently kissed my boyfriend. Andrew's words hung heavy in my chest, warm and comforting in a dizzying sort of way. As someone else started talking, Jack reached over and turned the radio off. We sat there for a long time, staring out the open window and listening to the distant sounds of crickets and the surf rolling in and out, a gentle reminder that the world carried on.

"The times are changing," I said softly, my voice startlingly loud in the quiet air. Jack nodded and rested his cheek on the top of my head.

"I hope for the better."

DAY THREE HUNDRED AND THIRTY

Twenty-five days later

    I arrived at work with a black eye. No one asked what had happened or questioned the fact that my knuckles were bruised. Instead, they handed me my bag and asked how my boyfriend was doing, voices innocent but eyes sympathetic. I told them fine, but they knew what I really meant. Sometimes, as much as it hurt me to do it, I needed to hit back when I woke Jack up because he was disoriented enough to seriously hurt me. Despite the fact that he couldn't use his legs, he was still pretty tall with a decent amount of upper body strength.

    That first night in the apartment was still fresh in both of our minds.

    Other than those few questions, my coworkers mercifully left me alone. We weren't particularly close beyond the friendly neighbor dynamic. They were nice of course, and I had no doubt that we could have been close friends at one point in time. But I wasn't quite ready for that yet.

    I was sorting mail into their respective bags for delivery when Casey's son Colin hurried into the room with a heavy box. He was tall and gangly, probably around fifteen years old with a shock of red hair and blue eyes that were underscored by a smattering of freckles. He was filling in for a girl who'd just quit to go have a baby.

    "Hi, Mr. Byrne." I nodded to him. "Some more mail came in."

    "Be careful," I said absently as he passed. "Someone spilled coffee over by the shelves, and the janitor hasn't come by to clean it up yet."

    He wasn't listening. Instead, he was engrossed in looking through the mail as he walked.

"Looks like some of it's addressed to you and Mr. Miller from someone named Marcel Jones."

Surprised, I turned to face him just in time to see him slip on the coffee I'd warned him about. As he went crashing backwards onto the ground, I felt my throat close up on me, and my heart pounded painfully in my chest. I dropped the bag I'd been carrying and sprinted around to him, unable to breathe properly, and skid to a stop beside him.

"Colin? Colin, are you okay?" I asked, voice unsteady, and he looked up at me, confused.

"Yeah, sir. I just slipped, I'm fine." Despite his reassurance, I couldn't get rid of the panic gripping my chest.

"Are you sure?" I asked, holding him down as he tried to get up. "No, take it easy." He frowned up at me, even more baffled.

"I'm *fine*." I suddenly realized that the air smelled heavy and musty, and I looked around myself, fear spiking again until it was hard to breathe. "Mr. Byrne? You okay?"

"Do you smell something?"

He shook his head, slowly getting to his feet and looking down at me.

"I know what's happening with you," he said slowly, awkwardly blunt but still kind. "You've got shell-shock."

I quickly got to my feet, ignoring my pounding heart as I struggled to get back to my work.

"Just give me the letters addressed to me and Jack," I said shakily and swiped the back of my hand across my nose.

"My mom works at the VA. You could go—" he began, unsteady, and I slammed my hand down on the counter, looking up at him in anger.

"Just give me the gods-damn letters and *get out*, Colin!" I shouted, and he quickly handed me the letters before all but running away.

I stuffed the stack of papers into my pocket and tried to even out my breathing. I had to finish up my shift. But all I could think about was Jack falling backwards as I screamed his name, and quite suddenly, it was all too much. The walls, the mail, the smell of the gods-damned coffee, all of it was too much. I hurried to the front door, ignoring Colin as he called out to me. I had to get out. Everything was closing in on me, and as soon as I was in the open air my heart was a little quieter. I pulled one of the letters from my pocket and looked at the addresses, but for some reason my eyes couldn't focus on the scrawled letters, couldn't make out their words.

"Hey, you okay?" I shied away from the man approaching me on the sidewalk and set off running, panic clamping down on my lungs again until I could barely breathe. "Kid!"

I didn't stop running until I got back to the apartment, and I nearly dropped my key as I hurried to open the door. As soon as it was open, I slammed it shut behind me and didn't even bother to lock it. I dropped my jacket and the letters on the table and stumbled into our bedroom, shoving myself into the cramped space between the bed and the nightstand, trying to make myself as small as possible and bracing my head against my knees. I felt like the walls were closing in on me again, as though there were eyes and voices pressing in from every angle. Shuddering breaths wracked my body as I tried to blot out the roar of war echoing in my ears, the tattoo of gunfire and the screams of people long gone.

I felt like screaming with them.

I had no idea how long I'd been there until I heard the door open.

"Tristan?" I took in a shaky breath and tried to curl in on myself even further. "Tris?" The bedroom door creaked open to reveal my boyfriend, and he quickly came over to me, maneuvering as close to me as he could using his chair and the edge of the mattress. "Hey...hey, what's going on?"

I shook my head, and he put a hand on my shoulder, trying to coax me out of the corner.

"Tris, come on. Talk to me." I took in a deep breath.

"Someone fell over next to me, and I couldn't catch him." My words were wavering on the verge of tears. "I just...I freaked out."

He stopped trying to pull me out and just sat there in front of me, hand comfortingly heavy on my body.

"No one's getting shot out here, Tris," he murmured gently. "Anyone who falls over is just tripping." I nodded shakily, shivering as he gently ran his fingers through my hair. "So, people falling, loud noises...anything else been triggering you?"

"How can you do this?" I asked weakly, still not looking up.

"You can't fight a war all by yourself and win, Tris," he said gently and leaned forward to kiss me on the forehead. I listened as he moved away and came back, paper rustling in his hands.

"Hey shrimp." I slowly looked up and saw that he had opened Marcel's letters. "I hope this letter finds you and Miller well. I don't know when you two will get this, but I'm hoping it's not a year from now.

"Things are going well. We went to the Mezitain outpost in Alama to look over their records for Kat's mother. It turns out we were a little luckier than most. We found not only her parents, but also her aunt and two-year-old cousin. Aliyah, Jayce, and I helped them find an apartment complex. It's a bit crowded and a bit pricey, but we're all helping them pay the rent while they find jobs. Kat's moved in with them while Jayce, Aliyah, and I are sharing a two-bedroom rental in the heart of the city. It's not the cleanest around here. In fact, it reminds us a lot of Norford.

"Tensions are running a little high. The four of us have caught some nasty looks from some of the white Amaerics here, but Aliyah and Katalin have attracted more glares than Jayce and I. It was worse at the Academy, but people are getting angry and frustrated everywhere. They're looking for someone to take it out on. I know the feeling.

"That aside, we've all found work in some form. Jayce and Katalin are working in the mining facilities since they tend to provide the most pay. I've found a job at a local construction company. They don't pay as well as the mines, but there's plenty to do. A lot of rebuilding left. And Aliyah, well she found a job at the local military outpost. Seems she wasn't bothered with staying in the business. Every day she's typing up those condolence letters, adding up numbers and organizing mailing addresses for vets. Putting them on file, you know? Tracking us all down. She gets paid even less than I do, but it's something."

Jack cleared his throat and continued.

"It's odd, seeing everyone out of the Academy. Out of the war. It's the first time I'm getting to see what everybody really likes. I'm learning about their tastes in music and food, what clothes they like to wear, what they like to do for fun. You're never going to believe it, but Jayce *loves* to go dancing. Part of each of his paychecks goes to the dance halls downtown. Aliyah still dresses real sharp, like G.A. Agathon, but she's been doing her hair up in all these intricate styles. She says it's how her mother used to do her hair when she was little. She's taught me a couple more, too. And Katalin's an amazing cook, which I don't know when she managed to pick up or where. I'm afraid to ask."

I gave a quiet laugh.

"As for me, I'm still trying to figure things out. Mostly I go walking, but I guess you know how it is, Miller. You're in limbo once you get out. You test the waters. I hope you're resting easy and taking care of yourselves, and

I definitely hope to hear back from you guys. The others say hi and wish you the best. Marcel Jones," Jack finished. I released a long, slow breath.

"Want me to read the next one?"

I nodded and closed my eyes.

"Hello again, shrimp. Miller, we really need to come up with a name for you." Jack laughed at that. "It's been two weeks since my last letter, but I figured I'd fill you in. There was an accident at the mines today."

My eyes opened immediately, heart pounding.

"Both Jayce and Kat are fine, but a couple of their friends died. My brother talked with me, and he decided to leave the business. He's working with me now. To quote him, he's 'not too keen on dying digging for rocks after surviving months of getting shot at.' Frankly, I have to agree, but Kat's staying with it. She needs the paycheck. In fact, she's managed to save up enough from her weekly pay to move her family to a slightly bigger place. We're all still helping out, of course, and her uncle and mother have jobs working at a soup kitchen, but she's insistent on pulling in a little more than the rest of us.

"And I've found a hobby. Looks like Harris was onto something with all of his poetry. Who would've thought? Have you seen him in the papers, by the way? Heard him speaking on the radio? I'd never have pegged him as becoming a big name diplomat, but it suits him. Oh, guess what? Jayce found a girl at the dance halls last week. They're going on a date tonight." My racing heart had calmed down a little bit, but it didn't last for long.

"There've been riots around here. Amaerics attacking people who they think are Mezitain, Xiangon, Arikaan, Rusikan...there was a Brettain kid here last week who ended up in the hospital. Jayce happened to be walking by when he saw some assholes beating the shit out of him. A couple ex-Academy kids came busting out of one of the shops across the street, and they kicked those racists' asses, thank the gods. Jayce carried the kid to the nearest emergency clinic, and he's okay. Seems to be a habit with him.

"But it's been worse in...well, the locals call them the shag towns. A few homes have been burned down, a couple bars. And it's worse for the people who aren't...I don't want to say white because Rusikan Amaerics have been targeted, too. Bottom line is if you aren't a born and bred white Amaeric, you better watch your back. In fact, a young Xiangon Amaeric girl was killed. It was brutal. She was a vet, graduated from the Academy four years ago. Aliyah had to contact her family, tell them that her daughter had been stabbed to death with the word shag carved into her stomach." Jack's voice shook a little, and he cleared his throat before continuing.

"It makes me so fucking angry and sick. Don't tell the others, but I've started walking a few rounds through that neighborhood on my way home from work. Just hoping that some homophobic, racist asshole will cross my path so I can knock their teeth in. I know it's not a smart move. I know I'm gonna get myself in trouble, but you know what? At this point the local police are just as prejudiced as the assholes who live here, so in my books I'm already in trouble."

"How the times change," I whispered quietly, and Jack nodded before continuing.

"I hope that things are going better for you two out in Estercliff. Jayce just yelled at me to say hello from our bedroom. So, hello, I guess. Marcel Jones." Jack set down the letter and looked at me kindly.

"There's one more. You still want to hear it?"

I nodded. I felt completely relaxed now as I listened to the words of my friends even if what they were saying wasn't all that cheerful.

"Hello Tristan. Miller. It's Aliyah." I let my head thump against the wall and looked at the ceiling. "Marcel was unable to write the letter this week due to the fact that she and Jayce are currently incarcerated for getting into a bar fight."

I snorted with laughter, and Jack grinned. But his amused expression quickly faded.

"She stabbed a man, broke another's arm, and shattered a third's ribs, so she is obviously in more trouble than her brother. Katalin is down at the sheriff's office as I'm writing this trying to post their bail. It is proving difficult since the local opinion on gays and those who support them is that they deserve what they get. I've received several particularly choice words from my employer about the Joneses' behavior, mostly along the lines of how similar vigilante actions will not be tolerated in his office."

Jack paused.

"Apparently, Marcel has made it a habit to go patrol the 'shag towns' as they're so crudely named. I wonder where she got that from, Byrne. Miller."

I managed a sheepish smile, and Jack rolled his eyes.

"Katalin just returned with Jayce. Apparently, they aren't letting Marcel leave just yet. He can better explain what happened, so I'm handing the pen to him."

My boyfriend cleared his throat, and his voice was a little more light-hearted than the somber cadence he'd adopted for Aliyah's writing.

"Hey, Tristan. Hey, Miller. I hope you're doing well. Or at least better than Marcel and I are at the moment. We were heading home and stopped in a bar – Aliyah just told me she already told you this. Oh well. Anyways, there was this couple sitting at one of the tables. Two girls, one of them was Rusikan, the other Mezitain. I thought they were just friends, but I noticed Marcel was keeping an eye on them, and all the other patrons were just glaring so I put two and two together pretty quickly. No one was saying anything to them, but the waitresses weren't giving them service and all of that. Then, these three guys came in and walked up to them, and things kind of fell apart from there.

"They said some pretty disgusting things that I'm not going to repeat *ever*, and then one of the bigger guys smashed a glass against one of the girl's heads. I didn't know what to do, but then I noticed Marcel wasn't next to me anymore. Next thing I knew, she'd pinned one of the asshole's hands to the table with her knife, and everything went to hell. I got the two girls out of the bar pretty quick, and Kat walked them to the nearest clinic. They were bleeding and shaken up, but they're fine now. You know, it's been a while since I've seen my sister in an honest to Mars, traditional, three to one odds fistfight. Even longer since I've seen her win."

I gave another small smile in spite of myself.

"She's got a swollen eye, split lip, sprained wrist, and a grin on her face. So, you know, she's fine." I laughed at that, and Jack snickered as well. "We told the sheriff we're vets recently back from the eastern front lines, so he said he's gonna let her slide just this once. He's still going to keep her in for the night, let her cool off or something, but we're all good. Don't worry yourselves, we're fitting right in!"

"Oh, Jayce," I sighed, wiping at my eyes and smiling. Jack continued.

"Aliyah just told me that that isn't particularly comforting. I think it is. Alright, I'm handing the pen back to her." His voice shifted back to that more somber tone. "It seems I should have just ended this letter where I'd written it. Do not worry about the others too much. I'll try to keep a closer eye on them, though, I can imagine that you are on some level pleased with their actions. Wishing you peace, Aliyah Moore."

I slowly extricated myself from my corner and sat on the bed, looking at my boyfriend with shining eyes.

"We have great friends," I finally said. Jack laughed and set the letters on the mattress next to me.

"So. Shall we write back?" he asked.

I nodded immediately. I already knew how our letter would start. *Dear dumbasses.*

DAY THREE HUNDRED AND FORTY-FIVE

Fifteen days later

The day started off like any other. Jack had another nightmare around half past six, and I woke him up, making sure that he was grounded once more in reality before getting out of bed and getting dressed. I headed to the communal breakfast just as Casey left her unit, and she helped me grab some food and bring it back to our apartment so Jack and I could eat in a more private setting – today's meal consisted of eggs and fruit and some milk. As we sat at the dining table, watching the road outside our window and the ocean beyond it, the newspaper boy cycled past with Ben's order of papers strapped to the back of his bike.

This time though, instead of just chucking the stack to the road and continuing past us, the boy jumped off his bike, shouting in excitement as he pulled one of the papers free and ran towards the front door.

"It's over!" he shouted and waved the paper in his hands so hard I was afraid it would rip. "Ben, it's all over!"

My heart froze in my chest, and I looked at Jack across the table.

"Go check," he whispered, barely daring to breathe, and I launched out of my chair, slamming my hip into the corner of the table as I did so.

"Ow, *fuck!*"

"Careful!" Jack scolded, and I ran out of the door towards the lobby, my dog tags bouncing against my chest.

"Tristan! What's going on?" Casey asked from her doorway. Colin was hovering behind her.

"Just a second!" I called as I ran past them into the lobby.

The paperboy was practically bouncing on the balls of his feet in front of our landlord, and the old man stared at the front page, nearly in tears.

"Ben?" I asked tentatively, hope shining painfully in my eyes and voice shaking. He turned to face me and grinned, hobbling over and hugging me tightly.

"It's over, son," he all but cheered, aged voice tearful.

He pulled away, showing me the paper. I put my hand over my mouth and nose, hiding my smile, and my eyes started to burn until my vision was uselessly blurred. The old man just started laughing at me in pure joy.

"Take it, my boy." He gestured to me with the paper. "Go on, take it. Go tell your boyfriend."

On the verge of tears, I took the paper from his eagerly offering hands and sprinted back towards our apartment, ignoring Casey as she called after me again. I briefly winced as I accidentally slammed the door open into the wall and ran over to Jack, tackling him in a tight, awkwardly angled hug. The paper was partially crushed in my grip, and I could feel both our hearts racing in our chests. My hip was going to be painfully bruised tomorrow, but I couldn't care less.

I could run a thousand miles right now. Could walk through hell, could do anything and everything, I was so filled with pure joy. I only let go when I was certain I wasn't going to break down in tears and sat back on my heels to look up at Jack with the biggest smile on my face since I'd kissed him for the first time almost two years ago.

"It's over, Jack," I whispered, tearfully grinning and laughing as I gave him the crumpled newspaper.

He took it from my hand, smoothing it out in his lap, and I laughed in breathless giddiness. He slowly grinned, hands steepling over his nose and mouth as he looked at the headline. I wanted to laugh at the tears of joy in his eyes, so I did, and he ran his fingers over the black ink as though to be sure that the tall words were real. I dropped my forehead to rest against his knees, just grinning like a gods-damn idiot, and he grabbed what was left of my arms and pulled me up into his lap, kissing me hard and wrapping his arms tightly around me.

The paper slipped to the floor beside us, headline up, and I heard the ecstatic screaming in the hall as Ben and the paperboy and the Romans no doubt spread the word.

WAR OVER

… — — …

That night, Jack and I sat on the couch next to a gently crackling fire, listening to the radio as the host wired in calls from all over the country about the fact that the war was over.

The thirty year war was over.

The once quiet Estercliff was chaotic with fireworks and cheering voices, and I looked at Jack over the top of my drink as he poured himself another glass of whatever alcoholic beverage it was we were sharing. As he sat back, his right arm laid across my shoulders, and I held his hand so my left arm crossed my chest. The radio had briefly stopped reporting the news and was instead playing some song that I vaguely recognized from years ago, a wisp of a memory from a time I'd all but forgotten.

I realized I was probably pretty drunk at this point, but I was actually quite okay with that. It was dulling my reaction to the booming noise of the fireworks that sounded alarmingly similar to exploding artillery shells. Every time one went off, I flinched, and Jack squeezed my hand. I took in a deep breath as I pulled away and downed another glass.

"*There'll be blue skies...*" I cleared my throat as I listened to the woman's voice on the radio. "*Shining above me, not a cloud to be seen...*"

I raised the glass to Jack, shakily smiling.

"To Idris Chance. Irina Korsakov. Alec Jackson…Maggie Burke–"

"Mia Banting." His eyes were fixed on something a million miles away. "To all of them – they should have seen this."

A firework exploded a block away, and I jumped, dropping the glass. It shattered across the floorboards into hundreds of crystalline shards as the thought "incoming" screamed over and over in my mind. I dropped my head into my hand and doubled over, trying desperately to somehow cover my ears with one arm. Jack quickly leaned against me, whispering reassuringly, and gently put his hands over my ears for me as he rested his head against my back.

"*Blue skies, my darling, blue skies for you and me.*"

DAY THREE HUNDRED AND SIXTY-FIVE

Twenty days later

"Okay, let's do this. Come on," I grunted as I shoved Jack's wheelchair forward in the sand, bracing myself against the left push handle and the prosthetic extension that we'd commissioned a local to make for my right arm. My feet dug and slipped back into the hot ground, but slowly we were moving forward.

Admittedly, it wasn't much, but we were going somewhere. Sort of.

"*Gods*, I hate your wheelchair so much right now."

"I'd help if you'd *let* me, Tristan," he responded. His voice was tinged with slight annoyance, but mostly playful challenge, and he looked back at me, neck arching and dark eyes meeting mine. The corners of his mouth curved up in the slightest of smiles as he reached back and tousled my hair. "C'mon. You know you want me to help."

"No," I said firmly, bowing my head to lightly rest against his forehead. "This is the start of our two year anniversary celebrations. You are doing *no* work. My orders."

He scoffed and rolled his eyes as he looked at the beach before us.

"Fine. I'll just laugh at the image of a one-armed man trying to push his wheelchair-ridden boyfriend through sand." Despite myself, I snickered and watched as Jack's shoulders started shaking in shared laughter as I struggled forward. "You know it'd be easier if you just dragged me wherever we were going and then brought the chair afterwards."

"Shut *up*, Jack."

He smirked and sighed, resting comfortably in his chair and staring out at the ocean ahead of us.

"I give you five minutes before you give up and do what I just said."

"Oh, a challenge then," I said and leaned into the chair, pushing harder. "You'll regret that."

Jack closed his eyes in the lazy heat and smiled.

"Oh, I'm sure I will," he murmured sleepily,

As I continued to push us forward, I looked down at him. I took in his angular features, the slight scar across the bridge of his nose from shrapnel, the worry marks on his brow, and the laugh lines at the corners of his eyes. His hands were folded in his lap, fingers entwined around each other in an intricate pattern of calloused yet slender joints. I looked at the invisible layers of grime, stress, and pain that war had coated over him and slowly began stripping them away until all that was left was *him*: his dark eyes free of worry and hurt, his mouth relaxed and not set in a perpetual grimace. His muscles were relaxed and for once it seemed he was sleeping in peace.

I sighed in contentment and leaned over him, gently kissing him on the cheek and letting my chin rest on his right shoulder as we continued on.

"You'll throw out your back if you push me while you're standing like that," he warned, opening his eyes and letting his head tilt to the side so it rested against mine. I scoffed.

"Don't you worry, old man. I'm stronger than that."

Jack smirked and shoved my face away with his left hand, and I stood up straight once more. A few minutes of silence passed as we continued on, broken only by the cries of the seagulls and the constant roar of the ocean as waves rolled in and out like the pendulum of a clock. A cold wind wound its way down the coast, burying itself in our clothes and chilling our skin.

"Almost there," I announced once the wind had died down a little, and Jack's eyes opened blearily. "Did you fall asleep?"

"No," he immediately retorted, defensive. I smirked, the small smile the only display of my amusement. "More like dozed."

"Well, our final destination is just around this dune."

I took in a deep breath and started running, sand spraying up from my feet as we jerkily bounced over the uneven ground. A couple times, we got caught and stuck on kelp and wood that had been washed up from the sea and buried beneath the sand during the last high tide. But despite that, we were getting places. Slowly.

"Three, two, *one*," I said and brought us to a grinding halt that rocked Jack forward a little bit. He laughed, leaning forward and bracing himself against his knees.

"Let's not do that again," he chuckled, the sound of mirth ringing false in my ears as he rubbed his neck. I nodded and massaged the stump of my arm where it had locked into the prosthetic brace.

"Yeah, I'm agreeing with you there. I'm pretty sure I rubbed my arm a little raw."

His playful manner vanished instantly. Jack twisted around as much as he could and reached for my right arm, pulling away the cap and lifting the cut sleeve of my green turtleneck to check on me. His eyes clouded with worry and pain once more, and I quickly put my hand over his, stilling it as he went to take a closer look at the reddened and angry skin.

"Hey. It's okay, alright? I'm fine. I *promise*," I added seeing the look he was giving me, and he sighed, letting go of my sleeve but still holding onto my hand. "Alright, let's do this." I walked around to face him and grabbed ahold of his belt as he linked his arms around my neck. "You count."

"Okay, on three," he said, took a deep breath, and pulled himself closer to me. "One, two, three —"

I rocked backwards and in practiced movements carried Jack to the side of the dune, easing him down as far as I could before I let the two of us fall, sinking back into the sand and laughing at the other's graceless collapse. But when I reached to help Jack arrange his gangly appendages, he pushed my hands away. He avoided my gaze and set about lifting and positioning his legs into a more comfortable position by himself.

"I'll get your chair," I said softly after a few moments of watching him, and he sighed in frustration.

"I'm not mad at you, Tris. I just…" I looked back at him so he knew I was actually listening. "I just have to do this myself. You understand."

"Yeah, I'm sorry. Just got excited," I said, smiling apologetically, and he rolled his eyes as he grabbed one of his legs and then the other above and below the knee to straighten the limb out.

I smiled gently and leaned forward, placing my hand at the back of his head and kissing his brow. He sighed and closed his eyes, leaning into my touch but still keeping his hands firmly wrapped around his right thigh. I pulled away, rested my forehead against his, and tightened my grip on the back of his neck.

"I know I hover. Thanks for putting up with me."

He laughed and gently pushed me away so he could prop up his legs a little. Now, they were slightly bent, feet buried halfway in the sand.

"Why *do* I put up with you?" he teased, eyes mischievous, and I looked at him dryly.

"Don't push it," I warned and sat against the dune beside him, taking his hand in mine and letting my thumb run over his knuckles.

We went silent, just watching the rolling waves while keeping ourselves grounded in each other's touch. We were happy, content in just sitting here side-by-side and basking in the warmth of the sun and the other's presence. That and we had limited topics to pick from.

There was no point in talking about friends. Friends were either dead or scattered across the world, and they tended to reopen old wounds and resurrect ghosts best left in their graves.

There was no point in talking about home. No point in talking about the Academy or a farm on the desolated plains or an orphanage in an overcrowded and polluted city. Right now, home was in the company we kept and a little apartment in the corner of an ocean-side building. And that was just a bit too close to nowhere – frighteningly so.

There was no point in talking about my missing arm or Jack's deadweight legs. Those had become parts of our daily lives, things we'd learned to adapt to. There was no point in reliving the stories behind every scar, no point in recounting my boyfriend's nightmares, and no point in talking about how I panicked at any loud noise and immediately reached for Jack, regardless of whether or not he was beside me. We already knew the stories behind those. We already knew why they happened, what they were.

There was no point in talking about how both of us sometimes broke apart. How I sometimes threw things I knew would break just because I needed to hear the sound of my hand doing something that I could control. How sometimes Jack was so tired of being confined to his wheelchair that, in his frustration, he messed up getting into it and fell to the floor, breaking down as I helped him back up.

Because while all of that was true, we weren't defined by it. We weren't defined by our troubles and lows. We didn't want them to be all we talked about or all we had at the end of the day. We weren't our traumas. We were how we survived them. But when we had these moments where we were left to reminisce about our pasts, I was always overwhelmed by just how much horror had happened in the mere twenty-odd years we'd been alive. Sometimes it seemed impossible to find any good moments.

But just when I thought we were going to lapse into another one of our hours-long sessions of quiet, the silence was broken.

"Remember..." Jack's voice sounded rusty, and he cleared his throat a few times to start over. "Do you remember when Idris told us that the meat in the rice was rat?"

I looked at my boyfriend in mild surprise, taking in how he stared at the ocean ahead of us with eyes that were too shiny and too wide. He sniffed, wiping at his nose, but still didn't blink. There was something set to his jaw, and a tragic smile pulled at his lips. I nodded and looped my arm through his. He gripped my hand tightly in mine.

"Yeah, and then she told us that the week before that it'd been cat," I said and snorted at the memory, my voice soft as I looked down at the sand beneath us. "Andrew had fished her out of the Lake just in time to eat."

"What was she doing out there again?" Jack asked after a few moments of silence. A sad smile pulled at my lips as I recalled the moment, the four of us laughing and smiling in our own ways.

"She was communing with the swans," I answered absently, entranced by the ocean before us. Jack smirked, making a small noise of laughter in the back of his throat.

"Yeah, that was it..." He shook his head and finally looked down from the horizon of silver glass, blinking. "She was a sweet kid. Odd, but sweet, you know?"

I nodded, thinking back to the Academy days when everything hadn't been exactly great, but certainly not as screwed up as it had all become. The days of aches and pains and bruises...was that all the good I'd left to remember my life by?

"When Jax railed off at us, he would get all red in the face. I thought he was gonna explode." The hurried words I spoke sounded foreign, the laugh that bubbled in my throat a stranger's. Or was it that I just hadn't genuinely laughed at the past in so long?

"Remember that time he busted a blood vessel in his eye when he was hollering at our troop?" Jack added, eyes distant and a faint smile pulling at his mouth. "I thought Alec was going to throw up. Jax just grabbed his eye and started swearing, and when he looked back at the poor cadet, his whole eye was just *brick red.*"

I started giggling uncontrollably, remembering the moment as though it were just yesterday.

"Alec literally went white, you could *see* the blood drain out of his face," I laughed, gesturing with my hands only to see the one. I went quiet, staring down at my lap in embarrassment and frustration. The merriment in Jack's eyes slowly faded away, and he draped his arm around my shoulders, pulling me into his lap and hugging me close.

"Remember Promenade?"

I looked at the silver water and glittering waves and heard the gentle music of "Sweetheart Waltz" in my ears again. I felt Jack's hands on me as we slowly danced, remembered the chaotic lessons in the attic and the way we would get hopelessly tangled up in each other.

"How could I forget it?" I whispered, and he kissed my temple.

"Those were the good old days, weren't they?"

I didn't trust my voice to respond, so I just hmphed in agreement. We fell into silence once more, but this time it was one that hummed with the need to be broken.

"I still can't believe we ate cat," I finally managed, the oppressive quiet shattering with my words.

Before I knew it, Jack was softly laughing again, a joyous sound that was heavenly music to my ears. Happiness, contentment – they were things that the world had come to lack as of late, and the people who'd made it through this far were only just starting to remember what they were.

"Jack, can I ask you something?" I asked, tightening my arm ever so slightly around the arms locked about me, and drew him over me like a protective shroud.

"Hmm?" His voice rumbled against my back. His eyes remained shut against the bright sun, basking in its warmth.

"What do you think it'd be like if there hadn't been a war?" I felt him move his arms to prop himself up, and I quickly grabbed one of his hands in mine, stilling his movement. "Don't turn this into a deep conversation. I just want to know off the top of your head."

I tilted my head back so that I could look up at him. He gently trailed his fingers through my hair as he settled back down and stared at the ocean moving in and out before us.

"Honestly," he began, voice tired and worn down, "it would have been the same. We just wouldn't have been out there fighting in trenches. We'd probably be fighting in other places, with different technology. Guns would be bigger, faster, stronger. We'd make clothing that could withstand bullets. Bombs and artillery could level entire cities and blocks instead of a twenty foot radius." He trailed off, waiting for a flock of seagulls to pass overhead, screaming in dissonant harmony to the sky. "Different settings. Different faces...but the same exact story."

"Bit cynical, isn't it?" I asked with a frown, but he just shook his head.

"No, it's just the flaw in the human design. We always like conflict, and we never like change. Put those two together, and we just do the same thing over and over and over again no matter how cruel or destructive or wrong it was the first time we did it." He paused, and I spoke up.

"Well, maybe we can learn." As we sat there, watching the sun slowly start its descent towards the horizon, I took in a deep breath. "So, our two year anniversary is tomorrow. You know, using the date of our first kiss after the Hunt." I looked up at him. "Your view on the folly of man aside, I assume you still want to do something?"

Jack adopted a thoughtful expression that I knew was a complete ruse. He had that sparkle in his eyes, that smirk on his lips, that told me he knew exactly what he wanted to do.

"Oh, you know...I was throwing around the idea of getting married."

I sat up and turned to face him so quickly I almost fell over. Naturally, the first words out of my mouth made me want to smack myself.

"You know you can't plan a wedding in a day, right?"

He shrugged, crossing his arms and smirking.

"Wasn't planning to. I was leaning more towards the eloping end of the spectrum."

My mind was stuck, trying to struggle through the logic and semantics of what he was saying to avoid actually facing the implied question.

"Uh, then who would we be running from? Because I'm pretty sure you need to be running or hiding from something in order to elope."

Jack rolled his eyes, laughing.

"That's a technicality, Tris, and you know it," he teased. I floundered again.

"I don't think the Horsemen, Jayce, Andrew, Jax, and Blackwell would appreciate it if we got married and *didn't* tell or invite them. Besides, we'd, like...need to find someone who'd actually want to marry us," I rambled, fidgeting and looking in what felt like every possible direction at once.

"Have you *seen* where we live?" he laughed. "That's not going to be a problem." I swallowed painfully.

"So..." Jack began, drawing my scattered attention to him once more. "Is that a yes?"

I looked at him, eyebrows raised in disbelief as everything clicked into place.

"No. Why would I want to marry you?" I answered sarcastically. At his hurt expression I rolled my eyes and grabbed the front of his shirt, pulling him towards me and giving him a slow, deep kiss. When I pulled away, I grinned and rest my hand at the back of his neck, tightening my fingers and laughing as a shy, hesitant smile slowly spread across his face.

"Of course it's a yes, you colossal idiot."

"Oh, good," he sighed, relieved.

"Were you seriously concerned I would say no?" I asked, voice taunting but not unkind, and Jack shrugged defensively.

"People change after a war. I didn't know if–"

"Two years!" I interrupted, torn between laughing or swatting his head. "Two years, and I haven't dumped you, Jack. We lasted through a godsdamn *war*. There's no way in hell that I'm marrying anyone else." He smiled at his hands, embarrassed, and I sat back next to him, suddenly feeling very excited.

"Well, we have the addresses of everyone who really matters, so we can set a date and start on the invitations tomorrow, if you like," Jack offered, bashful smile lurking at the corners of his mouth. "I've got the weekend off from work anyways. And joking aside, if we're doing this, we're gonna do it properly."

"I'll call the post office and tell them I'll be out sick," I suggested, and my boyfriend – *fiancé*, oh my *gods* – gave me a withering look. "What?"

"Don't skip out on your job," he scolded, but I pushed my point.

"How are they gonna know I'm not actually sick?"

"Tristan, that's lying. And it's a small town, come on."

We talked for a little bit longer, our voices climbing in volume as we tried to talk over each other as ideas came to us. I finally stopped speaking and took in several deep, content breaths to try and wrap my head around what was going on. Jack slowly stopped talking as well, expression serene. He leaned forward, holding my hand lovingly in his.

"You okay?" he asked, grin fading into a small, secret smile.

"I...I think so," I said. I nodded and smiled, wiping at my eyes. "Yeah. I'm okay."

"It's about damn time," he whispered and gently grabbed my shoulders. He pulled himself towards me while pushing me backwards at the same time until he was lying on top of me. I smiled up at him, and he brushed my bangs to the side. "You still good?"

In response, I quickly kissed him and looked into his eyes, filled with relief at how the brown irises were for once free of pain.

"How about you?" I asked, and he smiled, an easy, private expression. His gaze shifted downwards briefly, and his response was just as soft as his smile and even more heartfelt.

"Yeah. I'm good, too."

"We're gonna need a best man."

Jack burrowed his forearms into the sand on either side of my head as he pondered his response.

"Well, I was thinking we'd ask Andrew. But he's probably busy with the Summit – might not be available."

I shrugged beneath him, deadpan as I spoke.

"Well, we could always ask Blackwell. He'd probably be all for it–"

"*Tristan!*" Jack looked appalled at the idea, yet unwillingly entertained.

"Fine! We'll put Marcel in a suit and give her a fake moustache."

Jack started laughing so hard there were tears in his eyes, and I laughed with him as he pushed himself sideways to lie on his back in the sand. The sun was low on the horizon, and I looked at the upside down ocean, taking in the red across the sky and the golden fire reflected on the water. A cool breeze wound its way down the shoreline, burning against our skin and lining our clothes and hair with salt.

"Seriously, though. If Andy's not available, we should ask Jayce," I said. Jack readily nodded.

"Definitely." We were quiet for a moment before he continued. "Can you believe this? A gay wedding with all military guests? Hell, a gods-damn *gay wedding,*" he said with wonder, slowly growing serious once more as he pushed himself into a sitting position.

I shrugged and propped myself up on my left elbow while driving what remained of my right arm into the dune beside us for balance. He shook his head, marveling at our life with a long absent light in his eyes, and I looked at him with that same ridiculous grin on my face.

No more long silences. No more half-finished sentences. I was done looking to the past – my whole gods-damn future was right here in front of me.

"What can I say?" I breathed. "We're learning."

AND ONE MORE THING

I just wanted to say something, and it's something that's been on my mind since the beginning of all of this. It's about making your way through this maze of a universe that seems to go out of its way to make sure you're doomed to fail at every turn.

It's about surviving.

You see, it *is* hard to want to be loved by someone, be strong for the universe, and fit in all at the same time. And in the beginning, you *will* feel helpless. You *will* feel alone. And you sure as hell will be scared shitless of everything because the world seems so impossibly big and mean. You'll see the workings of existence and think that you have to fit in somewhere in the greater picture, that you have to do something with your life that adds up to something that can be measured on the grand scale of creation.

But that's just not true.

Because the truth is that the universe will keep turning regardless of whether or not you're alive. The universe doesn't care about the small blip of time that is our existence, but at the same moment we are not a grain of sand on an infinite beach. We are a bubble racing towards the surface of a stream, a fragile sphere that touches and encompasses so much more than just ourselves, but is just as fleeting as the rest of the world around it.

But we're not *nothing*. We're not *no one*, and we never will be. Because the grand play that is time is not where the actions of our lives matter; it's in the small realities that we shape during our own brief blips of existence that it all counts. Each one of us plays a role in the lives and destinies of others that we touch in our lifetimes, and that – *that* is our legacy.

That is the point of existence.

My life didn't change the future. I didn't alter history nor will my name be remembered throughout the centuries. Nearly the entirety of the human race will forget about me, but that's not what matters. It's not about who will forget.

It's about who won't.

My husband is blessed with a lifetime he should not have. My dearest, beloved Jack will never forget me.

The two children we will adopt in a year will have a life filled with love and family. And their children will. And their children's children will, too. They will never forget me.

Because you see, the valor of life isn't in saving the world. It's not in fighting and giving up your life for a unknown or warped cause. It's not in dying acts of bravery on a battlefield or in sacrificing yourself for someone else's greater purpose. It's not in going through the motions of a war in the hopes that your death will mean something. It's not in giving in to despair when the whole world seems to be against you and nowhere feels safe. The valor of life is *not* in how you can die or how spectacularly you can fail.

The valor of life is in how you succeed. The valor of life is in how you can manage to win even in the darkest of times, in the most fatal of failures, and in the moments when all hope seems lost. It's in how you can not just survive, but truly *be*.

It seems desolate, impossible – a fantasy, a pipedream that will forever lurk just out of reach.

But I have done it, am doing it, will always do it. I will not just survive. I will live and make sure that those I love live too, because there is nothing more honorable than that.

The true valor of life is living it.

And that is the hardest and most rewarding thing of all.

ABOUT THE AUTHOR

R.L. Stanley grew up in San Jose, California and has loved reading and writing since she was a little girl. She has pursued these passions throughout her life, from participating in annual short story competitions throughout elementary and middle school to joining her high school's creative writing club and newspaper. During her junior year, Stanley wrote a short story titled "Calm Before the Storm" about a gay couple in a dystopian military and, at the urging of her teacher, decided to pursue the idea further through National Novel Writing Month. This story became her first novel *Valor*. Stanley is now a sophomore in college.

Made in the USA
San Bernardino, CA
12 November 2016